Treasure.

Being a Tale of a Great Value.

Lost, or, Found.

George R. Mead

E-Cat Worlds Press

Comments and questions? –> gmead01@gmail.com

Treasure

Everything is fiction, nothing more, nothing less. No real people are in these tales nor do any real life clones of the characters exist.

LCCN 2009929089

Mead, George R.
Treasure. Being a Tale of a Great Value, Lost, or, Found./
George R. Mead.
p. cm. – (From Grandeville, a tale; Tale 10)
ISBN-13 978-0-9817446-2-9
1. Fantasy. I. Title. II. Series.

E-Cat Worlds established its publishing program as a reaction to the large commercial publishing houses currently dominating the book industry and the smaller intellectual clones. It is interested in publishing works of fiction and non-fiction that are often deemed insufficiently profitable or commercial or that are not necessarily reflective of literary trends and fads.

E-Cat Worlds, 57744 Foothill Road, La Grande OR 97850
www.ecatworldspress.com
SAN 255-6383

In the middle of nowhere - Creativity.

First Edition:
Printed in the United States of America

From Grandeville.

Portal
Lair
Search
Not Again
And Again.
Magiwitch
Rebirth
Offspring
Holiday
Treasure

A Tale of the Feyra

Jonathon and Dee

Nonfiction

A History of Union County
The Ethnobotany of the California Indians

Chapter One.

So? Now What's Going On?

It was a fine, early, summer day.

It was a fine, early, summer day, in the middle of the afternoon.

It was a fine, early, summer day, in the middle of the afternoon, not all that far from the small, rather isolated town of Grandeville located in the mountains of northeastern Oregon.

Grandeville. Tinker's Place.

They were scattered all over the place, inside and outside the large sprawling house. All the windows of the house were open. The mild, just right temperature, breeze gently passed here and there as it wandered in one window and out another.

Some of them were in the large swimming pool. Some lounged on the rear deck in chairs, or, in the hammock. A few cat-napped in the small living room.

He was crashed on one of the couches in the large living room. Soft classic music sang from the radio as he, more or less, dozed, and relaxed.

They had dug, and overhauled, and replanted the rear flowerbeds. Again. And the crew had showered and changed into more comfortable attire.

For lounging.

For sprawling.

For napping.

So that is exactly what he was doing.

He was sorta dozing, thinking about his life and those others that were his life and himself. So he was sorta dozing, or maybe, napping.

But he wasn't alone. Three of the six cats had decided to share the couch with him. They had grumbled, but had allowed him to do that, to share the couch.

Now one cat slept on his outstretched legs, one was curled into a ball on his stomach, and one was draped over his shoulder and hummed soft purr into his ear. The other three cats were in the barn looking for rodents to terrorize.

So, there he was, dozing, or napping, more or less, being used as a cat bed, listening to soft classical music and soft cat purr.

Relaxing. Really relaxing.

It was quiet.

It was peaceful.

Suddenly the cats came awake, jarring him awake. He turned his head to see where and at what the cats were staring.

Then he also stared. At this person standing there,

suddenly standing there, just standing there. In the middle of his large living room.

A stranger. A strange looking stranger.

"Now what's going on?" he mumbled to himself. He wasn't sure that he really wanted to know.

This person, this stranger, just stood there and looked at him with large, round, dark brown eyes. The face tapered down to the chin, a somewhat narrow chin. The ears looked to be slightly pointed and slightly long. This person was lightly built, and short, just about four feet tall, at least as judged by a sideways look while lying on one of the couches being used as a cat bed.

His garments, Tinker had decided that this person was a male, were soft tones of green and brown. He wore, did this male person, a loose brown-colored shirt, forest green trousers, high brown boots. And some sort of golden scale mail over his shirt.

He looked harmless enough. To Tinker. And to the cats. They went back to sleep, settling in their previous spots.

Tinker didn't. Go back to sleep. He sighed. This was not a way to spend a comfortable, quiet afternoon. Not at all. He cleared his throat.

"O.K. Who are you? And if you are selling anything, go away."

A soft calm voice replied, as the speaker made a short bow. "I am Helf. I am not a merchant. Who are you? What are those creatures? Guardian beasts?"

"Go away. Will you just go away?" He closed his eyes hoping that when he opened them it would be true, this guy would be gone.

"Many apologies," said Helf. "I must have come to the wrong spot in this elseplace. Can you tell me how to find The Chosen One? Would you help me locate that one?"

"Damnation," snarled Tinker, now staring up at the ceiling. "How did you slip in? We are blocked against demons and witches and things like that."

Helf twitched. And relaxed, realizing that the spell hadn't been cast in his direction. "I am none of those things. I am a warrior."

"Wonderful," grumbled Tinker, mostly to himself, now looking at his visitor. Again. "Now we need a warrior ward."

Helf nodded. "It is good to be a warrior."

"So, besides being a warrior, what are you? Helf?"

"Me?" He stared at this person and looked surprised, then a bit worried. "I am Hephira."

He looked around the rather strange room. It didn't look at all like what he had thought it was going to look like. Somehow, he must have gotten twisted around and come to the wrong place to hold a rather strange conversation with this rather strange individual in these rather strange rooms.

Chantal slipped into the room from the hall. She had felt his aggitation and heard his conversation with Helf in her mind. She stepped behind the couch and looked over Tinker and the cats at their visitor.

"Kinna cute." She raised one arm, rested her forearm on the couch back. The hammer clicked as it was cocked. She pointed the long-barreled forty-five revolver at their visitor. She was using high velocity loads and hollow points.

"But if he tries anything, I will blow his butt off."

Helf looked at her and the gun. "What is that thing?"

"A weapon." Smoke slipped in through the front door, dripping water on the floor. She looked from the puddle she was making to Tinker. "I was in the pool. And came around."

"What do you want?" asked Chantal.

"I don't want to know," mumbled Tinker.

"Help," replied Helf, staring at Smoke, especially her eyes. He nodded to himself. So he had come to the correct elseplace after all. He bowed. "Chosen One."

Tinker sighed. "Merde." He knew he hadn't wanted to hear something like that.

Helf waited. This was not what he had expected. Not from all the tales that he had heard. But that witch had suggested that the one to be sought was going to be different.

Tinker sighed. "Go away. Will you just go away. We are out of the adventuring business. Just go away." He waggled one hand loosely at Helf.

The small man stepped closer, fingering the hilt of the sword hanging from his belt. Maybe he really had made a mistake.

"How did you find us?" asked Tinker. "How did you find a way in?" He wished this guy would just go away. And he hadn't noticed that Helf wore a sword until just this moment.

"On Tandor's Vert, I met a witch. She told."

Tinker swung his legs around and sat up, displacing the cats who grumbled about being disturbed before rearranging themselves and going back to sleep. "Which blabbermouth was it?"

"What?"

"Who told you?"

"One of the ring adept witches."

"Who?" Tinker frowned darkly.

"Zwar witch Surlindar."

"I really am really going to have to have a talk with those guys."

"I saved her from a Pesak," explained Helf. "She told me. After. She was grateful."

Chicken walked in from the kitchen and sat on the couch next to Tinker, tugging the white robe she was wearing closed at the neck. "By nay testy so, My Lord, for We know not what this person do wish." She dragged one of the cats into her lap, fingers tickling through the thick fur. It was the large, black male. His eyes crossed in happiness.

Tinker sat straighter.

Fair Morn joined them, carrying a pot of coffee, handed him a cup and filled it.

The others began to filter into the room.

"Thanks," murmured Tinker to Fair Morn. He stared at Helf, sighed, and said, "O.K., you might as well tell us whatever it is that you think we have to know." *And I am probably not going to like what he has to say,* he told the rest of himself, mind to mind, as he waggled an arm at their visitor.

"Sit someplace. No sense in just standing there." Helf did. After pulling one of the chairs close to Tinker.

"I am Helf," he began, looking from face to face as they all settled around him. "I came to this elseplace to ask for help. She moved me to here."

He paused, saw no expression on any face, and continued. "All know of The Chosen One. And of them."

He waved one hand at the others. "And of the mighty deeds that have been done. All know of the evils vanquished and . . . "

"How about," interrupted Tinker. "How about we just skip over all the prologue and get right to the heart of the matter? Why are you here? Why are you here bothering us? Today? Now?"

Helf jerked back, bumping his head on the high back of his chair, and blinked at him, at them. "Nandau has been taken."

"Most dreadful," stated Chicken.

"Hephira," gurgled R-Bar, chewing on the tip of a sparkling silver wand, as she walked into the room.

"Ummm?" asked Tinker, glancing over. Dark was seeping out around her.

Ran slipped to her side, clenching a jet black chrystal clear sphere in one hand. She pointed. "That person thing is Hephira. One of them!"

"So?"

"Amtar, they are arn arn nik tik!"

"Wonderful," he grumbled, frowning at the witch pair. "Either of you care to explain, in clear plain old English as it is spoken hereabouts, whatever it is that you are grumbling about?"

"Mate'mer." Sha'gar turned from the window where she had been standing, looking out, carefully ignoring their visitor.

"Those," she pointed. "Those are the long ago evil spawn of elf and people mating."

Helf leaped to his feet, glowering angrily. "That is not true!" He looked at Tinker. "The part about evil spawn." He looked back at Sha'gar. "That tale is child boodar!"

"So, there," mumbled Tinker.

Messenger sat on the other side of Tinker and smiled at Helf. "He is kinna cute. Like one of our rabbits. Sorta."

Helf stared at them, at all of them, and wondered how he was ever going to convince them to help him. They didn't appear to be very interested in doing that at all. He began to wonder what sort of inducement that he might be able to offer. The witch hadn't told him anything that would be useful.

Grandeville. The Burger and Bowl.

They were eating.

Breakfast.

And dinner.

They had just finished bowling.

The guys had won.

Again.

This time.

Again.

Barely.

Again.

Two games to one.

Red and Green were the ones eating breakfast. Soon, they would go to work as the split night shift for the Grandeville Police Department.

Sandy and Janine were eating dinner. It was the end of the day for them. They had taken an early end of the day just so they could go bowling.

Sandy nudged her husband. He filled her tea cup.

"Me too, Red." Janine shoved her cup in his direction.

Both of the women looked like young girls sitting next to these two gigantic men. From a distance. It wasn't how they dressed or how they acted. It was just that Red and Green were so large.

Red stood. "Well, Counselor, let's go look at bowling balls. I'll buy you one of your own for your birthday."

Sandy jumped to her feet, smiling broadly, and hooked an arm around one of her husband's thick arms. "You trying to bribe me, copper?"

"Never," stated Red.

She leered at him. "Got something else on your mind, that it?"

"Take the fifth," he rasped in his usual tone of voice as he towed her towards the counter where the bowling gear was sold.

Janine laughed.

Green looked at her, all blank cop face.

"What?"

"I just gotta ask?" he rumbled, trying to keep his base voice from carrying all over the bowling alley.

"What?"

"You are taller."

"Than what?"

"Than when you were before you disappeared."

"What?"

"Stand up." He stood.

She did. Slowly. Very warily she stood. That statement hadn't sounded like a request at all. It had sounded just like a cop order. She frowned at him.

Green set his hand, gently, on top of her head, and moved it, edgewise toward his face. The edge of his palm touched the tip of his chin. "You are taller." He tapped his sternum. "Before you were only that tall. I checked with a Doc Red and I know from ER at the hospital. He said that people do not grow like that after a certain age. We are all beyond that certain age." He sat down.

Janine sat, reached over and lightly touched one of those large hands lying so quietly on the table top. "It is really hard to explain."

He nodded.

"Errrrrr," she said "I'll have to talk with John first."

He nodded.

"O.K.?"

He nodded

"Nothing to say?"

"Nope."

"Don't look so blank, Green."

He pursed his lips. "You grew, right?"

"Yes," she whispered. "Sort of."

His face relaxed. "Janine?"

"What?"

"I like you a lot."

"What?"

"I don't like secrets."

She smiled at him. "I'll go up there on my lunch break

tomorrow. I am sure that Sandy will let me go."

"You ought to see my new bowling ball," laughed Sandy as she and Red rejoined them. "It is bright green."

"Well, partner," said Red.

"Right," agreed Green standing.

They all headed outside to Green's truck.

The new bowling ball wouldn't be ready for a week.

Grandeville. Tinker's Place.

They had a late dinner. Helf included. He hadn't eaten in quite a while.

Tinker leaned toward Chicken and whispered, "For such a little guy, he can certainly put it away."

"Most hungry, it do appear."

Ran, R-Bar, and Sha'gar had settled down. They just ignored their visitor. As much as possible.

Helf finished the last of everything. Fair Morn had left some of this and some of that, having recognized a large appetite when she saw one. She figured that she could always get a snack later.

"Mighty One?" asked Helf. "Will you aid me in reclaiming my lands and my people? And finding Nandau?"

"Ummm," replied Tinker, his mouth full of cake.

"We are getting out of that business," stated Chantal, for him.

Tinker nodded.

Helf's eyebrows shot straight up. "You sell your services?"

"I am not sure that I like that question," snarled Chantal,

wacking a piece off her slice of cake with her fork.

"Prince Helf," said Chicken, "her comment t'was but local idiom. We do be merchants not."

Helf jumped up, his chair flying backward. "How did you know that? I wear no insignia." He gasped at his behavior, and bowed to her. "Most Royal Queen."

"Do seat yourself." Chicken waggled one royal hand at him. And looked at Tinker. *Mere word choice accidental, Me'Lord.*

He nodded. And looked down the table at their guest.

"Let's take our cups and ourselves to the living room and you can tell us what has happened."

So they did.

And Helf did.

And eventually Tinker yawned. "Bed time. Helf, the Princess will show you a room you can use. Tomorrow we can discuss this among ourselves. O.K.?"

Helf stared at him.

"All right with you?"

Chicken stood.

"I am in your hands," stated the Helf. He followed Chicken from the room wondering if all that he had been told was true.

Everyone headed for their beds.

He rolled his head sideways. Glowing red numerals spoke to him. They said, 01:23.

She mumbled. She was lying stretched along his side, using his shoulder and arm for a pillow. One of her arms was thrown across his chest. One leg over his. "Mate'mer, shall I cast sleep?"

He sighed. "No."

She blew warmth into his ear.

"How are you feeling."

Her fingers tickled across his chest. "Ribs."

"Health," he grumbled. "After whatever that was that happened."

"I have been healthy long and long. All of us. All are healthy. As you should know."

"Ummmmm. I really don't want to go out there again."

"We know." She kissed him.

"You trying to distract me?"

She hitched closer. "Yessssssssssssss."

He rolled onto his side, sliding his free arm around her waist. "You're succeeding."

They had a late breakfast.

All of them.

And idled away the morning.

There were waiting for him.

They were waiting on him.

Everyone had felt his mind jitter and jump as Helf told them his story and had felt his worry build and billow outward. They were staying away mentally.

But they stayed close, physically.

As close as they dared.

Then they heard a car enter their parking space, stop, a door slam, and the car drive away.

A young woman hurried up and onto the rear deck and walked in their direction. She was wearing ratty jeans, an old corduroy shirt, one of his, and a bandana wrapped around her forehead. "Hello, Father, Mothers. Oh good, lunch time." She dropped onto the wooden bench next to him.

"I had a nice time." She had stayed overnight with some other young women, all fellow graduates of the local high school.

"Good." He smiled at her. "This is Je'leel, our daughter," he said to Helf.

Helf bowed to her, as much as he could while sitting down.

Then they heard another car drive into the parking are, the engine stop, a door open and bang shut.

"Now what's going on?" mumbled Tinker.

She hurried, almost ran, down the deck, the sun making the white steak in her dark brown hair even more startling than normal. "Tinker, we need to talk!"

She started to sit across the table from him, stopped, and stared. "What's that?" Grabbing a knife from the table top, she jumped back, and watched this strange looking person, very carefully.

"Helf," said Smoke.

"He is a Hephira." Messenger dumped a jar of pickles into one of the small bowls.

It reached from somewhere.

And sucked them away.

Chapter Two

Well, This Is A Surprise.

Wag Half. Not A Bad Day.

They landed in a large meadow of tall grass surrounded by towering grey green dark forest. One moment the meadow had been empty, with the exception of a few small creatures doing their usual running and scurrying about, and then the meadow and its inhabitants had visitors. The visitors swore violently in a variety of languages and dialects. The local residents ran for their lives.

She grabbed him and rasped, "JOHN?"

He held her and patted her on the back. "I don't have the foggiest idea." And looked at their surroundings. "Does anyone?"

Smoke grabbed Helf by the back of his neck and half carried, half pulled him through the waist deep, waist deep on her, grass to Tinker.

He glared at the Hephira. "Did you do this?"

Helf shook his head as Smoke released him. "No, Chosen One, this is beyond anything that I can do. I am a warrior. Only."

Je'leel stepped close to them. "Father, why are we here?"

"Beats me. You all right?"

"Yes." She stared at their surroundings.

Everyone clustered around him.

"Well," he grumbled, looking pointedly at two of their group. "Any witchy ideas?"

Ran shook her head. R-Bar glared at Helf.

Chicken strode over, grinning at him. "Do pray tell, Sweet Prince, what soft bundle do be that which thee do now so fiercely a'clench?"

He dropped his arms. "You O.K.?"

She nodded and stepped back. "Sorry."

"By George!" gasped Chicken. "Tis Janine!"

"Yeah," she replied. "Where are we? And how did I get here?"

"Oh boy," observed Chantal. "Are we ever in trouble." She looked at the others. "No weapons. And we are not exactly dressed for the occasion either."

"No problemo," said R-Bar. "Ran, Sha'gar. Help!" She grabbed their outstretched hands.

The air shimmered around them and everyone else. And all were dressed in their usual traveling clothes.

Chicken wore a sword hanging from her belt. She yanked it out and peered at it. "T'will do."

Ran nodded.

R-Bar stepped close to him. "Best we can do, Tink. Ran, Sha'gar, and I are always armed." She lifted his hands. "And you still have those rings."

He nodded. "As far as I know, only the red one does anything. Kartz' gift." He looked at her. "Well, kiddo, take us home."

She shook her head. "Can't. I don't know where we are."

Ran nodded.

"Smoke? Anything?"

"No, MindMate. We are alone." She pointed. "There is a path over there."

He sighed. "O.K., let's go that way then. It is all we can do. See if we can figure out where we are." He glanced sideways. "Janine, you all right?"

She nodded, swallowed loudly. "Yes." Her voice cracked. "Yes." And tried it again. "I will be all right. Just shock, that's all. I didn't want to ever do something like this again. Or experience it either."

They hurried toward the path and walked into the forest.

Grandeville. Sandy and Red's Home.

Standing on her tiptoes, she kissed him. "Red, she didn't come back from lunch."

He nodded. "We'll go take a look. This is the second time." He turned and walked down the front walk and opened the door and settled into the passenger seat of the black-and-white. It canted back to normal. "We'll go by your babe's place first. Then visit Tinker."

Green nodded, set his cup in the cup holder, and headed them down the street.

"Sandy said that she didn't return from lunch. Supposed to go visit with Tinker. And didn't phone either."

"So she is worried."

"You too, partner."

Green nodded. "Second time."

Grandeville. River View Hospital.

She tapped him on the shoulder, several times.

Raj had been staring into the binocular microscope for minutes.

"Talk now," she demanded.

Jerking his head back, he spun around, the stool top making soft grinding noises. "What? What's the matter, My Dear?"

"Bad bad," she snapped, looking wildly around the room. "The home of him." And yanked.

Grandeville. Tinker's Place.

They walked from the living room, down the hall, out through the tub room, and onto the rear deck. And startled the two huge men dressed in blue.

"Nobody home," said Raj.

"What are you doing here?" asked Green.

"Just popped in." Raj threw his arm around Kartz. "For a visit."

"Didn't hear you arrive."

"House is empty," stated Red. "No sign of them." They had already searched the inside. "But their rigs, truck and van, are still here."

"Rah-ther strange," drawled Raj, staring at the lunch sitting on the table top. He began to gather things together.

Red nudged Green. "Let's go, partner. See you later, Doc." They clumped down the deck and across the parking area to their cruiser.

"Wonder where they parked," said Green.

"Time to get back." Red headed their unit down the driveway and back toward town.

Raj carried things to the kitchen, put away what he thought needed to be put away, and returned. "Circe, what is happening here?" He looked around the deck and across the flower beds toward the first pasture.

"Bad bad." She stepped over and began to carefully examine the deck and the benches. And took a slice of bread to eat from the basket he hadn't carried away yet. Then she walked back. "Bad evil touched here."

"Are they all dead?"

She shook her head. "Nowp! Far gone."

"Where did they go?"

She shrugged. "Sister ask help." And returned them to the hospital, to his laboratory.

The birds thought that the left behind bread was just fine.

Wag Half. Not A Bad Day.

They were walking along a trail, walking mostly in silence. Mostly. The low grumbling was coming from him as he thought about their present situation and walked along near the back of the group. The more he thought about it, the more he thought that somehow Helf was responsible for it. If he had stayed away from them, they wouldn't be here. They would be at home, relaxing, having lunch.

Chicken carefully nudged Helf to the front of the line as they walked along the narrow trail.

Smoke and Fair Morn flanked Tinker. All of them, the rest of him, kept carefully away from his mind. They would just wait. Eventually he would calm down. But right now he felt hazardous.

Je'leel and Janine walked at the back of the group, talking softly.

Janine looked at her. "You are his daughter?" And took another, much more careful look, and nodded. "O.K., I can see the resemblance, especially around the eyes."

Sha'gar interrupted as Je'leel started to explain. "We are not met before. I am Sha'gar." She pointed. "He is muchly bothered." She waggled her arm at their surroundings, and whispered, "He worries greatly for our safety." And smiled, a soft half-smile.

"Good." Janine nodded. "I worry about that too. What's so funny?"

"We are very safe."

"I don't know about that." Janine's eyes danced as she tried to watch everything around them at the same time. She tucked the butter knife into her back pocket.

Je'leel looked at her, eyes roving over face and body. "Mother did a nice repair."

"What?"

"Beautiful," stated Je'leel.

Sha'gar frowned at her.

Janine stared. "Mother?" And took another look, even more careful than the last one, and gasped. "I don't believe any of this."

"Mother wanted to," explained Je'leel.

Sha'gar shrugged to herself. It was too late to do anything now. Janine was about to find out.

Je'leel laughed softly. "She surprised him."

Janine nodded, slowly she nodded. "Right! I will just bet that he was surprised. I am surprised." And began to ponder what kind of a story Green might believe. Perhaps something to do with the thyroid gland and special hormones, and things like that. He ought to accept that. After all, he and Red were bigger than the average bear. Or man.

Grandeville. Near the Grandeville Police Station.

"Maybe she is on a trip with Tinker et al," suggested Red at the end of their shift. It had been two days since they had been up to Tinker's place.

Green shook his head. "I think that she ran away cause I asked her how come she grew."

"Well," doubted Red.

"Said that she had to talk to Tinker first."

"See," said Red.

"Nope. I think that she would have phoned at least. Besides."

"What?"

"Awfully sudden trip. Bad coincidence."

"Um," conceded Red. "Let's go to my place and have a few."

"O.K."

Bahn Duhr Tohr. The Quarters of the Royal Advisors.

Ripple had leaped from her chair, causing Hanred to gasp

and to wheeze. He had been her chair. They had been on the couch.

"Not possible!" She stared at Reep. "Sha'gar was a magician. That stops the bearing of children for us. After a magician."

"Look, see," whispered the faintest of dark shadows.

Ripple did. Very, very carefully, very, very gently. And sucked in her breath. "Strange strange."

Reep handed her a sack. "You will help."

"Of course. But not yet. Closer to birth."

"Home," sighed nothing as she disappeared in a soft puff of black.

"Amazing." Hanred sat up.

Ripple walked back and sat. In his lap. "Hold me. I am nervous."

He did. And worried. It took much to make this witch nervous.

Wag Half. Not A Bad Day.

In the twilight of the day, they made camp.

They were in another large meadow. This one had short grass. Other than that, it was a twin to the other one.

The forest surrounding this clearing, this meadow, appeared to be identical to all the forest that they had seen as they had walked along.

Ran and R-Bar waved in food. Sha'gar made carpet layers and called in cushions to sit upon. Helf stared at it all.

"Do join us, Prince." Chicken patted a nearby cushion. "Tis wonderfully tasty a'smelling food." She winked at Tinker.

Je'leel sat by her father's side. She heaped food onto his plate. "Father?"

"Whoa!" He grabbed her hand and stopped her from adding any more to a badly overloaded dish. "I am not Fair Morn, you know. What?" He picked up something and chewed thoughtfully.

"Prander platz," explained R-Bar. She had called in that dish.

"Pretty good." He swallowed. And took another bite.

Je'leel leaned close to him. "Was it wrong for you and Mother to have a child?"

He choked. Chantal reached over and began to thump him on the back. "Supposed to chew your food thoroughly."

"Who said that?" he growled.

"Everyone knows that, Cowboy."

"Mother always said that," stated Je'leel. "Janine looked surprised and startled and shocked when I told her."

"Oh my," whispered Messenger, hitching herself back, hiding behind Smoke.

He sighed. Loudly. And looked over at Janine. She stared back. "I didn't say anything." She shook her head.

"Eat, Prince." Chicken patted Helf's thigh. He had stopped eating to watch Tinker.

"I was just surprised, that's all," explained Janine carefully, setting down the knife she had grabbed when he glared over at her. "After all, she kept me alive. And all that."

Her face flushed. "Just didn't realize that you and her were, umm, parents." She began to eat again, not looking up at him.

He threw an arm around his daughter's shoulders, and looked at the circle surrounding him. "Oh well, nothing to worry about." And laughed. "Other than getting back home again in one piece, that is."

R-Bar suddenly sat bolt upright, eyes flying wide, rounder and rounder, mouth dropping open.

"You have some hot sauce over there?" He looked at the food on her plate.

"Reep is . . . " gasped R-Bar.

"What?"

"Going to have . . . a daughter," gurgled the short witch.

"What?" It was his turn to look surprised.

"A mother?" Sha'gar stared at R-Bar. "My Mother?"

"Not supposed to happen," rasped R-Bar.

"Strange strange," agreed Ran, fully aware of the reproductive system of the Faan witch clan.

"I thought that the birth of a magician stopped that?" he asked.

"A new sister," muttered Sha'gar. "What will she be?"

"It has never happened before," stated R-Bar, loudly, trying to relax. "Ever. Almost."

"How do you know?" He sipped from his cup.

"Faan sisters always know. After a certain point." R-Bar nudged Ran. Ran shoved over a bowl of green things.

"How about," he suggested. "How about that we finish dinner, set up camp, and go to sleep?"

So that is what they did.

Grandeville. Red and Sandy's Home.

She ladled the heap of hash browns onto the plate, right next to the mound of scrambled eggs, and shoved the dish over in front of him. Then she refilled their cups and sat down, across the kitchen table from him.

"That is an interrogatory stare, counselor," he said as he spread jam on a piece of toast.

She nodded. "What do you think, Red?" She tried to keep her tone neutral, to not let the worry seep through. It didn't work.

He swallowed. "I think that she went with Tinker and his mob somewhere."

"But Green doesn't?"

"Nope." He dumped hot sauce on the potatoes. "Thinks that she split on him. Just because he asked her how come."

"What?"

"She was taller." He was watching her.

"Stop that. I hate that dead cop face stare look."

"Ooops." He smiled. "Sorry, babe." And laughed. "Don't worry." He thumped his stomach. "Gut feel says that she is O.K. and will turn up when they do."

He laughed again. "And crawl all over Green when she does." He stood and headed for their front door. "Now, if the downtown late night crowd will just behave until then, no one will wind up in the E.R."

She joined him at the front door and waited until he bent over so she could kiss him. "What?"

"He is not in a mood to take a lot of nonsense from anyone right now. He is liable to hit someone." He shrugged.

"I'll try to keep him quiet." A black-and-white pulled up to the curb.

And Red walked over, got in, and went to work.

Sandy went back into the house and the kitchen to make her supper.

Wag Half. A Rather Nice Night.

"Now what's going on?"

He grumbled and sat up. Janine had placed her sleeping bag right next to him and had hitched even closer.

"Don't mind me."

Smoke thumped down on his free side. "She is nervous, MindMate." And smiled, great gold orange eyes staring at him. "I will keep her from pouncing."

"He is safe from me," mumbled the sleeping bag. Janine was well inside it.

"Damn well better be," muttered Chantal. "Cause I am going to sleep on his other side."

Smoke relocated and let her.

The camp settled down.

In their usual disorderly way.

All sleeping around him.

Two witches and one magician cast protection all around them, including Helf.

Just in case.

Smoke told them there was nothing to worry about. But they did it, anyway.

Chapter Three

Lots Of Changes.

Grandeville. Tinker's Place.

They appeared.

In the living room, the large living room.

Sedeem and Farth.

They just appeared.

They were tan and looking very fit. Actually, he was the one that looked tan. Her normal bronze skin tone had darkened somewhat. They were here to visit and to relax.

"Feels empty," she observed. "Must be in town shopping."

They went to the corner bedroom, dumped their gear and headed down the hallway to the kitchen. And were greeted by a horde of very hungry cats.

Sedeem scooped up the white female and scratched her behind the ears. "OOOF. Certainly getting heavy. And big."

Farth stared at them. "These are those little things?"

"Yep. It has been some time since we last visited." She located the cat food and filled their dishes and made six cats very happy. And then she rummaged around in the refrigerator. "Let's have something to eat. I'll cook pork chops."

So she did.

And they did.

It had been long after dinner and they were sitting on the couch. Accompanied by six happy cats. She had been reading back issues of the local newspaper. She had found a stack of them in the recycle bin.

Farth had provided something large and warm to lean against. And a lap for a few of the cats.

"There is something wrong," she said.

"They appear healthy." He gently rubbed one cat.

"Dad and the Moms should be home." She moved two cats from her lap to his, causing some grumbling from the others already there. "Stay. I am going to take a look around. See if there is anything to indicate where they have gone."

She walked from the large living room and began to make a careful search throughout the house.

Farth entertained an overflowing lap. And patiently waited.

A long while later, she stomped back into the living room, the air crackling around her. "Husband, something vile was on the rear deck. I felt the trace. We must visit Reep. Dump those cats from your lap."

Farth did. And stood.

She yanked him away.

The cats looked around, curled up, and fell asleep.

Grandeville. Doc's Place.

J. C. was sitting in the kitchen, just finishing his pizza,

about ready to go to bed.

"Whoops," he said.

"Hello, Uncle. Where's Aunt?"

"Hi, Sedeem, Farth. Gone." He shrugged. He was used to his wife disappearing for varying periods of time.

Sedeem sat and grabbed one of J. C.'s forearms. "There is no one there. I think that something bad is going on."

"Ummm?"

"I do not know."

Grandeville. The Home of the Hardcastle Family.

She kissed her husband on the forehead. "I have to visit Ripple. Clan business. "

He looked up. He had been sitting in his over-stuffed chair, reading and thumbing through a thick sheaf of papers. "What?"

"I won't be gone long."

He frowned at her. "You going somewhere?"

She knelt in front of him, leaned forward, arms crossed over his knees and said, "Yes. There is clan business with Ripple."

"Oh." He squirmed. "Do I have to go?" He waggled the papers at her. "This is a very complicated business deal."

"No. I should only be gone for a few of your days."

"Oh." He smiled. "O.K."

She stood, And was clothed in a dark robe. And disappeared.

Shem walked in. "Where did Mother go?" He had felt her leave.

Tajaar leaned around the door jamb. "It is dinner food, true mate, Ka-Father."

As they settled around the dining room table, Shem looked at his Father. "What did she say?"

Hard shook his head. "Not much. Just some clan business.

"Oh."

Wag Half. Another Not Too Bad A Day.

It was after breakfast.

And they were still on the trail.

Again.

Hiking along.

The surrounding forest remained the same. Tall trees, set not all that far apart.

Dark.

Dim.

The thick foliage kept most of the light away from the ground. It was slightly damp in this forest floor environment. But it was open. Other than for the trees.

Janine, now walking by his side, poked him in the ribs. "Look at me!"

"Huh?"

"Look . . . at . . . me!"

His head swiveled in her direction. "O.K. Now what?"

"I am taller than I was before all that happened to us."

"I suppose."

"And, erm, more, ummm, well developed."

"I suppose."

Je'leel looked past him at her. "Mother did it. She told me. And you have a certain indjinn look."

"WHAT?" Janine stared at her.

"It is, ahhhh, umm, your, emm, chest," he mumbled.

Chantal laughed as she drifted back to walk alongside her friend. "Relax, Streak, Dat just thinks that all females ought to poke out." She laughed louder. And rolled her eyes dramatically.

"It is not funny," snarled Janine. "Green has noticed and is starting to wonder how I could grow taller and larger."

Chantal nodded.

"So, what do I tell him? How do I explain all this?" She waved her arm and then plucked at her shirt. "Especially taller?"

"Ummm," replied Tinker.

Chantal smiled. "Right. A little surgery isn't really all that unusual. But I have never heard of cosmetic surgery for taller."

"Ummmmm," said Tinker.

"You really like that guy, don't you?" asked Chantal.

Janine nodded. "He is very nice. And gentle. Under all that cop layer."

"Ummm," added Tinker.

"No," said Chantal, grinning at him. "You may not get her shirt off."

"What?" Janine glared at him.

Tinker glared at Chantal.

She laughed. "Just kidding."

"Not funny," he mumbled.

"I'll say," agreed Janine. She stared at her friend. "What

caused that remark?"

"Ummmm," said Tinker.

"What, ummmmmm?" asked Chantal sweetly. "Joke," she said to Janine.

"I will tell Green." He sighed. "It should be all right."

"You will?" Janine stared at him. "Not funny," she snapped at Chantal.

"Umm," replied Tinker. "Sure."

"John," said Chantal. "You'll have to include Red. Those two are damn near twins. Besides, Sandy already knows. And she will feel better if Red knows."

Janine twisted her head back and forth, between Tinker and Chantal. "Sandy knew all along?"

"Not about you," said Tinker.

"About us," explained Chantal. "She never forgot. Like Freddie. Or you."

Janine suddenly lurched and staggered, grabbing Chantal's arm.

They jolted to a halt. The rest crowded around.

"Me Lord?" Chicken gently touched the pale forehead. And watched the tears stream down Janine's face.

"I didn't want to believe it," she sobbed. "All those thoughts, all those ugly monsters. Pain."

Chantal grabbed her in a tight embrace, and murmured low, "It's O.K., Streak. You're among friends. And Green will understand." She looked past Janine at Tinker. "Really, he will."

He cleared his throat, "He'll understand. So will Red. If we ever get home, that is. Let's start walking." He certainly hoped those two cops would understand. But it was a crazy story. He had lived it. And it still sounded like a crazy story.

Bahn Duhr Tohr. The Quarters of the Royal Advisors.

Ramp sat and stared at her sister.

Ripple looked back. "Hum."

Reep nodded. "Soon."

Ramp looked back at Ripple. "How can this be possible?"

Ripple shrugged and poked Hanred in the stomach with one finger. She was sprawling across his lap. "This clever illusionist found in one of those many dusty tomes of his, an ancient record. It has happened before. In the long past past." She paused.

"What?" asked Ramp.

Ripple's lower lip pushed out. "No one knew what to do."

"Hum."

"My daughter will be well behaved and Faan proud," sighed the soft breeze. Reep gasped, bent over, and wrapped both arms around her middle. "She comes. Now!"

Ripple leaped to her feet and beckoned a door open. "In there," she commanded.

Ramp helped Reep into the room. The door closed behind them.

Hanred stood. And decided that it was time to spend some time in his library. There was more searching to be done. This new niece was going to pose some unusual problems for the Faan witch clan.

Wag Half. A Pretty Nice Day.

"There is a clearing just ahead, MindMate."

Smoke pointed at an angle in the trail just ahead of them. "Just around that bend. With local folk."

"Friendly?"

Smoke shrugged. "I think that we are going to be a surprise."

He laughed. "I suppose so." And looked to one side. "Janine, stick close to Chantal." And hurried to the front of their group to walk with Ran and R-Bar. "O.K., nothing dramatic until I say so. We want to get home, not start a fight."

And so, they rounded the bend, and then another bend and another bend, and there it was! A village.

It was a sprawlmg collection of buildings, more or less neatly arranged along several paths leading in several directions. So they walked in and wandered along, just being tourist.

"See anything familiar? Anyone?"

"Nope," replied R-Bar.

Ran shook her head. "No, Amtar. This is new for your Ran."

Chicken nudged Helf. "Prince, be you here afore?"

"No, Princess. This is a strange land for me also. Of course, we Hephira do not travel much."

"When in doubt, ask someone," Tinker mumbled mostly to himself, as he watched one of the inhabitants walking along the street, in their direction.

As the man came closer, Tinker headed him off. "Pardon

me, can you tell me where we are? We seen to have gotten lost."

The man smiled. "Yes, I can do that." He looked at Tinker and the rest. And stepped closer to Tinker, and indicated with his chin. "What is that you have with you, lost fellow?"

"Prince Helf. What is the name of this village and this world?"

The last portion of the question drew a puzzled look from the man. He gestured. "Here is named Wag Half." He waved his arm in a grand gesture. "There is named Off By A Merk."

"Merk," said Tinker.

"Chaptung Merk, Explorer and First Traveler."

"*Nope,*" said R-Bar.

Ran nodded.

Maybe, said Sha'gar. *Have to think about it.*

"Get many visitors?" asked Tinker.

"Now and then. Never lost."

Tinker smiled and shrugged. "We seem to do that a lot. Someplace where we can get a meal?"

The man pointed directions. "Gap's Gap." He fished a rectangular piece of metal from a pocket and shoved it at Tinker. "I am Gap. Show this. Good meal." And patted Tinker on the shoulder and started slipping through the group, heading in the same direction he had been going. "Good meal, lost ones."

"Thank you," called Tinker at his back.

"Let's eat," said Fair Morn.

"Yes," agreed Smoke.

"Right." Tinker headed down the street, turning as they had been directed and found Gap's Gap.

Bahn Duhr Tohr. The Quarters of the Royal Advisors.

"She is pretty," said Ramp, admiring Reeps' new daughter.

Ripple, Raft, and Reptar agreed.

All the other sisters would arrive soon to visit and to see this new member of the clan.

Rekel faded in, looked, and said, "Hum."

Ranna swirled in. She bent over to take a closer look. "Strange eyes." She had left Anjan on Doth Lamex and told her to not wander off.

Reep's daughter, unlike all the rest of the clan, had pale grey eyes, not the jet pools of the Faan clan.

"Pretty," sighed soft shadow.

"Of course," hastily added Ranna. One did not agitate new witch mothers.

Raft pushed closer to the bed. She was almost as short as R-Bar. And reached out with one tentative finger and touched the baby. "Not witch."

Reptar noted the skin color. "Not magician." Her sister, Ramp the magician, had the light bronze skin color that indicated magician, not the moonlight pale skin color of a witch. This child was just a rather pink average skin color of a non-magic being. It was most unusual. For a witch clan.

Ranna looked at Ripple.

"Speak!" said Ripple. "Eldest sister."

"That daughter is Theurgist."

Witches hissed and twitched. And quickly settled down. Reep was watching them very carefully. Her daughter was now inside her robe, feeding.

"Witch true," agreed Ripple. "Mine, even now, searches through all his tomes for guidance. She must be trained well. Faan trained."

All the sisters nodded, including Reep.

Hanred leaned through the doorway and cleared his throat, "Ahem."

"Husband?" asked Ripple.

"Not much yet." He held up one dusty, cautious hand. "But I did find a mention of a Theurgist Manse on Ka'k Down."

Witches nodded.

"Well," said Hanred, jerking back and away. "Back to work."

"Raft," said Ripple to her quick traveling sister.

Raft nodded. And was gone. On her way to Ka'k Down. To seek out the Theurgist Manse.

"They will help train," stated Ripple.

The sisters nodded. And began to work on the appropriate spells. Just in case the Theurgist Manse might be obstinate.

Wag Half. A Nice Day.

They were all sitting around a number of small tables in a cluster of shoved together tables.

The meal was finished and they were relaxing over cups of what ever it was that the local population consumed for relaxation.

"So," he asked. "Where do we go from here?"

"Bed," purred Sha'gar, nudging him gently.

"Reep birthed," announced R-Bar.

"Amtar, we must find someone who travels." Ran looked at R-Bar and Sha'gar. "We require directions."

He nodded. "Smoke, any way you might be able to locate such a person?"

"I can try. When all sleep."

Messenger poked R-Bar in the side. "What is our new niece named?"

"Sgenn," hissed R-Bar.

"How do you know that?" he asked.

"Just do," she grumbled.

"How about using the same talent to get us out of here?"

She glowered at him.

"Well?" He glowered back.

"Ptar rak rak tak!" she snapped

Ran's eyes flew wide.

Sha'gar gasped. Witches could be so vile at times.

"Wonderful," he mumbled.

Janine nudged Chantal. "How do you stand it?"

"It is all me," she whispered back. "It is just all me."

Sha'gar reached in a long wand and began to carve an elaborate design into the table top.

"Ummm?" he asked.

She shoved his arm aside and began to widen the design.

Ran and R-Bar edged their chairs back and away from what she was doing. They could smell the mage magic in the acrid fumes boiling up toward the ceiling.

Sha'gar suddenly tossed the wand somewhere, grabbed a jug and poured the contents into the central portion of the design. Lightening crackled red fire across the ceiling. She said something to the carving.

It began to foam. The table began to burn.

Everyone leaped away, knocking over chairs, banging into other pieces of furniture. The two servers standing behind the counter, turned and fled out a side door, too frightened to scream. Just running, running, for their lives.

Sha'gar stepped into the fog mist shape and screamed at them, "IN! IN! QUICKLY!" She grabbed him by the shirt front and yanked him in and off his feet.

Ka'k Down. The Theurgist Manse.

The young woman in the flowing grey robes bowed deeply to the four figures in the golden robes.

"Ka'k a'qtar, ad'en nar b'dar dar." The words were the final phrase of the long and convoluted ritual of learning. Her tone was rigidly formal, her demeanor was just so, her gaze steady.

The Four smiled and nodded at her.

"We are few in number," said one. "Your training has been long. Your study has been hard. Your experiences have been hazardous."

"You are alive," said another. "Therefore, you have learned what you must know, what our lessons expressed."

The third nodded. "Now you must leave us. And return to your own kind. You may tell your Aunt that she did well to ever find us." She held out a glowing golden wand. "Give this to her."

The student in grey stepped forward, took, and slipped the wand up her left sleeve.

The fourth twisted a golden ring from a finger, reached out, took the student's hand and slipped the ring on the proper finger. "This is now your's. It is us as well. All, the few, who see and recognize this ring will understand. Remember the Values we follow. Strength and Restraint. Quiet Power."

She bowed deeply. "I am your words."

"We are always here. For you."

They were gone.

She was gone.

The great hall stood empty and filled with the quiet of vacant.

Grandeville. Riverview Hospital.

She tapped his arm as he leaned and peered into the eyes of his patient. He straightened up and looked at her. She beckoned him to the hall outside the room.

"Back in a tic," he told the patient.

Out in the hall, he leaned against a wall. "What?"

"Bad under magic. The sister Reep house." She tugged at his arm.

"We can't go now. We have to see to our patients."

"After," she demanded.

He nodded.

They went back to their rounds.

The Doctor and his Nurse.

Handat.

They were in the bottom of a v-shaped valley. It was dry. Bare. Sere. And arrow straight. Either end of this narrow gash through the landscape faded into the distance.

"O.K.?" he asked. "Now what's going on?" He stared into her eyes. She stared up into his. He had knocked her over when she had yanked him forward.

"Hum," she said, moving slightly.

"Behave! And answer the question."

"Shall we walk down this drainage?" drawled Chantal. "Or are you going in for spectator sport now, Cowboy?"

"Most crude," observed Chicken.

Ran and R-Bar stood side by side. And glared. And hissed. At Sha'gar.

"It was a seek elseplace spell. I think that we are now in Handat. At far end, there is a trading village town." She pointed awkwardly in the correct direction.

He rolled off and sat up. "Could have said something first."

"Yesssssss," agreed R-Bar. Ran nodded.

He stood, reached down, and hauled Sha'gar to her feet. "So you know this place?"

"Yes, Mate'mer."

"Which means that you should know how to get us home from here? Right?"

"Yes. Mate'mer."

He wrapped her in his arms and kissed her.

"Hum, hum, hum."

"That can wait," snapped R-Bar. Ran nodded.

"Oh, boy," gurgled Messenger. "We are going home."

As they started down the valley, Helf was the only one that didn't look happy.

"Don't worry," said Fair Morn. "After we get home, we

will figure out some way to help you."

Grandeville. Doc's Home.

She stood there, gently poking him in the side, just below the rib cage.

He was sitting, staring into nowhere. Thinking.

They were in the library. At his desk.

He was sitting, leaning back in his chair at a precarious angle, in the middle of a project for Doc, thinking it through.

She was standing by his side, trying to get his attention. At times it was very slow work. When he was thinking it was almost as if he wasn't there.

Then she saw it happen. Those small movements around and in his eyes that told her he was coming back. His chair thumped back on all four legs.

"What?" He turned and looked at her, eyes still unfocused, but rapidly beginning to see the outside world again. Then he smiled, hooked his hands around her waist, and tugged her forward. "Hi, there."

"Husband. A daughter is here."

"Which one?"

"Sgenn."

"Who?"

She hadn't told him. Or that she had been very worried about this strange event.

He looked deep into her dark eyes. "We have another daughter?"

She nodded.

"Why is this daughter a surprise?"

Soft shadows whispered to him, "I will tell you later." She

waggled one finger.

"I am Sgenn, Father."

"Holy cow." He laughed. "Another heart breaker."

"A strange oath." She frowned. "I do not have creature's internal organs injured."

He laughed again. "I meant that you very pretty."

"Unless they deserve it," she added.

He peered over Reep's shoulder. "Grey? Everything?"

"I am rejected?"

"No."

"She is Theurgist," breathed gentle whisper, now sitting on the lap he had quickly made for her.

He beckoned her to come closer. Sgenn did.

"What's that?" he asked Reep.

So she told him. Sgenn added explanations here and there as necessary.

"Certainly sounds different to me. You gonna hang around for awhile?"

"Theurgists have no need to do wander," sighed the darkness in his lap. "Much."

"Mother told there is a free room," she added. "Once Szaifeh's. Once Sha'gar's."

"Sure." He smiled at both of them. "Be nice for a change."

"May I meet my sisters?" She stood very close to her parents, one hand gently touching his arm.

"Szaifeh is with her husband, a Vander warlock, probably on Magevern, and Sha'gar is off somewhere with Tinker et al." He nudged Reep. "Let's go to the kitchen and get something to eat. I'll cook. Doc's project can wait. Boy, is he going to be surprised."

So they did.

Go to the kitchen.

And cook.

And eat.

And surprise Doc.

Chapter Four

O.K. Now They Know.

Handat.

Sha'gar suddenly lurched and stumbled. She turned to look at him, slowly she turned, and looked, her face going slack. She worked her mouth but no sounds escaped. She frowned. *HELP!* Her cry echoed through their minds.

He jumped forward and grabbed her as she sagged. "Now what?"

Smoke hurried up and stared. "She is exhausted."

"What?"

The rest clustered around.

"Spell spent," explained R-Bar. Ran nodded.

Sha'gar mumbled something low in her throat that no one could understand. In the distance something exploded.

Fair Morn lifted Sha'gar and cradled her in her arms, easily holding her. "I will carry her, One."

Sha'gar's arms hung loosely, her head rolled against Fair Morn's chest as she went limp. Her eyes were open, staring, seeing nothing.

Chantal stepped close, reached over and felt for a pulse in the magician's neck. "Certainly looks dead. She's out like a light."

He looked at the witches. "Now what's going on?"

"Curmmmmmmmm," said R-Bar.

"Zzzzzzzzz," added Ran.

"Spit it out!"

"Well, Tink," began R-Bar. "I don't know much about magicians, you know."

"True, Amtar. Witches really don't know much about magicians. They are rather strange folk."

"But," continued R-Bar, before he could say anything. "I think that she used up all her energies to get us to here."

"True," agreed Ran.

"And," added R-Bar. "I don't know how or what she did."

"True," agreed Ran. Magician incantations were rarely understood by witches who used spells of a different structure. Or vice versa.

"Can you get us home from here?"

"Yep." R-Bar nodded. "Can now. Been thinking about it."

"Do it. Now!"

R-Bar grabbed one of Ran's hands.

And twisted them away,

Grandeville. Tinker's Place.

They were in the living room, the large living room.

Janine had driven back to town the moment that they had arrived back home.

Sha'gar was lying on one of the couches, a blanket tucked around her. She was sitting up, looking unhappy.

Chicken was sitting , next to her, spooning thick soup into her mouth. "Eat it all!" she commanded.

"Kaz kik tik," she grumbled. But did as she was told. Barley soup was not a favorite.

R-Bar and Ran walked in through the front door, cackling, a very happy pair of witches.

He looked up from the book that he was reading.

"Protection," stated R-Bar.

"Many layered," added Ran.

Helf shifted in his chair and looked at Chicken. "Princess, how do I leave here?"

She leaned sideways, reached out, and patted his thigh. "Fret not, Prince. We will see you on your way."

"Relax," grumbled Tinker. "We have only been home for two days. When Sha'gar is fully rested we will take care of your problem."

"Oh my," gasped Messenger. "Gosh." She had felt his irritation anger build.

Je'leel refilled his cup. "Father?"

"Nothing," he mumbled.

Chicken looked at Smoke who winked and said in all their minds except for his. *I think that he needs some distraction.*

Chantal nodded. *That's a new word for it. Draw straws.*

Messenger bounced to her feet and hurried to the kitchen. And returned, clenching a number of straws, yanked from the kitchen broom, in her hand. Giggling loudly.

He watched her moving around the room, allowing each one to take a straw.

"Now what's going on?"

"You don't get one," Messenger said to Sha'gar. "You are resting. Really really."

"Hak karkle," suggested Sha'gar.

Ran gasped.

"Crude," growled R-Bar, yanking a straw from Messenger's out thrust hand.

"I won, I won, I won," chortled Messenger, twirling around and around. "Fair and square. Really really."

"What?" He was now frowning at everyone.

Fair Morn slid sideways, making a space next to him.

Messenger dropped into the opening and batted her eyes at him. "Purr, purr, purrrrr," she purred.

He sighed. "You gonna tell me?"

She dragged one of his arms up and around her shoulders and leaned close and whispered in his ear, "You need distraction. That's me." And kissed him.

"Oh? Whose idea is this?"

"Mom's."

Smoke leered at him. And laughed. "Mother knows best."

"You have a one-track mind, Big Cat."

Dat walked along the top of the couch back. "Kickle, kickle, kickle."

"What is so funny?" he demanded.

Dat sat on Fair Morn's shoulder and looked at Messenger. "I do not understand how he could have thought that you were a young male. You are very nicely formed for a short person of modest proportions."

"I am taller than R-Bar."

"I am not short," snarled the short witch.

"It was her native costume," he grumbled, glaring at the indjinn. "All that I could see was her face. And that was painted.

She was rather androgynous looking and spoke in a special tone of voice."

"He was surprised." Messenger giggled. "Really really."

"Nasty frown," observed Dat.

"He does that a lot," explained Fair Morn. "Doesn't mean anything."

"Merde," he mumbled, slipping his arm free, slumping deeper into the couch, and opening his book.

"Not fair!" Messenger jabbed him in the ribs with her elbow.

"OUCH! Stop that! What?" The book snapped shut.

"I won!" she stated firmly, giving his ribs another jab. Batting her eyes wildly at him, she gushed, "My Hero!"

He stared at her.

"You are," she carefully explained. "You are supposed to carry my compliant self away, in your strong manly arms, to some secret spot."

Chicken returned to the living room, having slipped away during all the conversation, and handed a bottle of champaign to him. "We do Ourself now declare, Most Royally, fair small living room do be A Most Secret Spot." She kicked the bottom of one of his feet. "Haul thy winnings thence, Handsome Prince, Great Hero!"

"Goofier and goofier," he mumbled, standing, scooping Messenger into his arms and heading for the small living room. She clenched the bottle by the neck.

Chantal yanked the door open and waved them grandly inside. And slammed it shut. "I'd say that he is already pretty relaxed. Let's go get our traveling gear organized. I'm gonna wear my gun until this is over. Don't want to leave home without it!"

Helf looked around the room and wondered what was happening this time. He didn't really understand their behaviors at all.

Somewhat later.

Her eyes flashed green as she hiccuped.

"Nice color."

They were sprawled on the large couch, gazing vaguely toward the large bay window.

A hand reached over the top of the couch and dropped another bottle onto them.

It landed on his elbow. "HEY!"

"We do but bring thee a'new." Chicken crawled back toward the door. She had decided standing up or looking over the top of the couch would be impolite.

"Oh boy," giggled Messenger, working the foil off the top of the bottle. The cork blew toward the junction of the wall and ceiling just above the door. "OOOOOOOPS!"

"Most welcome," replied Chicken as she gently shut the door behind herself, taking the cork with her.

"They're gonna be drunker than skunks." Chantal shoved the gear into the proper piles for traveling.

Smoke began stuffing food packets into the correct pockets on their packs. "We can dump blankets over them, later."

"You going to take advantage of me now that you have plied me with inhibition lowering beverages?"

"Might as well."

"Eeeeeeeek!" She squeaked, twisted around and kissed him. "I am so glad that you visited my elseplace."

"Worked out all right." He laughed as she glowered at him. So, he took advantage of her again.

"Eeeeeeeeek!"

"I am glad also, kitten."

She turned and took the bottle from his free hand and tilted it up. And then leaned back inside his arms. "I like everything about being us, and here, and . . . and everything."

"Me too. Well?"

"What?"

"Aren't you supposed to be distracting me?"

Smoke laughed, stood, and stretched. "Our kitten is a very enthusiastic distractor."

Chantal stood and headed for the door. "Let's get a cup of something. No hurry. Between her and The Princess he will be immobilized all day tomorrow."

Smoke threw a comradely arm over her shoulders and strolled with Chantal to the kitchen. "Sha'gar isn't going to be ready for traveling for another day or so anyway."

Finkle's Beek. A Faan Witch Training Spot.

Witches scattered in all directions, hissing and snarling. Except for one. That one was her cousin. The others were her Aunts.

Horror stood there and licked its lips. And reached for

the only witch that it could see.

"NO!" The command halted its motion. It was a voice that it could not disobey. She stepped over and kissed her cousin on the forehead. "Kak kak mer kar," she grumbled.

"Very coarse," observed her cousin, wondering where she had learned such witch vile expressions.

"They were making kar tar comments."

"Just being witch," suggested her cousin, plucking at her own black blouse.

"Hum." The horror was sent away. She nodded. "I shouldn't have done that."

The cousin stepped close, hugged and kissed her. "They will understand."

Grandeville. Green's House.

She knocked on the front door. Firmly. But gently. Until the door swung in and open.

"Hello," she said, all soft voice. "Wanna talk?"

He filled the doorway and stared down at her. "Sure," he rumbled. And backed up. "In the kitchen."

After pouring two cups full, he slid one across the table top to her and sat. He was wearing pajamas and a green robe. It was late afternoon, almost time for him to be up, getting ready for work.

She cleared her throat. "You might not believe what I am going to tell you, but it is true, absolutely true, every word."

He slowly nodded, watching her carefully.

She took a sip. Nodded back, and took a deep breath. "O.K. It all started up at Tinker's house."

Grandeville. Tinker's Place.

Fair Morn joined Smoke and Chantal and said to Chantal. "Janine said that she was going to tell Green everything." She made a sandwich and sat at the table. "Everything. "

He yanked the comforter around and mumbled, "Let's take a nap."

Messenger hiccuped. "Wumberful idea." She squirmed into a more comfortable position. And fell asleep.

He was right behind her. Sound asleep. Two breaths later.

Grandeville. Green's House.

"Ahhh," he said, filling their cups. Again. "That is pretty far fetched." And lowered himself into his chair.

"Well," she snorted. "I can't show you my scars cause there aren't any."

Green nodded.

She frowned, wrinkles forming around her eyes. "O.K. Let's go up there and talk to Tinker." Jumping to her feet, she headed for the front door.

"Just said that it was pretty far fetched," he rumbled, standing. "Gotta change into some clothes first."

"I'll wait on the front porch steps." She banged out the door.

So did the door.

Bang.

Shut.

Behind her.

Grandeville. Tinker's Place.

The sports car skidded to a halt in the parking area.

"Chantal's car, right?" He threw open his door and eased himself from the rather small, for him, seat.

"Right." She switched off the ignition and jumped out. "Let's go." She headed for the back door.

"S'blood!" snarled Chicken. Smoke had just told her who the visitors were. "Me'Lord do be fit not for a'visiting."

"We'll have to talk with them." Smoke ordered Dat to go back inside her ring house. Then she beckoned Je'leel to come over and to sit next to her side, but not to say anything.

Fair Morn adjusted the comforter around Sha'gar and then sat by her feet.

Helf was told to stay in a guest bedroom.

"John's napping," said Chantal as she ushered Janine and Green into the large living room.

"Indeed," added Chicken. "Most exhausted."

"I told Green everything," stated Janine as she dropped into a chair. "He doesn't believe me."

Green sat in one of the couches.

"Hum." R-Bar chewed on her lower lip as she and Ran joined the group and looked at Smoke who looked at Green and said, "Janine is telling the truth."

"She said that Sandy would tell me something similar."

Smoke nodded.

"What about Red?"

"He doesn't know," said Smoke. "She is our attorney."

"Un huh."

Smoke smiled.

Green looked at all the staring eyes and back to Smoke. "Janine said that a demon of some sort smashed her up and that somebody named Dat fixed her up, rebuilt, um, things. No. hospital, no nuthin."

"Most true," agreed Chicken.

"Mother is very good at it." Je'leel smiled at him.

Green looked at her. "Your Mother?"

Je'leel nodded. "Yes."

"Uh huh."

Smoke leaned forward, just a little, eyes totally focused upon the large man. "What will you do if we convince you of the truth of Janine's story?"

"Me?"

"Yes."

Green smiled. "Buy her dinner and some roses."

Janine stared at him, her mouth falling open.

R-Bar, get Dat out here, full size. Smoke winked at Janine.

Dat walked in from the hall, dressed in jeans and corduroy shirt, wearing sunglasses. "I am Dat." She sat on one arm of the couch and looked at Green. "I repaired Janine. She was messy."

"Repaired?"

"Yes. And made her a little taller." Dat cleared her throat. "And some other things."

"He didn't ask about that!" snapped Janine.

"What kind of a Doc are you?"

"Indjinn." Dat smiled at him.

"Interesting teeth."

"Beautiful," replied Dat, smiling even wider. Her upper canines poked down over her lower lip. Then she frowned at him.

"What?" asked Green.

"Why don't you believe what my Great Master's beautiful houris are telling you?"

"Who?"

"You."

"Ahh, Great Master?"

Chantal laughed. "She means John.

"Houris?"

"Us."

"Oh. Sure. Whatever."

Chantal could see the question in his eyes. "Strange as it seems, everything that Janine said is true. John just doesn't think that telling everyone was, is, such a good idea." She laughed. "Because it sounds so crazy."

"Uh huh. Why now?"

"Janine's fault. She really likes you and knows that you are bothered by her, ahh, physical changes. And John agreed that you should know." She nodded at him. "And now you know."

"Uh uh." Green shifted in the couch. "Except that I do not know anything. Yet."

"Ik dik dik," grumbled R-Bar, wondering which spell to dump on him. Ran nodded.

"Shhhhhh," hissed Chantal at them.

Je'leel stood. "Come with me, please. To the kitchen." She headed that way. "I do not require anyone else." Dat smiled at her.

Green heaved himself up and followed her.

In the kitchen, she stopped in front of one of the range tops, turned on a front burner, and pointed at the blue flame. "Put your finger in there."

"Nope."

"Why not?"

"Burn my finger."

"And if I do?"

"You will burn your finger."

"Do not move." She smiled at him and waggled her finger back and forth in the flame.

He reacted instantly. She was yanked back and away almost before her finger had touched the flame.

"Put me down."

"Sorry." He did.

"Do not do that again." She frowned at him.

He shrugged. "Your finger."

"Yes, it is. And I do not require rescuing. You just watch."

She stepped sideways so he could And slowly wiggled her finger back and forth in the propane fire.

Green watched, carefully he watched.

"Am I burning?"

"No."

"Should I be burning?"

"Yes."

She wiggled her finger around in the blue flame some more.

"Explain please."

"I can't."

"I am the daughter of Dat."

"Uh huh."

"Indjinns do not burn." She smiled up at him. "True?"

"Sure."

"I am the daughter of him."

"Who?"

"John Tinker."

"Oh?" He took another look, a more careful look, at her face. And nodded. "I see."

"What Janine told you about my Mother is as true as my finger." She was still waggling in around in the flame.

"O.K. You can stop."

She turned off the burner. "Now I will tell you about my Mothers, the eight of them who are him."

And she did. After starting the coffee.

They brought the coffee pots into the living room.

Je'leel and Green poured and then they sat down.

Green reached over and folded one gigantic hand over one of Janine's. "Other than height, and, ah, some other things, you still you?"

"Sure am. Just me."

He nodded. "Good." Then he carefully looked at the rest of them, weighing, appraising, seeing them with a new vision. "Really hard to believe."

Chantal laughed. "What I say every morning." She stood and walked over to her friend, bent and kissed her. "Well, Streak, that takes care of that."

Janine dragged one sleeve across her eyes. "Thanks."

"Sure."

"You might want to stay in town for a few more days. We don't really know what is going on. Yet."

Janine nodded. "I'll phone." She jumped to her feet and poked Green with one finger.

"Let's go."

He stood and smiled at them. "Unbelievable." And laughed. "But I like you guys anyway." He turned to go, turned back. "Oh. I won't tell anyone. Not even Red." He hurried after Janine.

Grandeville. Red and Sandy's Home.

He thumped into the house, ready for dinner. And kissed his wife, who was preparing her breakfast. And his dinner.

She filled his cup as he sat down. Then sat down across the table from him and smiled.

He looked the question at her.

"Cause you look so happy."

"Green and his jock babe are a thing again," he rasped. He always rasped. It was his normal tone of voice, a left over from his football playing days. An injury to the throat.

"Janine. Not jock babe."

"Sure," he started eating.

"What happened?"

He shrugged. "Talked. Green said that they talked." He smiled at her. "He said that he would believe anything that she ever told him. Forever and forever." His eyes squinted as he saw her expression subtly change. "It was private, Sandy. Is private."

She nodded, reached over and patted his hand. "Of

course." She stood, walked around the table, and wrapped her arms around him, at least as much of him as she could, and kissed him. "Good night, Red. See you later."

She hurried off to dress and go to her office. Her day was just beginning.

Grandeville. Chen's Chinese.

They sat in a corner booth, finishing lunch. The restaurant was directly below Sandy's office.

"So Green knows all about them?"

"Sure does," replied her secretary. She refilled her tea cup.

"Well, Streaker, think he will be able to not tell Red?"

Janine shrugged. "Why don't you tell Red? I am sure Green won't. He will feel that it is private."

Sandy nodded. "I guess that I will have to go visit my clients and see what they have to say."

Janine grabbed her arm. "Stay away from up there for awhile. For a few days."

Sandy jerked. "What?"

So Janine told her what Chantal had said.

Grandeville. Tinker's Place.

He slumped deeper into the couch.

And grumbled.

"I am not going anywhere. Or doing anything. Today."

"Me neither," stated Messenger, slumping alongside him.

Sha'gar joined them, slipping down so she could lean against his free side. "Me, also."

"Distracted to inertness," observed Chantal.

"You rest," ordered Smoke as she tossed a blanket around Sha'gar.

"Kak tak," she mumbled.

Chicken filled everyone's cups. "We will work elsewhere." And laughed. "We will bring most nourishing foods a'lunch."

So they did.
Went elsewhere.
And worked.
Until lunch.

Fair Morn put Helf to work. Planting shrubs. For him it was a new experience. A Prince didn't do things like this. Normally. But, as he was rapidly discovering, normally didn't seem to mean the same thing to The Chosen One and his Warriors.

Everything here was so strange and so different from what he had been told or thought. But they had managed to return to their own elseplace. And while he was warrior trained, these folk made him uneasy. There seemed to be a rather casual violence in many of their behaviors, especially that slim warrior Princess and those magic users.

Much Later In The Day.

It was late afternoon. Long shadows were creeping across this piece of the world. In the large living room, he woke, and yawned, and stretched.

Messenger wasn't there. Somehow, he had managed to

topple over and was now being used by Sha'gar as a large hot water bottle. Or something. She was radiating more heat than he was.

"Umm gummm," he mumbled, deciding that he did feel pretty good. So did Sha'gar.

"Mate'mer," she mumbled in return, as she twisted into a more comfortable position. And kissed his cheek.

Chicken walked in, carrying a large pot and two cups. "We do prepare most fine a'meal, Sweet Prince." She waited until they both sat up before handing them filled cups.

He nodded. "You need a sword for dinner? Something trying to escape from the kitchen?"

She beamed at him. "All do now believe as do fair Chantal. We do be arm'd till we all do Ourselves decide for to when depart." She grimaced. "T'was most unpleasant for to be so ill prepared in last bit."

Smoke joined them. She had a shoulder holster strapped on, the big 45 nestled under her arm pit, black handle gleaming soft polish. It was a gift from Master Chen.

"Looks like the beginning of a really low budget film."

"Taking no chances, Cowboy," drawled Chantal, dropping into a chair. Her long-barreled revolver, rigged for a cross-handed draw, hung from her belt. Two ammunition belts crossed her chest and each other.

He laughed. "You gonna wear a big sombrero too?"

"We want you to get into your black duds and get that evil sword of your's. Before dinner." She ran one finger along an ammo belt. "We are getting nervous with you being so unprepared. Now? Please?"

He reached out, mind touching minds. And felt the truth of her statement. "O.K."

Surging to his feet, he walked across the room and grabbed the great two-handed sword leaning in the corner. "Come on, you." And headed for his bedroom to change clothes.

He watched them file in for dinner. And smiled.

Chicken was still wearing her rapier. And had added two knives. One on her hip, one strapped to the outside of her left thigh.

Chantal had also added a knife strapped to the outside of her right leg.

Smoke still packed her pistol.

Messenger had put her hair into a fancy roll. A long black wand was poked from it.

Fair Morn wore her space cannon, as always, on the outside of her right thigh in its special holster.

Ran, R-Bar, and Sha'gar had wands stashed somewhere.

He looked at them as they sat and then at the expression on Helf's face, and laughed. "Certainly a lethal looking bunch, all right."

His great sword stuck to his back in its usual place. The hilt and some of the blade poked up past his left shoulder. He had to sit somewhat forward in his chair. It was uncomfortable leaning back against that thing.

He nodded at them and took a serving from a platter and passed it to Chicken. "Now if we only knew where we were going or what we were doing, we'd be in pretty good shape."

Chapter Five

Life's An Adventure.

Grandeville. Sandy and Red's Home.

"Pretty far-fetched story, babe."

He finished his breakfast and looked at his wife carefully.

"Don't give me that cop look," she snapped.

"Sorry. Habit." He stretched one arm over the table and took her hand in his, gently. "I'll just go up there and talk with them."

She shook her head. "Janine said to stay away from there for a couple of days. Said that we shouldn't get involved."

He smiled. "Green can come along."

"NO!"

He ducked his head.

She grabbed his hand in both of her's. "I know that you and Green don't worry about most things, but the stuff that they get into, you two have never met before." She squeezed. "And you do not want to either."

He nodded. "Sure, babe."

"Don't you dare!"

"Sandrew," he began, instantly making her start to worry. "I understand that you believe everything that you told me. But! It is still hard to accept." He held up his free hand, cutting off her comments. "And I bet that goes for Green also."

She yanked her hands away and jumped to her feet. "Stay there!" It was an attorney command. And hurried into the living room and back again, carrying the phone which she was dialing as she walked. And handed it to him. "Here." And sat and listened to his side of the conversation.

"Hi, Green."

"Yah."

"Janine talk to you, buddy?"

"Uh huh."

"Uh huh."

"Indeed she did."

"You do?"

"O.K. Later."

He handed her the phone. "She did. And they talked with a bunch of Tinker's babes. And Green accepts it all. Said that I wouldn't believe it. And that he told me that the other evening."

Standing, he hooked an arm around her waist as she joined him. "Guess we will have a lot to talk about this evening. He looked at his watch. "Time to go. Almost. You caught him on the way out the door."

She kissed him as he bent over. "Uh huh, what he said." And kissed him again. "See you in the a.m."

"Uh huh."

Grandeville. Tinker's Place.

The police cruiser slipped into a space next to the large van, headlights off, motor going off.

Two very large policemen got out and looked around.

"No lights on," observed Red.

Green looked at his watch. "Pretty early bed-time for them. It is only eleven. Let's go around to the rear deck."

They started that way. "Feel quiet to you?"

"Sure does, partner." Red rolled his shoulders. It was a little loosening up movement as they walked up to, onto, and down the deck.

Green opened the side door. And eased silently inside. Red followed. In the dim light they slipped on silent feet toward the living room doorway near the end of the hall. And looked in and then entered. And looked around.

"Nobody at home all right," said Green.

"Did they say anything about this?" asked Red, meaning the empty house and his wife and Janine.

"Nope."

There was a sudden pop of blue light. Then the room was illuminated with a soft yellow glow.

Two young women stood there and looked at them. One was dressed all in black. The other all in grey. Both carefully looked over the two huge men.

"Are you the estate paladins?" asked the one in black.

"No," replied Green. "We are G.P.D."

"Friends of Tinker's," added Red, shifting to one side, giving Green room to move. "Who are you?"

"Where are our Uncle Aunts?"

"Yessssss."

"No idea," stated Red. "We just got here." He moved a little more to the side.

"How did you get here?" asked Green. "And what was that blue stuff?"

One looked at the other. "Mother said that it was a primitive place."

"Hum. Mother told not."

"Where shall we look?"

"Mother said that The Mirf of The Monetary Control is a great friend of Uncle. And that M.C. watches, and records, everything."

"There, then?"

And away they went.

Winl Fzar.

"O.K., where are we?"

He looked around at the dense forest surrounding the small meadow opening where they stood. They had come from Grandeville, witched in by R-Bar and Ran.

Ornate arches, facing each other from opposite sides of the clearing, indicated where the trail entered and left. The trail was paved with large, greenish stone blocks.

Helf smiled. "We are on the edge of my lands." Then he frowned and glared at Tinker. "Why are we here? Nothing but dark evil lives that way." He pointed at one of the arches.

R-Bar stomped over and hanged him on the chest with a cracking bronze wand. "Do you want your lands back? Or not?"

He leaped backward. "CAREFUL!"

"Umm, kiddo?" Tinker stared at her.

She whirled to face him. "What?"

"You planning on just marching in and running the bad guys out of town?"

She nodded. "Yep."

"Let's talk about that."

"Sure." She sat on the pavement, and patted it. "Lots of room."

They all gathered around.

And sat on the pavement.

And they talked about it.

Dol Spar. An Office in Monetary Control.

"Hoo boy! A crowd of four!"

Mirf waggled one hand at her assistants who had leaped from their chairs, ready to attack these strangers that had suddenly appeared inside Mirf's office, telling them to remain calm.

"I am Mirf," stated Mirf. "Who are you?" She leaned back in her chair. "What are you?" She recognized the witch garb. Only.

"Sorry sorry," said the witch, waggling one hand at the various startled faces. "Mother said that you would help us, if we asked.

"So name me a mother. Or two."

"Faan witch Ripple."

"Faan witch Reep."

"Oi vay!" Mirf smacked her forehead with the palm of one hand. "Those mothers." She looked at her assistants. "So tell me trouble in cute packages isn't standing right here."

Then she looked at the two men.

"Big trouble. Big big trouble. Huge colossal trouble. So who, or what, are you two?"

"I'm Red," rasped Red. "He's Green. We are with the Grandeville Police Department. These two babes snatched us from Tinker's living room, somehow."

He looked at the two young women. It was a very blank cop look.

Mirf banged the top of her desk with the flat of her hand. "So put them in jail later." She looked up. "So you two shiksas can tell me your names. Then maybe we have a little business to do?"

"Faan witch Ripple daughter Sook."

"Faan theurgist Reep daughter Sgenn."

"Okey dokey. What help, Sweet Cheeks?" Mirf waggled her hands at both. "So sit, sit, sit, sit. That's one sit for each. And looking at me that way gets you bubkes."

As they sat, Mirf introduced her assistants. "Fred and Quan. She is a suk-dragon. He is a human, more or less, I think."

She banged something on her desk top and told her startled clerk, "Something to drink for everyone. For four other everyones."

After the drinks were fetched and served and everyone held a large mug, she leaned forward and peered at them. "So let's shmooz."

And laughed, loudly. "We can discuss bribery later."

Grandeville. A Small Apartment.

She banged, kicked, pounded, and rattled the door and the doorknob, until the door was opened.

Janine waved her inside. "Do you realize what time it is?" She was wearing an enormous t-shirt that had printed across the front in large purple letters, "So who worries?"

"One-thirty a.m.," replied Sandy, grabbing her friend by the shoulders. "Streak, they are both gone!"

"Both? Who? Who is gone?" Her eyes flew wide. "Oh, no." She grabbed her friend's forearms. "They went up there, didn't they?"

"Yes," sighed Sandy. "The Chief started searching for them after midnight when they hadn't reported in for a very long period of time. They were spotted headed out that county road. And he found their cruiser parked up at Tinker's place. There was no-one there. The Chief left their rig up there, just in case."

"What are we going to do?"

"I am going up there and search. Right now!"

Janine nodded. "Soon as I get dressed." She ran into her bedroom.

Winl Fzar.

"So, that's the plan?"

R-Bar nodded. So did Ran.

Tinker nodded back at them. "R-Bar makes us invisable and we just walk along getting rid of the bad guys?"

"Have'ta move fast, Tink. Before they realize what is going on?"

"Most true," added Ran.

Sha'gar inched closer to his right side. "These oppressors are very evil, Mate'mer."

He sighed. "Kiddo, call you get us out of here in a real hurry if we have to?"

"Yep." R-Bar nodded.

He stood. "O.K. Let's give it a try." He threw an arm around the short witch as she stood. "I'll bet that it doesn't work the way it's planned. Never does." He ruffled her hair. "Cutie."

She grumbled happily.

Dol Spar. An Office in Monetary Control.

She appeared, accompanied by a very large man. She held a strange looking wand of many rods in her hand. He held a very large silver sword.

"Where are my parents?" Her eyes fluxed blue. "We followed your trace to here." She waggled the wand at the two young women. "Speak tell!" she demanded.

Sook snatched in protection. Sgenn just looked at her.

"Kinder," snarled Mirf. "You damage my office and it comes out of your budget for repairs."

Sedeem reached through Sook's protection and shoved her into a corner and snarled at Sgenn, "If it moves, you die!" She turned and wacked the thing with her wand. "QUIET!"

Then she turned and looked at the two large men dressed in blue uniforms. "How did you get here?"

Sook and Sgenn stared at her, being still as still. For the moment.

"Your cousins brought them," explained Mirf.

"Cousinsssssssssssss," hissed Sedeem.

"If we don't get home soon, we're gonna lose our jobs,"

rasped Red.

"Hi, Sedeem," said Green. "Red's right."

Sook dropped her protection and tried to look as witch proper as she could. She had heard all about her cousin Sedeem.

Sgenn sent the thing away and looked this person over, very carefully, So this was his daughter, the owner of the three colors of magic. She tucked her hands inside her sleeves. And waited. Quietly.

"Cousin Sedeem," said Sook. "I am Faan witch Ripple daughter Sook."

Sgenn nodded. "I am Faan theurgist Reep daughter Sgenn. Cousin."

"Hum, hum," replied Sedeem, turning toward Red and Green. "Home," she said. They were gone.

Then she sat in a chair and smiled at Mirf. "So how's by you, Mirfeleh?" And waved at her husband to sit.

"Vunderbar," laughed Mirf, realizing that the condition of her office would remain unchanged.

"Sit," snapped Sedeem at her cousins, releasing their feet. They hadn't felt her fasten them to the floor. "And tell me what's going on?"

Grandeville. Tinker's Place.

They thumped down into the parking place. And walked over to their patrol car.

Red looked at his watch. "Not too bad. It's only two-o-clock."

Green nodded. "Start thinking up a good story, partner. We're gonna need one." He threw the door open and got in, behind the steering wheel.

Red laughed. "That's a big for sure, for sure." He walked to the other side, paused, and leaned in the open window. He had just heard a car racing up the long driveway that led from the county road. "Oh, oh, company's coming."

Green heaved himself out of their rig. And walked around to stand by Red. They watched the car lights coming up the grade.

"Car sounds familiar," said Red.

"We're in trouble," said Green. "It's your's."

"Oh, oh."

"Uh huh."

The car swung into the parking space and rocked to a sudden halt. Both doors flew open. Two figures leaped out and banged into the two huge men, wrapping their arms around as much of them as they could.

"Hi, babe," rasped Red.

"Janine," rumbled Green.

Sandy released Red and stepped back. "O.K., Goon Squad, where have you been? The Chief has been searching for you two since midnight."

"Missed us, did he?" Green nodded at her.

"Yah," snapped Janine. "What have you been doing up here?"

Green looked at Red over the top of Janine's head.

"Got lost," blurted out Red.

"Right," agreed Green. "Lost."

"I do not believe it," snarled Sandy.

"Ummmmmm, we got a report of a bear and went out into Tinker's wooded slopes to search for it. And, ummmmmnlln, got lost." Red looked at her. "We just now got back."

Green gently patted Janine on the back. "Wanna let go? I gotta radio in."

"I'll do it, partner." Red walked over to their black-and-white and reached in and yanked out the microphone. And shortly began to explain to Dispatch and The Chief how they got lost. It was a wonderful story.

Green scooped Janine up into his arms and walked over and sat on the steps to the rear deck. Red hung up the mike.

"What really happened?" she asked.

So Green told her while Red added this and that to the story and to Sandy.

The outside lights snapped on and a young girl walked down the deck and looked at them. "What are you doing out here?"

"Long story," said Red.

"Hi, Je'leel," said Green. "Where's your folks?"

Je'leel nodded at Green and Janine and the others. "Mother is in the ring, sleeping. Father and the Mothers are traveling."

"How come you didn't wake up earlier?"

Je'leel pointed. "My bedroom is way up there near that far corner. Very quiet. Very isolated from the rest of the house. There was no reason to, before."

Green stood, Janine still in his arms. "Time for us to go." He walked over and stood near Sandy's car and said softly to Janine, "I will believe anything you ever tell me."

"Those two cousin babes just snatched us to some other

babe's office," explained Red to Sandy. "I am gonna have a long talk with Tinker when they get back."

"Good idea, partner." Green gently set Janine on her feet next to Sandy. "We better get back and sooth The Chief."

As they cruised down the hill, Green smiled at his partner. "The Chief won't believe that we got lost. But I think that he will accept it."

Red nodded. "That's a big for sure, for sure. Let's stop for some doughnuts, first."

As they followed the police car down the hill, Janine turned in her seat. "How strong are they? It seemed to me that he acted as if he wasn't carrying anything at all."

Sandy laughed. "Far as I can tell, living with Red is just like having your very own Tyrannosaurus rex."

Winl Fzar.

It had been a long day.

They were still hiking along the main road following Helf. He had said that the dwelling cluster where the Princess lived was not too far away and that it should be liberated first.

Tinker grumbled, mostly to himself, mostly quietly. So far they hadn't seen anything except for rather run of the mill, rather ordinary appearing folk, going about their rather run of the mill, rather ordinary business.

"Thought that this place was supposed to be overrun by bad guy meanies," he mumbled to Chicken, who was staying close to his side.

"Tis most strange Me'Lord." She lowered her voice. "Think thee this Helf person do be ne'truth telling?"

Smoke shook her head.

They had this part of the road to themselves so they felt that they could talk out loud without frightening the inhabitants.

"That's it!" He halted, stopping their little procession. "Time for Plan B!"

"What was A?" whispered Messenger to Chantal.

"What we were doing, I suppose," came back the whispered reply.

"O.K, short stuff," said Tinker, hooking an arm around R-Bar's neck as she walked up to him. "Change in plans."

She poked him in the stomach, not too gently. "I am not short! What change?"

"We have done enough playing tourist. Jump us to this Princess's home, or whatever it is."

"Hum."

"Yah," he said. "Whatever."

"Risky, Amtar." Ran nudged his side.

"How risky?"

"Depends on what is there, Tink," explained R-Bar. "When we pop in."

Ran nodded.

He smiled at them. And intoned, in deep rolling tones, "We are armed. We are dangerous. We are the good guys from the planet Earth. And I am tired of all this messing around."

Sha'gar stepped closer. So did all the others.

"We will have the advantage of surprise," said Smoke. It sounded like a good idea to her. Surprise was a tactic that all predators favored.

"Right," he agreed. "So let's go surprise them."

Dol Spar. An Office in Monetary Control.

"So Mirf," said Sedeem. "You have any idea what is going on?"

"So I will just give a check," replied Mirf, banging on part of her desk and then issuing instructions to one of her clerks. "And give a run on this and don't dawdle," Mirf shouted after her. The door slammed shut as the clerk hurtled away to the appropriate archive.

"Just visiting," said Sgenn.

"But something not good had been there," added Sook.

"Hum," said Sedeem.

Sook shrugged. "Just a trace trace."

Sgenn looked blank. And then added, "It felt ugly."

"Hum," said Sedeem.

Mirf looked at the expression on her face and jerked upright. "Not in my office, kinder. Please?"

Sedeem laughed. "Just thinking."

"A thought like I just saw I wouldn't wish on my worse enemy." Mirf grinned, and shrugged. "So maybe I would."

The clerk burst into the office, dumped the report on the desk in front of Mirf and hurtled away. Mirf spun the report around, flipped open the cover. "So shall we see what we shall see?"

She started to read, flailing back and forth through the folder. And finally, she looked up, and stared into all those different eyes. "So vat's a Hephira?" She rapped the tattered report with one knuckle. "For some reason we have no information on a group of things called Hephira."

"We were told not-nice," stated Sook.

"I have never met one," added Sgenn.

"A hidden folk," stated Sedeem.

"Short, with large eyes," said Farth. It was that the first thing that he had said since he and Sedeem had arrived. "I can give you the name of their elseplace. The Silver Rangers have heard tales of their lands being overrun by vast evil, that scattered them far and wide."

"So, kinder." Mirf stood and stretched, her eyes slyly looking at Farth to see if he was looking at her. Farth fizzled softly. Mirf inhaled deeper and stretched some more.

"Kak lak folk," grumbled Sook.

Sgenn shrugged.

Sedeem shook her head. "Child tell tales."

Farth nodded. "They are told to be quiet and retiring."

"Well, Kinder." Mirf smiled at Sedeem.

Sook and Sgenn stared at Mirf. It was her smile, most unsettling. It reminded them of hobgoblin.

"So vat's the deal?" asked Sedeem.

"Vat deal?" Mirf tried to look all innocent.

"Heh, heh, heh, heh, heh."

"Should never have let you be my assistant," grumbled Mirf happily at her. She leaned back against the wall and waggled her arms loosely. "Anything you want. As long as we all go and visit these Hephira types. Together."

"Together?"

"Absolutely!" Mirf beamed at her. "You, me, that big lump you married, Fred, Quan." She nodded at the other two. "The kiddies can tag along if they wish, and, ummmmmm, you agree. Of course."

Sedeem laughed and laughed. "Hoo boy, such a deal. I'll

take it!"

Mirf stepped from behind her desk. "So you will probably steal my shoes. Let's go!"

Sedeem stood and nodded at her cousins. "You may come." She waited until they were standing.

And took them.

To the elseplace that Farth had named.

Winl Fzar.

"Looks like someone trashed this place."

He stared at the structures, at the many storied structures, that they stood before.

Walls bulged in strange places, Roofs sagged. Scorch marked holes punched through everything. Doors and windows were mostly blown out. Debris littered the roadways and the ground in all directions.

Chantal leaned in through a hole that appeared to have once been a wide doorway. "ANYONE HOME?"

Three bird-like things and something else fluttered out past her head.

Helf slipped inside. "Stay here." He disappeared into the interior gloom.

Tinker walked over to Messenger. "See anything?" He knew that she could see in the dark as well as if it was full sunshine. She had been watching Helf slip through the first room and out a far door.

She shook her head. "Just ruined stuff.

R-Bar joined them and pointed at the stains on the walls. "Those are magic splash marks. Terrible dark magic."

He nodded. "So, where are all the bad guys?"

She shrugged. So did Ran.

Sha'gar walked over. "The evil left after doing all this. Maybe Helf will know where they went." At least that was how it felt to her.

"Smoke? Anything?"

"No, MindMate, we are alone."

He sat on a large block of stone which had apparently fallen from somewhere high up in one of the battered walls.

"Looks like the goose we are chasing is pretty wild."

Fair Morn stepped close. "Are we going home?"

"Unless someone has a better idea." He looked at the rest. "Well, group?" All he received were head shakes and shrugs. "O.K." He looked at Chantal, who was still peering into the interior. "What's Helf doing?"

"Beats me, G. I. Can't see a thing in there."

"He is in another room," explained Messenger.

So they waited.

And waited.

And waited.

Ran leaned against his back and draped her arms over his shoulders. "Terrible bad evil, Amtar."

"I'd say so." He reached up and held her hands.

So they waited.

And waited.

And waited.

"Think we ought to go inside, take a look around?"

"No, Amtar, your Ran does not." She rested her chin on top of his head.

"O.K."

"Coming out," said Messenger, stepping back and away from the opening she was looking through.

In a few moments, Helf lurched from the structure. He, was dirty. He was filthy. He was a mess. He was a black smudge from head to toe. And made little dust puffs as he walked over to them.

He nodded at Ran who was watching him as he approached. Her head was still resting on top of Tinker's.

"I found a note, artfully hidden. From my Princess. We must go to the elseplace called Twice."

"Ummmmmm," replied Tinker.

Helf dropped to his knees. "Please, Lord?"

"Stop that!" snapped Tinker.

Smoke walked over and lifted the Hephira to his feet. "Not necessary. And doing things like that doesn't work anyway."

Tinker looked at R-Bar. "Know anything about Twice?"

"Nope."

"Anyone?"

"Nope."

"Nope."

"No . . . Lord."

"Oh, well."

"Guess that we are going." Chantal, yanked out her revolver, cocking it. "Gonna be ready the instant we hit the ground."

"Grand idea that." Chicken yanked her sword free.

"Yep." Fair Morn cradled her cannon in her arms, setting levers.

"Lemme go," said Tinker to Ran as he tried to stand up. She did. And stood. He did. And reached up and yanked down the great black sword. It sang a soft killing song. "Let's go!" he said. "We're ready."

R-Bar grabbed one of Ran's hand.

And twisted them away.

Not All The Much Later.

"HOO BOY! Really sloppy housekeepers." Mirf stared at the shattered structures.

Quan and Fred ran inside.

"So now what?" Mirf gazed at the mess.

Sedeem shrugged.

Sgenn looked around and walked over to look at something.

Sook rubbed a green and brown wand against her cheek. "Ugly bad."

"Vunderbar," gurgled Mirf. "That I don't need." Her eyes glittered. "Think that there is any little thing left in there? Valuable?"

Quan and Fred ran back outside. "No," said Quan.

"Chirp," added Fred as she handed an ornate box to Mirf who took it and looked inside. "Empty."

Quan nodded. "We found it in a secret place, recently opened. Clean. Not smudged."

"Soooo," said Mirf.

Sook walked over and stood near Sedeem. "Your father and his were here. There is a faint Faan witch trace mingled with a Tanpak witch trace. Shall we follow?"

"Hum," said Sgenn.

Mirf stared at her. "You too?"

"What?"

"Another hummer."

"Hum." said Sook.

"Oi," sighed Mirf.

"Family trait," explained Sedeem. "Remember?"

"Let's go," said Mirf.

"Where?"

"After them, of course. What else?"

"Hum," replied Sedeem, bursting into laughter at Mirf's sudden change in expression, She nodded at Sook. "Can?"

"Yesssssssssssssss," replied Sook.

And took them out.

Twice.

A large banner hung overhead, stretching from one side of the street to the other. Each end was anchored to a building.

The street they stood on was very neat. In fact, it was a very neat and tidy street in a very neat and tidy appearing town. At least that was the way it appeared from that portion of the town that they could see.

The place was all soft colors and rounded edges. A few of the inhabitants strolled casually here and there. They were dressed in clothes that shared the colors of the town.

They were stared at, but only from curiosity.

Not fear.

Not anger.

Just curiosity.

"Nice place." He swung the great sword up and over his left shoulder. It stuck to his back with a soft thump. He looked up at the banner.

It announced in large, red letters, to all who cared to read it:

Hooray, Hooray.

For Redundancy Day.

"Fest time, Sweet Prince." Chicken slipped her blade back into its scabbard.

He shrugged. "Guess so, Princess."

"Peers most innocent a'place."

"Yep." He beckoned over the two witches.

"Tink?"

"Amtar?"

"This look like a place that bad nasties might live in?"

"Nope."

Ran shook her head.

"Uh huh." One corner of his mouth puckered.

"Pik tik," grumbled R-Bar at his expression.

"Not nice," said Sha'gar, edging closer to them.

"We in the wrong place?"

"It came this way, Mate'mer."

He looked around and pointed at the banner. "Sure. Came for the party. Or whatever that is."

"Don't be gab dak." R-Bar glowered at him.

"What?" His arms flew wide. "Me? Gab dak? Heavens to Betsy, not me! Oh, no, not gab dak, not never!" He threw an arm around each witch shoulder and tugged them close. "So, what's gab dak?"

During all their conversation Helf had edged further and further away. Grumbling, glowering witches were not safe to be around. It was better to keep as much distance as one could between them and oneself.

Chantal stepped over and wacked Tinker on the shoulder. "Don't be such a grump, grump! We'll just have to look around. Ask someone or another. Things like that there." She shoved her revolver into its holster.

"Think they'll let us into their celebration?" Fair Morn leaned against his back and blew warm into his ear. "Get something to eat."

"Ah ha," he said.

Messenger nudged his side. "We are all hungry. Really really."

"Certainly are," agreed Smoke.

He nodded. "Time to eat, then. Which way?"

Smoke headed down the street and around a corner. Everyone hurried after her.

Including Helf

Some Few Moments Later.

"Nice place."

Mirf looked at the town. "Quan, keep notes." She spun around. "Well, bubeleh, which way? I don't see them. No signs of destruction."

Sedeem put her personal wand somewhere and looked at her cousins.

Sook sent her wand out as she and Sgenn tried to look as proper as they could.

Sedeem laughed. "Cousins, you will have to learn to relax."

Sgenn shrugged. She was relaxed.

Sook tried.

Mirf watched them and began to edge away. Just a little.

"Which way?" Sedeem looked at Mirf who shrugged and pointed. They went that way.

Some distance down the street, Mirf drifted back to walk with the cousins. "So, Grey Stuff, vat's a theurgist. I want to know. M.C. wants to know. Please?"

Sgenn began to explain what she felt Mirf and M. C. ought to know. Which was not very much at all. But it was all she was willing to tell.

And some small time into that small explanation, Mirf smacked her forehead with the palm of one hand. "Oi Vay! Such a bunch of trouble in such a cute package you are." She winked broadly at Sgenn. "So it's O.K. by me if it's O.K. by you." And whispered, "But you'll keep it under control, right?"

Sgenn nodded. She looked past Mirf at her cousin. Sook shrugged, and asked, "You are really that Mirf? The Mirf?"

She laughed loudly. "You betcha. There is only one! It'sa me! Every gorgeous inch. But don't worry about it, you are pretty cute also." She looked from one to the other. "Sooooo, how many are there? Kinder? Ahhhh, children?"

"Mother had three daughters, so far. Shitar, Santar, and me."

"I have two sisters. Szaifeh and Sha'gar."

Mirf's eyes popped wide. "Sha'gar is your sister?" She slapped her forehead with a palm. "So, I didn't pay attention."

"Yesssssss," replied Sgenn.

"She's Tinker. So I heard."

Sgenn nodded. "It was necessary."

Grandeville. The Home of The Hardcastles.

He reached down from the sky.

And grabbed them.

One moment Shem had been walking across the broad side lawn, arm in arm with Tajaar, heading from the house to a nice spot under the trees to have lunch, carrying trays.

And in the next moment.

They were gone.

The trays reminded behind.

Twice.

The numbers on the wall blinked at them. They were bright red.

02.23.6.61

"Wonder what that means?" Tinker stopped and watched the blinking numbers high on the wall.

"It is today's date." The man stopped and smiled at them. "Have you come for the celebration?"

"Ummmm."

"Redundancy Day. It happens twice a year. Once on 3.33 and 3.34 and then again on 6.66 and 6.67."

"Redundancy Day is on two days, twice a year?"

The man laughed. "Of course. It is Redundant." He pointed at the numbers. "Today's date, starting from the right. The sixty-first day of the sixth month of the twenty-third year of the second cycle. Today is 02.23.6.61. Tomorrow is 02.23.6.62."

Tinker nodded. "Thanks. Which way to a good restaurant?"

"May I guide you?"

"Sure."

They followed their guide.

As they walked along, their guide explained that this world was one of a Land Order of a Space Order. And that there were a number of Land Orders and Space Orders. This was the First Land Order, and hence, had been given the honorific title of Twice.

"We believe that redundancy is necessary for the long-term survival of the Orders." The guide indicated a door. "Your restaurant. R. D. celebration is in the Main Main. That way." He pointed, and left them, headed toward the Main Main.

"Let's eat." Fair Morn headed for the door of the restaurant

Grandeville. Greater Downtown.

"So, partner, what do you think?"

Red shoved the second brawler into the back seat of their black-and-white and slammed the door.

"These guys ought to know better." Green looked across the top of their cruiser at Red.

"Up at Tinker's."

"Oh. That." Green took a bite from the doughnut he held. The two of them had been interrupted during their coffee break by the pair now in the backseat who had started causing a ruckus in a nearby bar, Big Darlene's.

"That." Red nodded, poured his cup full from his thermos and took a sip.

"Hard to believe."

"Wonder who those two babes were?"

"The one in the golden suit said they were Sedeem's cousins."

Red nodded. "Any idea how a kid of Tinker's has cousins like that? And does the stuff that we saw?"

"Nope. Janine sorta suggested that there are a whole lot of worlds out there, somewhere, where people do stuff like that all the time. All kinds of weird stuff."

Red emptied his cup, shaking a few drops to the pavement. "That's a big for sure, for sure. Think this pair need to visit the E.R.?"

"Suppose we ought to take them up there. Wouldn't want them complaining about our hospitality. Let's go."

Red nodded and clambered into the front seat as Green slid behind the steering wheel, slammed the door, started the engine, and headed up toward the hospital emergency room.

Twice.

"Hoo boy, kinder, wonder how this place escaped our notice." Mirf waved her arms wildly and told Quan to take notes, again. Monetary Control needed an office here.

Fred kept her cape snapped shut so only the top pair of

arms were on the outside. Her multifaceted eyes glittered in the bright light.

The two cousins had decided to just stand and watch. And maybe in Sook's case to learn a new spell or two. Perhaps. Mirf and Sedeem appeared to know what they were doing. And it was obvious that they were old friends.

"So kinder. Have any idea, any way, on how to find Tinker et al?"

"Hum, hum." Sedeem smiled at her.

"You going to make a mess? Again? Blow a few buildings to pieces? Again? Little things like that? Again?"

Sedeem winked at her. "Do I do things like that?"

"Hee ho. I seem to remember an occasion or two of leetle things like that happening."

"Let's eat, And send a searcher."

"Vunderbar." Mirf headed them in the correct direction. At least she thought that it was the correct direction. "So vat's a searcher?"

"Just a leetle thing." Sedeem laughed. "No one will notice."

Eventually they found a place to eat.

Sedeem sent the searcher.

Over their meal they talked with the server about the history of Twice. Especially Mirf.

Airt Lak. A Bright Sunny Day.

Tajaar leaped in front of Shem, a long, glistening blade appearing in her hand.

Shem stared up at the towering figure who stared down and asked Tajaar, "Where did you have that?"

The man smiled at them. "A very protective wife, Shem."

Shem gently touched Tajaar in the middle of her back, between the shoulder blades. "Put it away. He won't hurt us."

Tajaar did. Shem smiled as she did. One moment the blade was in her hand, then it wasn't.

"She does that very well," observed the man.

Shem stepped up and slipped his arm around her shoulders. Her gaze remained fixed on this stranger, this enormous figure, standing there, smiling down at them.

"Tajaar," said Shem. "This is my grandfather, my mother's father. He is a great warlock."

The grandfather nodded. "And now it is time for Shem to expand his abilities. He has been ignoring his heritage for far too long, been sticking his head in books for far too long."

"Oh." Shem looked surprised and confused at the same time. A not unusual expression for him.

"Yes."

Then the training started.

Twice.

Sedeem jerked uptight. Something crackled around them and was gone.

"They are not here," she hissed.

"Who?"asked Mirf, looking around the room.

"Dad and the Moms. They are gone."

"Where?"

Sedeem stood. "We will have to go to where they were last and see if we can find a trace." She strode long strides for the front door.

Mirf ran after her, waving her assistants to follow,

yelling at the proprietor, "Send the bill to Monetary Control."

Sook paid the very agitated owner. Then she and Sgenn hurried after the rapidly moving group. Already far down the street.

Klop Nam Nam.

"Sorry, Tink."

She stepped to his side. "Had to hurry. That splash mark was almost gone. It came here."

"Really ugly." Chantal yanked her revolver from its holster and cocked it.

Fair Morn nodded and cradled her cannon in her arms.

The group slowly turned around, checking their new surroundings.

It was a dark place. Everything was a soft shade of grey and black. The ground rolled in brief undulations to far horizons. Dark stuff was draped over rock and vegetation, hanging in shreds and patches.

"This looks like that the bottom of a lake that just dried up." Tinker stared at the stuff.

"A rather stagnant lake, Me'Lord."

Sha'gar yanked in a glistening red wand. "An evil place, Mate'mer."

"Yessssssssss," agreed Ran, rolling a clear brown crystal sphere from hand to hand.

"Which way?"

"That way?" Smoke pointed at a wide smear of a track curving away from where they stood.

It disappeared around a nearby hummock. Beyond the hummock, some distance beyond, rose a high hill. The hill loomed over everything.

She looked at him, pupils dilated wide, black pushing golden orange into a narrow band. "Something is not too far away, that way. It is pushing back, hiding. Can't see it. But it feels . . . familiar."

"What?"

Smoke shook her head. "Too hard."

"Stop trying then." He frowned and reached up and pulled down the great black sword. "I am sure that we will find out all too soon." The tingle that said the sword was ready to take over, to start killing things, ran up his arm.

The group started down the wide path and then walked onto and down the flattened track.

They were headed for that high hill and whatever lurked there.

Chapter Six

Just A Little Rescue.

Grandeville. Tinker's Place.

She took the ornate ring with the gem that looked like an eye from the shelf and set it on the dining room table. And sat down and tapped it. "Mother, I am bothered."

A small figure appeared, yawned, stretched, and walked over and looked up at her. "What about?"

"Father. And the Mothers."

"And what does my daughter propose?"

"To find them. And help."

Dat sat down. And shook her head.

"Why not?"

"Because your father would be very upset."

"If something happens to them, I will be very upset. And so will you."

"He is still my Great Master."

"Mother, you know that makes no difference. He does not believe that way."

"True." Dat stood. "Where do we go?"

Je'leel smiled at her. "Indjinns can always find their Great Masters."

"Your devious nature must come from me." Dat smiled

back. "You are not properly dressed for traveling out there." She crossed her arms over her chest. "I will wait. If you do not take too long."

Je'leel ran from the room.

Twice.

"So, kinder, now what?"

Mirf spun around on the street and on top of the spot where Sedeem had indicated that her parents had used to exit from this elseplace. It was in the middle of the street, down a rather narrow side street.

Sedeem frowned. "There is almost no trace, Mirf, just a hint that tells that they were here. We can't follow them." She chewed on her lower lip, just a bit. "I suppose I could always ask Reep to come and take a look."

"Cousin," said Sgenn, very softly. "May I try?"

"Sure," replied Mirf. "So give a try."

Sedeem nodded.

It rose up from the deep down below. It was all odd angles and twisted joints.

Sook yanked in protection.

"Gak ptui," spat Mirf. "That is uglier than ugly." She looked at Sgenn. "And believe you me when I say that, cause chickee, boy oh boy, do I know ugly when I see it!" She pointed. "And that is ugly. Super duper ugly."

"Search find," said Sgenn.

Sniffing loudly, the thing moved here and there. And disappeared.

"Hum, hum," said Sook.

Quan and Fred stepped closer to Mirf, weapons held in

their hands.

Farth quickly scanned their surroundings and looked at Sedeem who looked at Sgenn.

"Soon," stated Sgenn. "There is a path." She tucked her arms inside her sleeves and smiled a soft half-smile. "We will wait. Here."

"So," said Mirf, sitting on the pavement. "She has a mouse in her pocket." And smiled at her assistants and at Sedeem. "So pull up some pavement and do a sit. Get comfortable. We are waiting."

Klop Nam Nam.

The strange path meandered around various of the hummocks and seemed to be slowly leading them deeper into a steep walled valley toward the high hill.

They stopped and stared. There was a great lump of stuff blocking their path. On the either side of it rose high hills, jutting straight up from the valley floor.

"Gee, Honey," gurgled a disembodied voice. "Look what came for dinner."

The center of the lump elongated upward, tilted to one side and burst open. She dangled by her arms high over their heads, wrists bound with shining black strands. The golden scales of her armor were stained and splashed with black. Her large azure eyes stared down at them.

"PRINCESS!" screamed Helf, hurtling a short blade at the black mass. It passed through and out the other side and bounced off the path.

The stuff sucked Helf inside.

"He is safe," said the voice. "For the moment."

Tinker leaned close to Chicken. "That voice sound familiar to you?"

She nodded. "Indeed, My Lord, tis that."

"What I thought," he mumbled, taking a cut at the mound with his sword. The blade flashed through it. To no affect.

"Tee hee, John. Tee hee."

"That you? Dram?"

"Very good, John, very good. Indeed, it is I, your old buddy buddy. Heh! Like this stuff?" A strand whipped around and dragged Ran under. There was a loud explosion.

"Urp!" said the lump. "Just kidding. Your witch is also all right for now."

"O.K.," snapped Tinker. "Now what? This time?"

Fair Morn fired. A great section of the stuff disappeared. And reappeared. She was sucked straight down.

"Tickle, tickle, tickle." It yanked Chantal backwards and in.

"HOLD IT!" shouted Tinker.

"I can think of more interesting things to do than that," gurgled the lump. "Shall I demonstrate on this Hephira? Heh."

"No. Forget it." Tinker swung the great sword up and over and onto his back.

The air was crackling and grumbling around R-Bar as she searched rapidly through her store of knowledge for just the right spell.

"Tell her to stop. Or these others become . . . appetizers."

"You heard, kiddo." The air settled down.

She stomped over to him. "It might work," she

whispered.

"Not yet," he whispered back.

"She loves me, she loves me not. Isn't that your child folk ditty, John?" A tendril began to pluck golden scales from the armor of the Princess.

"Leave her alone," snapped Tinker. "You have proven your point."

"You like lovely females, John. I just thought that I would unwrap her for you." More scales pattered down.

"Knock it off, Dram!"

"Oh, all right, John Boy. Just for you. Heh." It swung her back and forth. "Then I shall just keep her."

A tentacle swung around Sha'gar's waist. "Yummy. You have certainly been a busy boy, John."

Grandeville. Sandy and Red's Home.

She jabbed him in the gut with her elbow. It had as much effect as if she had hit the wall.

They were having dinner. Sandy, Red, Janine, and Green. It was Saturday. Red and Green had the weekend off.

It had been Janine's elbow. It had been Green's stomach.

Red winked at Sandy.

"What?" asked Green, really wondering about certain feminine forms of communication.

"I think that they are in trouble," stated Janine. "And need help."

"Who?" asked Green, looking at Red.

"Tinker," replied Janine. "And them."

"How do we do that?"

"Go up there and ask Dat."

Green slowly turned his head and looked at Janine. "You want to be even taller than you are, that it?"

"What?" snapped Janine,

"The last time that you helped," explained Green. "You lost bunches of yourself and Dat had to put you back together again. And you became taller, and, um, well, different, ahh, sorta."

Sandy rapped on the table top with her cup. "I am not going up there. And neither is Red. Again."

Red shrugged and looked at Green. He looked back.

"No! You are not!" It was Sandy's best professional lawyer tone of voice. "NO!"

"Sandrew doesn't think that it is a good idea," rasped Red.

Sandy glowered at him.

Green nodded. "Neither do I."

"Some cop," snarled Janine.

"Cops are noble and brave," stated Red.

"And show good sense," added Green. "Besides, you are fine just the way you are. Don't need your anatomy messed around with. Again."

"Streak," said Sandy, reaching over and grabbing her friends forearm. "We have no business up there." Her voice fell. "We don't know anything . . . useful."

"We could just go up there and talk."

Green shoved his chair back and stood. "Let's go. Talk."

Twice.

She growled.

Loudly she growled.

Sedeem stood and watched Sgenn. Carefully.

"It is The Evil One!"

"Who is?" asked Mirf. "Vat?"

"The Evil One has tricked Uncle. And his." Sgenn stood and yanked her arms from her sleeves.

Sook snarled. All around her the environment creaked.

"Settle, Cousin, settle." Sedeem had protected Mirf and all the others but she didn't think that it would help their surroundings.

Sook shook into existence her blue wand and told it to be quiet. It had been humming loudly.

"Kinder," said Mirf, addressing the group at large. "It is time to be hob-goblin sneaky." She smiled at them. Or maybe it was a grimace. It was hard to tell. "And believe you me, when it comes to sneaky being hob-goblin sneaky, I am an authority." Mirf's eyes seemed to be changing color as they glittered dangerously.

Sedeem steeped between her and Farth.

"So," said Mirf, "it is just me." She shrugged. "Take us to Harptz Krantz. There is something there we need to visit."

Klop Nam Nam.

"All this black mess really you?"

Tinker waved one arm at the lump.

"What you see is what you get."

"Really?"

"No. This is merely my persona of the moment, so to speak."

The black mass began to fade. And all tumbled free.

Helf helped his Princess stand and slipped a protective

arm around her shoulders.

The slight figure dressed all in light grey, just a slightly off-white grey, bowed and smiled a bent smile at them. "Is this butter. Heh. Ahhhh, is this better?"

Sha'gar twisted around.

"DO . . . NOT! Or I will pluck more than golden scales from her." He crooked a finger and watched more scales fall to the ground. Dram smiled. "I really think that I ought to remove all those things and let him see what she is really like. Heh."

"What's going on?" Tinker watched Dram and grabbed R-Bar by the back of her belt.

"Not much, John Boy, not much." Dram looked from face to face. "I am truly amazed at you and your collection. Heh. I really do not understand how you do that. Eight of them. Heh, eight! Is this the lot?" He winked. "Keeping a few in reserve?"

Then he strolled in and around the standing figures. "Heh. Two witches and one magician. Pretty strong combination. Heh. How do you keep them from clashing? Plus the usual ones."

He smiled at Smoke, Chicken, and Fair Morn, and stopped in front of Chantal. "How did you get involved. You are just . . . nothing."

She punched him in the mouth. And shot him. As he tumbled backward, she shot him again. The heavy slugs thumped into his body, jerking him backwards, and down to the ground. "Scum bag!" She jumped forward and kicked him in the side. And shot him again. And was frozen in place.

Dram sat up and stared at the bullet impact points, a tight cluster in the center of his chest. He nodded at Tinker. "Well, maybe not nothing after all."

He stood, stepped close, and ran his hands over her. "Very nice." And smiled at Tinker. "You do keep such a variety of shapes and forms. Heh." He stepped back and released her.

Chantal stuffed her revolver into its holster and punched him again. "Keep your damn hands to yourself, creepy!" She watched him, waiting for him to move.

Tinker walked over and said softly, gently. "Cool it, Cowgirl. You can't hurt him. And he enjoys agitating you."

Dram pouted at him. "Spoil sport."

"We done playing games?"

Dram nodded. "All right, John, no more games." He beckoned in a chair and sat. And waggled his eyebrows at Chantal. "Heh."

Grandeville. Tinker's Place.

"Still nobody home,"

Green looked at Red and shrugged one massive shoulder.

"Seems pretty quiet," he replied.

Janine stepped over to the book case and found the ornate ring. She picked it and rapped it on the shelf. "O.K., Dat, get out here and talk to us."

Green stepped over and peered over the top of her head just to see what she was doing.

"She lives in there," she explained.

"Dat? Je'leel's mother."

"Yes."

"Lives in that ring."

"Yes."

"Uh huh."

She whirled around and glared up at him. "It is true."

"O.K."

Sandy joined them. "Red went upstairs."

"Well?" asked Janine.

"What?" asked Green.

"What?" echoed Sandy.

"Do you believe me?"

"Sure," said Green.

"I don't believe you," snapped Janine.

"O.K." Green eased backward. "Whatever." And looked around the large living room. "Seems empty to me."

Sandy stepped close to Janine. "I think that they left before we got here."

Janine dropped the ring back on the shelf. "I suppose." And walked over and leaned back against Green. "Sorry."

He held her. Very gently. "So'kay."

"You sure?"

"Sure. Babes act funny. At times."

"That is not funny."

"O.K." He dropped his arms. "Glad that you are taller though."

Janine turned and smiled up at him. "That all?"

"Well, the, umm, rest is pretty nice, also."

She spun and fell back against him, and laughed, and asked Sandy, "Is that what cops call them? Um?" She laughed even harder

Sandy looked over. "Better hold her, Green."

"But not by the ummmmms," roared Janine. Just before she screamed.

Klop Nam Nam.

"Why are we here, Mother?"

They stood on a hilltop. Far below they could see small figures standing in a loose group apparently talking.

Dat stepped close to her daughter's side. "The one seated is called The Evil One. We must be very careful."

"He can not harm you."

Dat smiled and swung a comradely arm around her daughter's shoulders. "True. But he can harm your father and your many mothers. Although Sha'gar and the witches might escape with only some damage. But the Hephira would die also."

"Would I be safe?"

Dat smiled. "Yes. You are my daughter."

"Then I shall go down and join my Father and Mothers."

Dat smiled at her. "And I shall hide." She shrunk. "Pick me up. And do not tell them that I can do this."

Je'leel bent and did, and held her in the palm of one hand. Dat leaped to her shoulder and slipped down inside Je'leel's shirt.

"Mother, your claws are sharp."

"I shall just sit here, quietly nestled between your indjinn beauty, beauties." Dat peered out between two of the buttons.

Je'leel laughed and started strolling down the black slope toward the group below.

"So, why are you interfering again?" Dram slouched in his chair, his head propped in one hand, elbow resting on the arm of the chair. "Heh?"

"In what?" Tinker crossed his arms over his chest and

frowned.

"Oh," said Dram, waving his free hand airily. "The usual thing. Taking this and that."

"Ahhhhhh," replied Tinker. "What?"

Dram nodded and waggled one finger. A sleeve disappeared. On the Hephira Princess. The upper half of her armor pattered to the ground. "Her. Her elseplace."

"Oh. Well, we didn't know that was your doing. I, ahh, don't think that Helf knew that either."

"You still working for that pesky fowl, Big Red?"

"We don't work for anyone! Creep!" Chantal glared at him.

"Shhhhhh," hissed Tinker.

Dram laughed happily. "I like that one, John. May I have her? Heh?"

"Fraid not."

"You are greedy, you know that." He eyed Chantal. And watched as the buttons began to fall from her shirt. "Heh."

Chantal turned to Fair Morn. " You guys know this jerk from somewhere?"

Fair Morn nodded. "Yep. He is the greatest evil in all of the elseplaces. We thought that he had been destroyed along with his world."

Dram laughed. "Surprise, surprise."

Smoke edged closer to Tinker. She had just felt Je'leel move into her sensenet.

Dram winked at Tinker. "How about a swap, ol' buddy buddy? I will give you the Hephira Princess with the big eyes. And you give me that one," he pointed, "with the big . . . "

"TITs!" snapped Chantal. "They are called tits!"

"Ah . . . yes," said Dram. "I suppose they are."

Behave, growled Tinker at her.

Dram pointed. A large piece of the Hephira's blouse disappeared. "Very nice. Interesting skin tone."

"Damn juvenile," grumbled Chantal.

Chicken stepped to her side. "Tis that." Her mouth fell open as she stared up the hillside. "Ods blood!"

Chantal looked.

And they all knew.

"What are you doing here?" Tinker glared at the approaching figure so casually strolling along.

"I was worried," stated Je'leel as she walked past the seated figure, ignoring him. She kissed Tinker on the side of the face. "Frowning like that puts wrinkles in your face, Father."

"Merde."

"Father? Who is she, John?"

"I am Je'leel," she replied, turning to face Dram. "His daughter."

Dram smiled. "My, my. A lovely daughter."

Je'leel smiled back. "Thank you."

Grandeville. Randy's Truck Corral.

They sat around a corner table. In the back room. At this time of day, the truck drivers sat in the front room, eating, reading, swapping on-the-road stories, eating, joking with the waitress, eating.

"You all right?"

Janine nodded. "Yes, Green."

"Happens all the time," explained Sandy. "It is her stress

reliever." She refilled Janine's coffee cup, then Green's.

Then it happened.

The only witness, other than the participants, explained it this way to the Sheriff, this is way he explained it.

This witness was talking to the Sheriff, know by all as Two Gun. One Arthur Drill, known locally as 'The Driller,' explained it this way.

The Driller, who knew Red and Green on sight from their late night activities maintaining law and order downtown among the several bars and pubs, told Two Gun the tale, such as it was.

He, the Driller, had been sitting in the furthest corner of the back room from the party at the corner table. He had been hiding out, drinking coffee, as his missus was at that moment on the war path and as this was the safest place to be when one was hiding out.

Red and Green, and their ladies, had just been sitting and talking quietly until this really ugly flat-faced bear had somehow gotten into the restaurant and charged them

Red lurched to his feet and punched it in the mush.

Green grabbed up a table and shoved the creature backwards and out through the fire door exit, a glass door.

The door, the door frame, and the glass were scattered next to the side of the building.

The Driller ran outside to see what was going on and got there just in time to see Red run to their car with that ugly bear lurching after them. Red popped the trunk open, handed Green a riot gun and grabbed another. Then the two cops "just blew pieces of that bear all over the parking lot."

The Driller nodded at Two Gun who was frantically writing in his notebook as the frantically wound up Driller rattled out his story. Then, he told the Sheriff, they just climbed into Red's car and drove away.

The Driller cleared his throat. "Got all that, Sheriff?"

Two Gun nodded and shoved his notebook into a pocket.

The Driller pointed at the scattered remains. "Ever see a bear that ugly before?"

Two Gun turned away. "Nope." And watched as The Chief of Police drove his car slowly into the parking lot and over to them.

Klop Nam Nam.

Tinker slipped an arm around Je'leel. "What are you doing here?"

"I was worried, Father."

He sighed. Right now, at this moment in this place, he didn't want to get into any discussion as to how she had managed to find them.

The air broke and shattered.

They were there.

Farth. Sedeem. Sgenn. Sook.

"My, my," said Dram. "More of your's, Johnny Boy?"

Fred. Quan. Mirf.

"Hoo boy," said Mirf. "Such an ugly place this is." She looked at Dram and asked Tinker, "Who is this smuck?"

"Dram," he said to her. "My daughter and her husband," he said to Dram.

"Two daughters," said Dram. "Well, well."

"Ho, Ha! The worst of the worst, in person." Mirf rolled her eyes and signaled Fred and Quan to not do anything. Yet.

"Sister?" Je'leel looked at Sedeem.

"Dram," hissed Sedeem, yanking in her strange looking personal wand.

Sgenn called to the deep below. "I am Reep daughter Sgenn."

"Ripple daughter Sook." She yanked in a glittering yellow and red wand.

"What are you doing?" snarled Dram at Sgenn.

"Sister." Sha'gar's eyes flickered red flame as she gathered in mage fury. "I am Sha'gar."

"Stop that!" Dram hissed at Sha'gar.

R-Bar grabbed one of Ran's hands and started the spell, one of the ancient banned spells she had read in the book of banned and banished spells.

Dram leaped backwards, his chair toppling over, and disappeared. "You will all die," said the disembodied voice.

"No, we will not." Sedeem's eyes glowed a soft blue.

He reappeared and stared at her. "Ancient magic! How did you get that ancient magic?"

"I was born with it." She allowed green fire to trickle from her fingertips and crawl up her wand.

Messenger stared at Dram and gasped. Yanking her wand from her hair, she hacked it to the shreds. The bonds that Dram had been weaving fell in a heap at his feet.

"I remember you," he snarled. "You are that kid with Big Red's wand." He turned and glared at Tinker. And stomped his feet. And pointed.

The rest of the golden armor fell away. "Control these females, John. Or the Hephira dies."

Je'leel ran over, pushed between the pair and threw her arms around them. "NO!"

It oozed from the earth from far below below and towered over Sgenn and looked at Dram, and licked its lips.

Dram screamed.

Everyone threw protection.

The air banged and crackled.

"No one can control one of those," howled Dram. He twisted away. And stared at down.

His feet were anchored in place.

Sook nodded.

Sgenn smiled, a soft half-smile at Dram.

Red fire flickered around Sha'gar.

"Oh well," said Dram, smiling at Tinker. "You will still have one daughter." White fire blasted from his fingertips and enveloped Helf, Je'leel, and the Princess.

Levers clicked. "Full power," said Fair Morn.

"HOLD IT!" shouted Tinker.

The white glare faded as the spell ran water soft into the dark soil.

"You," stated Je'leel quite firmly. "You are really not very nice!"

"Am too," spat Dram, throwing a loop around Chantal, dragging her to his side. He began to sing to them, "We'll all go together when we go." And giggled.

Chantal stomped on his shin as her elbow smashed into his face. He snarled and released her. "You are not nice, either, pillow chest."

Jumping away and to one side, she spun, whipped out her revolver and rapidly fired.

"And short-tempered as well." He winked at her.

Then he looked at Tinker. "O.K., enough posturing, John. Go away. Let me be. I will take what I want or this world will cease to exist along with those Hephira."

"Ummm." Tinker's brow furrowed as he thought about what Dram had just said.

NOW, he told them all.

It all fell upon Dram as Fair Morn fired.

Red flame from Sha'gar.

Death maw from R-Bar and Ran.

Black destroy from Sook.

Pure hate from the creature.

Green blasted from Messenger.

And something unrecognized.

The elseplace ceased to exist.

And everything in it disappeared.

Grandeville. Tinker's Place.

The car slewed into the parking space and slid to a halt. It rocked just a little as four doors flew open. They scrambled out and looked around.

Red and Green opened the trunk and began to reload their riot guns.

"That was no bear," stated Janine. "Back there."

"Didn't think so either," rasped Red.

"Died anyway," rumbled Green. He grabbed a box and emptied it into a side jacket pocket. "Better take some," he said to Red.

Red nodded and filled a pocket. He smiled at Green.

Green nodded back. And started up onto the rear deck and began to ease himself along, very close to the wall of the house. "Stay behind us," he told Sandy and Janine. "And drop to the deck if anything starts to happen."

Red walked along the outer edge of the deck.

Sandy and Janine followed them, eyes darting every which way.

"Duck and shoot," said Green, halting by the side door.

"Right." Red smiled at him.

"On my count."

"Go." Red waved Sandy and Janine over against the house. "Shhhhh."

"One."

"Two."

The air over the first pasture ripped and tore in colors. And sparkled and flashed.

Red.

Green.

Blue.

White.

Yellow orange black.

"Fireworks?" asked Red.

Sandy gasped.

"LOOK!" shouted Janine, pointing.

Bodies were tumbling into the tall grass of the first pasture, falling from somewhere, rolling and sliding.

Then . . .

The large living room was littered with them.

Bodies.

Red and Green had carried them, two at a time, from the pasture. It hadn't taken long.

Sandy had ransacked the hall closet and hauled all the first aid supplies she could find to that room.

Janine brought towels and wash clothes and several buckets of warm soapy water.

Je'leel slowly wiped the grime from her father's face. Dat sat on her shoulder and watched.

"No dead ones." Green sipped from his cup. He and Red had made several pots of coffee.

"Meshuggener dummkopf," gurgled Mirf as she struggled to sit up.

Janine helped her lean back against the front of the couch.

"I'll go and find you a shirt."

Mirf glanced down. "Ho, ha, lots of me and not so lots of my clothes." Her eyes slid around the room, checking all the bodies that she could see and then back to Janine who had returned holding out a shirt. "So give us a tell, Florence. Sing like a nightingale. Vat happened?"

"I don't know."

Smoke's eyes popped open. "All alive."

Janine handed the shirt to Mirf and dumped the rest of the clothes into a heap on the floor. "Here."

"You fell from the fireworks display," said Green.

"Just after we got here," added Red.

"One of those bodies dressed all in off-white?" asked Tinker, staring up at the ceiling from his spot on the floor.

"Nope," replied Janine.

"Vunderbar." Mirf held out her cup. "You got something stronger than this black mud?"

"Sure." Smoke wobbled to her feet and headed for the kitchen. "I will make us all something to eat."

It took awhile. But not too long.

Tinker dragged himself upright and into his chair and looked around the room.

Everyone was either sitting on the couches, various of the chairs, or on the floor. Eating and drinking.

He laughed and thought to himself, what a crew. They all wore filthy clown faces with clear patches where the grime had been wiped away. Everyone wore clothes that were in various stages of tattered remnants. A few had on new shirts or trousers, depending upon their own personal sense of modesty.

"Me'Lord?" Chicken had been one of the less concerned ones. She had dumped the remains of her shirt on the floor. But put on a new one when she saw him glowering in her direction.

"Just admiring this group. You guys have taken the grunge look to new depths."

"Hum," grumbled R-Bar, glaring at her niece witch. Sook had followed Chicken's example and her mother's cavalier attitude. R-Bar threw a shirt at her.

Farth yanked off his shirt and draped it around Je'leel.

Sedeem quickly buttoned it up. And whispered to her sister. "They may do things like that, but you shouldn't. Our Father will get very, very grumpy."

Je'leel nodded. "Mother explained about that."

Dat smiled. "She is a very well trained daughter" She leaned forward and peered down. She had jumped from Chantal's shoulder to her daughter's shoulder. "Certainly developing an indjinn look."

Sedeem laughed.

"Mother, shhhhh." Je'leel yanked her shirt back up over one shoulder. It was a very large shirt.

"Mother?"

Dat smiled proudly at Sedeem. "I thought that you should have a sister."

"Jump down."

Dat did as Sedeem cast.

Dat was large.

"So I can hug you." Sedeem stood and did. "Mother."

Chantal sat on one arm of his chair. "So, how ya doing, lover?"

Tinker managed a smile. "Just fine." He swung an arm around and gave her a little pat. "Look's like Sha'gar and her sister are having quite a talk."

Sha'gar and Sgenn sat in a corner of the room, near one of the large windows, facing each other, on the floor.

Sedeem walked over and sat on the other arm of his chair. "Dad, you are an old sneak."

"Huh?"

"Je'leel."

"Oh." He ducked his head. "Wasn't exactly planned."

She laughed. "Lot's of parents say that."

"Not what I meant," he grumbled.

Smoke leaned against the back of the chair and ruffled his

hair.

"Knock it off!"

"Wonderful idea. We could draw straws or cut cards."

He sighed. "Think I'll go clean up."

Smoke pressed down on his shoulders as he tried to rise. "Nope. Prince Helf and his Princess are in there. Washing this and that."

Je'leel tickled his ear. "No peeking."

"Bad as your mothers," he mumbled.

R-Bar sat up and looked around the room. "Who put in the yellow black orange?"

"Red," called Sha'gar.

"Blue," said Sedeem. "And green. And black."

"Black," said Ran.

"Also," said Soak.

"Green green," said Messenger, violently nodding.

"I do not use magic," said Sgenn softly.

Dat stood and walked over to him. "I did, Great Master."

"Didn't see you there."

"I was hiding."

"Huh?"

Je'leel smiled at him. "Inside my shirt."

"In between," explained Dat. "Our daughter's beautiful indjinn . . . "

"All right," he quickly interjected.

"Pillows." Chantal smiled at him.

"Never heard them called that before, either." Janine sat down, near Sandy, Red, and Green.

Messenger looked over at Janine. "What?"

"Forget it," snapped Tinker.

"Ummms," said Janine.

"Oh." Messenger nodded. "I suppose."

"Go home," suggested Tinker.

The four stood.

"See ya later," rasped Red.

"It's been fun," rumbled Green.

"We'll talk tomorrow," said Sandy as she and Janine followed the men out the front door.

Chantal toppled into his lap. Sedeem stood.

"How about we shoo those guys out of the shower so we can get clean?" asked Tinker, hoping to start a new topic of conversation.

Chantal rocked her head back and winked at Sedeem, and nudged him with a elbow as she sat up. "Your bed? Or mine?"

"Cheat," called Fair Morn.

Sha'gar stood. "The shower room is free." She headed that way.

It became a mob scene in there.

"Well, Simba Leader?" She tickled some handy ribs. They were in her bed.

"Much prettier when you are clean."

"Grumble, grumble, grumble."

"Very nice."

"What is?" She squirmed. Just for him.

"Pillows, or whatever term you guys might wish to use this time."

"Not what I wanted to know!"

"Oh?" He tickled her in return. Just a little. Just for himself

"I think that it is over."

He laughed. "Maybe later."

"Not what I meant."

"Oh?" So he tickled her again. Just a little. Just for fun.

She rolled onto her side and jabbed him in the gut with one fingertip.

"Ooooof!"

"I meant that I think that all the ruckus that started when Helf turned up is over."

"Certainly hope so. Ummm?"

"What?"

"Wadda'ya want to do now, toots?"

"Let's go get a sandwich before they eat all the roast beef."

"Good idea."

They made it to the kitchen just in the nick of time.

[illegible]

[illegible]

[illegible]

[illegible]

"Go on."

[illegible]

[illegible]

"[illegible]"

[illegible]

[illegible]

Chapter Seven.

A Small Gift. A Pet.

Grandeville. Tinker's Place. Evening.

It was a dark and stormy night

The wind blew terror in its breath. Lightning flashed, pulsating bright in the thick cloud strands scudding across the face of a gibbous moon. Soft fog seeped moist wet across the grey moor making all sounds soft and tenuous.

Somewhere, not far away, hidden in grey blanket dim, it lurked. And crept in her direction, stalking on silent feet.

Far ahead, vaguely seen, stark building silhouette shape glowed faint outline with internal light.

And the thing came through the ooze.

She hiccuped.

Chicken laughed.

He marked the spot with a book mark as they fell apart into themselves becoming nine individuals again.

Tinker had been reading the book. All the rest were listening. The novel had been chosen by Messenger who was curled up next to him, an arm around his waist, as he sat slumped deep in one of the larger couches in the large living room.

The images that they saw were a combination of their various cultural backgrounds and imaginations all merged and shared as the nine minds flowed together into a single entity, having a single experience.

"HIC!" It was Messenger.

R-Bar walked over and touched her on the forehead, curing the problem.

"Thanks, kiddo."

"Most welcome, kitten." R-Bar headed for the kitchen. "I'll bring the cookies, if someone will help with the coffee."

Fair Morn went with the short witch. She was the tall, classic beauty of the bunch. And hungry as always. R-Bar was just slightly shorter than Messenger who tended to notify her, now and then, of the one-half inch difference in their heights.

"Me'Lord, most sorry." Bright blue eyes, framed by light sandy hair, twinkled at him from the other end of the couch. "For We do Us fair interrupt fair flow of tale Gothic."

"No problem, Princess." He smiled at her as she stretched, yawned, and smiled back at him as she saw him watching her stretch and yawn.

"Fair Prince?"

"Nothing."

"Thee did fair ravish Us with thy beady glance."

"Did not."

"Ogle, ogle, ogle."

He nodded. "Sure, Slim. Ogle, not ravish."

"Nay much for to ogle." She stood, a tall slim woman warrior. "Praps did We Ourself wear shirt most tighter?"

"Forget it," he snapped. "Everything is just fine as it is. Just won-der-ful." He wasn't ready for a flurry of activity revolving around them debating whose shirt was tighter or where ever her comments might lead.

Smoke rolled her head sideways and looked up at him. She was lying on her back on the floor, hands crossed over her stomach. She leered at him. "Tear her shirt off, MindMate."

"Burgle," he replied.

Chicken began to unbutton her shirt. "Sweet Prince Ogle, thee hast reason naught for to abuse Our Own fair raiment so."

He lurched up from his reading slouch. "Knock it off. Keep you shirt on."

Chantal laughed and tossed a pillow at him. "You lusting after her chest again, Cowboy?"

He sighed and sat back. The conversation was already getting out of hand.

Rapidly.

Again.

Ran straightened up in her chair. "Amtar?"

He looked over. "What? No!"

Ran looked disappointment at him.

Sha'gar relocated and dropped next to his free side. "Mate'mer, tearing the shirts off folk is not-nice."

"Merde," he mumbled.

"You could come down here and sneak off my shirt," offered Smoke. "I won't mind."

"No one," he grumbled loudly, making sure that he was grumbling loudly, very loudly. "No one is ripping or sneaking anyone's shirt off!"

"Spoil sport." Chantal laughed and waggled her eyebrows at him.

"Cookies," announced Messenger as she bubbled into the living room carrying a large canister. "Next!"

"And coffee," added R-Bar, carrying in two full pots. "Third."

Smoke jumped up. "I'll get the cups. Fourth!"

Tinker looked from happy face to happy face. And frowned from happy face to happy face. "What are we counting?"

"Shirt pillaging order," explained Fair Morn, handing him two cookies. "Our shirts. Your pillage."

"Five!" called Chantal. "Pass the cookies, please."

R-Bar helped Smoke carry in the cups. "Is pillage the correct term?"

"No!" He frowned darkly at them. Grumble didn't seem to have any effect. Maybe dark frown would work. But he doubted that it would. Not when they started up.

"Spoil is good." Fair Morn nodded. "Spoil," she intoned firmly. "To strip a person of goods, etc., by force." She winked at him. "Let's just call it an easy spoil." She filled his cup. "Heh, heh, heh."

"I am not going to read you guys any more stories like that one. You all get goofy."

"Indeed," agreed Chicken. "Tis most true."

He stared at her. "You agree?"

She nodded and smiled, a very sly smile. "For tis true Spoil Sport do be thy Verra Own title for thy sport do be for to a'spoil these, Thy Verra Own Most Pliant and most caring of hand-maidens of these Our Verra Own most fair shirts."

"Sport," snapped R-Bar.

Sha'gar leaned close and breathed soft warm into his ear. "Sport, to engage in amorous play."

"O.K., O.K., I get the idea." He finished his coffee and another of the cookies. And crooked a finger at Chicken. "Com'mer."

She shook her head. "Nay, Great King of Us All for t'would be most unseemly did thee strip this Thy Verra Own Beauteous Queen in front of all these most fair and most modest maidens."

"Blush, blush, blush," giggled Messenger. Then she hurtled toward the kitchen. "Run for your lives, the Mad Shirt Snatcher is ready to attack and steal us bare."

The room was suddenly empty. Except for Tinker who wondered, now what's going on?

Time passed in the quiet way that it often did.

He filled his cup.

He ate a few more cookies.

He slumped deeper into the couch.

And waited.

A large, six foot tall, red rooster walked through the front door, into the large living room, stopped in front of him, cocked its head, and stared at him with one glittering yellow eye.

"Cock-a-doodle-do," said the rooster, in well modulated tones.

"Hum bug," replied Tinker.

"You are no fun."

"What do you want?"

The rooster faded away and was replaced by a stocky, heavy-set man dressed all in shades of red. "Just came to visit."

"Have some coffee. And some cookies."

The man smiled and sat on a chair that had quickly slid over behind him so he could. Sit. He took a cup, filled it, and then three cookies. He munched happily. "Pretty good."

Tinker nodded. "Messenger made them."

Slowly, ever so slowly, the rest filtered back into the room. Chicken introduced those that Big Red had not met before.

"My, my," said Big Red. "Eight."

"Smoke assures me that we are done adding."

Smoke smiled at Big Red. "The Velvetmist usually stop when their groups attain this size in terms of the female-consort ratio." She winked. "Of course, he is not Velvetmist."

Knock it off," grumbled Tinker. "It has never been my idea. Never!"

"Everyone looks very healthy." Big Red looked from face to face.

"We take very good care of him." Messenger giggled.

Big Red looked at Sha'gar. "You have a younger sister and cousin, I believe."

She nodded. "Sister Sgenn and Ripple cousin Sook."

Je'leel joined them and sat next to Tinker.

Big Red looked from her to Tinker.

"Daughter," said Tinker. "Je'leel, this is Big Red, a friend of our's. He is visiting."

Big Red looked at Je'leel carefully, very carefully, and nodded to himself.

"Her mother is Dat, the indjinn."

Big Red's eyes flew wide. He laughed. "It takes a lot to surprise me, as you know John. But! I am surprised."

A small figure leaped from a book shelf, bounced off a couch top, and scampered over the cushions and up to sit on Chantal's shoulder, clenching a handful of Chantal's hair.

"Dat," said Tinker.

Dat leaned close and whispered in a handy ear, "I don't see how my Great Master could resist tearing off your shirt. Yum, yum, yum."

"Quiet," said Chantal.

"She is our size, now and then," explained Tinker.

Big Red nodded and cupped his chin in one hand. "I felt it when you, ahh, erased Dram, err, not all that long ago. Up till that moment in time, there had never been such an event."

Tinker slumped deeper into the couch.

"He was trying to kill us," said Je'leel softly, eyes focused on Big Red's face. "He was going to kill my father and my mothers and the Hephira."

Big Red nodded. "Dram is a nasty one all right. He needs to be eliminated every once in awhile."

"So?" asked Tinker. "Why are you here?"

"I watch the forces in the universe of universes, as you know. You have become one of those forces."

"I am retired. We are retired. Not a force!"

Big Red laughed, a very happy booming voice. He shook his head. "Look at you. You are the only polyorganism of your type in existence."

Tinker glanced at Smoke. "What about the Velvetmist?"

"Merely bands of telepathic carnivores on a hidden

world, a hidden elseplace, that no one can find or visit. What about Tinker et al?"

"Nothing."

"Damn right!" Chantal glared at their visitor.

Chicken nodded. "We do be naught but mere mortals, nay predatory carnivores." She smiled at Smoke. "Save one."

Big Red waggled his free hand. "Let me describe what I see, then you can tell me what I see."

Everyone looked at him.

"Nine individuals, one mind. Of the nine we have one physically changed telepathic carnivore, two witches, one who read a book of banned spells, one magician, one controller adept, one magical jest, the Princess Chicken, and two Homo sapiens, yourself and Chantal."

He held up one finger. "Added to that we may add those who would aid you in any manner that you might wish. The Golden Dragon of the House of Chen. Macabre, the Destroyer, and his companion, Gyre. The Vander mage guild and those magical others, $1.98 and Plum Duff, the Zwar and the Faan and the Tanpak witch clans. The Nagar sort. The demons: the a'demon and the predatory Tark. Monetary control, and the Silver Rangers. Ahh, what did I leave off? Oh, yes, Dat and myself. And of course, you daughter and son."

Big Red flopped back into his chair. He had been sitting more and more upright as he listed the various names, leaning more and more toward Tinker. "Oooops. There is also the Kingdom of Bahn Duhr Tohr." He laughed. "By anyone's reckoning, I'd say that makes you a force."

Tinker frowned at him. "O.K., so what?"

"And there is that ring, that piece of Ancient Magic,

BrenBand, and all those other rings that you wear." Big Red smiled, tapped his cup with one finger. The cup obediently refilled with hot, steaming coffee.

Tinker jerked upright and glared at their visitor. And stated firmly, "And . . . I . . . did . . . want . . . any . . . of . . . it!" He surged to his feet and stomped from the room "AT ALL!"

Chantal leaped to her feet and started to follow Tinker. "Damn trouble maker," she hissed at Big Red as she stomped past.

She found him sitting on one of the benches on the rear deck, staring out over the swimming pool. He had set the bench right near the edge. Sitting next to him, she nudged his shoulder with her own. "What's a'matta, Simba leader? We are what we are."

"He is up to something," he grumbled.

"So? Tell him to piss off."

He laughed. "Won't work. We won't like whatever it is. And it won't be nice."

She nudged him with her shoulder.

"What?"

"You wanna sneak my shirt off. Dat couldn't understand how you could resist tearing my garment away."

"Practice," he mumbled

"Yum, yum, yum, yum, is what she said."

"Four yums, huh?"

"I think that I deserve five."

"Umm, O.K." He reached over and popped a button loose. Then another.

She looked down at his hand. "You being sneaky?"

"Not very."

"I'll say."

"Well, well, well. Just you in there."

"Yep. No artificial pushing or pulling, just me."

The soft voice purred in his ear, "Soooooo, Vander Lord, up to your usual tricks, I see." She laughed softly.

Chantal laughed. He jerked.

She sat by his free side and smiled warmly into his startled expression. "Want to inspect me next?"

"Behave," he growled.

"I am always well behaved."

Chantal stuffed her shirt back into her trousers. And nudged Tinker. "Five yums, at least."

Sa'ar looked from Chantal to him. "Yums?"

"Chantal can explain," he grumbled.

"Sure." Chantal grinned. "It is a new U.S. Department of Agriculture mammary grading system. He is the first Official Inspector."

Sa'ar stared at him. "You are not going to start stamping, ahhhh, things with ugly purple stamps, are you?"

He glared at them both.

Sa'ar laughed. "Do I get a certificate?"

Then they both laughed, hugged him and kissed his cheeks.

"Andovar," said Sa'ar. "She is our newest member, said that you had caused a major magical disruption in some way off corner of the universes. She is a farseerer. Shall I call her in? For an Official Inspection?" Their laughter started up again.

Chantal grinned at him. "It is tough job, but someone has to do it."

"Ha," he said. "Ha. Ha. HA!"

"Just came for friendly visit," explained Sa'ar. "Wanted to see how you were." She started to loosen the fastenings on her blouse. "But . . . "

"Stop!"

"Pleasure before business." She started yanking at his shirt. "Let's see what we have in here."

Chantal joined her in her effort.

He lurched to his feet. It was a very bad idea.

"Well, Vander Lord," she said, bobbing in the water next to him, "that was a sneaky way to check." She heaved herself onto the rear deck and smiled down at him.

Chantal surged up after Sa'ar. "Certainly is. But he is that, all right, sneaky."

"I'm gonna stay down here. It's safer." He paddled over to the edge of the pool.

They reached down and hauled him out.

"O.K.," he said. "Five yums. Each."

Smoke stood and smiled at everyone. "Sa'ar is here. Five yums."

They all headed for the rear deck. Including Big Red.

By the time that they arrived Sa'ar had cast dry on them. She greeted everyone. Her eyes slowly wandered over Sha'gar. "Pretty yummy as well."

Tinker sighed.

Sha'gar looked mage proper. "I have heard of my cousin, The Heart of the Vander magicians. And her Vander Lord."

Sa'ar nodded mage greetings.

The rest crowded around, swapping hugs and kisses.

Except Big Red, of course.

Sa'ar slipped her arm under one of Tinker's. "Eight. Near Vander guild in size, Vander Lord."

"Faan mage Sa'ar, and Heart of the Vander. As you heard," she said to Big Red.

Big Red smiled at her. "May I visit? Some day?"

"Of course." She gripped Tinker's arm tighter. "Is it near lunch time?"

"Indeed," said Chicken. "We will Ourself fix most fine foods."

"May I?" asked Big Red.

"Thee may."

Big Red nodded. Both tables were covered with lunch and other appropriate items. "Buffet style," he announced.

Sa'ar nudged Tinker with an elbow and whispered softly to him as they filled their plates and then sat on one of the benches. "Eat hearty, we have business to discuss."

"Oh?"

"Yesssssss."

"Beef is good. What kind of business?"

She laughed deep in her throat. "Very pleasant business."

"Ummm?"

"After lunch, Vander Lord." She crunched on a celery stick.

Chantal leaned close to Smoke. "What is she up to? This time?"

Smoke shrugged. "Blocked off. She said that she will tell him after lunch."

Big Red sat next to R-Bar and looked past her at Ran. "I do not believe that I have met Tanpak before."

"We are few."

"Crystal adepts, I believe."

"Yesssssss."

"And how are your sisters?" he asked R-Bar.

She looked at him from the corners of her eyes. "Alive. Well."

"May I," he said as he lowered his voice to a conspiratorial whisper, "ask a personal question?"

"Hum, hum." Ran stared at him.

"Mere curiosity, witches, mere curiosity." He half-twisted toward them. "I didn't know that indjinns could do that."

"What?" hissed R-Bar.

"Have children. With dwellers of this elseplace. Or any other, for that matter."

"We were surprised."

"Also," added Ran.

They strolled.

Out into the first pasture.

Lunch was done and over with. All had scattered to do chores. Big Red had waved at them as they did. And vanished.

So Tinker relaxed. And allowed Sa'ar to tow him out into the first pasture.

"The Vander have talked long and hard."

"About?"

"It is why I am here."

"Ah ha."

"Tobtz, Our Soul, brought it up, this business."

"What?"

"Our archivist searched long and long and put to order all we have collected."

"I remember the mess in your library." He smiled at her.

"She found ancient history and protocols."

"About what?"

"Succession."

"Oh?"

"For the Vander to survive into the far future, we must have succession. Rorx gave us survival into the near future."

"Your group is certainly big enough, pick one."

She shook her head. "She must be a birth-child."

"She?"

"The next Heart, the next Broach Wearer."

"Ummmmmm. So?"

"Rorx is our warlock. Szaifeh is witch. Their offspring will not do."

"So?"

"The succession must be Vander born."

He nodded. "Well, I am sure that with the physical attributes your mob has that shouldn't be much of a problem."

She shook her head. "That will not do. The archives were very explicit."

"Tricky old archives."

"Tobtz made it very, very, very clear."

"That clear, huh?"

She nodded.

"She wants the job, that it?"

She spun and faced him. "She may not. Nor may any of the others."

"YOU?"

She nodded.

And smiled.

"Us."

"WHAT?"

She stepped close. "I told you that it was pleasant business."

It was a very long drawn out sigh. "Why me?"

"Vander Lord," she breathed gently.

"Merde."

"The Vander have many potions and ointments."

"Double merde."

"We can take days and days." She grinned.

"Find another stud."

"That is crude." She frowned at him.

"Makes two of us."

"You don't want to accept your responsibility." She poked him in the chest with one finger. "You wear the ring."

"You Vander certainly want a lot."

Her hand slowly rubbed up and down his chest. "You won't be doing anything you haven't already done on several occasions." She smiled.

"Your son and his mother talked. To each other. And to Tobtz and to me. He understands the Vander ways, the Vander need, the Vander culture." She laughed. "And your reluctance."

"What?"

"That you would squirm."

"Just a pawn again. Right?"

She shook her head. "No. You are the Vander Lord. You are The Heart of The Heart. You are free to do as you wish." She bowed her head. "To hear is to obey, Lord."

He grabbed her by the shoulder and gently shook her. "Damn, damn, damn."

She looked up and blinked away the tears. "I knew that you would agree."

"Oh?"

"Well, maybe I was worried. A little." She kissed him. "You do grumble a lot. The rest of you know that."

"Humpf." He frowned. "You really wanna do that, this, right? Become a mom?"

She nodded. "It is my obligation. My duty."

He sighed. Then wrapped her in his arms. And laughed, gently, quietly. "Do I get to see my daughter grow up? Or is it going to be like Rorx?"

"You met Rorx when he was small."

"Once!"

"We will try to visit more often." She leaned the side of her face against his chest.

He ruffled her hair. "Make you a deal."

"What?"

"I want all my children to meet each other, all at the same time."

"It will be done."

"O.K. Let's head inside the house and see what kind of trouble I am in this time. Or they are up to."

Chantal met then as they stepped up onto the rear deck. She frowned at him and glared at Sa'ar. "You owe me one hundred dollars."

"What?" He stared at her.

"Stud fee," she snapped. "I am the veterinarian and I set

the fee for my stallion!"

"Oh, my," gasped Messenger. "Is she going to punch Sa'ar? Again?"

"Probably not," replied Smoke. She watched Chantal carefully, just in case.

"Per attempt," added Chantal. "That is one hundred dollars a shot, no pun intended."

"Cool it, Cowgirl." He frowned at her.

"I should have talked with you first. I am sorry. Most." Sa'ar's forehead wrinkled as she worried what Chantal might do.

The air opened.

And they fell out.

"Oooops," he said, just before they, a man and a woman, hit the water. In the swimming pool.

Everyone ran that way.

"Hello, Uncle." He swam to the side of the pool and helped her out.

"Shem. Tajaar. What's going on?" Tinker stared at them.

"BROTHER!" Sa'ar wrapped him in a tight and a wet hug after he had clambered out and onto the deck.

Tajaar looked around and nodded. "Safe safe."

Sa'ar stepped back and snapped her fingers. They were now dry.

"Missed the deck," said Shem, eyeing the remains of lunch. Tajaar filled a plate and handed it to him, shoved it at him.

"Oh." He took the plate. "Thanks." His face flushed as he

sat. He waited until she had joined him, carrying another plate.

Sa'ar sat by her brother's side. "What have you been doing? You feel changed."

They all settled around the table to listen.

"Grandfather took us for training," said Shem, reaching for some radishes, somehow poking his elbow into the potato salad.

"Grandfather?"

"Yeth," replied Shem around his sandwich.

"Strong strong," said Tajaar.

"That's an understatement," said Tinker, remembering the one time that they had met him.

"Shem?" said Tajaar.

"Brother?"

"What? Oh."

"Yesssssssssssssss," said Sa'ar.

Shem ducked his head. "Grandfather said that it was time to become, ahhhh, what I am, so to speak."

Tajaar nodded. "Trained. Hard hard."

Messenger stared across the table at Shem. And gasped. "It sparkles."

"What color?" asked R-Bar.

"Bright yellow," giggled Messenger.

Tajaar stared at Messenger and then began to carefully check her husband, looking for sparks. She didn't see anything. Nor would anyone else. It was a unique skill that only Messenger possessed. The ability to see magical attributes and to manipulate them if she chose to do so.

Chantal sat next to Sa'ar, threw an arm around her shoulders, and kissed her on the cheek. "O.K., we agreed, all of us." The eight had been mentally linked, discussing what to do about Sa'ar's problem. The conversation had banged back and forth while they listened to the vocal talk around the table. And they had decided. He had an obligation, as the Vander Lord. Chicken had insisted that Lords had dynastic duties beyond the usual familial ones.

So, they had talked. And had decided. Besides, they had all thought that having another daughter would be all right.

Me'Lord? Chicken reached into his mind. She had the job of telling him.

Princess?

We decided, we did, one and all, that t'was most proper do Fair Sa'ar by thee have most beautiful daughter.

He looked in her direction and smiled. *Oh we did, did we?*

Indeed. She gave him a curt nod of her head. *Thee may take Most Luscious and Willing Vander Heart a'bed and with mighty thrusts . . .*

HOLD IT!

Me'Lord?

Don't need a graphic play by play description.

"Poke," said Smoke.

"Sport," added Messenger. "Thrust," she giggled.

"Rut," laughed Chantal as Tinker began to frown at them.

"Prong," suggested Fair Morn.

"Knock it off," he snarled.

"Your slang," suggested R-Bar. Ran nodded.

"Kop kop," added Sha'gar.

All eyes swung in her direction. She shrugged. "The Findak on Fal Wolbul say that."

Shem stood and stepped away from the table. "We

should be getting home." He grabbed Tajaar's hand as she stepped to his side.

They disappeared.

Sa'ar nodded.

Eyes popped wide all around the table.

She laughed. "To visit Mother and Father. And Shem some more." She stood and rolled her eyes at him. "I'll be back!" And was gone.

He looked around the table, at them, at the rest of himself. "O.K., smart guys, I am sure that we all have lots of things that need doing around here." He stood. "I'll be in my office. Working." And headed for the house and upstairs to his study.

They scattered.

Messenger decided to revise one of the flower beds and drafted Chicken and Sha'gar to help.

And time passed.

The door slowly swung open.

And she peeked inside the room.

The room was disorder personified. In an orderly way. Stacks of rough drafts and revisions sat here and there. Two walls were covered with charts and pages, all decorated in many colors with circles and arrows, all indicating what piece was to be moved and where it was supposed to go.

The printer rattled and dumped the rough draft into a box on the floor. He sat, peering at the monitor and hitting keys on the keyboard.

"Father?"

"Huh?"

"I brought coffee and cookies."

"Oh." He swivelled around, chair screaming loudly, and smiled. "Thanks." He made room for the tray on a small table and unpiled a chair so she could sit.

"Chantal said that it was time."

He looked at the clock on the wall and nodded, and filled both cups.

"She said to say, 'Eat hardy, stud.' And that you need to keep up your strength." Je'leel sat and took the offered cup and cookie. "Smoke made them this afternoon. The cookies."

He bit one. "Yep. Peanut butter." And took another. "It is nice to have a child actually living at home."

"Didn't Sedeem?"

"Nope. Neither did Rorx."

"I haven't met her."

"Him."

Je'leel sat straighter. "When will I meet my brother?"

He shrugged. "Ask Sa'ar. Rorx is the Vander Warlock."

She nodded. And frowned. "Smoke said that Sa'ar is going to birth your kitten. How can she do that?"

Chewing on his lip, he said, "Just a small dialectic problem. Smoke means having a child."

Je'leel nodded. "All of them do that, use words that I do not understand."

He smiled. "That is because there are eight different cultures each speaking their own jargon. Just like me."

She returned his smile. "Sa'ar is very pretty. All my mothers are." She laughed. "Now I have ten mothers."

"Not many people can say that." He stood. "Let's go

downstairs. I'm done up here for the day." He took the tray. "Thanks for the cookies and all."

"Sure thing, ah, Pop."

He laughed.

"Chantal said that it was an appropriate thing to say." She opened the door for him. "Isn't it?"

Sha'gar sat back and glared at Chicken. One side of Sha'gar's shirt had a large wet muddy splotch on it.

Chicken had reached over and rubbed her hand clean.

Sha'gar growled at her. "You have put mud all over my, ummmm."

"Ummmm," giggled Messenger as she wiped her hand on Chicken.

"Wench," snapped Chicken. "Unhand Our hindquarters."

Sha'gar nodded and flapped a cupped hand, digging in her fingers, over Chicken. The hand made a sharp slapping sound on Chicken's bare skin. Sha'gar's nod had sent Chicken's shirt somewhere else.

"Ga'zooks," yelped Chicken. "We have Ourself becomen unclothed and art being most muckly be'fondled."

"Gosh," said Messenger. "She got you."

"Indeed! In most firm and friendly a clasp."

Sha'gar released her and sat back. "We need a shower."

Chicken stood. "Most true. Let us away go."

The three gardeners headed for the house.

They bumped into Tinker and Je'leel at the entrance to the shower room.

"Princess?" gasped Je'leel. "Mother?"

"What's going on?" asked Tinker.

"This lanky wench do Us assault," explained Chicken.

"The Princess wiped her hand on Sha'gar's ummm first." Messenger nodded violently at them. "Really really."

"She caressed me," said Sha'gar.

"Me'Lord, We do Ourself plead non compos mentis au'temporare."

He laughed. "You sure that it is temporary?"

"She wiped her muddy hand on her. But Sha'gar got her back," stated Messenger. "Just clutched her, mud and all."

Je'leel giggled.

Chicken kissed her on the forehead. "Your pardon, Princess." Spinning away, Chicken hurried into the shower anteroom.

"Make us cocoa, please?" Messenger followed Chicken inside.

Sha'gar smiled, hooked an arm around his neck and kissed him. And followed the others into the shower room.

Fair Morn was shoved off the hay loft by Smoke, who watched Fair Morn drop and bounce on top of the great hay pile. They had been straightening up the barn and the gear stored up in the loft. Chantal shoved Smoke after Fair Morn, and leaped after her.

"Always thought that was fun," said Chantal. "Jumping down into the hay."

"The Princess is getting rowdy again," said Smoke, chewing on a stalk of hay.

"Yep," said Fair Morn, tossing hay at Chantal.

"No reason for you to start," snarled Chantal, grabbing Fair Morn by an ankle and yanking her off her feet.

Smoke stood. "Cocoa's almost ready."

R-Bar cast light further ahead. She and Ran were under the house, in the crawl space, squirming along. "See it?"

"In the far corner, I think," replied Ran.

They had cast a Naktar down here and sent it to seek out and kill the mice. And now, for some reason, it was loose and avoiding capture.

Ran pointed at the four glowing green eyes in the dense dark furthest corner. "There. The Princess shouldn't have grabbed Sha'gar like that."

"An tak," growled R-Bar as she cast, trapping the naktar as it made a dash for a different corner. "Like what?"

"Didn't you hear feel?"

"I was casting naktar hold," said R-Bar, now casting a go-back spell on the Naktar.

"Did you get it?"

"Heh, heh, heh. Sent it away."

"Cocoa is ready."

The two witches crawled back toward the opening into the wine cellar.

Tinker smiled at the pair as they clumped into the kitchen from their under the house chore. "Having fun?"

"Do dak," suggested R-Bar, patting dust clouds from her clothes.

"Eliminating mice, Amtar." Ran peered into the large cocoa pot.

"Almost ready." Je'leel gave the brown liquid another stir.

"Good," said the small figure leaping to the counter top and smiling up at Je'leel.

"I'll get the cups," said Chantal as the barn gang entered the kitchen from the back porch.

"I'll get the marshmallows," said Fair Morn.

"I'll get the cookies." Smoke tickled him as she passed by.

Sa'ar appeared, holding a large tray. "Date and walnut bars. I made them."

"Oh boy, oh boy, oh boy." Messenger hurried in wearing one of the thick white robes from the hot tub room, followed by Chicken and Sha'gar.

Everyone headed for the large living room. Dat rode on Je'leel's shoulder.

Several days had come and gone, all very quietly. No visitors.

Tinker relaxed. And spent a good part of every day editing and rewriting a revision of a new edition, to one of his first books. Editing and rewriting seemed to be something that he had to do often.

Sa'ar used one of the guest rooms.

Now, there he was, in the kitchen, having stopped work earlier than usual, making coffee, and rummaging around for cookies.

Sha'gar wandered in and kissed the back of his neck.

He twitched. "That tickles."

She breathed warmth into his hair. "Mate'mer, I have a gift for our new daughter."

"What?" He turned and looked into jet black eyes staring into his. Deep down he could see the deep red flicker flame, a faint pulsating glow.

Sha'gar smiled a soft half-smile. "A special thing."

"Ummm." His hands lightly settled on either side of her waist. "Kinna early for gifts, isn't it?"

"Nope."

"What sort of special gift?" She wasn't allowing him to see. So he started worrying instead.

"Anamaxtor."

"Sure." He smiled at her. "What?"

She stepped back. And called.

It appeared.

Sitting on her left shoulder.

It was an eagle-sized bronze yellow dragon with a happy smile and a very long tail.

"Anamaxtor," she said.

Green fumes leaked from both corners of the dragon's mouth.

"He likes chocolate chip cookies."

The dragon took the offered cookie with the delicate fingers at the corner of its left wing. And munched happily. Then it rubbed its muzzle clean on her shoulder.

Sa'ar came down the hall and washed her hands in the kitchen sink. "Messenger said that you were making coffee. "Nice dragon."

Anamaxtor watched her carefully.

"For your, our, daughter."

Sa'ar stared at her. "How did you know?" Her voice was all harsh whisper surprise.

"What? Know what?" He frowned at Sa'ar.

Sa'ar looked at him. "Our daughter is named Eulin.

Named after the first Vander Heart."

"Eulin." He smiled.

"She was also called Dragon Force, Eulin Dragon Force." Sa'ar leaned back against the counter. And looked from him to Sha'gar and back again. "You frighten me, John Vander Lord."

"Huh?"

Sa'ar nodded at Sha'gar. "You frighten me also."

Muscles at the side of Sha'gar's mouth twitched. "Big Red told me." She stepped up to Sa'ar and kissed her on either check, and then the forehead. Then she twisted an ornate ring from her finger and handed it to Sa'ar. And stepped back.

Sa'ar hugged her. "Sorry sorry."

Anamaxtor chirped.

Sa'ar whispered in Sha'gar's ear. "Is this is The Ring?"

"Yesssssssss," hissed Sha'gar. "He is your's."

"Coffee's ready," announced Tinker, beginning to wonder what shape the house was going to be in with that dragon running about in it. Then he thought that it was too bad R-Bar and Ran had gotten rid of all the mice.

Sha'gar spun away to get cups, the dragon riding lightly on her shoulder.

"Hum," said Sa'ar as she slipped the ring on one finger.

"Eulin Dragon Force?" He took a cookie canister from one cabinet.

"Yesssssssssss. It is an honored name. Don't you like it?"

"Nice name. Sound's Chinese."

She laughed. "She was from Dan ar N'Dak."

He headed for the large living room. She followed. And tickled the back of his neck.

"Eulin discovered the Vander principle," she purred.

"Uh huh. Stop that!"

"Will you come and visit, Lord?"

"Will the Vander behave?"

"Most Vander."

"Think that I will stay home." He set the cookie canister on the low table and picked up a cup already filled by Sha'gar, and settled on one of the couches. It was the dark blue plush covered one, ten feet long.

Sa'ar dropped onto the other end, tucked up her legs, and looked at him over the top of her cup, held in both hands.

He smiled at her. "Don't count your chickens before they are hatched. Maybe it will be a boy."

"No. It will be a daughter."

Sha'gar grabbed a handful of cookies and headed for the hallway. "Messenger wants help in a flower bed."

Sa'ar inspected The Ring. "Very ornate."

He nodded and swallowed the last of his cookie. "They chose it. It is just a ring, nothing special."

"Seems very special to me." She smiled at him.

He shrugged. "Umm, stops a lot of, umm, confusion."

She nodded. "How long is it mine?"

He shrugged again. "That is something they decide." He smiled back. "I really have no idea. Makes life interesting."

Sa'ar laughed.

Chicken drifted into the room. "Me'Lord, Sweet Vander Heart." She leaned over the back of the couch and whispered in Sa'ar's ear, one arm draped over Sa'ar's shoulder and across her chest.

Little creases formed at the corners of Sa'ar's eyes as she carefully listened and equally carefully kept her face blank.

Chicken straightened up. "Most impatient kitten do beckon Us for to return to flowery labors." She spun and headed toward the kitchen.

"Ummm?"

Sa'ar grinned. "Just received operating instructions for it." She rubbed the ring against her cheek. "The Princess has certain, ahh, Vander tendencies." She laughed.

"I think that you guys infected them all."

"Not so. They are just being themselves."

Chantal gently packed soil around the small shrub and glowered at Chicken. "Why did you tell her that she could keep it as long as she wished?"

Chicken glanced over. "Fair Vander do desire for to have daughter and thus insure dynastic continuity. Such matters may a'hurried be not."

"You ready for weeks?"

"Gosh," gasped Messenger.

"Shouldn't take weeks." R-Bar carefully emptied a container of six flowers ready to plant.

"What if she cheats?" Fair Morn glanced over at Chicken.

"Hum," said Ran nudging R-Bar.

"Magicians are sneaky," mumbled R-Bar.

Sha'gar stood and handed the watering can to Messenger and accidently dribbled water over Ran and R-Bar. "She will pass the ring in normal time."

"They went into the small living room." Smoke licked her lips. "I'll cook tonight. Steak." She stepped up on the rear deck just as Je'leel came outside.

"Mik dik," hissed R-Bar at the water sprinkle.

Ran tapped Sha'gar's ankle with the handle of her planting tool. "Not nice, magician."

Sha'gar shrugged and eyed the hose

Smoke and Je'leel walked over to clean the pool. Anamaxtor went with them.

Je'leel dragged the cleaning gear to the edge of the pool. "Mother could help her."

"Who?" Smoke shoved the cleaning device into the pool.

"Sa'ar. That way it wouldn't take weeks and weeks and the mothers wouldn't grumble so."

Smoke winked at her. "They like grumbling. It shouldn't take weeks. And I do not think that Sa'ar requires any help. Or wants it."

All the heads in the flower bed swivelled in the direction of the loud splash. Smoke had shoved Je'leel into the pool.

He sighed.

"Lord?"

"You are even more beautiful than the last time that I saw you."

"I am Vander. It is our way."

"Every one of you. Right?"

She poked a finger between his shirt buttons and tickled him. "Come visit. See for yourself."

"That is a deadly dozen."

"We added new rooms. The Council decided that the Guild talent was too restricted at twelve. We decided that the number could rise to eighteen, small, not too big." She laughed. "We still have some empty bedrooms."

"Not coming." He batted at her finger.

"We could build a wing just for your parts. All the new members want to meet them, those that were not present to aid us in our great battle."

"No."

She bowed her head, and looked up at him through her eyebrows. "As you command, Lord."

He sighed.

She leaned forward, lips lightly brushing over lips. "In the same bed that brought Rorx into existence."

"If you don't stop that we will never get there."

She pulled him over. "Oh, well."

Chapter Eight.

A Daughter. A Dragon.

Butterfly Horse Ranch. The Morgan Spread. Out in the Valley.

They were at a combination picnic bar-b-que and spaghetti feed.

The grass was newly mown, filling the air with pleasant cut grass odor. It blended nicely with the smells drifting from the kitchen.

In the distance, not too far, not too close, loomed the mountain range that defined this edge of the valley. Dark forest green dappled black shadow cloaked the steep slopes.

They were all gathered in the back patio area. The twin girls were getting spoiled by all their Aunts while Tinker talked with their hosts, one arm around Je'leel's shoulder. The hosts had both been startled but very happy to see that he had another daughter and that she was living at home. Both had began to accept that Tinker's affairs might be strange at times but, for all that, not too much stranger, most of the time, than many of the other folks hereabouts.

Chantal wandered over to the small group sitting around the table bringing Sha'gar with her. The tall magician looked at these new people with a face carefully held blank. Chantal made the introductions, "My brother-in-law, Deke Morgan, and my sister, Shannon. This is Sha'gar, J. C. and Reep's daughter. She lives with us."

Shannon stood and hugged Sha'gar and welcomed her to their home. Deke looked at Tinker, then he greeted Sha'gar and welcomed her to their ranch and nodded to himself. She had big, black eyes just like her mother.

It had been a week since Sa'ar had returned to her Guild. Life had been quiet, so Tinker had arranged for an outing, for the entire mob, as he put it. The mob had agreed.

The mob was having a good time. Especially after Red and Sandy, and Janine and Green, arrived. Red and Green had carried the keg and set it on the patio and had handed out filled cups to one and all. Je'leel said that she would have some of the punch stuff.

They ate.

Played horseshoes.

Red and Green won.

Shannon talked with her older sister about her life. Chantal assured her that everything was well 'up there,' as their place was frequently referred to by various of the local folk in Grandeville and the surrounding valley.

Deke took Tinker to one side to discuss what the current state of Tinker's and their corporation's, TINCO, finances were. Deke assured Tinker that they would not have to worry about money as, he, Morgan would do any worrying that was required for them.

Tinker cleared his throat and told Morgan that he would require a birth certificate for Je'leel. Deke nodded, didn't ask and walked into the house to make a phone call.

And finally, in the fading light of dusk turning into night, Tinker and the mob clambered into their large passenger van and headed for home. It was a very happy and relaxed group. Even he was relaxed.

Grandeville. Tinker's Place.

Once they were home, Smoke sat next to him on the couch he had selected, shoved an arm behind his back and around his waist. And kissed the side of his face.

He gave her a little poke.

"MindMate?"

"Cause you are there."

Smoke looked down her nose, inhaled, and said, "I am always there. But not as there as some of us are there, but there, none the less."

He sighed, a long drawn out sigh. Conversations around here always seemed to start this way.

She leaned heavily against him. "What?"

He shoved his arm around her shoulders just to get it out of the way. "Do you release how often you guys shift any conversation we might be having into talk about anatomical matters?"

"You poked my anatomical matter." She smiled at him.

"Umm."

"And even now, some sneaky hand is sneaking even lower to do sneaky things with some more anatomical matter."

"Sorry that I brought it up."

She smiled. "I understand."

"What?"

"You just have low will power."

"Huh?"

She laughed. "To paraphrase the literature favored by our kitten and Fair Morn, our feminine assets drive you into uncontrolled lust and your animal self takes over. Hence our anatomical matter is attacked whenever it is within striking distance,"

"Humbug." He frowned at her. "Just hum bug!"

"It is our fate." She laughed. "Mere putty in your hands, so to speak."

He yanked his arm away and slumped deeper in the couch. "Bug nuts."

She twisted sideways, pulled her arm free, and leered at him as she rubbed the side of his face with the ornate ring she was wearing. "Heh, heh, heh, heh."

He looked into those great gold orange eyes. "I am resigned to my fate. You guys are all bug nuts."

Her nose bumped lightly into his. "Not a bad fate. You get the pick of the litter."

"Oh?"

"Yep. Me." She kissed him. And purred. And laughed softly.

"Now what?"

"You are molding my putty." She twisted away and slumped against his side. "Just in case you didn't know that, it being, perhaps, some sort of habit."

It was another long, long sigh. It was him.

"Father," said Je'leel as she entered this room. "I brought coffee and cups for you and Mother." She set the tray on a low table and looked at Smoke. "Are you warm?"

"Nope. It just came undone." Smoke's shirt was open to her belt buckle. "Must be loose button holes." She smiled. "Of course, on hot days, it is very comfortable."

"Oh." Je'leel smiled back at her.

"Don't you even think about it," he growled at her. "Mothers may do that, but daughters may not."

Je'leel nodded. Then she laughed as she realized why Smoke's shirt was hanging open.

"Mother, is he trying to sneak your shirt off?"

"I am not," he grumbled, and frowned at his daughter.

"Intermission." Smoke poured their cups full.

The air shimmered.

They appeared.

Sedeem and Farth.

"Hi, Pop." Sedeem smiled at them.

"Mighty Lord," said Farth, by way of appropriate greeting, bowing to Tinker.

"Hello, sister," said Je'leel.

Sedeem walked over and hugged her. "Hi." She smiled at her father. "Rorx and Szaifeh are on their way."

"What?" He took a sip from his cup.

"My brother?" asked Je'leel.

"Yep," replied Sedeem.

There was a soft pop of black.

Rorx and Szaifeh stepped out.

"Father," said Rorx.

"Hi, Unc," said Szaifeh, grinning broadly at him and nodding at Je'leel. "Very pretty, but don't you think that she is rather young?"

"Our daughter," explained Smoke.

"Sister?" Rorx stared at her.

"Yep." Sedeem nodded. "Our younger sister."

Rorx looked from Je'leel to Sedeem to Tinker. "Sa'ar didn't say anything."

Smoke winked at him. "Surprise."

Chicken walked in and hugged Rorx. "Our Prince." She kissed Sedeem on the side of the face. "Loverly Princess Our's." And nodded at Farth and Szaifeh. "Fierce Warrior. Dark Witch."

"I thought that we ought to spend some time together," explained Sedeem. "Get to know our siblings. Sa'ar sent a call and suggested it."

Rorx sat. Szaifeh sat. In his lap and smiled at Tinker. "Always a surprise, Unc."

Tinker looked from face to face. "Everyone staying here?"

"We have lots of room," suggested Smoke.

"Indeed." Chicken beamed at Tinker, eyes twinkling.

"Corner room?" asked Sedeem.

"Most ready," replied Chicken.

"We'll stay at my parent's place," said Szaifeh. "But visit back and forth. Is my sister here?"

"Yes." Sha'gar walked in from the dining room. "But Sgenn is not."

Szaifeh stared at her. And blinked. "What?"

"Did you not hear?"

Szaifeh shook her head.

"We have a younger sister, Sgenn named."

Szaifeh clenched her sister's arm. "How? You are a magician. Mother couldn't have, shouldn't have, shouldn't have been able."

Sha'gar shrugged.

"It happens. Sometimes." R-Bar joined them, Ran at her side.

"In the best of families," laughed Tinker.

"Pik tik," suggested R-Bar, glowering at him.

"Mother!" gasped Sedeem.

"Im dip," hissed Szaifeh at R-Bar. "Aunt!"

"Witch vile," hissed Ran, bumping R-Bar with her elbow.

"Not too bad, kiddo," he grumbled. "You have managed to gross out our Niece and our daughter all in one fell curse, Ran included."

"Your fault." R-Bar kicked him lightly on the bottom of one foot. "Making dar remarks about my sister."

He patted the couch. "Join me. Please?"

R-Bar flopped next to him. "Hum hum."

Smoke leaned forward and peered past him at her. "Watch it," she whispered. "He is in a putty kneading mood."

"Knock it off," he mumbled at her, hoping to kill that conversational gambit before it managed to grow up.

"Dad!" Sedeem looked at him.

"Never mind." He glowered at Smoke.

So Smoke spoke directly to Sedeem's mind.

R-Bar nudged him. "Heh, heh, heh, heh."

He sighed. "Behave." It was probably a vain hope.

Smoke winked at Sedeem, who laughed. "Poor Dad."

Szaifeh stood. "I sent a call for Sgenn. Time to visit Mom

and Dad."

Rorx stood,

They disappeared.

Tinker slipped an arm around the short witch and the other around Smoke.

"See," said Smoke. "Told you."

Sedeem laughed. "Let's go talk, sister."

Je'leel nodded. They headed for the rear deck.

"O.K., you two, what's going on? This time? Goes for the rest of you as well."

Puzzled expressions and closed minds were his only answer. "Uh huh. Worse than I thought."

"I'll say." Chantal clumped into the room wearing blue overalls and big black rubber boots. "Now you are groping two at a time."

"He has been kneading my putty." Smoke winked at Chantal.

"Merde," he suggested.

Fair Morn came in from the hallway shaking her head dramatically. "Tsk, tsk, tsk."

Messenger bubbled in, giggling. "Next, next, next." And looked at Chantal. "Certainly getting to be a lot of terms for them."

Tinker frowned in her direction. "What? Now what? Them?"

Messenger looked at him, all round-eyed. She plucked her shirt front forward and peered down. "Them."

"Oh."

"Yep." She nodded violently. "Ummmms. Now putty."

He sighed. "You guys are corrupting the language. Bad

as politicians."

Chicken plucked the front of her shirt forward and leered dramatically inside it. "Forsooth, Sweet prince, We Ourself do pear most under supplied with this putty. Tis naught but mere handful." She laughed loudly. "Be this not so Great Lord?"

"Doesn't matter," he grumbled at her, at them all. "Everyone is just fine. Just fine the way you are. It does not matter at all."

"Right," agreed Messenger, spinning and staring pointedly at Chantal. "We can't all be globular shirt fillers. "She poked with one finger. "I think that you are trying to corner the putty market."

"Crazier, crazier, and crazier and crazier," he grumbled. And sighed, loudly. "What is causing all this?"

"Beats me, G.I." Chantal flopped into a chair. "I have been working in the barn. But it certainly appears that you have been working on Smoke." She filled a cup and leaned back, taking a sip. "Hot!" And glared at Messenger. "And watch what you are poking, Missy Green Eyes."

He tickled Smoke and R-Bar. R-Bar squirmed and Smoke said, "Giggle, giggle, giggle." She wasn't ticklish.

Messenger sat next to Smoke. "Is that foul fiend trying to torture you now?"

"Yep."

"Horrors!" Messenger leaned forward and stuck her tongue out at him. "What you get, foul fiend!"

"Where?" Sha'gar snatched in a green wand. "What?"

"Who is," he demanded as he began to wonder whether a trip to town might not be a good idea. They were really getting out of hand. Again.

"No sneaking off," ordered Fair Morn, catching his thought.

"No peeking," he ordered back.

"Thee may Us nay abandon." Chicken looked all Royal Stern down her nose at him.

"Yah!" agreed Messenger. "Fiendish tickle torturer putty fondling boogle!"

"Boogle?" Ran frowned at her.

"Him."

"Hum."

Sha'gar nodded and sent her wand away.

"Ah ha!" he exclaimed. "AH HA!" He had finally caught a stray thought. From them.

"What?" Chantal stared at him.

"Indeed!" So did Chicken.

"Eureka!" He smiled at them.

"Certainly did." Smoke patted his hand gently and slumped a little lower. "Putty grabber."

"All this bother," he stated, struggling to sit up. "All this bother is because of Sa'ar and Eulin." He couldn't get his arms free. "Isn't it?"

"I could have told you that." Smoke hung onto his arm.

He tugged. "Then why didn't you?"

She smiled. "This is more fun."

"Hum bug! Let me go!" He tugged.

"Buzz, buzz, buzz, buzz, buzz," buzzed Fair Morn as she flopped across all three laps and grinned crookedly up at him. She jerked. "Stop that!"

"Heh, heh, heh, heh, heh, heh," cackled R-Bar.

"That is his putty, not your's," growled Fair Morn at her.

Sha'gar leaned over the back of the couch, way over the back of the couch, sliding her arm down and around R-Bar.

"Im dik dik," snapped R-Bar, releasing his arm and flailing wildly at Sha'gar's hand

The rest joined in.

They all wound up on the floor.

In a tangled heap.

"With any luck," mumbled a voice from the bottom, "it won't be too long."

"What, Me'Lord?" Chicken had managed to wrap her arms around him.

"Eulin's birth." He kissed her. As long as she was there.

"Fair Prince?" she asked.

"What?"

"Be thee a'doing such a'Us?"

"Think so," he whispered. "Feels like you."

"Heh heh heh heh," laughed Chantal.

"EEEEEEEE!" Messenger jerked.

"OUCH!"

"Who ouch'd?" asked Chicken.

Messenger giggled wildly as she squirmed from the heap, away from Chantal.

"I did," he grunted. And wondered, once again, why he always wound up on the bottom.

The air swirled soft violet.

It filled the room with lavender hues.

She stood there.

With a young girl.

"Vander Lord?" She stifled her laugher. "Not even we do things like that." She began to laugh, unable to hold it in any longer.

"Off, off, off, off, off." Eventually, with much trashing about, he was able to sit up.

"Sa'ar." He smiled up at her, his eyes carefully looking at this young person that stood by her side. Then he stood. "Eulin?"

She stepped forward, dropped to her knees, crossed her arms over her chest, bowed her head, and said in her most formal tone of voice, "First Greetings, Vander Lord. To hear is to obey."

He stared at Sa'ar.

"The most formal greeting one may make to The Vander Lord," she explained. "She wanted to do that."

Eulin looked up at him, a tentative smile on her face. "Father?"

He laughed and out his arms. "Hi, Eulin daughter." And wrapped them around her as she lunged upward and thumped. against him. "Ooooof!" He glanced over at Sa'ar. "How old?"

"Ten of your years, Lord. We took a break from her training."

A St. Bernard sized dragon, all bronze gold, suddenly appeared and sat next to them.

Sedeem and Je'leel walked into the room, stopped, and laughed. "I don't suppose I ought to ask," said Sedeem, winking at her father. "But really young. Hi, Shar."

Sa'ar stepped over and kissed her cousin on the forehead. "You are looking very pretty, Deem." She hugged her, then

Je'leel.

"Let's sit down," said he. "On a couch?"

The rest began hastily tucking in shirts and sitting here and there. They watched him.

"Deem, Je'leel," said Sa'ar. "This is Eulin, future Heart of The Vander, called Dragon Force." She smiled proudly at them. "My daughter." And grinned. "Your sister."

Je'leel looked at him. "Father?"

Sedeem started to laugh. "Ooooooh, Daaaaad!" Then she hugged Sa'ar. "She is going to be a real beauty." She whispered very, very softly, "How did you ever manage to do that?"

"Later," came the whispered reply.

Chantal stepped over. "My turn. Gimme a hug, daughter."

The rest jumped up and crowded around. It was a well hugged daughter by the time that she was returned to her father, who by that time had sat down. In a couch.

"Father Lord?" asked Eulin as she sat by his side.

"Ummm?"

"Are all these beautiful ones your's?"

Smoke sat by his free side, leaned against him and looked past his chest at Eulin. "Yep. He is lucky that way." And winked.

Ran hurried to the kitchen to make cocoa. It was one of the few things that she enjoyed cooking.

"Is she witch?" Eulin watched her hurry away.

He nodded. Then he began to explain each of them to her.

Eulin frowned. "I thought all those stories about you were folk small tales."

He laughed. "They probably were."

"Not true!" Sa'ar sat next to her daugher. "We are not having our daughter's head filled with such fancy tales." She looked stern at her.

"Yes, Mother." It was a very weak reply. And a daughter dutiful look.

"Well," he said. "Your dragon has certainly grown."

Eulin grinned. "Anamaxtor was a very good gift."

Sha'gar joined them, kneeling, leaning her arms on his knees, smiling at her new daughter. "I am very happy that you enjoy my gift." She stood and leaned forward, to stare deep into Eulin's eyes. "Hum, hum, hum."

"What?" He frowned.

Sa'ar quickly cast protection over her daughter. "Sha'gar?"

"Dragon fire. Down deep." Sha'gar straightened up and nodded. "You are as you are named. Dragon Force."

Sa'ar sat straight, going rigid, staring at the tall magician. "How is that possible?"

Eulin giggled. "Anamaxtor gave it to me."

Sha'gar smiled. "It is your name right."

"And why wasn't I told?" demanded Sa'ar. Eulin pushed herself against her father's side.

R-Bar came back, empty handed. She had decided making cocoa this close to dinner wasn't a good idea.

"Dinner time," announced Smoke. Interrupting. "Almost. I am cooking." She reached past Eulin and handed a very ornate ring to Sa'ar. "I get it back." She kissed him on the side of the face and headed for the kitchen, saying to Sa'ar, "Watch your putty."

Fair Morn and Chantal went with her. "I'll change first,"

said Chantal heading into The Chamber and her bedroom.

Je'leel dropped into Smoke's spot. "Eulin may sleep in my room. And we can talk." She reached over and took one of her sister's hands in one of her's. "Let's go up to my room."

Eulin kissed him on the cheek and made her escape.

Sa'ar moved closer to him. "They are beautiful, our children." She would ask him about what Smoke had said later.

"Our?"

"Yes." She nodded. "Je'leel, Sedeem, and Rorx are my children now."

"I suppose."

She slipped an arm around his back. "Vander Lord, you have a very tangled familial structure."

He sighed. "My life used to be so simple before all kinds of folk started messing with it." He slipped an arm around her shoulders. "I can never get used to the trick that you guys use to raise children. They grow up. You don't age."

She nodded. "It is often a surprise to the mothers as well. But it is the way of many magic users and some other folk as well. Yet the generations do get spaced out."

Messenger bounced to her feet and tapped Sha'gar on the shoulder. "Help me make salad. Just lots and lots."

They hurried toward the kitchen. Messenger leaned close and said something. They all heard Sha'gar hum.

R-Bar nudged Ran. "Let's go visit with my sister, Reep." Ran nodded.

"We'll be back," intoned R-Bar in her best Arnold manner.

"For dinner," added Ran.

They disappeared in a puff of black.

Chicken stood. "Great Lord, We will Us away for to arrange thy quarters." Grinning broadly she headed into and down the hall.

"Just you and me, kid," he lisped.

"Yesssss." She wrapped her arms around him and toppled him over.

Umm?" he said after awhile.

"They do not mind," she replied. He had sounded worried about something.

"I know that."

"Oh. Of course." She kissed the tip of his nose. "What?"

"Ahhhhhhhhh, all that succession problem taken care of?"

"Yes." She tickled the tip of his ear with a fingertip. "Father Lord?"

"Ummmmm?"

She sat up as he did and arranged herself comfortably in his lap. "You do worry too much too much"

"Someone has to." He sighed. He didn't think that he did.

She poked a finger inside his shirt. "Tickle, tickle, tickle."

"Sa'ar?"

"Lord?"

"No more children, right?"

She grinned. "Not to worry. The Vander have absolute control over such matters."

"I wasn't worried," he grumbled and grabbed her pesky hand. "I just wanted to know, that's all."

"To hear is to obey." The side of her mouth jerked as she fought back laughter. "How many more do you want?" She burst into rolling laughter at the expression on his face.

Sha'gar ripped the head of lettuce to shreds and dumped it into a large bowl. "She shouldn't do things like that to him." Red flickered deep in her eyes.

"Shhhhh, shhhhh, shhhh," cautioned Messenger, heaving into the bowl other vegetables. "We are not supposed to be listening."

"He did not say that it was private." Sha'gar started to slice tomatoes. "Nor was he closed off."

"Welllll, just don't say anything." Messenger bumped her with a hip. "You will get us all into trouble."

"Hum." Sha'gar ordered the salad dressing into the bowl. She watched the bottle pour in the correct amount.

"Really really." Messenger nodded violently. "Trouble."

Smoke walked into the room, announcing loudly as she came, grinning widely, "If you are done assaulting her, dinner is ready."

Sa'ar laughed. "I don't think that he has started. Yet." She smiled at him. "Have you?"

"How is it?" he mumbled. "That in less than half an hour or so, you have managed to acquire all their bad habits?"

She moved away, stood, and smiled at Smoke. "I think that it is his bad influence rather than the other way around."

Smoke winked at her. "Probably so. He is really a bad influence all right. Look how fast he corrupted Sha'gar."

Tinker snapped upright, glowering at both of them. "All right, all right, we're not going to have one of those conversations, are we?" He certainly hoped that they weren't.

They all gathered around the dining room table, dropping into their chairs. Everyone was very polite and circumspect throughout the meal. Except every now and then, one would lean close to another, whisper, and then burst into gentle laughter.

"Merde," he mumbled to himself, wondering what it was that they were up to this time. He was really beginning to worry. This was a very bad sign, them being this well behaved and quiet.

And then.

Dinner was done.

All quickly cleared the table.

And with a great flourish, Smoke came from the kitchen and set a very large cake in the center of the table and then they all gave presents to Eulin. Then they all hugged and kissed her and Sa'ar. There was a short pause, then they hugged and kissed Sedeem and Je'leel as well. They just hugged Rorx.

"We all decided to merge their birthdays into one," explained Chantal, handing the cake server to Smoke. Chantal sat down, next to Dat who was large for the occasion.

R-Bar winked at him. "Three beautiful daughters."

"Three beautiful mothers," said Chantal, nudging Dat with an elbow and laughing. "Beat you to it."

"Yum, yum, yum, yum, yum," said Dat

"Mother!" gasped Je'leel. "You made a joke!"

Dat grinned at her. "And I will have some cake also." She beamed at Tinker. "Having daughters is fun."

"Cut the cake," he grumbled at Smoke before any of them could pursue that topic any further.

Smoke shoved the cake and the cake server in his

direction. "Your job." Chicken shoved the stack of plates at him.

She stood. "We will Ourself retrieve great ice'd cream tub."

So he cut the cake.

And Smoke handed around the loaded plates.

And they demolished the cake.

And the ice cream.

It was well after dinner. They sat, sprawled, slumped, or whatever, around the large living room. Rorx and Szaifeh had returned to her parent's place.

Sedeem sat and talked softly with Je'leel and Eulin about doing wander out in the elseplaces. Once in a while, Farth would interject a small comment.

Chantal read through her large stack of professional trade journals. Somehow that stack never seemed to shrink, week after week.

Messenger sat on the middle of Fair Morn's back, as Fair Morn sprawled face down on the rug, and massaged her shoulder, and flight muscles. She had shoved Fair Morn's shirt up above her shoulder blades.

Chicken was brushing Sha'gar's hair into a wave of shining darkness.

In the dining room, Smoke, R-Bar, and Ran sat at the table playing Hearts. The two witches had promised not to cheat. Or to magic the cards.

Into all this quiet, Sa'ar stood, walked over, opened the door to the small living room, and beckoned at Tinker with one finger.

"Umm?" He stood and walked over to see what she

wanted.

She tugged him inside, shoved the door shut and wrapped her arms around him.

"What?"

"Your eight are wonderful."

"Uh huh?"

"Eulin was so surprised and so happy that I almost cried."

He nodded. "You weren't the only one. There were lots of glistening eyes around the table."

"They really do love her, don't they?"

"Sure. She has very eight different mothers in that bunch, but they are all the same in that aspect. Nine of them if you count Dat. And I think that she would like to counted as one as well." He smiled. "This is the first time that we have ever had all the kids home at the same time." He kissed her. "Thanks."

She tugged his shirt loose. "They all look like their father." And shoved him back against the couch.

He fell backward. "Oooof! Actually they all look more like their mothers. Good thing, too."

She nodded, bathed the room in violet light, and settled next to him. "We all love you too."

"Who's we?"

"The Vander."

He sighed. He wasn't ready for something like that. It was a frightening thought.

"All will behave." She slipped her shoulder free from the shirt she was wearing, one of Smoke's. "Except Imdar and I. You are our's."

The three sisters sat around in Je'leel's room. They had relocated to there in order to talk privately.

"Bet Dad was unhappy to loose this room." Sedeem sat on the floor, leaning back against one wall, an arm around Eulin's shoulders. It had been his Den, an extra private space Smoke had built during one of the several remodeling projects.

Je'leel nodded. "He didn't say anything, not a word. I think that the mothers convinced him." She bounced on the edge of the bed. "But he insisted that there had to be furniture." Anamaxtor's head bounced. He was sprawling on the bed, but in such a manner that he could see and watch Eulin.

"Jel," asked Sedeem. "Will you be able to do wander?"

She shrugged. "I do not know. Nothing has been said. But I have no need to do that. I am indjinn." She looked at Eulin. "Will you be permitted?:

"Mother hasn't said. But if it is suitable for The Heart of the Vander, then it will be so."

Sedeem grinned and hugged her. "Tar, Szai, and I did wander together. And so did Shem and Sa'ar. I think that you will go."

Je'leel nodded. "If you go, then I will go. If you would like?"

Eulin grinned at her. "We could have fun." She frowned at the floor past the ends of her toes. "All I ever do to study and work and study and work."

Sedeem laughed. "It is all any of us did until we were around eighteen of his years old or so. Then we did wander to finish our learning. Most found their's that way, on wander."

Eulin nodded. "Is that where Mother found Father?"

"Your mother did things differently." Sedeem grinned.

"So did Dad." Then she began to tell her sisters various of the tales that she knew about him and the mothers and how they had come to be the multiperson that they are.

They spent the rest of the evening listening to tale after tale. Sedeem had spent considerable time gathering in these tales and verifying the truth of them.

Chicken leaned forward and peered down at Smoke who was now lying on her back on the rug, fingers laced together over her stomach, staring up at the ceiling. The card game had finished. Chicken nudged her with one toe. "All do peer most relaxed."

Smoke rolled her head and winked at her.

Chicken poked her again. "We do Ourself nay refer to most gentle administrations of fair Sa'ar."

Smoke grabbed the ankle of the still offending foot and reached over with her other hand.

"DESIST!" Chicken thrashed wildly as she was tickled.

"Oh, dear," said Messenger. "She is being tickle tortured."

"STOP . . . STOP . . . STOP ," gasped Chicken.

Smoke did. And was glared at,

"Vile wench!"

"Toe poker!"

"She is just bothered because Sa'ar is in there instead of a certain thin warrior person." Fair Morn poked Chicken in the side.

"Piffle," snorted Chicken. "Slim, not thin!"

Fair Morn gave her another little poke. "Huh?" And did it again.

"Leave off a'pushing Our anatomy, Wing'd Wench." Chicken jabbed back.

"Watch it!"

"Thee do Us so poke."

"That robe is so baggy that I couldn't tell."

Chicken snarled and poked. "Vile body slur cur!"

"That did it." Fair Morn shoved her hand inside Chicken's robe.

"Unhand Us, most foul clutcher."

"Stop poking people."

"EEEEEEK!" Smoke had just grabbed Chicken's ankle and foot again.

Chantal dropped the journal she had been trying to read. "Anyone want some cocoa?" She stood and headed for the kitchen having decided that they all needed something else to do.

"We have Ourself been abandoned," sobbed Chicken dramatically as she kicked Smoke with her free foot.

Smoke sat up and pulled, half dragging her from the couch. "Princess, that robe the only thing you are wearing?"

"Indeed, foul ravisher of the innocent."

Smoke let go of her ankle and looked up at Fair Morn. "Guess we had better release her before she is totally not wearing that robe."

Fair Morn grinned at Smoke. "She gets a very erotic urge at times."

"Bushwah!" snapped Chicken, shoving herself more upright.

"Hum hum." Ran leaned over the back of that couch and slide her hands down either side of Chicken's face and into her robe.

WATCH IT! shouted Chantal into their minds. *Sedeem and younger daughters are coming!*

Ran jerked her hands away, yanked Chicken's robe into order, and kissed her on the side of the face. "Can't fool us."

Just as Chicken reached for her, Sedeem, Eulin, and Je'leel walked into the room.

"We smelled cocoa," explained Sedeem, casting a quick glance at Chicken as she tugged her robe further closed. "And decided that after cocoa it would be bed time for younger sisters."

Messenger had decided that all required cocoa.

Farth is on the rear deck." Smoke looked at her. *Your Father is otherwise occupied at the moment.*

Sedeem stifled her laughter.

Everyone had cocoa and cookies including Farth who had been called in from where he had been sitting, enjoying the quiet of outside evening.

Anamaxtor had cookies only.

Chapter Nine

Friends and Traveling Companions

Grandeville. Tinker's Place.

It was the sobbing that did it.

The muffled sobbing.

It brought him up from deep sleep to awareness.

It was a slow trip.

"Ummmmm, huh?" He looked over at the clock. Red numerals told him, 03:42 a.m.

It was the only thing that he could see in the total darkness of his room. Rolling the other way, he reached out and slid an arm over her. "What?"

Her arm slipped over his side and tightened around him. "We are leaving tomorrow."

"Ah. Ummm?"

Soft lips brushed against his face. "Momentary lapse, Lord."

His fingers gently stroked over velvet smooth skin as he cleared his throat. "Gonna miss you, too," he mumbled. "Both of you."

"Eulin insisted and I agreed."

"To?"

"A wander. After training."

He sighed.

She kissed him again. "We know what happened to Sedeem and the rest on their first wander."

"It hurts to remember."

"Eulin will be well protected."

"We thought that they were safe doing that."

"She is dragon linked."

"Still . . . "

Her arm tightened. Just a little bit more.

"Oh, oh."

"Je'leel said she would go with her."

"What?" He tried to sit up. She wouldn't let him.

"She will be safe."

"I know that. I think. She is partially indjinn. Whatever that is."

She released, him so he could sit up. He did. So did she. "You don't know?"

"Nope. I don't think that anyone does. Even Dat. Who is one." He slipped back toward the wall, leaned against it, and sighed. Heavily.

She hitched herself closer and leaned against him. "Lord, how may I ease such worry as I hear in that sigh?"

He reached out and wrapped her in his arms, "Sa'ar, I don't know. I know less and less about more and more as time goes by. Look at my children. What are they?"

"Stop!" She felt his body shaking.

"Sedeem is some sort of a magician witch hybrid crawling with all kinds of magic. Rorx is your warlock doing whatever it is that he is supposed to do. Je'leel is more or less indjinn. And now Eulin is some damned dragon something or other."

"Stop, stop. Stop!" She crushed herself against him. He could feel the tears dripping on his shoulder.

"O.K.," he mumbled. "O.K." He gently rubbed her back, fingers sliding over tense muscles. "Just sorta catches up to me now and then, that's all."

"Come visit, Lord, come visit. We can search the archives and find some way to help. Your cultural beliefs fight with your personal reality. Your cultural beliefs keep trying to deny us all."

"I must be tired. Always happens when I get tired." He settled a little bit and leaned back again. There was a dull thunk as his head banged into the wall. "Ump!"

"Lord?"

"Forgot."

She laughed. Stood. Stepped down the bed. Tossing aside the covers, she grabbed his ankles and pulled.

"What?"

She lay down, arms and legs twined around him. "There is a Vander custom for the Vander Lord and The Vander Heart on their last night together."

"Ummmm, the last time we tried one of those Vander things we almost killed ourselves."

"Not to worry, Lord of Us All." She cast light Vander on him. "There."

Eight pair of eyes flew open.

Ran walked into R-Bar's bedroom and wrapped her in

her arms.

R-Bar hissed softly at her, "We will have to have a talk with her in the morning."

"Dark sister." She slipped into the deep recess that was Smoke's bed.

Strong arms yanked her down. "Princess?"

"Fair Sa'ar do touch us all."

"Certainly did."

Messenger burrowed under the blankets and nuzzled Fair Morn. "She shouldn't do things like that."

"The witches and Smoke will talk to her in the morning."

"Damn." Chantal slipped Sha'gar's pajama top off. "She needs her butt kicked,"

Sha'gar nodded and slid gentle palms over Chantal.

"You are so warm," sighed Chantal. "And so . . . "

"Tasty," sighed Sha'gar.

Sunlight had long before sent bright tentacles across the floor, over the bed, and up the far wall before there was any recognition that day had arrived.

"Ummmm," he said. "Suppose we ought to get up and go get some breakfast."

She smiled. "To hear is to obey." She kissed him. "However, at the moment, I find that I am not capable of doing that."

"Didn't mean at this very instance."

She laughed deep in her throat. "Certainly hope so."

They were all lounging around the dining room table dressed in pajamas and robes.

Smoke set several platters of cinnamon rolls on the table. Je'leel slid a platter over, took a roll, and shoved the platter to Eulin. "You'll like these."

Eulin took a roll, stared at it thoughtfully, and handed the platter to Sedeem. "Mother really likes Father."

Sedeem smiled at her. "She has loved him for a very, very long time."

Chantal nudged Sha'gar. "He is going to sleep for a week."

"Hum hum hum." Sha'gar pushed a platter over toward her.

Messenger yawned widely.

Fair Morn took two rolls and set another on Messenger's plate. "Eat, kitten." And shoved the mostly empty serving dish at Smoke. "Isn't there anything you can do?"

Smoke took the last two rolls and stood to get another pan full. "I could have. But I didn't think that we had anything to worry about here at home." She headed for the kitchen.

Chicken was emptying baking pans onto another platter.

"Better set some aside for him and her."

"Indeed!"

All the rolls, but their share, were gone, just a few crumbs here and there, when Tinker and Sa'ar strolled into the room. They had come from the shower and were wearing thick white robes.

He flopped into his chair and pulled his coffee cup over. Chicken filled it.

Sa'ar pulled the ornate ring from her finger and handed it to Smoke, bent sideways and kissed her cheek. Jerking upright, she gasped, "How did? Oh!" She cast hard and solid. "Sorry, sorry, sorry, sorry."

Ran looked at her. "That was not-nice."

"Sorry, sorry." Sa'ar bowed her head. "How may I atone?"

"Hum," replied Ran.

"Ran . . . fer!" snapped R-Bar. "That is also not-nice." She glared at Sa'ar.

Tinker stared at them. "Now what's going on?"

Chicken tapped his forearm and smiled. "Of no matter, Sweet prince. Tis ne'business of thee but of her and us."

Sa'ar walked around the table and sat in the empty chair. And smiled at her daughter. "Ready?"

Eulin nodded. "Do we have to?"

"We do. It is now time to begin to bring you to a higher level of training and knowledge, Young Heart."

"To hear is to obey," mumbled Eulin.

"When we are done with breakfast."

And soon, all too soon, for some of them, they gathered on the rear deck to say their goodbyes to Sa'ar and to Eulin who were now dressed, Vander proper for travel, in billowing lavender garb.

Everyone hugged and kissed everyone.

"Remember," whispered Eulin to Je'leel. "You promised"

"I will."

They were gone. In a soft flash of purple.

Sedeem grabbed and hugged him. "Us too, Dad. Farth wants to see if there is a Silver Ranger unit on Bandel's Finger, He is trying to locate all of them so they can be reunited in one place."

She kissed his cheek. "He is going to be a great General. I like my sisters." And beckoned Farth over.

He stepped close to Tinker and bowed. "As always, Great Lord, we have enjoyed your hospitality."

Sedeem smiled and grabbed Farth's hand.

They were gone.

Smoke reached over pinched Chicken.

"Eeeek!"

And handed her the ornate ring. "I get it back."

Chicken slipped the ring on a finger and leered at him.

He sat on one of the wooden benches, heavily he sat, leaned back against the table edge. "Anyone want to tell me why Sa'ar was telling everyone sorry sorry? What did she do? This time?"

Chantal walked over and sat next to him. "You sure that you really want to know?"

"Yep."

R-Bar and Ran sat by his free side.

"She was anxious for you to relax," explained R-Bar.

"Cause you were slipping into one of your deep grumbles," added Chantal.

"She cast light Vander on you, Amtar." Ran nodded at him.

"And it slipped from your mind to our's before I realized

what was happening." Smoke watched him closely.

"Vander lust!" exclaimed Fair Morn.

"Pant, pant, pant," giggled Messenger. She panted heavily at him to demonstrate.

"We will he guarded next time," stated Sha'gar.

Chicken slipped around to stand in front of him and lightly touched the tip of his nose with the ornate ring. "Tis thy natural state, Our King."

He sighed. "It is always something, isn't it?"

"Certainly was." Chantal nudged him with her shoulder. "Vander stud."

"How about we get our chores done so we all can take a nap. Or whatever. O.K.?"

Everyone nodded.

And headed off before he could say anything else.

Anxious to keep him from grumbling and worrying again.

Plana Dar. Late Afternoon.

He sat on top of a pile of rubble. He was a large, somewhat round man dressed in stained and scarred battle armor.

Popping his visor up, he smiled and admired the destruction stretching in all directions. Acrid fumes drifted in the air, grey bands feather floating on the slight breeze. Here and there, material not consumed smoldered dark columns upward.

Looking across the great plain of the shattered city, he watched a silver woman stroll from the open doorway of a large building, still standing, not too badly damaged. She clambered up the heap and sat by his side.

"Anything useful in there?"

"Yes. MechBots are taking parts to Ship. And a large collection of message discs."

"Message discs. Perhaps we may learn something useful after all. Even profitable." He looked from side to side. "Not much left to this place. Just that building. And the outlying hamlets. Them I didn't touch. It was just the overclass that had to go." He waggled one hand at the large structure in front of them. "Perhaps I ought to leave it standing as a little something for future visitors to see and to ponder."

"Scanning discs," she said.

"Connecting new devices to test circuits," she intoned.

He nodded, mostly to himself. "I think that I will leave it standing."

"Connecting new devices to viewing screens."

He fired, blowing away a large piece of the front wall. "There. Much better."

"Viewing next planet over."

He looked at her. "That good?"

"Fast scanning surface. Four large cities, advanced technology. All communication channels calm."

He rubbed his hands together. "A very good addition. We have always been limited in that capability before." He threw an arm around her waist. "Now ship has far vision."

She nodded. And kissed him.

"Let's go up."

Ship took them.

Up.

Ranzal. Mid-Day.

Anjan glared at the young woman dressed in orange and blue.

"Of no importance," said Ranna, eyes running over this person with such poor manners.

Anjan was frowning across the table at their uninvited guest who was sitting there, just sitting there at their table.

"Has that witch cast enchantment on you?" she growled at Anjan, admiring the arch of Anjan's eyebrows.

Anjan's hand slipped down to the semicircular thing hanging from her belt. The sharp edge and the jewels glittered in the sunlight.

She and Ranna had been sitting at an outside booth, watching the crowds of buyers and sellers. Ranna, after rejoining Anjan on Doth Lamex had brought them to this elseplace, where she had sought a certain purveyor of the darkest of arcana, without success.

They had stopped for refreshment and to take some time so Ranna could ponder this particular problem which was beginning to irritate her. Now they had been joined by this unwanted company, increasing her irritation. The air began to soft crackle.

Ranna stayed Anjan's hand. "This dak tar is brain soft."

Their visitor leaped to her feet and yanked in an orange and blue mage mace. "Dak tar! Scar ugly cheek witch, you must need punishment."

All around the booth, people shoved, making space, trying to get to safety before it was too late. No one wanted to be too close when magic users argued or fought. It was just not healthy. This was especially true when the combatants were a witch and a magician.

"Scar ugly cheek?" Ranna gently touched her cheek. A small, jagged lightning stroke ran zig-zag over it. Normally her hair cascaded over that side of her face. She left that scar there as a reminder to herself to be much more careful than the occasion had caused that wound. She gazed at this unpleasant mage and said something, softly, gently.

Fire blossomed on the mage's cheek as black wrapped her in midnight cocoon. Ranna cast follow and stood. "Let us go to our lodgings. We can play with her there."

People ran for their lives.

Ranna started toward their rooms. The air around them settled down. Anjan paid for the drinks, their's and the mage's and hurried to walk by Ranna's side. The black lump followed them, floating in the air.

Clear Bandler. Tripple.

"Dear?" She nudged him.

He had been sitting outside, on the garden bench. Just relaxing. Practicing. She had slipped up and sat next to him. A very small woman, half his height, dressed in clothing of soft pastel shades. He smiled and slipped an arm around her.

"We must travel out there. Tears is a grown man and should return to his own elseplace"

He nodded. "You are correct." He kissed her forehead. "Now?"

"Next day. Tears will pack this night. As will I."

"I still miss Sorrowful as well."

She knelt on the bench and kissed him. "Yes." And jumped down and left him to his thoughts.

Bahn Duhr Tohr. The Royal City. A Fairly Nice Day.

As the last petitioner backed away and out of The Audience Hall, the Queen beckoned over the Royal Scroll Keeper and told him to hold the visitors outside for a short while. Then she slumped into a more comfortable position in her portion of The Dual Throne and took her husband's hand in one of her's. "Great King, We have some small piece of business to discuss, We do."

He leaned sideways and kissed her. "Of course."

"Our children are ready for The Quest. They have returned not many dar past from Our Dark Advisor's witch training, full grown and most ready."

He frowned.

"It is necessary."

He nodded as his face darkened even more.

Her fingers tightened on his hand. "If thee should frown in such a manner at a petitioner, they would flee afear'd for their very lives."

He leaned back and stared into her eyes.

"They are warrior trained, many level trained," she stated. "And will have the latest design of armor and the very best of weapons. Much better than that which We did carry when We did The Quest." She lifted his hand and kissed it. "We survived."

He nodded. "Your brother did not."

"We two traveled separately. The Prince and The Princess have decided to quest together." She smiled.

"And."

"The Princess will wear white as did We, this Your Queen. And The Prince has chosen midnight dark. Thus he marks himself her opposite and yet complimentary other."

He cleared his throat. "When will they leave?"

"In one full set of days. It is a Most Royal Occasion and a Public Faire."

He nodded.

"A Quest is a prerequisite for rulers at all levels and stations. Every Noble in each and every kingdom has done this thing. Most survived. Some were never heard of again."

"I didn't do Quest."

"My King, thee were elseplace born. Making thee Our King was a special event."

The Royal Scroll Keeper carefully approached and whispered to them that petitioners were piling up in the outer hall.

The King nodded and sat up. So did the Queen.

The doors were reopened.

Grandeville. Tinker's Place.

It was a good month later, a good month since Sa'ar had returned to the Vander Guild house on Magevern. Life had been relaxed with the usual casual visiting here and there.

The young woman walked in from the hallway and stared.

At them.

In the large living room.

It was Sunday. It was mid-morning. All were lounging around in their pajamas, men's pajamas, more or less in their pajamas, as was their usual custom.

The Sunday papers were scattered around in the usual state of disorder. As was their custom. Each of them had claimed whatever portion of the papers that they favored. As was their custom.

They laid, sat, and sprawled. On the furniture. On the floor. Here and there, various of the cats had joined them. The cats were sprawling also. As was their custom.

Chicken was reading the comics to Smoke who had given up trying to learn this reading thing. After all, she felt that she didn't really need to learn this strange skill as telepathic carnivores had no cultural feel for it. If she needed to, she could just borrow the appropriate memories from someone else.

Tinker had finished those sections of the newspaper that he favored and had dropped them on the floor and was now sitting comfortably sprawled, slumped on one of the couches, just relaxing into the day.

Ran had, after much poking and prodding and piling of pillows, sat in his lap, her back propped against one of the couch arm rests. She was reading the Travel sections.

Fair Morn, sprawled face down on the rug, her pajama top off as Messenger sat in the small of her back, massaging Fair Morn's neck, shoulder, and flight muscles. Messenger liked doing it. Fair Morn enjoyed having her doing it.

Chantal was braiding R-Bar's hair and trying to talk her into letting it grow even longer.

Sha'gar and Je'leel were in the kitchen talking about what to make for breakfast

Smoke had felt the young woman arrive on their rear deck, had recognized her, and had decided that it wasn't necessary to say anything.

"Father?" The voice was a soft silken caress. She stared into the room. She knew that he had to be there somewhere. But she couldn't see him.

"What?" His voice came from one of the couches, the one facing away from the hallway.

She walked over and looked down, over the back of the couch. Ran nodded at her and smiled. She smiled back "I told Anamaxtor to stay on the rear deck."

He couldn't twist his head around enough to see so he used Ran's eyes. "Eulin?"

"Yes, Lord." She hurried around the couch and dropped to her knees, facing him. "First Greetings, Vander Lord. To hear is to obey." She bowed her head and waited. And waited, Vander correct.

The rest crowded around, yanking her to her feet, ending that. After eight hugs and kisses, she looked at him. "Father Lord?"

Messenger handed Fair Morn her top.

He stared at his daughter as she stood next to Chantal and cleared his throat. "You are now traveling alone?"

"I am Vander trained, Vander capable." Her bearing became subtly more self aware, more in control.

"I think," interjected Chantal, tossing an arm around Eulin's waist, "that your father thinks that anyone with a body like that and a voice like that will attract much too much attention, of the undesirable kind. Especially a single young female."

Eulin smiled at them. "I am eighteen of your years old. Besides I won't be alone. I will be with Je'leel and Anamaxtor." She slipped her arm around Chantal's shoulders. "And, I am the first child totally raised in the Vander Way. This is a new thing for our guild."

"What about Rorx?" He wondered what the Vander had done, this time.

Ran slipped from his lap. She felt his irritation starting to grow.

Eulin shrugged one shoulder. "My brother is our warlock. A male. I am The Heart To Be. A female. His training was tightly focused. Mine was general and all encompassing." She smiled. "I will be safe. Wander is something that I must do."

"And if I disagree?"

"Not even The Vander Lord may interfere." It was a no-nonsense statement, delivered by the Future Heart of The Vander. Slowly she pulled away from Chantal and slipped to her knees, and looked up at him. "But a daughter asks her father, please?"

He nodded, knowing that there was no use arguing the point.

She leaped up, spun, and flopped on the couch next to his side. "I will be careful."

Je'leel came in from the kitchen. Ran made room so Je'leel could sit by his other side.

"Nobody move!" snapped Chantal, hurrying from the room.

"Now what?" he grumbled.

She rushed back, yanked the cover off her camera, and started shooting pictures of the trio on the couch, of Tinker and his two daughters. "Just thought that I would record this moment. It's historic." She laughed.

Sha'gar walked in. "Lunch is ready. It is too late to call it breakfast meal."

Ranzal. Mid-Day.

She leaned back against a large table and made a slight gesture. The black faded away, uncovering the young woman's face.

"Name me a name and speak tell why you are bothering us so!" She reached out and lightly touched the newly scarred cheek. "Very nice."

Their prisoner growled at them.

"Speak tell," she demanded. Dark rumbled across the ceiling. Magicians could be so irritating.

"I am Hacto mage Adarlak," she spit, glaring at Ranna, wondering how that witch could touch her without causing an explosion.

"Hum hum. A small and minor guild of no record." She indicated her companion. "Anjan. I am Faan witch Ranna."

Adarlak's eyes flew wide. "The cross-tied witch clan?"

Ranna folded her arms over her chest and nodded. "More than once. Bother?"

"Dola," mumbled Adarlak. "I would not say."

"I would have you say," hissed Ranna. The dark shroud tightened, just a little.

"AK!" gasped Adarlak. "It was her. Strong seek want."

Ranna looked at Anjan. "You want our toy?"

Anjan shook her head. "Ena."

"If I release you, Hacto mage Adarlak, will you not bother?"

"Dola. As you wish."

The black faded and went somewhere. Adarlak stretched and waggled her arms. "Would you sell?"

"She is free given," snapped Ranna, grabbing Anjan's

arm to keep her from attacking. "The Faan do not deal flesh." She frowned. "Is that what Hacto mage do?"

"NATA! I would purchase freedom, not else." She nodded at Anjan. "Not else."

"Hum," said Ranna.

Adarlak touched her check with one trembling finger. "Take remove." It was a spell cast scar. Only the caster of the spell would be able to remove it.

Ranna shook her head. "A small lesson." And waved in a meal. For three. "Eat with us." It was a small concession.

Bandel's Finger. Green and Pleasant.

They poked through the decaying buildings and wandered the overgrown paths and roads. Then they began to carefully search the central structure.

"It looks like a deliberate move." Farth lifted a metal desk and set it to one side.

Sedeem stood in the doorway and watched. Everything. Staying out of the way. But watching carefully.

"It is here." Farth knelt and began to carefully search the floor, shoving rumble out of the way, rubbing his hand back and forth, wiping a spot dean. "Somewhere."

"Careful, husband." The air crackled faintly around her.

Farth nodded, cleaning an ever widening patch. Then he bent close and peered at something, face almost touching the floor. He tapped with one finger. "Here."

Sedeem stepped over and looked at the indicated spot. "Hum." She reached in her personal wand and gestured for him to move to one side. He heaved himself to his feet and did. She stepped back against the wall and waited for him to join her.

Then she did it.

The floor opened.

The guardian oozed out and stared at them.

Farth yanked his sword free and held it in front of himself, hilt up, clenching it just below the hand guard.

He reminded her of a priest warding off a vampire in one of the B-grade movies she had watched at her parent's home.

The guardian snarled and stared at the design etched deeply in the flaring side guard. It faded away.

"Very ugly," said Sedeem.

"Very effective." Farth banged his sword back into its scabbard, stepped to the opening in the floor, knelt, leaned over, and plunged one arm deep inside. He lifted out a scroll, unrolled it, and began to read the complicated script of the Silver Rangers.

"They were contacted by the Trayl Guard and relocated. This unit was the Dragon Crest Arm."

"Where?"

"Five Star Bar. We go to Plakdar first. There is an outpost with the Wryl Team there. They guard the passage." He smiled. "We have found three parts."

"Plakdar is a prak elseplace."

"Wife?" There were times when he didn't understand her at all. It was her Faan sub-dialect.

"A place of outcasts."

"It is the gateway."

She stood on her tiptoes and kissed him. "We will go. But you may not like what I do if we are attacked."

He frowned at her.

"Fiercely protective." She nudged him gently in the

stomach with her wand. And then grabbed one of his hands.

And took them to Plakdar.

Duraldin. A Darkly Shadowed Room.

The outer door burst open, Slim Shadow hurtled inside, slamming the door closed behind himself. He charged up the stairs and into the main hall. The group of four turned and stared at him. This was most unusual behavior for a member of the Thieves Guild.

The Guild Master, Dark Quick, nodded at this very agitated younger member. "Yes?"

"Ripped to shreds!" gasped Slim Shadow. "This, this thing . . . came. PIECES!" He ran into the proper room, bent double and lost his breakfast and lunch down the correct opening.

When he returned, the Guild Master sat in one of the chairs, waiting for the rest to gather, waiting for this young thief to settle down and to place himself into the proper state.

"Breathe deep, Apprentice. Tell us of this happening."

Slim Shadow sucked in a ragged deep breath, exhaled, and sat.

And told them.

He, Slim Shadow, had been skulking around the northwest gate, just outside it, waiting for a good chance to steal from the packs of the few travelers as they passed by, as they stood and talked with one another before entering the city.

Razor, Midnight, Starbright, and Slippery had arrived, very well hidden, had seen him, and had laughed at his embarrassment at being seen by them. Of course, this quartet were very high level and few folk could notice them. Casting multi-dark on the apprentice, they told him to stick next to the wall over there, and to watch them and to observe their technique.

And all went very well. So well, in fact, that five backpacks were almost full of coin and other valuables. The four had shared with the apprentice as this was his spot. The four were almost ready to head inside the city and to their bank, as there was almost no traffic and had been none for some time, when they saw in the distance, strolling down the Market Road, two young women. Two very relaxed young women

So, the quartet decided that one last bit of lifting would be in order and then the spot would be Slim Shadow's again.

The pair approached the gate, laughing softly about something. The one in grey halted her companion. The one dressed in black asked the other, "What?"

"Thieves," she replied.

"Where?"

The one in grey pointed. "There! Four of them." And pointed again. "One more, over there. That one is no problem."

The one in black snarled, yanked in a wand, and cast protection.

The quartet smiled at each other. This was a young witch. They had nothing to fear from a young witch. Her companion was unknown.

The one in grey looked right at the four. "Leave us be! We have nothing of value for you!" It was a command, not a request.

"She must have special sight," observed Midnight.

"I see no weapon." said Slippery.

Starbright nudged Razor. "They are a pair of beauties." And smiled.

Razor nodded. "You may have the witch. The hauty grey is mine."

The quartet circled around the pair.

"You are warned," snapped the one in grey.

Starbright slipped up behind the witch and grabbed her, yanking her backwards.

"TAK TAK!" she screamed, trying to stab with her wand. But seeing no one there.

Razor grabbed the other one.

She did not resist. She just leaned with him and said something under her breath.

Slim Shadow bent over in his chair, wrapped his head in his arms, and began to sob.

They waited

Patient as thieves.

Finally, gaining some control, he sat up, wiped his face with a sleeve, and cleared his throat And told them.

The thing rose up, rose up from the ground, all odd angles, bent and crooked. With one swing of a taloned hand at the end of a multi-jointed arm, it slashed Razor's back open from the base of the skull to his pelvis, and ripped his backbone free. Looping the grisly object around Midnight's throat, it yanked him to the ground, slashing his intestines out.

Straightening up, it grabbed Slippery and crushed his throat. Then it spun to one side, slipped past the struggling witch and plunged talons deep into Starbright's side and ripped away his rib cage.

"Just that fast," rasped Slim Shadow. "Four, five movements. Then it ripped them to shreds, throwing pieces, things to all sides. Everything was still cloaked in not-see."

Clenching the arm rest of his chair tightly, he stared at the Guild Master. "Then it came at me."

"STOP!" commanded the one in grey.

The thing did, and turned. She said something. And it sank back into the ground.

She walked over and looked into his eyes. "Make yourself visible! Your friends were warned. What is your name, young thief?"

"Sl . . . Sli . . . Slim Shadow." He no longer appeared vague.

She nodded. And turned as her companion ran over to them, snarling and growling. The air crackled around her. "Who grabbed me?" She glowered at the thief. "Him?"

"No. Four dead friends."

"Where are they?"

Smiling a small half-smile, the one in grey waved one hand lazily. "All over."

Slim Shadow felt his knees quiver, and threaten to buckle.

"It was that smile." He hiccuped. And looked embarrassed at The Guild Master. "Then she kissed me on the forehead, patted the side of my face, and walked away."

He watched them walk toward the city gate. The grey one

looped her arm over her companion's shoulders and spoke to her in low tones.

"WHAT ARE YOUR NAMES?" he yelled at their backs.

The pair stopped, turned and walked back to him.

"Our names will do you no good," said the one in grey.

Slim Shadow tried a weak smile. "It is good to know who spared your life."

"I am Sgenn."

"Sook," said the other.

The Guild Master nodded.

"And then they walked into the city and I ran here."

The Guild Master stood. "Warn our brothers. This grey Sgenn must be untouched. Until we decide upon this matter."

The thieves scattered to spread the word.

Chapter Ten

Plots And Plans.

Ebna Raint. A Pleasant Mist Shadowed Day.

"Majitar."

It was the proper, formal greeting. It was given by the Top Ranked selected for the mission.

They were in the room. The room was moderate in size, sparsely furnished. A few chairs, a desk which faced the door, and a small table with four chairs, all set toward a corner away from the door.

The First of The First nodded. "Majitar are we."

Formal greetings over, they sat at the table and allowed themselves to be served various of the foodstuffs by the attendant.

Naqua carefully swallowed. "There are no longer Plani'tar. That kingdom is gone."

The Majitar looked at him And blinked."Where?"

"Not relocated. Destroyed."

"Destroyed? With our treasure?"

Naqua shook his head. Carefully. One kept one's gestures refined. Or died. "I saw no sign. Only one structure still stood. Something took much from that building. And left the shell standing. The outlying villages were untouched."

"What do we know that could do that?"

Another carefully controlled head shake.

"Who do we know to take the Plani'tar contract?"

Naqua frowned, delicately. "The Mid Donae visited Calimus. The Caedi Syndicate speaks interest." Good news, well planned, kept one alive.

"New contract. With penalty clause. Survivor's debt."

Naqua stood and bowed himself out through the door. And in a little moment sent a message to the Mid Donae.

Dol Spar. An Early Mid-Morning Day.

Mirf looked up from the remnants of what had been a very short note and waved the tattered remains at her two assistants, Quan and his mate, Fred.

They were, as usual, in her office. One gigantic desk, chairs scattered along the wall. Doors in three walls, a large window behind her desk, behind her chair.

"The Plani'tar are kaputsky. Just a heap of rubble where their megatown once was. They must have grabbed too much, enslaved too many." She handed the shreds to Quan. "From the overall description of the place, it sounds Macabre to me. Although the small villages survived."

Quan read the note and handed it to Fred. Her multi-faceted eyes glittered in the light streaming in through the window. Two of her hands danced on Quan's shoulder.

"We think so, also," he said. "Wonder why he left one building standing like that? And the villages untouched?"

Mirf shrugged a shoulder. "So it matters? Pull a search, get us everything on the late and not so great Plani'tar. I want to know what they were doing, or planning. Let's see who might miss those late but not lamented no-goodniks." She stood. "So have a clerk do it Let's go eat! Something."

"Chirp," replied Fred. She was also hungry.

And after Mirf had adequately stirred up at least three bureaucratic layers of Monetary Control, they went out to get something to eat.

Duraldin. One of the Wooded Areas.

They strode down the dusty road, headed for the next large community, the one that they could just see, far down the white gravel road.

Their helmets, hung from their wide belts, banged soft metallic thump on their armor as they strode along. One figure in white, one figure in black.

"Brother, what is the first thing you will do when you become King?"

He laughed. "I will be old and grey and feeble by that time. Our parents are both very healthy and all their kingdoms, large and small, are at peace." He gave her a friendly thump on one shoulder. "My son, should I ever have one, should I ever find some lovely at court to attract my bonding sense, will inherit. I do not believe that the crown will pass to this generation." He laughed again. "And what of the lovely Princess? What be thy Royal plans?"

She kicked some small stone out of the way. "We do not plan on becoming the consort of one of those Lords or Princes such as hang around the palace. We do wonder about starting Our Own Kingdom anew."

He jerked. His sister often surprised him. "Indeed? And from where might this place come? The kingdoms stretch from edge to edge with no free space." He stared at her. "Surely those sparkling eyes do not cast glances covetous on the empty quarter?"

She shook her head. "Nay! That blasted land shall ever remain desolate."

He frowned. "Then? You plan on taking someone's throne from them? By force of arms?" He smiled. It was an interesting thought.

"Brother, what We are about to tell must remain between thee and Us."

"Certainly."

"We did find in some dusty, dusty scroll buried deep in our most disused Royal Library storage room, the writings of one Aah'n Tuh'r Rula'n, a long ago adventurer who sought knowledge of the waters surrounding The Kingdoms."

He nodded, knowing full well his sister's interests in all the records of The Kingdom, of all the Kingdoms.

"Those writings told of lands unknown and unclaimed far to eir-panee. When Our quest be done, We mean to fit out a ship or two of the best sea-folk and seek out these lands."

His lips pursed as he thought about that. He cleared his throat. "Would the White Warrior accept the Black Warrior on this expedition." It sounded to him to be much better than doing nothing as the-never-to-become-King just hanging around the Royal Court.

She gave him a hearty clap, armored fist clanking loudly off armored back. "Most willingly. Do we succeed, and those documents spoke true, there will be room enough for two kingdoms."

He laughed happily at that thought. It would be

something to look forward to be doing.

Kragkoptar. Dark Shadow Filled Hidden.

Ripple stood and stared into the dark encrusted room. The dark came from The Aunts, called by all The Old Aunts. The stuff moved slyly here and there, did this darkness.

She walked over and looked up at them. The two large. figures filled, over filled, their chairs. The chairs were set side by side. The Aunts hardly ever moved and rarely left their dwelling place.

"What is to be done with that niece?" Ripple tried to be as witch proper as she knew or had ever been. It would not do to irritate this pair. "She has already frightened most of my sisters."

A soft creaking came from one of the chairs as B'wass moved slightly. "There is nothing to be done. She will find her own way."

A faint rustle came from the other chair. "We know that she does wander with Faan witch Ripple daughter Sook." The slight noise stopped.

"The Silent One," added B'wass. "Has birthed a rarity. But she is Faan. Sook will keep her natural terror within bounds. And both will learn from this."

"It," stated Sh'lm. "It is why we do wander. To learn control. To learn of ourselves. That niece had no one like herself to teach her the craft that she requires."

"Sook told me," stated Ripple.

"We know of that," said Sh'lm. "She spared one. She learns."

"Your daughter is safe."

"Speak with your's, the clever Hanred."

Frenzel. Small, Private Rooms.

She waved away the remains of their meal. And waved in beverages. And looked across the table. "You may travel with us, Hacto mage. Dare you?" The dark eyes shifted sideways and fastened upon the blue speckled purple ones of Anjan.

"Dola."Adarlak tapped her right hand on the center of her chest. And blinked.

Ranna ran her hand up and down Anjan's back as she arched it and rolled her shoulders forward. "We are close-tied, this fierce warrior and I. Never have I traveled with a mage. It will be a new thing for me."

Adarlak filled their glasses and told the empty bottle to go away. And to send a full one back.

"Never met an orange and blue mage before." Ranna looked back and emptied her glass. "Tell us of your guild." She held out her glass, for a refill. "I know little of it."

Bander's Snatch. Oceans and Islands.

"Mother said to start here."

Eulin looked down the wide orange sand beach. Behind them, a short cliff of multi-layered fine yellow and red bands of rock defined this end of the waters edge.

Je'leel nodded.

Anamaxtor waded into the surf and took a drink. It was a gigantic fresh water lake.

The two young women were dressed in comfortable, loose fitting jeans and shirts and wore study boots.

All the clothing had been gifts from Tinker and the

mothers. But neither of them wore a pack or carried anything else. Eulin had stated that she would produce whatever they needed when they did need something.

The Six Lands. On A Path.

They stepped from behind a tree and out into the broad meadow of the surrounding forest.

Tears pointed. "That way lies the road." He started in the indicated direction, Duff and $1.98 followed. Behind them came the traveling bags, bobbling along, floating just above the ground.

As soon as they reached the road, Tears stopped. "It is here where Grandfather told me that we were about to have a grand adventure. It is from here that he sent me running to his dwelling to fetch his weaponkin." His hand patted the dagger and sheath hanging from his belt. "Gifted to me as he died."

Duff and $1.98 waited for the black memory to fade.

Tears nodded and started down the narrow track that was the road. "As we walk let me tell you a traveling tale. It is called 'The And'le-And'le That Ate The Umbra Fruit.' I think that you will enjoy it."

"Do," said Duff.

"Yes," agreed $1.98.

Tears nodded. And began.

"SO! In a time and at a time there was once an And'le-And'le who traveled through the land of Far And Wide . . . "

". . . and clenching its mid-section the And'le-And'le searched for the proper bush."

Tears halted and stared to one side of the narrow track

and then walked rapidly into a small clearing to stop and stare at it.

It was a vertical column of stone. At chest height a gleaming golden wand was set into the rock spire. The wand and the spire pointed at the sky.

Tears stared and blinked back suddenly wet eyes. "He is here, my grandfather. This is the spot that is Sorrowful Mistidings, Grand Master Teller of Tales."

$1.98 peered over the heads of his traveling companions. "That is my wand, the one I put with him just before sending him home."

Duff threw her arm around Tears and the other around $1.98. "It is a beautiful and peaceful spot."

Tears gulped. "Please leave me, for a moment. I wish to say a final farewell."

Duff and $1.98 drifted silently away. And then sat and waited. In the middle of the narrow track.

$1.98 slipped one arm around her. "Maybe now he will stop grieving. I thought that it might be permanent damage."

Duff kissed his cheek. "I think that he will rapidly heal now."

Bander's Snatch. Oceans and Islands.

"Let's visit. Ham Thatch is not far down this beach."

Eulin pointed at a vague splotch in the far distance.

Je'leel nodded. And started down the beach with her half-sister. "Father was very worried."

Eulin took her hand and swung their arms back and forth as they strolled along. "Mother said that he does that much much."

"We are safe."

Dull thumping came up behind them as Anamaxtor caught up with them.

Eulin laughed. "Very safe."

"What do we seek?"

"I do not know. Wander is a journey of discovery."

"True?"

"It is what Mother said. She said that she and her twin brother, Shem, found the brooch in a shop and with that she became The Heart of the Vander and brought the Vander mage guild back into existence aided by Shem."

She swung their arms again. "Maybe we will find or do something important like that."

Je'leel nodded. "A strange thing, wander."

Eulin smiled at her. "It is our way. All mage guilds and all witch clans do wander. As do other folk."

"Indjinns do not."

"True?"

"They have no need."

"Hum."

Je'leel smiled at her. "You sounded just like your mother when you said that."

Eulin laughed. "Tell me true, sister."

"What? Of course?"

"Am I as beautiful as my Mother?"

Je'leel stared at her. "Does it matter?"

"I am The Heart To Be."

"Sa'ar, The Heart, is pretty. Eulin, The Heart To Be, has a beauty that glows." Je'leel grinned broadly.

"What?"

"You are almost as beautiful as an indjinn." She hugged her sister. "That is what mother would say."

And then, they just wandered down the beach, laughing, and talking, about this and that.

Grandeville. Tinker's Place.

It was another quiet day.

It had been a fairly quiet six days since Eulin and Je'leel had gone on wander.

They had watched him very carefully and saw that he was slowly, ever so slowly, relaxing. Now Sha'gar had him cornered in one of the large closets that lined the hall.

Or, perhaps, he had her cornered.

She kissed the sweat from the joint of his neck and shoulder. "Mine," she breathed.

His hand drifted over the smooth skin, the light bronze smooth skin of a magician. "Mine," he breathed back.

"Sepanix is a strange name?" she mumbled, pulling him to the floor, sprawling on top of him.

"What? Strange name? This is really a strange place to be sprawling."

"Daughter name."

"What?" He jerked.

She tightened her arms and legs, a quick hug. She sat up. On him. "Calm, Mate'mer, calm."

"What did you say?"

She smiled, a slight half-smile, a trait that she shared with her youngest sister. And ran one fingertip around and around in small circles over his stomach. "I am . . . "

"What?" He was frowning darkly up at her.

She laughed. "Not bearing your child."

He sighed. "Then what are we talking about?"

"Sepanix."

"And why now?"

"R-Bar just felt heard."

He patted her thigh. "Speak tell Faan magician Reep daughter Sha'gar." He was finally catching onto their naming conventions, their formal nomenclature that signified who they were.

"Aunt Ripple witch daughter birthed, Sepanix named."

"Oh. Again? So soon?"

"Yesssssssss." She waggled her hand in front of his face so he could see the ornate ring that she wore on that hand. "Heh, heh, heh, heh, heh." And wound black over black across the opening to the closet.

"Most fertile." Chicken was fixing R-Bar's hair in a ornate braid.

Chantal dropped a veterinarian journal that she had been reading onto the floor and looked over. "Your bunch have rabbit genes?"

R-Bar growled at her. "Our Mother had twelve daughters. Sepanix is only the fourth for Ripple."

"Another witch?"

"Yessssss." Thunder rumbled across the room.

"Gosh," gasped Messenger as she looked over at R-Bar. "What's the matter?" The short witch was leaking dark in all directions.

"Thy hair do be nay tight," said Chicken.

Dark began to fill the corners of the room.

Ran hurried over and sat in front of R-Bar. "Stop!" She had felt the sudden witch agitation.

R-Bar growled.

Ran yanked in a gold crystal sphere and smashed it against R-Bar's forehead.

The black faded away.

"Gum tuk," growled R-Bar. "My hair is just fine. Raft is here."

Smoke rolled onto her side. She had been sprawled flat on her back, staring at the ceiling, listening to their minds. "Thought that you liked Raft."

"She found her's."

"And is coming here?" Fair Morn looked over. "What is wrong with that?"

"You'll see. Do tik ptar gak."

Ran covered her face with her hands. R-Bar was coarse even for a witch of that clan.

A disembodied voice asked, "Let us in, please?"

Ran peeked between two fingers at R-Bar. R-Bar nodded and growled, "Enter!"

They shimmered in.

The two of them.

Chantal leaped to her feet. "What is that?"

Smoke smiled. "Very handsome."

"He," stated Raft, very firmly, as firm as a witch can be when she is being very firm, slipping one arm around the figure standing next to her. "He is catfolk Rowrr Set, named Mrrinar. He is a healer."

Mrrinar stood a head taller than Raft. His fur was thick, jet black with light grey leopard spots. He had his tail looped over his free arm in a very casual stance. All his claws were retracted.

"Mine," stated Raft, staring at her sister.

R-Bar stood and faced her. Raft was slightly taller. "How?"

"I was on Fan Tangle," explained Raft. "Just passing through The Great Forest. And found him. Healing a slow creeper." She rubbed her hand up and down the fur on his arm. "Beautiful," she murmured.

Dat stood on the edge of the bookshelf where her ring was kept, yawned and stretched. "Who brought that catfolk here? We got rid of the mice with the kitten cats and that witch Naktar." She smiled. "Don't see markings like that very often. That is a rare pattern."

Chantal walked over to the bookcase. "That is Raft's, ummmm, husband."

Dat leaped up onto her shoulder and sat. "Different." And clenched Chantal's hair with one hand.

"Strange, strange, strange," mumbled Ran, looking from Raft to Mrrinar.

"Pik pik to," suggested Raft

"Sister!" warned R-Bar. Ran was getting that look in her face. Crystal adepts could be very dangerous.

Mrrinar watched Ran very carefully.

Smoke recognized the cat-folk's stare. It was the stare of a predator.

Raft slipped close to R-Bar, pulling Mrrinar with her. "Sister, we need your help," she whispered.

"Hum." R-Bar eyed Mrrinar carefully, still unhappy at her sister's choice.

"Please?"

"Speak tell."

"Come with us."

"Where?"

"Ripple's. She is clan head. And must need see our's when first taken."

R-Bar shook her head. "He does not want to travel out there."

"Make him," growled Raft. Mates did what witches wanted them to do.

Ran peered at Raft over R-Bar's shoulders. "It can not be done, it may not be done." She glared. "None would dare."

Sha'gar slipped over, clenching a glowing red wand in one hand. "Fast witch Aunt, you are close to leaving our home." Dark fire pulsed deep in her eyes.

Mrrinar's ears flattened back.

"NO!" snapped Smoke as she uncoiled smoothly, her great orange gold eyes fastening on his green ones. And, for just a moment, he saw a gigantic predator staring at him.

Mrrinar ducked his head. "One of them?"

Smoke nodded.

Mrrinar slipped his arm around Raft. "Den mate, you would kill us both. This band is many clawed." His eyes jumped at R-Bar. "Sister joined, she fears the clan head reaction."

"Ripple will just grumble." R-Bar leaned forward and kissed her sister's forehead. "Stay visit. We will talk of this." Then she frowned. "Reep and Ramp would have felt you arrive."

"Am m'an do!" gasped Raft. She had forgotten that those sisters lived nearby.

"WHAT?" Tinker had just stepped in from the hallway. "IS THAT?" His mind reached out. With the exception of two very agitated witches and a less agitated magician, the rest of himself felt fairly calm and relaxed. So it must be alright. Somehow.

R-Bar whirled around. "He is her's."

Tinker walked over to the little group, eyeing the creature standing next to Raft.

"Cat-folk healer Mrrinar," said Mrrinar, smiling properly. His canines were carefully covered.

"Pleased to meet you." Tinker looked at R-Bar, Ran, and Sha'gar. "Why is everyone just standing? In a little bunch?"

He spun and dropped into a couch, jostling Chantal, knocking Dat off her feet. She tumbled into Chantal's shirt which was not all the very well buttoned.

"Watch it!" yelped Chantal.

"Sorry." said Tinker.

"I am being very careful," stated Dat, crawling her way up and out, using the shirt material for claw holds. "Very globular." She regained her perch on Chantal's shoulder. "Yum, yum, yum, yum, yum."

"Quiet, Dat," said Chantal.

Sha'gar sat by his free side and patted his thigh. The ornate ring glittered.

He nudged her. *Silk, you ever see anything like that before?*

Mate'mer, he is the first one of his kind that I have ever encountered. Until now, I had never heard of these folk.

"I wonder if they are cross-fertile?" muttered Chantal, all veterinarian curious.

"I do not think so." Dat stood clenching Chantal's hair.

"Should I fix her?"

Tinker glared at the indjinn. "Sit down, busy body."

"Gimble, gimble, gimble," grumbled Dat, sitting down. hitching closer to Chantal's neck.

"Let's just hope that no one from town decides to come visiting," grumbled Tinker. "He would really be hard to explain."

R-Bar took Raft and Mrrinar down the hall to one of the guest bedrooms to talk.

Bal's Datar. A Pleasant and Sunny Day.

They had come here after leaving Tears at his Grandmother's house. It had been an emotional reunion. When Tears had left with his Grandfather, he had been a young boy. Now he was returning as a young man who had seen much, maybe too much, in too short a time. And had watched his Grandfather die.

Now the two of them stood in the small town of Prandle on Bal's Datar. They had heard of a small gathering of magicians here and had decided to visit it. They rarely attended such gatherings, so this was, for them, a rather unusual event.

Duff pointed. "Dear, lets go into that inn. Innkeepers usually know of such things."

He nodded. "If the place looks good, let's stay there."

Duraldin. One of the Wooded Areas.

"Brother," she said, shoving her visor up. "Why did these things attack us?" Her white armor was streaked with ugly stains.

Kneeling, he wiped his sword clean on one of the bodies.

"Hard to understand."

They had been hiking along this white graveled forest path, headed for the small town that they had been told was not too far that way, when it happened.

Partway through a large opening they saw, far ahead, a group of things running toward them. As that mob drew closer prudence indicated helmets on, visors down, swords drawn.

The mob attacked.

He stood, sheathed his sword. "Are they all dead?

She walked to one side and nudged a crumpled form with one boot tip. "I think that this one lives still."

He stepped over, bent, and rolled the figure onto its back. "You there, speak!" It was a command, a Royal command, a very Royal no-nonsense is expected command. Eyes flew open. "I am not dead?"

"Yet." She yanked her sword free, swinging it high above her shoulder.

It clenched a black armor clad leg. "Save me!"

"Speak!"

"Nothing," it snapped.

"Why were we attacked?"

"Orders. Had to."

The gleaming sword fell. The tip buried itself in the soil next to one furry ear. "Who gave these orders?" she snarled.

"Thieves Guild. Big price. Big big price."

She looked at her brother.

He shrugged and looked down. "Why? Us?"

It nodded. "A pair of strangers traveling this way. One black. One not black."

"Why?" she demanded.

"You butchered high level. Revenge."

She glowered at the thing. "We just shortly arrived to this elseplace and were seeking food and lodging. You and your dead companions were almost the first we did meet."

"Ag bu dug," it wailed.

"These things did attack wrong pair, Sister. Let us away from this vile elseplace."

She shook her head and slammed the sword back into its scabbard. "We are hungry, filthy, and dirty feeling, We are. Let us find lodgings, a good meal, and clean ourselves and our gear. Next, we two may travel elsewhere."

He nodded. She was obviously in no mood for discussion. He stepped around the bodies. She joined him.

They walked toward the next town.

The survivor ran into the woods.

Sgenn was napping.

As soon as they had entered their room in this quaint inn, she had dropped heavily into the bed. Then she told her startled cousin that it required great quantities of energy to keep a servant under control when one was called up. In this she was unlike her witch and magician relatives who seemed to never tire with the magical work. And this was something she had just learned and would have to learn how to regulate. "Mother said that wander was a learning process." She pointed at the door. "Go prowl while I sleep. I am safe."

Sook nodded and left. She put a ward on the door, just in case.

Sgenn dropped into a deep sleep knowing that Sook would have put a ward on their door, just in case. And that

Sook would have a hard time just sitting and waiting for her to come awake. Witches, almost everyone of them, did not wait well. And they were not every good at just sitting around either.

Much later in the day when her eyes popped open, she saw Sook who had just entered their room. Sgenn felt totally refreshed. "What?"

Sook ordered a chair over next to the bed and sat. "Soft rumor said that a mob attacked a pair in the wood and were butchered for their effort, all save one."

"Of no import."

"The pair were black. And not black."

Sgenn sat up and leaned back against the headboard. "Hum."

"It was also said that the mob was revenge hired."

"Revenge?"

"Four dead thieves."

Grey eyes poured into black eyes.

"CAREFUL!" snapped Sook She had felt something coming. From the deep below. Something horrible.

Sgenn blinked. The air in the room cleared as Sook waved away protection.

"Thieves," whispered Sgenn. She smiled a soft, gentle half-smile.

"Stop that!"

Sgenn exhaled slowly. She did. Stop that. "Hungry. Let's go eat."

Sook nodded, stood, and waited by the door. "Downstairs?"

"Yesssssssssss."

They took a table by a large window so they could watch the road outside. And ordered. And ate. And talked.

"I do not like this elseplace." Sook served her cousin from one of the large, food bowls.

She had jumped them to this small town far from the city. She had felt it. A new skill that this wander seemed to be bringing to the surface of her awareness. Now she wondered what other skills that the two of them might discover.

Sgenn was staring out the window, watching everything, eating automatically, looking for thieves.

Sook suddenly hissed and grabbed her cousin's arm. "Look! There!"

"Where?" Sgenn scanned the outside space

"In desk," hissed Sook.

Sgenn swivelled around. "Hum hum."

Two armor clad warriors were selecting lodgings. Their gear was dirty, stained ugly.

"One black," observed Sgenn. "One not-black."

The one in white yanked off a tufted helmet, set it on the counter, said something to the innkeeper who snatched up the keys and quickly handed her a different set.

"A female."

"Very pretty face," said Sook, looking at the other whose helmet now sat on the counter top as well.

"Look brother sister." Sgenn turned back to her food.

Sook poked her in the arm with an eating utensil. "Visit visit."

"Hum."

"Don't be nasty," grumbled Sook, not liking Sgenn's implication.

"Soon." Sgenn took another helping of the food. "Soon." She was still hungry.

Sook nodded. And began to fiddle with things on the table while her cousin ate.

Zantikpik.

It was a hot and steamy elseplace.

They had come to this elseplace seeking a certain weapon maker that they had been told lived here by a Sword Master on Far Far. Ranna was determined to properly gift Anjan.

The road they walked along led to the Minzor Mines. The mines were the source of that special metal that was required to produce the articles that this certain weapon maker crafted. It had been said that his shop forge was located adjacent to the mines.

Anjan altered her clothes to fit the climate. She strode along wearing mid-calf sandals, very short shorts, and a strip of cloth folded across her chest. The multi-colored design running from her left shoulder to her right hip seemed to have internal movements all its own as she walked.

Adarlak stared at the long scar running down the outside of Anjan's left thigh.

Anjan saw and nodded. "It is said that one cannot make a warrior without breaking the skin."

Ranna offered to cast cool over her, but Anjan refused. Her skin glistened soft sheen.

"Beautiful," observed Ranna.

Anjan wobbled her head from side to side.

"That," said Adarlak, pulling her upper garment higher, exposing more midriff and her lower ribs, staring at the white ring on Ranna's finger, "is a mage ring."

"Yesssssss."

"How?"

"Gifted."

Adarlak goggled at her. "How does a witch?"

Ranna frowned at the question. "Urh-witch given."

Adarlak snorted. "Urh-witch are child tell tale." Witches were known to stretch the truth.

Ranna shrugged. "Some gak need learn much," she purred.

"Hubtuk!" snapped Adarlak, not liking that purr.

"Tik tik," suggested Ranna, not caring whether Adarlak liked it or not. Magicians were not too bright, at times, it seemed.

Adarlak gasped. "Faan witch," she growled, the air beginning to shift in strange ways.

"Yesssssssssssssssss?" Ranna waved at Anjan, a gesture that told her to not interfere. "Hacto mage?"

The air settled. "Stop being mamdam," grumbled Adarlak. Witches could be very irritating it seemed.

Ranna's eyes squinted into the thinnest of slits. "You ask. I tell. Learn learn."

They started up the steep hill.

"Name me this urh-witch," said Adarlak, still bothered by a witch wearing a mage ring.

"Messenger."

"Guild?"

"Not." Ranna waved them to the top of the hill.

Adarlak sucked in her breath. "That was trivial." She knew about The Witches Code.

Ranna shrugged. "Tired of that rule."

Adarlak looked at her from the corner of her eyes. "Indo."

"We change," offered Ranna.

"How see visit this urh-witch not-guild?"

"It is not allowed. Only few few are able."

Adarlak laughed.

"Kaaaaaaa taaaaaket!" Anjan spun past Ranna, her arm flashing up and down in front of Adarlak.

The mage gasped as her upper garment fell open, neatly sliced from top button to knot. It tumbled from her shoulders. Her skin was unmarked.

"Hum," observed Ranna, looking over the now exposed parts of Adarlak.

Anjan stepped back, and watched Adarlak, the weapon once again riding on her hip.

Adarlak looked at Ranna. "See like?"

Ranna shrugged. "Pleasant smooth." She gently touched Anjan's arm. "Settle, fierce love."

Anjan slipped sideways, eyes watching Adarlak.

They started walking. Adarlak puzzled over her garment fixing, do it now or do it later. "Ring?"

"It was Parquor the White's. Then mine. Then Messenger's. Now mine again."

Adarlak growled low in her throat. "Parquor the White?" And jolted to a halt, the muscles in her face twitching.

Ranna nodded

"It is told," said Adarlak, "It is told that the White mage was done horrible. After that one did vile."

They started walking.

Ranna nodded. "Bad ugly."

Adarlak stared at the tall witch. "You?"

"No. My sister Reep. She delivered my sister Ripple's gift." She smiled. "And The Chosen One and his. They freed me from that one."

Adarlak staggered and stopped walking. She swayed, wobbled from side to side. "My brain is soft."

Ranna shrugged and held the mage in her arms and indicated that Anjan should do the same.

"Mage burn?"

"Sun sick?" asked Anjan.

"No," mumbled Adarlak, wondering why they had not exploded or died from witch-mage contact.

"Speak tell," said Ranna softly.

"Your sister is The Silent One? That Reep?"

"Yessss."

"The Chosen One is a . . . friend?"

"Yesssss."

Adarlak began to weep. Silent tears wet Ranna's blouse. "Kill me now. Gently."

"Hacto mage? Why?"

"I insulted you," mumbled Adarlak against her chest. "They will seek find. All know of The Silent One that looks death. The Chosen One and his are destruction terror." Her arms tightened around Ranna. "I am over, done, vanished."

"Be not child, Hacto mage Adarlak." Ranna pushed her away, just a little, and kissed her on the forehead as Anjan stepped away.

"I attacked," sobbed Adarlak, suddenly realizing the strength of this attractive witch. She gasped at the enormity of her behavior. "I insulted."

Ranna frowned at her. "I am alive. I am uninjured." She reached out and gently rubbed her thumb over Adarlak's cheek, brushing the scar into nothing. Then she slid her palm over the new skin. "Smooth, smooth."

"Forgive?"

Ranna nodded. And looked at Anjan who also nodded.

"Walk with us, Hacto mage Adarlak." She took one of the stunned woman's hands and tugged her into motion. "We will ask them for permission to visit and then you will see."

Adarlak jerked and stared at her. "Who?" She pondered over this very strange thing. She hadn't died when Ranna held her. Now she held her hand. Adarlak knew that contact between a witch and a magician most often blew their opposing magics into violent reaction, usually removing everything for some distance in all directions. And yet nothing was happening. It was confusing and very, very strange.

"The Chosen One. I have yet to pay witch debt. Think hard, mage. I must gift, but know not what."

Adarlak nodded, slowly. She wondered just exactly who this pair that she was traveling with really were. She had heard tales, here and there, told in many elseplaces of this Chosen One. The tales most often spoke of death to others.

Anjan stepped around them, and walked on Adarlak's other side. She reached out and gently held her other hand.

Bander's Snatch. A Warm and Sunny Day.

As they approached Ham Thatch they carefully looked it over.

The town had a low wall of thick vertical posts

surrounding it. As this wall was only waist high, they decided that it had to be decorative rather than functional. The entry was a Z-shaped passage, low walls on either side of it framing the way in. It was a narrow passage that forced them to walk in a single file.

As they entered the wide open space between the low fence and the outer walls of the first house, they stopped and examined everything that they could see.

"What is here?" Je'leel looked at the place and wondered.

Eulin shook her head. "Mother didn't say. Her exact words were these. Go. Seek. Learn." She smiled. "Doesn't look like much, does it?"

Je'leel smiled back. "We are being watched."

"Really?"

"Yes."

They passed between two buildings and stepped into the town. Eulin looked around as they walked deeper into it, down the narrow street. "Are you hungry?"

Je'leel nodded. "Let's."

Anamaxtor sniffed loudly and looked to the left at the first intersection.

They walked that way and followed the dragon's nose to a large food establishment. They walked in.

Just inside the entrance they were greeted by a green-brown person who edged away from Anamaxtor. "Pok, lovely ones. Food?"

"Yes." Eulin ran one hand down the dragon's neck. "He is well behaved."

Pok led them to a corner table. And in a moment or two the servant returned with two large yellow stiff sheets which were placed in front of them just so.

The sheet in front of Eulin snapped around her and tried to swallow her.

Je'leel slammed her hand flat on the table top and trapped the sheet in front of her. She held it in place.

Purple flare blasted bits and pieces of yellow throughout the room as Eulin surged to her feet.

Anamaxtor reared up on his hind legs, wings swinging wide open, deep rumbling coming from his throat.

The servant ran up to them, wringing his hands. "A small test, a small test. Nothing more." He winced as Eulin looked at him. Violet haze still floated around her.

"Sister, are you injured?"

"No," said Je'leel, rolling the yellow sheet into a tight tube, shoving it at the startled servant.

With a dull thump the golden dragon dropped to its front feet, wings folding in. He snorted orange fumes at the servant.

"Why do you test us?" demanded Eulin.

He watched the haze fade around her and nodded at Anamaxtor. "Dragon touched." Then he looking at Je'leel, his mouth open, nothing came out.

"I am her sister. You are not nice."

Before Pok could understand what was happening to him, a tall man hurried into the establishment, his red and blue robes billowing around him. "Release my servant. Now!" The air hummed.

Je'leel looked at Eulin.

Eulin looked at this new person. "Who are you?" The floor creaked. Purple seeped up through widening cracks, sizzling, crackling.

"I am Dargon," he stated firmly. "Stop that!"

"Why?" asked Eulin.

"You are dragon touched. But unskilled. I can teach you."

"Oh." The air cleared.

"Oh." Je'leel sat down.

Pok sucked in a deep breath. And dropped into a handy chair, waggling the yellow tube at Dargon.

"Astonishing!" Dargon looked at them. "What are you?"

"I am Je'leel."

"My sister," added Eulin.

"And you? Are?"

"I am Eulin. Vander Heart To Be."

"Those died many many years ago long past long past."

Eulin shook her head. "My Mother, Sa'ar Vander Heart, brought them back aided by her twin brother." She tapped a purple wand on the table top. "You know little."

"The Purple Mage do not mate."

"You know less," stated Eulin. "Vander Imdar the Healer birthed my brother Rorx, Vander Mage. My mother birthed me."

"Name me these powerful males that bed such as those."

"John Tinker called Lord called The Chosen One." Eulin frowned at this person who thought that he knew more than he did. "Heard you of this one?"

Dargon wobbled. "He . . . him?"

"Our father." Je'leel looked at him. "You had better sit down."

Dargon beckoned over a chair and sat. He stared at them. And nodded. And cleared his throat.

"Some die during training," he said.

"Some die during hard aspects," he stated.

He cleared his throat. "If you die here, will vengeance be sought?"

Eulin smiled. "Of course not."

"We will not die." Je'leel looked at him.

"Only the touched may train."

Je'leel sat straighter. "I do not require training. But I will be there."

Eulin looked at Dargon. "We are together," she stated, Vander firm.

"Unusual," snapped Dargon.

Eulin nodded.

"Strange," grumbled Dargon.

She nodded again.

"We accept," mumbled Dargon.

Eulin smiled at him

"We are hungry," said Je'leel.

Dargon jerked. "Oh." He waved over a food server. "Anything that they wish. Then adequate rooms." He jerked to his feet and pointed at Eulin. "You will have to sign a document releasing us of responsibility in case of accident or death. At first light we will start." His finger jerked sideways. "Bring him. Also." And hurried away.

Eulin hitched her chair over against Je'leel's. "Must be why Mother sent us here first. It sounds like fun." She leaned sideways and kissed her sister on the cheek.

The food arrived.

Including some for Anamaxtor.

Bal's Dartar. A Sun Filled Day.

The gathering was larger than they had expected it to be. It filled the Gather Place, a large grass covered area to one side of the town. A gaily decorated fence ran around all sides of this spot. Booths lined the outer edges while demonstrations were shown in the central opening.

The magician booths came from elsewhere, from as many elseplaces as there were booths. The food booths were all local. It is why the town maintained the Gather Place. Each Gather left much coinage in local pockets.

Two Members of Monetary Control, the entire office staff for this small outpost place, dressed in their rather severely cut golden uniforms, prowled from spot to spot. They were there to insure that the universal coinages of the universes were not debased.

Duff and $1.98 lounged in one of the refreshment booths. taking a break from visiting here and there, doing this or that. It was the third day of the Gather.

She tapped one fingernail on his thigh. "Dear?"

He head snapped around. "WHAT?" He didn't see anything that could be considered as dangerous or threatening.

She smiled at him. "You are beautiful."

He stared at her.

"I was speaking with Fage mage Bage from Hage."

Slowly he grinned, then he laughed.

"It. . . is . . . not . . . funny . . . Dear!"

"Oh." He sat back, frowning. "What are we talking about?"

She sat straighter. "Pay attention."

He nodded. It was a bad sign when she used that

inflection.

"I was speaking with Bage, a mage of the Fage Guild located in the elseplace Hage."

He nodded.

She frowned.

"What?"

"Bage told tale of a treasure search by the lowest of the low named The Caedi Syndicate."

He nodded. "Why would we be interested in such a told tale?"

She hitched closer. "This same vague word mentioned primitive beings from a primitive elseplace."

He nodded.

She frowned.

"We do not know any primitive beings. Do we?"

She nodded.

"We do?"

She squeezed his thigh. "We gifted the ring of ancient magic to some."

He jerked, snapped in a sharp breath, and shoved his right hand up his left sleeve.

"Leave that thing in there!" she hissed.

Slowly he withdrew his hand.

"Relax, Dear, relax." Nothing was safe if he started waving that wand of his around.

"How can we find out?" he whispered. "To know if true?"

"This evening we are meeting with Bage."

He nodded. "Duff?"

"Yes, Dear."

"Anything threatening them is dangerous dangerous."

She nodded. And smiled. "I know. We will just talk."

Chapter Eleven

Interesting Times.

09.09.00.63 DXA, In Ship's Notation. A Far Corner.

The great space craft hung there. Not all that far above the smallish planet. Not far away but not all that close either.

The ship didn't reflect light or most of anything else. It wouldn't be noticed, not by the primitive technology down there. It was just a short visit.

The heavyset man dropped into a chair, reached over and withdrew his breakfast from a slot in the wall. He smiled, a real smile with warmth in it. It was a very unusual thing to do, for him. "Gyre, shall we take a look with our newest acquisition?"

She nodded. One wall became all image. Which was rapidly enlarged. Until they could see the house, the barn, and other nearby structures, and the flower beds. And the individual flowers in those newer flower beds.

Filling a mug he took a sip and another helping from the food. "We had better wait until the terminator crosses their place. It appears to be early morning down there."

"4:32 in their morning, local time. Sensors indicate many sleeping forms." She looked at him. "One of those forms is most unusual."

"Can you tell?"

"No. Data banks have nothing similar. It is an unknown life form."

"Unknown?" He glanced at a wall covered with weapons of many and varied designs. "Is there a hazard? To them?"

"No signs of danger. Everything indicates very peaceful. Whatever it is, it is accepted it seems."

He nodded and watched the edge separating dark from light sweep across the lands below.

And finished his meal. And stood. "Shall we go? They will be waking soon."

She took his arm as they strolled from the room. Then he slipped his arm around her waist.

Plakdar. Dark and Ugly.

They stood and looked at the place.

Not one of the structures appeared to have ever been maintained. Everything was in an advance state of disrepair, some looking more abandoned than others. Every building tilted one way or another. Some had doors, some had doors hanging at odd angles. Here and there a window was missing, just a gaping hole with a piece of the adjoining wall missing as well.

"Even worse than I had heard." She scanned the area for the inhabitants. So far they had the street to themselves.

He looked up and down the street and pointed. "The gateway is in that direction."

She yanked in a wand constructed of a slender bundle of thin rods held together by narrow rings of various colors. It was her personal wand, crafted for her by Bissam. "Let's go."

"It is not far from here." He led the way.

Many eyes watched them. Many eyes watched the very large man with the great silver sword of a Silver Ranger hanging from his belt. And many eyes watched the woman walking at his side with such a confident smile. They noted, did these watching eyes, the light bronze skin color and the wand that she held, and decided that she must be a mage of some sort. Most the watchers decided that this pair ought to be left alone, left to their business, whatever it was, and not to be bothered.

But some did not.

They stepped into the street and halted the pair.

"What do you want?" asked the large man.

"Go away," ordered the woman.

"Pay to pass," said the spokesman of the small group halting this pair of strangers.

She laughed at them. "Is that all?" And tossed a gold coin at their feet. She gently set her left hand on her husband's right arm. "Told you that this place was a dump."

He fizzled. "It is not proper to pay thugs like these to use a public thoroughfare."

She smiled up at him. "Don't be so Ranger stuffy." Her fingers tightened, just a little. "They look like they can use the money. And we won't miss it."

"This is public way," he grumbled.

"Husband, this is an ugly elseplace."

"As you said." Shaking off her arm, he stepped forward. "Stand aside. You have been paid."

"Who are you," demanded the spokesman of the four, "to make such a demand of us?" The group began fingering their weapons and eyeing the woman just standing there so calmly.

"I am Farth. A Silver Ranger. Clear the way."

"Kill him," screamed one of the four. They attacked.

Farth punched one, kicked one, and threw one through someone's window. The fourth fled.

Sedeem smiled up at him. "Which way?"

"Left at the next corner. The gateway to Five Star Bar."

"Let's hurry."

He nodded. And stepped over the unconscious forms.

They did.

Hurry.

Grandeville. Tinker's Place.

He stretched and yawned.

Then he lifted the top edge of the pastel green blanket and peeked inside. "It's morning, Princess."

Bright blue eyes twinkled at him. "Indeed, My Lord, tis that."

Yanking the cover up and over his head, he rolled onto his side. "Yum, yum, yum, to quote a certain tiny indjinn."

She twitched. "Eeeeeeep!"

"Eeeep?"

"Thee does Us a'tickle."

So, he held her instead. Gently. "Pretty nice."

"LordLove, thee do a'all say this thing, pretty nice."

His fingers flexed, just a little. "Yep. Must be true then." He kissed her shoulder. "Cause you-all are all pretty nice."

"Thee do be also some pretty nice." She ran her fingers through his hair. And kissed him as they merged.

They walked from the pasture and along the meandering path through the flower beds and up onto the rear deck.

"Good morning," said Smoke as she slipped from the side door to greet their unexpected visitors.

"You are looking well," replied Macabre, smiling a real smile. "We decided to visit." He slipped an arm over Gyre's shoulders.

"We will have breakfast in an hour or so. He will be out of bed before then. Coffee?"

"Wonderful," said Macabre.

Smoke led them inside, through the tub room and the kitchen, the dining room, and into the large living room.

Macabre sat in one of the couches and looked at the room. "You have changed things since last we visited."

Smoke nodded and looked from one to the other. "Why are you here?"

He beamed at her. "Relax. Nothing is happening. That we know about or of. We just came to get rid of some stuff that is cluttering up Ship."

"What kind of stuff?"

"Oh," he waggled one hand lazily. "Just an accumulated treasure, gathered from here and there." He smiled at her. "You know how it goes."

"Treasure?"

"Yes," said Gyre. "We do not need it."

"I don't think that we need it, either."

"What?" Sha'gar wandered into the room, holding and sipping from a cup of coffee. "Don't we need?"

Suddenly the cup floated up toward the ceiling, headed for safety, as she noticed their visitors. "A Quannar!" It was a silver one. A flaming red wand flared into her hand.

Gyre leaped between Macabre and this person.

"No!" snapped Smoke. "These are friends of our's."

"Friends?" Sha'gar stared at Gyre. How could they be friends with a Quannar?

"Yes," said Smoke and Gyre.

"Certainly," said Macabre.

Sending the wand somewhere, she beckoned down her cup and watched them as they sat down. She took a sip. "I am Reep daughter Faan magician Sha'gar."

Macabre nodded, knowing that Gyre was logging everything into Ship's data bank. "I am Macabre and this is Gyre, um, ah, a companion. Not a Quannar, just a female person, ummmm, of a silver color."

Sha'gar's eyes popped wide. "The Destroyer?"

Macabre shrugged one massive shoulder. "You visiting John?"

Smoke shook her head. "She is part of us."

Macabre smiled. "A most lovely part. Wonderfully violent."

Chantal walked in, clenching a large steaming cup in both hands, eyes mere slits, and settled into one of the other couches, curled her legs up, and grumbled. "What is all the damn excitement about so early in the morning."

"This is Chantal," said Smoke. "Her also."

"Amazing." Macabre nodded at Chantal.

One of her eyes eased half open. "Who are you?"

"Macabre and Gyre," stated Smoke.

The other eye eased open as Chantal took another sip from her cup. She grunted. "You the guy that gave Fair Morn that cannon?"

Macabre beamed. "A beautiful device. Shoot holes in

anything."

Her eyes dropped back into slits as she settled deeper into the couch. "Ummm."

"Morning, morning, morning." Messenger bubbled into the room. And saw Chantal. "Oooops!" She flapped her hand over her mouth and smiled with her eyes at Macabre and Gyre. And whispered, a loud stage whisper, "You just get here?"

Then Fair Morn, R-Rar and Ran joined them. Fair Morn sat by Macabre's free side "You've lost weight. Morning, Gyre." And chewed on some toast.

R-Bar nudged Ran as they sat on the same couch as Chantal. *Macabre and Gyre,* R-Bar told Ran, mind to mind. Chantal liked quiet when she was waking up.

Macabre looked at Smoke. "Eight?"

"Yep. We are complete." Smoke smiled as she felt him and Chicken crawl from bed. "I think."

Ran beckoned in a coffee pot. It topped up her cup, then R-Bar's. Macabre watched carefully.

"I am," she stated firmly. "Tanpak witch Ranfer."

He looked at Chantal.

"Veterinarian, nosey butt," grumbled Chantal.

Fair Morn whispered in Macabre's ear. "She is pretty grumpy before she is fully awake." Macabre nodded.

Chantal's eyes opened fully. "I will make the damn breakfast. Who is helping."

"Me, me, me, me, me." Messenger smiled.

"O.K." Chantal yawned and stretched and then glared at Macabre. "Stop staring at my chest, tubby." She stood and clumped toward the kitchen.

"Globular shirt filler." Messenger giggled and hurried

after Chantal.

Tinker wandered in from the hall, through the room into the dining room, and returned clenching a cup, and dropped into his chair. Smoke snatched the coffee pot and filled his cup. Slumping lower, Tinker peered over it at Macabre, and mumbled, "Not going anywhere."

"Just visiting, John. Leaving you a little present." He nudged Gyre. Ship sent it down.

"Huh?"

"Tell you after we have breakfast."

Duraldin. Early Evening.

They drifted into the room.

Silently they drifted in.

It was large room with a large tub half-set into the paved floor. Steam drifted fog tendrils in the faint air currents. The pair in the tub were lounging, dozing in the warm water. Her eyes popped open and stared at them.

"Begone, witch and companion. This is a private room."

Sook stared at her. Few royal folk, which these must be to have armor such as she had seen, recognized a magic user on sight. Especially those from primitive elseplaces.

"Haute One, we wish some small information from you."

The female kicked her other awake and searched Sook's face with her eyes. "Know we you?"

"No, but I would know who you are."

"We are the Prince Frinda and the Princess Lurin. Who are you? Speak!"

"I am Ripple daughter Faan witch Sook. This is Reep daughter Faan theurgist Sgenn, a cousin."

He stared at Sook and smiled. "Yes, you have your mother's look. Why have we not met before?"

"We train, we wander." Sook nodded at them. So these are the offspring of the Queen that her mother advised. "We would have met in Bahn Duhr Tohr. Eventually. Now we are met sooner."

"Strange strange," stated Sgenn.

"Hum," replied Sook.

The young woman sank back in the water up to her neck. "What information do you seek? Sook?"

He smiled at Sook. "This is a large tub."

"BROTHER!"

He laughed. "On quest we may be less . . . Royal, if we so chose it to be." He nudged her with his foot. "Did not Our Mother, Queen and White Warrior, so tell this? And did she not tarry with some comely youth long before Our Noble Sire and King did appear?"

She nodded and chewed on her lower lip. "We will leave you, brother."

"No need," said Sgenn. "We only seek information."

"I am crushed." He laughed. "Ask."

Sook sat on the edge of the tub. "You were attacked. Why?"

He nodded. "Indeed we were. The survivor told us that it was revenge."

"Some pair," the Princess added, "killed some thieves. One black, one not-black. The gang thought that we were that pair. And suffered the consequences of their error."

His eyes jumped from Sook to Sgenn and back again. "It was you, wasn't it? You are the pair that they were hunting.

That is why you are asking of us these questions."

Sgenn nodded. "We will visit that guild of slow learners."

"No need," said the Princess.

"I will not accept thieves attacking my royalty," growled Sook.

The Princess surged up and thumped one fist on the rim of the tub. "If we are your royalty then you will do as We do say!" She gasped and quickly sank back into the water, up to her neck.

Sgenn smiled at her, a soft gentle half-smile. "You are not my anything. I will see to those lurkers in the shadows."

"Leave them be. Please?"

Sook stared at her. One just did not say please to one of the Faan clan. As far as she knew. Sgenn shrugged.

"Please?" repeated the Prince, echoing his sister.

"Hum," grumbled Sook.

"Hum hum," agreed Sgenn.

He laughed. "You two sound just like Our Parents' Dark Advisor Ripple."

The Princess glared at them over the rim of the tub. "If We wish something killed, We can do the deed Ourself!"

Sook nodded, turned, and headed for the door. Sgenn followed her.

"HALT!" It was the Princess, sounding all royal. Both turned slowly and looked at her.

"Yesssssss?" hissed Sook.

"What are you, Sgenn? We would know."

The grey eyes slowly looked over all that she could see. "I am, as was Sook told, Reep daughter Faan theurgist Sgenn, Princess someday Queen." She slipped an arm around Sook's waist. "We do co-wander as do you." It was all the answer that she was going to give. It was all the answer that she felt like giving.

The Prince surged upright. "Join us for a meal. Then, if we are most persuasive, you will join us, My Most Royal Sister Lurin and I, in a merged wander quest."

He smiled at his sister. "For in this manner we will learn much of witch and, emmm, theurgist, and," he looked at the pair, "you will learn much of royal folk, at least such as we are. Thus, the purpose of quest and wander will be doubly served as each will gather knowledge otherwise unlearned."

He smiled broadly at his audience. "How say you all?"

"A choice?" asked Sook.

"Enquest we be but mere citizens afoot." He looked at Lurin. "True?"

She shook her head. "Nay, Brother, nay. We are what we are. That cannot be changed."

"Hum," said Sook.

"Hum hum," agreed Sgenn

"Subtly bespoke," mumbled the Prince. He looked at their visitors. "Then I do pronounce thusly. This witch is given freedom from our request and may do as she wishes." He nodded his head.

"Thus do We speak and thus it will be." He waggled one hand at her. "You may leave us." He fell backwards, laughing loudly, sending waves over his sister. Who kicked him. Hard.

He wiped water from his face and smiled. "Do join us later. And wait until then to give your answer. Please?"

Sook nodded and turned for the door. Sgenn followed.

As they closed the door, he called, "Please?"

Bander's Snatch. The Earliest Part of the Day.

Dargon led them into the training space, many acres of trees and meadows and gullies surrounded by a very tall, log wall. He took them down a path. After walking some distance, he stopped and pointed. "Kill it!"

It was a cat-sized dragon sitting on top of a large boulder sunning itself in a morning shaft of sun beam. Its coat glowed red in the light.

"Oh," said Eulin walking toward it. "What a cute little fellow."

"Kill it!" hissed Dargon, edging to one side as the small dragon looked over at them.

Eulin knelt next to the boulder and held out one hand. "You are a cutey, you are." She gently rubbed it under the chin. The red dragon's eyes closed. It burbled softly at her. "Why?" she asked Dargon.

"That," he called, "is a Red Spitter. Very dangerous."

Anamaxtor peered over Eulin's shoulder and looked at the tiny dragon. She scooped it up and held it in the crook of one arm. "You wouldn't spit at me, would you?" She stood and turned to look back at Dargon.

The small dragon wrapped its tail around her arm. And spit. At Dargan. Who barely managed to block the fire ball as it blasted past his head.

"See," he yelped.

"It didn't spit at me." She scratched it behind the jaw.

"Sister," said Je'leel, stepping to her side. "Let us see what Lesson Two might be."

Eulin set the small red dragon back on the boulder. "Bye, little one." She turned toward Dargon. "Which way?"

They followed him down into the gully. Dargan was frowning darkly.

The small red jumped from the boulder and slipped into its tunnel.

Zantikpik. Warm and Sunny.

As they hiked over the last swell of the hilltop, Ranna released Adarlak's hand. In the not far distance they could see the mine works that they sought and the sprawling workshop of the weapon maker.

"Cloth yourself, Adarlak. These folk have no need to admire your beauty."

Anjan released the other hand. And nodded. Adarlak said something and her billowing blouse of orange and blue was there.

"Nicely done." Ranna smiled at her skill. "I see subtle magic twist there." She veered toward the weapon shop.

Anjan rearranged her clothes and followed them.

Dol Spar. Mid-Afternoon.

They eventually returned from lunch: Mirf, Quan, and Fred. And found, lying on top of Mirf's desk a report, the cover stamped in bold green, 'EXTINCT.' The smaller red letters read. 'Plani'tar.'

"Ho ha!" Mirf dropped into her chair and snatched up the report. "So let's give this a look." She began to read it, rapidly flipping back and forth through the pages. Then she dropped the badly mangled report onto her desk and looked at her assistants.

"The late, but not great, Plani'tar were messing around

with the Majitar, a gonif bunch of nogoodniks." She slammed her hand flat on the correct spot on her desk top. And snarled at the clerk who rushed into the room. "Dumbkopf, let's see everything we have on the Majitar!"

She squinted at her clerk, who went pale. "Rush, rush, rush," snapped Mirf. "Don't just stand there doing shallow breathing and turning green around the gills. Let's give a go!"

The clerk jerked, spun, and rushed from the room and down the hall, wondering what she had done to ruin her career. She had just been assigned to The Special Investigator. Her predecessor had asked for and been granted a reassignment after only two work periods.

Mirf nodded at Fred and Quan. "The Majitar are low level sleaze balls so them we didn't worry about too much." She squinted at the far wall. "But I think that they may be branching out into things we ought to worry about."

Fred indicated to Quan that she didn't know what a sleaze ball was either.

Mirf leaned her forearms on the desk top. "Quan, go get Prandam from his office. He has been loafing long enough." Quan stood and headed out the other door. "And send in that pasty-faced Keeper of Grades, Liactor Fimbee."

Quan nodded.

"Chirp?" asked Fred as the door closed.

Mirf nodded. "You are so right. Go get ready."

Fred hurried out and down the hall toward the staircase to the armory. The clerk, clenching a folder in one hand, ran past her, headed for Mirf's office.

Grandeville. Tinker's Place.

Macabre looked at Mrrinar from the corners of his eyes.

The cat-folk was holding a sausage rather delicately in two fingers and chewing on one end of it.

Gyre shook her head, indicating that Ship's data banks still had no information on that race of beings. She shoved the basket over to him. He beamed at her and took another one. A maple bar this time. And smiled at Tinker. "Everyone looks healthy and well."

Tinker nodded. His mouth was full.

"Indeed," stated Chicken, answering for Tinker. "Most healthy. Most well."

"Ahhhh," began Macabre. "We left some stuff in your structure out there." He waggled the remainder of the maple bar in the general direction of the building. "The one with the shiny roof."

Tinker swallowed. "What?"

"Treasure, John, treasure. Had to do something with it. It was cluttering up one of the cargo holds." Macabre smiled at him.

Chantal stared at him. "Treasure? In our barn?"

"Take it away," said Tinker.

"No," replied Macabre to Tinker. "Yes," he said to Chantal.

She stood. "I'll go call Morgan." She headed for the telephone.

"Our business manager," explained Smoke. "He married one of Chantal's sisters."

Macabre nodded, stood, stepped away from the table, and cleared his throat. "We have to be on our way. We have a little . . . business to take care of, here and there." He fished in a shirt pocket and pulled out a small credit card sized object and flipped it to Chicken. "Here. New and Improved. Calling device." He winked at her. "Just in case."

Chicken caught it, slipped it into her shirt pocket, and winked back.

Macabre threw an arm around Gyre who nodded.

Ship took them up.

Tinker slumped deeper into his chair. "So how are we going to explain that?"

Chantal returned and dropped into her seat. "Morgan said that he would be up soon."

"What?"

"Coming up here to examine the treasure. So, cool it, Cowboy." She refilled her cup and grabbed another doughnut, taking a big bite out of it.

He looked around the room. "Raft, you and Mrrinar go up to your room and stay there until we call you out." He wasn't about to try and figure out how to explain that to Morgan.

R-Bar jumped up and beckoned Raft. "Come, sister, we have to talk." Ran went with them.

Sha'gar walked around the table and sat on one arm of his chair, sliding an arm over this shoulder. "Mate'mer?"

He sighed. "We are getting sucked into it again. I can feel it. Too many visitors from out there all of a sudden."

Fair Morn looked at Smoke. "Shall we pack?"

"No!" He glared at her.

"Guess not," replied Smoke.

"We have no business out there," he added.

Messenger bounced out of her chair. "Let's go seeeeeee the treasure."

"Indeed." Chicken followed her into the kitchen and out the back door.

Chantal waved one hand at him. "Go ahead, Cowboy, I will wait for Morgan."

So. He did.

Head for the treasure.

They all went out to the barn to see what Macabre had left there.

Zantikpik. A Warm Day.

They stood in the small space and looked at the display cases and at the walls. Sharp edged weapons of every shape and form and color crowded every available piece of space. Cutting edges glittered in the light.

Something eased through the door behind the low counter, huffed air through cheek holes, and said, "We do not sell to witches or to mages. Of any color or type."

Ranna stared at it.

Adarlak glowered and reached somewhere and fetched in a large mace. Ranna stayed her hand.

"We," stated Ranna, "do not wish to buy anything. We will wait outside" She nudged Anjan forward and handed her a large sack that clinked. "Buy anything that you wish. "

Anjan nodded and began to browse as the others exited the room.

"That proztar," grumbled Adarlak, glaring at the door, kicking a small rock out of the way. Orange and blue vague crackled around her.

"Calm, mage, calm." Ranna nodded. "Anjan deserves a special weapon. Killing that proztar would prevent that."

"Ummmm," replied Adarlak. The air settled down. She sent the mace somewhere.

They waited.

Adarlak crossed her arms over her chest and watched the activities around the mine entrances.

Ranna walked here and there and back again, fingering this wand or that wand. Witches did not wait well.

But eventually, as it has to happen, the door to the shop opened and Anjan stepped out. She was wearing something on her left hip and had another something strapped to her upper left arm. The things were a deep blue shading into dark purple, almost black color, all high sheen.

She smiled at Ranna. "Sharp. Nice. Cut anything."

Adarlak walked over to see.

"Good gift?" asked Ranna.

Anjan stepped close to her. "Best gift." She leaned even closer.

Ranna reached sideways, grabbed one of Adarlak's arms, and took them elseplace.

Dol Spar. Late Afternoon.

Mirf pointed at a chair in the corner and nodded at the clerk who stood there sucking in deep breathes. She had run both ways. "Sit down, kinderleh. Give it a rest."

As her clerk dropped into the chair, Mirf began to paw through file making small sounds to herself.

A tall man strolled into the room, frowned at the clerk, and cleared his throat. "Ahem, ahem. Yes, Chief Inspector."

"Special Investigator, dummkopf!" Mirf waved the tattered folder in the clerk's direction. "So what is she, rank-wise, Fimbee?"

"She," he said, peering down his nose at her, reading her badge, "is a Clerk. An Apprentice, 5th Grade, Probation Period."

"Don't do stuffy with me." snarled Mirf, pawing through the folder again. "She is now, pay close attention, Fimbee, my very own Personal Clerk, 1st Grade, Special." She smiled at the Keeper of the Grade. "Hookey dokey?"

Fimbee blanched even paler than his usual pale complexion. It was that smile, or grimace, or whatever it was. He wobbled, just a little, and cleared his throat. "Ahem, ahem, ahem. Yes."

"Now! This very instant!"

His head violently bobbed up and down. "Yes."

She waggled the ever more tattered folder at him. "Send the correct shirt and badge. Go away. Push paper."

Fimbee rushed out of the room.

Mirf looked over at the staring clerk. "Sooooo, how's by you?" And frowned at her clerk. "You catching something?"

The clerk was slumped sideways in her chair. "I don't think so."

Mirf jumped up, hurried over, knelt next to her, and handed her a slip of paper.

"Here. Take the rest of the day off." She snatched the paper back and wrote something on it. "No! Take the rest of the week off. We are leaving on a little trip anyway."

She stood, lifted the clerk to her feet, aimed her at the correct door, and nudged her into motion, giving her a friendly pat on a rear pocket. "Nice tuchis. Bet the boy friend likes that."

She slammed the door closed as soon as her clerk wobbled from the room. She sat on the edge of her desk and mauled the report some more, finished reading it as a different door opened.

Quan walked in followed by Prandam. Prandam slipped into a chair.

"Time to go to work, sneak," Mirf said by way of greeting. She began to tell Prandam what she wanted to know and what he needed to know in order to get her what she wanted to know.

Bander's Snatch. Still A Pretty Nice Day.

They had run into, talked with, and passed by four additional kinds of dragons. Dargan was now twitching, every few moments, getting a strange look in his eyes.

Each and every time that they had met one of the dragons he had urged Eulin to 'kill it.'

Each and every time she had merely smiled at him, walked over and talked with the potential victim. Once she had hanged a horse-sized blue and grey monster sharply on the tip of its nose for burbling smoky grey fumes on them.

Now they were walking along a gully bottom headed toward a grime streaked vertical face of red orange rock, and the cave mouth from which the grime streaks originated.

As they walked along, Je'leel had slipped her arm under Eulin's, leaned close and mumured so low that only Eulin could hear. "Sister, I do not think that there is any training here for you to learn."

Eulin nodded, stopped and turned, freeing her arm as she did. "Dargon, you may stay here. We can look in there by ourselves." She spun and headed for the cavern.

Dargon nodded and made another note. He shrugged. No-one would be able to blame him if that pair died, especially angry parents or kin. He had ample documentation to show that he had tried to teach them and that they had disobeyed everything that he had told them.

He sat on the large boulder and waited for their extinction. It wouldn't be long now

Inside the cavern mouth, Eulin cast soft violet glow deeper and deeper into the great open space. "A very dirty place."

Anamaxtor bumped her with his head and looked worried.

"Stay here," she ordered. He sat.

Eulin and Je'leel slowly worked their way deeper and deeper and around a curve in the tunnel and stopped to peer at it.

"It is as big as our barn." Je'leel looked at the monster.

Actually it was bigger. But right now it was lying down, looking about as big as her barn.

One dinner plate sized eye opened. Then the other. They were deep red with green centers. It sniffed, tasting the odors. And watched them as they walked closer. A number of scars ran jagged lines across its forehead. Most of the trainees that had survived to get this far had not returned to the outside world. It grumbled deep in its chest at them, a low warning sound. Bilious green seeped from its nose. It licked its lips and wondered if they tasted good. It certainly hoped so. They often didn't. But these smelled fresh.

Eulin walked up to it, jumped, and sat down, using its

snout for a bench. The dragon grunted surprise. She reached up and scratched the wide space between its eyes and said to Je'leel, "We are closing this training place. Look at those scars. That is awful."

Je'leel sat on the large piece of the wall that had fallen out, crossed her legs, and nodded. "Wonder why your mother sent you here?"

It is strange," said Eulin. She whistled loudly.

Anamaxtor charged around the corner, glaring attack ready, and skidded to a halt, claws digging into the rocky surface.

"This is Anamaxtor," explained Eulin, rubbing her palm up and down in the flat spot between the monster's eyes.

Anamaxtor burbled something. The monster snorted.

"Don't you ever take a bath," scolded Eulin. "This cave is filthy and so are you."

It blinked both eyes.

Eulin jumped down and headed for the cave entrance. "Come with me," she ordered.

Je'leel and Anamaxtor hurried after her. The dragon reared up and up, filling the space. And followed them. Outside.

Out in the fresh air, Eulin stomped over to Dargon and demanded, "Where is the nearest large lake?"

He peered from around a tree and pointed. "That way."

She spun and pointed in the same direction and snapped, "Go take a bath!"

The dragon lunged into the air, vast wings flaring, and headed that way,

Je'leel and Anamaxtor walked over to join Eulin. Je'leel snapped at Dargon, "This school is not nice."

"Yessssss," agreed Eulin, pulsating lavender light. "Very not nice. Take down those walls."

Dargon stared at her.

Soft crackling wandered down the great tree and peered at them.

"A tree dragon," observed Eulin.

"Is that a command?" hissed the emerald one.

"Certainly," replied Eulin.

In the distance and from all around they could hear ripping sounds.

"But," gasped Dargon "What will I do?"

"Be my guest for dinner," hissed the emerald one. "The first course." It licked its lips.

"NO!" snapped Eulin. "He can learn guardian from all of you."

"Make a much better first course."

"NO!"

"As you wish." It disappeared back into the thick foliage of the tree.

"What is this place?" demanded Je'leel.

"Bander's Snatch," stated Dargon, back into his teacher mode. "The elseplace of many kinds of dragons. A very rare elseplace. It is the elseplace, ummm, was the place where those wishing to learn certain skills came to train."

He cleared his throat. "Our few graduates are known far and wide." He sighed. "Now what will we do?"

Je'leel tapped him on the chest with one finger. "Guided tours?"

Dargon's eyes unfocused. "We could charge great fees," he muttered. "Low overhead."

"Goodbye," said Eulin.

They walked away.

The emerald one slithered down the tree, coiled around Dargon, and began to talk business with him.

Far to one side, in the distance, a great gout of steam banged into the air.

Eulin laughed. So did Je'leel and Anamaxtor.

"Dax is nice," Dargon yelled at their back.

So they went there.

Five Star Bar.

They were all large men. They filled the meeting hall. Attentive, yet relaxed. Many were battle scarred. They admired the woman and listened to the man.

"It is a noble quest," said Nam, the Tadar of the Dragon Crest Arm, after some time.

Don Kaptax nodded his agreement. "We agree about that," he said, speaking for the Trayl Guard.

Pomon cleared his throat. He wore the wurm-sleeve tunic of the Wryl Team.

"Yes?" Farth looked at him.

"No offense, Ranger Farth," said Pomon, being very careful and correct in form of address. "But we have heard of a certain ranger who fled his unit and became, ahem, shall we say, umm, a rather light-fingered freelancer."

Men whispered to their friends.

Farth nodded and folded his arms across his chest. "When I met my noble wife, she made me see the error of my ways and I became, once again, a Silver Ranger." He smiled at her.

Sedeem sat far to one side of the room, partially to watch everyone in the room and partially to be as unobtrusive as possible.

Pomon sat straighter. He had been slumping in his chair, legs stretched out, listening to Farth's presentation. "How noble is this wife of your's, unaffiliated ranger?"

Someone sucked in their breath. It was a near insult.

Farth blinked and looked at Pomon. It was a cold, calculating stare. All eyes watched the pair. Everyone was ready to move, if necessary. Then Farth nodded.

"Brother to brother, I will answer your question." He looked over at Sedeem and noted that she had slipped her right hand up her left sleeve where she had placed her wand. "Stand, wife."

Sedeem pulled her hand free, stood, and turned to face the room.

"This," said Farth. "This is my wife, Sedeem. She is the First Daughter of the Great Lord Tinker called The Chosen One and many other titles. She will answer any question you may wish to ask."

His eyes scanned the room. "As will I." He leaned back against the wall and waited.

Pomon stared at her and asked, "How do we know that this is true, Ranger-mate?"

Nam surged to his feet. Don Kaptax grabbed him by the back of his belt and shook his head. Grumbling loudly, Nam sat down.

Sedeem walked across the room, stood in front of Pomon and looked up into his face. "What proof do you require, Zadar Pomon?"

Some whispered to others. She had recognized the rank patch on his grab.

"Farth tells us of your nobility. We would know this for certain."

The whispering grew louder. Pomon had not used a rank title. It was a deliberate taunt. Eyes watched Farth.

Sedeem nodded, turned, and addressed the room. "Pomon," she said, drawing out his name, leaving off his rank. "Wishes to have proof of my husband's claim. I will provide this Ranger his proof." She smiled at the room. "And you have my promise that he will be unharmed." She laughed. Pomon was twice her size.

They disappeared.

Sedeem and Pomon.

Folk surged to their feet.

"SIT DOWN!" bellowed Farth into the din.

And slowly they did.

"They will return shortly. My wife is not only noble, but a powerful magic user. We will wait."

He leaned back against the wall and crossed his arms back over his chest.

And hoped that it would be so.

Grandeville. Tinker's Place.

Suddenly they were there

In the barn.

Along with everyone else.

"Wow, Dad, where did you get all that?"

His head snapped around. He smiled and frowned. She was mobbed by all the others. All her mothers wanted to hug their daughter.

When she was finally released, she said, "Can't stay but for a minute or two." She laughed happily. "We are in the middle of an important meeting."

Pomon stared at the towering mound of glittering treasure. And at the women crowding around Sedeem. And at the male that she called Dad. Then his eyes searched the place for something to use as a weapon.

Disengaging from her mothers, she walked over and kissed her father on the forehead, turned and slipped an arm under one of his. "This is Ranger Pomon, Zadar of the Wryl Team, Silver Rangers. Zadar Pomon, this is my father, Lord John Tinker, The Chosen One."

Pomon nodded. "Easy to say." He waved one hand at the mound. "Impressive. But."

"Now what's going on?" asked Tinker, frowning slightly.

"Farth is trying to reorganize the Silver Rangers, bring them back to their old state, their once before strength and purpose. But Pomon is being difficult."

"And?" grumbled Tinker.

"He needs convincing."

"Of?"

"That you are really The Chosen One, Dad."

Tinker sighed heavily.

"Please?"

"Introduce your mothers to him," he mumbled.

She did.

Pomon nodded to each one. And shook his head.

"My Lord?" asked Chicken, being Royally Proper.

"What?"

"Let us to abode go. There thee might show this one thy most fearsome dark blade."

"Ummm. O.K., let's go." Tinker headed for the door.

They led Pomon toward the house and up onto the rear deck.

R-Bar glowered at Pomon. "I could put something on him." The air crackled around her.

Ran nodded.

Chantal stepped from the house and cocked her long-barreled revolver. "How about I just shoot him in the butt?"

Everyone, except Tinker, thought that doing something to Pomon was appropriate as this person doubted their daughter's words.

Tinker sighed. And looked at Sedeem. He felt all their intent. And wondered how long they would behave. "Any ideas?"

She told him.

He nodded and walked into the house. And rejoined them holding it.

She nodded at her father standing there, holding the great black sword, sword tip set on the deck. And looked at Pomon. "What proof do you wish?"

Pomon knelt and leaned his head close to the great sword, one ear almost touching it. Then he stood. "It is said that the man that wields a black death-singing blade travels with a shape shifter."

Smoke stepped around Sedeem. "Look at me."

Pomon squinted at those orange-gold eyes, vertical black pupils mere lines in the bright sun. "What would you like to see?" She reached deep into mind.

"Kan the Killer," gasped Pomon. "I killed you long ago." Then he saw her standing behind the ghost figure. He took another look at Tinker leaning so casually on that black thing.

He cleared his throat and dropped to one knee. "Mighty Lord, I wish to apologize to your Noble Daughter and to yourself."

"Rise, Zadar Pomon," ordered Chicken in her most Royal tone of voice. "To question is a mark of wisdom not often found in fighting men."

As Pomon did, she stepped over and kissed Sedeem. "Do come back and visit, soon, Our Verra Own Daughter, Our most Fair Princess."

"Sure, mom." Twirling around, she kissed Tinker on the side of his face. "Bye, Pop."

And they were gone.

Sedeem and Pomon.

Five Star Bar.

They appeared. They did.

Sedeem and Pomon.

Sedeem smiled at Farth and went back to where she had been sitting.

Pomon looked around the hall, stepped over to Farth, and dropped to both knees. "Tindar Farth, the Wryl Team is under your command."

Rangers gasped. Tindar was the title of The Supreme Commander of the Silver Rangers. They hadn't had such a person since their scattering.

"Select my replacement," stated Pomon, bowing his head.

"Rise Zadar Pomon. None can replace the brave."

As Pomon stood, Farth wrapped his arms around the large man. "You are my brother, Ranger to Ranger."

Nam jumped to his feet. "TINDAR!"

Don Kaptax leaped up. "TINDAR!"

Then they all surged around the startled Farth. When the group had finally settled down, Don Kaptax said, "We must have a home base, Tindar."

Farth nodded. "Let us begin planning our home base. And make preparations to relocate." He certainly hoped that the tale that Sedeem had heard was true.

Farth, Pomon, and Don Kaptax went into the adjoining room to make those plans. The rest scattered to pack and make sure everything was ready for relocation under the direction of Nam.

Smiling happily, Sedeem went outside to walk around. She felt very, very proud of her husband.

Chapter Twelve

Just A Wander.

Donae.

The Caedi Syndicate sent fast runners into selected elseplaces, seeking information. And then they hired more. The worse of the worst. It was the type of talent that they required to fulfill their contract. The Caedi Syndicate was in a hurry.

It was only not long ago that they signed the contract with the Majitar. While the contract was an exclusive contract, they knew that sooner or later word would leak out and the bounty hunters would begin to swarm. The Caedi Syndicate wanted to find the Majitar's treasure first. They wanted to receive the entire reward for themselves.

Plana Dar.

"So this place is a mess."

"So this place is a big big mess."

Mirf, Quan, and Fred stood on a rubble pile and looked at the desolation stretching in all directions. As far as they could tell, the entire city had been reduced to rubble.

"Ho boy when he destroys, boy does he destroy." She pointed at the front door of the only building still standing. "So let's give a look."

They worked their way over to and then into the structure and began to search, hoping to find some document that might have survived the destruction of the place.

Dax.

It was a nice place, all soft rolling hills covered with thick velvet green grass. Clear skies. Nicely warm, not too hot. A pleasant mild breeze.

"Nice." Eulin waved in lunch.

They sat on top of one of the hills and admired the view.

Anamaxtor admired the lunch.

"What is here?" Je'leel tasted one of the dishes. "What did you learn back there?"

"Don't know," mumbled Eulin around a mouthful. She swallowed. "Dragon call."

Je'leel looked at her. Eulin smiled. "The dragons told me how to call them." Her eyes twinkled. "Want to see?"

"Yes."

A small red popped in and sat in Eulin's lap. She scratched it under the chin. "Really fast." She fed it something and asked the small creature, "Do you know the way back to your home?"

It looked up at her and frowned a dragon frown. Dragons always knew their way back home.

She nodded.

It was gone.

Je'leel shrugged a shoulder. "Maybe we should return home as well."

Eulin frowned and put her hands over Anamaxtor's ears. "Don't go. Dragons are fun but not very exciting conversationalists. They mostly talk about eating. And the males, erm, talk mostly about female dragons."

"Those were all males?"

Eulin nodded. "Mostly. The females are very shy." She grinned. "They are actually smarter than the males. Please?"

Je'leel nodded.

Eulin removed her hands from Anamaxtor's head and then tickled him under one ear. "Let's sleep right here. Talking with all those dragons was really tiring." She yawned. "I didn't want Dargon to know that."

Je'leel looked at their surroundings. There was nothing to be seen but the low hills stretching away in all directions. And a large sun hanging very low on the horizon. She nodded.

Eulin waved in large numbers of blankets and pillows. "That should do it." She sprawled out on the sleeping area and smiled up at her sister. "Sleep with me."

Je'leel stretched out alongside her and rolled her head to look as Eulin rolled on her side and reached out.

"Vander spells have no effect," said Je'leel.

"Pooga." Eulin frowned.

"Mother is indjinn. I am indjinn aware."

Eulin slipped her sister's shirt open. "You are beautiful."

"I am my mother's daughter." Je'leel slid her hand under the loose folds of Eulin's upper garment. "As are you."

"Ermach," sighed Eulin.

"Sister, you must be careful. Being body proud almost eliminated your guild in the far distant past."

"Yesssss." Eulin rolled onto her back. "And you are a sneak."

Je'leel dragged blankets up and over them. "Let us sleep."

Eulin nodded.

Anamaxtor stretched out along their feet.

Plana Dar.

"So Mirfeleh, how's by you?"

Mirf leaped sideways, spinning around. "KINDERLEH!" She laughed loudly. "Don't do a sneak like that. It is hard on the nerves." Then she looked at the others. "Ho boy, a bunch of beefkins. You branching out? Taking after your father?"

Farth fizzled.

Sedeem stepped over to Mirf and introduced her to everyone. Then she slipped an arm under one of Mirf's and towed her over to where a large window had been.

As they stood and looked out the opening, Sedeem said, "Other than the small villages, this is an empty elseplace."

"Yas?"

"The Silver Rangers are looking for an elseplace for ingather, a permanent home."

"And?" Mirf looked hobgoblin-sly from the corners of her eyes at Sedeem.

"What if they came here?"

"Villagers?"

"They like the idea. I already asked."

"And?"

Sedeem tightened her grip on Mirf's arm. "M.C. fixes up the building. They get the ground floor free."

"Second floor and we remodel the lobby."

Sedeem laughed. "A deal?"

"A deal's a deal."

Sedeem hugged and kissed her. "Thanks, Boss."

"You could come and work for me again."

"Nope. Life is too exciting around you."

"So kinderleh, you fooling around with all that beef?"

Sedeem shook her head. "You know better than that."

Mirf shrugged. "Straight-laced Rangers, right?"

"Yep."

"Also," said Mirf. "We bring in a crew from Hamjam to rubble clear, repair, and in general make this heap respectable."

"For?" asked Sedeem.

"You keep our records up to date on the moose meat." Mirf indicated the large men watching them.

"Sure."

"A deal?"

"A deal sa'deal."

They both laughed.

"Let's explain it to them," suggested Sedeem.

So they did.

The elseplace was renamed, Fandor's Dan, after the first Silver Ranger.

Duraldin.

The Prince jumped to his feet as they approached. And smiled warmly at them, one by one. "Good," he said. "Good. We felt that perhaps a more public place than our rooms was proper."

As soon as they were seated, the server slipped up and waited to take their orders.

The Prince nodded at the pair. "Whatever you might wish."

"Hum," said Sook. Sgenn nodded.

The Royals wore loose, casual billowing attire. He was dressed in black, she in white.

"I will have whatever the house feels is best," said the Prince to the server. The Princess nodded. "Also."

"Yes," said Sgenn.

Sook nodded.

As the server left, the Prince leaned on the table. "May we get our business out of the way before we eat?"

"We have no business to discuss," stated Sgenn softly.

"Oh." The Prince looked unhappy at them.

"We will travel with you," said Sook.

Sgenn nodded. "Until we decide not to."

"We make no claim on your time," stated the Princess, looking from Sook to Sgenn. "You are free folk. As are we."

"Then," stated Sgenn, "as free folk we choose to travel some with you." A small half-smile tugged itself in place. "If you free folk will accept our companionship."

"Well bespoke." The Prince smiled at her. Then he looked at her cousin. And spoke to the Princess. "I think that our wander quest has just become ever much more, eeee, interesting."

"Indeed, Brother, indeed."

When the meal was over, and they had dessert, and some small cups of the local beverage, the Prince looked around the table and smiled happily at the others. "Where shall we travel from here? Is there some elseplace that one might wish to visit? Or shall we just bobble along and see as it happens?"

The Princess shook her head. "We have no goal in mind that one needs to visit. Our Mother changed the Quest Rules."

"Hum," said Sook. "There is a small foregather on

Wanderill."

"I heard of a special on Krag Far Reach." Sgenn set her hands in her lap.

The Prince leaned back and slumped just a little. His sister frowned at him just a little. Slumping in your chair was not considered as proper posture for future Kings or Queens. She never slumped.

"We might venture to each. First one, then the other?" he suggested.

Sgenn blinked. Sook wondered about that blink.

The Princess nudged him under the table and indicated the individual that had just slipped into the room, taking a corner table. He had quietly ordered a meal and was watching them intently. The man was dressed in clothes of dark tones of red almost black.

The Prince indicated that he saw. And slipped a long knife from his boot and up into his left sleeve.

Sook nudged Sgenn who gave a slight nod and stood, and said, "Prince, Princess, at first light, we will meet here and go to the foregather." She turned casually to see what the bother might be.

Sook rose and nodded to the royals. Then she walked with Sgenn from the room, casting lightly over this intrusive visitor as they left the room.

He forgot why he was there.

And wondered why he had ordered that meal.

Grandeville. Tinker's Place.

"O.K., John. I will take care of it."

Morgan stared at the great mound of glitter and sparkle.

And then looked at Tinker and all the rest crowding around and staring at the pile. "It will mostly have to go into storage. There is no way you could sell all that and not have it become big news everywhere. And you'd have every agency of government peeking and poking and wondering how you got it." He laughed. "I am not going to ask either. The first bunch was bad enough."

"We didn't ask for it," mumbled Tinker. "Could just dig a hole and drop it in."

"What?" Morgan looked past him at Chantal.

"Nothing," said Chantal.

"Well," said Morgan. "I will have some tight-lipped types come up and crate it and have it all sent to the Company's archives. We have a special storage place. It will just be more boxes among the many. Take a couple of weeks, that's all."

He threw his arm around Chantal's shoulders. "Well, siste-in-law, Shannon wants to know when you all are coming down for a picnic or visit or whatever?"

"Tell her to pick a date."

"Oh boy," gushed Messenger. She liked visiting down at their ranch.

"Sure," agreed Tinker. "We'll be there."

Rare Ranta.

They lounged on the steep grassy slope above the lake not all that far above the wide orange beach sand.

Anjan's skin had turned a rusty brown from the sun. Ranna had remained as pale as moonlight. Witches did not sunburn or suntan. Adarlak had merely turned a deeper bronze, the usual skin tone for a magician.

Ranna leaned over, her fingers sliding lightly down the slightly pebbled design running diagonally across Anjan's torso from left shoulder to right hip. "Are we rested yet?" She had been being as patient as she could be but was rapidly losing patience with being patient.

Anjan smiled and reached up. "You are beautiful, Pale Love."

"Hum hum." Ranna rolled back, pulling Anjan with her. Then she sighed. "That was most not-witch."

Anjan hitched just a little higher and kissed the hollow at the base of Ranna's throat, then her cheek, and then sang soft-song into her ear. She felt the tension leaving the witch's body.

"What are we to do with her?" mumbled Ranna.

"Doja?"

"The mage."

Anjan sat up and watched as Ranna rolled onto her side, facing the now sleeping figure. Adarlak was now wearing baggy orange trousers trimmed in blue and nothing else.

"Taste?" asked Anjan.

Ranna violently shook her head. "A witch that tastes mage cannot stop." She tugged Anjan back down. "Only mage."

"Ahhhhhh," sighed Anjan. "Haaummmjaaaaaaaaaaa."

Adarlak yawned widely and stretched. Ranna released Anjan and sat up, smiled, and slowly licked her lips. "Mine! My fierce warrior."

Anjan's finger lightly stroked across Ranna's stomach.

Ranna sighed. "If Parquor were still alive, I would thank him because he was responsible for us coming together." She smiled. "Then I would kill him."

Adarlak sat up, smiled at them, and waved in a meal. "I

am hungry."

And as they sat around eating, she asked, "Shall we journey elseplace? I am rested beyond rest."

"Where?"

Adarlak emptied her cup and looked at the witch. "It is said that a small mage gather occurs on Bal's Dartar. I would acquire a few spells more."

"Hum." Ranna slowly nodded. She was not exactly thrilled about the idea of being in the midst of large number of magicians but she understood the desire to learn and acquire more spells. She looked at Anjan who looked at Adarlak.

"As soon as we are finished." Ranna refilled her cup.

Dax.

They had wandered the low hills and eventually found a narrow wagon track which seemed to run, more or less, straight across the undulating topography. It appeared to be a little used road as it was mostly overgrown with grass and showed little erosion in the steeper places.

Now, late in the afternoon, they approached a small village. It was a collection of round cornered structures roofed in two-tone materials, Every structure had a tower. The towers jutted every which way, some from this corner, some from that. Some of them shot straight up from the center of the building. A few rose from the center of a wall. Every tower sported a large flag, all different colors and designs.

"Strange," observed Eulin.

"Different," agreed Je'leel.

They wandered the crooked streets and were stared at by the town's inhabitants. All the town folk were short and stocky, all dressed in various combinations of pale rose and pale green. Everyone wore their hair in two long braids.

"I don't think that they get many visitors." Je'leel stared back and looked around for an inn, or something like that.

After they walked a few blocks, she spotted one, she thought.

"That place with the red door. I think that looks like an inn." She headed that way.

It was.

They entered the large common room filled with appetite provoking odors that drifted through a wide door in the far wall. Must be the kitchen, thought Je'leel. She could see a long hall running off into the interior of the building at one corner.

They sat at one of the tables and waited. And soon a woman came from the kitchen door, walked over to stand by their table.

"We would like something to eat," said Eulin.

"Poota poota mage ukla," she sneered And glared at Anamaxtor. "Kakak tak flim flim." Then she stared at Je'leel. "You with this omdota?"

"Yes. We would like a meal and a room."

"Hook hook upta," snapped the woman.

Je'leel jumped to her feet. "Wait here," she said to Eulin.

"Come with me," she said to the woman, and hurried toward what she thought was the kitchen.

The stove ran the full length of one wall. It was flat topped with a series of grills holding pots with red flame licking up their sides.

Je'leel walked over, stopped next to one of the cooks, and peered into one of the pots. Then she waggled her hand through the flames. The cook stared at her hand. "Not as ticklish as propane," said Je'leel.

"EEEEEEEEEE UCKLA!" he screamed. "Fire bota, fire bota!"

Turning around, Je'leel nodded at the staring woman and pointed at the pot. "This smells good. We would like some." She walked from the kitchen and back to the table where Eulin waited. As she sat down, she gently laid her hand on her cousin's arm.

"Certainly warm," said Eulin.

Je'leel nodded and watched the woman approach, staring at Je'leel's hand. She carried a tray set with two bowls, two cups, utensils, and some sort of bread.

"Why don't you like magicians?" asked Eulin as the woman carefully set their table, always watching Je'leel.

The woman stepped back and glared at her.

"Why?" repeated Eulin.

"Sheta mage cause ugly, bistle bangtak." She pointed at the ceiling. There was a large scorched area right in the middle. "No pay, no fix. Just snicker snicker."

Eulin frowned and nodded. "I do not do things like that." She set a gold coin on the table. "And I think that will not be happening any more. We, err, changed that." She looked at her sister. "Didn't we?"

Je'leel nodded. "Dargon won't be graduating any more dragon hunters. Good thing too." She picked up her spoon and sniffed. "Smells good." And began to eat.

As they finished their meal, a man slipped into the inn and took a table and ordered a meal. He was dressed in clothes colored a deep shade of red almost black. He watched them closely as they headed down the hall to their room. Then he called over the woman and held a long conversation with her in very low, very private tones, passing her some coins.

Sprawling comfortably on the large bed, Je'leel poked Eulin in her side. "Better be careful around these folk. It sounds as if those trained by Dargon have caused all kinds of ill-will."

"She was certainly unhappy all right." Eulin stretched. And smiled. "Tell me what you did in the kitchen."

Je'leel did.

Eulin laughed.

Bal's Dartar.

"I am disappointed."

They were watching a demonstration not far from the outer fence. The small crowd of magicians were watching a mage in bright yellow robes showing a down-and-out spell.

The short woman poked him in the side. "Dear?"

"This is the next to last day and I haven't found anything new."

"It is a small foregather," said Duff.

"That is often the problem," said a mage wearing a green and red striped robe standing next to $1.98.

"I am the $1.98 magician," said $1.98. "This is Plum Duff."

"Hum ha," replied the man "I am Ra'am, Fulan Guild."

"No guild," said $1.98.

Ra'am shrugged. "Sometimes better." He looked past $1.98 at Duff and smiled. Duff nodded. And leaned against $1.98.

"Ahhhh," said Ra'am. Then he looked past her. And twitched.

"What?" $1.98 jerked and looked in that direction.

Duff banged him one hip. "Calm down, Dear!"

He stared at the trio. A Hacto mage had appeared with two female companions. The one was obvious witch. He couldn't figure the other. She was neither witch nor magician. The trio walked around the edge and slipped into one of the large tents.

"Kak pter tik tak," grumbled Ranna. She didn't like all those magicians staring at her.

Anjan grabbed her hand and held it tightly.

"Calm," hissed Adarlak. "No one is going to do anything here at gather." She rubbed her cheek with her finger. "I will not let them."

"Hum," mumbled Ranna.

They walked from the tent and began to wander around the gather, guided by Adarlak.

Anjan jerked on Ranna's hand and whispered very low in her ear. "Ran'na, look there."

Ranna looked.

They watched a man dressed in dark shades of red near black as he slipped through the crowds obviously searching for someone or something.

"Sneak peek," grumbled Anjan.

"Hum," said Ranna as Adarlak stepped away to talk with a tall mage dressed in green and red striped robes. He had crooked a finger at her. Ranna prepared a cast carefully, just in case.

"Fulan mage," said Adarlak, using formal address.

"Hacto mage," he replied. His eyes wandered over her face and body.

"What speak?" she snapped.

He shrugged. "It takes great strength and daring to travel with a dark companion."

"It is my travel."

He nodded. "Many pardons. I thought only friendly." He reached out and slid his hand slowly up her rib cage.

In one smooth motion she reached in her mage mace, jabbed him in stomach with it, doubling him over. She grabbed a handful of his hair, yanked him toward the outer fence and ran him headfirst into it.

"I decide who does finger play with me," she hissed and cast, paralyzing his hands. "Ask for help. It wears off in the morning."

She straightened up and glared at the circle of magicians staring at them and stepped through their ranks and headed over to where Ranna and Anjan stood watching, everyone and everything.

Duff tugged $1.98's sleeve and dragged him over to a refreshment booth. "That Fulan is fortunate. I would have made him an ugly spot."

$1.98 ordered and sat next to her. "I never saw a mage use a weapon before."

"Power mace."

"What?"

"Mace wand, Dear."

"Oh." He slipped an arm around her. "Guess I am safe."

"For the time being, Dear."

"Strange pair," observed Ranna, looking across the now almost empty middle ground.

Adarlak nodded. "Don't know of any guild of little folk

Or anyone that wears such tattered robes."

"Hum hum hum," said Ranna. "A sister did tell tale." She started across the open space toward that strange pair.

"Duff," hissed $1.98. "That witch and her companions are coming at us." He yanked a slender black wand from his left sleeve.

"Put that thing away!" she snapped. "We do not want half the gather removed." He did.

She patted his thigh and said, "One does not do vile at a gather. Unless necessary." She watched the approaching witch carefully.

Ranna stopped a respectful distance away, carefully testing for mage pulse. "I am Faan witch Ranna. This is Hacto mage Adarlak. And Anjan. May we speak?"

"The $1.98 magician and Duff, a magician also," answered $1.98.

"So, it is you."

$1.98 frowned. "Do I know you?" He looked at Duff. She shrugged.

"My sister and her's spoke of you."

"Sister?" He looked at her two companions.

"Faan witch R-Bar and her's, The Chosen One," stated Ranna.

$1.98 reached sideways for his mug and failed.

Duff pushed it into his hand. "Here, Dear. Welcome Ranna, sister of R-Bar. Welcome." She released the cast that she had been holding and sent it away. The air settled, the low hum faded away.

Adarlak exhaled.

"We were just relaxing after that last demonstration," said

$1.98, clearing his throat. "Join us?"

Ranna sat, not too close, and tapped the counter top with one fingernail, and told the counterman, "One of those for each." She pointed at $1.98's mug.

$1.98 looked at Adarlak. "What did Ra'am do?"

"Who?" replied Adarlak very carefully, studying this strange magician now that she knew that he had been involved in some manner with The Chosen One and with the Faan.

"That Fulan mage."

"His touch was unwanted."

$1.98 shoved his chair sideways.

Adarlak smiled at him. "Worry not."

Duff peered past him at her. "This wreck is mine."

"Of course."

Ranna ordered five more. "You helped kill The Evil One?"

$1.98 handed a mug to Duff. "Yes."

Adarlak's head snapped around, she had been looking out at the crowds. "You?"

Duff glared at her. "Nearly died."

Adarlak bowed her head. "I am mostly new."

"Learning," mumbled Ranna, ordering again, leaning against Anjan. She emptied her mug and slid an arm around Adarlak.

Magicians stared puzzlement from all directions. Nothing had happened.

"We require a room," said Anjan, throwing an arm around Ranna's waist, dragging the witch's other arm up and over her shoulder.

Adarlak stood and tried to do the same thing. Ranna

refused to relocate the arm from around Adarlak's waist.

"We will get you a room." Duff jumped from her stool. "Follow us." She took $1.98's hand and hurried him toward the place where they were staying.

"Hum, hum, hum," murmured Ranna, squeezing Adarlak gently. "Are my fingers safe?"

"Friendly safe," whispered Adarlak.

Duff tugged $1.98 to walk even faster.

Wanderill.

Witches spun.

Hissed. Growled and stared.

At them.

It wasn't the warriors that were causing all the consternation, it was that other one. The one dressed in grey. She was an unknown. Therefore she was bothering. An unknown was very bothering to witches.

Sook glared at all the black staring eyes and announced very sternly, "I am Faan witch Sook. This is my cousin, Faan theurgist Sgenn."

On all sides witches called down protection of every kind.

Sgenn tucked her arms into her sleeves and watched them. Very calmly.

Sook threw her arm around her cousin. "They will settle down."

And, little by little, the foregather did. Settle down.

"Perhaps," softly suggested The Prince. "We might find ourselves something to eat?"

"And a place to wait." The Princess shoved up her visor.

"Yes," agreed Sgenn. "There is little here for us."

The group ambled from here to there and eventually found what they thought looked like an appropriate booth to wait in.

Sook nodded to them and faded into the crowd of mostly black clad witches.

As they ate and watched the crowds milling about, the Prince said, "It is interesting."

"What?" asked his sister.

"Witches. This is an entire realm of which we know very little."

She nodded. "Other than Our Mother's Dark Advisor and her sisters, they do not happen in and through Bahn Duhr Tohr."

"Most quiet," observed the Prince looking at Sgenn.

"Yessss," she replied.

The Princess kicked her brother softly on one foot and indicated with a slight gesture.

He looked. A slender man was drifting through the crowds of witches. He was dressed in clothes of a red color almost black.

Witches nudged each other and watched this person and wondered about casting ugly on him. He was impolite. But they restrained their usual witchy reaction to such irritation. This was a foregather after all and one did not do such at a foregather. Most of the time.

"I wonder what he is searching for?" Frinda said, refilling his plate.

Sgenn watched the stealthy figure slipping along at the outer edges of the crowds. "I could find out for you, if you wish. Prince?"

He shrugged. "Oh, no. Just wondering, that is all."

They watched the figure disappear into one of the clumps of milling attendees.

So they sat and idled the day away. And sampled this or that food or beverage.

Until The Princess stood. "Let us away and look at trinkets. Perhaps we might find some small thing for Mother."

"Or Father," added the Prince looking across the table. "Join us?"

Sgenn nodded. "Sook will find us when she wishes to do so."

Dax.

They had been wandering around the village for most of the day.

The inhabitants had, for the most part, ignored them. The folk from the inn had been whispering in many an ear.

After their short tour of the place neither Eulin nor Je'leel could see any point in staying any longer and had been discussing for some time where they ought to wander next. They had found a low wall separating the road from someone's garden and now sat on it, kicking their legs idly as they talked.

"Mother didn't provide much in the way of guidance as to what one does on wander."

Je'leel nodded. "Why do we wander, sister?"

"I am supposed to. It is part of growing up. Or something."

"Other than that?"

Eulin shrugged and scratched Anamaxtor behind an ear. His head was lying in her lap. "To learn. To find out things."

"So?"

"What?"

"What do want to learn, to find out?"

Eulin chewed on a knuckle and stared into the distance. "I already know most everything Vander. And in spite of Dargon I now know dragon call. Sooooo."

"Yes?"

Eulin grinned at Je'leel.

"What?"

"I think that I would like more dragon skills and knowledge. They are nice beasts." She laughed. "And few folk are so skilled."

Je'leel nodded. "How does one find those skills?"

Eulin wrapped her in her arms and kissed her. "Oh sister, that is easy. We just have to ask a wild dragon." She pushed Anamaxtor's head away and jumped down. And called.

The sinuous green appeared. "Just as well that I didn't eat him."

"Who?" asked Eulin.

"The Dargon meal."

"Why?"

"Life is ever so much more pleasant since you were there. No more sneak mage trying to harm us. He guides visitors around for a fee and they laugh and throw food objects." It licked its lips, And whispered all silky secret, "Even my mate is happy."

Eulin patted it on the side on the neck. "I wish to learn more dragon."

The green coiled around her. "Really?"

"Yes."

"That is very nice."

"My sister and I do not know where to go."

"Really?"

"Yes."

It coiled three layers higher. And licked her face. Eulin giggled as the tongue slipped lower.

"Griz, griz, griz," laughed the green.

"Where do we go to learn?"

"Lair By Lair."

Eulin nodded. The sinuous green disappeared.

Je'leel pointed with her chin. "There is one of those sneaky men dressed in that dark red black watching us."

Eulin looked.

The man stood in the shadows and watched them.

"Ready, sister?"

Je'leel nodded.

Eulin grabbed her hand.

They were gone.

Golden dragon and all.

Fandor's Dan.

Hordes of workers sent by Monetary Control had completely refurbished the building, putting it back together, making it into a show piece. They had opened the road and stacked the rubble down either side, and made low walls around what had once been the central building and city square.

On third floor Pomon toured Farth and Sedeem through the various rooms that were now the Headquarters of The Silver Rangers. Standing in The Staff Room, he pointed out the features on the wall map, indicating the three small villages where the three ranger units now lived.

"Tindar, it is beyond speaking to have a single home again."

Farth fizzled and blushed.

"What's on the other floors?" asked Sedeem.

"Second floor," explained Pomon, pointing at a structural drawing, "is all Monetary Control. You have quarters on the third floor. Ground floor will be shops selling and dealing in armour, weapons, clothing, and other items. Except."

"What?" asked Farth.

"We have none of those guilds in this elseplace." He quickly pointed at the list on the map and cleared his throat. "We have spent what little we had paying the villagers for unit quarters and food."

Farth stared at the list.

"Dead broke, right?" asked Sedeem.

Pomon cleared his throat. "We are warriors, not merchants. Even if we do have some small staff of artisans for our own."

"Most true." Farth nodded. "It will be hard."

Sedeem laughed and jabbed him in the side. "No, problemo, Husband."

Pomon starred at her.

Farth gaped at her public display.

"Zadar Pomon," ordered Sedeem. "Tell M.C. to open an account for the Silver Rangers and to get ready for a very large, extremely large, deposit." She laughed again, and intoned, "I'll be back."

She took Farth with her.

Grandeville. Tinker's Place.

"Hi, Pop."

They appeared in the middle of the large living room, interrupting the conversation that Tinker and Morgan were having. She crashed down into the couch next to Tinker's side and kissed him on the cheek.

Morgan stared at them. "How did you do that?" He looked around the room and wondered how they had managed to enter the room so quickly and so silently.

"Tell you later," sighed Tinker.

"Sorry," said Sedeem. "Should have looked first."

"Great Lords." Farth bowed to both of them.

"Sit down, Farth," he said to Farth. "What's up?" he asked his daughter.

She laughed. "Have I got a deal for you."

"You working with Mirf again?"

"Nope. We are building a new home for the Silver Rangers."

"Sounds like fun."

"Daaaad?"

He slumped. "Oh, oh. What?" He wasn't sure that he wanted to know.

"Ummmmmm, what are you going to do with that great pile in the barn?"

"That is what Morgan and I were discussing when you, ahhh, popped in."

"Is it a problem?"

Morgan laughed. "The biggest golden problem that I have ever seen."

Sedeem sat upright and grabbed one of her father's arms.

"May I have it?"

"Huh?"

"That treasure pile."

"You want it?"

She shook her head. "It's for the Silver Rangers. They are broke."

"Wife," snapped Farth. "This is not proper!"

"You really don't need it or the associated problem either," said Morgan. He wondered what sort of a rock band The Silver Rangers were.

"Ummmmmm," um'd Tinker.

Sedeem smiled at him. "They will just be in your debt forever and forever." She kissed his cheek again, jumped up, and grabbed Farth by the arm. "Thanks, Dad."

They disappeared.

Morgan stared at Tinker. "How about explaining all that to your really confused Business Manager?"

Tinker sighed.

In Do Dak. A Faan Place of Training.

She swore, hissed, growled, threatened vile, and leaped, dragging the other down.

Black swirled everywhere, the air crackled and snapped electrical discharge.

Ripple appeared, grabbed a handful of thick, jet black hair and yanked the attacker off and away, and looked down at the figure sprawled on the ground. "Are you well, sister?"

Rumtah stood, her garment hanging in shreds. "Am tak tak," she snarled, slamming her open hand across the face of her attacker, now standing next to Ripple. The open hand banged her head back and forth. Rumtah's clothes shimmered and reformed.

"Pik tik do tak pak," growled the other.

"Sister," hissed Rumtah. "This daughter is bad bad ump dit dit!"

"Hum hum, " said Ripple, shaking the young woman, still holding her in a firm grip by her long hair. "Leave sister. We will speak."

Rumtah nodded.

And was gone.

Ripple released her grip. "Speak tell, Sepanix."

The young woman stepped away and turned to face her. "Mother," she tried to look witch proper. Unsuccessfully. "Aunt teaches tik tik."

"Hum."

Sepanix hissed at her.

Ripple smiled.

"DO NOT!" snarled Sepanix.

It banged into her, grabbing, clenching, driving her backwards. She reacted in desperation. She snatched out and cast horrid. The spell blasted over everything, including Ripple and Sepanix.

Ripple nodded. "You look Faan." She watched her daughter stand. Most of her blouse was gone and one trouser leg. Ripple stepped closer.

"Mother! Do not!"

Ripple stabbed.

"Ahhh," sighed Sepanix, staring down at the thin gold and red wand sticking at an odd angle from her chest. Her eyes rolled up. She stood, slack jawed, strangely tilted. Yanking the wand free, Ripple worked quickly.

"OUCH!" yelped her daughter.

"Clothe yourself, show off beauty," commanded Ripple.

The blouse repaired, whole and clean as did her trouser leg.

"Daughter, you are very strange twisted, yet Faan through and through."

"Hum hum."

Ripple nodded. "That helped." She crooked a finger. "Step closer."

Very cautiously her daughter did.

Reaching out, Ripple tilted up her daughter's head, she was a full head shorter than her mother, and kissed her forehead. "A very strong daughter. Listen to Rumtah. She knows much!"

Sepanix nodded. "I will try."

"Not try! Do!"

"Yessss, Mother."

Rumtah appeared. She stepped over and shoved a krartar under Sepanix's blouse.

"KAK PTAR!" bellowed the young witch, whirling away, blasting blouse and beast somewhere.

"Heh heh heh," cackled Rumtah at her sister.

"Hum." Ripple faded away.

"Always be ready, niece," stated Rumtah, deflecting the young witch's attack.

And the lessons continued.

Dol Spar. Mid-Morning. An Office in Monetary Control.

"Sooooooooo, Prandam, tell me someone's secret."

He settled into a chair, somehow managing to look inconspicuous. And smiled at her.

"The Caedi Syndicate have sent runners in all directions. They have been hired by the Majitar."

"Creeps, and creepier. Why?"

"They hunt for treasure."

"So, vat's the big deal. Treasure litters the elseplaces." Mirf's eyes glittered. "If you know where to look." The hob-goblin trace peered out. That wild look didn't bother Prandam. He understood hob-goblins very well.

"The Majitar are close guarded."

Mirf frowned. "But?"

"This treasure hunt is for a person."

"Ahhhhhhhhhhh. Who?"

Prandam shrugged. "So far, I can see not. The Majitar called this person treasure. In some manner they expect to gain great power."

"From this person treasure?"

"In some manner."

Mirf banged on her desk top and frowned at the young woman as she rushed in. "Who are you, shiksa?"

"Your, your, your, your . . . Second Clerk," she stammered, ready to flee for her life.

"Mine, mine, mine, mine?"

The Second Clerk nodded violently.

"So where is my clerk? My First Clerk?"

"You sent her home," she replied, eyeing the door out.

"Ah ho ha!" Mirf scribbled something on a slip of paper and shoved it at the clerk. "So do a search. Hurry, hurry. Machen schnell." She watched the clerk hurtle out the door and turned to Prandam. "So O.K., sneaky, go sneak some more. But be careful."

"Yes, Mirf." Prandam stood and faded out the door. A different door.

Mirf chewed on the tip of a fingernail and looked at her Assistants. "I think that the Majitar is going to cause trouble. Big trouble. Big big trouble. Grabbing someone to gain great power usually causes huge problems, monstrous problems. Not good."

They sat and waited.

Mirf gurgled.

The clerk crashed back into the room, waving a folder. Her blouse was half untucked. There were dirty streaks on her face and blouse. She was wild-eyed.

"Ho boy, what have you been doing? Fighting off file clerks?"

"Hurrying," she gasped. "Special Investigator."

"You related to my clerk? My other clerk?"

She nodded, her breath beginning to slow down. "Sister," she gasped.

Mirf stared at her.

She blanched.

Mirf thumped on the proper area of her desk. "Fimbee, you there?"

"Yes," oiled the response. "Special Investigator Mirf."

"I now have two, count them, two First Grade Clerks. Two sister First Grade Clerks. Understand? I added another one."

There was a loud gasp followed by a hasty, "Yes."

"Send the appropriate blouse, badge, etc., etc. Shuffle that paper!" Mirf banged the desk again and began to terrorize the report, ignoring her startled clerk.

Grandeville. Tinker's Place.

Morgan leaned back in his chair, stretched out his legs, and looked over the top of his coffee cup at Tinker. "Now don't take this wrong, O.K.?"

Tinker slumped deeper into the couch. "Sure."

"I don't believe it."

"O.K. No harm."

Smoke drifted silently into the room and stood behind the couch where Tinker was slumping even deeper and looked at Morgan.

"Don't do anything," Tinker grumbled at her.

She leaned on the couch back and blew warm air into his hair. "Treasure's gone." She dropped something in his lap. "Except for this."

Light flashed golden red from the necklace in his lap. "Sedeem thought that Shannon might like it."

"Sure." Tinker picked it up and tossed it to Morgan. "Here. Catch!"

Morgan did. He held it up in front of his face and looked at it. "We can't take this."

"It is your's. We don't need it." He smiled at his Business Manager. "Besides, Sedeem gave it to you."

Morgan opened his briefcase and slid it inside. "Rather exotic design."

"I'll bet it is," mumbled Tinker. He straightened up. "Well, that solves that problem."

Morgan nodded. Then he frowned. "Wait a minute." He looked at Smoke. "You said that the treasure is gone?"

"Yep." Now that Tinker was sitting up she could tickle his ear. So she did.

"Stop that!"

"Not possible. That mound must have weighed tons."

"Go look." Smoke shrugged and smiled at Morgan. "Maybe we turned it into straw, a reverse Rumplestiltskin. Or whoever he was." She leaned over and purred at Tinker, "Lunch is ready. Better late than never."

"Lunch?" He slipped from the couch and looked at Morgan.

Morgan laughed and stood. "Ahhh, no. Better get back. Conference call coming in soon." He headed for the front door. "Thank Sedeem, whenever you see her again. Maybe we can all get together for dinner? Soon?" He waved one hand and headed out and down the front deck to his car. There were times he really didn't understand what his client and friend was doing, or did. Not at all.

Tinker whirled around and glared at her. "Pesty butt Cat!"

"It is on the rear deck. Come on, we are all hungry."

He slipped an arm around her as they headed for the rear deck. "Not bad, for a big lump."

"I am not a big lump."

Lair By Lair.

Fog steam billowed cloud shapes and puffed upward with soft snorts. The vegetation was thick and broad-leaved.

The narrow road meandered with frequent side branches that headed every which way,

"Pretty warm." Eulin twisted a broad purple band across

her forehead and tied it in back. She inspected the road once more and pointed.

They started that way.

It fell from the sky.

It thudded to ground in front of them.

"OOOUOBA!" it grunted as it yanked each leg from the soft ground.

It was as large as a school buss, one of the large school busses. But it wasn't yellow but a very light blue with each scale edged in pale green.

As it was blocking the road, they stopped.

"What are you?" it asked. "Tasty bits?" It licked its lips.

Eulin pointed. "He is Anamaxtor. She is Je'leel. I am Eulin."

"Oh," it said. "The Vander immledid. I am Qrarzkor." Small red flame popped from its mouth as it spoke.

"What are you?" asked Je'leel

"What is immledid?" asked Eulin.

"Sky dragon," relied Qrarzkor, lowering his head to take a more careful look at Je'leel. "Young child."

"Nice colors," said Je'leel.

Eulin stepped closer. "I am not!"

"Think so?" Qrarzkor puffed flame over Je'leel's hand as she reached to touch his snout. "What I heard," he said to Eulin. "Mind if I roast your companion?"

Je'leel tickled him behind one flaring nostril. Qrarzkor snorted grey smoke. "You don't look or smell indjinn to me. How did you do that?"

"My mother is Dat."

Eulin layered on protection and nudged Anamaxtor to

one side.

Qrarzkor eyed Je'leel. "I met Dat once. Nice fangs and claws."" He looked down his snout at them.

"My Mother." She rapped a knuckle on one large dragon fang. "My father is The Chosen One. Eulin is my Sister."

He snorted fire over Je'leel. She grabbed one long whisker and yanked. Hard.

"OUCH! OUCH! OUCH!"

She yanked harder.

"OUCH! OUCH! OUCH!"

"You ruined my clothes."

"OUCH! OUCH!"

"My sister wants to learn dragon."

"OUCH!"

"Stop puffing."

"OUCH!"

She let go. Qrarzkor twisted his head around and rolled one eye at her. "Pretty Dat formed."

Eulin waved in new clothes for Je'leel.

Qrarzkor licked his lips. "I haven't had a meal, soft thing meal like you, since that last Slickta mage wandered this way." He eyed Eulin.

"That was your last one," stated Eulin. "There aren't going to be any more of those. We stopped that."

"What?" The sky dragon's head reared high above them. He stomped one foot. "Why would you do something like that?" He looked down. "You really picked a soft spot." The ground made sucking noises as the large foot was pulled free.

"Can you teach anything?" asked Eulin.

"Of course. All dragons can do that. If they wish to." The

head dropped low. "How about I eat you and leave the indjinn daughter alone?" He reached for her. "OUCH!" His snout banged into something hard in front of Eulin that he couldn't see.

"We are not something to be eaten," snapped Eulin.

"Why not?" grumped Qrarzkor, pulling his head back.

"I am here to learn dragon not to be someone's meal."

"Talk to The Dragon Master."

"Where is this person?" asked Je'leel.

"Third turning to the right." The sky dragon lifted into the air and sailed away.

Chapter Thirteen

Things Are Happening.

In Do Dak. A Place of Training.

Shitar dropped in lightly and watched them. "Hayou, Aunt. Hayou, Sister. Mother sent me to teach."

The pair were locked in combat. Sepanix was snarling, hissing, twisting. Rumtah was countering every thing the younger witch did, high and low.

"AM TAK TAK!" growled Sepanix as it grabbed her. She bit it and cast deep. It dragged her toward the hole. "IK TIK!" The ground exploded, blowing Sepanix one way, bits and pieces of the thing elsewhere. She leaped to her feet and banged ugly onto her Aunt.

Rumtah scraped it off. And tossed.

It struck her in the center of her chest, splashed upward and numbed her vocal cords. Her eyes flew wide. She stared at her Aunt in terror. Rumtuh was running toward her, a sparkling wand clenched in one hand.

"Hum," observed Shitar.

Rumtah halted in front of her and kissed her on the forehead. "Rangle niece?"

"I came to teach my sister."

Rumtah nodded. "This young Faan is twisted strange."

She disappeared. The spells fell away.

"Sister," croaked Sepanix, staggering over. "That Aunt is flic tik."

"She got you."

Sepanix growled deep in her throat. "I will win." Deep down her eyes flickered fire.

"Hum."

"Not nice," hissed her sister, dragging her fingers through her matted hair.

Shitar took them elseplace.

Dol Spar. A Very Fine Day. An Office In Monetary Control.

Mirf beamed at her clerks. They both were looking well, very rested. It had been a few quiet days.

"Well, chickeedudels, ready to go to work?" They nodded and looked at each other. Neither had any idea or had ever heard of this chickeedudel. Each wore a new patch over their left pocket that indicated the section where they worked.

That patch was enough to strike terror in anyone anywhere in the vast sprawling system that was Monetary Control. Few ever saw it. But every recruit was given a picture of it and told to memorize it. The Special Investigators Office was renown for having an often powerful effect upon an individual's career, one way or another.

So all knew that patch. And most hoped that they would never see either the patch or the one wearing it in person.

Mirf jabbed a piece of paper at each of her clerks. "Go get 'em." She bounced to her feet as her clerks rushed from the room, and chewed on the tip of a fingernail. "I wonder whether there are any more around like them?"

Quan shrugged.

"Chirp?" asked Fred while her fingers danced a pattern on Quan's shoulder.

"NAK!" he gasped.

Mirf looked at Fred. "I was not referring to their bodies, as luscious as they are." She headed for the door. "I am suddenly hungry. Let's go downstairs and see what kind of goo M.C. serves for food."

A door blew open and bounced off the wall as a tattered figure stumbled through. His clothes, the remains of them, were stained with various things and were mostly in shreds. He had a number of wet splotches that were slowly getting larger.

Quan ran for Medical Help.

"Prandam!" Mirf grabbed him. "Oi vay, such a mess."

His fingers dug into her arms. "I know, Mirf, I know." He started to sag. Four arms grabbed him from behind and held him up as the other pair starting ripping his shirt away from the multiple wounds.

"Vat? Vat? So speak to me already, sneaky one."

His head wobbled. "I know who the Majitar want." With an effort he straightened up, still mostly supported by Fred. "Lean closer. Just for you, Mirf."

She leaned close. He told her.

Mirf leaped backward. "Those meshuggener ding-dongs! They will cause a problem like you wouldn't believe or have ever seen before. An eruption like that wouldn't be nice."

She whirled away and slammed her palm on the desk top and shouted. "Forget the errands! Boy do we have some new business. And such a business it is, believe you me."

Fred released the limp body and gently laid him on the

floor. Medical Help burst into the room. And immediately took control.

Quan joined Mirf.

"So we will wait out in the hall," gurgled Mirf. "Wouldn't want my clerks running over you." Quan and Fred went with her.

"Oh me, oh my," mumbled Mirf. "We need a quiet place to talk. We need a no eavesdropping place to talk." Her eyes glittered. "I know just the place."

She pointed down the hall as her clerks rushed up. "Quan, everyone to the armory. Weapons, sturdy boots, etc., etc. Then meet me in my other room." She waggled her hands at them. "Go, go, go, go, go, go!"

Mirf spun and ran the other way, headed for her other room. The rest ran for the Armory.

Doth Lamex. The Land of Healing and Pleasure.

Santar strolled down the path to their space and turned in and sat in the soft plush grass. "Hayou, sisters."

A broad-shouldered man sat with his back to a tree. His shirt was green. It matched the deep green of the grass, and the color of the stone set in a ring he wore on his right hand.

Shitar sat under the same tree. In his lap. One of his arms provided support for her back.

They both held large mugs in their free hands.

Sepanix was sprawled flat on the grass, just now awake. She had felt Santar approach.

"Hum," said Shitar.

The man smiled at the newcomer. "Hello, Santar."

She knelt and poked the body with one finger tip."Hum

hum."

"I brought her here," snapped Shitar.

"Speak tell." Santar wondered why her eldest sister had sent a call. She wondered why her other sister was not here as well.

Mirf strolled down a path headed toward their assigned lodgings. And waved her arms wildly. They both appeared to be somewhat disjointed. They really weren't, they just appeared to be. "This place has security like you wouldn't believe. And believe you me, that is secure."

They walked around a tree and stopped. A large table was set in the middle of a large meadow. Not far away sat a small structure.

"Ta dah!" Mirf dropped into a chair. "So I ordered something to eat." She filled a plate and waved the rest to sit and to do the same thing. "Eat, eat!"

She waggled the leg of something at them and at the nearby structure. "Sleeping quarters."

Fred and Quan sat. Then the two clerks did, looking totally confused.

Mirf shoved plates at her clerks. "Eat, kinder, eat! Build up your, errmmm, energy." She shoved various of the serving dishes at them.

They carefully served themselves. They had never heard of mere clerks eating with the upper grades of M.C. And Mirf was very upper grade. They tried not to stare at Fred as she served herself from several dishes, filled her cup and Quan's and waggled her fingers on his shoulder, all at the same time.

When they had finished their meal, something took

everything away.

Then Mirf leaned forward and began to brief her troops on what she thought that the problem was, and what they were going to do.

Ebna Raint. A Normal Swirling Mist Day.

"Majitar."

It was the proper greeting, the proper formal greeting. It was given by the Top Ranked, selected for the mission.

The First of The First nodded. "Majitar are we."

Formal greetings over, they sat at the table and allowed themselves to be served various of the food stuffs,

Nanjure carefully swallowed. "The Caedi Syndicate runners are far and wide."

The Majitar looked at him, and blinked slowly. "And?"

Nanjure smiled. A small, careful smile. Just so. One kept one's gestures refined. Or died. "They report that the treasure is found."

"Ah."

A careful controlled nod. "They want to know which."

"Ah." The Majitar gestured dismissal, and smiled. "Take. Both."

Nanjure stood, bowed to the door, carefully not showing astonishment at that bold move. He hurried from the room to send a message to Donae.

Fandor's Dan.

She sat on his desk, on one corner of his desk, and looked out the window admiring the view.

"Most wild," he fizzled.

"Dad didn't really want it. And the Silver Rangers needed it."

Pomon entered the room and stared at them. The fingers of one hand fiddled with his belt.

"Zadar?" asked Farth.

"Tindar," gasped Pomon. "We . . . " He looked from Farth to Sedeem and back.

"What?"

"M.C. says," He looked at a slip of paper he held in his other hand, a badly crushed piece of paper. "Monetary Control says that we, The Silver Rangers, are wealthy."

"Yes," replied Farth. "It is so."

"They have sent for their Special Investigator."

"Oh?"

Pomon walked close to the desk and frowned darkly, mostly at Sedeem. "I think that they think that we stole all that value."

Sedeem slipped from the desk and stood, one hand on Farth's shoulder. "I will talk to Mirf. She will understand."

Farth smiled at Pomon. "Send two-man units to the guilds and have them tell the guilds on the list that we wish them to gather in what ever way it requires for them to become fully functional. Tadar Nam will loan troopers from the Dragon Crest Arm."

Pomon nodded. "At once."

Farth stood. "We are leaving. There is a rumor of the Black Talon Arm on Tion Forge. Follow our plan. This is a busy time."

Pomon saluted, spun and headed for the door.

Sedeem and Farth were gone.

Wanderill.

"Who is that imkak?" Sook indicated the figure over by the edge of the central spot dressed all in shades of red so dark as to be almost black.

It was the end of the foregather. Witches were leaving. Flickering out, each in their own fashion.

"It ends," said Sgenn. "I will speak with him."

"No need." The Princess drained her cup and stood. And strode across the open space pointing at the man. "HOLD! We would speak with you!"

He nodded. And waited.

She stopped in front of him. "We did see you staring and staring. What need you, Varlet?"

"Pretty Princess," he hissed. "You." He drew the capture down.

Her left arm flew up, her right hand reached across, snatching and drawing her sword. He fell in two pieces. The net in many more. Banging down her visor, she whirled around to face the heavy footfalls coming at her from behind.

It was the Prince charging her way. Jolting to a halt, he looked at the mess. "What?"

"This . . . thing," she snarled, "tried to take Us with that net."

Sook and Sgenn ran up. Sook kicked the remains. "Ptar tik."

Sgenn knelt and searched through his clothing. And stood. "Carried nothing."

"Hum," said Sook.

Sgenn nodded. "Bad bad."

"What is?" The Princess shoved up her visor.

"That." Sook pointed at the remains of man and net.

"Why?"

Sgenn looked at her. "Some . . . thing wants you."

The Princess frowned at the remains.

The Prince dropped one hand on her shoulder. "This Quest gets more interesting all the time, Sister Mine." He grinned. "Now we have a purpose."

"What?"

His face went all flat, expressionless. "We need to kill whatever would dare attempt to do that." He nudged the pieces of the net with one boot tip. "Whatever it is requires a hard lesson."

Sgenn nodded, a small half-smile forming at one corner of her mouth.

"Careful," hissed Sook.

The Princess knelt and wiped her sword clean on the grass, stood and shoved it back into its scabbard. "Are we finished here?"

Sgenn nodded.

Sook took them away.

Bal's Dartar.

Ranna stretched and yawned. She sat up, and looked left, then right. "Hum hum hum."

The bed was large. The covers were thick and fuzzy.

Anjan sprawled on her left side, Adarlak on her right.

Ranna waved in a refreshing beverage, slipped to the head of the bed, leaned back against the headboard, and sipped. And pondered, this and that.

This woke, reached over, and tickled her here and there.

"What are we doing?" asked Ranna.

Anjan blinked, sat up. "To?" She leaned back against the headboard next to her. Ranna waved in another beverage.

"The mage is a deep sleeper," observed Anjan.

Ranna nodded and kissed her cheek. "She is in our bed."

"No other." Anjan took a long swallow. "Only room."

Ranna reached around. "You are mine."

Anjan smiled and half-turned toward her. "Most true, lovely Ran'na witch."

Ranna send the cups away.

"Witches are interesting creatures."

"Oh?" Duff refilled their cups. They were seated at a small table, eating first meal. "You thinking of a certain lanky one?"

He frowned at her.

"Perhaps," she added, "a certain mage with strange companions?"

"Duff," he snapped.

"Sorry, Dear."

He pushed the food dish at her. "I didn't think that witches consorted that closely with mage guilds."

She smiled at him. "It is strange, Dear." She sipped from her cup. "The three of them together like that is strange."

He nodded. "Must be . . . friends."

"Dear?"

"That mage injured Ra'am but smiled at the witch."

Duff winked at him. "That witch was much more, um, personal."

"Today," he stated, "is the last day of the gather. What

shall we visit?"

"The Rando Guild. They are sharing a hard cast." She stood. "We need that spell."

Grandeville. Tinker's Place.

It was just after dinner.

They were in the large living room.

Relaxing.

She hit hard, stumbling, out of control.

And crashed.

Into the couch.

And its inhabitants.

HEY!" yelled Tinker.

"BY GEORGE!" gasped Chicken.

"AM KAK!" snarled Sha'gar.

Smoke sprang from the floor, where she had been lying flat, staring up at the ceiling, and grabbed her.

Chantal sprang from her chair and joined in the capture.

"Ahhhhhhh!" she screamed, struggling wildly as she was carried backwards.

"SHUT UP!" bellowed Chantal, leaning close, face to face, glaring angrily.

"Ahhhh . . . " She stared into grey green eyes. "Don't kill me, please?"

Tinker gently tugged Chantal back. He looked over her shoulder at this person. "Who are you? What are you doing here?"

Her eyes jerked to his. "I am First Clerk Nema. I was sent."

"Calming down," said Smoke, releasing her. Chantal

stepped away and dropped into a chair. Nema tugged down her blouse.

"Clerk?" He frowned at her. Nema nodded

"Most curve'd a clerk," observed Chicken.

"Stacked," added Fair Morn, walking in from the hall. "Where did she come from?"

Nema tapped the patch on her blouse. "I am First Clerk to Chief Special Investigator Mirf, Monetary Control. Which one of you is Tinker Bubbe?"

Messenger hurried in and handed Nema a cup of coffee. "Here. Take a seat."

"Mirf?" He looked at the patch, then at her uniform.

R-Bar dropped into the couch next to Chicken. "I think that he is drooling."

Nema sat and nodded at him, and carefully tried this strange beverage. "Are you Tinker Bubbe?"

He sat. "Just Tinker." And growled at R-Bar, "Knock it off."

Nema counted. "If there are eight, then you are him."

Ran came in from the kitchen via the dining room. And looked at R-Bar. R-Bar shrugged.

Nema searched each face then turned to him as she set her cup on the nearby small table. She stood and said, "Mirf said that I should give this to you. And then to run for my life." She tossed the message at him and actually took one full step before R-Bar's spell froze her in place.

Magevern. Deep Below the Surface.

They were gathered in the hall, after their first meal, to practice.

She hit hard, stumbling out of control, fell, slid across the smooth polished stone.

And crashed into some of them.

"Hok qat!" cried Tobtz, casting hard.

Aada, snarling, hooked one finger, calling the purple wrapped figure over, sliding across the floor.

"Ahhhhhhhh," she screamed, trying to get away.

"QUIET!" roared Moonda, bending over, staring into her face.

"Ahhhh . . . She stared back, into the violet tinged eyes. "Don't kill me. Please?"

Sa'ar nudged Moonda aside as the others stepped close and looked down at their prisoner. "Who are you? How came you to be here?"

Her eyes jerked to Sa'ar's. "I am First Clerk Rema. I was sent."

Aada knelt next to her, fingers sliding across Rema's cheek. "She is calming down." Tobtz released the bonds.

Moonda helped her to her feet. Rema tugged her blouse back into place. Someone had slipped it loose.

"Clerk?" Sa'ar frowned at her.

Rema nodded violently.

Aada smiled warmly at her. "Nicely formed. For a clerk."

Cazor lightly touched. "Near Vander." Rema jerked.

"Where did you come from?" demanded Cazor.

Rema touched the patch on her blouse. "I am First Clerk to Special Investigator Mirf, Monetary Control. Which of you is the Vander Babe, Sa'ar?"

Aada slipped an arm around Rema's shoulders and stroked her hair. "Mirf?"

Rema nodded. "Are you the Vander Babe, Sa'ar?"

Aada shook her head, reached around and popped the top button of Rema's blouse loose.

"Aada," cautioned Sa'ar.

Aada stepped away. A little.

"I am Sa'ar, Heart of The Vander."

Rema looked from face to face, then back to Sa'ar. And nodded to herself. "Mirf said to give you this. And to run for my life."

She tossed the message at Sa'ar, and turned. Moonda grabbed her as she collapscd and carried the limp clerk into the next room.

Bahn Duhr Tohr. The Royal City. Mid-Afternoon.

The Audience Chamber had just been emptied.

Now the Queen was massaging the shoulders of her King. The Dark Advisor hissed at her husband, who was looking quizzical at her.

"Nothing of mine requires massaging. In public."

He shrugged, and threw his arm around her waist instead.

They hit hard. He stumbled. She grabbed him. They jolted to a halt. And stared at the large hall.

Everyone quickly relaxed. They all knew each other. From the past.

"Great Queen, Great King," said Quan. "Mirf send this." He handed the message to the Queen.

The Advisor waved them all to the Royal Quarters.

The King pulled over a chair and sat next to his Queen as she unrolled the tightly curled message.

Ebna Raint. Dark. Swirling Low Clouds.

Mirf stepped around and looked up at the great dark structure. "Ho boy, such a pile of ugly this place is."

She clumped up the stairs, shoved the doors open, and walked inside. "Yoooooo! ANYONE HOME?"

The First of the First gaped at her.

She stalked over and dropped into a chair. "You the Head Chicken of this coop?" She filled a glass using the nearest jug.

"Who are you?" He sent for the guards.

She took a sip. "Ummm not too bad. Mirf, Monetary Control." She refilled her glass.

"Monetary Control? Here?"

She nodded. "You bet your boots, bubbe."

"Bubbe?" He stared at this crude person with the strange manner and strange dialect. "How am I to know that what you are saying is true?"

Mirf took something from a bowl and chewed thoughtfully. "So it's proof you need?" She fished a gold medallion from a shirt pocket and slammed it down on the table top and shoved it over to him, cutting a deep gouge in the wood. "Ooooops. So give a look."

He picked it up, looked at it, then looked at her, a very calculating look. He nodded. It was a carefully controlled gesture.

"Good," she said. "We need to talk." Shoving things to one side, she leaned forward and told him. After taking the medallion back.

Krag Far Reach.

It was a city of sparkle and glitter, crowded and busy. The

city was the center for trading, buying and selling, businesses of every kind in this portion of the universe of universes.

"Lodgings first," said Sook. "The Royals should dress more appropriately for this elseplace."

Sgenn nodded, and headed them down the street. As. they followed the pair, the Prince leaned close to his sister. "If we should see another of those fellows, let's grab him, not chop him into two pieces."

"Relax, brother, relax."

"Sword Master teach you that move."

"No. Mother."

"Learning. This quest is about learning."

"Brother?"

"Our Royal Mother Queen did not teach me that move."

"Praps she felt thee had no such need."

"Teach me that move."

She nodded. "When we have time. And, err, suitable surroundings."

He laughed, and nodded at the pair walking ahead of them.

"Brother?"

He leaned a little closer. "It is hard to decide which of them is more lovely."

"They wear baggy and hiding garb."

"I suspect that black cloaks fairer charms."

"Lust thee after commoners?"

"On Quest all are equal." He winked at her. "I do not believe that pair are common."

"Here," stated Sgenn, turning sharply into an ornate entrance.

They stood quietly while the Prince rapped on the counter top with one mailed fist.

A Checkin rushed up."

"Rooms," said The Prince. "For four."

The Checkin stared at him, his mouth dropping open.

"Well?" asked the Prince.

"We do not have sleeping furniture that large," gasped the Checkin, eyes jumping from person to person.

"Cretin," hissed Sook.

"One room for my sister. One room for them. One room for me," explained the Prince.

"Ahhhhh, ohhhh," said the Checkin. "Room 62-4-9." He swiftly found the key and shoved it across the counter top. "Register here." He waved over a short man who took the key from the Prince and led them to their rooms.

A man dressed is dark clothes, dark red almost black, slipped across the lobby and beckoned over the Checkin.

Lair By Lair.

They turned at the appropriate intersection and headed into the tunnel of vegetation that was now the path.

He leaped from dark shadow, grabbed her, and quickly wrapped the net around her.

Anamaxtor sprang,

"Don't!" shouted Je'leel. "Kill him."

Anamaxtor dropped the body and licked his lips.

Eulin cast, blasting net fragments into the shrubbery. They knelt next to the body and searched his clothing.

Je'leel looked at her sister. "If we see another of these, we had better talk with them. First."

"Wonder what he thought that he was doing?" Eulin stood and scratched Anamaxtor behind one ear. "Capture the next one," she ordered.

The golden dragon looked as sheepish as a dragon could. Which was not very much.

A motley green head popped from the thick growth. "Do you want that meat?" It eased itself onto the path. She was about horse-sized. The dragon winked at Anamaxtor. "Nice leap, cutie." And laughed. "Griz, griz, griz."

"All your's," said Eulin.

"Thank you. Who are you?"

"Eulin." She gestured. "Je'leel. Anamaxtor."

"Oh." She nodded. "Sky Drifter told me of you. He heard it from Qrarzkor." She reached down, grabbed the body, and eased back into the vegetation, and disappeared.

"Maybe the Dragon Master will know," suggested Je'leel.

"Perhaps. Really strange."

They hurried deeper into the jungle thickness, down the green lined tunnel path they were following.

Grandeville. Tinker's Place.

"What?"

His eyes flew wide. He glared at her.

Nema blanched and knew that she was about to die. She wondered why Mirf would do that to her.

Chicken grabbed one of his arms. "Steady on, My Lord."

Smoke pushed calm into his mind. But his mind was jumping around too much for this to have much effect. Yet.

Sha'gar shoved Chicken aside, grabbed his shirt front, dragged him to the floor, and fell on top of him, hissing into his ear, "Calm, Mate'mer, calm." She held him tight.

He blinked. He could feel the hear radiating from her. Then he realized that he was on the floor and that she was lying on top of him. He could hear the air in the room crackling and popping angrily.

Sha'gar released him and rolled off.

He sat up and saw R-Bar stalking back and forth, growling angrily.

Ran sat and watched her, sliding a clear crystal sphere from hand to hand.

Chantal was hugging Nema, trying to sooth away the terror she could see in Nema's eyes.

The clerk was afraid to look at her feet. They felt strange,

Smoke knelt next to him. "Don't you think that it would be more proper if you dragged her into your bedroom?"

He stood and frowned at her and growled at R-Bar, "Release her before she goes completely bug-nuts."

"Kap ptar ptar," hissed R-Bar. But she did. Release Nema.

Chantal guided the clerk into one of the couches and shoved her over, dragging an afghan from the back and over her, tugging it up and around her neck. "You are safe. Nothing is going to happen to you."

Chicken headed for the kitchen. "We will Ourself prepare coffee and cocoa."

Tinker lurched up and into his chair and rolled his head sideways and looked over at Nema. "Unlike some people who kill messengers that bring bad news, we don't."

Nema stared at him.

"Whenever you feel better," he said, "we can talk some more."

Magevern. Deep Below the Surface.

They gathered in the chamber around the great table.

"How do we find her?" asked Aada.

Everyone looked at everyone else.

Imdar laid a hand on Sa'ar's forearm. "I believe that she is safe. She is trained beyond us all. She travels with her strange sister and the golden dragon."

Moonda thumped a fist on the table top. "I think that we should visit this Caedi Syndicate in their elseplace. We could, ummm, talk with them." Violet haze shimmered in and out around her.

Sa'ar shook her head. "First we calm ourselves. Then we search the archives." She smiled at Elend. "Now that they are in order. Then we can decide what is to be done."

Moonda bowed her head. "To hear is to obey."

Sa'ar looked at Tobtz. "Call our warlock and his witch mate from wherever they might be. His skills are required here."

Tobtz began to make the call.

Sa'ar stood and headed for the smaller chamber. "Bring that messenger to me."

Everyone scattered to make preparations.

Bahn Duhr Tohr. The Royal Chambers.

The air crackled and snapped around Ripple. Hanred threw an arm around her.

The Queen frowned darkly. The King held one of her hands. "It will take a fortnight to raise a mighty army."

The Queen nodded her agreement. "We shall visit this elseplace of villains. But We do fear for Our children first. These folk will be punished, My King."

Ripple looked up from studying the floor or something that only she could see. "My Queen, I sent a call to all of my sisters, offspring and nieces. Perhaps one of them has seen the pair or has wandered across their path."

The King stood, walked into the adjoining room and told The Lord Of Arms what he wished to have done and by when he wished it to be so. The Lord Of Arms raced from the Royal Chambers and down to the Training Hall, calling for The Master Of Training and The Sword Master.

Toucan, The King, returned and said gently to his Queen, "It now begins. Soon My Own Queen Willawa, The White Warrior, will again visit bloody combat."

Ripple smiled, a true witch smile. "This time we are coming along."

Willawa nodded and gave her a warm smile. "It shall be so. Now, leave us. We would be alone with Our King."

Ripple took them back to her quarters, herself and her mate.

Krag Far Reach.

Once they were alone, after visiting the various interconnected rooms, and had gathered in the central rooms, Sook looked at them. "Royal armor is not suitable attire for this elseplace."

The Prince smiled. "Then We shall have to dress in appropriate clothing."

Sook nodded.

His black armor clattered in a heap in one far corner.

She nodded again.

A heap of white armor joined the black.

The Prince and Princess stared at her, clad only in their silk smooth under-armor garments.

He laughed as Sook stared at them. "Armor is hot and chaffing." He plucked at his top with two fingers. "These be most cool but protective."

Sook and Sgenn looked at The Princess.

"Yes?" she demanded.

"A surprise." replied Sook. Sgenn nodded.

The Prince grinned at his sister. "We think they did expect some square muscled lumpy bunched warrior did reside inside thy white container, not Our Most Shapely Princess in all the realms." She glowered at him. He shrugged.

He looked at the pair staring at them. "Praps one of you might call clothier for the garb we do wear is most unsuitable for to wander these wide thoroughfares. These are not public garments." He smiled at them. "Tis fine enough for private, how some ever." He shrugged. "Somehow we left other attire elsewhere."

Sgenn looked at Sook, who nodded.

The Prince and the Princess were now clothed in dress appropriate for this elseplace. Then she did the same for herself and Sgenn.

"Brother," chided The Princess, "thy mouth does hang most agape." She laughed.

"Most sorry." His face flushed, still staring at the pair. "Some small shock."

A small soft half-smile tugged itself into one corner of Sgenn's mouth. "Did you expect, Prince, some muscle lumpy bunched magic users inside our billowing robes?"

Sook hissed at her.

The Prince sat heavily in one of the chairs. "Nay! But tis still a surprise." He cleared his throat. "Most pleasant a'surprise." He smiled broadly. "Shall we go down and out and visit this fair elseplace now that we are all most appropriately begarbed?"

They headed down and out.

Tion Forge.

"So, Ranger Farth, you would have us relocate to Fander's Dan?"

"I would, Tadar Cipan Rae."

Cipan's brows rose. "Do I know you?" He squinted hard at Farth.

"No."

"We are safe here."

"What do you do, here?"

Cipan leaned back and crossed his arms over his chest. "Heal. Hide."

Farth jerked. "Hide?"

Cipan looked past him at something else, something only he could see in his memory. "We fought in the Clash on Imro and took a heavy battering. We were so victorious." He laughed bitterly. "That we had to drag our wounded and mangled selves to this elseplace, little known, little visited, to become whole again. Not long past we did become well. Yet our members are slight and fearful things strode that field of agony." His eyes refocused. He waved one massive arm in the air. "This small Ranger Arm would not stand long did such hordes descend upon us again."

"Join your brothers." Farth shoved a small, neatly folded

parchment at Cipan.

He took the parchment, unfolded it, and began to read. He smiled to himself. "So, Nam still lives. And I did hear tales of this Pomon. A stubborn fellow it was said."

He looked up and stared at Farth for long moments, then he nodded. "We will do it. How do we find this elseplace?"

Farth smiled. "Gather all and everything in one spot. When the Arm is assembled and ready, we will move everything."

Cipan stood. "As you say, as you say." He stepped from the room, telling his men to start packing and to prepare the Arm for moving."

"It will be a surprise," said Farth.

Sedeem kissed him. "It certainly will, my lovely General."

Farth fizzled,

Bal's Dartar.

$1.98 rapped on the door, one arm over Duff's shoulders. The door swung in and Ranna looked out. "Yesssss?"

"Just wanted to say that we are on our way elseplace."

The witch stepped out, forcing them to back up. "Do not go."

Duff looked up. "What!"

"I must speak to you privately. About magicians."

"Oh," said $1.98.

"Come to our room." Duff yanked him into motion.

In their room, Duff sat on the edge of the bed and looked at Ranna as she sat at the table with $1.98. "How can we be of aid, witch?"

"The Faan have changed. Greatly. We may now closely

associate with magicians do we so desire. As close as close can be."

$1.98 reached across the table and cautiously touched one wary fingertip to her arm. "Most true. And that explains what we saw."

Ranna nodded.

"And?" prompted Duff, just a little. She knew that to prompt one of them too hard was often likely to result in a witch twitch or anger burst.

"It is Adarlak."

$1.98 yanked his hand away. "The Hacto mage?"

"What about her?" Duff sat straighter, slipping her right hand up her left sleeve. She wasn't about to let some witch abuse a fellow mage. Not unless there was just cause.

Ranna stood, walked around, and sat next to Duff. She leaned close and spoke ever so softly into her ear, "My youngest witch sister did tell us all of this fact." And explained.

Duff gasped.

Ranna went back and sat at the table.

"Strange problem," murmured Duff. "Interesting problem."

"Help," mumbled Ranna. She cleared her throat and looked as unsettled as a witch ever could be, and uttered a word they rarely, if ever, used. "Please?"

$1.98 stared at her.

She stared back, deep fire flickering in her eyes. "I said that the Faan have changed."

He nodded.

Duff jumped down and walked to the table. "I must tell him. His knowledge is much greater than my own."

Ranna grumbled deep in her throat. And nodded. One quick nod.

Duff stood on her tip toes and whispered in his ear. His face flushed. He threw his hood over his head and jammed his arms into his sleeves.

Duff looked over and smiled at the obviously getting to be very agitated witch. "He is thinking, not hiding."

Ranna chewed on her lip and stared at him. And asked Duff, "What sort of a magician is he?"

"Big Red trained," she answered proudly. "One of the few."

Ranna sucked in her breath and layered on every protection that she knew. She waited. Not all that well. That aspect of the clan had not changed.

Suddenly $1.98 threw his hood back. He pointed at Ranna's hand. "Use your ring!"

"Which ring?" she hissed.

"The white one, of course." His face flushed. "The mage magic in that ring should affect, errrr, take care of your, ummmm, problem."

Ranna jumped to her feet. "Witch debt!" She spun and hurried from the room.

"Let's leave, Duff."

"Yes, Dear."

She took them out.

In her room, Ranna slipped soft silent across the room and stood near the bed and looked down at the sleeping form.

Anjan was still sitting up, back against the headboard. She watched Ranna pondering the other.

Ranna yanked the quilted cover down and snapped at the suddenly awake Adarlak. "Do not move, Hacto!" Adarlak froze, in place, eyes staring wide at her. Speaking softly to the white ring, Ranna slid her hand ever so softly, smoothly, over the bronze velvet skin. Adarlak's eyes popped wider.

"SILENCE!" growled Ranna as her fingers tightened. "No sound."

Adarlak twisted her head around, eyes pleading with Anjan to do something. Anjan stared at Ranna. She wondered what arcane horror she was putting on the mage and why Ranna was attacking her now.

Suddenly Ranna dropped to her knees next to the bed, leaned over and kissed Adarlak. After some time, she dragged her lips away.

Adarlak sucked in a deep breath, her fingers dug deeply into the bed.

Ranna sat back and smiled a very crooked smile at both of her companions. "Hum hum hum. Let us take a meal. Outside." She stood and waited as clothing shimmered onto Adarlak and Anjan as they stood and looked puzzled at her.

Throwing an arm around each of them, tugging them into motion, Ranna mumbled, mostly to herself, "That ragged magician was correct. We three owe him great debt."

Trib Scion. A Faan Training Place.

Shitar hugged both of her sisters at the same time.

Their clothes were stained ugly, tattered into shreds. Their hair was tangled and matted. Dark smudged weariness under their eyes, stark contrast to the moonlight pale skin showing through the dirt and other stains.

Sepanix wept silent tears onto Shitar's shoulder. Santar patted her younger sister on the back. Neither had the strength to do much else.

"Witch debt," murmured Santar.

Sepanix tightened her arms, and hissed softly, "Yesssssss, witch debt."

"Filthy dirty witches," said Shitar gently. She nodded at Mantara.

He was sweat stained and had a few rips in his clothes as well. But he wasn't as dirty as the pair. He smiled and joined the trio, standing behind Shitar. Then he swung his arm around her and carefully patted Sepanix on the shoulder with his free hand.

"Hum," said Shitar.

"Hum hum," answered her sisters.

Mantara kissed Shitar on the back of the neck. "They are fatigued into safety. Let us leave this training spot."

Shitar took them elseplace.

Chapter Fourteen

It Is Always Something

Grandeville. Tinker's Place.

He slumped in the couch and glared at the clerk who seemed to draw inside herself and further under the comforter.

"My Lord!" snapped Chicken. "Desist! Thee do a'frighten fair Nema."

"Huh?"

"Thy glarish countenance do scare one and all."

He frowned at her. "This better?"

She nodded. "T'will do, Grumpy Prince."

"Tink," hissed R-Bar, standing there, staring at him, Ran by her side.

"What?"

"Kill 'em," she snarled.

"Who?"

"The Caedi Syndicate."

"The whole bunch?" He stared at her.

Ran nodded.

"Yesssss," hissed R-Bar.

Ran nodded.

"Sieg Heil," he snapped.

"Kat tar im tik," she hissed, glowering at him. Ran

gasped.

"Well?"

Chantal settled next to him, slumping deeply so she could slide an arm behind his back. "I agree with you. I am not up to mass assassination. Beside, we don't know whether they snatched anyone or not."

Suddenly R-Bar grunted loudly and lurched sideways, eyes popping wide. "Dim dim dim dim dim," she growled. Ran grabbed her.

"WHAT?" Tinker lurched upright.

"That rangle mik ptar ptar sister is sending hard." R-Bar sat on one of the other couches.

Ran sat by her side.

R-Bar looked at him. "Ripple tells that the Prince and the Princess are doing wander with Sook and Sgenn. And that all are well."

"No news of Je'leel or Eulin?" asked Fair Morn as she carried in a tray heaped with sandwiches. "I got hungry. Figured that everyone could use a bite to eat. Also."

Grumbling loudly, he lurched to his feet and walked over to one of the bookshelves. He rapped one knuckle on the shelf where the ornate ring lay, the jewel looking like an ornate eye. "Dat! Get out of there!" He banged on the shelf. "Wake up in there!"

The tiny figure appeared, stretching and yawning. "Gimble, gimble gimble," she grumbled, staring up at him, hands jammed on her hips.

He snatched her off the shelf and walked back to his place on the couch and dropped heavily into it. "Time to join the group, snoozy butt."

She squeaked. "You are holding me too tight."

He dropped her into his lap. "Sorry. But we need your help."

"You are not nice." She glared up at him.

"Said that I was sorry."

"Pickle, pickle," she snarled.

"Sometime ago I believe you said something about always knowing where Je'leel is because of the indjinn portion."

Dat jumped into Chantal's lap and rapidly crawled up her shirt and sat on her shoulder. "Of course, Indjinn Mothers always can tell where their daughters are."

"Well?" he asked, twisting around so he could see her. "Do you know where Je'leel is?"

"No." Dat smiled. "But I could."

Chicken sat by his free side and wrapped her arms around him. "Take most deep a'breath, Fierce Lord, and relax." And kissed his cheek.

He sighed.

And did.

Relax.

Or tried to.

"Dat," he said, carefully being calm. "Can you, ahhhhh, talk with our daughter?"

"No. But they are on Lair By Lair." She kicked her legs back and forth. "Are we going on a trip?"

"Ummmmmmmm, anything exciting happening on Lair By Lair?"

"Don't know about that. But they are eating lunch, I think."

Smoke yanked over a chair and sat close. "Sounds pretty

normal to me."

"Hum," agreed R-Bar as she and Ran yanked chairs over so they could sit close.

Messenger sat next to Chicken. "Let's just bring them home. That way we will know that they are safe. Really really safe."

Dat leaped down and stomped across Chantal's lap, Tinker's lap, Chicken's lap, and glared up at Messenger. "My daughter is not safe?"

So Tinker told her about the message delivered by Nema from Mirf.

Dat leaped into the air.

And was gone.

"Oh, dear," gasped Messenger.

Krag Far Reach.

As they strolled along the wide street, the Prince smiled happily and looked from side to side.

"Fair Maidens, as you share Our Quest, and as We share your's, it is appropriate that you know our names as We know your's. I am Prince Frinda. My sister is Princess Lurin. And as We on quest wander are equal, you should call us Frinda and Lurin as We shall call you Sook and Sgenn." He laughed. "Oh, I already told you that!"

As they strolled along, past one of the many narrow alleyways, a man dressed in dark shades of red almost black, stepped out, hooked an arm around her face and yanked her backward into the dim passage.

Lurin spun in his grasp, bent, and shoved sideways. The attacker slammed into the wall and fell into the trash containers.

The loud noise caused the others to turn and run back toward the disturbance. They stood and stared. Lurin had dragged her attacker out of the trash piles and was sitting on him, both hands clasped around his neck, thumping the back of his head against the pavement.

"Why do your folk keep attacking us?"

THUMP!

"Speak, Varlet!"

THUMP!

"Or die!"

THUMP!

"Sister," said Frinda, very gently. "He can not speak."

THUMP!

"With his air cut off."

THUMP!

Lurin looked up. And released her assailant. And stood up. "You speak with him, Brother." And began to dust off her clothes.

The Prince knelt and peered down into the man's face. "You must have a very thick skull. You are still alive." He patted the man's cheek. Not too gently. "Who are you? Why do you bother Us so?"

The man rolled his eyes and stared at the man looking down at him, carefully not looking at her. "I surrender. Don't kill me."

"Who? Why?" snapped Frinda.

"Caedi Syndicate. By contract."

Lurin peered over her brother's shoulder. "Who hired you, thug?"

"Majitar," he whispered.

Frinda grabbed two handfills of shirt and stood, hauling the man to his feet as Lurin jumped back. He smiled at this battered person. "You will be our messenger. Tell your masters that we wish you to stay away. It is tiring to keep killing your associates."

Lurin shoved her brother aside, making him release the man, and grabbed a handful of shirt just below the attacker's neck. "Why Us, low muck?"

A very crooked smile wobbled into view and quickly fled. "We were told that you were treasure."

Thrusting him angrily away, she watched him bounce off the wall. "Go! Run! Leave!"

They all watched him scurry down the alleyway and around a far corner, wobbling badly from side to side.

"Hum," said Sook looking at Sgenn. Sgenn made an almost imperceptible nod back.

"Yes," said the Prince, smiling broadly at them. "This quest just keeps getting more and more interesting."

They walked out onto the broad sidewalk and continued looking for a good place to eat.

Which they eventually found.

Over the meal, Frinda hoisted his glass high and toasted his sister, the other two as well.

"To a real treasure. One and all." He beamed at them. "Our Most Royal Parents were quite correct. To do a quest is really the thing to do. Quite!"

Lurin lightly touched his arm. "Brother, We do worry bout these dark garbed creepers, We do." She began to serve the dessert.

"How so?" he mumbled around a mouthful, hastily

dabbing at his mouth with his napkin.

"Who ever hired them might get something smarter and tougher."

His gaze shifted instantly from happy to grim. "Ugly thought, Sister, ugly thought."

Ebna Rait. A Normal Grey Day.

"Soooooo, dummkopf, you going to listen or do something stupid?" Mirf waved in the general direction of the four guards that had slipped into the room and now stood carefully watching her. And him.

"What is there to listen to?" The Majitar sat back, a careful, studied move.

"ME!" Mirf flapped her hand on the table top. Guards twitched.

The Majitar stared at her. "Speak," he said. Such an unmannered person this one was.

"Forget the kidnaping scheme. It is not healthy."

"We would have our treasure."

Mirf's eyes glittered, hob-goblin wild. "Those kinder are not your treasure."

"We would have what we would have."

"Oi, yoi yoi, such a thick skull this one is." She leaned forward. "To me give a careful listen, nitwit. That's not a treasure. That's a short life. A very short life. And such an ugly death like you wouldn't believe."

"Monetary Control does not engage in such matters."

Mirf hissed. "Some parents do."

"We are protected."

She leaned back. And nodded slowly. "Soooooooo, you

have a death-wish."

The Majitar made a slight gesture. The guards stepped away from the door. "You may leave, Special Investigator Mirf. If you return, I shall have you caged."

Mirf bounded to her feet and headed for the door, stopped and spun around. "So O.K., I will say it now because I won't get a chance to do it later."

The Majitar looked at this horrid person, his upper lip curling slightly. "What?"

"I told you so!" Mirf spun and stomped away, slamming the door, cracking the door jamb. "Schmuck!"

Lair By Lair. A Warm Sunny Day.

Anamaxtor huffed and brizzled.

Eulin's head snapped up as she called on protection.

Je'leel smiled. "Hello, Mother."

Dat smiled at her daughter. "I am big."

"Oh! Aunt!" Eulin relaxed and poked the golden dragon with a finger just to calm him down.

Dat sat in the picnic circle. "Messenger said that you were not safe. What is there here that would do that?"

"Nothing," replied Je'leel.

"The dragons have been very understanding," added Eulin, scratching Anamaxtor behind an ear. His eyes slid half closed.

Dat looked at their surroundings. "Why would someone send my Great Master a note saying that you were not safe?"

Je'leel shook her head.

Eulin took another piece of their lunch, sharing a small bit with the golden dragon. "Maybe it was in reference to those strange men dressed in that dark clothing."

"Have they been making you not safe? Are they here?"

"There was one." Je'leel pointed back down the pathway. "That way."

Eulin smiled at Dat. "Anamaxtor killed him. And a motley green ate him."

"I will tell my Great Master." Dat leaped straight up. And was gone.

Eulin looked at her sister. "Why would anyone want to do that?"

Je'leel shrugged. "Maybe the Dragon Master will know."

Donae.

They appeared and strode up to the great gate.

One of the group stepped up to the gate guard and smiled very warmly at him. "Could you tell us where the Caedi Syndicate is located, we have some very urgent business there?"

The gate guard, a very large gate guard, beamed at her and told her. Aada stood on her tip toes and kissed him.

"Many thanks."

They slipped through the gate and drifted down the street following his directions.

Two blocks that way and one block to the left, to the building with the deep green-gold door.

They stopped and looked at that deep green-gold door. And walked inside.

"What business?" asked the man dressed in clothes so dark that the red looked almost black.

"We are here to renegotiate a contract," explained Sa'ar.

"Up two, first right." He gestured them through the open

space and pointed at the staircase.

She nodded. And they went that way.

The entry guard watched them go up the stairs. He wished that he worked for Contracting. He would love to bargain with them.

Dol Spar. An Office In Monetary Control.

She sat behind her desk and stared at nothing in particular. Especially at The General who sat in a chair and smiled at her. He indicated the message lying on her desk.

"Monetary Control does not meddle in other beings business."

"Biz baz," she grumbled.

"They filed a Formal Compliant."

"So sue me," she mumbled.

"They want restitution."

"Restitution schmestitution." She crossed her arms behind her head, momentarily distracting The General. "I am pulling our office from Ebna Rait."

The General's feet hit the floor, he had been leaning, tilting on the back legs of his chair. "WHAT?"

Mirf nodded. "Health and safety. Our people's health and safety."

Fred and Quan walked in through a side door. They saluted The General.

"The Prince and The Princess are safe," said Quan. "Chirp," added Fred.

"But," continued Quan. "The one called Ripple was very upset."

She fell into the room, leaped to her feet, hastily yanked

her blouse back together and into some semblance of order, refastening it, face blushing bright red. And gasped loudly, having just then noticed The General sitting there, glowering at Mirf.

"One of my clerks," explained Mirf.

Rema quickly saluted The General. "They left," she gasped. "Throwing me here."

"To where did they leave?" asked Mirf.

"Tobtz," answered Rema, yanking her belt around, flushing bright red again, "said that they were going to renegotiate a contract with the Caedi Syndicate on Donae."

Hastily scribbling something, Mirf thrust the slip at Rema. "GO! HURRY, HURRY!"

Rema read the note and hurtled from the room, forgetting the disorder of her clothes.

"Oh me, oh my," mumbled Mirf. She pointed at Fred and Quan. "Go after her. We want speed, not bureaucratic paper shuffling."

Fred and Quan raced in the direction that Rema had run.

"Such a life this is," hissed Mirf.

"Mirf?"

"Just evacuated the office on Donae."

"Another one? Tell me," demanded The General.

"Health and safety," she muttered. "If we get them out in time."

"Mirf," growled The General, leaning sharply in her direction. "Tell me!"

"You try to fire me again and I will quit," hissed Mirf. Then she leaned forward and stared into his eyes. "So O.K., I'll tell you." And she did. He winced.

Krag Far Reach.

She pointed. Across the street. At a dull grey door.

"The being I seek lives just there."

"Being?" Lurin peered at the door.

"A special thing," replied Sgenn softly.

She started across the street. The others followed. Standing in front of the door, Sgenn nudged her cousin to stay outside.

"I will come," stated Sook.

The Prince frowned at them. "What?"

"Stay." Sgenn lightly touched his arm. "Outside."

He looked at Lurin.

"No." She shook her head. "We will not stay outside."

The group stepped inside, and walked down the long curving hallway.

Into the inner chamber.

And faced it.

Grandeville. Tinker's Place.

They were sprawled, mostly, all around the large living room, having a snack and being very relaxed.

Dat was with them, standing with one arm thrown over the neck of the small calico female cat.

The cat was patiently waiting for Sha'gar to feed it some small tidbit.

Fair Morn refilled Nema's cup. "Pretty good, huh?"

Messenger popped a marshmallow into the cup. They were having cocoa.

R-Bar had said that after lunch, she would gently, aided by Ran and Sha'gar, send Nema back to Monetary Control

Headquarters.

Tinker looked over as R-Bar chewed on the corner of her lower lip. And bounced a marshmallow off her chest. "All right, short and sneaky, what are we up to this time?"

She caught it and ate it. "I am not short." And looked at Ran.

Ran nodded. "Amtar?" She and R-Bar had been discussing the appropriate spell to put on Nema as a little gift for Mirf for causing them so much agitation. Their minds had been locked away from everyone else. And they were not about to let him know what they had been discussing.

And then there they were. Golden scale armor glistening in the light.

"Prince and Princess," greeted Chicken, smiling at them.

"What are you doing here?" growled Tinker.

Smoke slipped from the room and down the hall.

"Hi, Helf." Messenger beamed at him. "Neato armor."

Helf nodded at them. His Princess made a low bow.

"We brought the Royal Band," said Helf.

"Five units," added his Princess.

"Not in the mood for music," grumbled Tinker. "Go away."

Smoke came back and sat next to Chantal. "MindMate?"

"Grumpy butt," grumbled Chantal to Tinker. She looked at the Hephira. "Sit down you two. Have a sandwich."

"MindMate?"

"What music?" asked Nandau.

"Thee look most healthy." Chicken smiled at the pair.

"MindMate!"

"We are," said Helf. "All is well at home."

Tinker glared at Smoke. "What?"

"The first pasture is littered with them." Smoke took another sandwich. "No sense is just letting the sandwiches sit there unattended."

"What?"

"The Royal Band," explained Helf, sitting on the floor.

"Five units," added his Princess, sitting next to him.

"It looks like an army to me." Smoke licked her fingertips and took another sandwich.

"WHAT?" Tinker jumped up and headed from the room, into the hall, and for the rear deck.

Helf stepped up to his side as Tinker stared out at his first pasture. Rank after rank of warriors stood there, glittering golden in the sunlight.

"The Royal Band," said Helf proudly.

"Five units," said his Princess, stepping up to his side.

Tinker sat on one of the wooden benches. He sat hard. And stared at the Hephira pair.

"Now what's going on?"

Helf sat next to him. "We heard that someone was after your daughter so we came to help."

Princess Nandau sat on Tinker's other side. "We are prepared and equipped for many, many, many, many, many days in the field."

Out in the pasture Tinker could see tents springing up all over the place.

In neat rows.

Donae.

The building occupied the corner of the block. The golden

door gleamed soft polish surface. The two ornate letters on its face contrasted sharply, dark black on gold. They told one and all who looked: M.C. The building next to it, its neighbor, was a large structure with a deep green-gold door.

The front door of Monetary Control flew open and they streamed out, the entire office staff, carrying just those critical files and ledgers. It was a drill that they all knew but had hoped never to have to do.

They quickly turned a corner and hurried to the node that would take them back to Headquarters. It was a very quick, but very orderly evacuation. No-one knew why they were doing this, not even the Station Chief. But they all knew who had sent the order as a double plus emergency. And knowing who had sent it was sufficient, in and of itself, to make them do exactly as they were doing.

Not long after the last low level clerk had stepped inside the node, it happened.

A large section of the building that was their neighbor blew into the street, into the air, and on top of the building just evacuated by Monetary Control. It blew up and on top of the buildings on all the other sides as well.

Then the shattered structure collapsed in upon itself. Taking down the buildings on either side as it fell into a great crater. A good portion of the street followed the buildings.

Dol Spar. An Office In Monetary Control.

The large man stepped into her office. And snapped to attention, hastily saluting. He had just seen The General leaning back against the wall, his chair tilted back on its two rear legs, sipping something from a large mug, something that Mirf had ordered.

"All are here," snapped the Station Chief. "Personnel and records."

A messenger rushed in and tossed a note at Mirf's desk and hurried away. Mirf read it. "So was the timing good or was the timing good." She tossed the note to The General. He read it and nodded.

"I think that we will be some time rebuilding in that elseplace," said The General. This meant that the elseplace would be economically isolated from all the others. He looked up at the Station Chief still standing rigidly at attention. "Hand over all your records, etc., to Files. We have a new office which up till now had only a skeletal staff in place. Any of your crew that wishes to transfer there may do so. It is a nice place. An opportunity."

"Where?" The Station Chief blinked and sucked in a deep breath. Things were moving awfully fast for him.

The General smiled. Which shocked the Station Chief. "Fandor's Dan. The Silver Rangers are gathering in." He nodded. "You may thank Mirf for saving all your lives."

The Station Chief stared at her.

"Your building is now a pile of rubble, burning and crackling and puffing great clouds of green and blue smoke into the air. Take the assignment. Its'a nice place, believe me, I know. And it is busy. It is in the process of developing. So it'sa career boost."

She waggled a loose hand at him. "Go talk with your staff." As the Station Chief turned to go, she said, "So thank me, ingrate. It's a promotion. Not a burial, which you just missed being a part of."

He swung back. "Mirf," he gasped. And snapped rigid. And saluted her. "Thank you, Special Investigator Mirf." He spun on his heels and marched from the room and down the hall.

Mirf gurgled.

"He will do well," said The General. "In his new assignment."

Bahn Duhr Tohr. The Royal City.

They had finished the first tour of each of the selected units camped around the Great Field located just outside and to the west of The Royal City. Many of the warriors were survivors of The Great Battle in The Empty Quarter during which The Horror had been vanquished by the greatest army ever assembled by the Kingdoms of the Realm. And those armies had suffered unspeakable losses in that great battle.

Now a new army was a'building, eager for battle, ready to assault any land that would dare kidnap, or attempt to kidnap, the Princess or the Prince of Bahn Duhr Tohr.

The King and The Queen strolled up the street headed for the castle, hand in hand, an act that caused no end of surprise and conversation among the population that saw them. Lords and Ladies just did not do that, even low level royalty. But it was happening. The King. And The Queen. Just strolling along, holding hands, quietly discussing whatever it was that a King and a Queen discussed, strolling along in the soft evening light that signaled the end of the day.

"All do appear most fit and ready," said the King.

"The games hone lethal skills," answered the Queen. "That mighty weapon a'gathering out there is near ready to use."

The King nodded. "Indeed. Yet I wonder."

"My King?"

"Little has actually happened. Mere excitement passing."

"Yes."

"Your brother died on his Quest. None died after that death."

Her grip tightened on his arm. "That was a hazard, not organized interference. Some foul group wishes to interfere in Our affairs. The Kingdoms are all agreed upon this one fact most plain. None may so interject themselves into Our Stately business. Nor may they tamper with Our Children, Royal or commoner."

"Does Our Dark Advisor know?"

"Not yet, Husband, not yet." Willawa, the White Warrior, smiled. "But her clan is widespread and clever. They will."

Krag Far Reach.

The Prince jumped in front of his sister, shielding her.

Lurin shoved him out of the way.

Sgenn grabbed Sook. "Do nothing."

Vague looked at them. Grey inside grey peered at them. Black smudge-stained eyes watched them and blinked. At Sgenn.

She held her hands in front of her face, fingers spread, one palm just before her mouth.

The gold ring on her finger glittered, taking light from the darkness.

It took her.

Into obscurity.

Lair By Lair. A Pleasant Warm Day.

The sun shone onto the vast green, flooding the meadow with warmth and comfort.

A rambling structure sat half inside and half outside the dense forest directly across the vast meadow from where they stood.

The road path that they had been following had dissolved into the verdant thick meadow covering.

They headed through the knee high stems and watched a woman dressed in rainbow hued garments step out of the only door that they could see. To stand and observe their approach.

"They said that you were coming." She nodded at Anamaxtor. "Very handsome." She looked from Eulin to Je'leel. "Very strange."

They stopped not too far away. Not too close.

"I would learn dragon," stated Eulin.

"Who are you?"

"I am named Eulin Dragon Force, Heart To Be of the Vander, daughter of Sa'ar Heart and John Tinker called Lord called The Chosen One. Who are you?"

"I am The Dragon Master. You could call me Master. Or Disamat Anig. I prefer Amat." Her eyes swivelled sideways, a little. "And you?"

"I am Je'leel Tinker. Her father is my father. My mother is Dat."

And you also wish to learn?"

"No. I have no need."

Amat slipped closer to them, clothes murmuring soft whisper secrets. "Unusual." She peered into Eulin's eyes. "Just you?"

"Yes."

Amat slipped closer, face almost touching face. Eulin could see minute scales covering The Dragon Master's skin. And the strange shape of her pupils. Dragon eyes. "I would see what I teach," she breathed.

Amat's hands slipped inside the billowing violet upper garment, rapidly loosened the fastenings and shoved the silken material away, letting it hiss to soft puddle around Eulin's ankles. "Do nothing magic," warned Amat, kneeling, stripping away the rest of Eulin's clothes. "A young Vander," she observed.

She stood and looked at Anamaxtor. "Well trained. He waits for your command, Eulin student."

She stepped sideways and began to unbutton Je'leel's shirt. "And the sister traveler."

Je'leel slapped her hand away and stepped back, yanking off her shirt, tossing it into the grass. And then sat and untied her boots. "I do not require help."

Standing, she stepped out of her jeans and looked at Amat. "Do all dragons have such prurient interest, old women?"

Amat stepped back and looked from one to the other. "Young, both young." And stepped close, eyes stroking over Je'leel. "Indjinn."

She stepped back. And back.

"I would see what I teach," stated Amat. "And what comes with what I teach. I would see no hidden magic. I would see no tricks." She folded her arms over her chest. "It is the way. Agree?"

Her eyes glittered. "Or flee."

"I am Vander." Eulin shrugged her shoulder, dismissing

the woman's stare. "I wish to study dragon." She smiled at Amat. "If you wish to gaze upon my body, it is of no concern. When do we start?"

Amat looked at Je'leel. "And you, strange sister of this unashamed Vander?"

"I will visit as my sister does. However."

"What?" hissed Amat.

"My Father is not to know."

Eulin laughed.

Amat nodded. "Enter my abode. There are robes just inside the door." She shoved Eulin roughly toward the house. "I believe that this young Vander Heart To Be will be a strong student."

Dol Spar.

She fell into the hall. And ran into the office.

"Mirf, Mirf, Mirf!"

"Vat? Vat? Vat?" Mirf leaned back and carefully looked over her clerk. "Well, you managed to keep your uniform on. John must be slowing down."

The clerk suddenly realized who else was in the room. She blushed, hastily brushed some small speck from her tunic, snapped rigid, and saluted.

"Relax, kiddo," sighed Mirf. "It is only him. So what's new with John and all his chickees?"

"They didn't say."

Mirf waggled one hand. "So Nema, do a sit." Mirf looked at The General. "Her sister, Rema, was the one more or less still in her uniform. Good thing that I didn't send a male there."

After the startled clerk sat, wondering what had

happened to her sister, Mirf leaned forward and lightly rapped a knuckle on the desk top. “So, cuddle curves, life there is nice and quiet and uneventful?”

“NO!” Nema blushed. “Oh, no.”

“So?”

“A tiny person named Dat visited with her daughter and said that they were just fine.” She held her hand out, thumb and forefinger close together, indicating the size of Dat.

Mirf leaned back in her chair. “They? Them? Who? Vat?”

“The daughter Je’leel, and the daughter Eulin, and the dragon Anamaxtor.”

“Ho boy,” mumbled Mirf. “So now it’s another dragon they have.”

“And the Hephira Prince and Princess brought an immense army.”

“VAT?” Mirf lurched forward. “What Hephira? What army?”

Nema jerked backwards. "Prince Helf. Princess Nandau. Their army. All dressed in glittering golden scale armor.”

Mirf ripped a piece of paper loose, scratched violently on it with her scribe, and shoved the tattered thing at Nema. "Nuff loafing. GO!”

Nema grabbed it and bolted from the room.

Mirf beamed at The General. “I like that pair. Hard workers.” And leered at him. “And easy on the eyes.” Then she said to herself, or the wall, or something, “Sooooooooo, what does he need an army for?” She shook her head. “So he doesn’t need one.”

Grandeville. Tinker's Place.

"What do I need an army for? I do not need one."

Tinker glared at the pair. And then at everyone else.

"Take two," gurgled Chantal, starting to laugh. "They're small."

"Ha. Ha. Ha."

"Not funny," hissed R-Bar at Chantal thinking that she was referring to all folk of short stature. The Hephira were shorter than she was, so she felt just a little better thinking about that.

Helf nodded. "We could bring in another Band."

"Five units," added Nandau.

"No way, Jose," growled Tinker.

"But there is," argued Naudau, wondering who this Jose person was.

"Of course," agreed Helf, looking around for Jose. He didn't see anyone else.

Tinker looked from one to the other. "Leave them at home."

Helf nodded.

Nandau bowed. "Lord."

"My Lord." Chicken slipped up to Tinker's side, sliding an arm around his waist. "Praps do we all comfort seek we might in vision become clear do we relax some?"

"Sounds like a leading offer to me."

Fair Morn nudged Chantal.

Chantal rubbed the ornate ring she wore on the front of her right thigh. "Better not be."

Fair Morn leaned close and said into Chantal's mind. *This must be private.*

What?

I think that we should contact Macabre.

WHAT!

Ouch! Fair Morn jerked. *Not so loud!*

What's going on, Butterfly?

I think that our daughters are in trouble and no one knows it. Just too many things going on, all af a sudden, that's all.

O.K. I'll get Raj to update our medical kits.

Fair Morn hugged her. "Smoke and I will pack in a very sneaky manner."

How are we going to contact Macabre?

Have to ask the kid witch.

He is really going to get angry if we do.

Not if we really need the help.

Chantal kissed Fair Morn and gave her a friendly pat. "Right! Let's get ready. But we'll wait on the Macabre invite."

He leaped.

It was an easy leap for him. From the doorway to the bed, catching her, pulling her down, fangs seeking the soft spot where neck joined shoulder. Razor sharp claws shredded her garments. His body weight flattened her to the bed, pinning her in place.

"Heh, heh, heh, heh, heh, heh." Laughing deep in her throat, she wrapped her arms around him and twitched as he gently nipped, here and there.

"Mine," she gasped. And dug her fingers into the soft plush fur as he rolled her back and forth.

Collapsing into a mutually entangled heap, he licked her cheek.

"You are mine," she sighed.

"What will your clan center think?"

Raft frowned and kissed him. "Lovely, I do not care what my sister thinks. She knows the Faan way. Each finds her own."

Ebna Raint. Clearing To Soft Grey.

The Majitar examined his visitor with careful, controlled glances. "The Caedi Syndicate is no more? For trying?"

The visitor leaned back, just a little, and looked right at the Majitar, his soft garments, grey with light touches of green and gold dancing a strange pattern, making soft slithering sounds. "The Caedi were inept. Hire cheap, bargain bad."

The Majitar touched the new contract with the tip of one carefully extended fingertip.

The visitor nodded, an almost imperceptible nod. "There are moments. And they are taken. Your guards are fierce and number vast. When properly armed, that handful of purple mage can not touch them."

The Majitar touched his fingertips to the contract.

"I will deliver those you wish. I will cast on your guards. My price, my bargain, is the best!" Some small emotion crackled here and there on the visitor's face.

The Majitar gently shoved the contract across the table top and authorized payment.

NOW!

Bal's Dartar.

They were halfway down the street, seeking some comfortable place to eat, when she hooked her arms around their necks, yanked them close, and kissed them, one after the other.

"Mine!" She kissed them again. "You are mine!"

Anjan smiled.

"What will your clan head think?" asked Adarlak.

Releasing Anjan, Ranna twisted around, fingers playing with the fastenings on Adarlak's upper garment. "Lovely One, I do not care a ptar tik what my sister thinks. She knows the Faan way. Each finds their own."

She slipped an arm around each waist and started them down the street again.

Bahn Duhr Tohr. The Quarters of the Royal Advisors.

Sprawling comfortably on the couch, back propped up against one large arm of the couch, he admired her.

Sprawling comfortably across his lap, back propped up by his knees, she admired him.

Two large tomes lay on the floor next to the couch, oozing dust.

"Husband," she murmured. "You are leaving dusty marks on my anatomy."

He nodded. Sagely he nodded, and smiled. "I do seem to be doing that." He carefully, with delicate touch, added a fingerprint here, a fingerprint there. He admired the pattern.

She leaned forward, just a little. "You are mine."

"Of course." He grinned. "I do believe, Dusky Midnight Handfuls of Delight, that things have grown, um, a little."

Tucking her chin against her chest, she peered down. "Things?"

He winked. "Must be having daughters that does it." And grinned. Again.

"What?" she hissed.

"Perhaps some small learned experiment, some small gathering of comparative data?"

"You are not divesting any court wench or courtier of their garments just to fondle them."

He laughed. "I would use calipers."

She jerked upright and growled.

"OOOP!" He yanked his hand away.

"Not you gentle touch mate. We are about to have visitors and I am dust besmeared."

"I will fetch soft cloth and warm water immediately. My pleasure."

She stood. "You will entertain. I will wash things." And disappeared.

He walked into another room and washed his hands and filled another basin. Just in case.

"May we enter?" asked a disembodied voice.

Stepping back into the main room, he said, "Of course."

They appeared.

He nodded. "Hayou, Ranna." And smiled at her companions.

"Hayou, Hanred. This is Anjan Trap Zahan and Adarlak."

Hanred nodded. "A mage and a . . . ?"

"Anjan is Death Warrior Guild. Adarlak is Hacto." She slipped an arm around each waist. "Mine."

"My," he said, quickly yanking a chair from the table and dropping into it. "My, my." He filled mugs and waved at them to sit down, shoving the mugs at them as they did. And took a sip.

And looked at Ranna.

She stared back.

"Your's? Faan your's?"

Ranna nodded, something crackled. Somewhere.

Hanred leaned back and smiled at the trio. "This clan never ceases to amaze me." He raised his mug.

"Welcome Anjan. Welcome Adarlak I am Hanred. Ripple's."

Adarlak stared at him. "The Illusionist? The one called Old Hanred?"

He nodded.

Then she was there. "Husband. you may not run comparative experiments on them either." She looked at her sister. "Sister? Traveling with a mage? And a . . . ?"

"Warrior," explained Hanred, tugging out a chair for Ripple. "Death Warrior Guild."

He nodded as Ripple sat. "Hacto."

"Small. Minor." Ripple waved over a full mug and sipped.

"Mine!" snapped Ranna.

Ripple choked and hissed, "What? Who?"

"Both," stated Ranna, sitting upright, black eyes glittering deep down fire. "Mine."

Carefully watching her eldest sister, she cast protection over Hanred. "Calm, eldest sister, calm." Her eyes danced from Ranna to Anjan to Adarlak and back again. "Speak tell."

So Ranna did. Then she looked from Ripple to Hanred. "Each finds their own. It is the Faan way."

Ripple nodded.

Ranna threw her arms around Anjan and Adarlak and tugged them close. "Mine. These are mine."

Wild dark crackled around Ripple. "Your's? These, erga na, these pik pit intik, are your's? Faan your's?"

Ranna surged to her feet, leaned on the table, plunged a flaming green wand into it, and snarled, "Watch your tongue, guanna dak!"

Anjan and Adarlak shoved themselves sideways and leaped to their feet. A glittering multi-edged weapon waggled in Anjan's hand. Adarlak held her mace.

"Guanna dak!" gurgled Ripple, rising to her feet, leaning toward her sister, caressing a deep blue glowing wand with her thumb.

"Suk suk meput," hissed Ranna.

"Hum," said Ripple. "That is coarse beyond vile, sister. The eldest is always supposed to be less so, not more."

"The Faan are fiercely protective," stated Ranna.

Hanred quickly refilled all the mugs, recognizing from long association, the calming down of the witches.

"Hum hum hum," added Ripple, sitting down, lower lip pushing out, appraising her sister's companions, again.

Ranna nodded, Anjan and Adarlak sat, weapons disappearing. "Hum hum," she replied.

"Do our sisters know?" The blue wand went somewhere.

"No. It is Faan proper to visit the clan head and center before all else." The green flaming wand disappeared.

Ripple leaned back in her chair and patted Hanred's thigh. "Most proper." And nodded. "They are lovely."

"Certainly are," agreed Hanred.

Ripple looked at Anjan, then at Adarlak. "Faan welcome, Anjan. Faan welcome, Adarlak."

She stood, walked around the table and stood behind

Adarlak. Sliding her palm over Adarlak's face and neck, Ripple ordered, "None may interfere." She plunged a long bronze wand into the mage.

Anjan sprang to her feet, weapon in hand and leaped at Ripple. Ranna's backstroke tossed her tumbling across the room.

Yanking her wand free, Ripple yanked Adarlak's head back by the hair and kissed her. "Now we are cross-tied, Faan-Hacto, clan to guild."

She watched the warrior lurch to her feet. "It cannot be done to non-magic folk."

Ranna patted the empty chair and waited until Anjan had reseated herself. "Now Adarlak' s sister are our sisters." Leaning sideways, she kissed Anjan's cheek, and murmured, "Fierce warrior." She sat back. "We are tired. Which are our rooms?"

Ripple sent them. Then she jabbed Hanred in the side. "Hold me, husband. I require comforting after that."

He grinned, "Our bed?"

"The couch will do." She stood. "And you might, somehow, slowly divest me of my blouse and leave dusty marks on, ah, . . . things."

"I washed my hands."

Dol Spar. An Office In Monetary Control.

The door crashed open and Prandam lurched in and dropped heavily into a chair. He nodded at The General and frowned at Mirf.

"Ho boy, to me you look a mess."

"I quit, Mirf."

"You can't quit. I just put you on vacation."

Prandam nodded.

"Doth Lamex," ordered Mirf. "When you are ready, come back."

"The Majitar," rasped Prandam, slumping in his chair, almost slumping out of his chair, "has hired a twisted mage whose name should not be spoken out loud." He tossed a crumpled sheet onto her desk. "Read it and destroy it."

Mirf did. She nodded at The General. And said to Prandam, "So, Sneaky Pete, other than a vacation, what else?"

"A raise."

"Done!" Mirf banged on the desk top and gave the necessary orders.

Prandam lurched to his feet and leaned heavily to one side. "I can't go back there ever again, I'd die."

Mirf squinted at him, eyes glittering. "So who knows, they might die, first."

"MIRF!" barked The General.

She waved an arm at Prandam. " Go! Rest! Loaf! Take that green-eyed slinky bod from files with you. Go! Go!"

Prandam stumbled from her office, slamming the door shut.

"Mirf?"

"Vat?"

The General sighed.

"What'sa matta? That one your's?" She laughed loudly. "I know. Besides, it is his friend."

The General rested his head on his hand, elbow on the arm rest of his chair. "How our agency ever, ever, ever hired you, much less gave you this office is a mystery."

Mirf leered at him. "All your's." The General had done the hiring and had put her in this office, specially created for her.

He nodded. "I know."

"Besides." She beamed at him. "I am the best for this kind of wiggle-waggle. Talented. Hard working." She sucked in a deep breath and threw her arms back. "Gorgeous." And exhaled. And leaned forward. "Let's schmooz."

Grandeville. Tinker's Place.

Morning.

Late morning.

Late breakfast morning.

He looked around the table and nodded. Helf and Nandau wore tunics and trousers of soft pastel blue material. He had convinced them that they need not wear armor nor carry swords in the house or anywhere in the immediate vicinity of the house.

Smoke watched him watching the pair. *Yum, yum, yum, yum.*

Knock it off.

"They went to visit Ripple. Ranna did," stated R-Bar.

"Huh?"

R-Bar took another roll, split it in half, and washed it around in her egg yoke. "Ranna found her's and visits Ripple, Faan proper. So Raft took her's to do the same thing." She ate the yolk drenched half and began to wallow the other part around on her plate. "I wonder what Ranna found?"

He took a sip from his cup. "Why?"

"Ripple sent unsettled."

He nodded, stood, and stretched. "Nice day outside. Good day for a hike, enjoy the sunshine."

Chantal nodded. "Care for some company?"

"Sure. Let's go."

They headed for their rooms to change.

Fair Morn smiled at Helf. "Your army going to behave if I flit about?" Her wings were beginning to itch from being closed too long.

"What?"

She stood. "Let's go talk with them. After I change." She hurried away.

The rest of them just drifted away to do various chores.

Krag Far Reach.

Grey vague sucked her inside. And tossed the empty husk into a corner. It eyed the other three.

"You are not," it hissed. And threw them into a different corner. The bodies tumbled and rolled in a loose-limbed disorder, one over the other.

They were alive.

Barely.

Lair By Lair.

She screamed and screamed.

And clawed at her robe.

It was molding itself to her body.

"IT STICKS! IT STICKS!" She spun toward them, eyes staring, running tears. "HELP ME, SISTER!"

Je'leel looked at the robe that she wore. It was just cloth of some kind.

"DO NOT!" bellowed The Dragon Master, one hand restraining Anamaxtor.

Eulin lurched and staggered a few short steps.

She stared down at the robe. The ever shifting colors and texture had stilled.

A young woman wearing glowing, pale green robes smiled at her. "Young Dragon, are you ready to learn? To become a Master?"

Eulin held out her arms and turned them back and forth. Her skin was multi-colored, multi-textured.

"Your strange sister and your dragon companion wait other well," stated Amat. "Are you ready to learn?"

"Yesssssssss," hissed Eulin, admiring her claws.

Amat look her to the training place.

Doth Lamex. A Place of Healing and Relaxation.

"Did you see that?" Santar pointed.

They were returning from a fast heal pond and had just turned the corner toward their spot. Everyone was feeling well and totally healthy, especially Santar and Sepanix. Their clothes were spotless, their footsteps light.

"What?" asked Sepanix.

"Hum hum," murmured Shitar.

Mantara laughed. "Your sisters are present."

"That was a grey sneak," explained Santar. "With a green-eyed slyph."

"Was she struggling?" asked Shitar.

"No."

"Then," said Mantara, "he is safe." He tugged Shitar against his side. "I prefer black-eyed witch."

Sepanix looked at Santar from the corners of her eyes.

"No!" Shitar frowned at them.

"It would be interesting." Mantara winked at Shitar.

"It would be lethal," she grumbled.

"I am hungry." Sepanix called in a server and ordered for them all.

"Dark hearts," said Mantara as he sat at the just appearing table. "I have nothing else to teach you."

Santar nodded, walked past him, dragging her fingers along his shoulder, and sat.

Sepanix stepped over, bent and kissed him. "Witch debt, Shitar mate." And took a seat.

Food and drink arrived.

Shitar served.

Santar emptied her cup. "Hardest training ever."

Sepanix nodded agreement and said to Mantara, "I am well healed, hard teacher."

Mantara smiled at the pair. "Perhaps a final inspection just to make sure, em, that everything is undamaged?"

Shitar tapped him lightly on the back of his hand with a pointed fingernail. "One may inspect the other. Or go find their's to do the inspection."

Mantara smiled at her. "We both know a mighty warrior with many, including your Aunt."

"Aunt is different."

"Heh heh heh." He tickled a rib or two.

Shitar looked at her sisters. "I will tell mother that your training is finished."

She nodded at Sepanix. "You have great strength and now great control over your wild magic. In your age-name group, in the pure Faan, you will become a most powerful witch." She frowned at her sister. "If you survive."

"It would be fun," he grumbled. [illegible]

[illegible]

Chapter Fifteen

A Little Change. Here and There.

Fandor's Dan.

They were walking back to their quarters after the turnout.

It had been the first time for the four units, the first time since they had come together. For practice and inspection.

Equipment had sparkled in the sunlight. Faces had glowed from the exercise, from their general healthy nature.

The Silver Rangers had banged and thumped upon one another with the gay abandon of very large men who enjoyed the rough and tumble mayhem of the warrior way.

She held his hand, her hand mostly enveloped in his. "They all enjoyed themselves."

He smiled. "They are becoming what they had once been. It is good to see."

She yanked at his arm. "Then why were you frowning before I spoke?"

"Many units are missing. Pomon and Cipan are making a list of everyone that they can remember and where they were last seen. But the M. C. Station Chief will not search his files for us. He states that by doing so it would be against M.C. rules and regulations."

They entered the building, the main building housing various shops on the ground floor, Monetary Control on the second floor and the Silver Rangers Headquarters and their personal quarters on the third floor.

"As long as we are here," she said. "Let's go visit with M.C." And laughed softly.

They started up the staircase, up to the second floor.

"Wife?"

She smiled. "I am sure that Mirf would help us. If she were here."

Soon, they stood in front of the wide desk that bared the way into the depths of Monetary Control proper.

"I wish to speak to The Station Chief." Sedeem smiled at the low level clerk. "We wish to speak with him."

"Who shall I say is calling?" She was one of the newest staff, just arrived.

"Tell him that Tindar Farth of the Silver Rangers and Sedeem. We were both with Mirf when she was with the Vander at their Great Battle."

"Mirf!" gasped the clerk, jumping to her feet.

"Yes," said Farth to her back as she hurried away.

"One moment," she called over her shoulder.

"You look very regal, Husband."

Farth was wearing the ceremonial garb of the Tindar of the Silver Rangers. He had grumbled about that and about not being allowed to join in the melee. But the Tindar was the ultimate judge and was not allowed to participate.

The clerk and The Station Chief stepped into the room.

"Yes?" asked The Station Chief.

Sedeem looked as innocent as she could. It was a very

practiced look. It was something her mothers and Mirf had insisted that she learn how to do. "We would like to send an official message to Special Investigator Mirf." She rattled off the priority code, the Headquarter's cipher, and the authorization series. "Please?"

The clerk hastily dropped into her chair and rapidly wrote it all in the correct form on the correct form.

The Station Chief had gone pale.

"We really do need your help?" explained Sedeem, smiling sweetly.

"Who are you? Really?" The Station Chief stared at them and wondered whether sending him and his staff here, to this new office, hadn't been some subtle ploy on Mirf's part to destroy his career.

Sedeem cuddled against Farth's side and blinked all innocence at The Station Chief. "Mirf is my Honorary Aunt and would help us if she were here. Of course, if you would help, I am sure that she would understand, being as busy as she is and everything."

The Station Chief stared at the clerk. "Get Friddle down here and tell him to search for whatever they wish. This is a building and growing elseplace and we should do all in our power to aid them." He spun on his heels and marched for his office.

As soon as the door closed, the clerk looked up and whispered to them, "Is Mirf really your Honorary Aunt?" She hit the appropriate button.

"You betcha," laughed Sedeem. "But she doesn't like being called Aunt."

"Friddle should be here shortly." The clerk looked up at

Farth. "Are all you Rangers so big, and so rugged, and so handsome?" And blushed.

Farth fizzled.

Sedeem winked at the clerk. "They certainly are."

Then Friddle arrived. Ready to go to work.

Krag Far Reach.

She shrugged up through vague grey shadow under dark from the deep below, a new being not new. The training had been long and hard.

Down there.

But she had gathered in all of the new that there was, had seen the many layers of the down below below, and had learned all the commands that few knew or dared to say or to think. Now she had only to think the thought for them to come.

She slipped mist quiet, vapor soft, from somewhere and poured into the husk of herself. And wondered at the strangeness of solidity, the crackle of joints, the hum of muscle and sinew.

She felt the hunger, the terrible hunger. She had been gone long. She had been gone long, longer than the mere passage of time that she now experienced. This body was ready to be fed. That feeling she could control, that feeling of hunger. Now she could control so much more.

She stood, stretched, and bent, and flexed. The body had lain in awkward repose, the limbs were very stiff. She was home. Grey eyes blinked, and focused. Slowly she looked at her surroundings and the three objects on the floor.

All the memories flooded back.

This room.

Her cousin.

The Royal pair.

Stepping over the bodies, she yanked Sook away and rolled her onto her back. Swiftly she unfastened her cousin's blouse and slid her hand over the midnight pale skin. Still warm, deep down flutter of heart beat, the faint movement of slow breath.

Calling one of them up, she watched it pour grey onto the exposed flesh. Sgenn leaned forward and watched Sook's face.

A muscle twitched at one corner of Sook's mouth, her eyes fluttered, and opened.

"Cousin?"

"Rest. Be still. I will see to the Royals."

Sgenn stood, walked over and grabbed a wrist. She dragged the limp body across the floor. Kneeling next to her, she tugged the ties loose, and yanked the garment from Lurin's shoulders, pulling it open to her waist. Sgenn nodded. This Princess would certainly attract males. Gently she touched here, here and there, mostly seeking life.

She knelt and took a taste, here and there, from curiosity. Straightening up, she directed the servant and watched it as it poured grey onto the still form.

Sgenn massaged it into the skin and brought Lurin thrashing to life.

"Foul wench," snarled Lurin, all rasp whisper. "Cease this wanton abuse!"

Sgenn sat back, a small half-smile tugging at one corner of her mouth. "Lovely Princess, your body is safe from me. It was a healing process, not an erotic one."

She stood and walked over to the Prince and heaved him

onto his back. "A heavy one." And yanked his shirt loose and sat on his stomach and threw the garment wide. "Hum hum hum."

She looked at Sook who had rolled her head in her cousin's direction. "A well muscled Prince." Then she set to work. And nodded at the surprised eyes that stared up at her.

"All are fortunate to be alive. And undamaged." She bowed her head. "Humble apologies to all. I did not know that this would, or could, happen." She sent the servant away, back down into the deep below below.

The Prince managed a feeble smile and cleared his throat. "Perhaps, Lovely One, we might try this later? In more proper quarters?"

Lurin gasped.

Frinda laughed, a small wheezing sound. "It was a thought."

"Hum," said Sgenn.

"Cousin," rasped Sook. "We must go to our quarters."

Sgenn lurched upright.

The Prince rolled onto his side and managed to wobble into a sitting position.

"MY!" His eyes jumped from Lurin to Sook. "MY!" And started to sag sideways.

Sook managed the spell, barely, and yanked them to their rooms.

Lair By Lair.

Eulin kissed Amat and bowed deeply. "Vander debt, Great Teacher." And stepped back.

Je'leel and Anamaxtor stood next to the front door.

The Dragon Master nodded. "Your mother was clever

and wise, young student, to set you upon the path you have so far followed. Remember! Think! And do not forget that dragons can be sly and devious." She stepped back and disappeared.

Eulin spun and shrugged off her robe and hung it on the peg. Je'leel had already done the same. They stepped outside into warm sunshine and green meadow.

"Sister," said Eulin. "Look at me."

Je'leel did. "What?"

"Am I different?"

"Besides knowledge?"

Eulin nodded.

"Yes." Je'leel smiled. "Everything looks the same as before. Maybe a little more . . . luscious."

Eulin snatched up her clothes from the pile on the grass and began to dress. "I was afraid to look. I didn't want to see fine scales everywhere."

Je'leel fastened her shirt. "Looks just like smooth skin to me."

Eulin sat and tied her boots. "Let's go to some elseplace and just have fun."

"Where?"

"Mother told of Doth Lamex."

"O.K."

Eulin stood.

And nodded.

And took them away.

The grab roared across the meadow.

One moment too late.

Krag Far Reach.

"Brother," snarled Lurin. "Your stare was most impolite, most ungentlemanly, and most vulgar."

"I humbly apologize," he replied. "To you and to fair Maiden Sook." He nodded at them. "I was startled."

He cleared his throat. "Perhaps if the owners of such mighty beauty would fasten their garments so sweet modesty would once again cover and merely hint?"

Sgenn knelt next to Lurin and tugged her clothes up and around. Then she yanked Sook's blouse closed.

Sook nodded at her. "We need some restful elseplace, cousin."

"Where?"

"Mother said Doth Lamex is safe comfort."

Sgenn stood and nodded.

Sook poured all her remaining energies into it and took them away.

The grab blew in one wall and exploded out the other.

One moment too late.

Bahn Duhr Tohr. The Quarters of the Royal Advisors.

They were sitting at the table eating the first meal of the day.

"How many sisters?" Ripple looked across the table at the pair flanking her eldest sister.

"I have five sisters," replied Adarlak. "I am the youngest and was on wander."

"Hum," observed Ripple.

"Nik nik," suggested Ranna.

Hanred stifled a laugh.

Ripple shrugged and looked at Anjan.

"Two," said Anjan. "I am the elder. And only warrior. My sisters are soft-curve. Menderes." She sat straighter. "It takes great strength to grade top."

"May we enter?" asked someone.

"Enter," replied Ripple, recognizing the voice.

They were there.

Anjan leaped to her feet, blade flickering into her hand, pushing between Ranna and this suddenly appearing pair

"Hayou, sisters," said Raft. "Who are they?"

"It is a cat-folk," gasped Hanred.

Mrrinar flipped his tail over his arm and bowed. And watched Anjan, carefully.

"Sit down," snapped Ripple at Anjan. She nudged Hanred.

"In my youth I traveled widely. Few visited that elseplace." Hanred looked at Mrrinar. "They do not like smooth skins."

"Mrrinar is different," stated Raft, pulling over two chairs, nudging him to sit in one. She served them both.

"Sister?" asked Ripple.

"Mine," replied Raft, filling both their mugs.

"What?" hissed Ripple.

"MINE!" snapped Raft, rapping a long purple wand on the table top.

"HAK TAK IMGAK!" exploded Ripple, dark billowing across the ceiling.

"Rim dim dik dik," gurgled Ranna, grabbing Anjan and Adadak, poking a large hole out, ready to flee, weaving witch spells around them. "Vile coarse," she snarled at Ripple.

"MINE!" screamed Raft. "MINE! MINE! MINE!" Horrible formed behind her.

Mrrinar's ears flattened back, his claws popped out.

Ripple dropped heavily into her chair, and mumbled, "Faan puz mer ptar kar." And waved in a large jug and filled her mug and emptied it. "This clan is going strange strange."

Ranna, feeling the tension ebbing, closed the hole and leaned forward and said gently to Raft, "Young sister, these are mine."

Raft stared at her. "Yours? Females? BOTH?"

Ranna nodded.

Raft gasped. "Female pik tik nap."

"Better than nook fon pla!" snarled Ranna.

"Witches?" asked Hanred into the gathering tension.

All stared at him, jet black eyes flickering deep down fire.

Hanred cleared his throat. "The Faan always find their own. It is their way. Correct?"

"Of course," snapped Ripple, sliding an arm around his shoulders.

"True," replied Ranna, staring at her sister and wondering at her doing such strange.

"Always," hissed Raft, wondering whether her sister Clan Head had gone head soft.

Hanred smiled at them. "Mrrinar meet Anjan and Adarlak. They are Ranna's. I am Ripple's." He looked at the cat-folk, a very close inspection. "Are you guild?"

Mrrinar smiled, carefully hiding his canines in a most proper and polite smile. "Healer." His ears rose, his claws disappeared. "Mrror tp House."

"Death Warrior Guild," said Anjan.

"Hacto mage," added Adarlak.

Hanred exhaled. The air was clearing.

Ripple stood. "Sisters, we must talk. Privately. Now!" She yanked them away.

Anjan looked at Mrrinar. "Touch?"

He nodded.

She carefully reached over and slid her hand over his arm. She nodded and sat back, leaned sideways and said something low to Adarlak. Adarlak blushed.

Hanred shoved his chair back. "Perhaps you would like to see the castle while the witches confer?" He ushered them from the room and down the main corridor. "Let's see if The King and the Queen are free?"

Doth Lamex. The Land of Healing and Relaxation.

Eulin stretched and yawned. "Sister, I think that I have had enough of wander. I want to go home and talk with Mother."

Je'leel smiled at her. '"Come visit. Father will be pleased. And proud. And he will be surprised that we have been gone two of his years. And aged accordingly."

Eulin smiled back at her. "But we are finally found."

Je'leel stepped close and kissed her sister. "I had nothing to find."

Eulin hugged her "I will miss you."

"Me too,"

Anamaxtor nudged Je'leel with his nose.

She laughed. "You too, handsome dragon."

Anamaxtor snorted blue smoke.

Eulin stepped back. "I can send you home from the

gateway."

They hurried that way.

Lurin finished serving and sat. "Brother, I am well rested."

"Sounds like it." He looked at the others. "Looks like it." He shrugged a shoulder. "As far as I can tell." And grinned at them all.

Sgenn nodded. So did Sook.

"Our Quest is over," stated The Princess. "We do wish to return home." Finishing the food on her plate, she dabbed at her mouth with her napkin, tossed it down and walked away to begin dressing in her armor.

The Prince stood and bowed deeply. "Fair Sook, fair Sgenn, your companionship was most pleasant, but I do fear we must now part. We, my Noble Sister Princess, and I, have a kingdom to seek, a voyage to make, in our own elseplace." He smiled at them. "Do visit. Please?"

"Hum," said Sgenn, leaning sideways and whispering in her cousin's ear. "He wants your body."

"Not mine," hissed Sook. She stood and walked away to help The Princess. And handed her the great white sword.

"Thank you."

"Princess, I would be your Advisor as my mother is to your Mother Queen."

Lurin stared at her. "True?"

"Witch true."

Lurin frowned at her. "If We fail in Our Search there will be little to advise as We will not marry some lessor Lord or Prince of one of the many kingdoms."

Sook shrugged.

Lurin smiled. "Then let us be on our way, and see what we shall see."

Sook nodded.

The Prince waved at them, black armor in place, shining, gleaming. "I am ready."

Sgenn stuffed her arms into opposite sleeves. "I have elseplaces to see attend."

"Visit?" asked the Prince. He laughed. "It is a Royal command."

Sgenn bowed her head, a small half-smile tugging at one corner of her mouth, and watched them head for the gateway.

Sepanix stalked back and forth. "I am ready to leave this place."

Santar nodded.

Shitar poked Mantara.

"I think that we all are," he said, recognizing the signs of well rested and healthy and restless witches.

"We shall visit mother," stated Shitar. "And the aunts Ranna and Raft. And their's."

Mantara tugged Shitar toward the gate. "I am curious also."

The four of them strode rapidly for the gateway.

Ebna Raint. A Fine Grey Day.

Soft grey mist blew up the slope, drifting wet just above their heads. They stood and stared down into the holding pit.

The mage tapped one fingernail on the railing and hissed, "Watch carefully, Majitar, watch carefully. This time I will do as

I promised."

A figure crashed down, rolling and tumbling across the soft soil, to crash and lay limp against the up curving wall.

The mage pointed. "She is not injured. It was subtle grab, separating her from her companions in the inbetween, necessarily violent. She will wake soon."

Another figure tumbled in, to lie in a crumpled heap.

"There." It was a very self-satisfied statement. "There." He turned toward the Majitar.

"Our contract is satisfied. My fee is due and payable."

The Majitar nodded, a small, carefully controlled nod. "It is all in the Red Tower."

The mage wagged one hand. The Red Tower disappeared. "I like that building." He leaned forward and peered down into the holding pit. "Now, one final payment for disbelief and for subtle irritations." He leaned further over, and wiped one sleeve across his mouth, and whispered to himself, "Lush lovely."

He disappeared, taking one of the figures from the pit.

A voice spoke to the startled Majitar from elsewhere. "One treasure is enough for you."

Chapter Sixteen

Treasures.

Grandeville. Tinker's Place. Warm and Sunny.

Bodies were sprawled everywhere.

In the late afternoon.

Sleeping bodies.

They had been straightening out the barn and the storage sheds. Somehow the barn and the storage sheds always seemed to need straightening.

Helf and Nandau had been ordered here and there by Chicken, a very new experience for the Princess. But the pair had enjoyed the hard work and the exercise.

Now, Tinker and the rest of himself and all their guests were having a siesta. Ran had joined Tinker in the hammock.

She appeared on the rear deck, looked at the bodies, silently slipped down the deck to the far corner and around and into the kitchen through the outside door, to make coffee and cocoa.

Smoke, lying flat on her back, at the edge of the swimming pool, mostly asleep, always watching, felt her arrive and smiled to herself.

Bahn Duhr Tohr. The Quarters of The Royal Advisors.

"AHEM!"

Someone loudly cleared their throat.

"AHEM!"

Both looked up at the ceiling from the tomes that they had been reading.

He carefully slipped the gigantic volume from his lap and eased it to the floor. It thumped heavily in spite of his caution and puffed a small cloud of dust into the air.

She banged on her shirt and put a mark on the page she had been studying. It was a particularly nasty spell.

"Enter, daughter." Ripple sat up. She had been lying flat on the floor reading from the open book that had been floating in the air, pages held open by something unseen, above her face. The book joined its fellow in a two book stack, and puffed a small cloud of dust.

They whirled in.

"Hayou, mother," they said.

"Hayou, daughters. And Mantara." She stood. And glared at Sepanix. "Daughter, leaving training is rak tak!"

Sepanix dropped into a chair, waved over a mug, and told it to fill. "Pook pook," she suggested, grumbling at her mother.

Shitar slipped between her sister and her mother. "Her training is finished. Sepanix is ready for wander."

"How finished?"

"Mantara and I. Santar and Sepanix. Trained in green."

"Hum hum," said Ripple.

Mantara laughed and slipped an arm around Shitar. "Of course not."

Santar dropped onto the couch next to Hanred. "Hayou, Father. Don't be an ik tit, Mother."

"My daughters will be witch proper!" snapped Ripple. She frowned from one to the other. "No matter how wild."

Sepanix ordered more mugs filled. And nodded.

Ripple sat next to her. "You learned green?"

"And Santar, Mother."

Ripple took her daughter's hand and held it in both of her's and looked into her daughter's face. "I have powerful daughters."

Sook blasted into the room, snarling and growling. Dark ripped across the ceiling. The room shuddered.

Shitar leaped in front of Mantara.

Ripple banged protection over Hanred, many layers deep, and yanked in a long black wand which crackled angrily. "CALM, DAUGHTER, CALM!"

The air flashed clear. "Sorry sorry," mumbled Sook. She snatched the mug from in front of Sepanix and drained it.

"Something took The Princess. While we were inbetween." She stalked around the room. The air still crackled around her. "The Prince is with The King and The Queen."

Shitar gasped. "From inbetween?"

Sook nodded. "It only took Lurin." She held out one arm and yanked up a sleeve. Her arm was motley black-and-blue-and-red. "It just touched in passing." She sat at the table. "What can do that?" She wiped heal over the bruising.

Ripple sent her wand somewhere. "I will ask Reep to look."

Santar looked at her. "Can Aunt do that? Inbetween?"

Ripple nodded. And yanked. Raft and Mrrinar were

there.

Raft blasted the air with unhappy witch and stuffed her blouse back into her trousers. Fastening it.

Three sisters cast protection. Sepanix leaped up, attack ready. Mantara grabbed Shitar by the shoulders and spun her away. Large ugly began to form behind Raft and Mrrinar, protecting them.

"DAUGHTERS!" commanded Ripple. "STOP!"

They did.

Ripple dropped into a chair by the table and snatched up a mug. "He is her's. He is a catfolk." She emptied the mug.

"On tik tik," hissed Shitar. "Aunt."

"Sister," said Ripple to Raft. "Someone took The Princess Lurin. Go to Reep and ask her to come quickly. Please?"

Raft nodded. "Ptar tak tak," she hissed at Shitar. "Niece." Then she kissed Mrrinar. "Stay here. I will be long not long."

She disappeared.

Ripple waved one hand at the cat-folk. "These are my daughters."

They popped in. "I felt you pull Raft." Ranna looked at the others, standing here and there.

"My daughters," repeated Ripple. "Aunt Ranna."

Daughters who had not met her introduced themselves. Ranna nodded at Ripple. Then said to the young witches, "Anjan and Adarlak." She paused. "Mine!"

"Females," gasped Sook.

"A mage," hissed Sepanix.

"Hum," said Shitar. "Were you Uncle touched?"

"What are you?" Santar looked at Anjan.

"Warrior," snapped Ranna. "Yes," she growled, "obvious

females. Hacto mage."

"Death Warrior Guild," added Anjan.

Sook crashed into her chair. "Muchly bothered."

Ripple looked at her oldest sister. "Princess Lurin has been taken. Raft fetches The Silent One."

Two daughters went still. They had only heard of this Aunt. And her daughter Szaifeh. Both had death stare.

"A mage," grumbled Sepanix.

Ripple wacked her shoulder with a bronze wand. "Cross-tied. First Vander. Now Hacto."

Adarlak's eyes flew wide. "Vander?" Something crackled.

Ranna grabbed her arm. "Calm."

"Long before before, Vander stole a Hacto warlock. The guild caught three Vander." She whispered, "And did things."

"They will do nothing," stated Ripple firmly. "You are cross-tied. Faan-Zwar-Tanpak-Vander-Hacto."

"Grenzanr," added Mantara, admiring his two sisters honorary.

Adarlak leaned against Ranna. "You told not."

"No need." She touched Adarlak's cheek. "The orange dot tells all."

"The Purple Ones never forget."

Ranna shrugged.

Ripple rapped on the tabletop with one pointed fingernail. "As soon as Reep locates the thing we will fetch The Princess back."

"And kill it," hissed Shitar. Nothing should survive that would dare do something like this. Especially to one that was Faan protected.

Anjan smiled at her.

Ripple ordered in food and drink.

Magevern. Deep Below the Surface.

Cazor ran down the hall and into the study. Sa'ar looked up from her work.

"Eulin is missing. Anamaxtor whirled in huffing fire."

Sa'ar jumped up. "How?"

Cazor shook her head. "Can't be Caedi."

Sa'ar headed for the doorway. "Fetch Andovar to the Soul Chamber. And Tobtz."

Halfway down the hall, she added, "Make sure Rorx gets here. I think we will need our warlock more than ever."

Dol Spar. An Office In Monetary Control.

Mirf beamed at her two clerks.

They winced.

Mirf looked at The General. "An almost matched pair. Rema must be the older."

She looked back at her clerks. "Soooooooo, kinder curves, you like working for me? Be honest." She jerked a thumb at The General. "He can reassign you just like that." Her fingers snapped, making a loud 'pop.'

Rema nudged Nema.

Nema nodded. "We do."

"It is interesting," added Rema.

Mirf sat and leaned back. "Kiddlelumps, today is the end of your probation period. Now, you either pass, or pass out onto the street." They blanched.

"All ready?" gasped Rema.

Mirf laughed. "With me the probation period is short.

Sooooo, you think a career with M.C., with me, is really for you?"

Nema nudged Rema. She said, "We do. Yes."

Mirf bounded to her feet and threw her arms wide. "Ta Dah! You passed. Go find Fred and Quan. I am hungry. I will buy whatever it is that we can find to eat."

They hurried away.

Mirf glanced at The General from the corners of her eyes. "So I cut a corner or two or three. Join us?"

He stood. "Back to paper shuffling. Keep me informed." He fished around in his pockets and gave her a pair of gleaming insignia. "For your clerks. They deserve it."

Grandeville. Tinker's Place. Warm and Sunny.

She carried a large tray down the rear deck and slid it onto one of the wooden tables. Pots, cups, cookies.

Tinker swung his feet over the edge of the hammock and looked at her. "How long?"

"Two of your years, Father." She handed him a cup and filled it.

"Everything go all right?"

She sat next to him. "Yes. By the time that Mother appeared we were almost at the end of Eulin's wander."

"Have a good time?"

She leaned against him. "Until the end it was dull, just wandering from elseplace to elseplace."

"Oh?"

"Yes. Eulin is now Dragon Master. Disamat Anig said that there were few and that they are widely scattered."

"Dragon Master," mumbled Tinker, working on fully

waking up, and wondering what his daughter had become.

Ran ran up, and sat next to him. She shot a quick glance at Smoke. Smoke pushed calm into him.

"Yes." Je'leel then told all of them that were now awake about the training on Lair By Lair, leaving out a few bits and pieces.

Doth Lamex. The Place of Healing and Relaxation.

The slender figure wearing the dark robe looked around the main gateway area and saw it.

The place where Sook had stepped into the inbetween.

Drifting silently, she followed.

And stepped out.

And fled.

Ebna Raint. Dim Afternoon.

She stomped back and forth, swearing and railing up at him. And described in vivid detail how she would slice his miserable self into small and smaller pieces and feed him to the kitchen beast.

The crumpled body of one of his Personal Guards lay in a heap, face down, down there, in the soft soil. The guard had been sent to take her weapon away. The guard's weapon lay on the stone pavement, some distance from the low wall he was peering over. She had hurtled it at him, almost striking his head off.

The Majitar stared down at her. He wondered why anyone would value a person like that. However, the return document was being prepared, aptly titled, "In Reward, In Return."

He jerked. And leaned back, just a little bit further. For just a flicker of a moment he thought that he had seen a dark shadow move down there. Then he hastily turned aside as the guard's helmet sailed upward and past his head.

Grandeville. Tinker's Place. Sunny and Warm.

Sha'gar dragged over a chair and sat facing him. "Mother searches. Someone stole The Princess."

"What?" His head jerked her way. And saw Chicken still lying face down on the deck near the pool, sound asleep.

"Not us," explained Sha'gar. "Princess Chicken's brother's daughter child Princess."

"Now what's going on?"

"I do not know. Aunt Raft came and Mother left, telling me."

"How about we don't think about doing anything until we hear something a little more concrete?"

She nodded.

He sighed. "I suppose that we will have to go out there?"

She shrugged.

Len Egat.

The Red Tower sat on the end of the brown-red ridge that was poking a rock finger out toward the open valley space far below. The mountains spread in either direction forming an absolute barrier along this edge of the far below valley.

The tower had been placed on the rock outcropping very deliberately.

He stood in front of one of the tall windows and looked outward. It was almost like flying. In all directions it appeared as if there was no support to this place. It was wonderful.

Spinning around, he walked over the unadorned floor to the bed. The body lay there, carefully asleep.

This would take careful thought. He had no idea of her skills. The Majitar had called them both treasures. He wiped his mouth with one sleeve. She was as beautiful as the Vander were told. A young woman. A young woman that had been traveling with a strange companion. A golden beast. With the grab he had seen it, a swift glance after they had gone their separate ways.

He gently touched her. "Luscious." And walked away.

Dol Spar.

They sat around the table that was now covered with the wreckage of the many part meal.

Mirf emptied her glass and ordered another. For everyone. And handed one of the insignia to each of her clerks. "Here bubelehs. Compliments of The General. He worries about my staff."

The clerks set the insignia inside the open spot inside the Monetary Control emblem on their tunics.

Mirf winked at them. "Any M.C. types that see those silver and green jewels will jump if you as much as suggest it."

She looked around the restaurant. It was the favorite spot for the M.C. types. And nodded at the third table over. "Rema, take a slow stroll past those guys over there, circle back, and watch their faces. You also, Nema. Take a watch."

Rema stood. And did as Mirf had suggested. And came back. And sat. "Their mouths fell open."

"Mirf." Nema looked over. "What do silver and green mean?" During training she didn't remember this color combination being mentioned.

"Silver is special as in Special Investigator. Green is general as in The General." Mirf shoved drinks at them. "So don't let it go to your heads."

Mirf popped the top button of her blouse loose. Her jacket already hung over the back of her chair. "So kinderleh, your total emblem tells one and all that choose to look, and how they couldn't is beyond me, Special Clerk, First Class. Senior Staff. The General's Staff. My staff. Makes you an elite. One of the few."

She laughed. "Like me." And waggled one arm. "And Fred and Quan." And nodded. "And others. Here and there."

Fander's Dan.

Pomon strode into the formal office and saluted smartly.

So did the three men with him.

Farth indicated that they should relax. And looked from face to face.

Stolid faces looked back. No expression faces, judging, waiting. Careful, impassive faces.

Pomon stepped to one side to announce them.

"Zadar Ran'l Zar, Raryl Team."

A heavy set man, thick in the middle, stepped forward and knelt on one knee. "We heard, we came."

"Welcome, Brother."

Zar rose and stepped back.

"M'Tadar Dar Dar M'da. Wing of N'Var."

A very tall man, the left side of his face warped and scarred, stepped forward and knelt on one knee. "We heard, we came," he rasped.

"Welcome, Brother."

M'da rose and stepped back.

"M'Tadar Az Zin, Wing of Pomar."

Zin stepped forward, his shoulders easily twice as wide as Farth's. And dropped to one knee and boomed in a basso window rattling voice, "We came, we heard."

"Welcome, Brother."

Zin lurched upright and stepped back.

Farth smiled at them, now that the formalities were over and done with. And waved one arm. "Food and drink next door. We can talk there, and I can explain this elseplace. Our home."

Grandeville. Tinker's Place. Night.

She drifted silently into the room, owl quiet, knelt next to the large bed set flush to the floor, and shook him.

"Ummmmm?"

And shook him again. "Mate'mer, wake up!"

"Huh?"

"Wake up."

"Timezit?" He looked over at his clock, glowing soft red digits in the night.

02:15.

It blinked.

02:16.

"Go away." He yanked the blanket back up.

She shook him again. "Wake up."

The other in the bed cast soft glow and mumbled, "Ptar tak."

"Pik tik im dit," snapped Sha'gar, giving him another hard shove.

"Magician coarse," grumbled Ran.

"All right," he said, awake enough to realize that there were two of them in here.

"Now what's going on?"

"Mother is injured. We must go."

"What?"

"Mother is injured," repeated Sha'gar. "We must go. To Bahn Duhr Tohr."

"O.K. We'll eat, get our gear together, and go." He yawned loudly and stared up at the ceiling.

Sha'gar sat back. "Chantal and Fair Morn prepare the meal now."

R-Bar hurried into the room. "Smoke and Chicken are packing everything not already packed."

He sat up. "You have any idea?" He thought that it was always something pulling them back out there.

"Nope." R-Bar shook her head. "Ripple didn't tell. Sha'gar felt it."

Bahn Duhr Tohr. The Quarters of the Royal Advisors.

They swirled in, into Ripple's rooms, into the main room, not bothering to announce themselves.

Ripple pointed. "In there."

R-Bar and Sha'gar hurried that way.

"What happened?" He looked at her and then at the others standing around. Raft, Mrrinar, Ranna, Anjan, Adarlak, and Rumtah.

"Reep was tracking that which took The Princess and got spell burned." Ripple shrugged. "She is mostly uninjured. She felt the twisted ward and fled."

"My Lord?"

"Let's go." Tinker followed Chicken as she hurried into the hall, headed for The Royal Chambers.

Chantal caught up with them. "Coming along."

They burst into the Royal Chambers. "Brother!" Chicken hugged Toucan, The King. "Most horrible."

"Indeed, Sister. We have gathered in the elite of all the armies in the realms. All the best of all the kingdoms. These soon will visit those villains."

The Queen stood. "Lord Tinker, will You and Your's join with Us in this battle?"

"Indeed." Chicken spun around and smiled at her. "Tis most true."

"Sure," he said.

A small figure ran into the chamber from the hall, gold armor glittering. "We came." Princess Nandau bowed to Tinker and looked at the rest.

The Sergeant of All Arms hurtled into the room. "Your Majesties, we are under siege!"

"What!" Tinker spun toward the Hephira Princess.

"What color?" demanded The Queen.

"Gold," stated The Sergeant of All Arms, staring at Princess Nandau.

Willawa, The Queen, frowned at him. "There is no kingdom whose house wears that color." Then she stared at the armor clad short person standing nearby. "Whose army is this?"

"It's mine," said Tinker, clearing his throat. "So to speak."

"Five units," stated Nandau.

"Highness?" Toucan looked at Tinker, a slight frown. forming above his eyebrows.

"Are they doing anything?" Tinker asked Princess Nandau.

"Tell your troops to calm down," he said to Willawa.

"They camp," stated Nandau.

"By the north wall." added The Sergeant of All Arms.

"My Helf is there," explained Nandau.

"Looks like we now have two armies." Tinker looked from Toucan to Willawa. "Anyone know what's going on?"

Toucan shook his head. "Nay. The dark sisters do search and seek."

"Better get your Generals in here." suggested Tinker. "They'll have to coordinate with the Hephira. And I will explain them to everyone at the same time."

Fandor's Dan.

They were walking back from the nearest ranger village. Arm in arm.

"You look very happy, Husband."

"Most true. It has been long and long since The Silver Rangers have gathered this way. All train and share. We are, once again, a force for good, a force to be reckoned with." He smiled at her. "It feels good to do this. And to be part of such."

Sedeem jerked to a halt and gasped.

"WIFE!"

"Husband, my mothers are greatly agitated. We have got to go to them. Now!"

She yanked him away.

Bahn Duhr Tohr. The Royal Central Room.

"Hi, Pop."

She smiled at him. "What's wrong with my Moms?" Then she looked at Princess Nandau. "Very pretty. Golden armor." She laughed. And laughed. "Oh, Daddie. A warrior? A short warrior?"

She hugged him. "Where did you find her?"

"No," he grumbled and held her out at arm's length. "Looking good." And released her. "This is the Princess Nandau, her Prince, Helf, is outside the city walls with their army. They are Hephira. Hi, Farth."

Farth bowed. "Mighty Lord. Is there some trouble here?"

Tinker dragged over a chair. "How about we all sit down and talk about it and about what we know."

Three Lords in armor burst into the room. "Majesties?" barked the one in front.

"Sit," ordered Toucan.

They did. And stared at this small person wearing golden armor. None of the known kingdoms wore that color. Their gaze shifted to stare at Farth. Nor bright polished silver.

Then they all discussed what little that they knew.

Sedeem went down the hall to talk with the rest of her mothers after giving Chicken and Chantal a hug.

Under Fanzle.

The awareness came to her and she stopped.

All around her were the remains of shattered structures. The inhabitants of the small village had tried to trap her. There was a fine trade in lovely young women. She had seemed to be exactly what that trade liked to trade.

Those still alive were fleeing the shambles in every direction open to hard running folk. Later they would argue and debate whose fault it was that this disaster had fallen upon them and who should have known better. Many would argue and debate about those things, those horrors, and wonder from where that terror had suddenly appeared.

Sgenn walked out of town looking neither right nor left. She had things to do.

Len Egat.

He fled.

And stood on a nearby peak and stared at the tower, his red tower. A patch on the wall was still melting and oozing downward.

He had gently woken her, ready to tell her how lovely she was, how badly she was desired.

She had stared at him as he had walked over to the large window, clearing his throat, preparing to say those things that would convince her that she should stay here. She had sat up, looked down at her open garment and looked back up at him, as he turned to begin his speech.

An orange dragon had suddenly appeared, orange and black with green splotching. It had spit at him. Acid.

So, now he stood, and stared at his tower and watched a piece of its outer wall slowly dissolving away.

He was confused. She was obviously Vander. So where did that ugly monster come from? He sat down to think. And tightened his hold on everything. She wasn't going to be able to go anywhere.

He hoped that the dragon didn't eat her. It would be such a waste. Then he wondered why the Majitar would keep such a beast in this tower.

Bahn Duhr Tohr. The Royal Quarters.

Sha'gar sat on the edge of the bed holding her mother's hand as R-Bar sat in a chair and whispered, "Sister?"

The large eyes stared at her. Deep pools of bottomless black. "I am well," soft shadows whispered to them. "That elseplace has twisted protection. Very powerful. But slow." Reep tightened her hand on her daughter's. "Calm, daughter, calm. I will explain."

Sha'gar nodded. R-Bar leaned close.

Reep carefully explained her search and the trace.

R-Bar grumbled at her as she finished. "Any arcana will cause this twist to attack?"

Reep nodded. "With many spells. It all felt very mage."

"Hum."

Sha'gar nodded.

"I saw a vast army, many protected as well."

R-Bar growled. The air darkened.

Sha'gar batted something away.

R-Bar stood and kissed her sister. "Rest. Heal."

Reep released her daughter's hand. "Princess Lurin is there. Elseplace Ebna Raint." She gave her careful directions.

The King read the label on the scroll, "In Reward, In Return." He handed the thing to the Queen. She unrolled it and rapidly read that which was written inside and looked up.

"Some person calling himself The Majitar is demanding a vast sum in exchange for Our Daughter. He warns us not to use magic as he is many guarded as is his personal army."

"What vast sum?" asked Toucan.

"Husband," replied Willawa. "He wants the grey jewels,

all the gems of that type in all of the Kingdoms."

Toucan frowned slightly. He had never heard of these things before. The Lords gasped.

"Grey jewels?" Tinker looked from face to face.

She nodded, stood, and began to pace back and forth.

"My Queen?" Toucan watched her walking back and forth. "What be these grey gems?"

She whirled around and walked back, to stand very close to him. "Our King, these gems are very rare and a closely guarded thing. They are placed double-guarded, deep in Our Treasure Vaults. And deep in the treasure vaults of all those that possess them." She dropped into a chair by the table and began to explain what these jewels were.

Grey gems were infrequently found. It was told, from far back and long before, that there lurks within each gem a latent power. What this power is, no one had ever been able to determine. But it was said in that long ago time, that a certain mage of great learning and many skills had tested one small gem with subtle arcana. And the power had flowed out around him.

And for one moment he had known. He smiled, a radiant smile that had permanently itched itself into the wall of the treasure vault. And then the power had eaten him. Alive.

Over the years others had tried but had never, ever, come close to understanding these strange jewels.

Willawa leaned back in her chair. "This Majitar person must know the secret else why ask for only them not vast golden treasure?"

"Why did he take your daughter?" Tinker sat next to her. "But not both. The Prince and The Princess? To make the bargain even more binding."

"Indeed, Highness, why not?" Toucan leaned on his forearms, now shoved onto the table top. "Why not?"

"Majesties," said Lord Zarh'n. "I will call the Men to arms and see to this Majitar!"

Willawa banged the flat of her hand on the table top. "We are to respond immediately. It will take a few days to organize the armies to travel to war."

"Tell him that the gems are on the way," said Tinker. "But that it will take a few days to gather in those from the outlying kingdoms." He reached out. *Everyone heard?*

Yes.

Chantal, ask Hanred to do a search on these gems. See why The Princess is the only one. She must have something to do with it other than just being a hostage.

Right. She hurried from the room.

"We will send a response this instance and a few of the gems." Willawa issued the necessary instructions to an orderly and sent him running

Magevern. Deep Below the Surface.

She stood. "I will go to Aunt's elseplace and ask for help."

Rorx stood and hugged her. "Be careful, something took Eulin inbetween."

Szaifeh nodded and kissed him. "I will not be long, husband." And disappeared.

He sat and looked at the others gathered around the table. "I can put a strong call on her dragon and layer harsh."

Cazor smiled, a warrior's smile. "We can all add harsh."

Sa'ar nodded. "But all Anamaxtor has to do is pop in, see her, and pop back. Then we will know the path."

Rorx looked at Tobtz. "Is the dragon healthy?"

"Yes. I will tell him in simple terms what we wish him to do." She stood and headed for the dragon's pen.

"We are decided," announced Sa'ar.

Cazor bowed her head. "The Heart controls The Body."

Sa'ar stood. "Come, Rorx. It is time to prepare." She held out her hand.

He stood and left with her.

As they left the chamber, violet mist flowed from her and wrapped them all in soft.

Dol Spar. An Office in Monetary Control.

Rema hurtled in and handed Mirf the folder. "Deep secure."

"Ho boy!" Mirf broke the many seals and opened the folder. "Such a nogoodnik this one must be." She waved her clerk to a chair. And after awhile, after almost destroying the folder as she pawed back and forth through it, she looked up.

"This guy is very dangerous. To everything." Her eyelids dropped halfway down. "Sooooooooo why was this person working for The Majitar? And what would The Majitar need this horror for?"

Nema zipped into the room and shoved a scroll at her. "Staff report. Urgent."

Mirf snatched it from her, eyes popping wide. "Raz baz!" She ripped it open. "Double ho boy! Double bad news. What could have stirred up that witch clan like that? And John and his bunch of bad news babes as well? Oh me, oh my. Send a note to our office staff on Bahn Duhr Tohr and one to that stiff neck on Fandor's Dan. We want to know what, if anything, is going on."

Nema ran out into the hall.

Mirf lurched up. "Let's take a walk, kiddie curves. I need to think." She stomped toward the outer door. Rema hurried after her.

Fred and Quan remained behind. Then they hurried down to the armory.

Len Egat.

He carefully, silently, eased the door open, tiny bit by tiny bit. Something inside the room flickered, a brief golden pulse.

He paused, not breathing, listening intently, every protection that he knew pulled into place. Hearing no sound, he pushed the door open just a little bit more. "Are you there? Alive?"

"Of course."

"Are you alone?"

"There is no person here other than myself."

He started to shove the door open. And caught himself "Are there any other living things in that room with you?"

She laughed.

He waited. Readied himself and shoved the door open.

She sat in one of the large chairs. It had been moved into a corner space. She watched him enter, close the door, and approach carefully.

"Release me!"

"I just received you." He smiled. "From The Majitar."

"What is that?"

"A not very clever person who strives high and thinks that he is very clever."

"This Majitar grabbed me?"

He shook his head. "I did. Under contract. Then I saw you." He wiped his mouth on his sleeve. "So I took you." He waved one hand. "And this tower as well."

He pointed at the soft edged hole in the wall that had been the window. "But I didn't realize that it was infested with dragons."

"It went away. Let me go."

"No. You are mine."

"I am not!"

"You should be."

"Get stuffed." Je'leel had told her about that statement. She had her heard Uncle J.C. use it.

"What?"

"Never mind."

He beckoned over a chair and sat, not too close to her. "Perhaps if I tell you what The Majitar is going to do to the other, you will be more appreciative."

He leaned forward and began to whisper the secret to her.

She screamed.

Magevern. Deep Below the Surface.

They were all gathered at the great table.

Anamaxtor sat next to Sa'ar, occupying several spaces.

She looked around the table. "Our Warlock sleeps still."

Imdar frowned at her. "You must also rest." It was a statement from The Healer to The Heart. It was a command.

Sa'ar nodded. "Soon."

Cazor stood. "We must test."

Zulan also stood. "No! I am the newest. My loss, if such should occur, will be the least damage to us."

"Sit," ordered Sa'ar. "Discuss."

The two sat And they all talked about the problem of testing the magical ward that the dragon had felt. And how to keep the one who tested it alive.

Bahn Duhr Tohr. The Royal Central Room.

They were gathered around the table and looking very, very unhappy. A group of very, very unhappy witches was a gathering to stay far, far way from and to worry much about if one could.

"Magic guarded?" Ripple crackled softly.

"Yes," sighed soft darkness. Reep sat with them, mostly healed. "A twisted ward, layers deep."

Sedeem sat up. "We have three armies."

"Couple of problems," said Tinker.

"What?" snapped Ripple.

"How do we get them there? How do we keep this Majitar from killing her while we try to find her in the midst of a great battle?"

"Tis conundrum, My Lord." Chicken laid a gentle hand on his forearm.

"Indeed, Highness." Toucan nodded.

"We can use a node," suggested Willawa.

"How big is it?" asked Chantal.

"Eight to twelve," replied Willawa.

"People? At a time?"

Willawa nodded.

"Not gonna work," grumbled Tinker.

"John," said Chantal softly.

"Ummm?"

"We could go and scout around, see if we can locate where she is being held. Then come back here."

He sighed. "I suppose we could do that." He looked around the table. "I doubt that those witch wards or whatever they are would work against guns or swords or Fair Morn's space cannon."

"Ready when your are, Gridley." Fair Morn smiled at him.

He nodded, slowly. "O.K., let's do it. No packs, no gear. We just get in, take a quick look, and try to find her. And we have to look as innocent as we can. That means that Ran, R-Bar, and Sha'gar do not try to do anything at all while we are there, nothing, not a thing!"

The trio nodded. They knew what would happen if they triggered those wards.

"Dad, take Farth with you."

Tinker shook his head. "Just us. Someone want to see us to this node thing?"

Willawa stood. "Follow me, Great Lord."

As they started for the door, he turned, waving everyone else to stay where they were.

"Give us a few days before trying anything else." He hurried after his group.

Dol Spar. Inside Monetary Control.

They were all back in her office. Fred, Quan, Nema, Rema. All the doors were closed and locked. Everything else was turned off.

"So," said Mirf. "We know where this skunk lives, so now we pay him a leetle visit."

Fred was wearing her travel cloak, only her upper arms poking out.

Quan had tucked his weapon into the small of his back, his jacket hanging loose, covering it.

Mirf shoved a long list at her clerks. "So keep the doors locked and run in and out a lot. Use this list to help keep yourselves looking busy."

She bounced out of her chair. "Shall we get this show on the road and see whether we are able to talk some sense into the senseless?"

The three of them headed for a side door.

Mirf waved at her clerks. "So make busy chickeepoos. If we don't return in a few, tell The General no fancy-schmancy service. He will understand."

She popped out the door followed by Fred and Quan.

Her clerks begun to run errands and tried not to look nervous or worried.

Len Egat.

"This Majitar must be stopped." She glared at him.

"How?"

"Release me. I will kill him."

He shook his head. "You can not. The ward protects against witch or magician."

She looked at him. "You could do it."

He shook his head again "I am magician. It works against all witches and all magicians. If any clan or guild attempts magic against the place, the ward reacts. And beyond that the Majitar has a magic'd army. He and his are well guarded, well protected."

"You are han kan," she hissed.

He smiled at her. "And you are beauty beyond beauty, Vander Princess. I saved you from horror torment. What is my reward?" His eyes wandered here and there, noting that she had unfastened her upper garment after having fastened it some time before. He wiped his mouth on his sleeve.

"You will not die."

He leaped to his feet and stalked to the door, the only door to this room. "I want you."

She watched him. He started to turn. She carefully watched him. "I choose," she snapped. "No one chooses for me."

"Eulin!" The woman gasped. And collapsed. And was gone.

He stared at the place on the floor where the body had been for just that brief instance. "Who was that? How did she escape? What else infects my tower?"

"Let me go!" she snapped.

He walked back, slid his hand over and around the collar of her upper garment, fingers gently stroking soft flesh, silken skin.

She grabbed his hand and bit him.

Screaming curse, he yanked his hand free. "Karpar Hag!"

"Let me go!"

He towered over her and glared down. "I will tie you up and do whatever I wish to do."

She glared back. "You will most certainly die if you do."

He jumped away and stomped around the room, checking here and there. "Why does it feel this way? We are alone."

The shadow dragon watched him from a dark corner of

the high ceiling as the mage circled the room and finally left, slamming the door loudly as he did.

Magevern. Deep Below the Surface.

Cazor scooped the limp form into her arms.

"Take her to Rorx's room," ordered Sa'ar. "Tobtz, Imdar, come with me. All the rest stay here."

The group hurried down the hall and turned into one of the bedrooms.

Sa'ar yanked the blankets away. "Szaifeh, we require his help. You have to leave this room."

Szaifeh rolled from the bed, dark witch garb clothing her she did. "He is not fully recovered from before."

"Zulan will die if we do nothing." Sa'ar nodded as Cazor gently laid her burden on the bed next to the sleeping man and dragged the covers over both.

Bowing deeply to Sa'ar, then to Szaifeh, Cazor left the room.

"Please, cousin?" asked Sa'ar.

Szaifeh nodded and left them.

"Imdar."

The Healer nodded and leaned over the pair and set to work. Then after not too long, she stepped back and shrugged. "She lives. A little." She walked from the room.

"Tobtz." The Soul of the Vander walked over to the bed, bent over and kissed him.

Rorx's eyes flew wide. Struggling wildly, he freed his arms from the blankets and wrapped them around Tobtz, crushing her against his chest. And in time released her.

"Very healthy," gasped Tobtz as she staggered for the

door.

"Warlock Rorx," commanded Sa'ar. "Zulan must be healed enough to tell us what she learned." Tears ran down her face. "We must know."

She touched Zulan's cheek and forehead and watched her eyes flutter open. Sa'ar spun on her heels and hurried from the room.

Ebna Raint. A Fine Day. Grey Lowering Clouds.

They stood, a small group dressed in long coats and over-coats of soft browns and blue.

The garments effectively hid the various weapons carried by those who carried weapons that were not magically driven.

He checked everyone and grumbled at her, "What are you doing here?"

Princess Nandau, wearing an earth brown robe, smiled at him. "I am your messenger. If the need does so arise. I shall run back and out and return with our army. We Hephira are quicker than most anything."

"Ummmmmm," he mumbled. "O.K., but you do whatever you are told to do."

"Certainly. I shall be one more female among the many, doing everything you wish me to do, My Lord and Master."

He sighed loudly. "I do not believe this. Less than one minute and she sounds as bad as the rest of you guys."

They stood at one dim corner of a large dim square surrounded by towering structures, all tones of grey upon grey. The heavy clouds kept the light soft.

"Smoke."

"We will have to wander about and see if I can touch her

mind."

He nodded. "All right. But remember, we are meek and mild folk. Especially two witches and one magician."

R-Bar grumbled.

Ran nodded.

Sha'gar stepped close. "We are not sharing with that Nandau."

He sighed and started down the street and headed them across the empty square. The rest spread out and followed. And after a little bit, he waved Fair Morn forward. "Mothra, that cannon ready to go?"

"Yep."

He stopped and waited for the rest to gather around. "We can't start anything until we find her. They might panic and kill her."

Everyone nodded.

"My Lord," said Chicken. "The King and The Queen do say they would send some few grey gems each day for to show good faith and for to make us as much time as possible."

"O.K. Let's assume that we have a day or two. Smoke, you lead, we follow." He winked at her.

She winked back. And did.

And they did.

Follow.

Chapter Seventeen

Endings. And Beginnings.

Len Egat.

"Griz, griz, griz," it laughed.

Dragons thought almost everything non-dragon was funny. The sinuous green was coiled around her chair, head resting on her lap, tongue tickling her arm.

"Take me from here." She scratched it under the chin. Then along the crest running from its head down its back. The bright green skin rippled.

"You are trapped here by twisted magic. Only the one who cast it knows how to untwine it. Griz, griz. Or someone even more clever than the designer. Or someone outside of everything."

"Unless he dies," she suggested.

The sinuous green smiled. "May I have the body?"

"Kill him."

The head reared up on the long neck, the emerald eyes stared into her's. "You know we do not do things like that. Unless he attacks you. Or us. Or means harm. To you or to us. That acid spitter was really very bad mannered and rather uncouth as well. Of course, she didn't hit him. So I suppose we could consider what she did as a warning."

She nodded. "I do not think that he will attack me. Or means bodily harm. To any of you or to me."

"Then you are trapped. Griz, griz, griz."

Magevern. Deep Below the Surface.

They helped her walk into the meeting room. Rorx on one side, Szaifeh on the other.

Tobtz jumped up and pulled out Zulan's chair and watched her carefully as she sat down, slumping to one side.

"We are going to Doth Lamex." Szaifeh yanked Rorx away.

Sa'ar looked around the table. "Our Warlock is badly drained." And then at Zulan. "Almost, sister. Almost near far."

Zulan looked back, moving only her eyes. "Yes," she whispered. "But I saw her. And him." She coughed.

Imdar hurried over and handed her a cup. "Drink." Standing behind Zulan's chair, hands resting lightly on her shoulders, The Healer looked at the rest of them, ending at Sa'ar. "We may not enter that elseplace. Only the call back and our protections, many layered deep, saved her. Barely."

Tears ran down Imdar's checks. "This brave one will be a long time healing."

Cazor leaped up and then dropped back into her chair. "There must be some way." She looked at Elend. "Something in the archives?"

Elend shook her head. "I do not remember anything like that in there. But I will search again." She stood.

"SIT!" commanded Sa'ar.

Elend did. So did Imdar.

"What?" asked Tobtz.

"We require help that is neither witch nor magician."

"Sorcerers are myth, although the Divineal seem to think that they are really witch of some sort. And demons wouldn't cooperate with us," stated Moonda.

"Who can we ask like that?" Aada patted Cazor's arm.

"The Chosen One," stated Sa'ar. "He is neither witch nor magician. The Vander Lord and his are mostly not-witch and not-magician. I think that he could rescue our daughter Heart."

Bant sat straighter. "Would he do this?"

Moonda looked at Sa'ar.

Sa'ar looked back. "Eulin is his daughter as well." She nodded. "I think so."

Aada stood and smiled. "I will travel there and ask." She faded away, humming quietly to herself.

Tobtz nudged Imdar. "She is not going to get what she wants."

Imdar smiled. "I think that she knows that."

Sa'ar rapped the table with one knuckle. "Zulan, tell us what you saw and what happened."

Zulan began her story.

Ebna Raint. A Beautiful Grey Day.

The Majitar gave his charm weaver one controlled small nod. "The grey gems are being delivered in small packets."

The charm weaver made an even smaller and more controlled nod. "We have enough of them now. We should take the bait to the crucible now."

"NO! We have only one chance. The second offering was taken from us. If she is used and the amount of grey gems is insufficient we will lose all our investment. We will wait."

The charm weaver stood. "It will be so." He turned and left the room.

Len Egat.

Release me."

"No."

She glared at him. "You will never have what you wish. I do not like you."

He sat across from her and leaned forward. "You do not know me."

"I know that you brought me here."

"I saved you from horror."

"I know that you gave The Majitar the power to do that. And protection."

He leaned back, elbows on the arm rests of his chair, hands held together, just in front of his mouth. "I was hired."

She mimicked his gesture. "Evil ugly may be refused."

"It is how I found you. And how I saved you."

"Because you grabbed me for The Majitar first," she snarled, all angry fury. "Go away."

He slumped, just a little. "You are beautiful."

She sat up. "You are not. Let me go. You may visit if you so desire."

He stood. "Vander sneaky. That guild would try to kill me on sight."

"No. I will guarantee it. If you release me."

He stepped close and lightly touched her garment. "You are just a young woman."

She slapped his hand. "I am Eulin, future Heart of the Vander!"

He reached, fingers digging into her neck opening and yanked, ripping the upper garment open, off her shoulders, and leaped back as she tried to bite him.

"Smooth skin. Beautiful skin."

His head jerked. He stared at dark shadow. "I saw something."

She surged to her feet, stomped over to him, and slapped his face, rocking his head to one side. "You almost saw death!" And kicked him in the shin. And jumped back.

Gasping, snarling, wobbling backward, he snarled, "You are witch nasty."

"I want to go home."

"NEVER!" He slammed the door shut as he thundered from the room, and stomped down the hall. He would search his books, find the want spell, and put it on her. And wondered what she had meant by that comment about death. He was safe here.

Ebna Raint. Grey Clouds Hanging Low. Another Nice Day.

They stood and peered over the low wall.

It was a large open plaza set into the side of the steep hill, just below an immense building of dark stone, more black than grey. The pit they stared into was large. And deep. Smooth walled.

Smoke stood behind him, arms wrapped around his chest. "Steady, steady," she murmured as she pushed calm into him. And held him tight.

"That her? Down there?"

Chicken stood close by his side. Chantal pressed against his other side.

Down there the figure sat slumped against one of the walls, apparently sleeping. The white armor was mud splattered and stained. Several bodies lay down there as well. In tumbled heaps.

Even from up here they could smell the odor of decay.

"That her?"

Smoke blew warm air against the back of his neck. "I think so, MindMate. But she sleeps deep."

"We can't climb down there. We'd never get out."

"Bet I could lift her out." Fair Morn leaned over the railing and looked down, measuring the distance.

He frowned. "It is too far to reach the top of the walls."

"Flap, flap, flap," she said.

"Oh. Think that you could?"

"Worth a try."

"CLEAR OUT! CLEAR OUT!"

They all spun around.

Smoke, Chicken, and Chantal stepped away, giving him room.

The speaker was one of the guards. A big, burly guard.

"CLEAR OUT!" he bellowed.

"Not supposed to be here, huh?" Tinker tried to look as puzzled as he was able. "Who is that down there?"

The guard stepped close. "Leave or die."

"We are leaving," said Tinker.

"Step closer, big boy." Fair Morn leaned against the wall and smiled at the guard.

He did.

Smoke grabbed one arm, Fair Morn the other. They yanked. And he flew up and over the low railing and into the pit.

The dull thud woke the sleeping figure, who surged to her feet, back scraping against the wall. Then she charged, the great sword swinging.

"Holy Cow!" he gasped, staring down.

The white clad figure wiped her sword on the guard's pant leg and looked up at them and screamed, "DAH'N DEMON SPAWN!"

Whirling around she hurtled her missile at them. The object bounced across the plaza, helmet thumbling one way, the contents of the helmet another.

Tinker jerked back. "Smoke, put her to sleep. We can't risk her attacking Fair Morn."

Smoke nodded.

Fair Morn unfolded and unfolded and unfolded her great butterfly wings. She lifted into the air and sailed down in a tight spiral to the spongy ground below. Landing lightly next to the crumpled figure in white, she scooped her into her arms and looked up. *Not too heavy. I hope. But really filthy.*

"Come on, come on," he mumbled. *Hurry up.*

Great wings pumping, Fair Morn lurched into the air, wobbling violently from side to side. *UGH!*

As soon as she was close enough, arms grabbed her and dragged her and her cargo over the lip of the low wall to crash in a heap on the pavement.

Chantal and Sha'gar grabbed Fair Morn and dragged her free and helped her stand. She began fold and fold and fold her wings. "Ouch, ouch, ouch!"

"What?" He stepped close.

Chicken and Messenger rolled Lurin onto her back.

"I think that I pulled my flight muscles." She blinked back tears.

He hugged her. And kissed her. "We can soak in the hot tub for as long as you want." He gave her a friendly pat. "Good job, Big Bug."

Smoke allowed Lurin to slowly come wake while Chicken knelt next to her, shoved the visor on the Princess' helmet up, and smiled as she saw her eyes open. "Fair Princess, we have from most foul a'pit freed thee."

Lurin blinked at her. "Father's Sister?"

Chicken smiled. "Indeed."

Smoke removed all the sleep. And nodded at Chicken. She and Messenger helped Lurin stand.

Tinker yanked off his robe and tossed it to Lurin. "Put this on, quickly. That white armor is a dead giveaway."

As soon as she did, they hurried down the zig-zag road, back toward the node.

And were intercepted by a portion of the Army of The Majitar.

Bahn Duhr Tohr. The Quarters of the Royal Advisors.

He leaned from the doorway, dust billowing around his feet. A dark smudge ran across his face. "Wife," he barked. "In here." And jerked back.

Witches sucked in their breath. No-one dared to address a witch that way. Especially Ripple, who was known to be even more short-tempered and dangerous than most.

She stomped across the room, the air crackling and popping around her. And into the room. The door slammed itself shut behind her.

Hanred grabbed her by the arm and pulled her over to one of the many open books and jabbed a nervous finger at one heavily illuminated page. "Read that . . . abomination." He stared at her from red-rimmed eyes, deep lines of fatigue etched across his face.

"I think that it explains the grey gems, And what that Majitar person intends to do with them."

Casting protection on, she stepped away and began to carefully read what was inscribed so boldly on the page. When she finished, she blinked, and turned slowly toward him. "Did you read this?"

Hanred shook his head. "Only the first bit. Just enough to know." He sagged dangerously to one side. "Was I correct?"

She stepped close and gently wrapped her arms around him. "Clever mate, you are, you are. Merely to read all that page in its entirety unprotected would have killed you. Come. First we shall bathe, then we will go to bed. I will send Rumtah in. She will explain it to others."

Holding his arm, she gently led him from the room as the door swung itself open. Then through the main room and into the tub room, all her attention focused on her mate-for-life, who was sagging more and more.

Not a witch dared say a word, not a single word, as the pair passed by. Once in the tub, arms wrapped around him, she summoned Rumtah and told her what to do.

Len Egat.

He had created a great and very festive meal and had shared it with her. But in spite of all his efforts, it was a meal eaten in silence as she refused to talk to him, even to ask for something to be passed her way. But he had enjoyed it, none-the-less.

The soft lighting had added to her beauty. Now he sat, relaxed, sipping from his ornate cup. He raised it in her direction. "Willing, or not willing, you are mine. Now."

He cast the carefully crafted want spell.

She smiled at him.

He nodded. At last.

She slowly licked her lips and leaned forward, and murmured softly, "We, the Purple Magicians, the Vanderlaine Guild of the Order Fanderlaine, have taken the love, want, desire spells beyond beyond. I am trained in our entire history and all our spell lore. I am the first of the new Vander to do so."

She thrust her hand at him, opened a tight fist, and rolled a sputtering ball across the table toward him. It scorched a trail into the polished wood. "Here is your feeble spell."

He batted the ball away and out.

Then he stomped from the room.

Grandeville. Tinker's Place. Early Evening.

They were lounging on the rear deck, in some of the more comfortable chairs, taking life easy, talking mother to daughter.

Dat was dressed as she preferred to dress. She was wearing mist fog soft billowing trousers, and nothing else. It was standard garb for an indjinn. She had convinced Je'leel to dress the same way as they were the only ones home and there was no-one to grumble and complain about it. Like a Great Master.

Je'leel had prepared their meal. They had eaten it out here, on the rear deck. Je'leel, being partially human, had gotten hungry. Dat, being all indjinn, had eaten just to be sociable.

She didn't have to eat at all.

"Did you enjoy traveling with your sister?"

Je'leel shook her head. "Not really. She is nice. But the traveling aspect was not very interesting. For me. Eulin was excited about most of it. She said that she had learned many new things, especially when she finally got to meet and study with the Dragon Master."

"But you didn't? Enjoy it?"

Je'leel shook her head. "The dragons are nice folk. But they are rather narrow in outlook."

Dat smiled. "Dragons are that way."

The woman appeared, stepping out of a violet haze. And smiled warmly at them. "Very pretty." She sat next to Je'leel, eyes wandering over her bare torso.

"Hello, Aada."

"I wish to speak to The Vander Lord, your Father."

"They are gone."

"To?"

"Bahn Duhr Tohr. Visiting the witches."

"We require his help. To rescue Eulin."

Dat sat up. "Rescue?"

Aada nodded. "Yes. She was taken to a place that we may not enter. It is twisted protected. Zulan near went far checking it for us." Then she explained all that they had learned.

Je'leel looked at her mother. "Isn't there anything, something, that we could do?"

"My Great Master, your father, would be very, very angry if he thought that I put you in the way of some harm."

Je'leel looked at Aada. "If we go, you must promise to never ever tell him. Never!"

"Vander oath," promised Aada, grabbing Je'leel and kissing her. "Vander debt."

Dat stood and tapped her daughter on the shoulder. "You must dress Grandeville proper first."

"Yes, Mother." She pulled from Aada's arms and hurried into the house.

Aada smiled at Dat. "She could join our guild."

Dat shook her head. "He would not like that."

Aada bowed her head, acknowledging The Vander Lord's wish. "To hear is to obey." She told Dat exactly how to find the elseplace, Len Egat. And reemphasized why they, The Vander, could not enter that place.

Ebna Raint. A Fine Day. Turning Rainy and Dark.

"Certainly a lot of them."

He swung the great black sword down off his back and waved them to stand clear. "All right, get back, and stay out of trouble." This comment was aimed at the three magic users. He stepped forward. "What do you guys want?"

"Strangers are not allowed in this part of the city."

"O.K., O.K. We are going home anyway."Tinker laughed. "Nice place to visit but I wouldn't want to live here."

Chicken stepped to his clear side, blade swishing back and forth as she warmed up. "Whish, My Lord, tis nay time for to be a'jesting."

He turned and spoke soft and low to Nandau. "If this turns into a brawl, do you think that you will be able to get back to the node?"

She stepped close, stood on her tip-toes, and kissed him. "I will bring our army." She slipped to the rear and to the right hand side.

"None may leave," bellowed the front soldier.

He turned back and nodded at Fair Morn. "Take out a bunch and let's see what they do."

She nodded and swung her space cannon up. The central portion of the mass facing them disappeared. No sound. They were just gone. The rest attacked.

"RUN!" Tinker, followed by the rest, hurtled into a very small alleyway. And whirled around to face the mob pressing in after them, their numbers jammed tightly by the very narrow space.

Bahn Duhr Tohr. The Quarters of the Royal Advisors.

She was suddenly there, handed in by something all black angles and strange joints.

Witches hissed and snarled, hastily leaping away.

She looked at the slight figure sitting so still at the table, watching her. "Hayou, Mother. I felt. Who would dare?" She nodded at the rest. "Hayou, Aunts, Cousins." Then she sat next to Reep.

"Strong daughter." Reep kissed Sgenn on the forehead. And then explained what had happened. Everything that she knew and had seen.

Nandau burst into the room, sweat pouring down her face.

Len Egat.

"Hello, sister."

Eulin jumped up and hugged her. "Did that zak dak drag you here also?" Something squeaked.

Eulin jumped back and stared at Je'leel. "What was that?"

Je'leel pulled the front of her shirt forward. "Mother. She is small and, ummmmmm, hiding in there."

A small arm shoved out from between the two buttons and waggled at Eulin, and then pulled back inside.

Eulin smiled. Then she frowned. "Why are you here?"

"We came to get you. Mother thinks that it will be no problem for her at all."

Je'leel looked very firm and stern at her sister. "But you must promise to never, ever, tell Father how you escaped. Mother thinks that he would get upset and very, very unhappy if he knew that I came along."

"Vander oath, sister, Vander oath. Do you think she can really do that?"

"Who are you?" he demanded, stomping into the room. He had heard their voices from far down the hall. "How did you get in here? Are you also part of the things that infest my tower?" He smiled at her. "It was a payment of a sort, this tower."

Je'leel looked at him and frowned. "Who are you?"

He glared at her, and waved one arm. "This is my tower, taken fair and square from the Majitar." He mumbled to himself, "I shall certainly have to speak to that Majitar about what he leaves laying around in his towers."

Then he refocused his attention on Je'leel. "Very pretty. You may stay."

She slipped an arm around Eulin's waist and shook her head. "We are leaving."

Waving over a chair, he dropped into it, and smiled at them. "No one leaves, no one enters. Unless I desire it."

"Not true," replied Je'leel. She nudged her sister. "Ready?"

"Yes."

"Mother," said Je'leel.

He stared around the room. "Mother? Something else lives in here?"

Something began to tear.

Something began to rip.

Screaming loudly as it came apart.

They were gone.

The spell shock of rupturing magic blew him and his chair across the unadorned floor, tumbling over the plain wood.

He was lucky.

The chair was not. It sailed through the soft edged hole in the wall and out into vast open space.

He merely crashed into the hard stone next to the opening.

Ebna Raint. A Fine Day. Drizzle and Heavy Clouds.

Battle cries sounded in the far distance from somewhere behind the troops. Commands and counter commands brought disorder to the attack.

Nandau ran up the alleyway from somewhere behind Tinker's group, golden armor glittering in the soft light. "Great Lord Tinker, Our Army and my Helf, attack your foes."

"What?"

She stood on tiptoes and kissed him. '"Five units. And the combined Army of Bahn Duhr Tohr. And the Silver Rangers."

She stepped back and waved her golden sword. "This foul kingdom will be taken shortly."

Lurin banged up her visor. "I want that Majitar for myself. Who are you? And what are Silver Rangers?"

"How did they get here?" Tinker frowned at the Hephira.

"My Lord," gasped Chicken. She pointed at their attackers. "They do flee."

She was handed up. Two witches and one magician hissed and growled loudly.

"Hayou, Aunts," she said. She grabbed and hugged Sha'gar. "Hayou, sister."

"Sgenn?" asked the startled magician. "Sister?"

"Yes."

"Muchly changed."

"I have traveled everywhere and then some and studied hard and long and much."

Sgenn released her sister and turned to face the others. "The wards on and in this elseplace are about to die."

Angry sang across the sky.

Things crackled and popped.

R-Bar reached out and yanked in a gleaming silver wand. Her eyes glittered. "They are gone."

Sgenn nodded. "I had the armies brought. Mother told me the find." She looked from face to face. "All look well enough."

R-Bar looked at Ran. Ran nodded. R-Bar hacked a vicious slash through the air with her wand. And there he was.

"Majitar!" bellowed Lurin, leaping toward him, great white sword swinging high.

Smoke bowled her over. "We need him alive." She helped the startled princess to her feet.

"To retrieve the grey gems," explained R-Bar, stepping

over to the Majitar.

"They are mine," he stated. "You can not touch me, I am many protected again witch and mage."

Sgenn stepped over and peered at him over the top of her Aunt's head. "I am neither witch nor magician," she said calmly, a small half-smile forming. "Shall I have something touch you?"

"What are you?"

"That which you ought listen to."

Something dark flowed up from the deep down below, all odd angles and strange joints. It stared at the Majilar and licked its lips.

"I am protected. Paid contract."

Sgenn stepped around R-Bar and over to him. The thing followed. R-Bar leaped away, hissing loudly at it. She was ignored.

"I had your contract nullified," said Sgenn. "I had your wards killed. I had great armies brought here to destroy your army. Even now the survivors are being chased into hiding."

She nodded and it jerked forward and touched the Majitar with one glowing claw.

The Majitar crashed backward to sprawl on the rock pavement, screaming as fire burst from his cheek.

"See," purred Sgenn. "You have been touched." She took a step toward him and looked down.

"STAY AWAY!"

"I want all those gems, Majitar. The next touch will not be so gentle."

"They are guarded deep."

Sgenn shrugged. The thing slipped past her and lifted the Majitar to his feet. Glowing silver eyes stared at him.

"Tell my . . . friend where this guarded deep is." She slipped her arms into her sleeves. "Hurry. It is hungry."

The Majitar did. His feet touched the pavement as the thing sank downward.

Two figures on large beasts came clattering over the pavement toward them from the mouth of the narrow alleyway.

They were followed by a large number of warriors.

Lurin looked and sank to one knee.

Willawa sprang from her beast and ran over, dropping to the pavement next to her daughter, and hugged her. Their armor clanged loudly.

Toucan dismounted and strode over, leading their beasts. "Daughter, thee did have Us muchly worried. Your brother leads a section of our army." He pointed at the town.

The pair stood.

"Father King," she said. "This Great Lord did Us free from most foul a pit."

"Actually," explained Tinker, banging Toucan on one armored shoulder. "Fair Morn did it." He jerked a thumb over his shoulder. "That's the Majitar. Sgenn sent something to gather up the grey gems."

Farth and Sedeem jogged up. "Hi Pop!" She smiled happily at them.

Farth bowed. His Silver armor was gore drenched. "Great Lords, that army is no more."

Helf ran up to them from somewhere and threw an arm around Nandau. His golden armor was badly stained and damaged. A bloody gash ran across his face. "Lost many. But we are victorious. Many are injured, some most badly."

R-Bar pulled Ran and Sha'gar aside. Then after some

conversation, they cast healing ever outward, pouring over the victorious and vanquished alike.

It surged to the surface. Swords whipped from scabbards. Sedeem yanked in her personal wand.

"That belongs to me," said Sgenn calmly. The thing clumped over to her and handed over a large sack. And faded into the deep down below. She opened the sack and peered inside. "These should be destroyed."

"We do agree," said Willawa.

"Indeed," added Toucan.

An arm reached up, took the sack, and yanked it deep somewhere.

With a loud sigh, Sgenn tilted heavily to one side, crashing into Tinker. He threw his arms around her, his sword singing wildly. People leaped back from that lethal thing. "What's the matter? Are you injured?"

She managed a small half-smile. "You are the only male that has ever dared to hold me." And mumbled, "Tired. Very tired."

She pulled from his arms and wobbled over to Sha'gar. "Very tired, sister."

"Let's go," he said to R-Bar.

Magevern. Deep Below the Surface.

She was home.

And they were there.

In the middle of the common room, they appeared.

Eulin.

Je'leel.

Dat, who was large.

The Vander crowded around, hugging and kissing Eulin and Je'leel.

Cazor ran down the hall to tell Sa'ar, Rorx, and Zulan.

"This is my mother," said Je'leel. "She freed my sister from that mage tower."

"How?" asked Tobtz, eyes wandering over Dat's bare torso. "Very nice."

"Of course," agreed Dat. Everyone knew that indjinns were beautiful. And very nice as well. "It was easy."

"She is an indjinn," explained Je'leel. "You all must promise to never tell Father how this was done. Ever!"

"Vader Oath." Tobtz kissed Dat thank you. "Vander debt."

Andovar, the Farseer, hugged Je'leel. "You may ask of us anything, sister of Eulin, sister of us all."

Suddenly the Vander made space as Sa'ar strode into the room followed by Cazor.

Eulin bowed her head. "To hear is to obey, Our Heart." She looked up. "Mother."

Sa'ar wrapped her daughter in her arms. And wept silently. "We were afraid that you were lost to us forever."

Rorx walked in, one arm around the still very wobbly Zulan, Szaifeh on her other side.

"Welcome home, sister." He released Zulan and hugged Eulin and then Je'leel. "Many thanks, sister."

She kissed him. "Mother did it." She looked around for Dat.

Dat was unfastening Bant's upper garment and running her hands over her. "Does your guild have indjinn influence?"

Bant smiled at her. "No. Elend, the archivist, has found

nothing in our records of such a nature."

"Mother!" snapped Je'leel.

Dat smiled at her daughter. "I think that an indjinn started this guild."

"If Father were here, she would be banished to her ring." Je'leel hugged Rorx one more time and stepped away. "Mother, I think that we should return home before Father and the Mothers do and find us gone."

Eulin wrapped her arms around her sister. "I will visit soon." She stepped away.

Dat released Bant and smiled at her daughter.

She and Je'leel went home.

Sa'ar sat and beckoned Eulin to sit next to her. "Now, tell us everything you know about this strange mage."

Bahn Duhr Tohr. The Royal City.

They had rested for a few days and had then journeyed to the port town of Trahn Bahn Hahn.

Now all were gathered on the waterfront at one of the large piers where three vessels made ready to sail. All personnel and supplies were aboard except for the leaders of this expedition. They were in the process of saying their goodbyes.

Frinda, The Prince, smiled happily and thumped his Father on the back. "We have all that we require. This will be ever so much more interesting than doing a Quest."

Lurin, the Princess, hugged her Mother. "We are well outfitted and My Ship's Master is agreed that this is the best time to sail." She kissed Willawa on the cheek. "We will have all the time we require to rest out there." She smiled. "We may return, Queen of a new land."

Sook stood near Ripple. "I am now her advisor as you are to her parents."

"Hum," said Ripple.

Sook shook her head. "He is handsome but will require a Princess Queen. I will find mine elseplace."

Santar, Sepanix, and Sgenn said their goodbyes. Santar swirled her sister and cousin out, looking very determined about something.

Soon, the ships sailed away.

When the small fleet had dwindled to dots on the horizon, Tinker looked around and said to their hosts, "It is time for us to go as well. Thanks for everything."

Everyone said goodbye to everyone else, and the two parties went on their respective ways to their homes.

Grandeville. Tinker's Place.

They clumped down onto the rear deck.

Dat hastily clothed herself and Je'leel.

Tinker spun around and smiled at them. "We're home. Things pretty quiet around here?"

"Very quiet, Great Master."

"Welcome home, Father, Mothers." Je'leel stood and helped them remove their gear and went with them to help put away things.

Chantal started the coffee makers in the kitchen and hugged Je'leel who had come in to help her. "Everything went smoother that we thought that it would. Were we gone long?"

"Four days here."

"Not too bad." Chantal looked at the kitchen clock. "Nobody's hungry. You have breakfast?"

"Yes."

"Good." Chantal opened a cabinet door and fished a large ornate ring from a small bowl and slipped it on her finger. "Heh heh heh heh heh, as the saying goes. Think that I'll go loaf on the rear deck. And a certain fella that we all know."

"I will bring the pots. You go ahead."

Chantal winked at her and left.

Soon all were lounging on the rear deck.

Chantal had talked him into joining her in the hammock.

It hadn't required much discussion.

Dol Spar. A Large Office in Monetary Control.

Rema ran into the office and handed Mirf a note.

Actually, she shoved it at Mirf. "Mirf!"

Then she straightened up and saluted The General. He had been sitting, his chair tilted back against the wall, talking with Mirf.

Mirf had been grumbling because he had intercepted them as they had been hurrying down the street. And had ordered them back to headquarters.

Mirf snatched the note from her clerk's hand and read it. "Well, well, well, one less nogoodnik dummkopf." She looked up, eyes glittering. "Can't say that I didn't try, ONCE, to tell him." She nodded at The General. "That Majitar is kaputsky. Some very angry individuals visited him shortly after his armies were decimated. Bet he lost more than one-tenth." She shrugged. "Too literate a pun?"

She waved Rema to a chair. "Be a long time before we need an office in that elseplace. Wonder if we will ever find out what he was up to?"

Nema rushed in and handed another note at Mirf. "Mirf!"

"Ho boy!" She grabbed it and read it. And looked around the room. "So vat else do we have on theurgist? She didn't tell me much! It was two witches and one theurgist that visited the late but not great Majitar."

She winked at her clerks. "So do a find or two, you two. I want to know." And winked at The General as the two clerks hurried from the room. "Best clerks that I have ever had."

"Who were they?" asked The General.

"Three terrors from that Faan clan. I told that thick-skulled Majitar that he didn't want to agitate that bunch."

She threw her arms wide. "So ignorance is its own reward."

The General stood. "Take a vacation. Take your crew with you."

"Good idea. Glad that I thought of it." Mirf slammed her hand on her desk top. "Everyone get in here now," she bellowed at it as she jumped to her feet. "I'll do it. We'll do it. And do I know a good elseplace or do I know a good elseplace?"

The General left as Fred, Quan, and the two clerks hurried in.

"Vacation time," announced Mirf. "So don't just stand there gawking at me. Let's get this show on the road."

Grandeville. Tinker's Place.

It was mid-morning and all had finally risen, had breakfast, and were all over the large living room. They were going through four days of newspapers and the accumulated mail.

They were also petting the cats and eyeing Tinker.

Chantal had two new issues of her professional journals to look through. She was reading one and leaning against him.

Sha'gar leaned against his other side and scratched the large black male under the chin. His eyes were crossed in happy cat bliss. He purred loudly.

The front door flew open.

"Hello, hello, hello! Guess who came to visit?"

"Well, it was quiet," mumbled Tinker.

Chicken jumped up, grinning broadly. "We will Ourself make more coffee."

Mirf grabbed a chair and dragged it over to sit near Tinker. "So you know almost everyone. My clerks, Rema and Nema. One you met already."

"What's up, Mirf?"

"Vacation time. You have room?"

"Sure."

"Vunderbar." Mirf shrugged off her jacket and popped the top button of her shirt open. "Might as well get comfortable." And leered at him just for fun.

Smoke rolled to her feet and beckoned the clerks and Fred and Quan to follow. "I will show you which rooms you can use."

Outside the house, the air sizzled, something exploded, and someone screamed.

"HO BOY!" said Mirf. "And we came here to relax."

R-Bar cackled. Ran nodded.

"What was that?" snapped Tinker.

"Spell ward," explained R-Bar. "Something tried to enter," explained Ran.

"Not on the list," added R-Bar, nodding at Mirf.

Fair Morn walked in from the dining room, coming from

the kitchen, and handed Mirf a cup. "Keeps unwanted visitors away."

"The magical kind," added Sha'gar. "Witches, magicians, demons. We are trying to figure a ward for other folk."

"Pretty bad coincidence." He glowered at Mirf.

"Not me, bubee. I am on vacation." She stood. "Let's go outside, admire the view." She winked at him. "I will admire the view. You can admire me and my clerks, especially my clerks. They will appreciate it." She headed for the rear deck.

So they all went out to the rear deck carrying cups and coffee pots and cats.

Magevern. Deep Below the Surface.

It was after last meal and all were relaxing in the large common space. Much time had passed since the rescue of Eulin.

Zulan, now mostly recovered, was talking with Eulin.

Elend, the archivist, was softly discussing with Sa'ar some ancient document that she had found packed away in a far closet with bundles of other documents.

"So," asked Sa'ar, "what have we done?" She indicated her daughter.

"Nothing harmful," replied Elend. "She will have to find her limits on her own."

"Are there limits?"

"We have no way of knowing or finding out." Elend waved the hand holding the document. "All we have are small pieces. The Dragon Master probably knows but I doubt that she would tell us or would summon."

"She grew."

"Beautiful," breathed Elend.

He appeared right in the middle of the common space. A great angry welt ripped across his left cheek. His garment on that side was torn and shredded down to his hip, a continuation of what had happened to his face.

Looking around the room, he nodded. "Just as I was always told." After checking each face, he stared at Eulin. "Ah, there you are." He smiled. "Something destroyed The Majitar and all his. Before I could. And whoever that meddler was, they are well protected. Very well protected." His hands gently touched his cheek and fluttered over the wreckage of his clothing. "Very well protected. Never ran into anything like that before."

Eulin slowly stood and frowned at him, her fingers making small signs, telling the rest to do nothing. "YOU!"

He bowed.

"Go away."

"You are mine. Time to return. Then you can tell me how you managed that escape."

"Leave!" It was a command, not a request. The Vander heard the voice of the Future Heart crackle through that order.

Rorx slipped into the room, Szaifeh at his side. The air billowed black around them.

The man looked over. "A mage? With a witch? Here?"

"I am Vander," stated Rorx. "You heard the command. Leave!"

"Mother," said Eulin, turning. "This is the thing that took me and the Princess Lurin to that Majitar creature."

"Shall I kill him?" asked Szaifeh.

Sa'ar shook her head and whispered to Eulin, "He is your's." She smiled.

"To hear is to obey," she whispered back. She turned to their visitor. "You are not welcome here. Not by any of us, especially by me. Leave now or die."

He looked around the room. "All this purple." And stared at Szaifeh. "And black is no threat to me. I will have what I wish to have. You. You will come. Or be injured. And then come with me."

She nodded.

The sinuous green wrapped him in tight coils and laughed. "Griz, griz, griz! It is not nice to threaten to injure her."

A motley green stood near him and bobbled its head up and down.

Anamaxtor trotted into the room, huffing small puffs of smoke. He stood by Eulin's side, the crest on his head raised, all dragon anger.

"Release me," he snarled. "Or die!"

The motley green looked at her.

"Yes," said Eulin.

She crushed his head with one snap of her jaws.

"May I have some of the rest?" asked the sinuous green

"Yes."

The two dragons disappeared, taking the body with them.

With a dull clink, a ring hit the floor and bounced. Eulin stepped over and picked it up. She waved away the stains on the floor. Then she turned, walked over, and knelt in front of Sa'ar.

"It had to be done, Mother." She looked at the golden dragon. "Sit."

"We would have done worse."

Eulin held out the ring. "May I keep?"

"Of course." Sa'ar smiled and patted the bench next to

herself. "Sit with me, young Vander. Sit with me, Dragon Force. Sit with me, daughter mine."

Eulin did. Then she held her hand out, palm up, the ring lying there. And blew. "Sent it to Je'leel." She laughed. And nestled under her mother's arm.

Grandeville. Tinker's Place.

Mirf had returned to her elseplace, telling her staff, "Nuff loafing. Too much vacation is not good for you!"

It dropped into her lap, a ring and a note, startling the calico female who hissed half heartedly and then closed her eyes again.

Je'leel read the note and looked at the ring.

"What's that?" Tinker looked at it.

She smiled. "A gift from Eulin." She crumpled up the note.

"Oh." He went back to reading his book.

Everyone relaxed.

He could feel it.

Life was quiet again.

For them.

Chapter Eighteen

Another Visitor.

IT WAS A SURPRISE ATTACK!

He was dragged down in the tall grass. Lying on his back, he looked at his attacker by his feet. He noticed how clear blue the sky was in the late summer. Not a cloud in sight. He squirmed to one side.

The attacker growled and pounced as he rolled, desperately he rolled to the side.

She missed.

So he counter-attacked.

The small group of tourists, standing on the rear deck. some 150 yards away, watched the tall grass thrash violently as the terrible struggle ensued. And nodded to each other as most of the motion stopped out there.

Grandeville. Tinker's Place

One of the tourists nudged another. "We might as well have lunch. She is going to be occupied for awhile."

Another laughed. "Fair wry a'pun that!"

They sat at one of the large wooden tables, on the wooden benches, and had lunch. Dressed in their pajamas. All had risen not all that long before after having stayed up rather late the previous evening.

"Ummmmm?" he asked.

"Lady lions do that just to get the males to do that."

He kissed her. "Pretty successful."

She sighed. "I'll say."

"Something wrong with beds?"

"Nope." She tightened her arms around him. "Warm days just make lionesses impulsive." She gave him a friendly pat. "Of course, you are fairly impulsive yourself." And laughed.

He sighed as he looked into those grey-green eyes.

She blinked at him. And laughed again. And twitched. He had just tickled her. "Don't!"

He rolled them onto their sides. And did it again.

"Don't!"

"Heh heh heh."

"Stop that!"

"Tickle, tickle, tickle."

"EEEEEEEK!"

He nodded. "Arching your back like that certainly does erotic things with those."

"Oh?" She arched her back again. "Those happen to be the way I am."

"Certainly are."

The tourists helped themselves to more food. "Good thing that she has the ring tomorrow," observed one. "He is going to go to sleep early."

The slim woman with the sparkling blue eyes set her sandwich down and shrugged out of her top and dropped it on the deck. "Tis most warm a'day this."

More tops dropped and made a soft heap on top of the first, more or less.

The young woman sitting with them looked around the table. "Mothers?"

"Just family here, no one else around." Fair Morn took another sandwich.

Je'leel shrugged off her top and folded it neatly and sat it on the bench next to herself. "Very comfortable."

"Yep," agreed Messenger beaming happily at her. "Really really is."

Sha'gar looked across the table at Je'leel and tilted her head to one side. "You have grown."

Messenger looked sideways. "GOSH! Certainly did."

"Very pretty." Smoke smiled at Je'leel. "No longer a kitten."

Je'leel nodded. "Eulin and I were gone two of your years in growth time. She is now Vander beautiful."

"Hum hum," said R-Bar.

A small figure scampered across the deck, leaped up onto the bench and then onto the table top. She walked over and sat on the edge of one of the platters. "If I were large you all could admire my anatomy."

"We are not doing that." Fair Morn reached past her and took another sandwich.

"Indeed not, Fair Dat." Chicken dragged over the potato salad bowl. "B'times we do know thy appearance so there be no need."

"Indjinns are beautiful," stated Dat. "And lovely to admire."

"Mother," cautioned Je'leel.

Dat stood and walked over to her daughter and looked up at her, smiling broadly. "Very beautiful. Especially the indjinn parts"

He lay on his back and watched a solitary cloud drift along. It had just come over the western ridge. She lay on her side, one arm and one leg thrown over him, using one of his arms for a pillow.

"Well, Simba Leader, what do you want to do now?"

"Ummmmmmmm?"

She laughed. "Really?" And blew warm air into his hair. "Maybe you ought to explain that before we begin."

He rolled his head to her side and frowned.

She batted her eyes at him. "Humor die with, ahhhh, everything else?" And hugged him. "O.K., let's just stick to the basics."

"Let's go take a shower."

She kissed his chest. "Right. You can ummmm me later." And laughed even louder than before. She rolled away, sat up and yanked her pajama bottoms on. "Let's go stud."

He did the same thing and stood. "That all you gonna wear?"

She stood. "Sure. It is a warm and sunny day and it is the costume de facto if not de jure."

He stood. "If you say so." He winked at her. "Pretty nice, all right."

Slipping an arm under one of his, she tugged him toward the house. "That's our cowboy."

Chicken looked at the pair strolling toward them from the first pasture and waggled a chicken leg in their general direction.

"Methinks yonder pair will shortly a'lunch come after fair showering and new attire."

"Looks like he survived the attack all right." Fair Morn took another sandwich. They had made lots.

"She is a strong pouncer," said Smoke, adding a couple more chicken legs to her plate.

Fair Morn shoved the potato salad bowl toward her.

"Don't eat it all," ordered Chantal as they walked past the food littered table and into the house through the side door, headed for the shower room.

Inside the shower room she poked him in the side. "And don't you get all grumpy and growly either." She twisted the levers, turning on all the shower heads.

"Burgle," he stated, stepping into the spray. "I don't think that daughters should do that."

She handed him the shampoo bottle. "Thought that we settled that argument a long time ago."

He took the bottle and worked up a thick lather in her hair. "Poo bah, as a certain green-eyed shorty would say. Turn around."

She arched her back as he scrubbed. "Ahhhhhhhh, HEY!"

"Heh heh heh."

She spun inside his arms and kissed him.

Fair Morn stood and headed for the back door to the kitchen. "I'll make more sandwiches. Guess that she didn't wear him out after all."

"Nasty peeper," gurgled Messenger.

Fair Morn shrugged.

Smoke smiled. "Chantal was a little slow in closing her mind."

"Hum hum hum," said a soft disembodied voice.

"You may," replied R-Bar.

Sgenn was handed up and in, all soft billowing grey robes, arms tucked inside her sleeves.

"Hayou, Aunts, Sister. And Cousin." A soft half-smile tugged at one corner of her mouth as she looked at the group seated around the table.

"Warm day," explained Sha'gar. "Sister."

Sgenn looked around, again. "May I join? Sister?"

"Oh gosh!" Messenger's eyes jumped to Smoke's.

"She doesn't mean us," said Sha'gar to Messenger.

Small winkles formed between Sgenn's brows. "I have never dressed . . . like that."

Messenger violently shook her head. "Better not! He will get all growley and grumpy and unhappy and not very relaxed. Really really."

"If you wish," said Chicken. "Do."

R-Bar looked at her niece. "Never?"

Sgenn plucked at her robes. "Theurgist proper. Always."

Chicken sat straighter, and stated in her most Royal tone of voice, "We do be most proper enow. How some ever We do choose to dress." She grinned at Sgenn.

"Or undress," added Smoke.

Sha'gar made room on the bench and dragged over an empty plate.

Sgenn nodded. Her robe unfolded, her arms sliding from her sleeves. "It is . . . pleasant." Sitting down she reached for the food dishes.

"OH!" Messenger bobbled her head. "MY!" She leaned close to Smoke. "She is at least four yums, really really."

Sgenn nudged Sha'gar.

"She means that you are beautiful, sister."

"True speak?"

"Mage true."

"Hum."

"Very," added Sha'gar.

Messenger stared across the table at them.

"Aunt?"

Messenger ducked her head.

"Kitten?" Chicken looked over at her.

"Just wondered," mumbled Messenger, pushing a finger back and forth on the table top.

"What?" Fair Morn set the sandwich platter on the table and sat next to Ran and took another. "Definitely four yums."

"Wellllllll," began Messenger. "I just wondered what hit Sgenn in the right, ahhhhhh, one?"

Sgenn looked down and touched a semi-circular scar curling down and around. "This?"

Messenger nodded.

"Small training accident."

"Who had a small training accident?" demanded Chantal as she strode from the side door wearing fresh pajamas, the bottoms, her hair wrapped in a towel. She walked over and sat in the space that Messenger made, mainly by scooting Smoke sideways.

Chantal looked and gasped. "Small?" She stared at Sgenn. "You almost had a radical mastectomy."

Sgenn shrugged.

Chantal glared around the table. "How come this babe is just sitting here flaunting herself like that? Are you-all up to something, again?"

"Nay!"' snapped Chicken. "Tis mere experience new for Fair Sgenn."

Chantal stared at the sandwich platter. Fair Morn shoved it over. Chantal took one and a big bite. "I see," she mumbled around mouthful. "She gets a new experience exposing herself and he gets a new experience goggling at her well developed self." She swallowed and nodded at Sgenn. "Very nice." And shoved and grumbled at Ran. "Make room." Then she waved at Tinker as he walked from the house.

"Over here, Lover." She laughed. "And before you say anything, just enjoy the view, raise your eyes, and notice that they are Sgenn, and think that you are experiencing life in ancient Hawaii. All the babes dressed, or undressed that way."

Tinker dropped onto the bench and glared at Chicken. "You care to explain what is going on this time?"

"Naught, Fair Prince." She smiled sweetly at him. "Tis mere fair niece Sgenn come a'visiting."

Messenger giggled. "Four yums." She looked over at him. "Right?"

"Sure." He figured that it was safe to just agree to whatever they were going off about. He bumped Chantal. "Gimme a sandwich."

She handed him one. "Damn grump."

"Bad enough when this kind of behavior spreads to daughters," he growled at her. "Now you guys are dragging in friends and neighbors."

"Fingers getting itchy?" She filled his mug.

"Huh?"

"Just look," she cautioned. "No touch."

He sighed. And wondered, really wondered, how this life could have gotten so strange in such a short period of time.

Sgenn leaned close to Sha'gar. "Does he wish to touch?"

"Shhhhhhhhh."

"What?" He looked at them.

"Nothing, Mate'mer."

"Her robes were certainly effective," mumbled Chantal to him.

"Ummm?" His mouth was full.

"Never would have realized all that was under all that. Not too bad for a debut."

He nodded. And swallowed. And said inside Sha'gar's mind. *What does she want?*

"Sister?"

"Eh?"

"Why are you here?"

Sgenn took one of her sister's hands in her's. "I have been on long wander and wished a soft quiet. It is known that here is such a place. Known among the Faan, that is. I am muchly tired. Most tired. That Ebna Raint used much. And then on the long again wander I did not rest often."

"Hum," replied Sha'gar.

"Father is working. Mother is out there."

She wishes a safe rest place, Mate'mer.

"We do have room," stated Chicken.

"You may stay," added R-Bar.

Ran nodded. "Niece."

"Deep thanks," said Sgenn. She kissed Sha'gar on the side of the face.

"Show me to my room, I would sleep now."

Sha'gar rose and led her sister into the house.

"She gonna walk around like that all the time she is here?" he grumbled to the table at large, hoping for once to get an answer.

"Nope," replied Fair Morn. "Unless we do, I suppose. She was just trying to fit in, to do what we were doing."

"To be polite, Amtar." Ran nodded at him. "I think that those theurgists don't have many opportunities for social engagement."

"O.K." He smiled at them. "If you guys just keep your shirts on until she leaves, everything will be just fine." He stood and wandered into the house and up to his office to work. He always seemed to have to edit something or other.

It was late afternoon when she eased into the organized shambles that was his office. She peered over his shoulder at the computer screen and then kissed him on the back of the neck.

"Huh?"

"All us kids thought that it was time for you to quit for the day."

"Oh." He spun around, his swivel chair complaining loudly, and looked up at her. She sat on his lap, tossed her legs over one arm of his chair. "You are sleeping in my bed, stud."

"Huh?"

"Not going to have any night creepers paying surprise visits."

He jerked. "Not again!"

"Don't think so. But you do not need any extracurricular activity. No intermural sporting events."

"Sha'gar can talk to her."

"Already did."

"And?"

"Just giving her the ground rules for visitors. That's all?"

"O.K." He smiled at her. "Pretty yummy yourself."

She kissed the tip of his nose. "Thanks. You can finish disrobing me after tea."

As they headed down the hall, headed toward the staircase down, he reached over, grabbed and tugged her close.

"John?"

"Now what's going on?"

She grinned. "Not much yet. But there is always hope. You have a certain gleam in your eye."

"That is exactly what I mean. Are we being affected by some Vander-like spells, stuff like that there?"

"Don't think so." Freeing her arms, she slipped them around his neck. "It is just you, in a manner of speaking. We have been resting and loafing and recuperating ever since we returned home from out there. And everyone is feeling very well and very healthy. No artificial stimulants of any sort."

Her lips brushed over his as she murmured, "Just normal robust Homo sapiens or whatever it is that we are."

"Ummm."

"Exactly." She gave him a friendly pat. "Let's go. Everyone is waiting." She laughed. "Besides, we have a house guest, so you will just have to behave."

They had tea and cookies.

Sgenn sat next to Sha'gar wearing the clothes that her sister had given her. Sitting side by side in the jeans and shirts, the family resemblance was striking in spite of the differences in skin and hair color.

Sha'gar had the light bronze skin tone and dark brown hair, almost black, of a magician. Sgenn had light grey hair and fair skin. Her eyes were a deep grey in contrast to the brown almost black of Sha'gar's.

All the rest were dressed in variations of the same theme. Same shirts, same jeans. Shirt tucked in. Or not so tucked in. Shoes, sandals, or bare feet. But, to his satisfaction, they were all wearing their clothes. He nodded. And sat in his chair. Chantal walked around the table and sat in her chair near the window.

Chicken filled his cup with tea. "Oolong. Strong." And pushed the sugar bowl and milk pitcher over to him.

"Oatmeal cookies," announced R-Bar.

"With wizen grapes," added Ran. "We made them. The cookies."

He smiled. "Really?" He knew that witches disliked cooking of almost every kind.

"Yes," replied R-Bar, sitting proudly. "We even used that oven thing in the kitchen."

"Raisins," said Fair Morn to Ran.

Then Messenger began explaining to him how 'neato' the flowerbeds were going to be when they finished the new plantings. She enjoyed gardening and somehow managed to get some or all of them involved at one time or another.

As she talked, he looked around the table. Judging from appearances they had stuck to the chores given them by Messenger and hadn't degenerated into the most often water, or something, fight.

Sgenn sat through all this food and discussion as Theurgist proper as she could given that she was dressed in this alien and rather exotic garb. She watched and listened and ate and drank, doing exactly as her sister did.

Tinker looked at Chicken who gave him a slight nod. "Methinks, Me'Lord," she whispered. "That fair wench wander and travel and training do ill prepare her for most social behavior."

"Well, I am sure," he murmured, "that exposure to this mob will take care of that." He sighed. "Just hope that she doesn't pick up too many bad habits."

"Piffle." She handed him a cookie.

And then, and finally, refreshed, they scattered, some inside, some outside, to finish working on whatever it was that they had been doing before the break.

Tinker and Chantal headed for the small living room, each carrying a stack of reading material.

Sha'gar and Sgenn went out the front door to sit on the grass and talk.

Fair Morn, R-Bar, and Ran headed for the kitchen to plan dinner and to clean up the cookie baking mess.

Fair Morn would do most of the cooking for this evenings meal with the witches mostly observing and helping at various chores as directed by Fair Morn.

The rest of the gang, more or less, headed for the flowerbeds.

He slumped into the couch and started through the several varieties of martial arts magazines, looking for ideas or inspiration for a new book. Hansen, his editor, was agitating for a new book.

Chantal sat lengthwise, back against a couch arm, legs

draped across his lap, and began to read through her veterinarian journals.

The door was closed, signaling to all that this was private time. All would stay away, physically and mentally.

The pleasant odor of roses drifted over them as they sat in one corner of the front lawn.

"Strange, strange." Sgenn plucked at her shirt with two fingers and then indicated the house.

"No," replied Sha'gar. "It is the way of here. This elseplace is different. Out there rules have no significance."

"Hum."

Sha'gar's eyes flared red as she leaned close. "Careful caution, sister."

"No offense. Startled." Sgenn's fingers fiddled with the buttons on her shirt, slowly undoing them. "I have never displayed myself . . . anytime, to anyone." Her grey eyes fastened on deep brown. "Sister, do you do this much?"

Sha'gar shrugged. "He is ours. It is antap."

Sgenn reached out and gently touched her sister. "He is not mine. Yet that blue-eyed Royal said so."

"The Princess Chicken is impulsive in manner and speech. You do not have to obey."

"It was comfortable."

"Yes."

"I did not mind."

"Yes."

"He gazed open hapquar."

"Who could resist?"

"I did not mind."

"Hum."

Sgenn leaned closer. "I have never male joined."

"Sister?"

"He, your's, is charm tempt."

"Careful," hissed Sha'gar.

"Curious."

"This place. Here." Sha'gar waggled her hand at the house and its surrounding. "It is tikzar. This male here is for magical ones strong lure want comfort. None understand this or know the cause."

Sha'gar gently ran her fingers over Sgenn's neck. "He is many protected, many guarded."

Sgenn nodded. "I am not magical. My presence is patr a'ar?"

"No not. You are here as one. This is sister sister true."

Sgenn slowly laid back on the thick grass. "Hold me, magician sister. I would not be solitary. I am greatly tired."

Sha'gar lay by her side and gently wrapped Sgenn in arms. "Rest comfort, strange sister. Here as long as you need."

"Oh my!" Messenger looked at Smoke who was carefuily patting the soil around a marigold that she had just planted. "Sgenn does not feel very good, really really."

Smoke nodded. "She just requires a lot of rest." She poked Chicken in the side, just above one hip, leaving a dirty soil blotch on the amply exposed midriff. Chicken had tied her shirt tails high on her chest.

"And," added Smoke. "That means that she does not need royal inducements to tease our mate with."

"Pish tosh." Chicken twisted around and glared at the

mud spot. She reached over with one grimy hand and drew a muddy line across Smoke's mid-section, Smoke having tied her shirt in much the same fashion as Chicken.

Smoke looked at her. And blinked.

"Dare thee not!"

"Not in my flower bed!" ordered Messenger. "You will crush all the baby plants."

"That theurgist better not think about crawling into his bed," growled R-Bar.

Ran nodded. And chopped the stem off the radishes she was cleaning. "Chantal wants him in her's."

Fair Morn stirred the sauce just beginning to boil in the large kettle. "Smoke said that after eight his attraction should not occur anymore."

"Theurgists are tik tik an abta!" R-Bar carefully stirred as Fair Morn started something sizzling in a large skillet. Ran nodded.

Tinker and Chantal sat and read in silence. All the conversations swirling around in their collective being were carefully held away from them. He finished the last magazine and dropped it on top of the others lying on the floor and stared out the bay window.

"John?"

"Hey there, Lover?"

Chantal slipped her hands around her mouth making a megaphone of them. "Earth to Tinker babe! Come in, Tinker." She waited. Then laughed quietly to herself and said in a lilting sing-song voice, "Hey G.I.! Push push zig zig! TWO DOLLA!"

"Huh?"

"Thought that would get your attention."

He looked at her. "What?"

"You got a foot fetish, Effendi?"

He looked down at her feet, in his lap. He was holding one of them. "Oh."

"You have been sitting there staring out the window for a long time. And fondling my pedal extremity."

"Just thinking. Got an idea for a new book." He grinned. "Nice foot, err, feet." He grabbed her ankles and pulled her his way. "Nice legs. Nice shorts." And pulled. "Nice belly."

She exhaled loudly.

"Ummmmmmmm," he said, fingers tickling.

"Oh!" She twitched. "You going to join me?"

"Huh?"

"In puris naturalibus."

"She is really going to be hungry," stated R-Bar.

"He will need to eat much also," added Ran.

Fair Morn laughed. "I am making lots."

The garden crew entered the kitchen from the back door.

"Smoke?" asked Fair Morn.

"We are just all feeling well rested and very fit. She has The Ring and is taking full advantage of both." She peered into one of the pots. "When do we eat?"

Fair Morn glanced up at the clock. "About thirty, forty minutes. Plenty of time for you dirt clods to shower."

"Jolly good idea." Chicken headed for the shower room, shedding clothes as she went.

Smoke followed, gathering up the clothes.

"Smells yummy." Messenger giggled as she followed the other two.

The water gushed, the steam billowed out the open doorways.

"Unhand me!" commanded Chicken.

"No plants in here to crush," observed Smoke.

"EEEEEEEK!" screeched Chicken.

"Gosh." Messenger took the shampoo bottle from its holder.

"DO NOT!" yelped Chicken. "AAAAAAaaaa!"

"Rowdy bunch." Fair Morn looked at her helpers. "Set the table please."

The two witches hurried away. Fair Morn began to slice the french bread.

"Something is going on. I can feel it."

She kissed him on the tip of his nose and breathed softly. "I know. Me too."

"That is not what I meant!"

Her fingers tickled a few ribs. "Too heavy for you?"

"Nope." He looked up, past the side of her face. "Do you know that there is a crack in the ceiling?"

"How do you do that?"

"Pretty easy."

"Oh! Not what I meant."

"What?"

She clenched his shoulder. "Never mind."

Ran nudged R-Bar. "Has her sister brought something? I

feel taste nothing."

R-Bar set the last knife and fork in place and straightened up, casting lightly. And waited. It floated back. R-Bar shook her head. "Nothing." She nodded. "But some will sleep early tonight."

Ran nodded. Her braids curled themselves around her neck in loose folds. "That Theurgist is many spent."

R-Bar nodded. "She is safe here. The ward keeps out the uninvited."

Ran nodded. "Except Theurgists," she whispered.

Chapter Nineteen

Visitors.

Grandeville. The House of Raj and Kartz.

She blew into the house and tumbled across the rug, landing in a heap just short of the wall. Orange fumes seeped from her clothes and drifted oil heavy across the room. With a loud grunt, she sat up and peered around at this strange looking room. She stood, wobbling slightly from side to side, and listened. This dwelling was empty. The furniture was certainly not zp tek, so she knew she must be in the correct place.

She wandered through the house, from room to room, stopping at every window to peer outside. The house was on a hillside. The town sprawled out and away, down the slope. It was much larger than home.

Stopping in one room she looked at the strange things and yanked open the door on one of them. Cold air flowed down and across her feet. Various foods stuffs sat on the shelves.

The sight of the food reminded her that she was hungry. So she tried one or two of the things from inside this peculiar box and sat. It glowed light across her and the floor. As she ate, she knew that this was the home of her sister and of her sister's chosen mate.

Finished, she stood and placed those portions not eaten

back on the shelves and shut the door to the box. Then she headed toward the room with the soft furniture to sit and wait.

Grandeville. Doc's Place.

The slight figure floated silently from the house and down across the patio to the table with the large umbrella over it. She stood. Next to the man slouched in a chair, reading a book. She poked him in the side with one finger. And waited.

And poked him again.

And waited.

And did it again.

And waited.

She knew that it would take some time before he realized that she was there. When he concentrated, all else disappeared. So she waited. Very patiently. It was a very un-witch thing to do, to be patient. It was a special skill. For her.

Then it happened. He put a piece of paper between the pages of his book, snapped it shut, and turned his head, smiled at her. "Been waiting long?"

Shadow soft breeze whispered to him, "Not long, Husband."

"Lunch time?"

"That also."

"Ahhhhhhhhhhh. Also? What?"

"Your daughter stays with them." There was the faintest change at one corner of her mouth in an otherwise devoid of expression face.

He noticed. For her, it was an expression of great emotion.

"She is part of them," he said.

"Sgenn."

"Oh." He smiled. "Problem?"

The huge black eyes blinked. Once.

"Let's take my van." He stood and threw his arm around her shoulders as she straightened up.

He was 6 feet 4 inches tall. The top of her head came to the top of his shoulders. He laughed. "Good enough." He was referring to her clothes.

She was wearing a large man's shirt, one of his, fastened in the middle by one button. Tattered shorts. Gigantic sunglass were pushed up and nestled in her thick black hair.

They strolled around the house to where he usually parked his van.

Grandeville. Tinker's Place.

Smoke felt them approaching and reached out. *MindMate, Chantal. J. C. and Reep are coming up our driveway. They just turned up the slope.*

Chantal sat up and patted his stomach. "We have time for a quick shower."

"O.K., let's go."

They grabbed their clothes and ran through the large living room and down the hall and into the shower room dumping their clothes in the hamper as they passed it.

Smoke met the battered van as it coasted to a halt next to their truck. "Afternoon," she said, smiling at them as they clambered out. "Let's sit on the rear deck. He and Chantal are taking a quick shower."

The trio wandered around the corner of the house and up onto the rear deck and walked down to sit at one of the large tables near the swimming pool.

Slowly the rest of them filtered from the house. And settled here and there. In a few minutes, Tinker and Chantal joined them dressed in jeans, shirts, and wet hair.

"Hi guys," said Tinker, greeting them. "What's up?" He and Chantal sat across the table from them.

J. C. shrugged.

Sha'gar and Sgenn walked from the house dressed in jeans, shirts, and bare feet.

Sha'gar had pulled back Sgenn's hair and fastened it into a long ponytail.

"Hayou, Mother," said Sgenn, being Theurgist proper. She was the youngest of the three daughters. "Father."

"Mother, Father." Sha'gar released her sister's hand and walked around the table to sit by Tinker's free side.

Reep tapped the bench by her free side. Sgenn sat there. Reep looked at Tinker. "Is my strange daughter," asked the faintest of breezes, "a problem?"

His eyes jumped from Reep to Sgenn and back again. Then he looked at the rest of himself. "I don't think so."

Nope, said a chorus in his mind.

He smiled at Reep. "Guess not. Why?"

"Theurgists," breathed Reep. "are many layered trained deep. Such persons tend to be indirect and to make demands without thinking."

Sha'gar leaned on the table. "My sister has been quiet quiet."

"Most peaceful a'week," added Chicken. "And most welcome for to visit."

Tinker glanced at Chicken. "As well behaved as anyone

here." He smiled. *Not counting running around with their shirt off.*

Pish tosh, Grumble Lord. Chicken looked at Reep. "Be there some worry?"

Reep looked at her sister. R-Bar gave the slightest of head shakes. "Mother concern," sighed the afternoon breeze.

J. C. laughed. "I think that she just wanted to get me away from the books for awhile." He slipped his arm around Reep and hugged her close.

Sgenn watched her mother from the corners of her eyes. "I would rest here. With Sha'gar."

Sha'gar nodded. "Mother, I would have my sister here, with me, with us."

"Hum," whispered the quiet.

Sgenn jerked her head and hissed, "MOTHER!"

R-Bar stared at her sister.

Reep shrugged. And looked at Tinker. "If my youngest daughter and her sister and you feel that this may be done, then it will be so."

Tinker looked at the rest of himself. "Sure," he replied. "Why not?"

Chapter Twenty

Another Faan Problem?

Grandeville. Tinker's Place.

"Let me in! Let me in!"

Two pair of eyes popped open in the pitch black that was midnight dark.

"Who was that?" he mumbled.

"I do not know."

He sighed.

She rolled his way, sliding an arm and a leg over him, skin making soft silken whispers.

"Mate'mer." Her lips delicately fluttered against his neck as she rolled further onto him.

"What?"

"My sister . . . "

"You have two." His arms looped around, crossing loosely over the small of her back. "Ahhh?"

"Theurgists are different folk, very different."

"Really warm." He tickled her, just a little.

"No. I think that her temperature is similar to your's."

He gave her a friendly pat. And then another. Just for the fun of it. "I was referring to you."

She hitched a little higher. "Hum hum hum."

"Really warm."

Her eyes fluxed, a deep red black glow.

"LET ME IN!"

"What?"

"What you said."

"I didn't say that."

"It wasn't one of us." She kissed him. "We are private."

A small patch of grey light formed in one corner of their ceiling. He could see it past her ear. "Something's happening."

"Uh . . . huh."

"Really."

"Uh. . . huh."

"Bad."

"Uh . . . huh."

"Timing."

"Uh . . . huh."

Up there, the spot flared white, blue, and orange.

She shuddered violently and clenched him even tighter. And the room went dark again.

Something thumped to the floor making a very large thump. "KAN KAKTO!"

Soft yellow light billowed around her as she stood, looked around the room, this very strange room, and then glared down at them.

"Debaucher!" she snarled, stalking over to the bed set flush with the floor, crackling mace clenched in her hand.

"Rapist," she hissed.

Sha'gar sat up, head snapping around. Scarlet blasted this stranger into a far corner of the room where she sprawled in a loose-limbed heap.

The yellow light went out.

Doors banged open all through The Chamber.

Sha'gar bent and kissed him.

"Who was that?" he mumbled, reaching over, snapping on the light.

She shrugged. "A soon to be dead person." And stepped from the bed.

He reached over and dragged on his pajama bottom. "Better get dressed. We are about to be invaded."

Shrugging on her top, she reached out and gently nudged him with a foot.

He twitched. "Watch it!"

"Heh heh." She yanked on the bottoms.

He pulled on his top as the door banged open.

They poured into his bedroom, snapping on the room lights. Ready to attack. Whatever the problem might be.

Chantal waggled her long-barreled revolved at the body in the corner. "Just something that you've been hiding in the closet, Cowboy?"

He stood. "She just dropped in. Literally." He frowned darkly at the short witch. "You wanna explain that? How could she do that?"

R-Bar glared back. "The ward is still in place."

"So?"

Sgenn slipped quietly into the room, dark something oozed up from the down below to stand ready, waiting for her command. "Who threatens him?"

"You wanna wear the rest of your pajamas?" he demanded.

She nodded. Something strange handed her the top. She

shrugged it into place.

"And," he pointed, "I don't think we need that."

She nodded. It sank into the deep down below.

Smoke knelt and peered at their visitor. "Still alive."

Je'leel ran into the room. "FATHER!"

"I am fine. She didn't do anything."

"She attacked," stated Sha'gar. Then she leaned close to her sister and whispered in her ear, "Stay clothed around him, sister."

Sgenn nodded. And whispered back, "Others do not."

"I will explain about that later."

Smoke grabbed an ankle and dragged the limp body into the center of the room.

Chicken straightened out the body's limbs and brushed the hair back from her face. "Who be this young woman? Me'Lord?"

"Beat's me."

Messenger stared at the body. "Gosh! Orange and blue magic."

"Hum," said Ran. "One of those."

R-Bar nodded. "Why would she attack him?"

"Dead to be," grumbled Sha'gar, peering over Chicken's shoulder at the body.

Fair Morn returned, now wearing her top, and winked lewdly at him. "We can just throw her back if you don't want her.

"Good idea." He decided to ignore her wink and most of her remark.

"Wait!" snapped Chantal, easing the hammer of her revolver down. "Let's find out how she got in here first. And what she was up to. Then we can send her where ever, when ever."

Chicken nodded. "Most clever a'thought."

Smoke looked at Sha'gar who snapped her fingers.

"Ooooooooooooooo," moaned the young woman, limbs twitching and jerking. "Ag zig zig top top!" Her eyes popped open.

R-Bar stepped over and kicked her in the ribs. "Vile coarse." She kicked her again.

"UK!"

Tinker yanked R-Bar away. "Hold it."

R-Bar grumbled loudly.

He looked down. "You have a name?"

She looked up at the group standing around staring down at her. "Indo."

"Interesting name. Well, Indo, how did you get in here? What do you want?"

"No!" She started to sit up. Sgenn stepped on her, holding her in place.

"Stop that!" he snapped.

"I am Adarlak," she stated, carefully watching the grey haired one as she stepped back. "I came here to find The One. But all I found is you!" She glared up at him.

Chicken looked from him to Adarlak. "Why for do you glare so?"

Adarlak pointed. "He, that debased filthy figt tik, was despoiling," she pointed at Sha'gar, "that young woman."

"Ummmmmm?" asked he.

Chicken laughed. "Nay true. In part."

"Gosh!" Messenger, stifling her laughter, looking at

Sha'gar.

"My Father," stated Je'leel, kneeling next to Adarlak, "is neither debase nor filthy nor figt tik."

"And I was not being despoiled," grumbled Sha'gar.

"So there," he mumbled.

"Much," added Sha'gar.

Sgenn nudged her sister and whispered soft soft, "That person watched you? And him?"

"A short moment."

Je'leel helped Adarlak sit up.

"I am . . . I was with Anjan and Ranna. But I escaped. To here. As Ranna directed." Her eyes darted from face to face. "How do I find The One? Do any of you know how?"

The loud sigh, the loud slow sigh, was Tinker.

Chicken headed for the door. "We will Ourself make coffee, Me'Lord."

Chantal and Fair Morn followed her.

"We will start breakfast," said Fair Morn. "An early breakfast."

Je'leel helped her stand. "Come with me. You are safe." She led the stunned young woman away and added as they headed for the large living room, "My Father is The Chosen One you seek, I am sure that he will help you."

Adarlak jerked. "Him!"

Je'leel pulled her back into motion. "Sha'gar is his, ah, um, wife."

"Oh. I see."

Sha'gar pushed Sgenn toward the door. "We will talk. After we eat."

As she eased out the door, Sgenn looked over her

shoulder and smiled a soft half-smile.

Messenger giggled. "May I be despoiled next?" And ran from the room.

"Merde," he grumbled.

Tinker slipped his arm over Sha'gar's shoulders. "How about we don't beat her up? Again?"

"She was attacking you."

"Point conceded."

"Despoiler of young women," gurgled R-Bar, leering at him.

"How about we drop that topic of conversation," he mumbled.

"We should talk with that mage," suggested Ran.

"Yesssss," agreed R-Bar.

"Just talk," he ordered.

The witch pair left the room, cackling softly to each other.

Sha'gar spun and wrapped herself around him. "I will ask Dat to repair her." And kissed him. "If necessary."

"Who?"

"Adarlak. That was death spell." And kissed him again. "But I stopped it. Now."

"Let's go eat."

She released him and walked by his side, arm in arm, across the common space of The Chamber, heading for the dining room via the kitchen.

As he dropped into his chair at the dining room table and watched Sha'gar walk around to her place, Adarlak straightened up, and said to him, "Your others explained. Everything. Sorry sorry."

R-Bar came from the kitchen and set two baskets of toast

on the table and said softly in his ear, "She is Ranna touched. That is why she could slip past the ward."

"Did Dat fix her?"

"Yes. I heard Sha'gar. She is healthy." She kissed his cheek. "Not bad looking for a mage from a minor guild."

"Don't start," he snarled.

"Heh heh heh." She headed for her chair.

Then they all ate breakfast.

At 1:00 a.m.

Then all decided that naps were going to be in order later in the day.

Finally they settled around in the large living room. Smoke checked Adarlak, pronounced her truly healthy, winked at Tinker, and dropped into one of the large chairs.

Sha'gar and her sister joined the already slumping Tinker on the couch.

Chicken refilled his cup. "Fret thee not, Our Prince."

"I am not fretting," he grumbled. "Thanks." He took a sip. "Too early in the morning for that."

"Damn right," growled Chantal as she dragged an Afghan up and over her lap, legs curled to one side. She glared at Adarlak and wiggled into a more comfortable position.

Tinker looked around the room. "Where's Dat?"

"Sleeping," replied Je'leel, setting the ornate ring with the eye-like gem back in its place on one of the bookcase shelves.

"Mother said that it was a very uncivilized hour to be doing things." She laughed softly. And sat by Fair Morn.

"What else did she say?" whispered Fair Morn.

Je'leel leaned close. "She said that dik dik mage should have things done to her."

"Dik dik?"

"It is a very coarse indjinn term."

Fair Morn laughed.

Sgenn dragged over a comforter, yanked it up to her neck and leaned against Tinker, eyes dropping half-closed. He was forced to slip his arm around her shoulders as she squirmed lower and nudged her shoulder under his arm. She pushed the comforter over his arm until only her upper face was showing.

R-Bar dragged over a chair, close to Adarlak.

Ran sat on one arm of that chair and leaned slightly, arm thrown loosely over R-Bar's shoulders.

"Tell me of my sister," ordered R-Bar.

Adarlak nodded. "We were doing a wander, Ranna, Anjan, and I. Ranna wished to find information on the Zar House of the Reit Guild of Ferufoken Mind Twist.

Sgenn's eyes flew wide open, her fingers digging into his thigh.

"Ouch!" he whispered to her.

"Sorry sorry." She hastily pulled her hand away and then reached up under the comforter and grabbed his left hand where it dangled down past her shoulder.

Chapter Twenty-one

Faan Wander Search

Rak. A Weird and Twisted.

Ranna, Anjan, and Adarlak were working their way down the twisted and bent sometime tunnel that was the street called Kabal Dir in the warped city of Rak on the elseplace aptly named Dark.

Five days earlier the trio had arrived from Plan Tan where Ranna had finally found a person who told them how to find a person who might be willing to help in her search. The person was highly placed in the Below Bight Guild. It was told that this certain person had knowledge of the unmentionable. And might, just might, provide Ranna some of that knowledge she sought. And that certain person had told them of this street.

For four days the three of them had searched across Rak for this street. And this morning they had finally located the dark hole that was the spot where Kabal Dir joined the garbage strewn gutter of a street perversely named The Golden Way.

The air crackled around Ranna and Adarlak as the three of them stalked deeper into the entrails of the warped space of Rak.

Anjan, multi-curved weapon in hand, slipped silently along, witch on her left, mage on her right. During the hours of their passage they had seen no other beings.

"That fondo sent us dar dar," grumbled Adarlak.

"Then that one will die," hissed Ranna.

"Just so." Anjan smiled.

Many spaces away, in a small square, the crowd gasped and whispered to each other as they stared at the mess that had been Handle the Bag. Even for Rak, they told each other, this was extreme. Pieces of Handle decorated every light stand in the small square.

The folk doing the staring wondered what secret the Bag had whispered in whose ear. And wondered where that person, or persons, would be found.

Those persons, or person, the ones of all that speculation, stood and carefully inspected the huge carved wooden door with the moving runes on it. The images shifted and changed. And the door carefully inspected the three figures standing there inspecting it.

"Hub dub," said the door.

"Hum," said Ranna.

The blue and orange mace sprang into Adarlak's hand

"Speak nice," ordered Ranna, kicking the door on a lower panel.

"Ouch," replied the door, cackling deep dirty. "I suppose."

Clenching a glowing red wand with a flaming yellow tip in her left hand, Ranna leaned forward and cautiously touched a middle panel with one fingertip of her right hand.

"Aaaaaaaa," moaned the door. "Stroke my in . . . lay."

Her hand jerked away.

"Rapture anatomy, don't stop," it rasped.

"Step close," it whispered.

"Press those appendages against my panels," it sighed.

Ranna stepped back and stared at it. "Hum hum."

"Retik bag bag," suggested Anjan. She had never heard of a door like this one.

"Magic'd weird," observed Adarlak.

Ranna shook her head.

The door blew warm, sweetly scented air at Anjan. "Straddle my knob, fine warrior."

Snarling angrily, Adarlak leapt forward and brought her mace down on a side panel. The mace bounced wildly back, flinging her arm up and away.

Anjan caught her as she stumbled backward.

The door laughed. "Slither against me, brave one. If you dare."

"Hum hum hum." Ranna threw her wand somewhere. "Watch watch," she said to the others. She stepped up to door, held her arms out and away from her sides, and pressed her body against the door. And began to move slowly.

"Beautiful," sighed the door. And sucked her inside.

Anjan looked at Adarlak who looked at the door. The door made sucking noises at them.

Shrugging her shoulders, Anjan sheathed her weapon, stepped up and mashed herself against the door.

"Lovely," gasped the door, slowly dragging her in.

Adarlak hung her mace from her belt, sucked in a quick breath, and flung herself at the door.

"Don't be so rough, sweet meat," whispered the door. "Be kind." She was drawn inside.

Ranna and Anjan caught the mage as she stumbled

forward, wrapped her in their arms, and kissed her on the sides of her face.

"Strange, strange, strange," mumbled Adarlak.

Ranna's lips fluttered lightly against her ear. "Sweet meat," she breathed.

"I want to kill it," growled the mage.

Ranna gave her a gentle pat. "Later." And stepped away.

Anjan released her. "We will." She stepped away and began to look around.

Adarlak nodded and fastened her garments. "Where are we?"

The room was large. Far across the bare stone floor, on a far wall, was another door.

Closed.

Adarlak stared at that door and looked at Ranna. "I will not be used like that again."

Ranna nodded. "It was vile."

They walked across the stone floor and stopped and carefully examined the huge wooden door.

"Hub dub," said the door.

Adarlak looked at Ranna. "Never again."

Ranna nodded. "Let us through, door."

"Certainly. Step up."

Ranna kicked it. "Open wide."

"Most unkind, tasty witch." It gurgled wetly, "Zugdar, over there, told me. Everything."

"Open. Or die."

The door swung slowly open, hinges wailing rust torment.

"Ouch, ouch, ouch," cried the door.

Ranna nodded and stepped into the next room.

Followed by Anjan.

Followed by Adarlak.

Who almost made it.

The door swung shut.

Grabbing her.

Holding her, pulling her.

In.

Adarlak screamed, blasting magic in all directions. Door parts pattered down into both rooms as she fell through the opening, sagging to the stone floor.

Ranna grabbed her. Anjan leaped past them, guarding.

There was nothing left. Smouldering embers, blazing splinters, half-melted hinges.

"Ranna," she gasped. "It tried to take me."

"Safe safe, my own," soft sang in her ear as Ranna stroked Adarlak's hair. "You are safe safe."

Dark eddied against the ceiling, answering the agitated witch's call. She kissed Adarlak's forehead and held her close.

"Lovely mage, sweet mage, my mage, I share with no-one, we share with no-one. There is only you and I and Anjan."

Anjan sat next to them. "This room appears empty."

"Hidden clever." Ranna sat up. "Stay with her. I will seek." She began to prowl around the room, carefully checking.

"How do you kill a room?" Anjan looked past Adarlak at the ruined doorway into the other room.

Adarlak nuzzled Anjan's neck. "I will find a way. After I kill that other door."

Across the room, in a corner, Ranna gestured, ripping

open the floor. Kneeling next to the ragged hole, she reached down into it and extracted a scroll wrapped in an ornate outer sleeve.

She walked back to them and nodded. "We have what we need." One corner of her mouth twitched. "From this elseplace." She tugged the others to their feet. "Ready to leave?"

Anjan nodded.

Adarlak shook her head. "It needs killing."

"Of course." Ranna dropped several small, black spheres on the floor. She smiled. "Fire dragon eggs. Ripple told me of them."

One egg popped open and released a tiny black dragon. It belched fire on the floor, ate the tiny cooked spot. And grew.

"These rooms are dead," said Ranna. "The city Rak is dead. We must leave."

"Indo," agreed Adarlak.

Anjan kissed her, then Ranna. "Leave."

Smiling a true witch smile at the destruction soon to be, Ranna grabbed them and yanked them away.

Another egg popped open.

Frar Top. Distant, Lush.

They startled the innkeeper. He had been dozing lightly, not expecting anyone to walk in at this time of mid-morning. Jerking upright, he stared at this stranger pair. Their clothes were travel worn and much used, obviously slept in. He wasn't sure that this pair of traveling females ought to be allowed into his establishment and to use his facilities. While few ever traveled to the town of Far Ferlax, the long road was around and about, narrow and twisting, few used these many generations since the old road had been abandoned, he still felt he could be selective. So he eyed them with an appraising glance.

"Room, bed, wash, food," said Magna, stopping in front of him. She opened her hip pouch and handed him three glittering gold coins.

"Apla," said the innkeeper, biting each coin, then nodding. Heaving his bulk up, he guided them to a room with facilities and went to tell the food folk to prepare meals.

Magna examined the room, the bed, and the great tub filling with steaming water. She nodded and turned to her companion. "Will do." And began to shed her garments. Later they would buy new. Kicking the last aside, she tugged Phonta's garments down, running delicate touch over soft curves, and drew her over and into the pleasant water.

Fair Ernet. Sunny and Warm.

They faded in.

Ranna pointed. "There." And hurried them into that establishment. It was the closest place.

"Rooms! For us! Big, comfortable bed! Large and roomy wash facilities! Food!"

She glared at the clerk as she barked her orders at him.

"NOW!" The air sang angrily around them.

"Instantly!" yelped the clerk, gesturing wildly. The porter rapidly walked up the staircase, beckoning them to follow. They did.

He raced through the rooms explaining everything and then ran out the main door, slamming it shut.

Ranna walked into the correct room, pointed at the bed and nodded, tossing Adarlak and Anjan into the middle. Then she ordered off their clothes, crawled over to them, smiled and rolled onto her side, her hand sliding across Adarlak's waist.

"Shall we get comfortable?" She tugged Adarlak closer, hand sliding up that smooth, bronze magician skin. Adarlak. sighed. And hooked her arm around Anjan.

The clerk and porter warned all the staff about their three guests. A witch and a warrior traveling together was understandable. A mage and a warrior traveling together was understandable. But a witch with a mage and a warrior was magic twisted and a group to tread lightly around

Grandeville. Tinker's Place.

Adarlak looked around the large living room at her rapt audience.

"We . . . rested there for four days." Her cheeks flushed.

Smoke winked at Tinker.

Sgenn, still holding Tinker's hand, pressed it against warm soft swelling flesh. "Continue," she said to the mage, a soft half-smile tugging at one corner of her mouth.

Star Burst. Small and Isolated.

They faded in.

Following the scroll directions.

"Nice lodgings first." Ranna headed down the broad street. "A certain mage and a certain warrior are spoiling a certain witch."

People scattered. All knew that a smiling witch was one step from mayhem. None could know, of course, that in this case, this smiling witch was smiling from happiness. This was a rarity among witches. Ranna was in a state of very not-witch.

In the lodgings place they allowed the front desk to select their rooms. In the restaurant they allowed the server to select their meal. Then they strolled down the broad street, sharing a very happy glow of togetherness.

"Somewhere along here," explained Ranna, lightly tickling the waist her arm was around, "is the shop of the one we seek."

Anjan twitched. It was her waist. And batted gently at that pesky hand on the other side, sliding up her rib cage.

Adarlak frowned, a very gentle frown.

So, they strolled very casually down the broad street and then turned into another.

This one was not as broad as the main street nor as narrow as the narrowest of side streets. This street was a way of pedestrians only. Nothing else allowed. Shops were randomly scattered along the street, on both sides. Of every kind.

The trio wandered along, meandering from side to side. Looking, prodding, poking, and occasionally, eating some of the food stuffs on display at the many food booths.

Ranna looked at her companions. "Do you see anything?" She indicated the places selling objects of all sorts.

Anjan shook her head. "I have all that I wish." She smiled.

Adarlak nodded. "A few spells are always nice."

"Of course," agreed Ranna, who knew magic users were always looking for new spells. "When we are alone I would like to try something new."

Adarlak's cheeks flushed.

Anjan patted her on the hip. "You may try something new on me after."

Ranna frowned at them. Just for show. "I wish to teach Adar a witch spell."

Adarlak gasped. "The magics will twist. Blow back will injure ugly."

"Hum," replied Ranna. "We shall see."

"There." Anjan pointed at the small shop just down the street from them. "Just there. The one with the blue door, the pale blue door."

Ranna consulted the scroll. And nodded.

They went that way and inside.

The inside of the small shop was neat. And tidy. Very neat and tidy. It had two doors in the rear wall. Both were closed. One door was a pale yellow, the other a soft green.

"Hum," said Ranna. "This one likes colors."

"Mage or witch?" asked Adarlak. Ranna shrugged. There hadn't been that kind of information in the scroll.

"This shop reeks of magic." Adarlak began a careful search as Ranna slipped to the other side of the shop. Searching.

Anjan stood in the exact center of the open space. From here she could watch both back doors. And hear anything coming through the front one. And began to move with small, careful steps toward that pale green door. There was something about that door that felt different.

"Ran'na, Adar, look see!"

The others hurried over.

"Hum."

"Blur hide," stated Adarlak. "Very subtle."

"Very good," he said, stepping out.

The speaker was a small man dressed in garb of several colors, the same as the doors, pale green, pale blue, and a touch of pale yellow. "Come back here. We may talk private."

The door swung open as he stepped backward, gesturing for them to follow him. They did.

Inside this room, a comfortable looking room, a small comfortable, very neat looking room, he motioned them to the chairs and sat. He waited until they were settled before speaking. "I am Ap Kar, Hinta warlock. What do you seek? Here?"

"Information," replied Ranna. The scroll had brought them to the correct place for the information that she sought.

"Perhaps," answered Ap Kar as he looked from face to face. This was a strange group, unusual even. "Name me some names."

"Faan witch Ranna."

"Hacto mage Adarlak."

"Death Warrior, Anjan."

"Faan! Many hear about that clan. Your, ummmmm, companions are unknown. To me."

Ranna shrugged. "Hinta are unknown to the Faan."

Ap Kar nodded. "Three very attractive females seeking information."

Ranna nodded.

"What will you give?"

"What will you ask?"

Ap Kar looked at Anjan.

"She is mine," stated Ranna. "So is Adarlak."

Ap Kar steepled his fingers under his chin. "Love bent? To, ummmm, death warrior? And a mage? Also?"

"True."

"The Faan are told . . . different."

Ranna nodded.

"A large number in that clan."

She nodded again. He was slowly coming to the point. A most cautious warlock was this Ap Kar.

"Most, umlah, unmated?"

You may seek, you may not find."

"Ahhhhh."

"We find our's. Once! Never to change."

Ap Kar smiled.

"This shop is neat. Tidy."

"I prefer order."

"Hum. Witch strange."

Ap Kar shrugged. "We are each strange, then, in our own manner."

Ranna nodded. "Business?"

"As you wish."

"I, we, seek information."

Ap Kar propped his chin in one hand, leaning his body to one side.

"Of a sensitive nature."

"Large cost," he suggested.

"Special reward," suggested Ranna, sitting upright. "After."

Ap Kar's eyes squinted into slits as his brows furrowed. His eyes glittered. "How special?"

Ranna leaned back. "You may seek, you may not find."

"Ahhhhhh. Ask."

Ranna ordered her chair closer to Ap Kar. Then, knee touching knee, she told him.

He jerked back, head thumping against the high back of

his chair. "The Zar House of the Reit Guild of Ferufoken Mind Twist?"

She nodded. All their work had been for the good. This warlock could tell them exactly what she wanted to know.

He stared at her. "Special reward?"

She nodded. Once.

"Lips forever sealed?"

"Witch word, witch oath."

Ap Kar waved in a small book, thumbed through it, and made her a small scroll. And handed it carefully to her. "A many turns trail. There are . . . things . . . in the way."

She put the scroll somewhere.

"You may die. Horribly."

"Hum."

His eyes caressed her. "A waste."

"Mine to waste." She began to unbutton her blouse.

Ap Kar straightened, licked his lips. A nervous gesture.

Removing her hat, Ranna reached inside her blouse and pulled it out, slipping the fine chain up and over her head. Then she carefully reset her hat and handed the object to Ap Kar.

Ap Kar clenched the chain in his fingers and dangled the orange stone in front of his eye.

"Orange magic?"

"Rekel has the twin. Wear it, Hinta warlock Ap Kar."

Cautiously he slipped the chain over his head and carefully settled the orange stone inside his shirt. Then he smiled as she told him of Rekel.

"Just so," said Ranna when she was done explaining. "Now you may seek." She waggled a cautionary hand. "The

Faan chose their's. None choose them." She leaned back. "Special reward?"

He nodded. "Just so. However it does, we are mutually satisfied?"

"I am." Ranna stood.

Ap Kar pushed his chair back and rose to his feet. "I am."

As soon as they outside the shop, Ranna sagged against Adarlak. "Food. Rest. Now." She had burned up much energy working against him.

Anjan helped her into the nearest shop. And placed their order. A very large order.

Grandeville. Tinker's Place.

R-Bar bounced to her feet. "My oldest sister sent a Hinta warlock seeking Rekel? Seeking Rekel's body?"

Adarlak nodded.

R-Bar sat down. "Hope that he is made of sturdy stuff. That Rekel is a bother." She thought that her sister was a pik ptar meddler.

Sha'gar leaned forward and looked past Tinker at her sister. "Release his hand," she whispered.

Sgenn whispered back, "I did, some time past." She smiled a soft half-smile. "Your male does soft touch."

"Mate'mer," Sha'gar hissed in his ear.

"Oh!" He released her. "Forgot who it was."

Sha'gar stood and gestured for her sister to follow. "We must talk."

Sgenn followed her from the room.

He looked over at the couch where Smoke and Chicken sat. *Smoke, you wanna check Adarlak? Then Sha'gar and her sister?*

????? Smoke blinked at him.

Something is going on.

Well there certainly was. She winked at him.

And I do not want anyone to know what you are doing either. That shouldn't have happened.

She didn't mind.

That is not the point!

Heh heh. Smoke began to filter inside his mind, searching for something that was not the way it was supposed to be.

He sighed. And listened to Adarlak continue her story.

Uant Wze.

The village was called Zan Wze. It was built from the same grey and black rock that it was nestled in. The cluster of houses were three-quarters stone, the uppermost portions wood and thatch.

Far above the village, up the sterile landscape, near the peak was Zar House, tall towers visible from the town. The Reit Guild had Houses perched on many of the crags in this mountain range. Below each house was a village that functioned as the supply center for that nearby house and as its guardian.

Ap Kar had known about the supply function. None knew of the guardian function.

It was small inn, with no other visitors. Few came to Uant Wze and traveled to the high villages, such as the town of Zan Wze. Ignoring the stares, they had arranged lodgings and ordered food sent to their rooms.

As they ate, sitting around the small table, they talked about tomorrow.

"First light," said Anjan. "We are high, the way is steep."

Ranna nodded and refilled their cups. "This guild is muchly hidden."

"Maybe they do not want visitors," suggested Adarlak.

Ranna looked at her. "They have some now."

"Cautious, cautious." Adarlak wobbled to her feet. "Tired." She stepped over and crashed into the bed.

They had hurried through three other elseplaces just to get here. And had removed a number of things that had gotten in their way.

Anjan walked over and dragged the limp body further up the bed by the shoulders. Ranna had the ankles. Between them they put her in the middle of the bed.

As Ranna turned, Anjan jumped lightly to the floor, slipped her arms around the witch and tugged her blouse open and free.

"Hum hum hum," purred Ranna, leaning back. They slowly sagged to the floor. Out of sight of the carefully concealed peep-holes strategically placed to watch the table and the bed.

A messenger ran up the trail to the great structure high above the town with the news. Three would approach at first light.

Preparations were made.

Adarlak woke to soft lips brushing here and there. Warm breath caressed her skin as tongues tickled goose bumps into existence.

"Firstlight." Ranna kissed her.

"New day." Anjan nipped her shoulder.

Adarlak smiled. "We could go tomorrow."

"No." Ranna rolled from the bed waving on clothes. "Now!" She nodded at Anjan.

"There." Ranna pointed at the table, now set, platters filled with steaming foods.

So they sat and ate.

Then they headed out of the village and up the hill. On their way they passed the marker stone.

Whirling dark hurtled down the trail upon them.

Grandeville. Tinker's Place.

Adarlak looked at R-Bar. "Ranna screamed fast instructions and threw me here."

Then she looked at Tinker. "I battered at that ward until it let me pass. And tumbled into your bedroom."

Hunching forward, hands over her face, she began to sob. And after a minute or two, she pulled her hands away, and looked at the rest. "Ranna said that I should seek The One for a great need." Her eyes beseeched them as she rasped, "I have a great need!"

Fighting for control, she wiped her eyes with one sleeve. "A great need." Tears continued to trail down her face.

Tinker sighed. "This is the second time for her."

Messenger sat next to Adarlak and held her hands. "He means Ranna."

R-Bar nodded. "My oldest sister does wild wander."

Tinker frowned in their general direction. "Think that they are still alive?"

R-Bar nodded. "The clan most always feels death shock. Ranna lives." She tapped Adarlak on the knee. "Can you take us to Uant Wze?"

Adarlak jerked. "Yes. We worked the way very carefully. For revisit."

"Hum," said Ran.

Chantal stood. "Couple of days, Simba Leader."

He nodded and yawned. "Let's go back to bed."

They all stood and headed for their rooms. Messenger took Adarlak to a guest room.

Heh heh heh, said Smoke, winking at him as the others went ahead.

Huh! He looked at her. *Now what?* She winked again.

She threw a comradely arm over his shoulders as they headed down the hall. "She is very nice."

"Uh huh. Seems like it."

"Sgenn."

"WHAT?" He halted and glared at her.

Shoving him back into motion, she said, "Shhhhhh, you'll get them all involved." Through the common space and into his bedroom she led him and stopped at his door. "Just be your usual warm bodied comforting self."

He looked inside. "I'll sleep in your room. Or Sha'gar's."

She shoved him into the room and slammed the door shut. And walked around the corner to her room, thinking about this. Among her kind, The Velvetmist, it was not unknown. This was unusual, most unusual. She would think about it as she, as they all slept.

Chapter Twenty-two

Rekel Wander

Krandel's Pot.

She sat in one of the chairs at one of the outdoor tables, one foot propped on another of the chairs. Leaning forward, buffing away the smudge on the tip of one gleaming boot. She was using one of the napkins.

The cause of that smudge lay not too far away, in a crumpled heap, moaning softly.

He had sat at her table, uninvited. And had made certain suggestions to her, also uninvited. He was a member of one of the lesser, rather minor, witch clans. And as he strolled along he had recognized that she was witch and had decided to be sociable. In a manner of speaking. He had thought that he was being sociable. She did not.

A waiter hovered nearby, anxious to retrieve the napkin, get his bill paid, and remove the moaning body which was frightening away customers. But he knew better than to say, or do, anything, just yet. Not until she was finally ready to notice him standing there.

Finally she was ready to notice him, now satisfied with the shine on her boot tip, once again restored to its glass-like perfection. She stood and walked over to the body on the ground. And kicked him again. "Cretin!" She snapped her fingers and sent him elseplace. Unpleasant. And returned to her table, glancing down at her boot tip. It was unmarked.

"I would like the specialty of the house," she told the waiter. "And a new napkin. Make that two new napkins. And some of that pleasant tasting blue stuff."

The waiter nodded violently and ran for the kitchen.

She reset her hat, just so, straightened out her smock, putting it back into its military sternness, brushed some small speck from a sleeve and sat. And watched the folk passing up and down the street. And frowned. Now there was a man dressed in three colors standing there, staring at her.

Just standing over there, staring. Then he came her way. And nodded at her. And stopped, a correct distance away. At least he not as obnoxious as her last visitor.

"May I join?" He looked expectant.

"No."

His face fell.

She waggled her hand at him. "Go away."

"Erb," he said. "You are Rekel? Faan witch Rekel?"

Black eyes stared at him from a blank face. "Who . . . are you?"

He bowed. "I am Hinta warlock Ap Kar, and have traveled long just to meet you."

"Hum." At least this one knew his manners and was polite. "You have met me. Go away."

Unfastening his shirt, he fished around and yanked out the orange stone. "I received . . . "

In a flash she was on her feet, one hand clenching him by the throat, banging him flat on the adjoining table, dishes and utensils scattering across the pavement. "You will answer my questions," she snarled, the air crackling wildly around them, "or die!"

Behind them the waiter nearly dropped the tray bearing her order. She was assaulting another customer. At this rate they might as well close for the day.

"Yes," he rasped. "Ask."

"That stone belonged to my eldest sister Ranna. How came you by it?"

"She gave it to me. In exchange. For information."

Releasing his throat, she waggled a silver wand in front of his face. "Why?"

"I, ummm, wished, ahhh, to meet you." He rubbed his throat. "She said that the stone would lead me to you. And there you are and here I am."

Turning away, she returned to her table and sat. As he regained his feet, she waved over a chair, pointing at it. Across the table from her. "Speak tell!" she demanded.

As Ap Kar stood he carefully dusted and straightened out his garments, then walked over and sat.

And did.

Speak tell.

He left out the private information that he had told her sister. It was private after all.

Rekel leaned back and threw her wand somewhere. "All that to meet me."

The waiter quickly set her order on the table and hurried away.

Ap Kar nodded. "It was a long twisted journey."

"Why?" She began to eat.

He cast protection over himself. "I have never met Faan before witch Ranna entered my small shop. She is very attractive. But had found her's, she said."

"Hum hum," mumbled Rekel, looking up. "Is he very handsome? Which clan?"

"Neither. Your sister took two."

Rekel's eyes flew wide.

"Females."

She gasped.

"A Death Guild Warrior and a Hacto mage."

She stared at him. "True?"

"It is so. Witch oath." He nodded.

"You said Hinta?"

He nodded. Again.

"The witch clan of colors from Din Widdle?"

He nodded yet again.

"Hum." She looked him over, what she could see.

"You have heard of Hinta?"

"It is told that Hinta are proper proper."

"It is so." He carefully set one hand on the table top. "Ranna said that Rekel is order neat."

She nodded. One short nod.

"May I visit, Faan witch Rekel." He was being as witch proper as he could be. This Rekel appeared to be a very stern person. A very neat, very stern person. And very, very witch proper.

"Hum hum hum." She chewed on her lower lip. Then she yanked the waiter in.

"Another meal, another jug."And sent him flying to the kitchen.

"You may, Hinta warlock Ap Kar." She watched him relax. Just a little.

"Perhaps," suggested Ap Kar, seeking safe conversational ground, "we might spell share?"

"First tell me of the multi-colored ones."

So he did, all through their meal. And several jugs later. And watched her relax. Just a little.

"Now," said Ap Kar, refilling her cup, a daring move, but not improper, "tell me how you came by that orange magic."

So she did, all through several more jugs. And a meal or two. And into the dark evening, the tale swapping taking most of the day and a part of the evening.

"May I pay?" asked Ap Kar, hiccuping softly.

"Yes." She patted the back of his hand. "Where do you stay?"

"Forgot to do that."

Rekel heaved herself to her feet. "Come! Where I am will provide you with a room." The air began crackling.

Ap Kar hurriedly paid the bill and followed her.

Two doors down, they turned into a well cared for inn. It was neat. And orderly. Rekel banged on the counter top and announced to the clerk, "This is Hinta witch, err, warlock, Ap Kar, who requires a room."

"I will check," stammered the clerk.

"NO!" corrected Rekel. "You will provide!"

"OF COURSE!" shouted the clerk to the room assigner, snatching a key from a drawer and thrusting it at her.

Rekel handed the key to Ap Kar, the badly tilting Ap Kar. "Here. Follow me. It is just down this way."

"Anywhere," mumbled Ap Kar.

"You will join me for first meal?"

"Me also." Ap Kar hiccuped.

At his door, she stopped him. "I an early riser."

"I will be there," he mumbled, throwing the door wide, falling inside. "Rekel."

Humming to herself, she headed for her room, thinking that this Hinta warlock was turning out to be fairly pleasant company. He was polite, neat, orderly, witch proper. Tomorrow they would spell trade.

Ap Kar rose early and hurried downstairs.

Rekel sat at one of the outdoor tables, sipping from a mug from which grey green fumes drifted lazily into the still morning air. She was leaning back, one leg crossed over the other. Her boots were highly polished, the black trousers draped neatly over the high tops. The high collar of her black blouse was buttoned to the top. Her hat was set on her head, just so. He hurried over and bowed.

"Sit," she said. And waved in another fuming cup.

He sat and sipped. It was quite good.

"Where do you go from here?" Her eyes watched him carefully. Jet black, they seemed bottomless to him.

"In no special direction of no special purpose."

"Hum hum." A careful person was this Ap Kar.

He cleared his throat. Carefully.

She watched him as he set his cup down, just so.

He cast every protection he knew. And sucked in a deep breath and said, "I would do wander."

"Hum."

"With Faan witch Rekel."

Her eyes squinted into narrow slits as she sat straighter, legs uncrossing. "Exactly what did my eldest sister, Ranna, tell you about me? Hinta warlock Ap Kar."

The air soft crackled around them as she carefully set her cup to one side.

Reinforcing his protection spells, he cleared his throat and sat straighter. "She said that her sister, Faan witch Rekel, was prickly, irritating, and the most alone of her sisters, most travel alone. Also she said that you were very clan proper. And Faan value conservative. Very witch proper."

"And?" she sizzled.

"And," he cleared his throat again and pulled in the deepest purple barrier that he knew, "ahem, that wearing the orange made soft contact, feel, touch, aware of the other." Shoving both arms onto the table top, he leaned forward and peered into those midnight eyes. Deep down he could see the flicker of red flame.

"It is true," he whispered, reinforcing the orange. "I am there. You are here."

"Take that stone off," she ordered. "Sneak peek." And glared at him.

He jerked back. "I am not!" He quickly unbuttoned the top of his shirt and jerked it open, yanked the chain from around his neck and banged it and the stone on the table top, shoving all toward her. "HERE!"

She picked up the stone and the chain and dropped them into a blouse pocket, fastening the flap on that pocket. And looked at him. "What are you staring at?"

"Only the witch that you are." He fastened his shirt.

"Which is?" The air crackled louder.

"I would say nicely formed, most witch attractive." And tugged his shirt into its proper order.

"You would say that, you would?"

He nodded. "Yes, I would."

"Hum hum hum." She leaned back. Her frown faded away. She waved in a meal. "Eat! Nicely formed?"

He began to eat. "Yes."

One corner of her mouth twitched. "Then you may stare at my chest, Hinta warlock Ap Kar, if you feel the need to do that. Or my face, if you so choose."

Ap Kar snatched up his cup and took a long swallow. She hadn't attacked. Yet. Then he worked on his meal, looking up, now and then. Every time that he did, she was staring at him.

When they finished their meal, she sent everything away, except for their drinking vessels, which were refilled.

"Soooooo, Ap Kar," she hissed.

"Erm?"

She rolled a long green and black wand between the palms of her hands. The tip of the wand glittered red angry. "You figured out how those itchy fingers of your's are going to sneak inside my blouse, yet?"

Ap Kar gasped. And leaped to his feet, glowering angrily at her. He smashed his fist into the center of the table, bending it badly. "THAT IS QUITE ENOUGH, REKEL WITCH!"

She blinked.

Dropping heavily into his chair, he waved at the table top, restoring it.

"Hum," she said.

"Sorry sorry."

"I would visit a certain Fingl witch on Tar Tar Tak."

He nodded. Carefully.

She stood. "You may come . . . if you wish . . . Ap Kar."

He stood. "I wish."

She took them to Tar Tar Tak, leaving four gold coins on the table top.

Tar Tar Tak. Green and Golden.

Vaccby felt them arrive in her small village, the faint witch pulse of two blowing in. It was a special skill. And very handy skill to have.

Her village was well off the main road and rather isolated. The small products made here were carried to the market town. Few strangers, that is, folk other than the villagers, ever came to visit this village. There was no need.

So, she thought, two witches arriving meant that they would seek her out. And that meant one must be well prepared. She walked outside to sit in the shade of the hamtil tree. And prepared for her visitors.

"Been here before?" Ap Kar looked around, at the buildings lining both sides of the street where they stood. It was a very small village.

"I have not," stated Rekel, reaching over and straightening his collar in the back.

"Why are we here?"

"It was told that Gaz witch Vaccby of the Fingl sub-order has an under sneak spell of some deviousness. I would learn. that spell." She gently brushed some small speck from his shirt front.

"Oda." He nodded. "Eh eh eh."

She banged him on the shoulder, not too hard. "I thought so." Turning slowly, Rekel sought and sent a seeker. "Shouldn't take long," she mumbled.

He stepped away, giving her room, and admired her, in profile, and tightened his protection. The Hinta were known for their protection spells.

She watched him from the corners of her eyes and pretended not to notice. And pushed back her shoulders, just a little, feeling her blouse tighten, just a little.

It returned. She pointed. "That way. Not far. Not close."

Ap Kar hurried to her side as she strode into a side street. "Cautious, cautious."

"Cautious, cautious," she agreed.

Vaccby watched them coming down her street. One black, one many colors. She had never seen one of many colors before. One male, one female. She nodded to herself. And waited under the Hamtil Tree in her chair. She was prepared.

The pair stopped. Not too close. Not too far away.

"You are Gaz witch Vaccby," stated the woman. It was a statement, not a question.

Vaccby thought that this was an interesting statement. She nodded, stood, and thought that this female, being witch, was the more dangerous of the pair.

The tangle struck from an odd angle, bearing the female down, choking off any attempt at spell casting. The male slipped sideways and forward, eluding the second attack. The third attack exploded, rainbow shards raining down around them.

Then he did something Vaccby had never seen or had ever known any warlock to do.

He dashed forward and struck her in the forehead. With

his fist.

She hit the ground, sprawling. And struggled as green things pinned her in place, as yellow things crept over her body, as blue wisps hovered over her face, whispering terror to her.

She screamed. A silent scream.

"Release," he commanded. "Release!"

She did. Instantly.

Ap Kar knelt by Rekel and gently brushed her hair from her face. "Rekel?" He picked up her hat and ordered it clean, and bent closer. "Rekel?"

Her eyes fluttered. And opened. "Gaz tak der dak dak," she snarled.

He helped her sit up. "Wonderfully coarse."

Her eyes jerked and settled on his face. "You should hear my sister, Ripple."

Someone thrashed weakly.

Rekel turned her head and smiled. "I require her alive."

Ap Kar nodded and helped her stand. And handed her the hat.

She walked over to the form on the ground and stared at the colors passing rainbow patches over the sprawling figure on the ground. And kicked her. Then she set her hat on her head, just so.

"Very sneaky, Gaz witch Vaccby," she growled. Kneeling on one knee, Rekel yanked in a flaming red wand with a glowing blue tip and jabbed Vaccby with it.

The Gaz witch jerked and screamed. But no sound came out. Ap Kar had frozen Vaccby's vocal cords.

"I came," explained Rekel, "to learn Gaz indirect. I did hear that Vaccby of the Fingl suborder was the most adept."

She jabbed again, admiring the result as their captive thrashed. “Before I would request and bargain. Now, I demand.” She leaned close to Vaccby’s face and slid the tip, the glowing blue tip, of her wand just below one staring eye, caressing the skin. “Will you agree to teach me, aaaaaahhh, aaaahhhh, teach us?”

Vaccby blinked, afraid to move her head.

Rekel stood and kicked her in the side. “Ap Kar, dear, release this witch. We are about to become Gaz adept, you and I.” The corners of her eyes crinkled as she looked at him.

He nodded.

The colors faded away.

Vaccby sighed and struggled into a sitting position. “Who are you?” she gasped.

Jet black eyes fastened on her. “I am Faan witch Rekel. He is Hinta warlock Ap Kar. We do wander. Together.”

“Many tales are told of the Faan,” said Vaccby. "The Hinta are unknown.” She stood and straightened her clothes.

“Now you know. A little.” Ap Kar stepped over and gently stroked Vaccby’s forehead with his fingertip. The swelling and discoloration disappeared.

“Yes,” she agreed. “A little.”

“Teach” stated Rekel, in no mood for idle conversation.

“I would rest. A little,” replied Vaccby.

Rekel looked at Ap Kar. He nodded.

“You may,” grumbled Rekel. “A little.” She waved in chairs, for two, and a snack, for three. And sat. And carefully watched the Gaz witch as the three of them ate.

“You are safe, Faan, for I did agree.”

“Tak tak,” rumbled Rekel, being as impatient as all the

Faan witches were, save one.

Ap Kar lightly, gently, feather soft, touched Rekel's hand. "It is a wander, after all." It was a daring thing that he was doing.

"Hum," replied Rekel, not moving her hand away.

Vaccby emptied her cup, set it down and stood. "Very well. I am ready. To teach." She nodded at them.

The pair stood. Rekel waved everything away and waited. And nodded.

Vaccby beckoned in a very large bowl, a very large flat bowl, filled to the lip with an oily grey brown paste. "Flerk. A necessary ingredient." She pointed at Ap Kar. "Bare to the waist, warlock."

He nodded. His shirt went somewhere. He was well muscled thought Rekel. And he had wider shoulders than she had thought. His clothes had hid much.

Vaccby slowly began to rub the stuff over his bare torso, starting at his neck. She worked slowly, caressing, stroking, massaging his muscles. And left his arms bare. Then she stepped back and made a careful inspection of him and what she had done, walking all the way around him. "Yes. It is nipto!"

She looked at Rekel. "Now you. Take it off!"

"WHAT!"

"Yes."

"The Faan do not expose themselves."

Vaccby shrugged. "Then the Faan do not learn."

"Hum."

Vaccby shrugged again. "Just so." And watched her.

"Close your eyes, Ap!" snapped Rekel. "Tightly."

Vaccby shook her head. "No. He will watch. What there

is to watch. One cannot train with closed eyes." One corner of her mouth twitched. It was a small revenge, to be savored.

Rekel sizzled anger.

"Are you so ugly?" asked Vaccby sweetly. "Rekel?"

Growling deep in her throat at the familiarity of this Gaz witch Fingl sub-order, Rekel snapped her fingers.

Ap Kar gasped. And tried not to stare.

"Begin!" demanded Rekel, glowering at both Ap Kar and Vaccby.

Vaccby started at Rekel's neck. Taking her time. Smoothing the paste on. Caressing, massaging. And finally, stroking Rekel's stomach, she said, "Very beautiful. As is told of the Faan."

"Flar ptar," sizzled the angry witch, unsure of Ap Kar's very frank and admiring stare. He was trying to keep his face carefully blank.

Vaccby sent the bowl somewhere, cleaned her hands and stepped back and away. "A handsome pair." She nodded at Ap Kar. "When you finish wander perhaps you would come back for some more, um, friendly visit?"

"NO!" snapped Rekel. "He will not. Proceed!"

"Um um," replied Vaccby. "Follow the spell and repeat exactly. And watch my motions closely."

Then Vaccby slowly led them through the afternoon long training.

As the sun settled low, she nodded at the exhausted pair. "It is done." Vaccby looked at Rekel. "We are debt settled."

Rekel nodded. So did Ap Kar.

"Remove this gib tir," demanded Rekel.

"Wash yourself, witch." Vaccby spun on her heels and

headed for her house.

"Gib tik dir dir," hissed Rekel, waving her clothes on over the gooey mess. "Lodgings."

Ap Kar nodded, carefully setting his clothes on. Then he took them. Back to the central spot.

Rekel pointed. "There!" She hurried into the closest inn, demanding loudly, "Rooms, food, bath. Starting with bath. A large bath!"

The clerk nodded and ushered them in the correct direction.

"Go away," she snapped at the clerk, grabbing one of Ap Kar's hands. She yanked him forward as she stepped into the large tub.

The clerk fled, slamming the door shut.

She released his hand as she sank into the water. As her clothes went somewhere, she grumbled at Ap Kar, the water now lapping under her chin. "You may scrub my . . . back."

He nodded and sank into the water.

A long time later, after relaxing some, relaxing for them, and a very complicated meal, eaten outside, Rekel had ordered a table outside, explaining to him that she preferred taking her meals outside, if possible, she sat up and stared over the table at him.

He watched her carefully, chewing slowly on some last tidbit.

She reached up and unfastened the top pocket of her blouse and fished out the chain and the orange stone and tossed it to him. "Here."

He caught it. It was the orange magic.

"Wear it. It is your's."

He did. Stuffed it inside his shirt. And carefully fastened the shirt and tugged it back into order.

"Well?" she demanded.

"Imbl?" He hastily swallowed.

She sat straighter. "Very beautiful?" One sharp fingernail tapped on the table top. It made soft popping sounds and little holes in the table top.

He frowned. "Who? Vaccby?"

"Nik tik tik," she snapped, beginning to frown darkly.

"What?"

She hissed at him. "When that Gaz tar kar was fondling my anatomy and you were staring so hard, she said that I was beautiful, very beautiful."

"Oh. Ah."

"Well?"

He slipped his chair back, just a little.

"True true speak!" she demanded.

He nodded. "Yes."

She growled.

"REKEL! STOP!"

"Tar ptar," she grumbled. "Speak tell."

He sat straighter. "It is told that the Faan, of all the witch clans, the many many, are the most beautiful."

Her eyes watched his.

"When I saw the eldest sister, Ranna, I saw that this was true tale."

She chewed, just a little, on her lower lip.

He cleared his throat. "When I saw Faan witch Rekel standing there, with Vaccby, I knew that it was true tale." He cleared his throat. "Rekel, she spoke what had to be said. You are very beautiful. To me, you are more beautiful. Than all."

"Than Ranna?"

He nodded.

"Hum hum hum," she murmured. And unfastened just the top button on her blouse. On the collar.

"I have traveled long just to see," he said softly. "A face."

"And the rest?"

He shrugged. "Unplanned." A small smile tugged at one corner of his mouth. "But . . . a nice surprise."

"Hum hum hum." She stood. "We must visit my sister, Ripple. She is the clan center, the head. And the most rangle of all."

He stared at her.

"Come."

"What?"

Rekel stepped into the open space of the town spot. And demanded, "Come here, Ap Kar, warlock of the Hinta witch clan."

He stood and walked over. "Rekel?"

She stepped close, reached up, and unbuttoned her blouse to her belt buckle, pale witch skin in sharp contrast to the velvet black of her clothes.

"That is not proper," he gasped.

She grabbed his hands in her's. "There is only us."

"Still. It is not proper. In public!"

"Mine," she whispered, stepping closer, still clenching his hands.

"Rekel?"

"You are mine," she growled.

"Me?"

"Yessssssss." His hands were mashed between their bodies as she pressed against him.

He gulped. "True?"

She kissed him. "Most true."

"Certainly," he said.

"Ripple will be surprised," she said, spinning, taking them elseplace.

Chapter Twenty-three

Always A Surprise

Grandeville. Tinker's Place. Night.

"Not sure that I like this idea," he grumbled as he laid down and yanked up the covers.

"Hum," said Sha'gar, hitching closer to him, using as a pillow one of his shoulders for her head.

"Hummmmmmmm," murmured Sgenn, ever so carefully easing closer to his other side.

"Sooooooooo," he asked as Sha'gar ordered the light to go away, "anyone want to tell me what exactly is going on, this time? In here? In my bed? This time? Here?"

"Mate'mer, relax," said Sha'gar.

"I am relaxed," he growled, wiggling into a more comfortable position.

She tugged at a fold of skin on his side with a thumb and forefinger. "No, you are not. I can feel your muscles all taut. And mentally as well."

He sighed. "O.K., so I am not relaxed. I have good reason for it, a very good reason."

"What is your reason, sulda?" Sgenn rolled onto her side and feather soft touched his chest with her fingertips.

He twitched. "Stop that! That is."

Her hand ever so gently slid over his chest. "Very erba," she murmured.

With some struggle, he managed to grab her hand. Sha'gar had been lying on that arm. He didn't want to move the other one. "Will you behave?"

She kissed the corner of his shoulder. "I am. Sha'gar told this so."

"WHAT?"

"She wanted to know . . . things." Sha'gar patted his stomach.

"So you told her," he snarled into the darkness.

"Of course. Sister to sister."

"That all?"

"You have nice taste," she murmured.

"May I make a suggestion?"

"Yesssssssss, sulda, you may." She hitched a little higher and a little closer, her body just lightly touching his.

"How about," he sighed into the black of his bedroom, "that when we go out there to help Ranna et al, that we grab the first guy that Sgenn likes. Then she can haul his butt into some dark corner and do whatever."

"Poo duk quar," hissed Sgenn, jerking away from him.

"Faan do not do that," growled Sha'gar.

"Bout the only thing," he mumbled, yanking the covers back into order.

"Flik tik," stated Sgenn, kicking the covers into order. For her.

"Not so," stated Sha'gar, pulling the covers into the proper order.

"Hap tap tap!" Sgenn jerked into a sitting position, the

covers flying.

"No." Sha'gar lurched upright.

"Na sulda an tan," moaned Sgenn.

"NOOOOOO!" screamed Sha'gar, lurching over the top of him, wrapping her arms around her sister.

"Oooof!"

"Eh?" asked Sha'gar.

"Eh?" echoed Sgenn.

"Get off. Both of you! Off, off, off. OFF!"

"Sister," ordered Sha'gar, "you will not!" She sat back, her eyes flashed red fire. Soft crimson glow pulsed across the ceiling.

He struggled and finally managed to sit up and back, against the wall. "Who is crying?" Someone was sobbing.

Sha'gar flooded the room in soft faint light.

"Amda," whispered Sgenn, looking down, eyes glistening wet. She plucked at the front of her pajamas. "Fibt dim."

"Hold her!" snapped Sha'gar.

"What?"

"In your arms, Mate'mer. Hold her."

He stared at her.

She leaned close. "Please?" she whispered. "My sister is thinking of going far."

"Merde," he hissed. Then he looked and crooked a finger at Sgenn. And patted the bed by his side, shoving a pillow out of the way. "Come over here. Please?"

Sgenn nodded and hitched over and back until she was sitting next to him, leaning back against the wall.

He slipped an arm around her waist. "Ummmmm, you wanna explain what the problem is? In English? As spoken around here? I really didn't understand most of what you two were saying." He tugged her against his side. And wiped the tears away with the sleeve on his other arm. "Better?"

"No," she grumbled.

"Why not?"

"Sulda tar ptar," she grumbled, slumping.

"AM TAK!" shouted Sha'gar, lurching past him again, slapping her sister on top of the head with the palm of her hand.

"Hold it!"

"Eh?" asked Sgenn.

"Eh?" echoed Sha'gar.

"You guys wanna go into another room and argue?"

"No, sulda." Sgenn looked at him from the corners of her eyes.

"Nope," grumbled Sha'gar.

"Then knock off whatever all that flailing of hands is about."

"She said not-nice about you," mumbled Sha'gar.

"So?" He looked from one to the other.

Sha'gar sat back and glared at her sister. "The Faan do not like their's being so said!"

Sgenn nodded.

"Even from sisters," Sha'gar stated firmly.

Sgenn nodded again. "Sorry sorry." She slid a cautious arm behind his back and around his waist. "Sorry sorry."

"No problemo." He patted her side and really wondered what was going on this time. He was beginning to get nervous.

Sha'gar nodded. And wiggled so she could sit back against the wall by his free side.

"O.K." He sighed. "Now . . . explain. Please?"

"Sulda," breathed Sgenn.

"Start there," he suggested.

"Eh?"

"That term you keep using. What does it mean?"

Sgenn tightened her arm around his waist. "It is a special term of meaning for a theurgist." And leaned her head on his shoulder.

"Uh huh?" He looked at Sha'gar, who nodded.

"A person, sulda, is the all. The essential reason for existence." Sgenn inhaled deeply. "For the Faan or any magic user, witch, or mage, a threat to their's is a reason for death. For a theurgist, a threat to sulda is a reason for chaos."

Sha'gar sucked in her breath and gasped.

"It is our way," stated Sgenn.

"Ando tak tak," mumbled Sha'gar, clenching his arm tightly.

"Sulda," he suggested gently.

"I feel," began Sgenn. "I believe, I am, I . . . " She wiped another tear away. "You . . . sulda."

"Me?" He jerked.

"Hum." Sha'gar stared at her sister.

"It is so," she stated. "In all my wander there was never such a feeling. Only here, healing, did I see this."

"Noooooooooooo!" He sighed, slumping down the wall, pulling his arms free. "Not possible."

Sgenn twisted toward him and nodded. "True speak."

"We are done," he mumbled, looking up at the ceiling, now flat on his back. "Aren't we?"

MindMate?

Aren't we?

Sgenn looked at the ceiling, wondering what he was looking at. Then at her sister who shook her head.

I think that there was something about her that started this.

Is it possible?

Among my people it happened. Very rare.

Nine?

She is nice. Quiet.

But nine.

We have room. She smiled inside his mind.

He sighed. *We have to talk about this.* And grumbled at her, "But you are Sha'gar's sister."

Sgenn nodded. "Of course."

"Folk in this elseplace, your elseplace, have done so," stated Sha'gar. "I have read much of your history lore."

"But."

"I would not be unhappy, Mate'mer."

"But."

"I would live," whispered Sgenn. She bent over him and stared into his face.

"I am not a thing to be divided up," he growled at them, once again staring at the ceiling, past their faces.

"Of course not." Sgenn sat back. "Who would dare?" Vague dark shifted up from the down below.

"No need," hissed Sha'gar.

Sgenn nodded. It went away.

"Ummm?" He looked up at her.

"Yes, sulda?"

"You really want to stay here, that it?"

"Yes."

"With us?"

"With you."

"It is us."

"Dak tak!"

He reached over and patted Sha'gar. "You get to explain it to her. In some way, and I do not understand how, I feel that you are responsible for all this." He glanced from one to the other. "Go somewhere. Talk. I need sleep."

He slid deeper into the bed, tugging the blankets into some sort of order. "And turn off the light."

Sha'gar stood and beckoned her sister to follow her. Sgenn did. Sha'gar darkened the room.

They heard him mumble as the door closed, "I can't believe that this can be happening, not again."

They sat in the dark on one of the couches, in the large living room. And Sha'gar explained exactly what sort of complicated organism they really were.

"Nothing told of this," said Sgenn.

"Few know. In any elseplace. It is our private knowledge."

"Sulda is sulda."

"We understand" She hugged her sister. "Do you understand?"

"Yes."

"You will be changed forever."

"Yes."

Smoke slipped predator silent into the room and sat on the couch next to Sgenn. "It cannot be undone."

"Sha'gar told."

Smoke flowed inside. *Do not resist. This will take some time.*

Yes . . . Smoke.

As he slept, they all knew.

Then the sun, having finally crawled up and above the high mountain ridge that defined the far side of the valley, sent bright lines of gold through the many-paned windows in the living room and tickled their bare feet with warmth.

Smoke stood and stretched. "Done. For now." She turned and bent and kissed Sgenn. "Welcome to us." She smiled as she straightened up. "You are a very interesting person."

Sgenn nodded and tossed an afghan over Sha'gar who was slumped over, sleeping soundly.

Smoke wrenched an ornate ring from a finger and handed it to Sgenn and winked Then she slipped from the room and headed for her bedroom.

Sgenn stood, walked over to one of the large windows and looked out. And all around. Feeling the rest of them, all the parts that were now her as well. And felt the other arrive.

"Morning Light, Mother," she said.

Reep drifted over and stood by her side. "Strange daughter, what have you done?"

"He is sulda. Dark Smoke has joined us together. As was my sister."

Reep drifted closer and tapped her tall daughter on the shoulder. "Look at me."

Sgenn slowly turned. "I will not resist." She knew that death would stare from her mother's eyes.

"Bend your head down."

Sgenn did.

Reep kissed her. "My daughters will do as they do."

Sgenn released a held breath.

"He is a nice person. Your Father will understand. Also."

"Yes, Mother."

Reep floated higher and gently touched Sgenn in the center of her forehead with one finger. "Faan well." And Reep wasn't there.

Sgenn slipped from the room, through the dining room and into the kitchen. Her kitchen, it was now her kitchen, her everything. Now. And walked on.

She stepped into The Chamber, admiring Smoke's design and then into his bedroom. And stood there and looked at him. Then she slipped into the bed, tugging the covers back into order, snuggling next to his warmth and comfort and fell asleep.

Safe.

Healing.

Complete.

Frar Tap. Distant, Lush.

They wandered the town of Far Ferlax for days, exploring every road, every byway and alleyway.

On their first outing, Magna had bought all new clothing, outfitting them in local garb, local in cut and style, all more tasteful than what Phonta had been wearing. The long days of walking to get to this place, and the good meals had added some weight to Phonta's figure. And it was all to the good, thought Magna. Her companion was even more attractive than before.

Now, Phonta stood straighter and was much less nervous. This also pleased Magna.

Then, when they knew the town like one of the natives, and no-one paid any more attention to them, Magna began to think of what to do next. Those pursuing her would not rest and would eventually come here after eliminating all other possible places.

But, for now, they stood at the far end of a narrow pier gazing out at the dark green water.

Behind them was a fisher shed, shielding them from all eyes. They were alone.

Magna idly ran her hands over Phonta's skin, sliding her hands down smooth skin and lovely curves, pondering her next move, wondering did she dare do such a thing.

Phonta leaned back against the railing, arms dangling toward the water, arched her back and mumbled as Magna continued.

"Ohhhh," she sighed.

Magna nodded to herself. She would do it. Releasing her selected companion friendlover, she gently tugged Phonta's clothes back into order. "We are taking a trip," she said. "To elseplace, elsewhere."

"Yes," sighed Phonta. "Yes, yes."

Heading down the pier toward the small restaurant they both enjoyed, Magna slid her arm around Phonta's waist and gently reached up, caressing her ribs. "First, room go." She wanted to fetch the Black Scroll, the thing she was being hunted for.

She had a sudden urge to keep it with her, She always obeyed these sudden urges. They kept her alive.

Bahn Duhr Tohr. The Quarters of the Royal Advisors.

Ripple stared at her sister.

Her sister stared back.

Hanred beckoned Ap Kar over to the table and filled two cups, shoving one at the warlock. "Here. Welcome to the family."

Ap Kar sat, look the cup, and carefully sipped. "Hanred?"

"Yes."

"I heard that name elseplace."

Hanred smiled. "Probably."

"Mine," snapped Rekel, crossing her arms over her chest, glaring at her sister.

"Hum," said Ripple. She was rather surprised.

"Mine is witch clan." Rekel stressed the word witch and stood taller, arms dropping to her sides.

"Zik tik," suggested Ripple. "Tar tak." And shrugged.

Rekel glared at her.

"Come join us," called Hanred, interrupting them. He thought that it was time to interrupt them.

Ripple spun and beckoned over a chair and sat next to Hanred. She snatched the cup hastily filled by Hanred and took a long drink. And looked at Ap Kar, carefully looked at Ap Kar.

He carefully returned her stare. "Humble greetings, clan center." It was the most proper of proper greetings.

Ripple nodded, relaxing some small amount.

"We came, duty bound, to visit," added Ap Kar.

"Hum," replied Ripple, nudging Hanred, who quickly refilled her cup.

"Hinta," said Hanred, recognizing the colors that Ap Kar wore.

Ap Kar nodded.

"The color spinners."

"You know of us?"

Hanred nodded.

"He is widely traveled," explained Ripple, casually sliding her arm over Hanred's shoulders. "A very knowledge laden, arcana and otherwise, person."

Rekel sat and stared at her sister, and her not-witch behavior, doing that in front of others.

"You are him?" asked Ap Kar.

"Who?" asked Hanred, smiling.

"The one called in the elseplaces, Old Hanred."

Hanred nodded.

"Mine," stated Ripple, looking at Rekel, running her fingers through Hanred's hair.

Rekel gurgled.

"Many tales are told of Old Hanred," added Ap Kar.

"And some of the Hinta, here and there," replied Hanred, slipping his arm around Ripple's waist, tugging her close.

Rekel gasped and leaped to her feet. "May we stay visit?"

Ripple nodded.

Rekel yanked Ap Kar to their rooms.

Ripple kissed him on the cheek. "Well done, clever mate."

"Thought that is what you were up to."

"Heh heh heh heh heh."

His hand slithered higher.

"Hum hum hum." She relocated them to the couch.

"Hum it is," he agreed, tugging her blouse free.

"Are you up to no good?"

"Of course."

"Good! After that Rekel, I am in the mood for no good."

Rekel stomped around the large bedroom, boot heels popping. "That Ripple is flik tik."

On the second cycle around the room, Ap Kar stopped her.

"Husband," she gasped.

"It seemed deliberate to me." He kissed her forehead, crossing his arms across the small of her back.

"She has always behaved not-witch," she grumbled.

He kissed the bridge of her nose and gently tugged her blouse loose. "Calculated."

"And he helped her," she grumbled louder.

"Of course." His hands slid up her back, crumpling her blouse upwards. "He is her's."

She told their boots to go somewhere as his lips brushed over her's. "As I am your's." His black eyes gazed into her black eyes.

"Yesssss," she sighed, ordering her upper garments to follow their boots.

"Beautiful," he said. "You are beautiful, Rekel mate-for-life." He nudged her backward, toppling her onto the bed.

"Mine," she purred. "Mine."

She tumbled to the floor and was instantly overwhelmed by a multi-tentacled Harpa Frin from Ckran. One groping arm wrapped around her waist and slowly dragged her into the mass. Others whirled around her arms, pinning her in place as a great feeding disk rose on a thick stalk, darted forward, and fastened to softness.

She gasped as it struck. And gasped again as others followed. Pulsating slowly, they drew her in and in and down.

The beast folded over her, enfolded her, overwhelmed her senses.

With a loud outward rush or breath, she collapsed.

On his chest.

"Illusionist mate," she mumbled.

"It seemed just the thing for a very agitated witch." He gently rubbed her back. "Especially such a dark heart as witch Ripple." He wrapped his arms around her and gently held her.

"Hum hum hum," she sighed, resting her head on his chest, listing to his heart beat.

"Will she stay long?"

"Three days. At least three days. Rekel will be ever so witch proper and follow Faan custom exactly."

One finger slowly ran up her backbone and caressed the back of her neck.

She grumbled softly.

"What?"

"I shall try to be agitated at least once a day for three days."

He laughed. And kissed her.

Uant Wze.

"Ran'na," she whispered, kneeling by the body. She patted the limp form on the side of the face. "Ra'na," she demanded, shaking her by the shoulders.

Jet black eyes fluttered open. "Anjan," she rasped. "How long."

"Long," she replied, bending over, kissing her. "Long. This is the first we have been together."

"We live."

"Yes."

"It is their mistake."

"Where is Adar?"

Ranna clenched one of Anjan's hands. "When they attacked, I sent her elseplace beyond elseplace. Where they cannot reach."

Using one ripped sleeve, Anjan wiped Ranna's face, taking away some of the grime. "You should have gone."

"Both would have died. And I would have been alone."

Anjan nodded.

Ranna shivered. "Hold me, my warrior love."

Anjan yanked the two blankets over, the only furnishings in the bare room, and lifted Ranna into her arms, swinging the blankets around her.

"Adar will free us," mumbled Ranna as she fell asleep.

Anjan slowly rocked back and forth. And blinked away her tears.

Bahn Duhr Tohr. Somewhere At Sea.

The small fleet had been sailing for days.

And days.

And days.

Always in the same direction.

They had long ago left the land far behind them, something that the seafaring community never did. And much to the surprise of the sea folk, the ships had not shot over the edge of the world and disappeared into the void.

This simple fact raised The Royals in the crew's esteem, especially the Princess, as all knew that this expedition was her idea and her order.

All the crew, on each of the ships, had volunteered, even knowing what she planned to do, even knowing that they were looking certain doom in the face. And yet, here they were, still sailing along, still headed in the same direction, still alive. It was a wonder one told another. And they also told one another how brave and clever they had been to come along. None mentioned that she had promised twice-wages and full support to their families if they did, in fact, pitch over the edge of the world.

So they sailed. On and on and on.

For days and days and days.

Then, one day, far ahead, much to their surprise, there they saw them, sitting on the far horizon, they saw them there.

Clouds.

A long line of them.

Clouds.

And the more experienced of the crew said those clouds looked like the clouds one saw forming along the sea edge of land.

The Princess, standing in the bow of the lead ship, thumped her brother on the shoulder, rocking him sideways. "That tale was correct."

He grinned. "Even if there is nothing there, you will have made history."

"Our new kingdom, Brother."

"What name, Great Queen, for this new land?"

She frowned. "That will take some thought." She propped her head in her hands, elbows on the railing, and stared at the cloud band.

Sook approached them and stood the correct distance back.

The Prince noticed and smiled at her. "Always so formal." He pointed. "Land."

Sook nodded. "Aunt R-Bar sent a call to all Faan. Aunt Ranna and one of her's has been taken."

"By whom?"

"Aunt did not say. Mother will ask."

The Prince smiled even broader. "We could ask Father and Mother to send an army."

The Princess straightened up and turned toward them. "Are you leaving us?"

"No, Princess. I am your advisor."

"You may if you wish."

"Aunt told that they were going to help. I shall stay."

The Princess nodded.

"Good," said the Prince. He smiled happily.

Sook stepped to the railing and looked out across the water. "A new land?"

"Yes," said the Prince. "New land. New kingdoms." He laugh happily. "And maybe even new rules as well. New ways of living."

The Princess turned her head and stared at him. "Interesting thoughts, Brother."

"It is true, Mighty Princess, soon to be Queen. These are new lands. And soon they will have new kingdoms, large, or small." He stepped sideways, closer to her. "Surely there are certain rules, certain customs, certain restraints, that you would like to change. This is our great opportunity."

She nodded. "This, Mighty Prince, soon to be King, requires even more careful thought."

"Sister, I would wed who ever I would choose, not some

simpering wench who happens to be highborn."

"You may do that now."

"I would be King."

"Mother married Father."

"He was Royal from elseplace."

She nodded. "Those rules insure a certain order in the kingdoms."

"I would have my people strive beyond their station. If they wished to do so."

She nudged his arm. "Come to my cabin. I would discuss this idea with you in private, in some detail." Her eyes flicked to a nearby seafolk who was pretending that he wasn't listening to their conversation.

The Prince smiled. And spun the other way. "Sook, would you ask the Ship's Master to have a jug or two sent to the cabin of the Princess?"

Sook nodded. And walked away.

He watched her until she headed below deck.

Bahn Duhr Tohr. The Quarters of the Royal Advisors.

They were in their great tub, relaxing. Hanred was very relaxed. Ripple was as relaxed as witches ever got, especially witches of the Faan clan. She was not very relaxed. But, for her, it was very heavy relaxing indeed.

"Hum hum hum," she murmured, leaning forward, kissing his forehead.

He stared into the bottomless black eyes with the deep red fire flicker and asked, "Midnight Delight?"

"You are starting another daughter."

"Just me?"

"I am helping a little."

He reached up. "Very nice."

"Nicer than the Queen's Third Handmaiden?"

He smiled. "Perhaps I should take a closer inspection, a very close inspection, of that fair form? Ahem, just for comparative purpose and learned study. Where are my measuring tongs?"

"Husband," she growled. "You are not inspecting, or measuring, anyone's anatomy. Other than mine."

He nodded and gave her a very sage look. "These handfuls are wonders to behold."

"Just behold?" She leaned closer.

He tugged her even closer. "There are other, ummmm, activities."

"Hum hum hum." There was a soft pop up near the ceiling. The scroll bounced off her back.

"An tak tak!"

Releasing her, he fished the scroll from the water and handed it to her.

"It is from the runt," she said, unrolling it.

"What is she and all of them up to now?"

Ripple hissed. Dark swirled around the ceiling, rumbling loudly.

"WHAT?"

"My eldest sister has been taken along with one of her's. The other, the magician Adarlak, was thrown to them asking for help."

"Again?"

"Hum duk duk," grumbled Ripple. "This is the another time for her."

"Any way to keep her out of trouble?"

"Witches do as they please."

"One of these times she will die."

"We will talk with Rekel later." She nodded. They fell into their large bed.

"We are wet," he observed.

"Of no import." She grabbed him. "I would have a daughter named Szart, named after a powerful witch of legend."

Chapter Twenty - Four

Quiet Interlude

Grandeville. Tinker's Place.

Adarlak strolled from her bedroom, down the hall and into the large living room. And stared at the sleeping form on one of the couches. It was the magician, Sha'gar. She wondered why she was sleeping there rather than in her own bedroom. The Royal, Princess Chicken, had explained about The Chamber and their bedrooms located in that portion of this structure.

Turning away, she walked outside onto the front deck and looked at her surroundings.

They were obviously isolated, there was not a neighbor in sight. And far across the valley she could the mountain range looming up. The sun was high enough to flood the valley floor with light. She sighed. This place did have a most comfortable feel to it. This must be why Ranna had sent her here, although she couldn't understand what there was about this place that made it feel this way.

She shook her head. She certainly didn't understand how this male person, who surrounded himself with females, could be of any help. Although the witch one was certainly powerful and she supposed that the magician must have skills as well. And that Dat creature certainly was skilled in strange ways.

So she stood and thought about everything she had encountered so far. To one side, through the open dining room windows, she heard someone making faint noises in the kitchen area. And then that someone leaned out of one of the windows. She was bare to the waist.

"OOOOPS! Thought that you were someone else. Want some breakfast?"

Adarlak nodded.

Fair Morn smiled. "Be right back." And ducked back inside. To start breakfast. And to shrug on her pajama top. Otherwise he would start grumbling the moment he got up, all because they had this visitor who happened to be female and shouldn't really care one way or another.

As she worked at the large range, Chicken walked in from the hall and stepped up behind her, sliding her arms around and under Fair Morn's top. "Fair morn, Fair Morn," she said, kissing the back of her neck.

"Coffee's ready. Adarlak is on the front deck."

Chicken walked away, filled two cups and headed that way. "Most early a'riser."

Sitting on the edge on the deck, she began to talk with the magician, searching for any piece of information that Adarlak could remember that might be useful to them when they went to free Ranna.

In the kitchen, Fair Morn filled the large skillet with diced potatoes and gently reached out with her mind. Most of them were coming awake. Smoke was back from her morning run and easing through the side door headed for the shower room. He was still asleep. Sgenn was sitting up, staring at him.

Morning, said Fair Morn.

OH! Sgenn jerked. *First Light . . . Fair Morn?*

Yep, it's me. Hungry? I am making breakfast.

Yessssssss. She stood, slipped silently from the bedroom and down the hall to the kitchen. As she passed the shower room entryway, she heard the shower start up.

You are learning fast. Smoke smiled in her mind. And worked up a thick lather in her hair.

Sgenn stood next to Fair Morn and watched what she was doing. Fingers slid across her backside as Chicken passed by. "Me'thinks we do require pot pon front deck. Fair Morn, Sgenn."

"First light, Princess."

Fair Morn nudged Sgenn with her elbow. "Better put your top on. We have a visitor and we are cooking."

Sgenn nodded. Something black handed up her garment. She took it and shrugged it on and looked down. Something was tickling her ankle.

Dat looked up at her. "You going to make cocoa?"

Sgenn bent over and picked her up. "I do not know the formula for that . . . Dat."

"I will tell you," said Fair Morn.

Sgenn set the tiny figure on the counter top.

Dat walked across the range top and peered inside the large skillet. "Fried earth tubers. Not too bad tasting." Then she leaned against the pan and idly kicked one foot through the blue flames curling up the sides of the frying pan and stared at Sgenn. "You his new houri? Does he like to play with your body?"

"Shhhh, Dat," ordered Fair Morn.

"Emel. Yes. No, he has not."

"Yet," laughed Fair Morn.

"Morning, morning, morning." Messenger bubbled into the kitchen, a large white towel turban wrapped around her head. She had taken a shower with Smoke. "Oh boy, oh boy, oh boy, hash browns." She filled two cups and headed for the living room. Sha'gar was waking up.

Bouncing into the living room, she handed one cup to Sha'gar who was sitting up, afghan draped over her shoulders.

"Morning, morning, morning." And dropped into the couch, somehow managing to not slosh her coffee in all directions. Sha'gar carefully sipped from her cup.

"Your sister is really nice," gushed Messenger. "But she is really quiet." She smiled. "Really really."

"Theurgist," replied Sha'gar.

Smoke walked into the kitchen and hugged the cooks. "Nice morning for a run." She smiled. "Good morning, Dat. Cocoa ready?"

Dat poked her cup into the brown liquid and took a taste. "Almost."

One of the coffee pots suddenly disappeared.

Ran and I are on the rear deck, explained R-Bar.

"Where's a damn cup?" mumbled Chantal as she came to a stop in front of the coffee makers. Her eyes were barely open.

Sgenn hurried over, grabbed one, filled it, and poked it into Chantal's hand. "Here."

Chantal headed down the hall. "Thanks," she mumbled.

Sgenn looked at Smoke.

"She doesn't wake very fast. Even slower than he is." Smoke smiled. "You have to let them wake slowly and leave them alone, in the morning until they do."

And sometime around thirty minutes later or so, they all

settled around the table in the dining room as Smoke, Fair Morn, and Sgenn set plates and pans around on the table top.

Chantal, eyes half open, awake enough to eat, pointed. "That is your chair, toots."

Sgenn nodded and sat in the indicated chair.

Adarlak watched them as they ate and held soft conversations.

Tinker wandered in and dropped into his chair, dragged over a cup and took a sip. Chicken had filled his cup when she had felt him approaching.

"Fair morn, Me'Lord." She or Chantal were the only ones who talked to him as he was waking up.

"Gumpf," he mumbled, eyes mostly shut.

Sgenn nudged her sister.

"Not awake. Yet," murmured Sha'gar.

"Watch those claws," grumbled Chantal as Dat climbed up her pajama top in order to sit on Chantal's shoulder.

"His new houri needs to eat much."

"Why?"

"She is still recovering. And lost much weight." Dat leaned lose to Chantal's ear. "A little more weight would make her four yums for sure."

"Only four?"

Dat laughed. "Kickle, kickle, kickle."

"Yes?"

"There are only a few five yums around." She grabbed Chantal's hair so she could lean forward without slipping down. "Me of course."

"Of course."

"Fair Morn."

"Comes from having been a magical jest."

Dat peered into Chantal's top. "You are pretty yummy."

"I think that we have had this conversation before." Chantal refilled her dish.

"Gimble, gimble, gimble," grumbled the tiny indjinn.

He sat up a little, picked up his cup just refilled by Chicken, and looked around the table.

"Soooooooo, we did it again." He sighed heavily.

"You wanted to," said Smoke.

"My sister would have gone far," stated Sha'gar.

"D.O.M.," grumbled Chantal.

"What?" Messenger looked her way.

"Dirty Old Man."

Sgenn looked at him. "You are not old."

Fair Morn laughed.

"Thanks," he replied.

Fair Morn winked at him. "She left off the dirty part."

"Heh heh heh," cackled R-Bar. Ran nodded and cackled.

Sgenn looked around the table at them all. "You should not do that," she commanded.

"Oh my gosh!" Messenger slumped in her chair until only her eyes were peering over the top edge of the table.

"What, sister?" Sha'gar stared at her.

"Denigrate him."

"They joke," whispered Sha'gar.

"Do what?" asked Tinker.

"Put down, John, put down." Chantal grinned at him. She was awake. "Your new tootsie is defending you."

"Bout time that someone did," he grumbled.

Sgenn looked at Chantal. "Tootsie?" It was the second

time that she had heard this strange term or something like it.

"A term of endearment," explained Fair Morn.

"Smoke?" he asked.

"By tomorrow she will have all the memories, especially the language ones."

He sighed. "How about we lounge and rest today?"

"Or whatever." Chantal leered at him.

"And pack what we need tomorrow."

Messenger popped upright. "Oh boy! I can finish the flower garden."

And then.

They all scattered.

Chicken, R-Bar, and Ran took Adarlak out front, to sit on the lawn and talk about what they needed to plan for.

Tinker looked at Sgenn. "Let's take a walk out through the pasture and talk."

She nodded.

And some time later, they strolled out through the first pasture, dressed in shirts, jeans and hiking boots.

"By tomorrow," he said, "you will have all the memories and experiences except for the really private stuff."

"Strange strange," she replied. "It is strange to be me and everyone else."

He nodded. "Takes a lot of getting used to."

They stepped over the edge of the great depression, a gigantic bowl shaped place where the land had sunk.

"A favorite place to sit and talk," she said, pointing at the slope just below the lip of the hole.

At the bottom of the steep slope, as they walked along the

western edge, she pointed. "The cavern where Macabre put your first treasure."

"See," he said. "That is how it works."

She stopped, turned and stared into and out of his eyes. "I see you seeing me seeing you." She touched the tip of her nose with one finger. "I have never seen myself as others see me."

He blinked.

She was gone. Just herself again.

He started walking, working up the slope, heading up to the narrow trail that ran up and out onto the long ridge.

As they walked along the narrow path on the spine of rock, toward the far end, she pointed back toward the house, small in the distance. "We are now at the edge of their awareness."

"Yep."

"It is learning a new."

He nodded. "Smoke explained private, didn't she?"

She nodded, and smiled. "Yesssssss."

He blocked his mind.

She frowned at him.

"That is what it feels like." He released.

She did it. "Ermel. It gets so quiet."

"Yep."

She released. And he blended in. *Now. Do it.*

I see. Now we are together, sulda. Just you and me. Her half-smile tugged at the side of her mouth as she stepped close and wrapped her arms around him. *Just you and me.*

He held her and gently rubbed his hands up and down her back. And sighed.

What?

"We stopped adding quite a while ago. Eight was supposed to be it."

She leaned against his chest and listened to his heart beat. "The Smoke said that she was thinking about that."

One of his hands ran through her hair. "I know."

"Oh! Of course." She leaned back and looked into his eyes. "Sulda?"

"Ummmm?"

"You are the first male that has handled me."

He tugged her shirt loose. "Ummmm."

She reached down and yanked it free. "Theurgist training is long and hard and dangerous."

She stepped back and unbuttoned his shirt. "I like your hands sliding over my skin, sssssssulda."

"Nice skin." He slipped her shirt from her shoulders and stared.

"Am I ugly?"

He shook his head. "No. No, you are not. You are lovely, very beautiful." One fingertip gently touched her. "What have you been doing?"

She looked down. "What?"

"Scars. There are little scars all over the place. And that great big one."

She slipped her shirt back in place. "I will stay clothed." And began to button it.

"What caused all that?" He reached out and undid her top button. "It is all right."

"True speak?"

"Can't lie to ourselves, can we? And we are all kinna beat up, here and there."

"Ermel." She leaned her forehead on his chest. "It was only my training, sulda. Just that. Nothing other."

"Kinna hard on the bod."

Plucking his side with two fingers, she breathed soft. "Many many die. It is why there are so few of us."

He gently brushed back her hair with one hand. "You must be pretty tough."

"I am Faan. I am the first theurgist in many generations." She looked up. "Mother taught me before I did wander. Before I trained with the few. She is very powerful. For a witch."

He smiled. "Certainly frightens most of her sisters."

"I am not frightened."

"Shouldn't be."

"Of anything."

He felt the air shift and change around them. Something moved. "Careful."

She kissed him. "I like that, also."

So he kissed her back. "Me too." And felt the environment return to normal. "Let's head back to the house."

She released him, buttoned her shirt, and tucked it into her jeans. "See. I know your elseplace proper." And crashed into him, swinging her arms around his waist.

"OOOOOF! What?"

"It is good. To be us."

Tilting up her head, he kissed her. "I know," he murmured. "I know."

They headed back toward the house.

"EEEEEEEEEK!"

It was Chicken.

"Better put your shirt on, they are on their way back."

They had been lying on the side lawn, sunning themselves. Smoke's normally tan skin never seemed to burn, just tanned ever so slightly.

Chicken's fair skin seemed to be immune.

Both of them just enjoyed the warm sun on bare skin.

"Piffle," commented Chicken, rolling onto her side, pinching Smoke back.

"Eeeeek," said Smoke, just to be polite. "I didn't pinch you there."

"We will pinch, We will, where err We do so fancy," announced Chicken in her most Royal rolling tone of voice.

Smoke grabbed her.

"Unhand this, Our Verra own anatomy, wench!" She squirmed.

"Just consider it as a large pinch."

"Desist!"

Smoke released her and leaped to her feet, pulling on her shirt.

Chicken stood and stared down her nose at herself. "Do thee leave prints of fingers thereon?"

"Of course not."

"Wench," reiterated Chicken as she pulled on her shirt.

"Royal pincher." Smoke tied the tails of her shirt across her lower ribs.

So did Chicken.

"He has become very Velvetmist. This time it went easy."

Chicken grinned. "Most true. And most passing strange."

"I think that he just knew, this time. Some of the consorts had that ability."

Chicken threw her arm around Smoke as they headed toward the house. "We will Ourself sweet cocoa make."

"I will take the cookies out back. Made lots."

Chicken laughed.

They all gathered around one of the large wooden tables on the rear deck. Many had cocoa, some had coffee. They all had cookies. Then they made room for Tinker and Sgenn as they walked through the path in the flower bed and up onto the rear deck.

Chicken handed him a cup. "Coffee, My Lord." And one to Sgenn. "Cocoa, Sweet Sister Self."

He sat. "Thanks."

Sgenn sat next to him and nodded at Chicken. "Thank you."

Chicken walked around the table and sat next to Smoke.

"SOOOOOOOO," he asked, "are we ready?"

Chicken nodded. "We are that, Fair Prince. Most ready."

Ran nodded. "Adarlak told us all that she knows of that elseplace."

R-Bar grumbled, "Which was not much."

"We were not there long," explained Adarlak, looking at him.

Sgenn curled her hands around her cup. "That guild is very dangerous. They shouldn't have gone to that elseplace."

All eyes looked at her.

She looked at Adarlak. "You are fortunate that Faan witch Ranna was strong enough to save you."

"What do you know about that guild?" he asked softly.

"They are on The Death List," stated Sgenn.

"The what?"

"The Theurgist Death List. Any theurgist that meets anyone of that guild should instantly kill them."

"Holy cow!"

Steady, My Lord. Chicken had felt his mind lurch and jump.

"No sulda, they are evil, not holy." She looked across the table at her sister. "Evil, evil, evil. And not cows, either."

Tinker leaned his forearms on the tabletop. "Well that certainly complicates things a bit."

"Indeed, My King, indeed." Chicken frowned and began to dig a fingernail into the wood of the tabletop and looked up at R-Bar. She was staring into somewhere.

"My eldest sister is still alive," she stated. Suddenly she jerked and began to cackle. Ran jabbed R-Bar with an elbow.

R-Bar looked across the table at him. "Rekel has found her's. A Hinta warlock. Ripple just told all."

"The same Rekel that was here?"

"Correct, Tink. Rekel, the Irritating One. Wonder how she found anyone that would put up with her and her tik tik behavior? Especially from a witch clan. Most have been the same one that Adarlak mentioned."

Sgenn looked at R-Bar. "I did not meet that sister when I witch trained."

R-Bar shrugged."She tends to stay away."

He rapped a knuckle on the table top to bring them all back to the more important question. "How are we going to do this? We want to get Ranna back, not start a war."

"And Anjan," added Adarlak.

"Oh!" He smiled at her. "Sure. Her too."

I could put her to steep, MindMate.

Think you could?

Smoke smiled at him. And all the rest wondered why they were mind talking private.

Then what? We can't just lug her around.

If that guild house is not too far away, we could leave the Princess and Chantal with her while we go get Ranna and Anjan.

Sounds good to me.

Smoke told Chicken and Chantal.

Chicken looked at him and nodded. As did Chantal.

O.K., we'll do It. And hope that she understands why, afterwards. How long will she sleep?

I will just hold her there. It will only work as long as I am not overly distracted. Smoke winked at him.

He yawned. "I am going to take a nap." He stood and headed for the side door, And wound up in the small living room, sprawling on the couch.

Sgenn slipped silently in, closing the door. "Sulda?"

"Ummmm?"

"I will nap with you."

"Sure, lots of room." He made room as she stretched out alongside him. He had been staring up at the ceiling. He rolled onto his side. "Do you really have to attack those guys?"

"It is a strong command."

He popped a few of her shirt buttons loose and slid his hand over her mid-section. "Oh well."

It was some time later and she leaned over the back of the couch and said softly, "Tink?"

"Umm?"

"Ripple is having a daughter named Szart."

His eyes opened and looked up. "Latest news flash from

Bahn Duhr Tohr?"

"She didn't say anything about the expedition of The Royals."

"Who?"

"Ripple."

"Ah."

"I really wonder how that Rekel could find one."

"Worlds beyond counting out there. There had to be someone, somewhere."

She looked doubtful even though it had happened.

"Someone that carries a big stick."

She growled at him.

He smiled. "Just a thought."

Sgenn's eyes opened. She smiled, a soft half-smile at him and at R-Bar. It was very much like Sha'gar's smile. She slipped her hand inside his shirt and mumbled, "Mine."

R-Bar reached down and poked her in the side. "Our's!"

Messenger came in. "Lemonade on the rear deck!"

Chapter Twenty-five

Things Turn Strange. Sometimes.

Grandeville. The Knock'em Down Bowling Alley.

It was very late in the afternoon.

"Partner," said Red as he stepped back to admire the pins still standing at the far end of the bowling lane. "I think that I have finally figured it out."

"The secret of the universe?" Green watched as his ball crashed through the pins leaving the six, nine, and ten pins standing.

"Almost," sighed Red. "What's going on with our bowling game. But not with why this bowling alley keeps changing its name."

They headed back for their refreshments after their second attempts. Their opponents stepped around them, smiling broadly.

"I think that the term is no talent." Green sipped from his pitcher. It looked like a mug in his hand. He meant their game, not the name changing.

Red did the same. "They cheat."

"No way to cheat in bowling other than if they are keeping score, which they are. Maybe."

Red lowered his voice to a raspy bass hum. It was always

raspy, but usually never held this low in tone. "They are deliberately letting us win."

Green watched the taller of the two women caress the alley with her ball as she sent it on its way. "Think so?"

"That's a big uh huh, partner." Red stepped closer. "I think that they think that if they win all the time that we won't invite them to come along any more."

"Well," said Green, "your lawyer babe wife, being both a lawyer and a babe as well as your wife, is overly endowed with deviousness, three times worth."

"So, what ya think?"

Green carefully watched their opponents, all cop stare. He watched them bowl and watched them hold discussions before and after the first ball and then hold an even more animated conversation just before the second.

"Uh huh. They just let us get ahead by two pins."

"So, Partner?"

"So I think," said Green, "that we will let them think that they are being clever and not say anything. They'd probably quit if they knew that we had figured out what their little con game is all about."

"Wouldn't want that."

The taller of the two stepped closer to her friend and indicated with her chin the two immense men standing there sipping from their pitchers. "What is your moose talking ever so carefully to my monster about?"

"No way to tell. But they both have that cop look on their faces. And Green has been intently staring at you while you were bowling."

"Not just gawking at my butt?" Janine laughed.

"Nope. That was a cop stare, a searching cop stare, a wondering what is going on cop stare."

They two gigantic men walked down to the lanes.

"Pardon us, ladies," rumbled Green, "but you two are holding up the game."

"You drink all the beer?" asked Janine.

"Nope. We ordered three pitchers. One for Red, one for me, and one for you two."

"Let's get something to eat," said Sandy as she and Janine headed up to their table.

"O.K., Partner," said Red as soon as their opponents were out of ear shot. "Let's see what happens after we are done with this frame."

"They won the first game," said Green, watching his bowling ball as it hurtled down the lane.

"So," replied Red, sending his second ball at the few pins left standing. "That means that no matter how poorly we do, they will have to be just slightly worse."

"Let's go watch." Green shrugged. He had missed.

Janine took a hasty bite from her burger and mumbled around it as they walked down to take their turn. "Certainly going to be hard to do that badly."

Sandy laughed and banged her on the shoulder. "You can do it, Streak. Just let me go first."

Janine swallowed and grinned. "How about we just take them, three zip!"

Sandy laughed with her. And shook her head. "Ladies don't do things like that. Besides, it is more challenging this way."

Janine hooted and looked back at Red and Green. They

seemed to be talking about something and not watching their opponents at all.

"Bet you a beer," said Red.

"Sucker bet," replied Green.

"Even if they pull ahead, it will only be two to four pins max. Nothing that we can't overcome. With luck."

"And their help," added Green.

"That's a big un huh, Partner." Red tilted up his pitcher and took a long swallow.

And when the monster pair had finally won the third game, squeaking by, by one pin, Green gave his partner a barely perceptible nod of his head.

Janine and Sandy laughed and giggled and happily paid for the beer.

"Close game," said Janine, dropping her hand on top of Green's massive forearm still curled around his plate. Sandy and Janine looked like two young girls sitting by their fathers, they were so dwarfed by the massive bulk of the two men.

"Certainly was," grinned Red, carefully draping his arm over Sandy's shoulders.

She grunted. "Careful, moose."

"Sure, babe." Red started on another pitcher.

Janine looked at her hand, still resting on Green's forearm. She didn't think that she could wrap her fingers around. So, she tried.

"What?" he asked.

She couldn't. "Let's get some chili at Big Darlene's Place."

"Sure," said Green. "We have tomorrow off as well."

"Tomorrow's Saturday. We can all sleep late," stated Sandy, nudging Red in the ribs. "So we can go to a movie as well. It is still early."

"We will buy the chili." Green shoved back his chair. Janine yanked her hand away. "And the popcorn," added Green.

As they stood, Janine said, "Hold my wrist," to Green. And held out her arm.

"Sure." He did. Using his thumb and forefinger. His fingertips touched each other. "Nice wrist." There was lots of room inside his fingers for Janine to waggle her wrist.

She looked up at him. "I keep forgetting."

And shortly thereafter, Slick William, new to the town, made the biggest mistake of this day. For him.

Red and Green were standing out of the way, watching Janine and Sandy pay for the beer and burgers. Red and Green had paid for the bowling. And they watched William step up to the counter next to Janine.

"My, my, my," observed Slick William.

"Buzz off!" snapped Janine, pushing his hand away.

"Don't be unkind," he replied, giving her a little pat, a little friendly pat on the rear pocket.

"Get lost, creep!"

He leaned closer.

And suddenly rose into the air.

"HEEEEEEY!"

Green shook him, just a little.

"If you hit him," rasped Red, "we will have to fill out all that paperwork and we will miss having that chili. And the movie as well."

"Good point," replied Green. "Back in a minute." He headed for the door, still holding Slick William in the air.

"What's going on?" demanded Slick William. "Put me

down!"

"Stop squirming," demanded Green in return. "We are just going outside."

Sandy looked at Red. "What is he going to do?"

Red shrugged. And winked at her. "Nothin' illegal, counselor."

In a moment Green returned. "Let's go get that chili."

He smiled at Janine. "That fellow apologized." And gently slid his arm around her shoulders and gave her a very careful hug. "Don't frown like that. It puts wrinkles in your forehead."

Green looked at Sandy. "Counselor, I just showed him my badge and suggested that he was close to disturbing the peace."

They walked out the door, across the parking lot to Green's truck, and then drove over to Big Darlene's for that chili.

Before deciding which movie to see.

Uant Wze.

They swirled in.

Suddenly.

They were there.

Filling up the central room. The inn keeper's eyes bugged out as he gasped and looked for the shortest way from the room. His fright was partially due to their sudden appearance, here in the central room of his establishment. The rest was due to his sudden recognition of Adarlak.

She strode up to his table and rapped on it with her mace. "Rooms. We require rooms." And, as soon as he handed her the appropriate keys, she paid him. And then smashed him alongside the head with her mace, As he slumped behind his table, she cast, binding him several layers tight. She turned to the rest of them.

"He must have told else we would not have been surprised." She jerked a thumb over her shoulder. "He will not tell this time."

Tinker nodded. "Shall we store what we don't immediately need in our rooms?" They headed upstairs and dumped their belongs wherever they felt like doing so.

"My lord, shall we away?"

"Sure, let's go. So far, we have surprise on our side." He nodded at Smoke.

Sgenn began to sag. Smoke caught her and laid her on the bed. "She will sleep until I release her."

"Good. Princess, stay here. And Chantal. That ought to do it."

The rest headed outside and gathered on the path.

Tinker looked up the mountain side. "Adarlak, lead the way. And tell us as soon as we get close to that spot where you were attacked. I want everyone ready. Now!"

He reached over his left shoulder and swung down the great black sword. He could feel the urge crawling up his arm from the hilt as the sword hunted for something to kill. "Guess we're ready," he mumbled.

They headed up the slope, the air crackling around the witches and the magicians.

Messenger walked alongside Tinker. "She is really going to be unhappy with us. Really really."

"Who?"

"Sgenn."

He shrugged. "Better than having her attack these guys the moment we see them. I'd rather convince them to just hand over Ranna and Anjan than start a brawl."

"Grey-green-blue," gasped Messenger. She pointed up the hill. "There is stuff coming toward us."

Everyone looked up the slope. There was nothing there that they could see.

"How close?"

"Twenty feet."

"Kill it!" he ordered.

Ran, R-Bar, Sha'gar, and Adarlak cast up the slope. Something screamed and made loud thumping thrashing noises.

"It ran back up the hill," said Messenger.

"What was it?"

"A vague thing. Sort of like a cloud."

"Hum," said R-Bar. Ran nodded. "Bad bad."

Adarlak slowed up. "Just ahead, by that stack of rock."

"See anything?" asked Tinker.

"No, MyTinker." Messenger's eyes jumped from place to place. "Nothing."

"O.K. But slowly. Smoke?"

"Nothing, MindMate. But I couldn't feel anything when Messenger saw that other stuff."

Ran nudged R-Bar. "Strange bad."

R-Bar snatched down a jet black wand with a glowing green tip. "Time for angry, Ranfer."

Ran reached out and fetched in a clear purple sphere. Red streaks wandered across the shiny surface. She nodded at R-Bar.

"Careful," hissed the shorter witch.

Ran nodded again.

Sha'gar joined them, Tinker and Messenger, and walked alongside Messenger, staying away from the weapon that floated so easily in his hand.

"Mate'mer, the witches call in terrible ugly."

He shrugged and looked over at her. Red flame was crawling up and down the ruby wand she was holding. Deep in her eyes, deep down in the jet black, he could see red flickering.

They passed the spot with the stacked rock and walked slowly upward.

Messenger gasped and pointed.

A building was slowly appearing, just ahead of them. It had nothing to do with the spires and towers that they could see further uphill, well beyond.

"Tricky, tricky," grumbled R-Bar. Ran nodded, and shifted the clear purple sphere from hand to hand.

As they walked closer, the door opened.

"Inside," said Smoke. "They are inside. Six." She grunted. "Twisted, ever twisting minds."

"STOP!"

Smoke pulled herself back. "Never met anything like that before. They wait for us."

"How are the rest?"

"Sgenn sleeps. The Princess and Chantal watch and wait and talk. The inn keeper is inert."

"Fair Morn?"

He heard levers click as she made adjustments. "Ready, One."

He sighed. "O.K., here goes." He stepped through the door. Into a large, rather pleasant appearing room. It was flooded with soft golden light. Six figures sat in large chairs along the far wall. They were dressed in heavy green and yellow robes. The six watched their visitors approach.

One stood. "Why came you here, strangers, to this our land?"

Tinker stopped, keeping distance between himself and the speaker. "To find our friends."

The speaker waved his hands, providing chairs for all. "Sit." He sat.

Tinker couldn't tell from the tone of voice whether that was intended as a command or a request or a suggestion. He sat, figuring that it didn't really matter what it had been. The rest remained standing. He rested the great blade across his lap, still holding the hilt. "How come you grabbed them?"

The speaker frowned. This strange fellow spoke a strange language. He looked at the other five. They indicated the same confusion.

"Respeak, Dark Warrior." It was a command, this time.

Tinker sighed. "You, or something that you control, attacked three females not too long ago." He indicated Adarlak. "She came to us for help. To get her two friends back. We would like to have them freed."

"And we would like to know why you did this," added Adarlak. "We only sought knowledge."

The speaker tapped one of the rings he wore against the arm of his chair. "We do not share knowledge."

"Then why attack rather than warn?" Adarlak glared at the speaker.

"We do as we please." He launched the attack.

It caught Ran in the side, hurtling her into R-Bar. The pain blasted through their collective being, momentarily stunning them all. Tinker lurched to his feet.

Smoke's minds damped down, protecting them. She staggered into Messenger.

Three of the six disappeared, including their chairs and a large section of the wall behind them. Fair Morn had fired. The speaker tumbled in two pieces as the great sword leaped to the attack. Red flame roared from Sha'gar, shriveling another into ash as he tried to run.

The survivor banged out, escaping. And the twisted spell took them deep down into the dungeon's holding pen.

"Merde," cursed Tinker.

"Ranna," gasped Adarlak. "Anjan."

Anjan leaped to her feet, stood in front of the figure lying on the floor, and crouched in a defensive stance. She stared at them. Then she slowly unbent. "Adar?"

Sgenn's eyes flew open. She sat up and looked at Chicken and then at Chantal. "That was not-nice. He, they, require our help."

Her feet banged on the floor. "Come or stay."

Chantal hurried after her, waving for Chicken to come, yanking her long-barreled revolver from its holster. "Let's go!"

"Well," said Tinker to R-Bar, "take us out of here."

"Can't, Tink. They put a twice ward on this dungeon."

Sha'gar nodded. "It is true, Mate'mer. We are locked in."

"Not good." He knelt next to Smoke, who was sitting on the floor and holding Ran in her arms.

"She is still with us," grunted Smoke. "We must leave."

He stepped over and banged on the door with the hilt of

his sword. "Solid metal. Shoot it open, Butterfly." And stepped to one side.

Before he took another step the door was ripped loose, door jamb and parts of the supporting wall tearing outward.

Sgenn stepped through, ordering something to remain outside. She grumbled at Smoke. "That was not-nice, putting me to sleep."

Chantal ran in and began to rip her medical kit open, taking out the package with Ran's name written on the outside in black felt tip pen. "Gimme room to work."

"His Ran is going far," mumbled Ran as Chantal bound the grey stained wound in Ran's side.

"Damn well better not be!" snapped Chantal, stabbing the syringe into Ran's thigh and slowly depressing the plunger.

"WHAT?" He whirled around.

"Calm down, Cowboy, calm down," grumbled Chantal, fastening another large bandage in place. "You're gonna confuse us."

Chicken grabbed his arm. "Steady on, Our Heart."

He glared at Ranna, now held in Anjan's arms and at Adarlak. "I am gonna disown the whole lot of you!"

Adarlak snapped protection around Ranna, Anjan and herself, stepping between them.

He looked around. "Where's Sgenn?"

On the next peak over, the figure dressed in soft grey robes knocked gently on the great door.

"Open," she said

Inside, the six, and the one from the other house, looked out and decided that one young woman never before seen was no threat and opened the door.

Within moments she stood before them.

"My sister Ran requires healing from that spell." Grey eyes stared at them from an expressionless face. She slipped her arms into her sleeves and stood, arms crossed over her mid-section, patient quiet.

"There is no cure for that spell," cackled the survivor. "The rest of your group will die after you."

"If there is no cure," she said calmly, "then you are all dead as well." Something dark reached up and yanked the survivor into the floor. Over his cries they could hear bones crackling. Things rose from the down below, blocking all the doors, open or secret.

"You are all dead."

Dark vague rose behind her, higher and higher. And watched as the six tried to escape or to attack her.

"What are you?" screamed the last.

She smiled, a soft half-smile. "I am Reep daughter Faan theurgist Sgenn, sulda to John Tinker called The Chosen One, that you tried to injure."

"There are no Theurgist Manse."

"We are few. But greater than you in numbers."

Yanking himself away from the thing holding him, he stepped one step toward her and laughed. "We are many!"

She nodded. "Few are greater than none." And watched as he came apart. Then she turned and spoke softly, sending her servants on their mission. And told the last one to return her to the first house. She knew that by the time she talked with her sulda that all the houses would be smoking ruins and that this twisted guild would be gone from the elseplaces, only alive in tales told on dark nights.

Stepping through the hole in the dungeon wall, she dropped to her knees, and wrapped her arms around his legs, pressing her cheek against one of his thighs. "Sulda," she wept, "our Ran self can not be cured."

Tinker growled at R-Bar and Sha'gar. "Get us home. Maybe Dat can do something."

"Outside," commanded R-Bar. "We must be outside this thing." She ran out the hole in the wall.

Fair Morn stepped over and snatched Ranna from Anjan's arms, easily cradling the witch in her arms. "Come on, let's get out of here."

Adarlak helped Anjan stand and walk after the rapidly disappearing group.

Smoke followed them, holding Ran in her arms.

"I am fading," whispered Ran.

"Stay!" growled Smoke.

As they stepped from the structure to the outside, Ran sighed. "Lovely Smoke, his Smoke, I do not think that I can." Her head flopped back. Her fingers loosened and a black crystal sphere dropped to the ground, shattering into pieces beyond counting.

At that moment R-Bar and Sha'gar yanked them home.

Grandeville. Tinker's Place.

They came spilling down, a whirlwind of bodies and equipment, down across the front lawn.

"An tak tak," snarled R-Bar as she rolled over a bed of marigolds.

"Damn rough landing," snapped Chantal, shoving at Adarlak who was lying half across her. "Get off, lard butt."

Messenger hurtled past them, pelting for the house, banging open the front door, charging into the large living room.

"WE NEED HELLLP! HELP, DAT!"

As Tinker lurched to his feet, Smoke staggered by, carrying the limp form of Ran.

Smoke's face was contorted with pain. "Can't hold it back much longer, MindMate."

Inside she crashed over a chair and tumbled into one of the couches.

"Oooooooo," wailed Messenger, shoving Dat that way. "Dooooooo something!"

Dat lifted Ran from Smoke's arms and laid her on another of the couches and began to inspect her wounds. Je'leel joined her. "Mother?"

Dat straightened up and wrapped her daughter in her arms. "I do not think that I can restart this houri." She kissed her daughter on the cheek. "Your father is going to be very upset."

Tinker lurched into the room, tears running down his face. Chicken walked by his side, her arm around his shoulders, frowning with worry.

"I think that I will kill that trio," he mumbled. Sgenn nodded.

"Please, Our Lord." Chicken towed him toward the small living room. "Come. Sit with this, thy Verra Own Queen." Her head snapped around, glaring at Sgenn. "Do nothing, wench!"

Dark grumbling was coming from the deep down.

"They must pay," stated Sgenn, very, very calmly, grey eyes watching Tinker carefully as Chicken gently moved him away. She blinked back tears. The rumbling sounds stopped.

Fair Morn walked around Sgenn and dropped Ranna on another couch.

"Pik tik," hissed Ranna as she thumped and bounced.

Fair Morn dragged her into a more comfortable position. "You are lucky that I didn't shoot you!" She headed down the hall. "Going to my room."

Chantal sat next to Smoke and wrapped her arms around her. "Release it. We are all home." And crushed Smoke to her chest and began to sob. "Let it go, let it go, let it go." And Smoke did.

Separation shock, pain, loss, ripped through their collective being.

R-Bar dropped to her knees and sat staring at Ran, dangerous crackling rippling through the air around her. She held one limp hand against her cheek and slowly rubbed it up and down.

Sha'gar held the wildly sobbing Messenger and gently stroked her hair. Sha'gar's eyes flared bright red, and brighter.

Adarlak hastily dragged Anjan into a far corner and crouched over her, sheltering her from the mage flare she could see building around Sha'gar. She could feel all of them, his magic users, and the strength pulsating wildly. Kissing Anjan, she sang a farewell song, knowing that they were all going to die. They were all doomed.

A window, one of the large living room's windows exploded outward, scattering itself across the front lawn.

"Smoke," hissed Chantal, "do something. Please. Before this place blows up."

Smoke's eyes opened, mere slits of orange. "Hard," she

mumbled.

Chantal gently shook her. "We can't have gone through all this just to wind up killing them." She shivered. "You have got to keep us together."

Red seeped across the floor. It was coming from Sha'gar. And it was reaching for Ranna.

Sgenn crashed into a wall, falling sideways, muscles in her cheeks jumping. Dark surged up from deep below. To protect her. To destroy anything that was causing her such pain.

Chantal shook Smoke. "Hurry, hurry."

Reep stood there. "I felt all arrive," sighed the slight breeze. She slowly turned around. "My daughters," whispered the soft light, "will behave."

She drifted over and peered at Sha'gar. "Tall daughter, stop! Settle!" The great midnight pools that were her eyes watched the flames die in her daughter's eyes.

Then she turned and drifted over to Sgenn. "Strange daughter, send that away." Sgenn stared back.

"Now," whispered the quiet.

Dark vague settled into the deep down below. Sgenn lurched up and over and wrapped her arms around her mother. And began to cry. "Terrible pain. Help me, mother."

Reep freed an arm and reached up, gently touching Sgenn in the middle of her forehead with her index finger. "This is all that I may do. Go sit with him." Reep gently, softly, pulled herself from her daughter's arms and drifted over and settled next to R-Bar.

"Favorite sister," sighed the air. "Our eldest sister is debt tied to you and your's forever."

"Hak ptar pik tik," growled R-Bar, wiping her eyes with

one sleeve.

"Yesssss," agreed Reep.

R-Bar looked sideways and gasped. A single, solitary tear was trickling down Reep's face.

It was the greatest show of emotion that R-Bar had ever seen from this sister. It was unheard of.

"I will speak with my husband. Now." Reep was gone.

R-Bar stood, walked over, and stared at Ranna.

Ranna looked up.

R-Bar's palm cracked across Ranna's face. Over and over and over, alternating hands, rocking her sister's head back and forth. "Reep cried. She cried for us." R-Bar spun and ran from the room.

Ranna ran her hand over her face sending the pain away. "Ummmmm do dar," she mumbled. Nothing, no-one, would ever dare upset Reep like that. If she had the strength she would twist them away now and hope. But she knew that would be futile. Reep had the ability to follow any trace, no matter how faint.

Feeling all the danger draining from the room, Adarlak helped Anjan stand. They lurched over and sat on the couch with Ranna.

"Ran'na," sobbed Anjan.

"We will wait." Ranna took one of Anjan's hands in her's. And then held one of Adarlak's. Adarlak was frightened to see that fierce warrior Anjan cry.

Smoke blinked and kissed Chantal. All their collective being felt the calm flowing out from Smoke, flowing through them. And the healing that would come from that.

Then they all wandered into The Chamber and up to Fair

Morn's room. To sit. To merge. To become a single organism. To share their loss. And their pain.

And, long after long after long after the sun had set, they walked out into the first pasture and laid Ran next to their long before losses, Ferrelden and Flar. And said their final farewells. And watched Ran fade away.

.

come strong. To sex. To emerge. To become a single organism. To share their loss and their pain.

And their attention [illegible] longed after the end, and they [illegible] into the first [illegible] and Ran [illegible] their love [illegible] and [illegible] said [illegible] [illegible] away.

Chapter Twenty-six

New Things

Bahn Duhr Tohr. The New Kingdoms.

The Prince came striding down the central lane between the tents. He was dirty. He was more than just dirty, he was filthy. But, through all the layers of grime, in all the many colors of the local soil, he was smiling and very happy.

He and a party of seafolk had left five days before to explore in a direction directly away from the shore and the meadow where the camp was located. And now, they were returning. The Advisor to The Princess and the Princess stepped from the Royal tent and watched them approach.

"Most badly be'grime'd," observed The Princess.

"Congratulations, Mighty Queen Sister." He laughed happily. "We have found a great source of fertile flat lands and all manner of trees and other material that craftsmen do desire." He grabbed her in a most un-Royal hug. "Thee did it, Sister. We shall great celebrations in Bahn Duhr Tohr have when those folk do hear. And we have much great planning to do."

She kissed his cheek. "We ordered baths for all when thee were first spotted returning. Now We shall require one as well."

He stepped back and grinned. "We, thee and I, shall build great kingdoms in this new land. Here will be The New

Kingdoms of Bahn Duhr Tohr. The first ones in many, many generations to come into existence."

Lurin laughed with him. "It will take much time."

He grinned wider. "It is the first time in my life that I have truly enjoyed being Royal." Then he looked at his sister's Advisor. "Sook, lead me to that hot water."

Sook nodded and headed for the next tent over, followed by the Prince.

Lurin called at his back, "Clean attire does await thee as well." She beckoned over one of the seafolk who clenched the scrolls of the expedition in his arms. "Come with us. Explain briefly what you saw, then go clean yourself." He bowed, and followed her into her tent.

"Ahhhhhh," sighed the Prince as he sank in the hot, perfumed, soap frothy water. "You may turn around now, Sook."

She did, slowly she did.

"Step over here. Please?"

She did, carefully she did, and looked at him. "My Prince?"

He reached up. "Give me your hand."

Carefully she held out one hand.

He grasped it. "Does that feel any different than any other hand you have ever touched?"

"No, Great King, it does not."

"Am I ugly, hard on the eyes?"

"No, Mighty Warrior, you are not."

"Then, look at me, lovely witch."

Her eyes slowly rose and looked into his. People did not call witches lovely. Ever. Except for their mate-for-life.

"Would you like to be Queen?"

She gasped and tried to step back. His grip tightened.

"Well?"

"It has never been done! It is never done!"

He laughed. And tugged her closer. Her knees banged into the edge of the large tub.

"Do not," she cautioned.

He sighed. "Every kingdom, major and minor, has dangled lovely Princesses in front of my face, each wanting to be Queen. Lovely maidens of all stations have rolled their eyes at me, all wanting to be, ummmm, favored, their station in life enhanced. With these new lands it will even be worse."

"It is the way," she intoned.

He sat up, water surging violently over the tub edges. "NO LONGER! This is a new land! Mine will be a new kingdom! There will be new rules. I will find a better way!"

Sook bowed her head. "To see such great daring is an honor beyond honor."

He yanked hard. Water splashed in all directions.

"PTAR IM TAK!" she snarled, sitting up, wiping water and her hair from her face.

The Prince smiled broadly. "That sounds very bad." Then he grinned. "It appears that there is nothing under that blouse but you."

She started to stand up. He yanked her back down. "Sook, I would have you as my Queen."

She frowned at him. "I can not be ordered to do that. It would be tar tar!"

"It is not an order," he whispered. "It is a desire. It is a wish."

"Hum hum hum."

He released her, and looked deep into those dark, dark witch eyes. Far in, somewhere, he could see faint pinpoints of red fire flickering.

"I know your custom, Faan witch Sook. The choosing is your's." He smiled. "However, the asking is mine." He leaned back against the tub end and waited, watching her face.

She leaned forward and lightly touched the side of his face with her fingers. "What will The King and The Queen, your Mother and Father, say and do?"

He snorted. "They will probably be as upset as your mother."

"Hum."

He reached up and trapped her hand against his cheek. "The Queen and The King will have to accept what ever I choose to do. This is My Kingdom, this is Our Kingdom." He pulled her hand around and kissed her palm. "And I believe that Ripple will accept this as well for I have heard that the Faan have changed muchly from the old ways."

She nodded. "Witch true."

"I want you, Sook."

"Lovely Prince, Lovely Daring Prince, now King of a New Kingdom, the Faan mate for life and are fiercely protective of their mates."

"Wonderful."

"Kings are often tempted. For political reasons."

"With you at my side all else pales by comparison." He laughed. "And with your cultural values, I will have all the excuse required to politely decline all such offers and inducements."

"Witch true?"

"King true." He tugged her closer. "Husband-to-wife true."

His forehead gently bumped into her's. "I have wanted you from the first time I saw you, Lovely Witch. We will have to have children to guarantee succession."

"Your children will all be magic endowed."

He slipped his arms around her and tugged her against his chest. "A new line of royal for a new kingdom. What kind?"

"Witch, if female. Mostly. Warlock, if male." Her voice dropped to a low whisper, "Aunt Reep had a female theurgist. You met her, my cousin Sgenn."

"Let us exit this wet environment and discuss all these and other matters over a fine meal."

She nodded.

They landed in bed.

She nodded.

They were dry.

He laughed. And kissed her. "My Queen?"

She nodded. "My King. Mine!"

Sometime later they burst into the tent of the Princess. He was clean and dressed in his best. She wore standard black witch garb.

The Prince dropped to one knee. "Great Queen, I do hereby, now, in this place, request thy blessing pon my nuptial plans."

She smiled. "Of course, Brother Mine. Rise." She looked at him. "Which of the many many is it to be?"

He rose to his feet and cleared his throat. "Ahem, prepare

thyself Sister and I will so say." He beckoned Sook forward as Lurin frowned at him and settled herself in her chair.

"Brother?"

He held one of Sook's hands tightly. "This fairest of maidens has so consented." And laughed loudly at Lurin's expression. "Be not so shocked, Sister Queen, for did I not say that this, Mine Own New Kingdom, was to be different?"

"But?" she stammered.

Sook looked at her.

"We are as one in this resolve," he stated, most Royally positive. "And none may change that."

Lurin surged to her feet. She hugged the startled witch. "Welcome to The Royal House, Fair Queen Sook."

Frinda kissed them both. "I would have gay celebration here in our new lands, then sail to have a more Royal one. And then gather those stout hearted folk who would seek adventure with us, and bring many supplies for both Our Kingdoms."

Lurin stepped away from them. "Indeed! We will stay and continue our work here. T'will be a good time for to remain far from blustering storms that this Royal Pair are about to unleash."

She grinned at him. "What say thee to this proposal, Brother? All that way," she pointed, "from this great river be your's." She pointed in the opposite direction. "And all that way be Mine?"

He laughed. "As we know not in detail what lies out there, in either direction, I say tis as fair a compact as was ever drawn. We do most humbly agree. The New Kingdoms are thus created!"

Grandeville. Tinker's Place.

A number of weeks had passed in quiet activity. All were finally healed. Ranna, Anjan, and Adarlak from their physical damage. Tinker and the rest of them from their psychological damage.

It had happened during the flurry of painting and cleaning, and heavy relaxing in the evenings. Now all were sprawled here and there on the rear deck lightly dozing.

Tinker was in the hammock. He had been joined by Messenger who was at this very moment gently plucking at the buttons on his shirt. Undoing them.

Suddenly R-Bar jerked into an upright position in the lounge chair. "Ptar ptar pak to!" she snarled.

"Vile over vile," mumbled Sha'gar shifting into a new position in the other lounge chair.

Ranna hissed loudly. "Foul, foul." She sat up.

Sgenn joined Tinker and Messenger.

"Now what?" he murmured, wondering what disaster was about to appear.

"Really nasty," whispered Sgenn, lying close against him. "That witch."

R-Bar glared at Ranna. "Sook just found her's."

"Not my daughter." Ranna frowned back at R-Bar and shrugged.

"What did she find?" asked Sha'gar, wondering what strange combination her Faan relatives had made this time.

"How do you know that," asked Sgenn.

"Ripple told," snapped R-Bar.

"So what is the excitement about this time?" Tinker rolled his head and peered past the top of Messenger's head at the agitated witch. "You guys are always doing something like that all the time."

R-Bar stomped across the deck and glowered down at him. "That indo Sook took The Prince Frinda, the son of Willawa as her's."

"So?" asked Tinker.

"Witches do not marry royalty!" stated R-Bar.

Sgenn yanked his shirt loose and patted his stomach. "You did. Sha'gar did. I did. For this one is a Prince."

"Indeed!" Chicken walked over and joined them. "Most true."

"We are not witches," hissed Sha'gar at Sgenn.

"Dim dim dim dim dim," growled R-Bar.

"What did Ripple say?" asked Tinker.

"Nothing to repeat," mumbled R-Bar.

"That's the afternoon's news from far away Bahn Duhr Tohr?"

R-Bar shook her head. "The Princess and The Prince are organizing new Kingdoms in some new land far across the waters that they found. And Ripple birthed Szart, a witch."

He smiled and batted at Sgenn's hand. And then at Messenger's. "Life goes on, it seems."

"Sure does," called a voice from the third floor balcony.

It was Fair Morn, leaning way out and over the railing.

The water balloon hit him in the chest.

Grandeville. The Home of Raj and Kartz.

They entered the house each carrying bags of groceries.

He had convinced her that they ought to do this most of the time. It was a small town and people would notice if they didn’t buy groceries.

“By George!” gasped Raj, staring at the young woman sitting on their couch.

“Nowp name By George,” she said. “Name Reslar.”

“Sister,” added Kartz.

“Oh,” said Raj. “Of course.” He hurried into the kitchen to put away the groceries. They had been on a trip and had just returned. He wondered how long she had been sitting there.

“Sister?” asked Kartz.

“Stay visit.”

Kartz nodded.

Raj returned and stopped next to Kartz. “What?”

“Sister wants to visit.”

“Oh. Of course.” Then he frowned. “Will you mind sleeping on the couch, ahhhh, Reslar?”

Noticing the look on her sister’s face, Reslar quickly nodded. “Yeel.” And looked puzzled.

Raj pointed. “That is the couch.”

Reslar was sitting on it. She bounced. Just a little. “Yeel.”

“Here why?” asked Kartz, sitting next to her sister.

Raj sat in one of the two chairs after emptying it of medical journals.

“It is told,” said Reslar, “that theurgist here came.”

Kartz eyes popped wide. “Here?”

“Yeel.”

“Told?”

“To me. By Flinder the Flik.”

Kartz gasped.

“It owed favor.” Reslar smiled. And eyed Raj.

“Nowp!” snapped Kartz.

Reslar pouted.

"Here why?" Kartz demanded again.

"It was told to this sister that a mother lives in this elseplace here. Theurgists are witch terrible terrible paz kop!"

"My dear?" asked Raj.

Kartz looked at him. "Theurgists are blacker hearted than witches."

"And?"

"Not nice," she added. Reslar nodded.

Raj stood, left the room and quickly returned. "Here." He handed a can to Reslar. "We always have one before dinner."

He looked at Kartz. "I put something frozen in the microwave."

Reslar turned the can around and around, end for end. Kartz showed her how to open it.

Reslar took a careful taste.

"A flik?" asked Kartz.

"Hammat Jam, Over Below." Reslar produced a small grey wand with green banding and proudly showed it to her sister. "Flik crafted." The wand grumbled.

"Psssssss," snapped Reslar.

The wand stopped.

"Amazing," said Raj.

Reslar put the wand somewhere, emptied her can, and peered inside it through the hole.

"Another?" Raj stood and looked at Kartz. She shrugged.

"Yeel." Reslar handed him the can.

So he got everyone another. Reslar opened her's and nodded at her sister.

Kartz pulled off her shoes and leaned back in the couch.

"Reslar is the youngest."

Reslar ordered off her boots and flopped back. And tilted up her can. "Urbie," she observed. And unfastened two buttons on her blouse.

"Ummm?" said Raj.

Kartz nodded. Reslar emptied her can.

"Any idea who this theurgist person might be?" asked Raj. "Or where they might be living?"

Reslar tossed her can to him. "Flik mentioned sister mage Sha'gar." She sat up and began to tug her blouse from her trousers.

Raj leaped to his feet. "I had better check on the food in the oven." And hurried into the kitchen.

Kartz sat up and banged her sister on top of the head with the flat of her hand. "Sha'gar is his, the one who released me. He ended the witch-bane war."

Reslar rubbed the top of her head. "Leave?"

"Stay. It is am lept to have sister visit."

Reslar sniffed at the odors drifting from the kitchen.

"Lagzana," said Kartz, standing. "Come. Eat."

They joined Raj in the kitchen. He corrected Kartz pronunciation of the main dish.

Grandeville. Tinker's Place.

The small sport car, bright shining blue, slipped into the parking space and stopped next to their van. The top was down.

Kartz turned the ignition off and handed the keys to Raj. She drove. He had been giving her lessons for days and days. She thought that it was a quaint but interesting custom of how to move from here to there.

Kartz chewed on her lower lip and frowned at Reslar. Her sister had insisted on sitting in Raj's lap, claiming that the back seat was too small.

Raj open his door. "They are probably on the rear deck."

As the trio started around the corner of the house, Raj said to Kartz, "I shall sit in the back on the way down."

Reslar looked unhappy at him. Kartz kissed him on the cheek.

Walking down the rear deck they could see people at the far end. Reslar stepped behind them and hissed softly, "Witches."

Kartz nodded. "The short is R-Bar. The tall is her eldest sister. All safe safe."

"Urm," said Reslar.

Chantal hurried toward them. "Hi Raj, Kartz. See you later. Got to visit a sick cow." She clumped past them, zipping up her coveralls, rubber boots thumping as she walked past. Reslar stared at her back as she disappeared around the corner of the house and wondered what she was doing.

Tinker looked up from his reading. "Morning Raj, Kartz. Coffee?"

"Very kind," said Raj, sitting on one of the wooden benches at a table. "This is Reslar, the youngest sister of Kartz."

"So, how's the medical business?" asked Tinker, sipping from his cup, just handed to him by Chicken. "Hi, Reslar."

"Mostly the same." Raj dribbled honey into his cup. Reslar stared at the thick liquid as it oozed from the spoon. When enough had dribbled in, he handed the spoon to Reslar. "Lick it."

He looked at Tinker. "She came to warn Kartz because

she heard that there is something called a theurgist in the area."

"Hum hum," said Sgenn, surging from the pool, quickly swinging a towel around herself, unsure about these others looking at her. She was wearing a swim suit. She dragged on her thick grey robes.

"I am Sgenn," she stated, sitting on one arm of Tinker's chair. "Faan theurgist. His."

"Nothing to worry about," said Tinker. He smiled at Reslar. She nodded back, the spoon tucked in one corner of her mouth.

"What I did so say as we came this way," said Kartz, looking at her sister.

Ranna walked over and sat on the other arm of Tinker's chair. The chair creaked louder.

"Careful," he warned.

Ranna nodded. "Great One, Anjan, Adarlak and I must leave. We are healed and well. We are forever witch debt, mage debt, warrior debt, tied to you and them."

"Ummm. Ahhhh." He didn't like all these comments about debt, beginning to worry about whatever she might have in mind for paying off that debt she was stressing. The Vander were bad enough.

She leaned close and kissed his cheek.

R-Bar goggled at this most un-witch behavior of her eldest sister.

"Anj and Adar insist that I stop spell searching." She kissed him again. "I agreed." Yanking his shirt open, she quickly drew a twisted and interbent design on his chest.

"YIPE!" Her fingers were cold, icy cold.

"Heh heh heh heh heh," cackled Ranna. "Adar and I

designed it." She stood and banged elseplace, taking Anjan and Adarlak with her.

Tinker stared at as much of his chest as he could see. "What? What did she do?"

R-Bar hurried over, dragging Sha'gar by one hand.

"Hum," said R-Bar.

"Hum hum," added Sha'gar. "A sly devious thing."

Kartz grabbed Reslar as she started forward. "Stay."

Reslar growled.

"What?" he snapped. "What is it?"

"Sulda," said Sgenn very softly, very gently. "I know that sign. She did not exactly design it. She merely altered it some." She touched his shoulder. "The Nagar recognize it as well." She looked at Smoke.

"Now we will really have to stay home," laughed Smoke as she shared Sha'gar's and Sgenn's thoughts with the rest of them, save Tinker.

Kartz struck Reslar with a bright red wand, releasing the spell effect. Reslar shuddered.

R-Bar knelt in front of him. "Promise that you won't get excited."

"I don't like the sound of that statement."

"Just hafta keep your shirt on," laughed Fair Morn.

"You are The Vander Lord," stated R-Bar.

"So?" he grumbled.

"The Vander Lord may command any Vander to do anything that he wishes," added R-Bar.

"Anything," gurgled Messenger, stifling her laughter.

"What . . . did . . . she . . . do?" He sat up, grabbing R-Bar by the shoulders. She tried not to laugh. "Ranna, Anjan, and

Adarlak had great life debt. So they gave you a great gift. And hurried away."

He sighed.

"Maybe I can remove it," grumbled Sha'gar.

"It is him. Now!" snapped R-Bar. "It is permanent."

"Merde." He flopped back. "All right, all right, give me the bad news."

"And we can't do anything about it either," chortled Messenger, holding her hands over her mouth. "Really really."

"Worse and worse," he mumbled.

Kartz stepped over. "That spell has never before been activated. All were afraid. Afraid afraid."

"Tell me, Kartz." He sighed. "Please?"

She knelt next to his chair. "Of course. Chosen One. You have now become a . . . Witch Master." She bowed her head. "That design will fade. It is now in your voice."

He sat up and looked down, rubbing his fingers on the skin of his chest. The design was fading. "What is it?"

"Like being Vander Lord," said R-Bar.

"What?" He looked at Smoke.

She grinned.

"Witch Master?" he asked.

"Of every witch clan," stated Kartz. "None can resist. None can disobey your every command."

He smiled. "So I can tell Ranna to remove it, and she will have to do it."

"Nowp!" snapped Kartz. "It is you now."

"Tink," hissed R-Bar. "You will just have to be careful what you say from now on, that's all."

"Magicians? Theurgists?" His eyes jumped from face to

face.

"Nowp!" Kartz stood. "Witch Master. Only."

Raj stood. "We will see you later, Tinker old boy. I think that you need some time to yourselves."

"Sure," said Tinker. "When you have time, come up for dinner."

"Yeel," said Kartz.

"Yeel," breathed Reslar.

Raj hurried them down the deck to their car. He drove.

"Damnation." grumbled Tinker. "It is always something."

R-Bar leaned against his legs. "A great gift."

"I don't need it."

"Heh heh heh heh," she cackled.

"What?"

"Certainly will surprise Ripple. Heh heh heh."

"We are staying home."

R-Bar nodded.

He squinted at her. "Kiddo?"

"Staying home," she echoed.

He sighed. "Boy, is this going to be tricky." He smiled at her. "Never mind, it was just a grumble." He sat up. "Ahhh, anyone want lunch?"

Chicken joined him. "Thee will become most Royally indirect, Me'Lord." She twisted the ornate ring she was wearing on her left hand. "We would with thee nap in fair hammock after fine repast."

He winked at her. "Sure, Slim. After lunch. I have a lot of thinking to do."

"Twenty minutes," called Fair Morn, hurrying down the deck toward the kitchen. "Super Stud." They could hear her laughter all the way into the kitchen.

"Boy," giggled Messenger, "wait until Chantal hears about this. She is really going to be a grump, grump, grump."

He sighed, long and heavily. "It just keeps getting worse and worse."

Chicken tickled the side of his neck. "A Mighty King commanding uncounted legions."

He nodded. "At least they can't visit. We have enough trouble with the bunch that can, including the Vander."

"Indeed, My Lord. But they do but obey thy every wish. And thus, Mighty Lord, do nay problem be enow."

He struggled up from his chair and wrapped her in arms. "And now all those witches as well. You know, I feel better about that already."

Chicken kissed him, moving a little as she pressed against him. "Indeed, fair Prince, thee do feel so."

He laughed. "I am ready for lots of R-n-R."

"So do be we all, LordLove."

And that is what they did.

Lots of rest and relaxation.

Chapter Twenty-seven

One Problem Solved

Grandeville. The Home of Raj and Kartz.

As soon as they entered the living room Kartz wrapped herself around Raj. "Hold me, husband."

"Certainly." He did. "What is it, my dear?"

She nuzzled the side of his neck. "He is a Witch Master."

"You know that I do not understand most of the cultures out there and all the matters relating to them."

"No witch is able to disobey," she whispered in his ear, "a Witch Master. That Ranna should have not done that!"

Raj gently patted her back. "I am sure that Tinker is probably as upset about that as you are. From what Chantal has told me, he doesn't like things like that either." He hugged her. '"Besides Circe, my love, Tinker is a perfect gentleman and would never abuse such an ability."

Reslar stepped close to them. "He looked very nice."

Her sister's head snapped around. "You will go up there alone nowp!"

Reslar winced. "Yeel, Elder, it is so."

"Let us sit out in the back yard and sip a little scotch and relax," suggested Raj.

Kartz nodded.

So they did.

Reslar wondered about her sister's taste in alien liquids.

Grandeville. Tinker's Place.

He lay in the hammock staring up at the sky, at the few clouds drifting along, all so cute and fluffy, across the sky. He grumbled up at them. They were just being clouds. He wasn't in the mood for cute and fluffy clouds, or anything at all.

Chicken lay on her side, using one of his arms for a pillow, her arm thrown across his chest.

He sighed, a long, drawn out sigh.

"Fret thee not, Sweet Prince." She ran her hand up and down his ribs, just a little.

"Damn witches," he grumbled.

"She thee do wish great reward for to be a'given."

He rolled his head toward her and looked into those bright blue sparkling eyes. "Princess, now what are we going to do?"

She kissed him. "Be naught but thy Own Loverly Self, My Lord."

"My life is really and truly messed up big time, this time." He frowned darkly. At this close range, it lost most of its effect.

She kissed him again. "Heavy weighs the head that wears the crown, Mighty King."

"I am not a King!" he growled. "I am just plain old John Tinker of the unbelievably complicated, getting worse all the time, life."

"PISH TOSH!" She sat up and glared down at him. The hammock swung wildly.

"WATCH IT!"

Messenger wandered over and peered down at them through the webbing. "Thought that you wanted to take a nap in the hammock." She giggled at them, at the tangle of limbs that was them, lying on the deck under the hammock.

"Pish tosh," he mumbled.

"Fierce thing," explained Chicken, "do us throw out."

"You did it all by yourself, wiggle butt."

Fair Morn joined the discussion group. "Care for some coffee and cookies, assaulter of the skinny?"

"Might as well," he grumbled. "Can't get a nap."

"We do be nay Skinny," retorted Chicken. "We do be merely warrior slim, most pleasingly so."

He stood, reached down and yanked her to her feet. "N.C."

"Nice couch?" asked Messenger, smiling broadly at him.

"No comment!"

"Heh heh heh." Chicken yanked him across the deck to one of the large wooden table. "Me'thinks t'will be nice couch soon enough."

Smoke shoved a cup of coffee in front of him as he sat, as she dripped water on him.

R-Bar shoved a platter of cookies at him.

Sgenn walked over, towel wrapped around her head. She had been in the swimming pool with Smoke.

Chicken sat by his side and nodded at R-Bar.

"Tink?" The short witch looked at him, frowning.

"Ummmm?" He was starting on his second cookie.

"All you have to do is be just a little careful about how you say things when you are around witches."

"I suppose."

"It is true."

"Kiddo?"

"What?"

He leaned on the table, cup held in both hands. "If I told you to ignore my, umm, commands, would that work?"

She shook her head. "Nope."

He sighed.

R-Bar leaped up, ran around the table and threw her arms around him. "Sorry, sorry, mate-for-life, sorry, sorry."

"Don't?" he said. "Please?"

"Of course," she replied, instantly releasing him.

"Merde," he growled.

She hugged him again. Tighter.

"Kiddo!"

"Yesssssss."

"Unless I say, this is a command, at the beginning of the sentence, you are not to understand what I say as a command."

"Of course."

"Sing and dance."

She hugged him, fingers digging into his shirt, and sniffed loudly.

"You crying?"

"Witches do not cry," she mumbled, releasing him and wiping at her eyes with a sleeve.

Yanking his legs from underneath the table, he swung around and pulled her into his lap. "OOOF!"

"I love you, Tink."

"It worked, didn't it?"

"Yep." She slipped her hand inside his shirt. "That was very witch devious of you."

He ran his hand through her thick black hair. "Now all I have to remember is to tell it to everyone that we meet."

Chicken reached around and handed a large ornate ring to R-Bar. "Here, Sweet Witch."

R-Bar shoved the ring onto her thumb and grinned at him. "Heh heh heh heh heh. But not everyone."

He tugged her shirt loose and ran one hand over smooth midnight pale skin. "Nice belly, kiddo."

Fair Morn moved sideways. So did Chicken. R-Bar stood and sat in the space that they had made next to him as he swung his legs back under the table.

"Certainly glad that worked."

"Me to, Tink." She leaned against his side.

Sha'gar refilled his cup.

"Most clever, Our Heart." Chicken pushed the cookie platter back in his direction.

"Yep," agreed R-Bar, taking two cookies, slipping her free arm around his waist.

"Boy, am I relieved." He laughed. "That could have really messed up our lives." He hooked an arm around her neck and grinned happily. "And not only that, but now I am not worried about any of those witches visiting, either. Not any more." He stood and ruffled her hair. "Come on, short and cute. Let's take a walk across the pastures."

"Poo tik," she grumbled, taking two more cookies.

"Wonderful." He look a few more as well.

She stood and kicked his ankle, not too hard. "I am not short."

"Certainly." He took her hand, the one free of cookies, and led her down the steps and out through the flower beds.

R-Bar growled loudly.

They all watched the pair as they walked out to the forested edge of the pastures, where slope met pasture, and the shade provided cool.

"Sounds normal to me," laughed Fair Morn.

"Absolutely," agreed Smoke. "Pass the cookies."

Fair Morn did. After taking a few first.

Then they all scattered to do this and that.

"Well," he said as they sat on the edge of the great depression, legs hanging down the steep slope.

"Tink?"

"Cutest witch around."

"Hum."

He sighed.

She leaned against his side.

"Can you somehow tell Ranna how much I appreciate her gift, their gift? Ummm, now that we know how to control it."

R-Bar nodded. Something shot into the sky. And flashed out into the elseplaces.

"Can you tell a certain short, grumpy, beautiful, kid witch how much I appreciate her?" He twisted around and slipped her unbuttoned shirt from her shoulders.

"I am not short or grumpy," she grumbled. And tugged his shirt loose. And looked down at herself. "Or a kid!"

"Warm afternoon," he said.

"Yep," she replied, freeing her arms, sending her shirt and his shirt, to the house. And glanced at him, waiting for the usual grumble.

He stood, tugging her to her feet. "Let's walk down

through the depression, over to the spring, and then back around to the house."

"Sure."

"I want to admire our place and your bod." He laughed happily. And rolled his eyes at her.

"That all?"

"There is a nice and cool grassy patch over near the spring."

"Heh heh heh."

"My idea exactly."

They strolled down the steep slope.

In no hurry at all.

"Bout time you got back, Cowboy." Chantal mock frowned at him as the pair came through the flower beds and up on the rear deck. "Damn casual," she said as she eyed their bare torsos.

"'Mother?" Je'leel began to fill the plates. Everyone had been waiting supper until he and R-Bar had returned.

"Warm afternoon," replied R-Bar, taking a filled plate and sitting next to him.

"Thanks." He sat at one end of the large wooden table, pulling his plate over. And smiled at them all. "Where's Dat?"

The tiny figure scampered down the table and leaned against the edge of his plate. "Great Master?"

"You oughta be large," he mumbled around the roll he was eating. "But get off the table first."

Dat jumped to the deck and wrapped her arms around him and kissed the back of his neck. "Many thanks, Great Master. Shall I take off my upper covering?"

He began to make a ball of spaghetti on his fork. "If you want."

Chantal leaned close to Smoke. "R-Bar bounce his brains into jelly?" she whispered.

"Nope. Our consort is fully relaxed."

"Damn slow."

He smiled at her, at all of them. "Now that we, I, don't have to worry about demanding witches popping in all the time, I suddenly realized that I ought to take you guys just as you are."

Chicken pouted. "T'will be most dull."

He laughed. "O.K. Then I will growl, now and then." He looked around the table and shook his head. "What a mob." And grinned at them.

Chantal bounced a dinner roll off his chest.

Chapter Twenty-eight

Lots of Relaxation. Mostly.

Grandeville. Tinker's Place.

He woke.

Later than usual.

He woke.

Alone.

He woke.

To silence.

He lay there.

And stared at the ceiling.

Whatever it was, he didn't think that it was good.

It was three strange things in a row: later, alone, quiet. He reached out with his mind. And sighed. All but one were closed off. That makes four strange things in a row. He reached out with his mind, again.

Morning, Princess.

Fair morn, Sweet Prince.

What's going on?

Naught, My Lord. She laughed, tickling softly across his awareness.

Straight flush! He sighed and sat up, grabbed his pajamas and yanked them on. Then he grabbed a thick white robe, stood and headed for the rest of the house, tugging on the robe as he walked across the open space of The Chamber.

He walked on silent, bare feet down the hall and into the large living room. And dropped into his favorite chair.

Chicken strode in from the dining room and handed him a cup of coffee. "Frown not so, LordLove."

He frowned at her. "I am not frowning." And took a sip from his cup. "You gonna tell me?"

"What, pray tell?"

"Think that I'll just go back to bed," he mumbled. "Try again. Tomorrow!" And took another sip.

She stared at him, a slight frown wrinkling her forehead. "Me'Lord?"

"This day is only a few minutes old and I am already worried."

"Morning, morning, morning." Messenger bubbled into the room, giggling happily and flopped onto his lap.

"Oooof!"

"Stop frowning, MyTinker, it puts wrinkles in your face." She kissed him.

"Already have wrinkles in my face, lots of them. Wanna tell me what is going on, kitten!"

"Sure." She nodded vigorously. And kissed him again.

"O.K.?"

"What?"

"Tell me."

She slid one hand inside his robe and under his pajama top and tickled him. "About?"

"What's going on?"

"Oh." She tickled him. "Nothing."

"Merde," he mumbled.

"Damn grouchy." Chantal walked in and stood behind his chair and tostled his hair. "What's your problem, Cowboy?"

"Eight," he hissed, waving one hand wildly around his head.

"Nine." She laughed. "Just saw you and raised by one."

"Ten," stated Messenger, joining in. "What are we playing?"

"STOP THAT!" He flailed with his free hand, trying to fend off one tickler and one hair messer. The other hand held his cup of coffee. "BOTH OF YOU!"

They did.

R-Bar leaned over Messenger and kissed him. "Bout time that you crawled out of bed, Tink."

He sighed and slumped.

Sha'gar tapped the small witch on the shoulder. As soon as R-Bar stepped aside, she leaned over and kissed him. "Don't frown so, Mate'mer, you are getting wrinkly looking." Then she stepped away so Sgenn could kiss him.

Smoke slipped into the room, smiled at him and tapped Messenger on the shoulder so she could take Messenger's place.

"OOOOOOF!"

"I am not heavy, MindMate."

"Heavy enough," he grumped.

She kissed him. "Guess what, wrinkles?"

"I gave up. What?"

"Happy Birthday," they sang.

"It is not my birthday."

"Happy Father's Day," they sang.

"Happy Poo Tak Erb Day," they sang.

"What?"

Laughing happily, they mobbed him.

And, as per usual, he wound up on the bottom. Somehow his cup had escaped without sloshing coffee everywhere.

From beneath the happy mob there came a loud, long sigh. It was Tinker.

"Me'Lord?" asked Chicken in his ear.

"Sulda?" whispered Sgenn in the other.

"What'sa matta, Simba Leader?" asked Chantal. "You are awash in babe bodies, how can you grumble?"

"Eeeeeeeeeek!" squeaked Messenger. "I've been clenched."

"What you get," he grumbled.

Fair Morn poked him. "We baked a cake. Just for you."

Sha'gar twitched.

"Oooops," laughed Fair Morn. "Thought that was him."

"What, exactly, is going on? This time?"

"Heh heh heh heh heh heh," cackled R-Bar.

"Oh my gosh!" gasped Messenger.

"Just being friendly," said Smoke, giving him a little nip.

"OUCH!"

They all unpiled, sitting up, smiling happily, all around him. He stared up at the ceiling and really, really wondered about his life.

Chantal leaned over and kissed him. "Just your Lady Lions showing their appreciation, Simba grumble butt. Ready for breakfast?"

Messenger buttoned her pajama top. "We made just lots and lots."

They all trooped into the dining room and quickly set the

table. He dropped into his chair and watched all the happy faces. "Pass the pancakes, please."

"We made a big chocolate cake," said Messenger, scooping sliced strawberries onto her plate from the bowl.

"Many layers," added R-Bar.

"Just for you," explained Fair Morn, snagging several of the pancakes and shoving the platter toward Smoke.

"We do believe thee ought have fair surprise," stated Chicken.

"That's it?" He shoved his cup sideways for a refill. Chicken refilled it.

"Yep," said R-Bar.

"Happy Poo Tak Erb," giggled Messenger, wiggling a pancake piece around in the syrup on her plate. "Erb erb erb erb Day."

Je'leel joined them. "Everyone felt that you needed a Special Day, Father."

"So we made one up." Fair Morn took the last three pancakes. "Just for you, Poo."

"Ah," said Tinker.

"Ha," said he.

"What's that mean?"

"Tis thy day, Fair Prince. What do be thy wish?" Chicken lightly touched his forearm.

"Beat's me."

"MyTinker?"

"Ummmm?"

"May we go to the County Fair?"

He looked around the table. "That time of year already?"

R-Bar nodded. "Yep."

"All?"

"Why not?" asked Chantal.

"Everyone will behave, right?"

"Of course," said Fair Morn.

"Well then, let's get dressed.

He watched them hurry away. "You wanna come along?" he asked Je'leel.

"Yes. This will be my first County Fair to visit."

"Go get dressed." He started for The Chamber. "Oh, and tell Dat to come along as well, if she wants. But to dress properly."

Je'leel ran around the table and kissed him on the side of the face. "Mother will be so pleased." And hurried from the room.

Everything had worked just like Smoke, Chicken, and Chantal had said it would. He had gotten over the unsettling nature of the gift from Ranna.

Eventually, they all piled into the large van. Everyone was wearing corduroy shirts, jeans, and cowboy boots. Including Dat. She and Smoke were also wearing sunglasses to hide their rather unusual appearing eyes. Tinker dressed as he always dressed. The same as all the others.

At the gate, they agreed that they could scatter around as the fair grounds weren't all that large and Smoke could keep them all in sight inside her sensenet.

They broke into pairs and trios and wandered into the crowd of fair goers.

"An interesting celebration, Great Master." Dat strolled by his right side. Je'leel walked on his left side, eating cotton candy. "Interesting stuff," she said.

"Tradition," said Tinker.

Suddenly Dat grabbed his arm. "Great Master, listen! That is barbarous."

"What is?"

"People are being tortured horribly over there." She pointed. "I can hear them screaming in terror."

Slipping an arm around her waist, he headed that way. "Let's go watch."

She gurgled at him.

He laughed.

Je'leel gasped. "Father!"

"Those things are just rides, amusement rides. People do that for fun." He pointed as they got closer.

Dat stared at the machine as it whirled around and around and up and down. Je'leel stared at it also. "May I do that?"

He handed her some money. "Sure. Go ahead. But I will stay right here. I don't like those things."

"Mother?"

"I will come!" Dat walked away with Je'leel. She would kill it, if it hurt her daughter.

Soon the machine swallowed them and took them around and around and up and down.

And, after awhile, it spit them out.

"Well?" he asked.

"It was interesting," replied Je'leel.

Dat kissed him and whispered, "I am behaving just like all the other females leaving that device." She kissed him again.

"Let's go look at the livestock," he suggested.

So they did.

And then, after awhile, they wandered over to the bandstand area, to sit on the grass to get ready to listen to the entertainment, eating food that they had bought in any number of the food booths.

And little by little, all the rest arrived, and settled around him.

Chicken was carrying a very large teddy bear. "Dark Smoke do win fair prize," she explained.

"It was easy." Smoke shrugged. "All I had to do was knock down those little things." She handed Tinker a calling card. "I was asked to join a baseball team."

He slipped the card into his shirt pocket. "Everyone else stay out of trouble?"

Chicken handed the teddy bear to Je'leel. "A gift, fair Princess, for many of the young maidens hereabouts in this fest do carry such things."

Je'leel looked at the stuffed animal, then at all the other folk around them on the grass. "Thank you, Mother." She tucked it under one arm. "But what do I do with it?"

"Keep it on your bed," explained Tinker. "It is a local custom."

Je'leel nodded.

A young woman flopped down next to her. "Wow, Jel, how'd ja win that?"

Je'leel smiled at her. "Mother did it." She looked at Smoke. "This is Mary Carter, a friend from school."

Smoke smiled.

"And my Father," added Je'leel.

"Hi," said Tinker, starting to worry a whole bunch.

"Geeeeee, Mrs. Tinker," said Mary to Smoke. "I wish my Mother could win one of those."

Grinning wickedly at Tinker, Smoke uncoiled in one smooth motion. "Come with me, Mary." And led her in the direction of the amusement zone.

Je'leel handed her bear to him. "I will watch." And hurried after them.

"Merde," he grumbled, shoving the bear at Dat.

Nothing with happen, MindMate. She really wants one of those things.

"Stop grumbling, Cowboy. Smoke won't make it look too easy." Chantal sat next to him and frowned at him. "And Je'leel knows not to say anything either."

"My daughter is indjinn clever," said Dat.

"You call her your daughter again and you will get bopped," he snarled, yanking his arm from around her waist.

"Gimble, gimble, gimble," grumbled Dat.

"Husbands do not sit with their arms around other babes in public. And stop grumbling."

And, after awhile, Smoke, Je'leel, and Mary returned. Smoke and Mary were smiling broadly. Mary was holding a very large teddy bear. Her's was pink, Je'leel's a bright blue. Dat handed her bear to Je'leel. "Here . . . Niece." She smiled at Tinker.

Smoke flopped down next to him and kissed him on the cheek. *Heh heh heh heh heh.*

Tinker handed Je'leel some money. "Here you go. Both of you go get some popcorn. We will wait right here, watch the bears."

As the two young women walked away, talking happily, he looked at Smoke. "Well, Mom?"

"Mary doesn't have many friends. Her father died last year. And her mother is just managing to get by."

Chicken moved sideways and kissed Smoke on the cheek. "Most kind a'heart, Dark Sister."

"I thought so." Smoke nudged Tinker in the ribs with her elbow. "Mary is very nice. And a good friend to Je'leel. And very intelligent." She kissed him. "And I gave that game person some extra money when we were finished. So he is a happy person also." And then the music began and they all felt him begin to relax.

And much later, they wandered toward the side gate and the parking area, and their van.

"Where's Je'leel." He stared around the parking lot.

"She walked Mary home," explained Smoke. "I will give you directions."

Once they were in the van, she did.

As they turned the correct corner into the correct street, they looked at the area.

"Damn run down part of town," observed Chantal.

"Indeed," agreed Chicken.

They pulled up in front of a rather small unpainted house.

"Everyone stay in the van," warned Tinker, as he climbed out. "They won't understand this mob scene."

Smoke joined him. And winked at him. "Father."

He knocked on the front door and waited. The door opened and Mary and Je'leel came out. Mary hugged Smoke.

"Thanks a bunch, Mrs. Tinker."

"Call me Smoke," she said, hugging her back. Then she kissed Mary on her forehead. "Good night, Mary. And don't worry." She stepped away and tugged him back toward their van.

"Night, Mary," he said hastily. "Smoke," he hissed, "Cut it out."

Mary and Je'leel talked for a few more minutes and then Je'leel hurried to the van.

As they headed for home through the mostly dark town, he grumbled at the group at large.

"O.K., what's going on? Now? Smoke?"

"Mary didn't want us coming inside," explained Smoke.

"She thought that Mother was absolutely amazing," said Je'leel, pushing her arm behind Smoke's waist. Then Smoke told them all that she had seen inside Mary's mind and her mother's mind.

"Oh my gosh!" gasped Messenger.

"Me'Lord, we Ourselves must do something!"

"We are going to be damn careful," he stated. "If we do something."

"We have a very sneaky attorney," suggested Chantal.

"O.K.," he mumbled. "We can talk with her in the morning."

It was in the middle of the next morning when he finally hung up the phone. "O.K., our very sneaky lady attorney said that it will take her a week or so. She said that she would talk with Morgan and his legal eagles."

Chantal grabbed him and hugged him. "You are just an

old pussy cat, Cowboy."

"Gimble, gimble, gimble," he replied.

"Can't kid me. Let's go outside and lay about in and around the swimming pool."

So they did.

And about a week or so later, more or less, in the local newspaper they saw a small article about the amazing "inheritance" and "educational endowment" that Helen Carter and her daughter, Mary, had suddenly received.

"So there," said Chantal, tickling his ribs. "You have done your good deed for the year."

They were lolling about in the pool.

Again.

So he tickled her ribs.

Again.

"Fresh," she snorted, bobbing closer.

He tickled her again.

"Fresher." She kissed the tip of his nose.

"You guys really worry me a lot, you know."

She laughed. "Nothing to worry about, we'll protect you."

GUESTS! shouted Smoke in their minds.

"Damn," growled Chantal. "You keep them away from the pool while I hunt for my top which you have somehow managed to sneak off and to lose."

He surged from the pool. "I'll get you a towel, a big towel."

The woman hurried down the deck, laughing at his expression. "Just me, your ever so busy attorney." She walked over and looked down into the pool. "Hi, Shooter. Lose something?"

Chantal glared up at her. "Not funny, Sandrew."

Sandy took two steps back and knelt at the edge of the pool, and fished out some blue cloth. "Here it is." And handed it to Chantal. "Well, I don't blame him."

Tinker walked from the house holding a very large towel. "Oh."

"She'll be properly modest in a moment." Sandy laughed.

Tinker led her to a table. "What's up?"

She sat facing the house, popped open her briefcase and fished out some paper. "Need your signature. Here! Here! And here! There, that wraps up your gift giving."

Chantal joined them. "I oughta toss you into the pool." She sat next to him.

Sandy grinned at her, then at him. "If she does, you going to sneak off my blouse and bra?"

Tinker sighed.

Sandy stuffed the papers back into her briefcase and snapped it closed. "Just kidding. Life has been rather dull around the office lately." She stood. "Red wants to know if you are up for a bar-b-que this coming Saturday. He and Green have the weekend off."

Her head snapped sideways. "Who is that? One?"

Sgenn had just slipped from the house. She walked silently over and stood next to him and stared at Sandy. She was wearing a bathing suit.

"Sgenn," he said. "This is Sandy, our attorney and our friend."

Sgenn nodded, walked away and dropped into the pool.

More or less.

Sandy leaned over the table and stared at him and Chantal and said in a very low, low tone of voice, "That was the most frightening look that I have ever seen. She makes a psycho killer look like Santa Clause. Where did she come from?"

Tinker sighed. "Never mind." He watched Sgenn slowly sink into the water. She had walked out on the surface to the middle area first. Something dark underneath had been holding her up.

He sighed again.

"Ahhhhhh," said Sandy. "O.K." She looked over at the pool. Sgenn was bobbing up and down, head just above the water. "Morgan wanted to know whether there was anything else he could do?"

"Nope."

"Sure," said Chantal. "Ask him and Shannon and the kids to come up for the bar-b-que."

"O.K." Sandy hugged her. "Well, back to the office. See you on Saturday." She waved. "Bye, Sgenn. Nice to meet you."

"Thank you," replied Sgenn.

Sandy hurried down the deck.

Smoke, snarled Chantal, *that wasn't much warning.*

I didn't know that he was going to do that. Smoke laughed.

"Now what do I do?" called Sgenn. "The Princess didn't explain."

Chantal stood and tickled his ribs, then stepped over to the pool and dropped in. "You can fetch the coffee pot, Cowboy."

In the kitchen, he found Smoke and Fair Morn making sandwiches, wrapped in thick white robes. They had been reroofing the building housing the dojo and the generator shed and had just stepped from the shower room.

"You did that deliberately," he grumbled

"It was only Sandy," replied Smoke. "They roomed together when they were at college and she knows all about us."

"I know that," he mumbled, taking one of the coffee pots.

R-Bar joined them. "Like my suit?" Her two piece swimming suit was bright red.

"Yep," said Fair Morn.

"Nice color," added Tinker.

"Filling's all right." Smoke winked at him.

R-Bar frowned at her. "I am a little better than just all right." She poked him in the side. "Right, Tink?"

"Sure." And he wondered what was going on this time. Or starting to get ready to go on, this time.

R-Bar hissed at him.

"Let's not start one of those conversations, shall we?" He sighed and took the filled pot and coffee cups and headed for the rear deck and the pool side.

"Ger tik," suggested the short witch at his back.

"Let's make some cocoa," said Fair Morn.

The pool had acquired more occupants by the time he set the pot and cups down.

Chicken, Sha'gar, and Messenger had joined the other two. Messenger was trying to teach Sha'gar how to float on her back.

"Ptar ptar kap tak dindo nik nik," snarled someone.

R-Bar shot from the side door, a glowing green wand clenched in her right hand. "THAT IS VILE GROSS!" she yelled.

They appeared. A man and a woman.

"Yikta ta pikdo, sister!" snapped R-Bar.

Rekel frowned at R-Bar and her costume. "Most un-witch." She nudged the man standing by her side. "This short person displaying herself boldly in that ugly color is my youngest witch sister, R-Bar." She nodded at Tinker. "He is her's. The Chosen One."

Rekel stood witch proper and announced, "This is mine! Hinta warlock Ap Kar!"

Ap Kar stared at Tinker, grabbed Rekel by one arm, and yanked them away.

R-Bar's wand bounced them back.

"Hak nar nar," snarled Ap Kar, wrapping them in multi-layers of protection.

"Husband!'" gasped Rekel.

"Look at him," hissed Ap Kar.

Rekel did. And moaned, "Ando ando." She stared at R-Bar. "Sister, how can this be?"

R-Bar whirled on Tinker. "Quickly, Tink! Tell them to not obey!"

"Huh? Oh." He did. "Sorry about that."

"Ranna gift," grumbled R-Bar.

"Zig ptar dik!" growled Rekel.

"WATCH YOUR MOUTH!" snapped R-Bar, shadow dark gusted around her feet.

"Ptar tik," grumbled Rekel. She tugged Ap Kar over to where Tinker was still sitting, watching Tinker, wondering what was going on with him and the rest. Rekel sat directly across the table from him.

"None told of this," stated Rekel.

"Ahhhhh, it just happened," he replied, now wondering why she was here.

Smoke and Fair Morn arrived with large pots of cocoa and a tray filled with cups and a box of cookies. So, everyone sat around the table and had some.

"Most strange," said Ap Kar, referring to the cocoa, the cookies, and the rest of the group.

Tinker introduced everyone. R-Bar sat next to Tinker and eyed Ap Kar. Chicken joined them.

"Just visiting?" asked Tinker, hoping.

"Three days," stated Rekel. It was the correct time for showing a mate to a sister. R-Bar nodded.

"My," said Messenger, smiling at Ap Kar. "Many colors."

He jerked and stared at her.

Tinker sighed and looked at R-Bar. "Kiddo, how about you explain everything?" He stood, walked over to the edge of the pool and slipped in. Sgenn joined him.

"Sulda?"

"R-Bar will explain enough to calm them down, I hope."

She bobbled over and kissed him. And then frowned.

"What?"

"I do not know. Is it because we have those other witch folk here?"

"Huh?"

She blinked.

"What?"

"Chantal said that you would not be able to resist."

He frowned. "Resist what?" he demanded.

"Untying my upper garment."

Chantal plunged into the pool and surfaced near them.

"Not funny," he growled at her.

"Sorry. It was a joke," she said to Sgenn and explained what had happened earlier.

"I understand." Sgenn nodded at her. "This pool behavior is not mate lure."

Chantal slipped her arm around her. "Only sometimes. But not when we have visitors."

The air hummed a soft puff of violet. And she stood there, on the deck. Smiling happily at them.

"Fair Princess," greeted Chicken, jumping up and hugging this newcomer.

"Mother."

"Eulin sister." Je'leel walking over smiling.

"Now what?" He twisted around in the water and looked at her.

She walked to the edge of the pool. "First Greetings, Vander Lord. Mother."

He scrambled from the pool, smiling happily. "Hi."

Eulin waved dry over him and hugged him. "Mother sends her love." And whispered in his ear, "And who is that one, Vander Lord Father?"

He watched them come from the pool, throwing an arm around Sgenn when she stepped close. "This is Sgenn. Eulin, our daughter. She is Vander."

"I see," said Sgenn, nodding. "The daughter of the Purple Magicians."

"Sa'ar coming?"

"No. They are in a special ingather. Rorx and his were sent long way out. I came here."

"You may share my room," offered Je'leel.

Eulin smiled warmly at her. "Show me your room."

They walked off, arm in arm.

Ap Kar nudged Rekel. "Perhaps we might be alone and you can explain all that I am seeing?"

Rekel nodded. "Sister, show us our room."

R-Bar headed into the house, waving for them to follow.

"That warlock is muchly confused," observed Sgenn.

Chicken walked over. "Me'Lord, We would Ourself and others a'town go for to fetch foodstuffs for great feast to be."

"Not dressed like that," he grumbled.

"We will, of course, in attire proper dress." She hurried away, followed by most of the others.

He sat and refilled his cup. Sgenn sat next to him. "I will remain here." And soon, they heard the van leave and felt the others pass from their awareness.

"Wonder what's going on? This time?"

"They are buying food."

"I meant the sudden influx of visitors. That usually means that something is about to fall down around our heads. Something that we really don't want."

"Ummm." She nodded, stepped into the pool, and beckoned at him.

He dropped in alongside her. "What?"

"Hold me, sulda. Deep water standing is a new thing. It was not part of my training."

He did. "But it is all right, isn't it?"

She nodded. "The Princess and Chantal did instruct me most thoroughly. Tell me of your magic'd daughter, Eulin."

"Long story."

She tickled his ribs, ever so gently. "I would know.

Totally. From you. Directly." She smiled, a soft-half smile. "We are alone.

"Well," he said. "I had better start with Sa'ar, Eulin's mother."

So, he began to tell her the long story.

And tickled her, ever so gently as well.

They were stretched out in the large bed. He lay by her side, admiring her profile. She lay on her back, staring at the ceiling.

"And so, husband, that is all that I know of that which my youngest sister witch has entangled herself and us." She rolled onto her side and looked into his black engulfing eyes.

"Nowhere had it been told that the Faan were so daring and adventurous," he said.

Rekel hitched closer and slipped an arm over his chest. "Lovely One, we keep our business to ourselves and trust the linked clans to do the same."

"It shall be so." He tugged her closer.

"So," said Eulin, hugging Je'leel, running her fingers up and down her sisters back. "Much time has passed since we did wander."

"Yes. And now you are even more Vander than before. How fare them all?"

"We have a new one, Galron by name." She tugged Je'leel's shirt loose. "This one came to us glowing arcana, studied in an ancient way, begging to join, as no guild would have her."

"She was dangerous?"

Eulin shook her head. And yanked the shirt from Je'leel's shoulders and gasped. "More lovely than ever. No, she was magic bent strange strange. None knew what."

Je'leel smiled at Eulin's compliment. "Mother would be pleased if you told her, ummmm, without Father hearing. What did you do?"

"The Heart and The Soul counseled her and took her in, daring to do so, saying that the Vander are the experimenters of the mage guilds, and saying that being so we shall do this thing."

"And what has my sister done?"

Eulin dropped her hands and yanked her upper garment open. A small strange mark glowed darkly on the otherwise golden toned skin.

"What is that? What did that?'

"Dragon bite. The blackest of the black, faster than lightening, bringer of storms." Eulin smiled.

"What?"

"It took away all the pebble coarse Dragon Master skin. It had started coming back. Yet I remain and retain all that and more in the minds of the dragonkin. I may walk unafraid with or around them, now truly Eulin Dragon Force."

Je'leel shoved her sister onto the bed. "Tell me of your adventures since last we parted for I have done little but lose a mother and gain another."

Eulin nodded. "After you tell me of that."

Sgenn leaned against him. "It is good to be us."

"Yep." He ran a finger down her backbone. "It has taken us years, but I agree. It is good to be us."

Then they felt the rest returning from town as the van started up the long drive to their home.

Heh heh heh, said Smoke.

Damn sneaky, added Chantal.

Fair sly a'wench, suggested Chicken.

"Sulda? Where is Chicken's cloth piece?"

"Don't worry about it. Let's get inside and get changed before they get here." He surged from the pool and helped her out.

Eulin ducked back from the window. "Our Father has partially unclothed that new one and even now pulls her into the house. He is very Vander."

"All the Mothers return from town," explained Je'leel.

"I would splash in that great tub."

Je'leel sat up. "Swimming pool. I will loan you a suit."

Eulin smiled. "Oh yes. I remember. Now."

They made it to the pool just as the others arrived.

He finished drying her hair. "There. All dry. And fluffy."

"Thank you." She spun around and wrapped her arms around him."

"Ummmm. OOOF!" She had backed him into the wall.

"Mine," she said, deep in her throat, lips seeking lips. "My room!" She pulled, tugging him in that direction.

Chantal stepped to the side of the pool. "Want some ice cream? We bought a bunch."

"Yes, Mother. Come sister, you will like it."

Eulin followed her up onto the rear deck and looked at them all. "Father is very Vander."

"What flavor?" asked Fair Morn.

Je'leel pointed. "Neapolitan. Eulin will have the same."

Fair Morn handed them each a large bowl, filled, and a spoon. "Sweets for the sweet."

"Good thing that she doesn't live here." Chantal plunked down her bowl of chocolate as she sat next to Smoke.

"Forsooth," agreed Chicken, sitting by Smoke's other side, a gigantic mound of vanilla in her bowl.

"Six yums," giggled Messenger. She had several kinds of ice cream in her bowl.

"Vander magic," observed Sha'gar, licking her spoon clean.

R-Bar nodded. "Hum hum."

Everyone watched their daughters as they sat side by side, eating ice cream and talking low.

"Where's mine?" demanded a tiny figure standing near Chantal's feet.

"Move away," ordered R-Bar nodding at Sha'gar.

Dat was large.

"What flavor?" Smoke smiled at her. "I'll scoop.

Dat sat next to R-Bar. "Chocolate." She nodded toward Eulin. "I'll bet that males really want to play with her body."

"Shhhhhhh," hissed Chantal.

R-Bar waved her spoon. "Have some ice cream."

Rekel and Ap Kar had just walked from the house.

"What is that? Stuff?" Rekel stared at their bowls, her expression suggesting vile.

"Sit! And eat! Dik do!" R-Bar thumped to her feet and stalked over to the ice cream tubs. She carved great chunks of lemon lime and thrust them into two bowls. Then she banged the bowls down in front of the pair and stabbed spoons into the ice cream. Flopping heavily back on the bench where she had been sitting, she began stir her ice cream violently with her spoon.

Rekel took a careful taste. "Hum hum." And nodded at R-Bar. "Thank you."

R-Bar choked, coughed, and gasped. Ap Kar twitched.

"Ripple," explained Rekel, in her most pleasant of voices, "told that all should so speak, sister to sister."

"Im pir pir," mumbled R-Bar. Then she rasped softly, "You are welcome, sister."

Ap Kar wisely decided to remain silent and to eat his ice cream. It was quite good, this stuff.

"Sssssssuldaaaaaaa," sighed Sgenn as she toppled forward and lay on his chest.

He wrapped his arms gently around her and stroked her hair. "Fluffy grey."

"Theurgist color," she mumbled.

"Pretty nice." He rolled them onto their sides. "Better than that even."

She smiled a soft half-smile.

"What?"

"Messenger will be upset."

"Why?"

"She has the ring."

"Oh." He reached up and tickled along smooth skin. "She is very understanding."

"That grey haired sneak," snarled Chantal.

"Certainly is," agreed Messenger. "Really really."

"Ought to know better," suggested Fair Morn looking at Smoke.

She nodded. "Has all the memories."

"Hum," said R-Bar.

Sha'gar waved a cautionary hand at her. "I will speak with her. Sister to sister."

"Oh my no," said Messenger. "I will." She grinned broadly.

"What do be thy plot, kitten." Chicken pushed her empty bowl toward Fair Morn.

Messenger giggled. And twisted the ornate ring on her finger. "She was next. Now she owes me her turn!"

"Heh hell heh," cackled R-Bar.

"Nasty," said Rekel, glaring at her sister's comment.

"Heh heh heh," replied R-Bar, ignoring her sister. "Bet that she doesn't do that again."

Ap Kar looked the question at Rekel. She indicated that she didn't know what they were talking about either.

"Heh heh heh heh heh," gurgled R-Bar.

Eventually, Tinker and Sgenn joined the group around the table.

Messenger leaned sideways and whispered in Sgenn's ear, who gasped, and glowered, and agreed.

"Heh heh heh heh heh," cackled R-Bar.

Tinker took his bowl with him, deciding that it was safer to go over and talk with his daughters.

Eulin smiled at him.

Je'leel nodded.

And slowly the day wandered into evening.

And movies.
And popcorn.

Chapter Twenty-nine

A Vander Problem.

Rand Nar. Stark and Bare.

Far across the universes, far, far from the small star on its isolated planet.

They struggled.

Many many elseplaces away and many, many elseplaces up.

They struggled.

Here on this small, rocky bare place they struggled.

Sa'ar, The Heart, and Tobtz, The Soul.

Here they struggled.

With Galron, The Bent.

All around them, in a silent, distant circle stood and watched the others of the guild.

Magic billowed in great waves outward from the struggling trio. And crashed back inside the restraining circle.

None could tell how this would end for this was a new thing that they fought, never before seen or told.

In one great downstroke, the magic roared silent as Sa'ar

and Tobtz bore Galron down. In a tangle of limbs and tattered garments they crashed to the hard stone, thrashing and heaving. And then they lay still as still.

The circle tightened.

And drew near.

All wondered did any survive this terrible hard thing they had been striving for. The three bodies lay limp and unmoving.

Aada burst from the circle and gestured for their Healer to come forward for she saw soft breathing and fluttering eyes. They pulled one free and knelt by her side. Aada bent close and stroked the sweat tangled hair from her face as Imdar began.

"Our Heart, speak to us."

Eyes fluttered open and stared upward into the dark overhead sky. Sa'ar moistened her lips with her tongue. "How are . . . the . . . others?"

Aada bent and kissed the sweat streaked forehead, tasting salt, rock dust, and something else.

"Moonda checks Our Soul. Cazor, the other."

Imdar, The Healer, pulled the ripped and stained garments aside and began to smooth on the salve, fingers kneading and stroking.

Sa'ar smiled up at her. "The most gentle hands of all has Imdar."

Imdar handed the jar to Aada. "She will finish." She stood and moved over and knelt by Tobtz, The Soul of The Vander.

Moonda had rolled her onto her back and straightened out her limbs and was now sitting, stroking Tobtz' hair, cradling the limp form in her arms.

Imdar yanked the garment off Tobtz' shoulders and stared. "Strangely marked. Sa'ar was not so affected." She reached somewhere and fetched in a glittering silver and blue wand. "Hold her tight, fierce warrior."

Moonda wrapped her arms tightly around Tobtz and watched as Imdar slowly ran the thin wand into soft flesh. Tobtz' arms and legs twitched and jerked. Her eyes flew open as she screamed.

And screamed.

And screamed.

And sagged limply, eyes blinking away tears pouring forth.

Imdar threw her wand somewhere and ran her palms over soft swelling. "As pleasant as ever, Our Soul."

"Sa'ar?" mumbled Tobtz.

"More alive than ever," replied The Healer, standing, handing Moonda a jar of salve.

"Caress her with this." And turned to the last one.

Cazor sat next to her and was slowly peeling the sweat soaked garments away. "This lovely breathes most slowly."

"Then," said Imdar as she knelt next to them, "she lives." Imdar slid her palms here and there. "Most beautifully endowed is Galron of the long limbs."

Slowly Galron's eyes wobbled open. They blinked and focused on Imdar's face. A slow smile formed. "A loving hand," she whispered.

Imdar fetched in a clay vessel and handed it to Cazor. "With gentle fingers and a lover's touch, rub this on." She stood and walked over to where Sa'ar was sitting.

Cazor bent and kissed Galron.

Sa'ar smiled at Imdar as she sat on the stone pavement. "Cazor favors Galron over all."

Imdar nodded. "She will be healed."

"As am I for Aada did with gentle loving touch your salve stroke me to health and well being."

Imdar bent forward and kissed Sa'ar greetings. "In not too short a time we should return home, Our Heart. To rest and finish healing."

"Yes. And there, in comfort, we may examine, most carefully, that which we just did birth in this hard and rocky place."

Grandeville. Tinker's Place.

It was a great bar-b-que.

Red and Green and Sandy and Janine came in Green's truck. Red and Green brought a keg and lots of ice and two pitchers. After setting up the keg, they filled their pitchers. They preferred them to cups. For them, cups were too small.

Janine poked Green in the gut. "Leave some for us little people!" It had felt like poking a wall.

Green nodded. "Sure." And winked at her.

She strolled off to talk with Sandy and Chantal.

Red and Green walked over to peer at the grills.

Tinker was helping Smoke and Fair Morn finish setting bowls and platters on one of the wooden picnic tables when they heard J.C.'s old, battered van rattle to a halt in their driveway.

"Be right back," he said, hurrying down the deck to meet them.

As he stepped off the deck, Reep grabbed J.C.'s arm and hissed loudly. For her.

"What?" J. C. stared around but didn't see anything out of the ordinary. Reep carefully watched Tinker approach. "Hi, guy," said J. C.

"Hi," said Tinker. He looked at Reep. "Unless I say this is a command, nothing I say is to be taken as one. Understand?"

"Yesssssssss," hissed the morning air.

"Good. Let's go mingle."

Another car pulled in and spilled out two girls, followed by their parents, Deke and Shannon Morgan.

"Tinkle," giggled the twins, crashing into Tinker.

"Hello, Uncle J. C.," said one.

"Hello, Aunt Reep," said the other.

Shannon kissed J. C. on the side of the face. "Hi there, big guy." She smiled at Reep. "Hello, Reep." She looked at Tinker. "Everybody on the rear deck?" She headed that way, taking the twins with her.

Morgan tossed an arm around Tinker's shoulders as they walked down the deck. "Small piece of business?"

"Sure. What?"

"Just a couple of details about that, ummmm, gift of your's."

"OK. Let's sit at the pool end."

They walked that way.

Shannon, after cautioning the twins to behave, went over to talk with her sister, Chantal, and the others. Reep slipped over to talk with R-Bar, while J. C. stepped down to see what Red and Green were staring at.

After a short time, Shannon came over to Tinker and Morgan carrying two foaming glasses. And handed them to the two men. "Enough business talk."

"We are done," said Morgan.

"Hard, Ramp, Shem and Tajaar are supposed to come," said Tinker.

"Who's that grey haired woman?" asked Shannon. "The one talking with Sha'gar."

"Her sister, Sgenn."

"Sister?"

"That's J. C.'s youngest daughter?" asked Morgan.

"Yep."

They watched Reep approach the pair and kiss each on the forehead. They had to bent down.

"Certainly look different," observed Morgan.

Suddenly the twins were hurtling down the deck toward them. They crashed into Shannon's legs.

"Mommy, mommy, mommy," cried one.

"A tall lady just appeared," said the other.

"Down there," said the first twin.

"At the end of the deck," explained the other.

Tinker looked. "Certainly tall, all right."

"Who is she?" asked Shannon.

"No idea," replied Tinker. "Ummm, wait here." He hurried toward this stranger and wondered why she was here. Her soft lavender garments told him that she was one of the Vander but not one that he had met before.

She watched him approach. When he was close enough, she dropped to her knees and bowed her head.

"I am Galron, the Bent, Great Lord, Heart of our Heart, Sire of our Warlock and of our Heart To Be. To hear is to obey. My body is your's."

Tinker sighed. She looked up at him.

"Stand up."

She bounced to her feet. "Lord?" And smiled warmly at him.

Eulin walked up to Galron, hugged her and kissed her. "First Greetings, Our Heart To Be."

"First Greetings, Galron. Why are you here?"

Chantal joined the group. "This lanky babe one of the Vander?"

"Who are you?" asked Galron.

"One of my mothers here," answered Eulin. She began to point. "Those are his, and they are my Mothers. Smoke, Princess Chicken, Messenger, Fair Morn, R-Bar, Sha'gar, and Sgenn. And Chantal."

Galron smiled broadly. "Most Vander, Lord."

"You said that your name is Galron?"

"Galron, the Bent, Lord." She stepped closer to him. "As those are all your's and thus Eulin's mothers, as you mated both Sa'ar and Imdar, then we also are your's as well. Twice, your's, as you are The Heart of Our Heart and the Vander Lord as well."

"Ummmmmmmm. O.K., I guess."

"Galron, answer my question," said Eulin.

She turned and smiled at Eulin. "I bring word from Our Heart, your Mother." And nudged up against him. "And word to you, Vander Lord, who could mate with all did he but wish it to be."

"That was settled," snapped Chantal.

He nodded. "Certainly was. Behave, Galron."

She frowned. "I am most well behaved, Lord. How have I failed?" She looked at Eulin for help.

"Come with me," said Eulin. "It is time to eat. We may converse at the same time. And I will explain."

Chantal slipped an arm under one of his. "Come on, Stud, time to eat."

"Don't start that stuff."

"To hear is to obey," she snickered.

"I wonder if Ranna could give me a witch spell that would work on you guys?"

"Don't be such a grump, grump."

Messenger and Fair Morn called everyone down to the grills to get something to eat.

Hard, Ramp, Shem, and Tajaar arrived, piling from Hard's car, and hurrying down the deck. Hard and Shem each tripped on something that wasn't there.

"Sorry we are late," Hard called, stumbling over something else not there. "Some business at the last moment." He and Shem walked over to talk to Tinker as Ramp joined Reep in the line. Tajaar stayed close to Shem.

Red and Green admired the grilled food. "Shem's babe is packing a blade," said Red.

"Don't be such a cop," commanded Sandy, handing him a plate.

"Certainly is," agreed Green.

Janine banged a plate into his mid-section. "Don't eat everything on the grill."

Messenger giggled happily and heaped Red's plate full as he held it out. "Oh," she said, "we cooked just lots and lots." And violently nodded her head. "Really really."

Green looked over the top of Janine's head at Red. "Think she'd be upset if I called her Tranquil?"

"No comment, partner." Red moved sideways to collect salad and other things.

"Down here, T. Rex," commanded Janine, handing Green several napkins.

He looked down. "You are very relaxing to be around."

"Some compliment," she snorted. "Let's get some salad."

At the back of the line, Eulin told Galron that they would talk with her father after all his friends had left and that until then Galron was to be not-Vander.

"The Heart commands The Body," stated Galron. She gently touched Eulin's arm.

"Yes?"

"Who are all these magic users that I see? Tell me again?"

"The short woman in the red trousers and t-shirt is Faan witch R-Bar, one of my mothers. The tall women in black is Faan magician Aunt Ramp. The slight woman with her arm around her waist is Faan witch Aunt Reep, called The Silent One."

Galron gasped. "How does she touch?" Then she nodded. "I have heard of The Silent One."

"I will explain later. The tall young woman is Faan magician Reep daughter Cousin Sha'gar. The grey haired is Faan theurgist Reep daughter Cousin Sgenn. Also my Mothers."

Galron's face went blank, a carefully controlled blank. "Theurgist? His? Your mother?"

"I will explain all." Eulin did. As much as she knew.

"This was not told," gasped Galron.

"Much has happened to them since last the Vander did visit here." Eulin pushed Galron forward. "That tall man is Ramp son warlock Shem, trained by Ramp's warlock father, The One Who Travels Alone."

"They gather together so casually."

Eulin nodded. "All you see are my father's friends."

"And that one?" Dat had just joined the group, dressed appropriately for the occasion as she knew Tinker would want her to do.

Eulin smiled. "Dat, mother to my sister Je'leel. She is an indjinn."

Galron's cheek twitched as she whispered low, "Protect me, Our Heart To Be."

"You have nothing to fear here."

"They will do things to me."

"Of course not," snapped Eulin.

Galron looked at her from the corners of her eyes. "I slipped Anila on him. His many loves will hold me down and do things."

"NO!" stated Eulin. "All who visit this elseplace are safe protected comfortable. It is the attraction of this elseplace?" She leaned close to Galron. "Although he will be very upset if he finds out. But I shall say nothing."

They stepped up to the grills. Fair Morn filled their plates. Messenger waggled a drumstick at Galron. "Naughty, naughty." She giggled. "But you are very pretty."

"Kitten," cautioned Fair Morn. She began to heap Eulin's plate full. Then they watched Eulin and Galron walk down the deck to the pool end where Je'leel joined them and introduced Shem and Tajaar.

Galron leaned close to Eulin. "How did that green-eyed one know?"

So Eulin explained Messenger.

Galron sat down heavily. And stared. "Never," she

mumbled. "Ever."

Shem stepped over. "Are you ill?"

She shook her head.

"She is knowledge shocked," explained Eulin. "I told her about Father and my cousins."

Shem slipped an arm around Tajaar. "I can understand that. My Uncle is a surprise for most of the folk out there in the elseplaces. And few really know anything except those standing around here." He looked at Galron. "You are Vander, correct?"

"Yes."

"Newest," added Eulin.

And the day passed.

Filled by little conversations.

And then.

The guests filtered away.

The left over food was put away.

Things were made neat and tidy.

More or less.

Then it was mid-evening. Tinker and all were lounging in the large living room.

Sprawling, relaxing, reading.

He was editing a manuscript. Chantal sat next to him, scanning trade journals. Messenger curled against his other side wiggling the parts of one of Chicken's wire puzzles.

"Father?" asked Eulin.

"Huh?" He looked up.

"Galron brings a message from Mother."

"Oh?"

Galron leaped from her chair, hurried over, and crashed

to her knees in front of him, bowing her head. "Our Heart," she intoned, "did tell speak thus. Vander Lord, mate, lover, father of our daughter, friend, please come to us."

He sighed and looked from face to face. All were looking at him. Then he looked at the couch where Eulin and Je'leel sat. "Eulin?"

"I know not."

He looked back at Galron still kneeling there. "How come she didn't come herself?"

"Imdar the Healer would not allow it."

He jerked upright. "She is sick?"

"No."

"What then?"

"Some injuries."

"Oh my!" gasped Messenger.

All eyes focused upon Galron.

"Galron," he said gently. "You don't have to kneel like that."

"I would not be improper," she said to the floor.

"How about you just sit in a chair and look at me and tell us what is going on this time?" He leaned back and slumped

Chicken headed for the kitchen. "We will Ourself start pots of coffee."

Galron stood, dropped into a chair and sat, facing him. "To hear is to obey." She watched his face carefully.

"What have the Vander been doing now?" he asked, beginning to worry.

So, she told them of her training in deep, ancient arcana, the twisted and the bent, and of how no guild would admit her, Galron, The Bent, so named for her magic. She told them of deep and wide travel always seeking a place to be until one day, in a ruin, horrible to see, inhabited by a few crooked things, she had heard of the mage guild called Vanderlaine, an order risen from the dead. She had traveled and hunted for those who knew of these women often called The Purple Mage. And as she traveled and hunted, she learned of their Great Battle where they had finally vanquished their ancient enemy, the battle where they were aided by The One called Chosen, a dark warrior and his fierce others.

And, in this elseplace and in that elseplace, she had heard other tales. This dark warrior had taken Imdar the Healer and produced a male, Rorx, Vander warlock, thus insuring that the Vander Guild would last into the next generation.

And, in this elseplace and in that elseplace, she had heard of this dark warrior who had also taken Sa'ar, The Heart, to his hidden abode and there they had produced Eulin Dragon Force, Heart To Be, thus insuring that the Vander Guild would live into the future. This person was also called The Vander Lord, the only male who could command each and every Vander to his very wish.

And in this elseplace and in that elseplace, she also had heard whispered tales about these Vander saying that of all the mage guilds in the universe of universes, that these mage were called The Daring Ones, as they would study what none other would.

And so, Galron had traveled and had finally come to that place wherein this guild lived, on an elseplace called Magevern.

Then, one day not long past, Sa'ar had said that the Vander should gain knowledge known by this, their newest sister and all had agreed and journeyed far from their home to do so.

Galron had instructed The Heart and The Soul and had described the great danger on what Sa'ar wished them to do. And to all the guild.

So, on that hard rock, they had struggled. And had succeeded, nearly dying in the process.

"I healed quickly," explained Galron. "In the care of Cazor." She smiled And bowed to Eulin. "You were sent far distant, just in case. One had to survive if the Vander were to survive. To stay alive. To rise again. If need be."

"The Heart and The Soul live. But heal slowly." Galron looked around, then at Tinker.

"Sa'ar begs. Not for herself but for Tobtz who weakens. Imdar says that you are required, Vander Lord."

Messenger wrapped her arms around him. "MyTinker?"

Eulin stared at him. "Father?"

Galron slipped from her chair to her knees, throwing her arms wide. "Anything that I have, anything that you wish! Anything . . . anything."

He looked at Chantal.

"Might as well pack our bags," she said. " You know that we have to go."

He sighed. And nodded. "O.K. In the morning." And stood. "Bed time." He slipped an arm around Messenger's shoulders as she stood. "Someone show Galron her room." He headed down the hall, Messenger at his side.

Chantal stood. "Smoke, Fair Morn and I will pack. Everyone else might as well get some shut eye."

They scattered

His eyes popped open. It was dark, very dark. Someone's soft hand slid back and forth across his chest. Warm breath and soft lips caressed the corner of his shoulder.

"Oh my gosh!" gasped Messenger, sitting up. "How did you get in here?" Two green orbs glowed in the dark.

"Who?" he asked.

"Galron," they both replied.

"What are you doing in here?" he demanded.

Messenger lifted the covers. "And where are your clothes?" To her there was no darkness, only light.

Galron yanked the covers back. "None told that the Vander Lord consorted with a green-eyed demon childettan."

"Get out of here," he grumbled.

"I am not," stated Messenger. "Whatever that is."

"I would offer all the pleasure that Our Lord would wish as thanks for his assistance. Is that so wrong?"

Tinker sighed.

"Yes," snarled Messenger. "Creep sneaky!"

Galron sat up. "I am rejected?"

"Not exactly," he said. "Sa'ar can explain. Tomorrow. For now, just go back to your room."

"To hear is to obey." She stood and walked from the bedroom.

Messenger laid down and tickled him. "She is very pretty."

"Dun care," he mumbled, rolling onto his side and tickling her back.

Her eyes flared brighter as she squirmed.

"Wanna turn off the lights?"

The green glow slowly faded away.

"Doesn't that affect your vision?"

"No. And our daughter Sedeem taught me how to control the eye color flare. She learned how on Randle's Fair from an undermage named Zipta." She demonstrated, eyes glowing and fading. "Galron really wanted you to. Really really."

"Damn Vander," he grumbled.

She wrapped her arms around him.

Chapter Thirty

Is The Cure Worse Than The Illness?

Magevern.

They swirled in, down onto the bare rock surface near the entrance to the Vander Guild Home.

"So here we are again." He looked around. Sha'gar and R-Bar were casting illumination.

Galron pointed. "Down, just there. I will go first and control the door spell ward."

Sgenn shrugged and stepped closer to Tinker.

R-Bar hurried over. "Rekel and Ap Kar went to Bahn Duhr Tohr. Sook has the clan upset with her mate choice. Rekel said Ripple told all are summoned."

Tinker sighed. "It is always something with your bunch."

"We will there go!" stated Chicken.

"After we finish here," he added, once again resigned to his fate. Which was always getting stranger.

They trooped after Galron as she descended the steps into the steep entryway that led down to the main gate. Purple light flared as she passed inside. And died to a soft glow. They followed her in.

And were greeted just inside the gate by Cazor, Moonda, and Imdar. Cazor grabbed Galron in a tight embrace amd murmured, "Well done, lovely one."

Moonda bowed to Tinker. "Welcome, Vander Lord. How may we serve you?"

Imdar hugged him and was hugged in return.

"How's Rorx?" he asked. "And Szaifeh?"

Imdar kissed him and breathed softly in his ear. "Your son and his witch-wife are well." She stepped back and smiled. "Later you may tell me of the changes that I see." She watched Cazor and Galron walking away, down the passageway, talking softly.

"Come, Sa'ar is this way." She led them into a different corridor. And explained to them as they strolled along all about the changes that they had made to their abode since the last time that Tinker and his had been there.

"You've been working hard."

"Yes." Imdar hugged his arm. "We have kept the number of guild members small, being very selective as to who we chose to take in. But we did have a need for special chambers and rooms. The archives alone have been expanded twice."

"You look . . . well."

"Only well?" She smiled at him.

"Beautiful," he stated. "But different. What have you been doing?"

"Perhaps Our Heart will explain." She touched a door open. "In there."

They stepped into a large chamber decorated in soft tones of lilac and violet. Sa'ar lay, half propped up by large pillows, on a long couch. Two young women in billowing purple garb were standing near. They smiled warmly at all and bowed their heads.

Eulin stepped past Tinker and Imdar and bent and kissed her mother. "Heart To Heart, Mother."

Sa'ar kissed her in return. "Heart To Heart, Daughter." She waved her hand. "Perhaps I could be alone with Imdar and them?"

Eulin nodded. And left, followd by the silent pair. Sa'ar smiled at him and patted the couch. "Sit here, Love. I will introduce all later. Who are these that I do not know?"

He took her hand and made introductions. Sa'ar nodded. "Very Vander, Lord." Then she peered deeply into his eyes. "Such a loss."

He nodded. And blinked. And swallowed. "Yes." And looked back. "Now what's going on?"

Sa'ar laughed. "You are the constant factor in all our lives."

"You are avoiding the question."

She smiled. "None may disobey you, Lord of the Vander, not even me." She lurched upright and swung her legs over the edge of the couch and leaned against his side. "Hold me in your arms while I tell you our tale of special magic." She kissed his cheek. "Then Imdar will tell you what must be done. For myself. And Tobtz."

They pulled chairs around and settled themselves as Sa'ar twisted around until she was curled inside his arms, head leaning against his chest. "It all began," she started, "from the time when Galron appeared at our guild door, weeping . . ."

" . . . and so you see, Galron healed fast because it was her magic we tamed and altered and brought in. But, in some strange way not fully understood, yet, it bent our Vander nature, Tobtz and I. Not even Rorx can affect it. Imdar has prowled the archives, searching our ancient history for an answer."

Imdar nodded. "There is something that we must try."

Tinker stared at her. "Try? You don't know whether it will work or not?"

"Do," amended Imdar.

Chicken jumped up and sat next to him. "Hist, My Lord. Do calm thyself." And smiled at Sa'ar. "We will try this thing."

"Oh we will, will we?" He frowned darkly at her.

"Grumble Butt," growled Chantal. "Let's find out first what it is. You can grumble after."

"Indeed!" agreed Chicken.

"O.K.," he said. "What?"

"It is Vander private," stated Imdar. "All must leave."

"Oh, oh." Chantal stared at them.

"Oh my gosh!" Messenger looked at Smoke.

"And you may not tell them. Ever!" Imdar leaned toward him, looking Vander stern.

Chantal stood and stomped from the room. The rest trailed after her. Smoke turned and winked at him as she stepped through the door.

Sgenn turned and walked back to them. And said in her usual calm voice, half-smile tugging at one corner of her mouth. "If he dies, or is injured, there will be no Vander or Vander home until the end of forever." She turned and walked out, gently closing the door as she did.

"What is she?" Sa'ar rubbed her hand up and down his chest.

"Theurgist. That is about all anyone seems to know."

Sa'ar looked at Imdar. "Have the archives searched! I would know what he has mated with, this time."

He stroked Sa'ar's hair. "Well, am I going to be injured or die?"

"No," replied Imdar. "We are safe. From that." She stood. "Come, husband to us both, Moonda prepares a special meal. For you. For me. Will the rest behave?"

"Sure." He laughed. "I hope."

Sa'ar tightened her arms around him. "Kiss me, John, and tell me that you love me."

He did. "I really do, you know. And they all know it. And love you also."

He winked at Imdar. "And you too. They just don't show it very well." Then he helped Imdar as she resettled Sa'ar. "See you later." He took Imdar's arm and walked with her from the room.

Chantal thumped down into one of the chairs in the large gathering room they had been given to use. "I don't think that I like what these Vander babes think they are up to. And I don't even know what it is."

Messenger sat near her. "Sa'ar is really not well." And wiped at the tears in her eyes.

Smoke nodded. "Imdar will take care of him."

"Those purple babes have been panting after him for years," grumbled Chantal.

"Can't let them die, can we?" Fair Morn stretched and stood. "Let's look around, like Smoke said. Maybe find something to eat."

"Indeed." Chicken joined her. "We would see, We would,

what these Vander have wrought. Last time we do here come, we do make most big a'mess."

Imdar stopped them in front of her door. "Vander Lord, from this point on all that you may be is The Vander Lord. All are prepared to play their part in this most complicated healing process. It is the Vander way, very ancient, from our very beginnings. Sa'ar and I believe that it will succeed."

He nodded. "Sure."

Imdar wrapped her arms around him and rubbed herself slowly against him, lips enveloping his, waiting until his arms wrapped around her, and slid here and there.

"Yes, Lord," she whispered, and gently bit his lower lip. "Dinner awaits. Inside." And pulled from his arms. And touched the door open.

Moonda stood there, smiled warmly at him, and hugged Imdar. She spun free and wrapped herself around him. "Long have you denied us, Lord. Now you are us." Yanking her head back she laughed, a deep throated laugh. "Dinner is set there, Lord. I will wait through that open door and provide anything that you might wish." Slowly she pulled her arms free and backed away and then walked through the open door.

"Sit, Lord." Imdar served there both. "Eat hardy." She bent, kissed him, and then sat by his side and began to eat.

Every now and then, she leaned sideways and kissed him. And refilled his dish and his cup until all the food and drink were consumed. Then she stood. "Come with me, Lord." And took him out another door.

They were met by Cazor. "Lord." She laughed gaily and slid inside his arms, kissing him, hands tugging his shirt loose.

Leaning back in his arms, eyes sparkling, she laughed. "It was a good wine that you drank." Spinning away from him, she grabbed Imdar, tugged her upper garment loose and kissed her. And then strolled away, down the corridor.

Imdar yanked him into motion. "My private room is just down there." And just down there, she stopped and touched her door open, just as someone came up behind them. Her arms wrapped around Imdar, ripping Imdar's garment open. The Healer arched her back and moaned. And was released.

"I am Imten, the Artificier," she laughed as she hugged him. And yanked his shirt from his shoulders, pressing him back against the wall. "We are well met," she sighed, "for first meeting." She shoved herself away, pushed them into the room. "Imdar awaits, Lord." The door closed behind them.

Imdar walked over and lay back on the bed. "In that purple jar is a special slave. Rub it on my body. Everywhere."

He turned, picked up the jar and turned back. And began to do as he was ordered.

They walked down a long corridor, touring the Vander home. Sha'gar nudged Sgenn. "The Vander cast longing glances at all who pass."

"Most wicked a'look," observed Chicken.

"Hum hum hum," said R-Bar.

"First one that grabs me gets her butt kicked," grumbled Chantal.

"They are just being friendly," said Fair Morn.

A Vander slipped past them, smiling warmly at one and all.

"Really really friendly," said Messenger, tucking her shirt

back in.

"Those babes have one-track minds," grumbled Chantal, even louder.

"That one fondled me!" snapped Sgenn, grey eyes watching the receding figure.

"Sister," cautioned her sister, rebuttoning her shirt. "Do nothing!" Sgenn nodded.

"Most friendly, indeed," laughed Chicken. She tugged her shirt the rest of the way loose and tied the ends just above the bottom of her rib cage.

"Brazen Queen," said Smoke.

"When in Rome," replied Chicken.

The Vander walking toward them suddenly jerked and sagged sideways, eyes rolling wildly.

"GAZOOKS!" cried Chicken, running toward a crumpled form. "Fair Vander do around us tumble."

Sha'gar and Sgenn hurried back down the corridor toward the figure slumped against the wall.

"What is wrong with them?" Chantal looked one way, then the other.

"Nothing," said Smoke. "It was some kind of sudden shock." She joined Chicken in peering at the figure she was bent over. "See, her eyes are refocusing."

Chicken nodded. "Fair heart do itself race." Her hand under the Vander's upper garment moved.

"Erotic Princess."

Chicken's hand wandered. "Fair smooth skin do be most hot and moist."

The Vander straightened up, smiled at Chicken, and

grabbed her.

"YOIKS! She do Us clasp."

"Turn about," laughed Smoke, spinning away. Just in time to see Sgenn yanking another Vander away by the back of her collar.

Sha'gar snapped angrily at the Purple Mage, "I am not to be Vander touched."

"Leave her be," ordered Smoke, running up to them.

Then everyone looked up and down the corridor. They were suddenly alone.

"Whither?" asked Chicken, standing, her shirt flopping freely. She frowned. "We do Us now begin to understand Our Lord."

"Seek Sa'ar," rasped Imdar as the gold glowing shape slipped from her limp form. "Seek . . . Sa'ar!"

As the group stood staring up and down the corridor, something bright yellow flashed across a far intersection, the light fading in the direction that it had loped.

"What was that?" Chantal jerked around.

A Vander ran past them and barred their passage that way. " Do not interfere!"

Smoke tapped Chantal on the shoulder. "Let's go the other way."

Chantal spun and glared at her. "What is going on? You know, don't you?"

"No. Only what I was told. We were told that it was Vander private. My awareness is no larger than this group in this corridor. I cannot feel him at all."

A Vander slipped into their cluster, her arm sliding around Smoke's waist. "I am Tinlee, bronze skinned one. Tinlee, the Adept." She smiled and looked deep into Smoke's eyes. "Very, very interesting." Her hand gently ran up and down Smoke's rib cage. "Just ahead we have refreshing liquids. Join us."

Smoke nodded. "We will do that." And blinked. Tinlee twitched. Smoke smiled at her. "You are a clever kitten, but have much to learn."

They wandered down the corridor and into a large room. The Vander smiled at them. All were sipping from tall glasses.

"Oooo," sighed Sa'ar, as she sucked in deep breathes.

He twitched, jerked, and gasped, "Sa'ar?"

"Who . . . else . . .," she managed to rasp, "do . . . you . . . know . . . that . . . feels . . . this . . . nice?"

"I can't move anything," he mumbled.

She managed to kiss the side of his face. "Not true, Lord."

"What did you do to me?" he rasped.

She managed a weak smile. "That should be my question."

He toppled sideways. "OOOF!"

She rolled her head in his directions. "No time for modesty, Love."

The door opened and two Vander walked in. They lifted him and carried him to a large bed. Then they carried over Sa'ar and laid her along his side before covering them both with soft lavender colored blankets. Then they bent and kissed Sa'ar and him.

"Lovely Lord," breathed one.

"Beautiful Lord," breathed the other.

They left, closing the door quietly.

She reached over and held his hand. And fell alseep. So did he.

Galron smiled. So did all the Vander.

Eulin marched in looking extremely unhappy about something.

Tinlee sat next to Smoke. "How are you called?"

"Smoke."

She leaned close and sucked in a deep breath. And kissed her. "Neither smell nor taste."

"It is my name from my homeland, a number of years past."

"Tell me of your home, soft hued, lovely one."

Smoke nodded. And began to tell her of her past life. She slipped her arm around Tinlee as Tinlee leaned against Smoke, laying her head on Smoke's shoulder.

Vander mingled, speaking softly, welcoming them.

Chantal snapped her arm back, fist clenched.

Fair Morn hastily grabbed her. "Don't!"

"If this babe . . . "

"Imten," she said. "I an Imten, the Artificier."

"Well," growled Chantal, "if Imten cops another feel, I'm gonna bust her face."

"John," laughed Fair Morn, "said that we were supposed to behave."

"Just can resist not thee," suggested Chicken. "Round, gobular."

"Lovely," interrupted Imten.

"Loverlies," finished Chicken, shoving her empty glass at Galron.

Eulin leaned close and whispered in Imten's ear. Imten nodded.

"What?" demanded Chantal.

"Sorry, sorry," murmured Imten, grabbing one of Chantal's hands and kissing the back of it.

"Oh, hell." Chantal leaned forward and kissed Imten on the forehead. "Forget it. But don't get any ideas. The only one sleeping in my bed is Fair Morn."

His eyes popped open. He stared upward. At the soft unfocused ceiling. At least he assumed that it was a ceiling, that the blue up there was a ceiling. He felt like he had melted into the surface of the bed.

Someone sat next to him and lightly rested a hand on his forehead. Then yanked the blanket down and touched his chest, his stomach, brushing lightly.

His eyes focused. "Imdar?"

She smiled, leaned over and kissed him. "First Greetings, Vander Lord. You are merely tired, very tired." Then she reached across him and laid her hand on the woman's forehead. Yanking the blanket away, she checked.

"UMMMMMMMMM!" she gasped. "IMDAR!"

Imdar smiled, leaned across him and kissed her. "First Greetings, Our Heart." Then she sat back and hauled the blankets back into place.

Sa'ar reached over and grabbed one of his hands and squeezed.

He cleared his throat, several times, and finally managed

to speak. "Well?"

Imdar wiped at her eyes with one sleeve. "Our Heart is all Vander again."

"John," sighed Sa'ar. "Imdar did not tell me what would happen."

He swallowed hard. "Me neither." He looked up at Imdar, and rasped, "I have to go through that again?"

Slowly Imdar shook her head. "No. Tobtz died."

Somehow he managed to hold two sobbing women in his arms.

Smoke's eyes popped open. She reached out and woke them all. She shoved from the bed, as the blankets spilled onto the floor. "Hurry, Princess, get dressed. All the Vander gather on the surface." Smoke and the others hurried up the stairs and gathered to one side.

Tinker stood, dressed in pale lilac grab, his arms around Imdar and Sa'ar. All around them clustered the Vander. Everyone looked across the bare rock at the neatly constructed pyre. The body lay on top draped in purple cloth.

The Vander waited for the sun to reach the appropriate spot.

Galron ran from the cluster, climbed up onto the pyre, stood feet straddling the form, and glared up at the sky. Ripping her upper garment to shreds, she arched her back and thrust both hands upward, clenching a gleaming violet wand. "My life for her's," she howled.

The wand slowly lowered. "AHHHHH!" Blue green fire crackled electric flame, toppling Galron from the pyre. The fire spread from her body and enveloped the pyre and the body on top.

"DON'T!" screamed Smoke. "SHE IS ALIVE!"

Sgenn burst from her group, dashed to the thrashing, groaning woman, and knelt by her side. "Not nice," she said, ordering something to reach through the spitting green, yanking the wand from Galron's hands. And snapping it in half. The fire flickered and was gone. The wood of the pyre smoldered, threatening to burst into flame.

Smoke ran over and yanked Sgenn back. Fumes were seeping from the pyre.

Chicken and Sha'gar grabbed Galron by the arms and dragged her from the side of the pyre as Fair Morn clambered up, snatched the body from on top, and leaped to safety.

All around them purple angry billowed from the Vander.

R-Bar knelt next to Galron, inspected the pieces of the wand, and slapped Galron's face, rocking her head back and forth. "Don't you Vander listen?" she snarled. "Our Dark Sister said that one is still alive." She poured silver grains onto Galron and slammed her hand against the Vander's forehead and mid-section.

"Kaffff karpppp!" gasped Galron.

R-Bar grabbed the Vander's face with one hand and violently shook her head. "Speak, speak, speak!"

Galron's eyes wobbled and finally settled on R-Bar's face. "You?" she rasped.

"Good enough," growled the witch, standing, kicking Galron in the side "Ter ptar!" She turned and looked at Sgenn.

"I am fine." Sgenn kissed her on the forehead.

Smoke stepped over to Fair Morn and looked at Tobtz. "She is still in there."

Moonda stalked over. "How dare you?" she demanded, warrior angry.

Chantal shoved her roughly aside. "Cool it, tough babe." And glared at the rest of the Vander. "You almost burned her alive."

Imdar joined them as Vander hurried Tinker and Sa'ar down below. "Alive?"

Smoke nodded. "Deep inside there is a spark. A very small spark."

"Will you help me?"

"Indeed," said Chicken.

"Follow me." Imdar walked off.

They were taken to a large room, stripped of their clothes and placed in a large bed. "What's going on?" he asked as all the Vander left the room but one. She walked over and ran a fingertip down their bodies. Then she pulled the blankets up.

"Rest, Our Lord. Rest, Our Heart." She bent close and breathed warm on him. "I am Xanx, learning from Imdar. To fully heal, you must rest." Soft lips caressed his. She straightened up and smiled. "You may enoy each other as you wish, and as you are able. It is part of our healing process." She spun on her heels and left the room, gently closing the room.

"Better follow the doctor's orders," laughed Sa'ar, yawning widely.

He slipped an arm around her as she rolled toward him. "Right." He fell asleep.

Imdar led them down and around and into her room for healing.

Fair Morn laid Tobtz on the high platform and stepped back. "Certainly looks dead."

"Not yet," said Smoke.

R-Bar burst into the room snarling wildly. "Dim dim dim dim dim dim dim!"

"Help me," asked Imdar. "There are witch skills that a mage may not touch."

R-Bar looked at Smoke.

"Still there," said Smoke. "But very, very faint."

"Hum." R-Bar stepped over and peered at Tobtz and reached out to loosen the lilac garments. Purple flame roared up.

"OUCH!" R-Bar leaped back. "Get that ptar ptar tak tak off her." She glared at Imdar, dark swirling around her legs.

Imdar stared from Tobtz to R-Bar. "It seems that Our Soul is still wrapped in the sending spell. None have ever had to release one before."

"Gar dik dik!" snarled the short witch. Dark began to billow and form above her, red eyes popped open and stared out.

"Do not," hissed Imdar. "You would destroy us all."

"Do dar dar," she growled, angrily waving the stuff away.

Chicken looked at Smoke.

Smoke pointed. "That way!"

Chicken banged the door open and charged into and down the corridor. "KITTEN!" And in a few minutes raced back into the room, Messenger right on her heels.

"Gosh!" Messenger looked around the room. "What have you been doing, kiddo?"

"Nothing, yet!" snapped R-Bar, stabbing her finger at Tobtz. "That purple flarp flarp is protected and no Vander dar ptar flim knows the undo speak."

Imdar stared at her. She had no idea what this witch was saying, her dialect was so strange.

"Im tik tik," suggested R-Bar, not liking any mage to stare at her that way.

Messenger looked at Smoke. "Mom?"

"What our coarse self means is that we need to take something protecting Tobtz away so she can be healed. Can you do that?"

Messenger stepped over and looked at the still form. "Gosh! She is wrapped every which way in purple stuff and it is angry." She nodded her head violently. "Really really."

"Kill it," growled R-Bar.

Smoke stepped up behind Messenger and gently laid her hands of the shorter woman's shoulders. "We have to hurry kitten. Tobtz is very faint."

Xanx burst into the room. "Imdar?"

"Watch and learn."

Smoke turned to Xanx. "Bring Tinlee."

Xanx nodded and ran out the door.

Messenger turned to Imdar. "Who put that stuff on her?"

"All," replied the Healer. "All sang the final parting."

"Oh my," she said. "No wonder. Maybe Sgenn can help."

"We will Ourself fetch her." Chicken charged from the room.

And shortly returned with Sgenn and Tinlee.

Smoke beckoned over Tinlee. "I will show you something and we will see whether your talent will grow." Tinlee nodded and stood very close to her.

Messenger smiled at Sgenn. "I need help."

"How?"

"Look through my eyes and I will show you." Sgenn did.

"See it?"

"Yes."

"Can you help me get it off?"

Deep grumbling came from beneath their feet. Vander jerked and stared.

"Don't you dare do anything," hissed R-Bar, waggling an angry green wand at the Vander.

"Can you guide?" asked Sgenn.

"You will have to give me control."

Sgenn grimaced. "Like . . . this?"

Messenger giggled. "My! What have you been doing with yourself?"

"Training," whispered Sgenn. Darker than dark oozed from the down below and blurred over her arms and hands.

Messenger kicked her in the ankle. "LET GO! I can't do anything if you don't let go."

"This is strange strange," mumbled Sgenn as she allowed Messenger to direct her and the black thing.

Also, said Sgenn-Messenger in Smoke's mind.

Smoke grabbed Tinlee by the shoulders and stared into her eyes, great orange gold eyes seeming to grow larger and larger. *Follow me in, Tinlee. I will keep you from getting lost.*

"You are here?" she gasped.

Yes, I am. Speak to me.

Like this?

You are learning. Now follow me. Throwing one arm over Tinlee's shoulder, Smoke turned them so they both faced Tobtz. Then they followed what Messenger directed them to do.

Black something swiftly sank into the deep down below as Messenger swung around and hugged the dazed Sgenn. "We are done, mom," she said to Smoke.

Smoke's minds plunged deep, searching for the spark that was Tobtz. One of Tobtz' hands twitched.

Our Soul, said Tinlee. *Come back to us.*

I am Vander no longer, wept Tobtz. *We failed.*

NO! Our Heart even now sleeps in the arms of her Lord. Imdar spun great, taking energy from many. He is, he was, he did.

Is this beyond beyond? Have you gone as well?

No. I live as well.

Smoke smiled in her mind. *I brought her. She is a fast learning kitten. Come back, your guild needs you.*

How?

Follow Tinlee. And Smoke began to back out.

Imdar stared, and yanked Xanx away. Color began to appear in the pale under pale skin of Tobtz' face.

Tinlee wobbled, quivered, and began to collapse. Smoke held her up and then scouped her into both arms. "Very tired," she said to Imdar. "I will take her to her room."

Tobtz slowly rolled her head and looked at the people standing there. Imdar and Xanx stepped close and gently set their hands on her.

"I heard the farewell song," rasped Tobtz. "Do I live?"

"Yes," replied Imdar. "But we have much to do to finish the healing."

"Do it," she sighed. "I would stay."

Imdar nodded and turned to the others. "We will all thank you properly, later. For now we have much to do. In Vander private."

Chicken opened the door. "We will visit more of this abode vast." She waited until Messenger and Sgenn joined her in the hall. Before hugging and kissing them.

"Stop, stop, stop," giggled Messenger, pulling herself free. "Sgenn did it. Really really."

"Strange strange," mumbled Sgenn, wobbling from side to side.

"She needs rest also." Messenger led Sgenn down the hall, yawning widely.

Chicken followed, seeking the rest of herself.

Laughing softly, she bit the side of his neck.

"HEY!"

"Not at all. Tastes like The Heart of The Heart."

"I'd say that you must be feeling pretty good."

"I'd say," she said, squirming. "That that is an interesting comment."

"You are healthy," he mumbled.

She trapped his arm and laughed again. "You feel very healthy also, Our Lord Vander."

"May I ask you something?"

She gave him a gentle pat. "You were wonderful."

"Not that!"

"No," she said, lips blowing warm at him. "I will have no children."

He sighed.

She heaved them onto their sides. "Those are the usual concerns of your culture."

"Tobtz."

"Our Soul?"

"Right. Am I going to have to go through that again?"

"Only Imdar knows that." She smiled. "Was it so bad?"

"Explain what is going on? What went on?"

"I know little." She hitched closer. "Imdar told us, Tobtz, Galron, and me, that we were Vander bent by our endeaver. Galron healed quickly as it was her arcana but Tobtz and I lost much." She kissed him and moved into his arms. "The cure was to take energy, special energy, unique energy, unique Vander energy, from each, and then." She smiled. "Transfer it to me."

He kissed her gently. "So I am, was, just an animated battery?"

She threw a leg over his. "Of a sort, I suppose." And rolled him onto his back. And grinned. "Shall we see if there is some small current left?" And fell on top of him.

They stood and looked at Galron, stretched out on the bed.

Sha'gar laid her hand on R-Bar's shoulder. "She heals fast."

"Hum." R-Bar looked at the faint trace of the wound.

Galron smiled up at them. "Great debt. Name your desire."

"Hum hum," said R-Bar.

Sha'gar tightened her arm around the shorter witch's shoulders. "Par tak!"

"Not her," hissed R-Bar. "But perhaps some small Vander spell?"

"Hum."

"Heh heh," replied R-Bar.

Galron threw her legs over the side of the bed and sat up,

her ragged garments falling from her shoulders.

"Clothe yourself," snapped R-Bar.

"Nothing to hide that was not already well gazed upon," replied the Vander. "What may I teach to two so well versed?"

R-Bar shrugged off Sha'gar's arm, leaned close and told her.

Smoke tugged the blankets up and grabbed Tinlee, arms and legs wrapping her in tight embrace. "Now, Vander kitten, we will train you further." Her minds poured in, enveloping Tinlee.

She struggled and moaned, but couldn't resist.

Xanx slipped into their room, gently tugged the blanket down, bent over, a lip tickled soft flesh.

"Xanx," sighed Sa'ar.

"Imdar calls Our Lord to her. To Tobtz."

"Take him," gasped Sa'ar.

Tinker's eyes popped open. "What? Huh?"

Xanx straightened up, licking her lips. "Follow me, Lord." She turned and left the room.

"Go, Lord, with Xanx," mumbled Sa'ar. "Leave me now."

He sat up and looked at her. "Now what's going on?"

"Imdar calls." She tugged the blanket up.

Chantal and Chicken walked into the room.

"What's for breakfast?" Fair Morn looked at the gathered Vander as she followed them into the room.

"Fine foods." Cazor scooped several bowls full and handed them to each. "For fine friends." She leaned forward and kissed Chantal, hands slipping here and there.

"Damn friendly," snapped Chantal, sitting, then elbowing Imten in the ribs as Imten sat and slipped an arm around Fair Morn's waist.

Imten grunted. "Such a narrow waist."

"Way I was made." Fair Morn took a second helping from several of the bowls. "This is pretty good stuff."

"Very nourishing. High energy producing." Imten gently rested her hand on Fair Morn's thigh.

Chicken pulled from someone's embrace, laughed, gave her a wack on the backside and joined Fair Morn and Chantal, dropping into a chair across the table from them. "Fair erotic a'bunch." She retied the tails of her shirt just along the lower edge of her rib cage.

A Vander walked over, yanked Chicken's shirt from her shoulder and kissed the exposed skin. "Sweet Queen."

"This lissome wench do be named, Marl." Chicken yanked her shirt back into place.

"Duty beckons," said Marl as she headed for the door and into the hall. Cazor smiled at them and followed Marl. Imten watched Fair Morn refill her plate yet again, nodded, and walked from the room.

"Most brazen a'bunch." Chicken pulled over a bowl and served herself.

Fair Morn reached over and filled Chicken's cup. "Certainly didn't behave this way the last time we visited."

Chantal took just a little bit more from some of the bowls. "Maybe it is their breeding season."

"Think thee so?" Chicken's brows furrowed as she pondered this idea.

"Beat's me," replied Chantal. She didn't know if the Vander were the same type of female as she was.

As Imdar entered the room, they grabbed her, pulling her backward into the bed and ripped her garments open, hands and mouths taking her.

Cazor grabbed him as he stepped around the corner. "Great Lord," she sighed. "I, of the first, am twice favored." She sagged sideways against the wall. "Leave me, Lord."

He started up the corridor, toward the far end, Imdar's room. A door opened and Aada stepped out and watched him approach. She grabbed him, yanked him into the room. "Mine at last, Lord."

"Heh heh heh heh," cackled R-Bar as Galron finished explaining, teaching the spell.

"Hum hum," agreed Sha'gar as she helped Galron to stand.

Galron threw one arm over Sha'gar's shoulders and sagged heavily against her. "Do not use it here, where we live. It would be too dangerous."

"We will wait," replied R-Bar.

"Until we are home," added Sha'gar. "If it is, ah, needed."

The pair guided the very wobbly Vander to the room where all the food and drink was waiting.

"Hi there." Chantal looked over as they walked in. Sha'gar gathered plates and cups for all.

"Anyone seen Eulin anywhere?" asked Chantal as all seated themselves.

"Nope," replied R-Bar looking at Galron.

"She visits her mother now," stated Galron.

Eulin yanked herself from her Mother's embrace and gasped, "First Greetings, Mother."

"Some after touch, it passes."

Eulin carefully sat on the edge of the bed. "Why have I been contained in my room? None would obey!"

Sa'ar sat up and took one of her daughter's hands and held it tight. "Eulin Dragon Heart, it was, and is, for your own safety. All events are under Imdar's control. But unchecked Vander force races our corridors and halls, sparing none save the extra guarded, which now includes me and Galron."

Eulin sucked in her breath. "Unchecked?"

"Yes. Unchecked."

Eulin sat straighter, eyes flashing. "How dare she do that!"

Sa'ar smiled. "Calm, Our Heart To Be, calm. I will carefully explain. And then you will understand."

Aada gasped, eyes rolling wildly. "Go," she mumbled, thick-tongued. "GO! Seek Imdar! Leave me, leave me be. NOW! Else I die!" She stared up at the golden thing hunched over her.

"Imdar," she moaned, "go to Imdar." It flashed from her room.

And into Imdar's.

"Loooooord!" she screamed as it dropped over her. She pounded it with her fists. "Obey . . . my . . . command! Seek . . . Tobtz!"

Moonda staggered into the room. "Madness," she gasped. "It is all madness." It turned, sprang and pulled her down, overwhelming her defenses. "Nooooo."

"Tobtz," rasped Imdar. "Go now!"

The thing hurtled from the room and down the corridor.

Moonda dragged herself, slowly, slowly, over to the bed. "That ravenger will kill us all."

Imdar lay half off the bed, head and arms dangling down. "No," she whispered as she licked dry lips. "I do not think so. Protect yourself."

Moonda's arms gave out. She thumped flat on the thick carpet. "I can not," she mumbled into it, sobbing softly.

Tobtz gasped as it fell on her, shredding bed covers, blankets, and her garments.

They tumbled to the floor in a tangle of limbs.

And rolled thrashing against the far wall.

Galron suddenly jerked, gasped, and sagged sideways.

"Gazooks!" cried Chicken. "Tis happening a'new!"

Marl staggered into the room and dropped to her knees, barely holding herself up with her arms.

Eulin coughed and slumped, staring at Sa'ar as she shivered. "Mother?"

The feeling passed.

"Tobtz," mumbled Sa'ar, pushing herself more upright. "It took Tobtz."

Eulin straightened up. "Who did? Who would dare? It?"

"In time, speak with Imdar. For now, sit with me, daughter. I need your company."

Fair Morn rolled Marl onto her back. "Are you all right? You just toppled over."

Marl smiled up at her. "Lovely One, I am. Help me stand."

"Sure." Fair Morn stood and easily lifted Marl to her feet. "There."

Galron leaned heavily on her forearms sprawled over the table top. "Never told this."

Cazor joined them, fastening her garments, and took a number of orange jugs from a cabinet. "Here! Refreshing liquid. All must drink and rest."

"Many days," mumbled Marl, emptying her mug in one long swallow.

Aada lurched into the room, her garments hanging in shreds. "Moonda," she mumbled. "In Imdar's room. Take liquid there." She dropped heavily into a chair next to Chantal. And drank straight from the container.

"Whatever you have been doing," observed Chantal. "It doesn't look healthy to me."

"Indeed." Chicken nodded. "Most unhealthy a'look."

Soft warm hands rolled them apart and laid them gently in the bed. And sponged their bodies with soft cloth and soothing lotions scented with special fragrances.

Xanx ran feather soft fingertips over her, stroking her awake. "Our Soul," she mumured as Tobtz' eyes opened and focused on her face. "First Greetings." And bent and kissed her.

"First Greetings," mumbled Tobtz.

"The Vander are whole again," said Xanx. "Rest and rest well."

Marl upended a jar and stroked the lilac liquid over muscles with her palm. "He moves not."

Xanx walked around the bed and bumped Marl aside with her hip. She massaged his stomach and chest. Then she bent and kissed him, and breathed into his mouth. "Vander drained. Bring liquid and remain. Feed Our Lord and Our Soul whenever they wake." Marl hurried from the room as Xanx tugged blankets into place.

Long time after long time past, his eyes opened and stared up at the ceiling. He wasn't sure where he was, not the time, not the day, not anything at all. He wasn't even sure who he was. But he did know one thing. He was certainly tired.

Soft hands carressed his chest. "May I help you sit up, Lord?"

"Sure. Who are you?"

She did. "I am Marl, Marl the Seeker." And lifted a mug to his lips. "Drink."

He did. "Thanks." And frowned at her. "Have we met?"

She shook her head. "I am one of the missed." Her face floated close, her lips brushed against his. "The floor is amply soft and I shall make no cry or sound did you wish."

"What?"

"Marl," cautioned a soft voice.

She sat back. "Our Soul?"

"Help me sit."

Marl walked around the bed and did. And held a large mug to Tobtz' lips.

"Most refreshing," said Tobtz. "Do you not agree, Lord?"

He nodded. And began to remember.

"Long before, long after," she said. "When the Great Battle was over with you and your's at our sides, you refused our debt payment."

He nodded. "I remember."

A smile tugged at one corner of her mouth. "Of the original guild brought back into being by Sa'ar, all have given, in this our efforts to heal. Cazor, Aada, Moonda, Cazor again. Sa'ar. Tobtz." She lifted his hand and kissed his palm. "Imdar." Releasing his hand, she touched her throat. A fine chain of purple appeared, a glittering violet gem nestled just below the hollow at the base of her neck. A small ring of the same violet formed on the little finger of his right hand. "Now each Vander will recognize those who gave so much. And your ring."

"Not sure that I want anyone to do that," he grumbled.

She smiled. "It is done."

"And," he mumbled, "I suppose that this ring won't come off either."

"It will only appear in the presence of Vander, Lord."

"Small consolation, I suppose."

"You are changed."

"I am?" He stared at her, not sure he liked that idea at all.

"Yes."

"Ummmmm?"

"Muchly."

"How? Muchly?"

She laughed, a soft chidding laugh.

"O.K., you win. This last year changed a lot of things with me, with us."

Tobtz slipped down deeper into the bed, and yawned. "Lie with me, Lord, for I sink into sleep."

He slumped down and wiggled into a more comfortable position. "Me too."

She rolled and kissed his shoulder, sliding an arm across his chest. "Rest. Rest and rest well."

"Xanx," he grumbled. "I don't think that we need a watchdog."

"I will be near," she whispered, ordering the room dark, stepping into the adjacent room and sitting in a chair. She wondered what kind of thing this watchdog was.

"By George!" Chicken gasped as the gem appeared on a chain around Aada's neck.

Then Cazor's neck.

Marl looked at Galron.

"I was healing," replied Galron.

Sa'ar and Eulin strolled into the room, arm in arm. The gem sparkled in the opening of Sa'ar's garment. She smiled at Cazor and Aada and sat at the beginning to become crowded table.

"Where's John?" asked Chantal.

"Resting," said Sa'ar. "Until next day."

Eulin checked Marl's neck, then Galron's. Marl shook her head. And pouted, just a little.

Smoke walked in, her arm around Tinlee, and smiled at everyone. "This kitten has learned much." They sat across the table from Sa'ar and Eulin. Smoke nudged Tinlee. "Tell me how Sa'ar is?"

Tinlee looked. And smiled. "Rested. Well. She created the gems and the chains and his ring and now believes that he has become fully Vander."

"Our Lord?" gasped Chicken.

"Now what did you do?" demanded Chantal.

"Vander secret," replied Sa'ar. "He is just more, ahhhh, understanding." She fingered the gem. "A token, as it were, of that understanding."

Chantal looked at Smoke who was filling her plate and Tinlee's. Smoke shrugged. "I only helped Tinlee develop her skills." And began to eat.

Messenger bubbled into the room, Sgenn striding all calm beside her. "Oh boy, oh boy, oh boy, oh boy," laughed Messenger. "Food. We are hungry, really really hungry." Then she sat and stared around the table. "OH MY GOSH!" Her eyes darted from Sa'ar to Aada to Cazor. She giggled.

"Mother," said Eulin. "It is a Vander secret."

Messenger nodded and began to eat.

Sgenn filled two mugs and shoved one over to her. Then Sha'gar joined the group.

And more Vander arrived.

None wore purple gems.

Imten pushed past two Vander, looking unhappy.

"Imten?" asked Sa'ar.

Imten touched the base of her throat. "I was too hasty."

Sa'ar smiled, and shrugged.

Chapter Thirty-One

Not Bad, For A Disaster

Bahn Duhr Tohr. The Quarters of the Royal Advisors.

They came down in a swirl of heavy thumps and muttered oaths. They also smashed the table and interrupted Ripple who had been striding back and forth blasting the air in the room with a string of adjectives that her husband hadn't heard before.

He sat on the couch and watched. He had become quite accustomed to sudden arrivals, that being the rather normal behavior of his wife's mostly witch clan. And he recognized the snarl of one of her younger sisters. So he knew that there was no cause for alarm.

Ripple glared at them all. "You are supposed to knock," she snarled at them. Most of her sisters had finally accepted this rather novel, for them, behavior.

"Dim dim dim dim dim," growled R-Bar, kicking pieces of the table in all directions. For some reason they always seemed to come down right on top of it. "You need better control."

Sha'gar nodded and looked at the tall women dressed all in black. "Hayou, Aunt. Sorry sorry."

"Hi, Ripple, Hanred," said Tinker. "Sorry about the

table."

"Of no matter." Ripple, waved them to one side, snapped her fingers. The table reappeared, whole, set with mugs and tall earthen ware jugs. Hanred walked over and sat, rapidly opened one of the jugs and filled all the mugs. He quickly shoved one into Ripple's hand as she sat. "Good to see you again." He looked from face to face.

"Tell you later," replied Tink sitting, leaning close to him. "When's the wedding?"

"In two days. Most everyone had arrived."

"Which rooms?" asked R-Bar.

"Usual," said Ripple. "The Queen insisted."

R-Bar yanked them away.

Hanred refilled Ripple's mug. "Midnight Delight, were those not Reep's daughters with them?"

"Hum," said Ripple. "He took the middle one."

"So perhaps the younger as well?"

Ripple emptied her mug. "I do not think anyone alive understands theurgist behavior."

"This is a wedding of surprises."

"Ptar tak," grumbled Ripple. "In tik do surprises."

He smiled. "Wonderfully coarse, Dark Luscious."

She tapped his forearm with one fingertip. "Empty that mug. The Queen calls."

He did.

They disappeared.

As she entered the room, he sprang, catching her in mid-flight, pulling her down, back into the bed, His claws shredded her clothes and resheathed as his arms wrapped around her, clenching, kneading. Growling deep in his throat, he nipped at her throat, tail lashing, and forced her further back.

"Help, help, help," she cried. But not very loudly as she locked her arms and legs around him, feeling the erotic arousal from the thick fur pressing slow strokes across her smooth skin. "Husband, you are very hard on my clothes."

Crushing her flat, he mumbled purred against her throat, tail curling around, the tip ticking ever so slowly. "It is good that witches can recreate any garb that they wish."

She kissed him. "My sisters are accepting you."

He tickle licked the base of her throat. "Witches do not mate with cat-folk."

"This witch did."

He chuckle purred. "Because my fur is so beautiful?"

"Because, lovely one, you are the only one I have ever met that can see me move."

"All cat-folk can see you move." He hugged her just a little tighter. "It is our eyes. But no one had ever seen a witch before. You were the first to come to our elseplace." He tickled with gentle claw tips and felt her wiggle beneath him. "And you were, you are, the most beautiful being that I have ever pounced upon."

"May we enter?" asked soft shadow.

Ripple tugged her blouse back onto her shoulders, and grumbled, "Husband, you will have to finish molesting me later. Enter!"

Reep and J. C. faded in.

Ripple stood and greeted them. "Welcome, sister."

"Hum hum," said Reep looking at Ripple's unbuttoned

blouse.

"Of course," replied Ripple. "We were relaxing after Court business."

"Hi, Hanred," said J. C.

"Are all gathered in?" whispered soft shadow.

"All sisters are here except Reptar. My oldest and her's have not arrived."

"Here we come," sang someone wildly.

They banged in.

"Hi, Mom," said the young woman in black, hugging Reep. "Hi, Pop." She hugged J. C.

"Tall daughter," sighed soft shadow.

"Hi, Szaifeh," said J. C. as he hugged his daughter in return. And looked over the top of her head. "Hi, Rorx. How have you guys been?"

"Well." Rorx turned, and bowed. "First Greetings, Aunt, Uncle."

Hanred stood and slipped an arm around Ripple. "Both look very happy, very healthy."

Szaifeh turned, stood with her arms around J. C. and Reep. "Aunt, did that old hunk, my uncle, and his collection arrive yet?"

"Just not long ago," said Hanred.

"And Shitar?"

Ripple frowned. "My oldest daughter is being slow." Green light crackled across the ceiling.

They hurtled in.

"Ptar dar tak," snapped Ripple.

"Hayou, Mother, Father," said the woman dressed all in black with a deep green belt tied around her waist. "New spell,

Sorry sorry."

"We were many many over and one layer deep," explained the man dressed in deep shades of green. "Shitar wanted a Grenzanr quick spell. Most sorry, Ripple."

"Hum hum."

"Mother," cautioned her oldest daughter.

"Hi, Shar," said Szaifeh, bouncing over and hugging her. Rorx nodded at them. "First Greetings, Shitar, Mantara."

"Vander warlock Rorx," responded Mantara, being very proper. "Witch Szaifeh." He nodded at Reep. "Humble greetings, Faan witch Reep and your's, J. C." Then he looked at Ripple. "Are all gathered in?"

"Almost." She kissed Reep on the forehead and told where her rooms were located. Then she told Szaifeh and Shitar.

Reep and J.C. faded away.

Szaifeh winked at Shitar. "R-Bar just told that I may visit. See you later, cuz." She pulled Rorx away.

"Sit and talk," said Ripple. "I would know how my powerful daughter fares. She visits little." Something near the ceiling grumbled.

Shitar sat at the table. "We have traveled muchly."

As Ripple sat Hanred stood. "Let me show you this wing of the castle, Mantara. Much has changed since last you two were here."

They shifted in and stood in the middle of the room. She hurtled forward and wrapped herself around the man who had been standing and talking with one of the others in the room.

"Hi, Unc, you old hunk," she laughed, mashing her lips over his. "Ummmmmmmm."

"Szaifeh," he gasped.

She pressed herself against him. "In the flesh . . . Vander Lord."

"Szaifeh," cautioned her husband.

"Yes, Rorx." She released Tinker. Then she kissed him again and whispered ever so softly, "I know all about you and them, the first Vander." She stepped back and hugged the shorter woman dressed all in black. "Aunt." Releasing R-Bar, she beamed around the room. "Hi, Aunts." And stared. "Sgenn?"

Sgenn looked at her, all calm quiet. "Yes, sister?"

Szaifeh grinned. "Just surprise. You look well. You all look well."

"Happy niece," said Chicken. "We do be that. And so do look thee and Our Prince."

"Hello Father, Mothers." Rorx smiled at them. "We are well. We traveled while Our Heart and Our Soul ran that experiment. And passed through there before coming here."

He reached into somewhere and withdrew a small chest all carved and decorated with purple and lavender incising. "Mother sends these broaches as small tokens of her love." And handed it to Chicken.

She carefully opened the box, and gasped. "Tell Imdar many thanks for this noble gift." Pale lavender chains held lilac gems edged in dark velvet metal. As Chicken held out the chest, each took one and hung the sparkling gem around their necks.

"Most Royal, indeed," said Chicken, admiring them. "Do tell Imdar many thanks."

Chantal hugged Rorx and said very softly, "And tell her and Sa'ar and the others that we all understand."

"Thank you, Mother. They were greatly worried that all

my Mothers here would hate them forever and forever. There was no other way to save Tobtz and Sa'ar."

She kissed his forehead. "Let's talk about something else. Come sit and tell us what you and Szaifeh have been doing. It has been a long time since we have seen you two."

He nodded. "And you." His eyes flashed to Sgenn and back.

Chantal tugged him over to a couch. "That is a long story also."

Bahn Duhr Tohr. The Castle Fitting Room.

Sook glared angry at them. "White is not-witch tak ptar," she snarled.

"Of course, Princess," said the First Seamstress, backing away.

" The Royal color," added the Second Seamstress, leaping to one side. "Of this, The First Kingdom of the Kingdoms."

"A Must custom," stammered the Third Seamstress, wondering who would care for her husband.

The white wedding cloak trailed in soft folds behind Sook. Dark fluttered around her legs and peered hungrily at the quivering trio.

"Don't be tik do," said Santar from the corner where she had been practicing shadow merge as the trio had fitted her sister.

"White!" snapped Sook.

"Perhaps," suggested Santar, "with some midnight black trim and ornamentation to emphasize your luscious self?"

"It is un-custom to add a color," said the Third Seamstress.

"The blue kingdom of Frahn Nahn Sahn had a pale green artfully added," offered the Second Seamstress.

"It would take but a few moments more," stated the First Seamstress.

"Try it," said Santar watching Soak relax, a little, the air clearing around her.

"You will hurry," said Sook to the trio.

They did.

"Most regal a witch," said Santar as Sook twisted and turned, watching her image in the mirrors held by the trio.

Sook nodded. "I like it."

The trio fled, silently offering blessings on that one's dark sister. Then, far down the corridor, they slowed up and relaxed. They were the first to ever garb a witch. All Royalty would bid for their services. They ran to their homes to tell the news.

"Mother is still not-calm," grumbled Sook, now dressed in comfortable soft black, her ceremonial dress carefully set aside.

Santar kissed her forehead. "She will. The Faan have already changed greatly." She smiled, a rare thing of warmth for one of her kind. "Princess, nearly Queen."

"I am witch," growled Sook. "And know nothing of princess or queen."

Santar flopped into a chair. "You took The Prince who now glows with happiness in your presence. You will learn. He will also learn much." She nodded. "You could not do otherwise."

"Mine," snapped Sook. "He is mine."

"Witch true," observed her sister. "Stop grumbling, rap tap."

Sook stalked back and forth across the room. "I do not like waiting."

Santar nodded. No witch did, not in this clan. Except for her Aunt Reep who was a legend for her patience. "It is only short time longer."

Messenger tickled his ear and giggled happily at his reaction.

"Kitten?" he mumbled, waving one hand loosely around and swatting, more or less, at her hand.

"MyTinker." She poked his ear again. "You slept all through yesterday."

He rolled and trapped her arm. "I did?"

She nodded. "Really really."

"Morning?"

"Yep."

"You sleep that long also?"

She grinned. "Oh, no! We went shopping and bought Sgenn some beautiful shirts. And some for Sha'gar. And then we found lovely things for the wedding." She sucked in a deep breath. "And The Princess visited with The King and The Queen and R-Bar with Ripple and we talked with Rorx and Szaifeh and Eulin cause she came to be with you at the big big ceremony and Smoke said that you needed to sleep and everything was all right and all slept with you and all you did was sleep sleep sleep." She looked at him, all round-eyed seriousness. "Really really slept."

"Wedding is in the mid-afternoon, right?" He tickled her here and there and then unfastened her pajama buttons, tugging her close.

"Eeeeeek!" She tickled him in return, pushing his pajama top open. "Yep."

"Let's have a late breakfast."

"Heh heh heh," she laughed happily, wrapping her arms around his chest, shoving him over.

"Most well rested do be Our Prince," laughed Chicken.

"Peek Queen," said Smoke, giving her a poke.

"Wench," snapped Chicken. "I do but feel him awaken and do naught else." She jabbed Smoke. "Touche!"

"Royal Peeker Poker." Smoke stepped out of range.

"Just keep your fingers to yourself," grumbled Chantal. "Had enough of that from the Vander."

"For awhile," laughed Fair Morn.

Suddenly Sgenn grabbed Sha'gar's arm and pointed.

R-Bar whirled in, one arm around a witch, just a little shorter than herself. "Tink not up yet?"

Chicken laughed. "Most up We do so suspect yet still a'bed."

Smoke winked at R-Bar. And smiled. "A lovely kitten."

"My newest niece, Szart, Ripple's youngest. Just finished training."

"Loverly," observed Chicken. "Witch?"

"Yes, Aunt," replied Szart, all witch proper. She had heard all about these Aunts and especially R-Bar during training. She carefully looked at the grey-haired one, the therugist. Sgenn looked back, sitting all calm quiet.

R-Bar introduced each of them in turn. And said to Szart. "You will meet Messenger, and him, later."

"Yes, Aunt." She cleared her throat, just so.

"Yessssssssssssssssssss?" replied R-Bar.

"It was told that Uncle is now Witch Master. Is that true told?" Dark eyes fastened on dark eyes.

"It is so. Ranna done."

"I met Ranna and her's yesterday. Strange lovely."

"Rik tik," observed R-Bar.

Szart nodded.

Eulin floated in, startling Szart, who gasped, "A Purple Mage!"

"Ripple daughter Szart," said R-Bar, introducing her niece.

"Hello, cousin. I am Eulin. Where is father, we must talk."

"Busy," said Fair Morn. "They will join us for brunch."

A small green gold dragon appeared on Eulin's shoulder. She whispered to it. It disappeared.

R-Bar clamped one hand on Szart's forearm. "Behave, witch."

"What was that?" asked Sha'gar.

"Messenger dragon." Eulin dropped onto the couch next to Chicken.

Messenger sprawled, all soft contented on top of him, her breathing now slow and gentle, one finger idly playing with his side burns. "Yipe," she said, and twitched.

His eyes popped open and stared past her ear at it.

The small green gold dragon peered down at him from its perch on the back of one of Messenger's shoulders.

"What is it?"

Messenger peered from his eyes to see. "Oh, it is cute." She giggled. "It is a messenger dragon."

"What do you want?" he grumbled at it.

The tiny dragon hopped down and whispered in his ear and disappeared. He laughed.

"MyTinker?"

He hugged her tighter.

She giggled. "What?"

"It said that the Vander had masked Ranna's gift in such a way that it is only visible if I wish to use it."

"See," smiled Messenger. "They are really really nice."

"Ready for something to eat?"

"Yep." She rolled to one side, looking outward. "R-Bar brought Ripple's new daughter to visit."

Szart watched them walk from the bedroom. She stared at Messenger and watched him carefully. During her training she had been told all about the green-eyed controller. But in person she looked so . . . innocent. And he just looked . . . ordinary.

"Hi, Szart," he said, his eyes flicking to R-Bar.

Confused, explained R-Bar.

Messenger beamed at Szart. "Hello, Szart. You are very pretty." She poked him in the ribs."Isn't she?"

"Sure." He smiled at Szart. "Very pretty. Runs in the family, I'd say."

A voice asked, "May I?"

It was Ripple, determined to make everyone understand that they ought to ask first, not just pop in.

"Sure," replied R-Bar.

Ripple appeared.

"Hayou, Mother."

"If my daughter bothers, send her," said Ripple.

"Most well mannered a'daughter," stated Chicken.

"Hum," said Ripple, looking at Szart. "Few witches are called well mannered."

Szart frowned at her.

Ripple handed a gaily beribboned scroll to Tinker. "This passes you into the wedding hall and to your seats. First right, with The Queen and The King. The first bell calls all to come. The second tells small time. The third announces closing of the Great Doors."

She looked at R-Bar. "Sister, may Szart sit with you and your's?"

R-Bar nodded.

"We will visit during the after celebration. The Royal Wedding starts soon." Ripple faded away.

Chicken beamed at Messenger and Tinker. "Sit. Eat. We will all dress in new finery and set out thy own. Do hurry, My Lord."

Everyone hurried away. R-Bar tugged Szart along by one arm. Szart gasped, "Aunt."

The bedroom door slammed behind them.

As Tinker and Messenger ate they could hear an occassional burst of muffled laughter from the bedroom. And, about the time they had finished their meal, the door banged open and out, in a rustle of bright costume and happy laughter, they came.

Tinker stood and smiled at them. "WOWIE! A bevy of beauty, a clutch of cuties, a . . . "

"O.K., Cowboy," interrupted Chantal. "We get the idea."

All of them had gaily colored ribbons woven through ornate hair styles. The clothes they wore were a medley of colors and patterns with bright sashes tied around their waists. The skirts touched their ankles. Their blouses were cut low with broad straps over their shoulders. More of the bright ribbons were tied around their upper arms, long tails flying freely.

"Come on, kitten. The Princess and I will help you get dressed. He can take care of himself." Chantal and Chicken went with Messenger into the bedroom and began brushing Messenger's hair and working the ribbons into it.

"Well," said Chantal, "we can't do much with hair this short. Shuck your duds. These fancy clothes all fasten up the back."

Tinker tossed his shirt on the bed and sat down to yank off his boots. "Just got dressed," he grumbled. "Someone could have said something."

The door slammed open and R-Bar stomped inside. "Niece, stop all that hiding and get out here with the rest of us."

Szart stepped from a corner, a cloak of shadow wrapped around herself up to the neck. "Aunt," she growled, "this is not-witch."

"Ptar flik tik," snapped R-Bar, yanking Szart from the room and out of that dark shadow cloak.

"OUCH! AUNT!"

The door slammed shut. Chicken tugged Messenger's top into place while Chantal tucked it in and fastened the skirt. Then she wound the bright sash into place.

"Not bad," observed Chantal. "Not bad at all. Shove your tootsies into those shoes and let's go."

They joined the others in the middle room.

"Holy Cow," said Tinker.

"Pretty nice, right?" R-Bar winked at him. And wacked

Szart on the backside. "Turn around and let him admire everything."

Looking angry, upset, unsettled, and not very witch pleased, Szart slowly turned around.

"Mouth's open, One," laughed Fair Morn.

"Not a kitten," observed Smoke.

"She is twenty-two of your years, Tink," explained R-Bar. "She had longer than usual training."

Tinker shook his head. "I will never get used to that idea. Or how you guys do that."

Szart looked at him. "I am nice, Uncle?"

"Certainly are." He cleared his throat. "We better get on our way. Lead on, kiddo, you know where we have to go."

R-Bar headed out the door, yanking Szart along by an arm.

"Kar pak pak," snarled Szart as she looked back over her shoulder at Tinker.

Sha'gar slipped an arm under one of his and tugged him into motion, gurgling softly, "Mine."

In the wide main corridor, Sgenn hurried up and took his other arm. And said, loud enough for all to hear, especially R-Bar and Szart just in front of them, "Sulda, that brazen witch is mik tik ar pak tak." She smiled a soft half-smile.

"Certainly," agreed Sha'gar, tightening her grip. "Ptar mar mar."

"O.K.," he grumbled at them. "Nuff of that."

Soon they were outside and approaching The Great Hall of Ceremony.

The vast space in front of The Great Doors was mobbed. Yet, there was clear space leading to the entry. Royalty from every Kingdom passed inside, each holding their scroll so all could see. Everywhere outside the hall wandered vendors selling all manner of food, drink, and objects.

Everyday folk commented loudly on this costume and that manner as the scroll holders passed by.

Most gasped and gaped as Tinker and his crew passed by and inside. None had ever seen a Lord with that many Fine Ladies in close attendance. Nobles and Lords stared and whispered behind their hands and wondered from which frontier Kingdom they had come. Mouths popped open and sudden breathes were sucked deep when "those folk" were led straight up the central aisle and to the right. And the whispering thickened when The Queen and The King rose to their feet to greet them, smiling happily.

"Serves them all," laughed Willawa, the Queen, White Warrior of Bahn Duhr Tohr. A wide space separated their high backed bench from the rest. She knew few would be able to overhear their conversation. "The court will worry for days until word does filter down as to who you are."

Toucan bowed to Tinker. "Highness, thee appear most well. Will you, and your's, sit here by me?"

"Sgenn, Sha'gar," said Tinker, introducing them as they sat on Toucan's right side. Willawa moved over and patted the space between herself and The King. "Sit just here, Princess Queen, and thee may speak with both myself and your brother."

Chicken bowed neatly, formally, and did.

The rest arranged themselves on Willawa's left. R-Bar plunked Szart down next to The Queen and sat. And growled softly at Szart. "Ripple will not do anything either. She knows that I did it."

Szart nodded. And thought that everything that she had been told about this Aunt sitting next to her must be true if even Ripple would put up with such behavior.

Messenger nudged Smoke, and whispered, "She is even shorter than R-Bar."

"Yep."

Over the din in the Great Hall they heard the First Bell.

Outside, everyone hurried toward the hall that could be admitted, the rest filled the great space in front of it.

"How does Willawa like your son's choice?" asked Tinker.

Toucan smiled. "Mine Own Queen was fairly well shocked." He laughed. "And the Kingdom even more so. Especially as he and Our Princess have found unheard of new lands and do claim all there as their just due, adding two New Kingdoms of unknown value to the greater realm."

"How fares Thy King?" asked Willawa. "He does appear well."

Chicken smiled. "Most well. And most generous."

Willawa nodded. "Yet it does appear to Us that some are new and some no longer with thee."

Chicken leaned closer. "One fell in battle dark and dire. T'were Us, we would say naught as he do still feel some great loss."

"Indeed," agreed Willawa. "Boon companions that fall in battle are mourned most heavily. Non-warriors this do not understand."

Over the din the Second Bell boomed.

Willawa took one of Chicken's hands in her's as she half-turned in her place. "Queen to Queen. Our Prince takes to His

Royal Self and to His Throne as unusual a choice as has ever happened in all of this Our Kingdom."

Chicken leaned over and kissed her cheek. "Mighty Queen, Warrior to Warrior, this We feel to be most true, for Thy Prince, and now King of his own lands, this choice will be the best of choices. What says His Sister Princess and soon to be Queen of her own lands?"

Willawa laughed. "My daughter did say in her scroll that the Princess Witch Queen was her brother's own choice and none else could make him as happy."

Then Willawa wanted to know what they had been doing since last they had met.

The Third Bell echoed through the Great Hall and the Great Doors thudded shut. The audience hissed to a proper low murmur. The Royal Wedding was about to start.

The New Kingdoms.

The Princess had pushed deep into the interior, coursing east of where her brother had wandered and mapped. She had taken the men-at-arms with her and one of her sea-folk who knew and had map-making skills. Her primary goal was to find thick wood and fine stone, necessary materials if they were to build a new kingdom with permanent settlements and little outlay of a very small treasury.

All the sea-folk from the other ships had been left behind and ordered to build quick quarters, all identical, as all would be equal. They would worry about ceremonial buildings and more elaborate habitation later.

The other primary task was to use all available stone to build a quay large enough to handle the ships and supplies that her brother would be bringing.

And, as the accuracy of the map was the first concern, they traveled at a pace set by his need, the map maker.

Nine long days they had wandered creating the map of their new world, their new kingdom.

Nineteen great bubbling springs had they found, three hot to the touch. The weary party had sampled one of these and soaked long in the soothing waters. And all had been very startled when The Princess had plunged into the deep pool. They had hastily averted their eyes.

She surfaced not far from them, blowing water and wiping the hair from her eyes.

"Fear not," she laughed. "For we are all warriors, save one. And may not warriors share such a welcome treat?"

The Armor Captain dared look. All he saw was a smiling face and vague white beneath the surface of the water.

She laughed at him. "Such a fearful expression on such a fierce warrior."

"Highness," he said sternly. "All do fear the wrath of Our Noble Queen, thy Mother, did we treat Her Daughter, Our Queen, in too familiar a manner."

"Well spoken, clever Captain. And as you speak true, this grand soak in warming and relaxing waters we do now proclaim Court Secret and do swear all to silence. Thus your fears are erased." Leaning back, she drifted away.

The Captain's First swam close. "This Queen is sly and does honor us greatly."

"Indeed," replied The Armor Captain. "And I now tell to you and all present, this plain fact. To that Queen do I now swear forever allegiance come what may in this her new land."

"And I do follow as well," stated his First.

And thus began The Queen's Own, The Royal Guard, save one. That one became The Queen's Cartographer and over the years devised many clever tools to aid him in his endeavors.

And for nine more days did they wander, mapping in portions of a wide river that the map maker felt was the same one whose mouth they had anchored their ships near and where the first town was now being built.

As they strode down a wide game path in a forest of tall trees and open underspace, The Princess looked at her Captain.

"What think you of this? Great water course is the first boundary. All lands east must be mine. All lands to the west to be Mine Own Brother's."

"Highness, none know what lands or treasure may lie more favored, east or west. Be this a wise choice before we know. It might be most poor a choice."

"A merchant's thought, a merchant's worry."

He frowned at her. "It would be an ill beginning did My Queen start by kneeling at Her Brother's feet begging for support."

She laughed. "Captain, We shall neither kneel nor beg. Ever!" She raised a hand cutting off his reply. "Hear Us in this. We feel, We do, that Our choice is both wise and fair. In this do We have faith. Will you not share your fortunes with Us as We do play such a guessing game?"

"Warrior Queen, from now to the end of forever however that may be."

She slammed his shoulder in a comradely gesture, rocking him slightly. "Then Our bargain is well struck and is sealed. Enough worry. What think you of these Our Forests?"

And so they talked of all they saw until they left the woods and entered the great meadows behind.

And far to the north and east across the great plain they saw it, nestling against the forest edge, a gigantic conical mountain wearing a crown of clouds.

Bahn Duhr Tohr. The Great Hall.

"ALL HAIL!" intoned the Highest of the High, bouncing the Ceremonial Sword off the shoulders of The Prince, and handing it to Hanred, who stood close to The Prince's left side. "The King in Aahn Duhr Tohr, The New Lands."

As The New King and The New Queen stood and turned to face the vast crowd down below, the courtiers, the Lords and the Ladies, Princes and Princesses stood and cheered. The New King had named his lands and that of his sister, the ancient and revered first name of Bahn Duhr Tohr, thus implying both an understanding of their history and a binding of the New Lands to the Old Lands.

Throwing his arm around his Queen, Frinda motioned for silence, and then spoke to them all. "My new Kingdom is hence forth named Bahn Aahn Tohr, and this My Queen does wear the colors of that New Kingdom, the purest of white, the darkest of midnight."

And with that he started down the long stair and out the long aisle to the carriage waiting to tour them around the city so that all could see them.

Later, at the Great Fest, he told The King and The Queen that he didn't know what his sister was going to call her share, or what colors she might select.

And then the next weeks passed swiftly as he gathered

ships and supplies and those daring souls who would trust their families and their fortunes to the unknown.

Prince Rahn, the younger brother of Kahn, of Hahn Dahn Bahn, offered his allegiance, his personal army,, and a great collection of artisans, volunteers all, if this daring King would have him and them.

The King smiled and looked at His Queen, who searched Prince Rahn's face with the darkest eyes he had ever seen.

"Honest and true, My King," she said.

"Then, Rahn," said The King, clasping him by the shoulder, and laughing. "You are my new lord, The First Lord, my right hand." And leaning close, the King said softly, "We have many long and hard days ahead of us, you and I, with Royal lands making us as battered and weather worn as the simplest held hand in all the kingdoms. Do you accept this most unroyal duty?"

Rahn dropped to one knee. "No task too low, no challenge too great, Highness."

"Rise, Lord Rahn. We will give you lands when and if we know what lands we have to bestow. You have made a great gamble."

Then, they all gathered at the harbor and saw the greatest fleet ever assembled sail away.

The Lord of Hahn Dahn Bahn and Prince Kahn had gifted the now Lord Rahn with a great number of their finest beasts, and the finest stores of food as befits a Lord. His father wondered whether he would ever see his youngest son again.

They were in their quarters some days since the great fleet had set sail. It had been a day spent visiting the main bazaar.

Szart had been with them. R-Bar had been adding to her spell lore and skill every day. This day had been no different. Szart's knowledge and skills were being pushed to ever higher levels.

Messenger had whispered to Tinker, as they ate some fried thing at one of the many booths, that Szart just billowed magic in great waves. She had never seen anyone do that, not even their many magic daughter, Sedeem.

"Is that what they are doing?"

Messenger nodded. "They are being very careful, both of them. But R-Bar is building and building Szart's abilities and skills greater and greater, far beyond where most witches ever go."

R-Bar and Szart had gone into another room to be by themselves.

"Anyone have any idea what's going on?" He looked around the room.

"About what, worry butt?" Chantal shoved another pillow behind her back. "All we have done is watch a wedding, wave goodbye to the Prince, now King, and his Queen, go shopping, and lounge about."

"What is R-Bar up to?" A sea of blank faces turned in his direction.

"Smoke?"

Smoke shrugged. "She has put that into a private area that is locked away from us."

He frowned. "She all right?"

"Very healthy, MindMate. But I feel anxiety concern."

"About?"

"That part is also locked away."

He sighed.

"She trains her niece hard, very hard," said Sha'gar. "Hardest that I have ever seen or heard of."

Szart folded her hands just so and said in the most proper proper witch perfect that she could. "Witch debt, Aunt, witch debt beyond payment. Why do you do this?"

R-Bar smiled, causing Szart to wince. "There is a payment."

"Aunt, you have taught me and trained me in every spell you ever learned." Szart leaned close, face almost touching face. "Even those from the Book of Banned Spells." She sat back. "My training has now excelled all my sisters and has gone in many new directions. This is never done, witch to witch. Why?"

She jerked, realizing what R-Bar had said. "What," she gasped. "Payment?"

R-Bar gestured for Szart to sit on the couch beside her. "Niece, the reason is because I have had a witch feeling."

Szart sucked in her breath and slowly exhaled. "Oh, Aunt!"

R-Bar shrugged. "Of no import, for you now know all that I know. And have an even greater skill and power." She threw her arm around Szart's shoulders and leaned close and began to whisper in her ear what the payment entailed, what Szart must do and say, and what that would mean to her, forever.

And when she was done, Szart hugged her, and did a most un-witch thing. She began to cry.

Aahn Duhr Tohr. The New Lands.

The Princess and her party were halfway around this singular, free standing mountain when they found the crack of a cave in a deep valley, carving into the mountain from the south flank. A path disappeared into the darkness.

After making camp some distance down the narrow valley from the dark opening, the Princess ordered three sets of three torches to be made for she intended to go inside and wished to have sufficient light to do exploring for some time. Then she ordered The Captain and the Map Maker to detail the map of this place that it might be easily found again, putting marker stones some distance from the narrow valley mouth.

In the morning she selected the men for her party and told the Captain to return by nightfall on the following day as she intended to further around the mountain and then return to their first town.

Waving jauntily to the Captain, she and her party headed into the darkness, torches flaring bright yellow light. And soon they passed into a huge central chamber.

"Highness," said one of the men. "This space is larger than the Great Hall of Bahn Duhr Tohr."

"Indeed. It is a wonder. Let us inspect each of these smaller holes, starting on the left. One hundred paces in, then out. Some other day shall we send a proper expedition to chart all in detail."

They had entered the fourth of the smaller tunnels and had just wandered around a sharp turn when it woke and bared their way.

Handing her torch to one of the three with her, she yanked her sword free. And pointed.

"You two that way while we go this. We believe it will come at us, thus you two hurry fleet of foot and seek the Captain down dark hole. Tarry not for we do so command you to go.

NOW!"

The Princess ran in her chosen direction, telling her warrior to hold that torch high and to give her plenty of room.

The dark thing came at this small figure hurtling battle cries at it.

The other pair were smashed against the wall by the enormous tail.

The Princess danced back and forth, her great two-handed sword clanging and bouncing off the reaching talons of midnight jet. The thing forced them further back into yet another of the small tunnels, ever deeper into the mountain, the great tail flailing, collapsing the roof behind, burying the way out. From behind them somewhere red light flared and flickered.

"Run, man, run. For your very life, run, all is for naught before this gigantic thing. We must find some small hole to hide in or die in the trying."

She whirled, yanked her companion into motion, and raced for the red light far ahead.

And in short moments, all sound behind them faded into silence.

Frar Tap. Distant. Lush.

They dawdled over their meal and the local liquid, enjoying everything. Then Magna, The Mind Predator, removed the Black Scroll from her side pouch and carefully unrolled it and reread it. The scroll had been neatly liberated from a library that few ever visited.

The first two lines were lines of command written in a strange and difficult language.

The next explained the why of the scroll. This was the first chance that Magna had time to read the scroll since she had first come by it. Rechecking every line she nodded, knowing why she was being hunted so. To command such a power was to be a power commanding anything. The first part took her to another world. The last part gave her control over a vast beast of great power. Those that once had owned this artifact would do anything to get it back.

She reread the first two lines again and again practicing the difficult words. Now, even if she should lose the scroll, she would be able to do it. Rolling it, she returned it to her side pouch and gazed across the table at Phonta, her most recent selection, thinking that it was time for them to return to their rooms.

The Herzla, a thief seeking monster, crashed through the entry door snarling angry as patrons and waiters scattered in all directions. And saw Magna leaping to her feet.

"Run rear," Magna snapped at Phonta as she spun and raced for the food preparation space at the back of the establishment. She chanted the first line and looked back, intending to grab one of Phonta's hands.

The Herzla lifted dripping fangs from the limp body and threw Phonta tumbling limply through a window and leaped at the fog becoming Magna.

Magna turned and ran for the rear area, hastily chanting the second line, and faded vapor thin as the beast hurtled through the spot, where she had been, smashing tables, chairs, and the rear wall.

Aahn Duhr Tohr. The New Lands.

In the fading light of day, the Captain and the mapping

party returned to their camp and were surprised to find cold ashes where they had expected to find welcoming fire.

Suddenly worried, the Captain ordered the map maker to stay, to prepare food and fire, and wait while they went into the caverns to see what their Queen was doing.

In the flickering light of the torches it was obvious which way they had gone as their foot prints were all that had disturbed the dust in here. And soon they came to the rubble blocking their way.

"We can not return without the Queen, dead or alive. Here we camp and labor long and hard until this rock is cleared away. Outside, all to prepare torches aplenty for our work in here appears to be days long."

The gigantic beast waited for them as they raced from the tunnel toward the red light.

"Be'trapped," snarled the Princess.

The beast, tired of playing with them, puffed smoke over these small creatures that would dare enter its space and watched them crumple to the ground. Delicately picking up one in her claws, she ate it. And pondered the taste, thinking that it reminded her of something. Perhaps if she chewed the other one slowly she would remember. Picking up the limp form with two talons she dropped it into her mouth. Then the thought came to her. Outside. That is what the taste reminded her of, outside. She had been in the interior of this mountain so long that she had forgotten about that. She decided to save this taste for later now that she had remembered and spit it out, into a corner.

The rock of this mountain was ever so much more tasty. She gnawed off a large chunk and chewed contentedly. All the tunnels and chambers were the result of her appetite. Then a new thought popped up. Water. She decided to try that stuff again. A great stream of it was nearby. She had bumped into it long ago. Scooping up her tidbit in her mouth, she walked off in the direction of the stream, scaly hide rasping silk soft hiss on the sides of the tunnel.

Bahn Duhr Tohr. The Royal City.

They sat around the table having a light snack, waiting for R-Bar and Szart to join them.

The pair were the other room where R-Bar was showing Szart a short, thin green wand and explaining some minor bit of arcana.

Eulin walked in and sat at the table. "Father, Mothers."

"Shouldn't be long," said Fair Morn. "Then we'll go down to that shirt shop."

Magna formed in, fog soft, and saw the two standing close, speaking softly. Both were short, pleasantly formed, dressed in black, exactly the female forms that she enjoyed.

Slipping up behind the one whose back was to her, she slid her arms around, caressing ribs, and grasping soft swelling, her fingers incurving, gripping hard. Her palm fang ripped easily through the fabric and sank into the lovely flesh, glands pulsating, injecting the mind control venom. She had a new selection. One that would do all that she desired.

"PTAR AP TAK!" snarled R-Bar, plunging the green wand into one of the those hands, stabbing deeply.

"AUNT!" screamed Szart. Her palm struck forward, past R-Bar's head. The blast hurtled Magna across the room, crashing into the far wall. She thumped to the floor, a limp tangle of arms and legs.

Szart's scream brought everyone to the locked door, pounding upon it.

R-Bar had crumpled to her knees. "Strange strange," she mumbled. "It is a fast spreading poison."

Szart crashed down beside her. "Poison?"

"Too fast to stop," gasped R-Bar.

Smoke grabbed all their minds, fighting off the shock, the sudden shock of losing another so soon after Ran. Minds jittered and jerked all around her. Tinker's body shook, strong spell residue surged and pulsated through him

Magna's eyes wobbled open. She had heard the word and was confused. "Who was poisoned?" Her hand was agony. But it didn't feel like poison.

Szart slammed her hand across R-Bar's cheek, then she poured healing into her Aunt, using every spell that she knew. "Fight it, Aunt," she commanded.

"Remember," whispered R-Bar. "The . . . pay . . . ment." She forced her eyes open, and smiled. "And . . . kill . . . her. . ." And fell limp.

"Yaaaaaaaah!" The pieces of the door flew into the room as he hacked it open and hurtled inside, separation shock, blood lust, and something else roared through his mind. His eyes darted around the room, seeking the one to kill. He saw, and charged, the great sword swinging high over one shoulder.

Magna screamed the two sentences and faded as the massive blade arched down, carving a wide notch in the wall, sinking deep into the wooden floor.

"ESCAPED!" howled Tinker.

"I can follow her," yelled Szart.

Chantal yanked her to her feet. "Then do it. Take us now. She must know the antidote." She grabbed Eulin's wrist.

Szart ripped them away.

Aahn Duhr Tohr. The New Lands.

She became, wisp soft. And looked around. The space was vast. Somewhere, high overhead, had to be the ceiling. Not far away lay a crumpled body, once dressed in white, now mostly grey with other stains. A great thing was hunched over, drinking from a swiftly flowing stream contained by the rock channel that it sped through. It was larger than the largest building she had ever seen. Sensing her presence, it lifted its head, turned a long neck to look at her.

The intelligent eyes stared at her. They were a deep green.

Magna quickly chanted the lines of command. Nothing happened. The monster cocked its head and began to turn its body. She tried again.

The monster stared at this small being, surprised that she knew a tiny amount of the language even though her accent was wrong and the words were garbled and some phrases mis-spoke, meaningless babble.

Suddenly a whole herd of them appeared, all highly agitated, leaping and jumping in all directions. The first one, the funny speaker, pressed herself back against the wall.

Purple light, near black, flooded from one of them. She was about the same size as her carefully hoarded taste.

"My Lord," gasped Chicken. "Tis Greater than the Great Hall."

"One," said Fair Morn, clicking levers on her weapon to new settings. "Even with wide focus I can only take a small portion with one shot."

All heads tilted back, following the long sinuous neck up to where the head was.

"No one move," commanded Eulin. "This must be a Great Black." She strode toward it.

"If that mountain moves, try for its head," hissed Tinker at Fair Morn. "It is our only chance." He glanced at Szart, "Where is that assassin?"

"Here somewhere," she snarled.

Deep rumbling under their feet announced some things, or things, coming up, summoned by Sgenn.

Sha'gar cast protection on everyone, her eyes flaring bright red.

Chantal cocked her revolver. "If I hit it in the eye we might be able to make a run for it."

Magna watched them and wondered what manner of folk these were. The one had died when none had ever done that before. Her arm now ached up to the shoulder. She tried but she couldn't pull that green thing from her hand. It wouldn't come out.

Eulin touched one large foot and looked up.

She looked down.

"Do us no harm," said Eulin, gently.

"Of course," she said. It had been long before long ago since she had last met a Dragon Master. "Would you like to have something to eat? All I have is that one over there wrapped in dirty white metal." She smiled. "Perhaps the other one who repeats and repeats just those few lines so very badly. It must be crazed."

Magna sagged heavily. Something was very, very wrong.

All stared at the monster as it slowly settled onto the floor, nestling its immense head on one clawed foot, one yard wide eye held close to Eulin. It was obvious that the pair were talking to each other. No one recognized a word that they said.

Everyone relaxed a little and scattered, searching for their enemy.

"Oh, My Lord," cried Chicken. "Here tis The Princess." She knelt next to the limp form and straightened out her arms and legs.

"Here," called Sha'gar, kicking something in the side. "Here is the one we seek."

Magna lay on her side gasping for breath.

Sgenn stepped up and peered at her. "A female."

Almost dead," said Smoke, dropping to one knee, gently touching the side of Magna's neck.

"Why?" mumbled Magna, eyes fastening on Smoke's. "Never . . . before . . . happened."

Smoke's minds sank in, following memory traces in the rapidly fading and very unusual mind. She slid hastily free.

"It must have been because R-Bar was a witch. Something about her body chemistry," said Smoke. "This person injects a control venom in those that she selects as companions."

"What is witch?" sighed Magna, exhaling, slumping.

Smoke straightened up and told them all. *It was an accident.* Then she shared what she had learned. Of the stolen scroll and the strange body chemistry of those folk where Magna had lived. She hurried over to where Tinker and Chicken were now standing. Sitting on the floor, Smoke leaned over and peered at the limp form. "A very strong warrior. She is still alive, but requires care."

"Captain," said one of the men, "she will starve before we remove all this."

The Captain leaned against the wall and nodded. "You are correct. What an evil thing this exploration has become for Our Queen is dead even before she knew her new lands." He walked away from them and sat on a large boulder, hunched over his knees, shoulders heaving in silent sobs.

And then, some time later, the soldier yelled, "Captain, the rubble moves! Flee!"

All ran to the first bend, and stood peering back to see what was coming their way, ready to bolt for the outside and safety.

The blockage was pushed aside.

The Captain rubbed his eyes and looked again. A large number of people were coming out. One carried a body in its arms.

"Captain," whispered a soldier, "is that Our Queen?"

"Back, back," he hissed. "Too many for us. Let us hide and watch."

They ran on silent feet and slipped into the next tunnel mouth.

As the group passed by, one soldier gripped the Captain's arm. It was The Queen these folk carried.

Suddenly the group stopped.

"They are the Queen's men," said one of the women.

One of the shorter turned and looked right at them. "It is all right," she said, smiling at them. "We won't hurt you. And she is still alive. Really really."

The Captain and his men stepped from the tunnel mouth, carefully watching this strange group for any hostile movement.

Then they led them to their camp.

They watched from a discrete distance, prepared food, as Chicken and Smoke held the Queen while Szart did strange things. The warriors stopped fingering their weapons when the Queen gasped, coughed, and said weakly, "Noble Queen, how came you here? And how did all escape that great beast?"

"Hush, hush, Fair Queen," said Chicken. "On the morrow we shall discuss all. Now allow this one to feed thee. And then urge sleep."

Tinker sat surrounded by the rest of the group.

Smoke had managed to ease their collective pain, partially held away by their concern for Lurin, the Princess, partially by something she felt but didn't entirely understand. She explained what little else she knew of this Magna person.

"I have never heard of such a thing," said Sha'gar.

Sgenn shook her head. "Unknown."

Szart walked over and joined them. "That warrior Queen is lucky endowed. She is badly battered and greatly bruised. The Queen Chicken and Dark Smoke still bathe away grime. I put much healing in her." She looked at Tinker. "That one will wear soft clothes for many days and a new scar on her face."

He looked around. "So these are the new lands?"

"Yes, Our Own," replied Szart.

Tinker jerked. "Where's Eulin?"

She walked into camp from the dark. "Here, Father. I told M'ban to stay out of sight until we were properly, ummmmm, prepared."

"M'ban?"

"The Great Black Dragon." Eulin sat next to him as Fair Morn filled a plate and handed it to her. She started to eat. "This is very delicious."

"Tell the Captain," giggled Messenger. "He prepared it."

Eulin took more. "She wishes to apologize to the Queen. She had no idea, of course, that she was a Queen. M'ban has been in there for hundreds of your years and had lost track of outside affairs."

"Hundreds of years?" Chantal leaned forward, hands on her knees. "You are kidding?"

"No, Mother. Dragons tend to loss track of time unless they are doing something where time matters." She smiled. "They have very narrow interests."

Szart waved in mats and large tents as soon as she saw Tinker yawn.

"Thanks." He said, stood, and headed for the nearest one. '"I am bushed. See everyone in the morning." He stepped into the blue one.

Szart called a pavilion around Chicken, Smoke, and Lurin.

"Rest, Sweet Queen," said Chicken, gently tucking silken blankets around her. "Smoke and Mine Own Self will here this night sleep by thy side. Rest and heal."

The camp rapidly quieted down, the Captain and the soldiers marveling at these friends of their Queen.

Messenger wiggled into a comfortable spot and slipped her arm over his chest. "We all miss her, MyTinker, we really really do." And sniffled.

His arm tightened around her shoulders. "I know, kitten, I know."

He lay a long time staring into the darkness of the tent roof. Trying to understand.

The roof was lightening and he realized that he had been

asleep. He stretched a little and bumped into a warm body on either side. So he lay there and reached out with his mind to see who had joined them.

She grunted, tossed the blanket aside, and sat up.

"SZART!"

"It is." She was wearing pajamas bought for her by R-Bar, a soft orange rust tone.

"What are you doing in here?"

Messenger sat up. "Morning, morning, morning." And leaned across him and kissed Szart. "First Greetings." She giggled happily. Then kissed him. "First Greetings. I like that Vander thingee custom."

"I gathered," he grumbled.

Szart handed a steaming cup to Messenger and looked down at him. "If you will sit up, there is one for you."

Tinker heaved himself upright, took the offered cup and sipped. "Thanks," he mumbled. It was his favorite blend of coffee.

"R-Bar told me," explained Szart. She gently ran her hand over his chest. "She told me everything."

"Stop that."

She nodded. "Of course, Witch Master."

"You can see that?"

"No. It was R-Bar told." She sat with her hands folded in her lap, very witch proper.

"What is going on? This time?" He looked from Szart to Messenger.

"You were Aunt's mate-for-life," explained Szart. "Most die when their witch mates die. It doesn't always happen to a witch mate, but it can. But you are multi-tangled. R-Bar thought all would survive. Even so." Dark eyes fastened on his. "She worked very hard."

"What?"

"R-Bar had a witch feeling that her end was fast approaching."

He jerked more upright. "WHAT?"

Szart nodded. "And she wished to not excite you all, so she held it close. She made me witch-duada and taught all she knew rush fast." She leaned close. "Even the banned spells. We worked very hard. Very, very hard.""

"What did she make you?"

"Duada." She said it carefully. And nodded.

He sighed. "You gonna tell me what that means?"

"It is your right to know," said Szart. And nodded again. "Yep. She told me that term for affirmation. Yep. I am duada, you are arnab. Faan terms."

"Ummmmmm?"

"R-Bar told," she continued, "that in all the self there must be a witch mate." She sat straighter, throwing her shoulders back, spine straight. "I am R-Bar made duada. The one. It is a rare thing for a witch who felt close death to choose a new mate for her's. She knew that she was near going far. But not in the manner or by what means." She nodded. "You are very witch attractive." And shrugged. Her eyes flashed deep down points of golden fire. "You are mine, arnab. The one who mates the duada. It was R-Bar told and did strong strong."

His eyes jerked away to stare at Messenger and then around the tent. "Oh, no." And then he stared at Szart. "You have got to be kidding."

She frowned at him. "I am no witticism." And gently

touched his knee. "R-Bar made one mistake."

"Only one?" he gurgled.

"Yesssssssssssssss, arnab. She said that I was only twenty-two of your years. To wait until," she frowned at the tent floor, "until twenty-five is probably to be not taken, not selected, not wanted."

"Oooooo," sobbed Messenger. "That's terrible."

"Old maid, huh?"

Szart blinked. "Just old . . . twenty-six."

He slipped back against the side of the tent and leaned heavily. The tent wall bulged outward. "Boy, am I confused."

"BUT YOUR HIGHNESS!"

"OUT OF MY WAY, SOLDIER!"

"OOOF!"

The tent flap was violently yanked aside and she stomped inside. She wore a large bandage around her forehead, down over her left eye and cheek bone. Her bare right arm was in a sling. Her left arm was in the sleeve of the pajama top. She was wearing a pair of Chantal's. The right side of the top was pulled off her shoulder. The top button was the only one fastened. The open gap ran a sharp diagonal from the left side of her throat.

"LORD KING TINKER!" she snarled.

"What?"

She glared down at him. The glare lost much of its ferocity by being a glare from one eye only.

"What?" he asked again, wondering to himself, now what's going on?

"Your . . . personal guard refused our orders!"

Chicken, Smoke, and Chantal hurried into the tent.

"This Royal wench needs a'bed be!" snapped Chicken.

Smoke winked at Tinker. "Don't know why we bothered with the top, it doesn't cover much."

"Damn near punched her," grumbled Chantal. "Stop drooling, Cowboy! One new beauty bod at a time." She smiled at him, then at the Queen. "Pretty plush." Lurin looked at Chantal and curled her lip.

"Very healthy and well muscled," added Smoke. "Comes from her training. A strong pouncer."

"What are you doing out of bed? Princess." He looked up.

"We have much work to do."

"In those duds?"

"Duds?"

"Clothes."

She stared down her nose at him. "We wear what We do chose." She whirled around and leaned her head out the tent opening. "CAPTAIN, FETCH US OUR RAIMENT!"

In a few brief moments, the Captain's arm shoved through the tent opening clenching her clothes and dropped them. Then he handed in her boots. They landed next to her clothes.

The Queen waved her good arm. "Dismiss these churlish guards of your's and thy concubines, I would dress."

"Don't," he snapped at Chantal. He had recognized her expression. She was about to punch the Queen.

Szart growled, dark swirled into the tent.

"You too," he said.

"Yes, arnab." She waved it away.

"O.K, everyone out." He stood and made shooing motions. And headed through the opening as all ducked outside.

"STAY!" commanded the Queen. "Please, Highness, for

We do require some small aid."

"Damn cheeky," grumbled Chantal.

"Don't start," he growled, half out of the tent. "I don't need any more of that this morning."

Chicken smiled at him and looked at Szart. "What do be this that, pray tell?"

"You tell 'em," he muttered to Szart. "Maybe they can figure out what's going on." He pulled back inside the tent. "All right, Lady, what do you want?"

She had lain her garb neatly out on his sleeping mat. Yanking the tie loose, she kicked her pajama bottoms off. "Most pleasant a'garb. Hold Mine trousers up, Majesty." Placing her good hand on his shoulder for balance, she neither felt or saw the purple light that leaped from his shoulder to her hand. Or the faint golden flash. She paused, eyes flying wide, then sighed. And stepped into the trousers as he did as ordered.

"Hold still!" He yanked them up, tugging them over her hips, and partially fastened the front, leaving the top fasteners loose, her belt dangling. He took her shirt and ripped the right sleeve to the elbow. "There, that ought to work. Now, hold that arm still."

He slowly removed the sling and began to work the sleeve over her right arm. He stepped behind her. Smoke was right. She was well muscled in a smooth sort of way.

"O.K., now stick the other arm in."

She did. He yanked the shirt up and over her shoulders.

"Turn around."

She did. And smiled at him. "That endowed fierce warrior did say that We do be plush. Be this true?"

"Sure," he said, tugging her shirt closed, fumbling with

the fasteners, trying to not stare at the soft swelling pressing the blue material taut.

"Overly so?"

"Nope."

"Most fair?"

He stopped, and sighed, and grumbled, "O.K., O.K. Lovely long legs, nice waist, great hips, beautiful breasts, nice rib cage, nice gut, good shoulders, nice neck, lovely hair, beautiful eyes, good arms, new scar on your cheek." He stepped back. "Did I leave anything off the list?" he growled.

Her eye twinkled at him. "Fair ankles?"

"Right! Great feet."

"No male has ever so dared to even attempt to view that which you have just listed."

"Right." He managed to tuck her shirt into place once he had it fastened up. He tugged her belt tight. "Narrow waist, too." He fumbled her trouser buttons into their holes. "Sit down, we'll get your boots on."

"We would have Our hair brushed."

"Messenger will do it. She likes brushing hair." He tugged the last lace and tied it and stood. "Stand up, you're ready, Princess."

She rose, stepped close and kissed him, gently. "Fair Lord, Now We do know why thy personal guard be so fiercely loyal. You are most gentle."

"Breakfast," giggled Messenger, poking her head inside the tent. "Really really. I'll brush your hair while you eat. It is short."

Lurin stepped outside, followed by Tinker.

Stop ogling her butt, said Chantal.

Most bold a'Queen, added Chicken.

Old babe magnet is still cooking. Chantal smiled at him.

I would say brazen, not bold. Fair Morn nodded.

Sha'gar looked at him. *Are you taking another queen?*

"Oh my gosh," gasped Messenger. *Are we going to move here?*

Knock it off, he snarled. *And settle down.*

"I am most settled," said Sgenn, handing him a plate.

"I know," he said. "It's great." And then he noticed that all her soldiers were carrying bare swords.""Now what?"

The Captain knelt on one knee near his Queen as she sat on a fallen tree and began to eat with her left hand, balancing the plate on her legs. Messenger stood behind her and began to carefully brush her hair.

"Highness, this is a be'witched land."

"How so?"

He pointed. "Yonder hill was not there as sun set yesterday."

She looked at where he was pointing. A great black hill rose just beyond their clearing, its base obscured by the intervening trees. "Indeed." She handed the plate to him. "Would fetch Us more?"

Messenger finished and walked over to sit next to Smoke and to eat.

He jumped to his feet. "At once." And hurried away, marveling at her calm when notified that a hill had just wandered in from somewhere.

She was not calm at all, but taking her cue from The Lord King Tinker who sat calmly and chatted with his personal guard who laughed at something as they ate and whispered to each other.

The one dressed all in lavender saw her glance at the strange hill and approached.

"May I sit?"

The Queen patted the log. "Do." She was very hungry, strangely so, and took her plate, just refilled, from her Captain who stepped away, but not too far.

"Princess, please order your men to lay down their weapons and to sit down and not do anything unless I tell them to."

"Why?"

"Someone wishes to meet you and apologize for their behavior but doesn't want your men to attack or to run away."

"Indeed?" Lurin smiled. "A most fierce person is it?"

"No," said Eulin, smiling back. "Not a person. Order your men, please?"

"You are one of his?"

"His daughter, Heart To Be, of the Vander, called Eulin Dragon Force."

"A purple mage?"

Eulin nodded.

"Be this magic, this not a person?"

"No." Eulin decided that this was not the time to discuss the various abilities of the dragon folk.

"Captain," said the Queen, "order your men to do as she says and Mine Own Map Maker as well."

He saluted. "My Queen." And hurried away.

"Now call this fierce friend to us." Lurin smiled.

"Her name is M'ban, Princess." Eulin stood and called softly.

The nearby hill moved and shifted and stretched and headed their way.

"STAY!" bellowed the Captain. Two had almost bolted. He clenched his belt with both hands, twisting to watch his Queen and hoping that she knew what she was doing.

Then the front end shoved through the trees as the long neck stretched across the clearing and lowered the immense head close to Lurin and Eulin.

"This," said Eulin to the dragon, "is the Queen, who wishes to claim these lands for her's."

"I have no use for them," replied M'Ban, speaking in the language that these small beings could understand. "But I will wander as I wish."

"This is M'Ban," said Eulin. "She is a Great Black Dragon. They are very rare. I will leave you two to visit. I need to speak with my Father." She walked away.

The Queen stood and began to talk with this terrifying beast.

"I apologize for almost eating you," said M'Ban, after awhile.

"Humbly accepted," laughed Lurin. "Humbly appreciated."

"Griz griz griz," laughed M'Ban. "I ate your warrior though. And squashed two others."

The Queen shrugged. "There be naught that we might do about that now." She was hardly in a position to argue that point with this gigantic dragon beast looming over everything.

"Did they have a family?"

"Nay." Lurin carefully reached out and touched the tip of M'Ban's snout. "Be these your own lands? We have no desire to contest them for we did think none lived herein."

"No. I have only been here for a millennium or two." M'Ban snorted soft smoke. "More or less." She blinked. "I will be very unhappy though if you despoil them."

"Of that, rest assured, great M'Ban. We enjoy beauty in all things." Her eyes jumped to Tinker and back again.

M'Ban nodded. Warrior hands jerked, reaching for weapons, then stopping as The Captain glared at them.

Lurin smiled at her. "Great Dragon, how may we and thee coexist in most peaceful harmony, for this We do most humbly wish?"

"May I have that dormant volcano? It has a pleasant taste."

"It shall be so and henceforth named M'Ban's Mount."

"Thank you, lovely Queen," rumbled M'Ban, trying to look sly. It didn't work as dragons were not good at being sly. "May I ask a boon?"

"Thee from us, a boon?"

"Yesssss," hissed M'Ban. Green fumes spurted from the corners of her mouth.

"Ask and it shall be so."

"I wish to be your Royal Dragon. I have never been a Royal Dragon before."

The Queen reached out with her left hand resting it on the long, bony snout and proclaimed in rolling tones, "Hear ye, Hear ye, attend all present to these Our Very Own Words for We do proclaim now in this place and at this time to all ears, that this be M'Ban, Great Black Dragon, henceforth to be called Royal Dragon, and thus to be so addressed forever. Let no one break this Our Law for the penalties shall be swift and painful."

She sucked in a deep breath. "All hail, M'Ban, Royal Dragon, all hail. And it shall be so to the end of Our Kingdom's Days."

The warriors not already standing jumped to their feet and bellowed with all the others, "All hail, M'Ban, Royal Dragon, all hail."

M'Ban blinked back a gigantic tear. "Thank you," she said, beginning to back away. "I will visit you, now and then." Extending mighty wings that she had kept close folded, she flapped once and soared high into the air, and coasted toward the north. Dirt and leaves and twigs blew over everything.

"All hail," shouted the warriors, "all hail, the mightiest Queen in all of Bahn Duhr Tohr, the Old and the New Lands."

She bowed to them, as well as she was able. "Break camp for we have lands to map." She strode over and sat next to Tinker and laughed. "We would love to see Mine Royal parent's faces and that of Our Noble Brother when they hear of that amazing beast."

He laughed with her. "You are pretty amazing as well."

She grinned. "More than mere plush body, Great King Lord?"

He nodded. "Definitely."

She stood. "Then We would wish thee to visit Our bed, at your convenience, warrior lover." She whirled around and walked away, shouting orders at her men. In a very short time, the camp was packed away and they were ready and headed down the valley and out, to finish their circumspection of M'Ban's Mount, now so named on the map.

"Most brazen a'Queen," said Chicken.

"Merde," sighed Tinker.

Chantal frowned at him. "Now I suppose we will be making lots of trips between here and Grandeville?"

He glared at her. "Szart, Sha'gar, take us back to Bahn Duhr Tohr. We have to take R-Bar home." His face fell as he looked away. He didn't notice the worried glances that he was receiving from all of them.

Chapter Thirty-Two

Oh Well

Grandeville. Tinker's Place.

They swirled in gently onto the rear deck in the twilight of the day. Dropping gear and weapons in casual heaps they walked slowly out through the flower beds and out into the first pasture. There they laid R-Bar next to Ran. And watched as she faded into the meadow.

Slowly, quietly, easing one another's sorrow, they walked back and into the house and settled in the large living room, and sat in mutal comfort and watched night fill the house.

And, long after after, finally, rising sun filled the room with golden light.

He popped one eye open.

Chicken pushed a cup of coffee into his hand. "Fair Morn, Me'Lord. How fare thee."

"Goomp," he mumbled, eyes closing, taking a sip from his cup.

"Most fine," observed Chicken. She looked down. "Release Mine foot, Dark wench." Smoke, lying on her back, on the floor, close to the couch, had grabbed Chicken's ankle.

"Pretty early for you," suggested Smoke.

"We do think Us for to prepare most sumptuous

a'breakfast."

"Good idea." Smoke flowed to her feet. "I'll help."

Fair Morn eased Messenger over, sat up and grinned. "Me too." Messenger had been sleeping in her arms all night. Standing, she covered Messenger with the afghan and followed the pair into the kitchen. "Let's have waffles with lots of sour cream and sliced strawberries."

One eye opened to the narrowest of slits as Chantal slumped against him, reached over, took the cup from his hand, and took a sip. "Damn noisy for early morning," she grumbled.

"Ump," grunted Tinker.

"Shhhhh."

Chicken returned, set a small table near them, and a large pot of coffee on a warmer. And another cup. She refilled his cup. Then she slipped around the couch, leaned over and lifted one edge of a large quilt forming a mound by Tinker's other side.

Szart was curled up against him. She was wearing black pajamas. The bottoms. Chicken gently replaced the quilt. Returning to the kitchen, she watched as Fair Morn ladled waffle batter into the second waffle maker while Smoke sliced strawberries. "Fair Witch do be most curvaceously endowed."

"Early in the morning to be grabbing people, Vander touched Queen," said Smoke.

"Poof piddle," suggested Chicken. "We do naught but mere peek under quilt mound. That witch do wear pajamas in Fair Morn mode."

"Shows good taste and a great idea for comfort," laughed Fair Morn.

"Fry lots of these sausages," ordered Smoke. "A large breakfast ought to dampen down his grumbling. When she wakes, you can help her rearrange R-Bar's room." Smoke, dropped handfuls of sausages into large cast iron skillets.

"Morning, morning, morning," bubbled Messenger, bouncing into the kitchen, grabbing two jugs of orange juice from the refrigerator and beginning to fill tall glasses. "She is very nice." She giggled and wiped up a spill. "Now I am not the shortest cause she is at least two inches shorter than me."

"Dark Sister?" Chicken turned and looked at Smoke.

Smoke shrugged. "It was R-Bar's last thought." She looked at the others. "She is us now. I worked all night. Saved a whole lot of debate." She smiled at them. "Sha'gar and Sgenn agreed, said that R-Bar was correct. Witch, magician, and theurgist combined guard him well. All Faan, all fiercely protective. R-Bar's idea and doing."

Sha'gar and Sgenn walked into the kitchen.

"It is good." Sgenn kissed Smoke on the forehead.

Sha'gar nodded. "I cast great calm on him."

"Gimme some blanket, damn it." Chantal yanked one up over her shoulder and nudged him. "And fill my cup."

He, eyes now fully open, had been staring into nowhere, waking, feeling some difference in them. Bending, he reached for the coffee pot. "Grumpy butt."

The cover and the quilt were dragged with him and what they had been covering toppled, no longer having him to lean against.

Chantal lurched upright and watched Szart sit up and stretch.

"Bright sun," said Szart.

"Not bad, babe-magnet. You already got her top off."

"Huh?" He turned. "YOU!"

"Bright sun, arnab."

"Where's your top?"

Szart shrugged.

"Jiggle, jiggle, jiggle," said Chantal, sipping loudly from her cup. Then she sniffed. "Guess breakfast is about ready."

"Why aren't you wearing anything?"

"I am wearing something. Witches wear as they choose." stated Szart. "Your, our, Fair Morn, does not wear differently."

"Our . . . ?"

Chantal stood. "Come on, short stuff, let's go set the table. And don't mind him. He will be all right in an hour or so."

Szart stood, looked at Chantal, and waved in a top of similar design, in black, of course. And went with her.

"Our?" he mumbled.

Yep, said Smoke. *Whatever R-Bar did, it was an absolute to Szart.*

Me?

All your's, so to speak.

He sighed.

It is just as R-Bar told, said Szart, marveling at this new ability to know and feel, at the multi-merged being that she was now part of.

"Me'thinks," said Chicken to the kitchen crew. "That R-Bar do be more devious than do any suspect."

"Protecting her mate," explained Smoke.

"Let's eat." Fair Morn carried some platters into the dining room. "He is awake."

And then.

A long time later.

They sat.

On the rear deck they sat, in the warmth of the mid-morning, thinking about R-Bar. And about the Fall they could all feel fast approaching.

Sha'gar and Sgenn had talked Szart into a swimming suit and into the pool where they bobbled, quietly talking.

Chantal decided to sprawl on his lap, so she did. The lounge chair creaked warning about overload. "Well, Lover," she said, making sure that he saw the ornate ring she wore on one hand. "How ya doing?"

"Huh?"

She laughed. "Just trying to make small talk while you decide which part of my anatomy to grab and fondle." She smiled at him. "Of course, knowing you, you'll start at the top and work your down."

"Chantal?"

She kissed him. "O.K., bad joke."

"We took a real beating this time."

She leaned against his chest and slipped her arms around him. "I know, John. We are all sorta numb. Just thought that we ought to think about something else."

Something glittered in the air and bounced on the deck, clanging loudly, bringing everyone not already standing, leaping to their feet.

Sha'gar, Sgenn, and Szart hurtled from the pool.

It was a shield, a round shield made of shining silver. The center was enameled with a disc of soft rose. Over that disc was a stylized black dragon in full flight. A scroll was tied to the shield.

Sha'gar carefully approached the shield and scroll, flaming red wand clenched in her right hand, and gingerly removed the scroll with her left hand. She looked at it and handed it to him. "For you."

They settled around him as he sat and unrolled it.

"Out loud," said Fair Morn.

He nodded.

And began to read.

To The Great King Lord, Greetings, from Her Most Noble Majesty, Queen of the Realm of the Dragon, The Princess Lurin.

Most Gentle Handed Prince, we do have this missive clearly written by Our Own Court Scribe as Our Own Script be crabbed warrior scrawl.

Greetings.

Take this small token of Our Most Affectionate Thanks to thy Noble Self, to thy Personal Guard, lovingly attended to, and to Your Beautiful Mage Daughter Eulin Dragon Force, for all that company did for this Humble Princess.

We have chosen, We have, for our Kingdom, the rose color from silky garment given to Us by The Chantal of the globular form, and imposed the dragon image of Our Own Royal Dragon, M'Ban, for Our Royal Kingdom and Lands rank design.

We have named these lands, yet unexplored and mapped, Hahn Dohr Kahn.

Both Kingdoms are teeming with activity and those folk who begin anew with Us.

Great guilds do produce abundant and all do feel safe and secure err foul Ice Time does come.

The Chief of the Seafolk does say great snows will fall pon us as these lands do protrude further into the icy regions than do The Old Kingdoms. We do heed his advice as does Mine Own Noble Brother.

Most great bridge is designed and construction does start at first sign of Our Warm Time past Ice Time.

Tinker cleared his throat. "Here the hand writing changes. It must be her's." He rolled the scroll further open.

Great Lord King, We do wonder greatly, We do, pon when thee and thine here again will visit. Our Court Craftsmen have wrought great bed for Mine Own quarters. This has a most comfortable and most pleasing softness and warmth. We would be Most Royally pleased (to make some slight courtier word play pon words) did thee so enjoy that which We do offer.

Lurin, Princess Royal.
The Realm of the Dragon.
(The Plush).

Chantal patted his hip. "Sounds like an offer that you can't refuse."

The scroll rerolled with a pop as he released it and dropped it on the table. "How did this stuff get here?"

"Sook sent," said Szart.

He sighed. And looked at them all. "My life just keeps getting weirder and weirder."

Szart suddenly jerked. "Mother just told."

"What?" He frowned at her, expecting some additional problem.

"Eulin went home. The King and The Queen give thanks for aiding The Princess. Raft and her's, Mrrinar, the cat-folk healer, went to his lands to help his folk. All the sisters have gone out. And Mother says she understands as R-Bar left a long message for her. She also said that she would gift you if you needed anything but she doubted that you did."

Fair Morn smiled. "She have any Princess repellant?"

"Ha. Ha. Ha. Ha. Ha," said he.

"Let's have lunch." Fair Morn stood.

So they did.

And then they bustled in various directions.

And life settled down.

As much as it ever did.

Chapter Thirty-Three.

A Royal Visit

Hahn Dohr Kahn. The Realm of The Dragon.

The great map covered a large section of the long wall of The Hall Of Progress. The Hall was always open and anyone could enter, day or night, to view the map. The left hand edge of the large map was bordered by a wide river that had been drawn up the side of the map from the sea at the bottom to the unknown territories at the top. This river curved one branch to the east and passed by a nearly circular mountain labeled M'Ban's Mount.

Dotted lines indicated unknown land and boundaries further north. From the mouth at the river the dotted coast line wandered east. Dotted lines ran from the first town toward the north indicating a proposed road. The Royal Town, the first town, was shown in proposed detail, as well as the Coast Road and the River Road, neither constructed very far from town. The Great Bridge was drawn in, spanning the river, connecting the two kingdoms, linking the two Royal towns.

The great quay was shown and the many dotted lines of planned harbor construction. Her brother had agreed that she would have the seaport while he developed the armor and weapon works.

All along the coastal plain had been drawn in the farms and the farm road connecting them and the Royal Town as well as the planned farm villages.

Everywhere else, the map was stark white, blank space, labeled as unknown. Except for the green forest running some distance from M'Ban's Mount.

She stood, dressed is black trousers of soft material draped artfully over tan boots, rose colored shirt tucked in, blousing over the wide silver and gold belt. A great white sword hung from her belt. She was conversing with a large man who wore her warrior's garb, all rose and soft black. He was now the First Lord of The Realm, once Captain of her guard.

Once the two of them, and a handful of advisors also agreed, the First Lord saw to it that things happened to bring these plans into existence.

The Hall and The Map were items of pride to all in the land. Here were the visible signs of the new kingdom that they were all building. And here the humblest could argue for a change in some detail, in some aspect that affected them directly.

And if all agreed upon the final decision, honestly arrived at.

"So," she said, "we are agreed? Once the icy fingers pull away, we push along the coast till we can pass no further."

"Indeed, My Queen. The First Seafolk of your Royal Ship believes, based upon all his years of experience, that more rivers are to be found. If true, they will offer swift access to the interior and mapping parties may quickly color in the white blankness."

"Then this we will do." She smiled. "With one small change. Send some small fleet along ahead of our land party carrying supplies for the road builders. Thus we may move even swifter."

He smiled and nodded. "We shall begin preparations now. Thus, at first chance in the beginning of Warm Time, we are off."

They bent over a table and began to make plans and to draw up lists.

The door banged open and two men dressed in white and black hurried in, carrying a long roll of material, followed by a third who quickly shut the door on wind and snow.

The third hurried forward and bowed, and said in deep rolling tones. "Hail, Dragon Queen, thy Noble Brother, Our Great King, does send his love and this to adorn thy wall."

"Came you in great storm, across roiling river, just for this?" She frowned at him as he straightened up.

"Nay," he cried, alarmed at the look she cast in his direction. "We were magic'd here by Our Queen."

"An interesting thing, that," she murmured, more to her self than to her audience.

"Show Us Our gift."

Instantly, the three men scurried about rearranging tables and chairs until they had most of the floor open. And then they unrolled it.

"A map," observed The First Lord.

"Thy Noble Brother, Our King, did say... gift this to Mine Own Sister and request that she hang it with her map so all in both kingdoms may see what is planned everywhere. Her idea was great and we wish all to share in it. Once the mighty bridge is open, all our folk may journey back and forth and plan our futures together, as will we. Thus the kingdoms are linked in friendship forever." The spokesman cleared his throat. "If the

Queen does agree."

"We do," she said. And ordered the map hung and cleverly joined so that the two became one. "And do tell Mine Own Brother this was most clever an idea as We have been much too focused pon only here and not there. We wait most impatiently for great bridge to be constructed."

The three men hurried to one side as carpenters arrived and began to hang the new map as directed.

Then all stepped back and admired the new map of The New Lands.

"He pushes west and north," observed The First Lord, stepping close to her side. "And does explore that great jumble of mountains."

"See there." She pointed. "Mines. And a great cart road."

"We must be careful, My Queen," said The First Lord, softly.

"How so?"

"Some small kingdoms may be sorely tempted to relieve us of our gatherings."

"Who would dare?"

"Greedy men. There are always some. And we have military few."

"We will counsel with Our Brother when bridge does open. Few dare sail as did we. None in this icy time of year. We have time to make plans."

He nodded. "Work calls loudly. By your leave." He bowed and hurried from the hall.

Crooking one finger she beckoned over the spokesman. "Tell Us, Noble Sir, how Mine Own Brother's Queen, did move you from there to here?"

"I know not, Majesty. T'was some witchy trick."

Whirling around she bent over the table and wrote a short note, folded it thrice and handed it to him. "To Mine Brother take this."

He bowed, touched a black ring, and they were gone, all three of them.

She smiled. And tugged her shirt into order. And began to study the map of The New Lands. Planning.

Grandeville. Tinker's Place.

They had finished various chores early and were all gathered around the dining room table shoving maps back and forth, except for Smoke, who was making cocoa and coffee. They had decided to take a three day trip, a little vacation, and were deep into the chaos of deciding where to go.

He sat in the living room, reading, staying a safe distance away from all that energy.

"May a visitor enter?" asked a disembodied voice.

He looked up. "Huh?"

So the voice repeated the question.

"Who is this?"

"Sook."

"Oh. Sure. Come on in." And she stood there, smiling at him.

"YOU?"

"As thee did not deign travel to us, We did travel to thee."

"Gazooks!" yelped Chicken, staring across the table and into the large living room. "Tis her."

Everyone looked. Sook popped out.

"How did she get here?" Chantal frowned. "Think I ought

to get my gun?"

Szart stepped into the large living room and looked. "Sook sent."

"Indeed," said The Queen. "At Our request." She looked around. "Most cosy a room this." Then she looked into the dining room at the table littered with maps, then at Tinker.

"Great Lord King, be thee preparing for battle?" She clasped the hilt of her sword.

"No. You wanna put that over there, in the corner?" He pointed.

"As thee wish." And walked to the corner, unhooked her belt and stacked sword and belt where indicated and stuffed her shirt back into her trousers. Then she walked over and looked out one of the large picture windows. "Most fair a'land.

She turned back and looked at him. "Thy season does be different than Our's. We be fairly covered in icy white."

Smoke walked in and handed him a cup of coffee. "Coffee?" she asked.

The Queen nodded. "We will try this beverage."

Smoke gave her a cup and filled it.

Lurin watched Smoke fill other cups as some headed for the kitchen to get cocoa instead.

"Servitor warriors? Most unusual these personnal guards of thine." She dragged over a chair and sat facing him. "We were told, We were, that they do dwell with thee and that thee do them all service."

"What?"

She leaned forward and set one hand on his knee. "Think you, did We treat Our Royal Guard so that they would to us be as Fiercely loyal as these to thee?"

His sigh was heard all the way into the kitchen.

"Praps not," she said. "T'would be a mighty task."

He watched her face carefully. "Who have you been talking to?"

"We did by Sook travel to Mine Own Parents, the Noble King and Queen, and there we did visit with them and thy Princess, Eulin Dragon Force, and Ripple, Dark Advisor. Prior to that We did speak with the witch Raft."

She nodded slowly. "Thee are most mighty a'King, Lord." She emptied her cup.

HELP!

Chantal charged into the room, making trumpet calls, followed by a giggling Messenger.

"General Custer," announced Chantal. "I think that you are surrounded."

"Really really," agreed Messenger.

"This is not funny," he growled at them.

The Queen frowned as well. "Indeed, for We do miss fair jest as well."

Chantal crashed down into the couch, jostling him. "I think that this is going to be a tough one, John."

Lurin leaned back and waved one hand. "Begone, for thy Master Lord and We would speak pon matters of some private nature."

I'm gonna punch her lights out, snarled Chantal. *This hot bod is worse than all of the Vander ever thought of being.*

A spell would work, suggested Szart.

I could put her to sleep, offered Smoke.

And have Szart sent her home, added Fair Morn.

Nay, commanded Chicken. *For We will with this Queen*

council. She walked into the room. "Fair Queen, with Us do come, for We have gentle business to discuss."

Lurin stood and bowed her head to Tinker. "As thee wish, Fair Queen. Lead on." She followed Chicken from the room.

He slumped even deeper into the couch and watched them as they all came in. "What is she doing here?"

Smoke winked at him, a long, slow languid wink. "Pounce on her, MindMate."

"Well," drawled Fair Mom. "She certainly wants him to."

"Smoke, Messenger, check her out, see if something has been put on her."

Smoke nodded and reached out. And smiled. "A very healthy female."

Messenger shook her head. "I didn't see anything. But there is some trace of Vander purple spell residue and some other golden stuff."

Most determined do be this Queen, said Chicken.

"Merde," grumbled he. "What?" he asked Messenger.

Messenger blushed. "You did it. Something stuck to you from that Vander trip."

Chantal threw her arms around him after casting a fast glance at Smoke, kissed him, and toppled him over. And after awhile she said, "That was just the warm up, Cowboy. We are all going to go to town and shop until we drop, etc. Three hours ought to be enough time for you to pummel her into exhaustion." She sat up. "Use my bed. It's that bouncy one Szaifeh gave us, remember."

Smoke set a brown bag next to him. It clinked. She dropped a cork screw next to it. And smiled. "Should be enough."

Szart stepped close. "R-Bar taught me a Vander spell."

"Put it on him," snorted Chantal. "She deserves it."

"Hold it," he snapped. "What is going on? This time?"

Fair Morn grinned at him. "We are making the supreme sacrifice."

"Indeed, My Lord," agreed Chicken, walking in from the hall. "Royal wench do have most strangely a'focused intent. Most powerfully driven!"

Smoke nodded. "There is something very deep driving her."

He stood, sack under one arm. And sighed.

"It's a tough job," laughed Chantal. "But someone has to do it."

He frowned at her. And then told Szart, Sha'gar, and Sgenn. "You three figure out how to keep her away from here. We are not going to do this again. She has Lords, Princes, and whatever, by the hundreds, by the thousands, back there."

"She is moon-struck," stated Messenger. "Really really. It is some left over purple and gold magic."

Sha'gar, Sgenn, and Szart headed outside to the van, talking quietly.

Chantal leaned close to him and kissed his cheek. "I know that this is all pretty crazy, Love. But somehow, it is O.K. We'll buy steaks." She pecked his cheek again and spun away. "Come on, let's go," she said to the others.

He walked into the kitchen and then headed into the Chamber and upstairs.

Standing on the balcony of Chantal's room, he lined the bottles up on the railing, including the additions he had made. Yanking all the corks out, he tossed them and the corkscrew into a corner. "We'll be crude, drink straight from the bottle." He handed her one, slid an arm around her waist and turned her so they could look out over the flower beds and out at the first pasture. He tilted up his bottle and took a long pull, wondering why it was always happening to him.

Lurin tilted up her bottle. "Most tasty."

"Drink up. We have lots."

So she did.

He yanked her closer. "Nice waist."

"Be that all?"

"Nope," he said. "We'll get to the rest in a while."

Chantal looked at her watch. "Let's go home."

Smoke nodded. She was tired of shopping.

Sha'gar had tried explaining to Szart why they did this thing shopping.

Szart told her that it was strange strange. She could wave in anything that they would want.

Sgenn agreed. Shopping was a strange way to acquire things.

He lay on his side and poked a pillow under his head and squinted into the dim light.

She lay flat on her back, head turned his way.

"I . . . am," she said, slowly rolling onto her side, smiling crookedly at him, her arm sliding over his waist. "No . . . longer the. . . Princess . . . chaste." She hiccuped.

"Home," he mumbled. "They are coming home."

"Whoooooo . . .?" She sighed, blinked, and fell asleep.

"Them," he replied, closing his eyes, and falling, down,

down, down.

"Sleeping," said Smoke, snapping on the lights in the kitchen. "We better talk softly in the morning."

"I'll use his bed," said Chantal. "Mine's occupied."

So, they made dinner, talked about this very strange behavior, watched two movies, ate popcorn, and went to bed.

Chapter Thirty-Four.

Finally, Quiet At Home

Grandeville. Tinker's Place.

He woke, flat on his back, and stared up at the light on the ceiling. It must be morning.

He yawned.

And stretched.

And wondered how his life had gotten so strange. No-one lived like this, absolutely no-one. Then he sighed.

He wasn't Velvetmist. He was just good old Grandeville, U.S.A. There had to be some way to put some normalcy back into his life, such as it was. Pondering how he was going to accomplish that, he fell back asleep.

Chantal crooked one finger at Smoke, grabbed a pot and two cups. "Outside, we need to talk Private." She clamped her mind shut.

Smoke did the same thing and followed her outside and onto to the front lawn and sat facing her, taking one of the cups.

Chantal frowned at Smoke as they sipped. "Thought all this babe stuff was over when this mob reached critical mass?"

Smoke nodded.

"Well?"

"I don't know. For sure. But Messenger did see Vander

traces and gold magic as well." She smiled at him. "She told you that. I really do think that he infected that Queen into doing what she was driven to do.""

"WHAT? How could you not know?"

"Ran died. Then the Vander did something he won't release. But Messenger does believe that this is responsible. Then R-Bar died. Major system shock, all these things coming so close together. I do not understand why he didn't come apart, all mind madness. Then he is Szart, something that R-Bar planned."

She looked at Chantal, great gold orange eyes seeming to swallow her. "Things like this do not happen to Velvetmist." Smoke shivered. "It is hard being the Hub when this much happens, one event after another."

"Smoke?"

"We are . . . alive." Then she was calm, relaxed, again.

Chantal leaned toward her. "This has got to stop. It is not right."

Smoke sipped. "What?"

"That!" Chantal jabbed a finger at the house. "That! That horny Princess babe."

"Oh."

Chantal glared at her. "Don't you oh me." She refilled her cup, the pot rattled wildly on the cup's lip as she did. Setting down the pot, she held the cup with both hands. "I want it stopped." She stared at the grass, forgetting her coffee.

Then she slowly raised her eyes. "John is losing it. I can feel it. He needs stability. He needs something closer to his cultural values, not your's." She waved one arm wildly. "And not all those bitches out there either! Where ever out there really is! Understand? His values. Mine!"

Chantal blinked fiercely to stop the tears. She picked up her cup and mumbled. "Not your values. Not Messenger's values. Not Sha'gar's values. Not Sgenn's values. Not Szart's values."

"You forgot the Princess and Fair Morn."

"They don't have any, damn it! They were created!" Coffee sloshed onto the grass.

Smoke sat predator still, watching.

"And you know it," added Chantal. "They are Big Red things."

"We are eight females. He was getting used to it. Before all this disaster happened."

Chantal sat back. "True. But, on this world there are societies where this can occur. And he knows that. Multiple wives. So it is not alien."

She set her cup down. "But all the rest certainly is. And that is the problem."

Smoke nodded.

"And that," whispered Chantal, "includes Sa'ar and Imdar."

Smoke blinked.

"Do you understand?"

"No. Let me in."

Chantal did. "O.K. Take a look."

Smoke flowed in and became Chantal. They became one.

The coffee was cold long before they parted.

"Well?" gasped Chantal.

Smoke swallowed loudly. "Never have I gone that deep. Yes, I see."

"At least a year. We need peace and quiet for at least a

year."

Smoke wobbled to her feet. "I will talk with the magical ones." She headed for the house.

Chantal flopped back on the grass and stared at the sky, watching a cloud. It was the only one up there.

"What are you staring at?" she asked it.

It didn't say anything. It was just a passing cloud, after all.

His eyes popped open. It was the same ceiling up there. And it was quiet, very, very quiet. He reached out. Suddenly worried.

Messenger was directing Chicken and Sgenn at some task in one of the flower gardens.

Sha'gar was taking Szart on a hike, showing her their lands.

Smoke and Fair Morn were cleaning and straightening things in the barn. Chantal was close.

She slipped quietly into the room and set the tray on a side table and stepped up to the bed. "Sit up, Lover."

He did. She fluffed up the pillows and stuffed them behind his back. "Skootch back."

He did, leaning back against the pillows and the headboard. She set the tray on his lap.

"What's this?"

She sat on the edge of the bed and lightly rested one hand on his knee. "When I got married, John, I always thought that I would give my husband breakfast-in-bed. Once in a while. So there you are. B.I.B." He took a sip from the glass.

She stood and turned toward the door.

"Don't go," he said softly. "Wife."

"Left the coffee pot and my cup in the hall."

She fetched them and then sat facing him, filling his cup, then her's.

"Where's Lurin?"

"Pressing business. She had to hurry home."

"Why'd we do that?"

"What?"

"Lurin."

Chantal shrugged. "Seemed like the thing to do. Smoke doesn't know. Szart thought that she felt some sort of magical trace that tasted Vander as Messenger had said. Sha'gar said that the Princess wasn't magic capable." She held his hand. "Don't dwell on it. Please? No one really seems to know. At least not yet, for sure. But we all think that her behavior is all a result of whatever you did to help the Vander."

He ate in silence for some time. Using his free hand. Not wanting to let go of her hand. And then looked at her. "It is true, isn't it? You are my wife."

"You betcha."

"Eight wives," he mumbled.

"If you had vast petroleum deposits and wore floppy clothes no-one would even think about it."

He ate the rest of his toast and nodded. "You make it sound so normal."

"It is, John," she said ever so softly, ever so carefully. "It is." She took his tray. "Let's go downstairs and enjoy the fall day."

He slipped from the bed, quickly dressed, and caught up with her in the kitchen. He slipped an arm around her and gave her a little pat. "Thanks, wife."

She kissed his cheek. "Just don't expect to get spoiled."

And the day wandered into peaceful.
As did the seasons.
In Grandeville.

Individuals Of Note

Grandeville.

Tinker's Place

John Tinker -- the individual used as an intermediary by Big Red in his ongoing activities to maintain the balance of the universes. During his initial time on Mirk Wild Weald, Tinker was told by The Thought that he is The Chosen One of legend. Now merged telepathically into an entity with the rest following the cultural values of Smoke's people.

Smoke of the Velvetmist - a gigantic, telepathic carnivore, now transformed into a human shape by Big Red. She was selected from her home, a hidden and never visited elseplace, to be one of the original companions to aid and journey with John Tinker. Now MindMate to Tinker, Chicken and the rest.

Princess Chicken - an Easter Season fluffy chicken toy from an Easter basket, transformed by Big Red and placed as a traveling companion and aid for John Tinker.

Messenger - Once "The Messenger" of her people but joined with Tinker and the rest when she began to fold inside herself believing Tinker and crew were monsters and demons from her folk's mythology come alive.

Fair Morn - a one-time mythological jest created by the magical force, Big Red. Messenger severed her magical bonds changing Fair Morn from a jest into a real person.

R-Bar - a witch of The Faan clan, joined into the polyorganism of Tinker and the rest by Smoke. (Deceased).

Sedeem - her daughter, a magician.

Farth - Sedeem's mate-for-life, a Silver Ranger.
Ferrelden - of the Risshar, a Night Runner from Zhorndar'h. (Deceased).
Flar - one time owner of a Magical Items Shop. (Deceased.)
Chantal Baire - a Veterinarian with a clinic near Grandeville.
Ran - witch of the Tanpak clan. Preferred to be called Ran. (Deceased).
Sha'gar - Faan magician, daughter of Reep and J.C.
Sgenn - Faan theurgist, daughter of Reep and J.C.
Dat - an indjinn, gifted to Tinker when the group bought a ring, The Eye of Dat.
Je'leel - her daughter.
Szart - Faan witch - chosen by R-Bar to be Tinker's mate-for-life.

Chantal's Friends
Frederica Hensler - "Freddie" - lives in Portland.
Ralph Andervante - her husband
Sandrew Sherl Sandermeyer now **Anderson** - "Sandy" - Tinker's Attorney.
Red - her husband, a member of the Grandeville Police Department.
Janine Teacate - "Streak" - Sandy's secretary.

Chen's Chinese - The Building.
Adam Lieu Chen - Master Chen owns and operates *Chen's Chinese,* a restaurant located in Greater Downtown Grandeville. He also trains Tinker in the martial arts.

Dragon Ranch - not far from Tinker's Place.

Prince Goose - a windup plastic toy transformed by Big Red into a traveling companion for John Tinker. He is a brother of Chicken.

Chen Gum Lung - The Golden Dragon of the House of Chen. A sometimes amulet gifted to Tinker by Master Chen.

Doc's Home

Kappa "Doc" Heckmann - anthropologist and adventurer. A friend and neighbor of John Tinker's.

J. C. Smith - one of Tinker's close friends. He works for Doc in many capacities.

> **Reep** - of the Faan witch clan, married to J. C.
>
> > **Szaifeh** - her daughter, a witch.
> >
> > **Sha'gar** - her daughter, a magician.
> >
> > **Sgenn** - her daughter, a theurgist.

Membrane - one of Doc's "associates." He run Doc's stores, *Cactus Spine,* specializing in cacti and succulents.

Badnews Treefalls - another of Doc's "associates." He is Doc's constant companion.

The Hardcastle Residence.

Alandale Fredrico Hardcastle IV, known as "Hard" by all his friends.

> **Ramp** - of the Faan witch clan, a magician, his wife.
>
> > **Sa'ar** - her twin daughter, a magician.
> >
> > **Shem** - her twin son, a magician, also known by his parents and grandparents as **Alandale Fredrico Hardcastle V.**
> >
> > > **Tajaar** - his wife.

Grandeville Police Department (GPD)

Red and **Green** - two very large men who once played football together on the local college team. They function, usually, as the late night patrol. They are good friends of Tinker, J. C., and Hard.

The Elseplaces

Paradise.

Big Red - a pure force of magic personified. He is primarily concerned with maintaining the balance and order of the universe of universes. And, more often than not, has some influence over the events that plague Tinker.

Dancing-All-The-Day - Big Red's wife.

Silly-All-The-Day - their son.

Treena - the wife of Silly.

Various - depending upon mood.

Dram - an individual often called The Evil One. He began life on Murk Wild Weald as a magician-in-training. But after long and secretive study in The Library of Arcana he slowly was transformed by his knowledge and his ambitions into one of the few pure forces in the universe of universes. Dram has a tendency to work at living up to his title.

Stumpf.

The-Mountain-That-Walks - an individual most often addressed as Mountain by his traveling companions. He is one of the original companions selected to aid John Tinker.

A Place Unnamed.
Macabre - who specializes in killing things. He is usually accompanied by his pets: The Vipers, and the Sparkling Tigers.
Gyre - his female companion, created by his vessel, Gyreship.

The Six Lands.
Sorrowful Mistidings - a professional Teller of Tales, selected from The Six Lands, as one of the original companions to aid John Tinker. He lived with his wife and sons. Now deceased.
Tears Trimblechin - his grandson, a growing Teller of Tales, trained by his grandfather.

Clear Bandler - The Land of Magicians
The $1.98 Magician - trained by Big Red and told to aid Tinker in whatever manner he could.
Plum Duff - a magician and consort to $1.98.

The Old Lands - Bahn Duhr Tohr.
Willawa, The White Warrior, Queen of all the lands, New and Old.
Toucan, The King - he is the brother of Prince Goose and Princess Chicken and once was Tinker's advisor.
Hanred, Ripple's mate-for-life - he is a Master Illusionist who once traveled widely through the universe of universes and is also known by many of the folk as "Old Hanred."
Ripple, Advisor to the Royals - she is the Clan Head of the Faan witch clan.
The New Lands - Aahn Duhr Tohr
Frinda - son of Willawa and Toucan, now King of Bahn

Aahn Tohr.

Sook - a Faan witch, now his Queen.

Lurin - daughter of Willawa and Toucan, now Queen of Hahn Dohr Kahn, The Realm of The Dragon.

Dol Spar - Headquarters of The Monetary Control and Mirf's home.

Mirf - The Special Chief First Inspector, often sent on special assignments by The General, the overall director of The Monetary Control and her boss.

Fred - a suk-dragon, her Assistant.

Quan - Fred's mate - Mirf's Assistant.

Magevern - home of the Vander mage Guild.

Sa'ar - the Heart of the Vander, who made Tinker The Lord of The Vander.

Clans, Guilds, and Other Organizations.

(known individuals listed)

Anaza sorcerer Phylota located in Far Corner.

Netanada -- Elixa (Clan Head), Sorceress.

Abadoda -- Three Rank Sorceress.

Hatopa -- Three Rank Sorcerer.

Important Artifacts.

The Ancient Book of Songs.

The Divineal of Thantala located in Murklan Obscuratan. A Place Never Visited.

Lady Grimtouch - The Glimmer (Clan Head) of The Divineal of Thantala.

Lady Fairdeath - traveling with Sluba mage Ransapal.

Lady Dawnmort

Lady Softtouch

Lady Nightreaper

Lady Final Kiss

Lady Lastgift

Clan robe color - forest green almost black; carry a short gold staff.

Important Artifacts

The Book of Death.

Potri witch Clan

Turintor

Clan robe colors - grape and green design.

Faan witch Clan - scattered widely throughout the universe of universes.

Ripple - Clan Head - The fifth Born.

Hanred, the Illusionist, her Mate-For-Life.

Shitar - their daughter, a witch.

Mantara - Grenzanr warlock - her mate-for-life.

Santar - their daughter, a witch.

Sook - their daughter, a witch.

Sepanix - their daughter, a witch.

Szart - their daughter, a witch - mated to Tinker.

Ranna - The First Born

Anjan - her mate, Death Warrior

Adarlak - her mate, Hacto mage.

Riz - The Second Born.

Rekel - The Third Born.

Ap Kar - a Hinta warlock, her mate-for-life.

Rbat - The Fourth Born. At one time thought by many to have gone far.

Reptar - The Sixth Born.

Rumtah - The Seventh Born. Known as The Lucky One.

Reep - The Eighth Born. Known as The Silent One. Married to **J. C.**

Szaifeh - their daughter, a witch.

Sha'gar - their daughter, a magician.

Sgenn - their daughter, a theurgist.

Rotak - The Ninth Born.

Raft - The Tenth Born. Known as The Fast.

Mrrinar - a Catfolk Healer, her mate.

R-Bar - The Eleventh Born. (Deceased).

Tinker - her Mate-For-Life

Sedeem, their daughter, a magician.

Ramp - The Twelfth Born. A Magician.

Married to **Hard**.

Sa'ar, their daughter, a magician.

Shem, their son, a magician.

Important artifacts.

An immense collection of volumes dealing with the arcane collected by Hanred during his many travels through the universe of universes.

Talair witch Clan - located on Tanadra.

Motaiss - a warlock

Mendurra - a witch.

Clothes colors - black with just a hint of faint grey in an ornate design that runs down the outside of each sleeve.

Sluba mage Guild, one member located in Three Trees Town.

Ransapal- studied the Dark Under and ancient witch history. Traveling with Lady Fairdeath.

Vander mage Guild - located in Magevern.

Sa'ar - the Heart of the Vander.

Eulin Dragon Force - her daughter by Tinker, a

mage and Dragon Master.

Tobtz - the Soul of the Vander.

Cazor - mage warrior.

Moonda

Aada

Bant

Andovar - the Farseer.

Imdar - the Healer.

Rorx - Vander warlock - her son by Tinker.

Szaifeh - a witch, his Mate-For-Life.

Imten - the Artificer.

Tinlee - the Adept.

Xanx - Apprentice Healer.

Marl - the Seeker.

Galron - The Bent.

Eulin - The Brave.

Clothes color - they are always dressed in garb of the faintest purple. It is from the color of their garments that folk often call them "The Purple Magicians."

The Wood With located in Newlar, relocated from Blurratha. Hidden. In Plain Sight.

Fairlan - Cluster Head

Ringlan - Cluster Head

Clearlar - Cluster Head

Faerlar - Cluster Head

Flerlan - The Observer

The Wood With are always accompanied by their beast. When the Wood With are present one might notice the smell of blooming flowers on the air.

The Garden Gnomes located in Growing Green.

Phineas Grass

Hiram Toadstoll

Franny Waxflower

Franelken Vetch

Tiny Rosebud - the emissary

Rose Perrywinkle

Monetary Control - located on Dol Spar.

The General - Head of Monetary Control.

Mirf - Head of the Special Investigations Office.

Fred - a suk-dragon - First Assistant.

Quan - Fred's mate - First Assistant.

Rema - First Clerk.

Nema - First Clerk.

The Nagar

Kartz - Head

Raj - a Medical Doctor - her mate.

Reslar - youngest sister.

The Silver Rangers - located on Fandor's Dan.

Farth - Tindar (General) of the Silver Rangers.

Sedeem - Faan magiwitch - his wife.

Bits and Pieces of Cultural Data

(From the files of Monetary Control)

The Garden Gnomes.

The Garden Gnomes are a small folk, perhaps the smallest of all the folk. As their name implies they are fascinated by gardening and frequently visit those gardens that they recognize as being above the average in terms of arrangement and care, whether ornamental or functional.

At some point, in their past, one of them had been seen while visiting a particularly well designed ornamental garden. This kind of happening was not something that they liked to happen nor did they like to talk about it. This garden, as things seem to happen to this folk or that folk over their histories, belonged to a sculptress of some skill and very fast eyes. She made a statue of what her eyes saw as just a fleeting glance and set this statue in and among a artfully organized patch of flowers.

And as things so often happen, a visitor saw this statue and asked the owner to make one for him. And so it went. And so it went. Much to the consternation of the Garden Gnomes.

And eventually an entire industry sprang up around these statues and their production. People even wrote fanciful books about the culture of these things. They were all wrong, of course. None of the authors had ever talked with one of these small folk or had ever visited a Garden Gnome village.

The end result of all this was that the Garden Gnomes retreated deeper and deeper into areas where they would not, or could not, be observed.

Young Garden Gnomes, every once in awhile, on a dark, a particularly dark night, would steal one of these statues and hide them away.

Of course, this had no effect on the overall population of these fake garden gnomes. That industry was to well intrenched.

The Divineal of Thantala.

In time before time almost before memory it is told that the Divineal were there, passing through the universe of universes upon business that none dared ask about and few would dare challenge. The few that did, died. This rare occurrence, challenging one of them, and the result of that challenge, was told one to the other, and thus was the tale spread, and The Divineal were left to pursue their own interests. Most of these interests appeared to have something to do with Death. Death as a being, not merely as the end of something.

All the folk of the elseplaces recognized them as none else would dare to wear a deeply hooded robe of dark forest green that was almost black. And none else would presume to carry a short gold staff.

It is said among the many cultures in the universe of universes that few have ever seen the face of the individual hidden in the blackness of the deep hoods. It is also said that to see that face is to die. But, if one had ever done so and survived, none had ever so stated.

It is known and understood by most folk that one does not approach one of The Divineal and start a conversation. One does not watch one of The Divineal closely. One tries as much as possible to ignore their existence. One hopes to stay alive. It was this understanding that brought into being the label used far and wide for them, "The Sisters of Death." But it never, ever, was used when of them could hear it.

None knew where their elseplace, their home place, was located. None knew which of the many elseplaces, numbers beyond counting, would be the one wherein they resided. And even if one could find out, in some mysterious way, none would dare chose to go to such an elseplace.

The Divineal were polite and very soft spoken, if and when they might chose to speak to someone. And all, but the foolish and soon to be dead, would do all that they were capable of doing, if asked to do something. That is what the folk in the universe of universes believed. And none knew of anyone that had been asked and who had refused and survived.

None knew how many Divineal there were. None knew why or what they were about and most folk felt that the best place to be when one of them was around was to be somewhere else.

The Divineal were like a pebble dropped into a still pond whose action caused ripples to flow out in all directions. And like that pebble, they were totally unconcerned about those ripples.

The Witch Clans.

The Potri witch clan came into existence, as did all the witch clans, during what all the clans call "The Great Migration." From where this migration came is a great matter of debate and argumentation, but not why.

The ancestral clan, or clans, also a matter of intense debate and argumentation, had, through arcane knowledge, come to understand that a disaster beyond the control of any user of magic was about to happen to their homeland.

So they fled out into the universe of universes and over

time the witch clan, or clans, splintered and grew into the myriad of clans that are now present.

The long ago seen disaster happened in a single violent explosion that removed their homeland as their sun erupted and ate everything within reach.

Some thing, some event, during that long ago migration and scatter brought into the witch culture a sense of authority coupled with a powerful magic that each clan cultivated. Each clan developed their own clan interests and evolved their own unique concept of magic. The end result of this was a somewhat provincial sense of proper witch attire and proper witch behavior. The pairing of these beliefs with their sense of authority meant that the folk living in the many elseplaces in the universe of universes knew that any witch tended to be rather short-tempered and had a predilection toward violent behavior when the behavior of other folk, witch, magician, or non-magical user, was felt by the witches to be engaged in improper behavior, undesirable behavior, or were just plain irritating.

Most witch clans dressed in wardrobes of midnight black, the exact style of their clothing varying widely. Some of the clans, in the long before before, had, for reasons they chose not to reveal, settled on wardrobes of other colors.

The Faan witch clan is unique. Among all of the witch clans scattered across the universe of universes, they are the only one that does not maintain a clan house. And, unlike all the other clans, the members are all and only generationally linked. The magic of the Faan flows down the female line from mother to daughter.

The Faan clan, unlike the other clans, are trained almost exclusively by their female relatives, mainly by their mother and their aunts. But if a sister has learned some new and unique twist, it may be shared, sister to sister. It is due to this multi-generational sharing and training that has made the Faan noted throughout the witch clans as being the most powerful clan and to be avoided if at all possible. And some few understand that at some point in the long ago long ago, in their mating with their chosen mates-for-life, from other witch lines, that something unusual happened that twisted and transformed their genetic material.

The result of this event was that, at times, their offspring are born with new and unique abilities. This tends to explain why the Faan do not maintain a clan house. Members of their clan, most often, prefer to wander mostly by themselves and to study and collect magic and magic spells. And other things.

The Mage Guilds

The mage Guilds apparently came into existence in the long ago long ago in a manner none understand or thought to record as this event was in a time when such occurrences were not seen as being important enough to warrant special note.

Magicians are, in one sense, at the opposite end of the magical spectrum from the witches. That is why the magicians and the witches tend to avoid each other whenever possible, especially physical contact. The magic of each tends to be unstable in contact, often resulting in fatal results. However, there is the fact that, at times, in a manner none truly understand, that magicians and witches may have close association, even mates of the others, without dire affects.

The **Vander mage Guild**, as written in the *Histories of the Arcane,* was once a sub-Order of the Fanderlaine mage Guild. Little is known of the Fanderlaine and what they thought to specialize their skills upon. The Vander sub-Order eventually split away from the Fanderlaine and pushed deep into the arcane knowledge that was of particular interest to their members. The Vander became the most radical of the experimenters of the mage Guilds and explored many areas of interest to them. This was considered most strange in the mage communities as the Guilds tend to be extremely conservative in their outlook and mage knowledge. Unlike most Guilds, the Vander are almost exclusively female, each member carefully selected for skills and aptitude.

The Anaza Sorcerers.

The Sorcerers were, and are, a small clan and have forever lived in small isolated elseplaces rarely relocating. Small isolated elseplaces were more common in the universe of universes than most of the folk realized. And that suited the Sorcerer clan quite well.

Why they preferred to live this way is lost in the dim reaches of an ancient history begun in a time almost before time itself. Various of the First Sorcerers at numerous points in time in their long, long history had searched their book of lore and learning, The Book Of Songs, for clues as to why this was the way it was. But each had failed. None of them realized, or knew from the oral traditions of the clan, that the Book Of Songs had come into existence long past the time when the reason why could be remembered.

So, as these things happen, the Sorcerer clan has remained reclusive and unknown to the larger universe of universes, not really hidden so much as just being very remote and private.

There was one piece of information known to the clan, a piece of information never allowed to be transmitted to anyone not a member of the clan. And similar to the reason for their preferring small, isolated elseplaces, the acquisition of this piece of information, the how and the when and the why of it did happen, was lost in the time long before before.

Someone, way back then, had learned to recognize the presence of a folk never seen and poorly understood. This recognition was not visual but rather a matter of odor, the odor of blooming flowers. With such an olfactory clue, this small clan of magic users, the Sorcerer clan, knew when the Wood With were around. They had never seen one but the delicate and pleasant odor told them when these folk were about.

The Wood With knew of this strange thing. So they tended to keep a watch on this small group more from a matter of curiosity than of any fear of what that clan might do.

The Sorcerer clan, of course, knew when these other strange folk came and went so they, the Sorcerers, tended to keep Sorcerer business very carefully hidden from these others. And in some strange and subtle way, the clan felt that the Wood With were not to be trusted. It was a cultural tradition, never to be questioned. The reason for this was also lost in the dim historical past. And, of course, they would never attempt to affect the behavior of the Wood With. Tradition also stated that this was not to be done.

The True History of the Magic Users as Discovered by the Divineal.

Many of the witch groups, whether the Witch Clan, the Sorcerer Phylota, the Nagar sort, or the Divineal, have a tale from a time long before long before, and long before written records, of fleeing their homeland before it was destroyed by an event that no magic could prevent. This tale was passed member to member as an oral tradition and eventually was written down. It appears that this event happened.

But, as the magic users scattered into the universe of universes, their knowledge and identities became unique, group to group, and most felt that they were different than all the others.

However, all the groups so far mentioned are witch, even though some felt that others were not and needed to be hunted down and destroyed.

What none of them knew, or understood, is that the magicians were also from this same single event. Witch and magician fled from the same homeland, although, in some manner not understood, the magicians lost the remembrance of that past happening.

The witch and magician groups on that homeland attempted to cast a great spell of prevention. It failed and they fled. None knew that the failure of that spell caused a great change in their magic, with witch and magician forces becoming polar opposites of each other, hence the great danger, now, of mixing, one with the other, magic or personnel, most of the time.

The Wood With.

The Wood With are a small folk. If anyone saw one of this secretive group from a distance, an event so unlikely as to be in the realm of never, it might be thought that what was seen was a very young human child of ten or twelve years of age. Of course, few human children are accompanied by a beast as tall as they are.

The Wood With, from a time before forever, have remained unobserved and unknown, which is exactly what they wish. As a group they are, for the most part, uninterested in the affairs of other sapient beings in all the universe of universes.

But, every so often, there occurs a one that attracts their attention. This event is a rare, but not unusual, happening.

The Wood With prefer to live in and among the big trees, taking comfort one from the other. They and the environment blur together where ever they might be. This skill, this cultural attribute, is the main reason, but not the only reason, why they remain unseen and unnoticed.

Their beasts are as unique a species as the Wood With. From an early age one finds the other and from that instant the pair are inseparable. The beasts blend into their surroundings with the same ease as their constant companions.

It is a peculiarity of the Wood With that their presence leaves a faint odor of blooming flowers in the air. In all the time of their existence only one small group have ever realized this fact. But that group's mythology and cultural values are such that the fact that they know this is all that they know. Every thing else they believe, everything else are tales from antiquity with all the error that derives from that.

The Kingdom and Kingdoms of Bahn Duhr Tohr.

The Kingdom of Bahn Duhr Tohr had been, until its most recent merging into a whole, a series of large and small kingdoms, each with a unique name and a unique color scheme. These color schemes were relegated to their Royalty and to their armies. It was very useful to combatants to be able to recognize friend from foe in the chaos of massed combat.

Many of the kingdoms, but not all, could trace their existence back into the dimly remembered past. Some even argued that they existed long before written records came into use. The kingdoms large and small, frequently merged, or broke apart, as the normal political intrigues and royal wheeling and dealing created large kingdoms out of smaller ones, or as so often happened, smaller kingdoms out of larger.

But, in spite of the usual turmoil over boundaries and royal household alignments, all the kingdoms were dependent upon each other as no single one had all the resources necessary for true self-sufficiency.

The bonds between the rulers and the ruled are tight and mutually advantageous. Rulers who did not keep the needs of their folk foremost did not last long. Of course, the occasional battle with a neighbor was accepted as just part of life. Battles were, for the most part, short. This was due to the usual approach to warfare that assumed that most of the fighting would happen between the royalty of the houses in contention. The knights and lessor troops often suffered nothing worse than broken bones. Most of the time this occurred during the first melee and charge.

Grandeville.

Grandeville is a small, rather isolated, rural community of 8,000 population (more or less) tucked away in the mountainous corner of northeastern Oregon. It survives in a provincial unawareness of many things, being overly conscious of the ancestors who settled the place long after the westward migration brought California, Washington, Oregon, and Idaho into statehood.

The town sprawls down from "The Bench," a shallow bench along the edge of the next door mountain slope, to The Blue River, named after the color it has after the first snow melt surges from the canyon and out across the valley proper, always threatening to jump its banks and flood the surrounding farm land.

There are two newspapers published in town, a weekly and a daily (except for Sunday). The Daily, The *Grandeville News,* tends to ignore anything happening outside the edge of town. The weekly, *The Mountain View,* tends to ignore anything happening in Grandeville and prints whatever the publisher happens to feel like publishing.

There are a number of local establishments of note:

- The Two Bags Full - a grocery store.
- The Railroad Bar and Grill - also known as The Rail.
- Big Darlene's Bar - the home of the Annual Chili Cookoff and Arm Wrestling Championship Event, All Comers Invited.
- Johnson's Everything Shop.
- Chen's Chinese Restaurant.
- Leonard's Outdoor Supply Shop.
- The Always Open Gas Pump.
- The Romp and Stomp Motel
- Randy's Truck Corral.

About the Author

George R. Mead began to study anthropology in 1962 after being discharged (honorably) from the U. S. Army, Combat Engineers. He eventually received a B.A., M. A., and Ph. D. in his chosen field. And many years later an M. S. W. in Clinical Social Work. He was worked in aerospace, taught at the college and university levels, worked in a community action agency, ran a restaurant, been unemployed, and worked for the U. S. Forest Service. He is now retired from the work-a-day world but does a certain amount of consulting, writing, and research. He lives seven miles outside of the small town of La Grande, Oregon, with his wife, one cat, and a German Shepard dog named Katy who firmly believes that staring into his face at nine-o-clock in the evening is a statement that popcorn should be made. A new dog joined the house as an eight-week old puppy found by Katy under some brush in the middle of the American Southwest desert. Rez is now four years old and weighs 93 pounds (some puppy).

www.ingramcontent.com/pod-product-compliance
Lightning Source LLC
Chambersburg PA
CBHW052337020726
47503CB00001B/4
9780981744629